DAWN OF FURY

Ralph Compton

BERKLEY
New York

BERKLEY
An imprint of Penguin Random House LLC
1745 Broadway, New York, NY 10019

Copyright © 1995 by Ralph Compton
Excerpt from *The Killing Season* copyright © 1995 by Ralph Compton
Penguin Random House supports copyright. Copyright fuels creativity, encourages
diverse voices, promotes free speech, and creates a vibrant culture. Thank you for buying
an authorized edition of this book and for complying with copyright laws by not
reproducing, scanning, or distributing any part of it in any form without permission.
You are supporting writers and allowing Penguin Random House to continue to
publish books for every reader.

BERKLEY and the BERKLEY & B colophon are registered trademarks of
Penguin Random House LLC.

ISBN: 9780451186317

Signet mass-market edition / December 1995
Berkley mass-market edition / July 2019

Printed in the United States of America
41   43   45   47   48   46   44   42   40

Cover art © Hiram Richardson
Cover design by Steve Meditz
Logo art by Roberto Castillo / Shutterstock

Prologue

The James River Plantation, near Charlottesville, Virginia. November 15, 1865:

"Seven riders comin', suh," said the old black man.

"Thank you, Malachi," Joshua Stone said. "You're a free man now, and you'd best hide yourself. If they're Yankees, there could be trouble."

Malachi left the room, taking refuge in the loft where he could observe the parlor. Neomie Stone and sixteen-year-old Rachel peered nervously out a window at the approaching riders.

"Perhaps they're Confederates and mean us no harm," Neomie said.

"Perhaps," said Joshua, but he knew better. The men rode good horses and none of them wore the threadbare gray of the Confederacy. They all carried saddle guns, and beneath their coats, holsters attested to the presence of sidearms. The seven looked exactly like what Joshua Stone feared they were: renegades who had probably fought on neither side, but had taken advantage of the war to pillage and murder. The lead rider, a tall man with a shock of white hair, dismounted and pounded on the door with the butt of his pistol. The rest of the riders dismounted, and Joshua eased the door open just a little.

"We're needin' grub," said the white-haired stranger.

"We can't spare any," Joshua said. "We have little enough for ourselves."

Joshua tried to close the door, but the stranger was too quick for him. He kicked the door, slamming it against the wall.

"We'll have a look for ourselves," the intruder said.

The seven surged into the parlor. One of the men seized Neomie's dress at the throat and ripped it to the waist, while a second man threw Rachel to the floor and got astraddle of her. Joshua slammed a right to the jaw of the man who was stripping Neomie, and the renegade hit the floor with a crash. Drawing his pistol, he shot Joshua Stone in the belly. Stone fell backward onto a sofa. He tried to rise, but could not. Tears rolled down his cheeks as he saw his wife and daughter stripped, violated, and brutally murdered. Their passion spent, the men looked at one another, shaken by the enormity of their crime.

"We'd best get the hell out of here," said the white-haired renegade. "Snider, Dillard, Foster, check out the barn and be sure there's no livestock. Jenks, Tull, Withers, sack the kitchen for anything worth takin'."

The others needed no urging, anxious to escape the grisly scene. Finding the barn empty, the trio skirted the house and mounted their horses.

"The old fool wasn't lyin'," shouted one of the renegades from the kitchen. "There ain't enough here to fool with."

"Then take what there is," the albino said.

The three quickly took what little food remained in the house, bounded off the front porch, and joined their mounted comrades. The man with the mane of white hair remained in the house.

"Hankins," bawled one of the impatient renegades, "you ridin' with us or not?"

"Somebody's got to think for this outfit," said Hankins when he finally stepped out the door. "Never leave any evidence behind."

By the time old Malachi recovered from the shock enough to creep down from the loft, flames had gobbled up the drapes and were biting into the papered walls and the ceiling. The heavy carpet was afire in a dozen places. Malachi couldn't fight the fire, but there was one thing he could do. The Stones had been his family, and although they were dead, there was one last thing he could do for them. He could save their earthly remains from the fire and see that they had a proper burial in the family graveyard. But Malachi was old and tired, with the miseries in his back.

"Lawd God," the old Negro prayed aloud, "gimme de strength to git 'em out of here in time."

He took Neomie and Rachel first, gritting his teeth to

avoid crying out at their ravaged bodies. When he returned for Joshua, he was startled to find a spark of life remained.

"Malachi," Stone whispered. "Malachi."

"De house is burnin', suh," said Malachi. "I got to git you out."

"I'll be ... dead ... then," said Joshua Stone. "Malachi, Nathan will ... will be coming. Tell him ..."

"Tell him what, suh?"

"Remember ... these men," said Joshua Stone. "Tell Nathan .. tell him to ... hunt them down ... and kill them ...to the last ... man."

"I tell him, suh," Malachi said. "I tell him."

* * *

Miles away, the seven renegades reined up and looked back. A spiraling column of gray smoke dirtied the blue of the sky. Satisfied their heinous crime had been concealed, they rode on.

* * *

Richmond, Virginia. January 3, 1866.

Nathan Stone had gone to war with the Confederacy when he had been only fifteen. Now barely nineteen, his dark hair was graying at the temples and his pale blue eyes said that he had seen more than his share of hell. He wore Confederate gray trousers, a faded gray shirt with both elbows out, and no hat. His belly was gaunt, and lacking a coat, he shivered in the cold wind. The Yankees had turned him loose afoot, weaponless, without a scrap of food. He had scrounged a little food, but mostly he had gone hungry. For three long years he'd had no word from home, and his longing to return was somehow tempered with an uneasiness he couldn't explain. Nobody had escaped the privation and suffering wrought by the war, and he wondered how it had affected his own family. He approached Richmond with the hope that he might find some food, but that hope died when he beheld the devastation of the city. Debris littered the streets, while in stark contrast the capitol building stood undamaged. He limped on in worn-out boots, his blistered feet in agony with every step. He had only to follow the James River eighty-five miles, to the point where it swung north toward Charlottesville. There would be his home. Or what remained of it . . .

*   *   *

The James River Plantation, near Charlottesville. January 12, 1866.

Mighty oaks surrounded the Stone home, and leaves crunched brown and dry beneath Nathan Stone's weary feet. Through the barren branches of the oaks, he could see only the standing chimneys of what had been his home. He stood there in shock, his legs trembling with weariness, while that which had been only nameless fear became full-blown reality. There was no point in delaying the inevitable, and he trudged on. Somewhere ahead a hound bayed low and mournful. The hound bayed again, closer, and by the time Nathan reached the burned-out house, he could see the dog. It looked as gaunt and as starved as he felt. The animal glared at him suspiciously, its hackles up, growling.

"Cotton Blossom," said a familiar voice, "hush yo' mouth."

"Malachi," Nathan shouted. "Malachi!"

"Mist' Nathan, suh," Malachi cried, "do it really be you?"

"What's left of me," said Nathan wearily. "I expected . . . hell, I don't know what I expected, but not this. Let's set, and you tell me what happened. All of it."

Malachi talked for almost an hour. Nathan Stone sat with his face buried in his hands. He wept as the old Negro haltingly described the shooting of Nathan's father and the violation and brutal murder of Neomie and Rachel.

"I couldn't save de house, suh," Malachi said, "but I was able to git de folks out. Dey be in de fambly graveyard. I lay 'em out as fittin' an' proper as I know how, an' I speak from de word of de Almighty God, prayin' he take they souls to rest."

"Thank you, Malachi," said Nathan. "That helps. I reckon the Yankees took all the livestock during the war."

"Ever'thing, suh," Malachi said. "De springhouse ain't been hurt, nor de barn. Me an' ol' Cotton Blossom sleep there. He catch him a rabbit ever' now an' den, an' I eat from de garden. Frost kilt de rest, but dey's still plenty of taters.''

"God,' said Nathan, "I could eat them raw."

"I fix a fire pit near de barn," Malachi said. "I go roast a bunch of dem taters.''

Nathan walked down the hill to the springhouse. It was of stone, and had literally been built over a spring. It had provided clear, cold water, and a year-round coolness that had preserved their milk, butter, eggs, and meat. But within its stone walls was a legacy old Joshua Stone had set aside for just such a time as this, and never in young Nathan Stone's life would there be a greater need for it. Nathan found the familiar yard-long piece of hickory, beveled at one end. From the springhouse door he counted the flat stones in the floor until he reached a specific one. Using the beveled piece of hickory, he dug around the edge of the stone until he could get beneath it and raise it. The hole beneath was just large enough for a small canvas bag. Nathan emptied it on the stone floor, and the gold double eagles gleamed dully in the dim light. There were ten of them. Two hundred dollars! Strong in Nathan's mind were his father's dying words.

Remember these men. Tell Nathan to hunt them down and kill them. To the last man.

He'd have done that on his own, had it taken the rest of his life, but his father's cry from the grave seared this quest for vengeance on his very soul. He would need a good horse, a saddle, a weapon, ammunition, some decent clothes, and a little money for food. But what of old Malachi? The faithful Negro had buried Nathan's family and had suffered great hardship so that he might deliver Joshua Stone's final message to his son. But old age had caught up with Malachi, and he could never ride the trails that Nathan Stone believed lay ahead. But even with his father's plea branded on his heart and mind, he couldn't leave old Malachi to starve. The Yankees had won the war and were boasting they had freed the Negro, but for what purpose? To wander a war-ravaged land, pursued by the spectre of starvation? While Nathan could not and would not leave Malachi behind, he knew the old man would never survive the trail that Nathan Stone must ride. Now, though, he needed rest and food, even if that food were only roasted potatoes. He could smell them as he neared the barn, and his empty belly lurched in anticipation.

"De taters don' be big," Malachi said, "so dey don' take long, cookin' 'em. Dey be ready d'reckly."

Malachi had a blackened pot three-quarters full of water, and as he dug the egg-sized potatoes out of the ashes, he dropped them into the water.

"When dey cool some," said Malachi, "jus' wash 'em off an' eat 'em skins an' all."

The potatoes were bland and the centers a little raw, but Nathan wolfed down a dozen of them. Malachi buried more in the ashes and stirred up the fire. Cotton Blossom sat on his lean haunches watching them eat, looking deprived as only a hound can.

"We must have meat," Nathan said. "Have you tried trapping rabbits?"

"No, suh," said Malachi. "Ain't seen none. But we got de bait. Dey be carrots in de garden."

Despite Malachi's pessimism, Nathan managed to trap two rabbits, and on the second day after his return, they had roast rabbit for breakfast. Hungrily they devoured everything but the bones and hide.

"Sorry, Cotton Blossom," said Nathan. "You'll have to catch your own."

*   *   *

"You be going soon," said Malachi, on the third day following Nathan's arrival.

"No," Nathan said, "I'm not leaving you behind."

"I cain't go, suh," said Malachi. "I be too old an' tired. I jus' stay alive to tell you what yo' daddy say. I be goin' home soon."

Nathan was awakened sometime after midnight by the baying of the hound. It had a bone-chilling finality that got Nathan's attention, and he found Cotton Blossom in the next stall where Malachi slept on a bed of hay. It was an eerie scene. The dog stood over Malachi in a protective manner, growling at Nathan as he approached.

"Malachi," Nathan said. "Malachi."

Malachi was silent. The sound of Nathan's voice had some calming effect on Cotton Blossom and the hound backed away, allowing Nathan to get close enough to take

Malachi's wrist. There was no pulse. Old Malachi had gone home.

*   *   *

Nathan dug Malachi's grave next to that of Joshua Stone, laying the old man to rest with remembered words from the Bible. He lingered by the graves, his heart heavy. He could go now, riding a bloody trail that would lead him he knew not where. Cotton Blossom sat beside Malachi's grave, baying mournfully as Nathan walked away. Charlottesville was the nearest town, twenty miles to the north, and he headed that way. Leaves rattled behind him, and Nathan turned to find the hound following. They were outcasts, two of a kind, their loneliness drawing them together for the long trail ahead.

Chapter 1

Charlottesville, Virginia. January 16, 1866.

Nathan spent two miserable days and nights reaching Charlottesville, only to find it as war ravaged as Richmond had been, and lacking all the things that he needed. One of the few buildings left standing was—or had been—a blacksmith shop. Nathan eased one of the double doors open and stepped inside. The forge was cold and a bearded old man in patched overalls sat on an empty nail keg. A second man hunkered next to him, and the pair of them eyed Nathan curiously.

"Howdy, gents," Nathan said. "Would either of you be knowin' of anybody with a horse or mule for sale?"

"Mister," said the bearded man, "we been through hell, and we been picked clean as Christmas geese. Them as has a horse or mule ain't sellin' at no price. Even if some high roller come along and had the money."

"I can understand that," said Nathan. "Thanks."

He stepped out the door and moved on, Cotton Blossom plodding along behind. One thing the man said had struck a note of caution. Each time he inquired about a horse or mule for sale, he was implying he had the money to buy. There were desperate men who would kill for just one of the double eagles in his pocket, and that left him facing a new dilemma. How was he to buy a horse, a mule, a saddle, a weapon, food—or anything—without revealing his gold? He trudged wearily on. He had roasted a few potatoes and had brought them with him, but they were not enough. Weak from lack of food, he stumbled.

When he came to a wind-blown oak, he sat down to rest and collect his thoughts. He now knew he must travel beyond the devastation of the war before buying a horse or mule. He could follow the Blue Ridge, crossing into Ken-

tucky somewhere south of Roanoke. But he must have
food, whatever the cost. He forced himself to his feet and
continued west, the evening sun in his eyes. Three hours
later sundown left him facing a chill west wind, and he
settled down on the lee side of a rocky knoll near a shallow
creek. There he ate the last of his roasted potatoes, Cotton
Blossom watching hungrily.

"Sorry, pardner," Nathan said, "but you need meat, and
so do I. Tomorrow I'll be at the end of my rope if we don't
find some decent grub."

With nothing but cold water from the creek to sustain
him, Nathan was on his feet at dawn, bound for the mountains that never seemed to come any closer. More and more
often he stopped to rest, leaning against an oak or pine,
lest he be unable to get back to his feet. By the time the
sun began to slip toward the elusive mountains, he was
dizzy with weakness. Stumbling, he fell and was unable to
rise. When he finally came to his senses, he was shocked
to discover that sundown was only minutes away. Cotton
Blossom eyed him sympathetically. Suddenly the hound got
to his feet, growling. Nathan sat up, listening. The wind
had died almost to nothing, and somewhere to the west
there was the barking of a dog.

"Cotton Blossom," said Nathan, "where there's a dog
there's people, and where there's people, there's grub."

Nathan got to hands and knees, and with a supreme effort staggered to his feet. Another day without food would
be the finish of him. Somewhere ahead there was a camp,
a cabin, and food, and he must reach it before dark. In his
weakened condition he might stumble off a bluff. He set
off in a lope, a shambling run, ignoring thorny underbrush
and last summer's blackberry briars dried fierce and hard.
Cotton Blossom was now forging ahead, barking a challenge to the other dog. His opponent responded, sounding
much nearer, and Nathan could smell wood smoke. Nathan
could see the shake roof of a barn, and by the time he
reached it, Cotton Blossom was headed for the cabin beyond. He was brought up short by a snarling yellow hound
who didn't relish the company of another dog.

"Ichabod," bawled a female voice from the cabin, "you
or Immanuel see what's roused up that fool dog. My God,
you'd think Grant and the Union army was a-comin'."

Growl for growl, Cotton Blossom was facing up to the

other dog, and Nathan waited for Ichabod or Immanuel to end the standoff. Neither did, and a big woman in bonnet and homespun dress opened the door and stomped out on the porch. She spoke to the hound and it slunk under the porch, continuing to growl deep in its throat.

"Ma'am," Nathan shouted, "I'm hungry. I have a little money, and I can pay."

"Emma Meekler never turned away a hungry man," she said. "Come on in. You're invited to supper, and you keep the little money you got."

By the time Nathan reached the cabin, Ichabod and Immanuel had stepped out on the porch. Both were brawny, bearded, over six feet, with long sandy hair. Nathan judged that either of them could have caught and soundly thrashed a bobcat with one hand. They wore patched overalls, faded flannel shirts, and brogan shoes. The pair eyed Nathan without friendliness, stepping aside to allow him to enter the cabin.

"These are my sons, Ichabod and Immanuel," said Emma.

"I'm Nathan Stone, and I'm half starved. I haven't had a decent meal since the war ended."

"Which side was you on?" one of the bearded men asked bluntly.

It was a touchy question, one that could cost Nathan the meal he desperately needed. But Emma came to his rescue.

"Ichabod, that's not a proper question, and it's none of your business."

"It sure as hell is, ma," Ichabod shouted. "Them damn Yankees . ."

"Ichabod," Emma snapped, "you watch your tongue."

"Sorry, ma" said Ichabod, not looking sorry at all.

"I was with Lee," Nathan said, "and spent six months in a Yankee prison."

Ichabod and Immanuel were silent, and Nathan thought Emma was a little uncomfortable. He doubted that either of the men had ever been off the farm.

"I'll have supper on the table in a few minutes," said Emma. "There's a pan, water, and soap on the back stoop if you'd like to wash up."

Ichabod and Immanuel took their seats at the table, while Nathan continued on through the kitchen to the back door. The very odor of frying ham left him staggering. It had a similar effect on Cotton Blossom, for he was already on the back porch.

"After supper," said Emma from the kitchen, "I'll give you some leavings for your dog."

"Thank you," Nathan said. "He's about as used up as I am."

Nathan sat down on the bench next to Emma, across from Ichabod and his surly brother. There was fried ham, fried eggs, cornbread, and molasses. At each plate was a mug, and there were two pitchers of water on the table.

"Sorry we have no coffee or milk," said Emma. "Not much variety, but for what there is, we have plenty."

Nathan found himself unable to eat very much. One thing that distracted him was the predatory look in the eyes of Ichabod and Immanuel. There was little doubt the pair had heard him tell Emma he could pay for his food, and if Nathan Stone were any judge of men, these two were contemplating the money he had and pondering a means of getting their hands on it. It seemed Emma was the only one with an appetite and there was an enormous amount of cornbread and fried ham left.

"You're welcome to sleep in the barn, Mr. Stone," Emma said. "There's hay and I'll get you a blanket. There's a mess of ham scraps for your dog, but take him with you. That no-account varmint of Ichabod's won't leave him alone."

Nathan said nothing, but when Ichabod's eyes met his, there was a hostility that put Nathan on his guard. When Emma returned, she had a blanket and two cloth-wrapped parcels.

"This is for your dog," she said, handing him the smaller one, "and this one is leftover ham and cornbread. Being long without food, you couldn't eat much, but you'll be getting hungry during the night."

Nathan took the two packets of food and the blanket and headed for the barn. There, he paused only long enough for Cotton Blossom to wolf down the food, then took the dog with him into the shadow of the lofty pines nearby. Nathan chose a small ridge from which he could observe the cabin and the barn. There he settled down, wrapping himself in the blanket, and waited. While he waited, he ate as much of the ham and cornbread as he could, silently thanking Emma for her generosity. He would need all the strength he could muster. Nearly two hours later, as he watched in the starlight, two shadows separated themselves from the cabin and started for the barn. Ichabod and Immanuel! In Nathan's weakened condition, either of the pair was capable of killing him with their bare hands. Nathan wrapped the blanket about his shoulders and headed west, Cotton Blossom following.

"Cotton Blossom," Nathan said, "I reckon we'd best spend the rest of the night getting some distance between us and that pair of varmints. Come the morning, I wouldn't put it past them trailing us. At least for a ways."

Fortified with food and having had a chance to rest, Nathan was able to travel what he believed was at least ten miles before a rosy dawn swallowed the darkness of night. The weary pair followed the shallow runoff to a spring that gurgled out from beneath a rock ledge at one end of a narrow valley.

"Here's where we hole up and rest awhile," said Nathan. There was no wind, the sun was up, and for a January day, it was pleasant. Nathan lay down, having folded the blanket into a pillow, and Cotton Blossom stretched out a few yards away. The dog had proven himself not only a worthy companion, but an edge that might mean the difference between life and death to an unarmed man. The sun was noon-high when Nathan awoke. Cotton Blossom was about halfway done devouring a rabbit. Taking advantage of the cold spring water, Nathan finished the rest of Emma's ham and cornbread. He must take full advantage of his renewed strength, finding more food before weakness overtook him again. Hereafter, he wouldn't be so quick to reveal that he had money to pay. It was hard times. His being afoot in threadbare clothes was evidence enough of his need. Nathan got to his feet and shook out the blanket.

"Bring the rest of that rabbit with you, pardner," he said. "We don't know how far it is to the next grub."

Just before sundown, Nathan stopped awhile and rested. The night would be cold with frost, likely. Better that he keep moving than sit huddled in his blanket awaiting the dawn. He walked steadily the rest of the night, covering his head with the blanket to protect his ears. Despite his exhaustion, he went on until the sun had time to burn away the chill. He was traveling southwest now, and being at the foot of a mountain range, there was no problem finding

water. Springs abounded, and the wary travelers took refuge near one for a day of rest. By early afternoon they
were again on their way, Nathan's belly growling. He had
begun to believe he'd made a bad choice, keeping to the
lowlands. Settlers who had escaped the ravages of the war
were likely deep in the mountains, and in winter, with snow
a possibility, he dared not venture there afoot. The first
stars were blossoming in a purple sky when Nathan paused.
He smelled smoke, and with a slight breeze from the west,
he was downwind from it. He moved cautiously on, Cotton
Blossom at his heels. It was a violent time when a man
knew not whether he was encountering friend or foe.

Nathan was hoping for a settler's cabin, but those hopes
withered and died when he saw the glow of a camp fire.
The man or men in the camp had kept the fire small, so
that an approaching stranger couldn't tell if there were one
man or a dozen. Nathan sighed. He had but one option.

"Hello the camp," he shouted. "I'm friendly and I'm
hungry."

"Come on up to the fire," a voice responded, "and keep
your hands where I can see 'em."

Nathan obeyed the command. On the opposite side of
the fire, a man stepped out of the darkness. He was about
Nathan's height, and his mackinaw was unbuttoned,
allowing access to a tied-down Colt on his right hip.

"You got money?" he asked.

"If I did," Nathan said, "would I be afoot, begging a
meal?"

"I reckon you wouldn't," the stranger said. "I got beans
and bacon."

"I'd ask nothing better," Nathan said.

Skewered on a stick, a rasher of bacon simmered over
the fire. But then everything went wrong. Cotton Blossom
took a dislike to the stranger and cut loose with his most
formidable growl.

"I don't like dogs," the man shouted. "Git that varmint
away from me."

Cotton Blossom moved like a striking rattler. His lean
neck arched out and he swallowed the rasher of bacon in
a single gulp. The man was quick with a Colt, and his first
shot barely missed Cotton Blossom. Before he could fire
again, Nathan caught his arm and they fought for the pistol.
Still weak from the lack of food, Nathan lost his grip and

the stranger swung the muzzle of the Colt like a club. It grazed Nathan's head and he went down, his adversary on top of him. But Nathan had an ace in the hole. Like a clawing, snarling cougar, Cotton Blossom leaped on the gunman's back, and the man screamed. This allowed Nathan to gather his wits and hump his assailant off. Seeing that Nathan had control of the situation, Cotton Blossom backed off. The two men had the Colt between them, fighting for possession of it. Suddenly the Colt roared and the stranger's struggles ceased. Nathan rolled away from him and lay there gasping for breath. Cotton Blossom crouched in the shadows, growling. Nathan sat up, holding his aching head.

"My God," he said, unbelieving. "My God."

He sat there until his head stopped pounding and then got unsteadily to his feet. He had killed a man over a dog, and unintentional as the act had been, he was still shaken to his very soul. Finally reason took over. While the fight had started over Cotton Blossom, it had ended with a stranger doing his damndest to kill Nathan Stone, and Nathan had resisted. Whatever the dead man had, he wouldn't be needing, and that included a horse, a saddle, a Colt, a warm coat, and food. It was time for some cold-blooded straight thinking. He searched the dead man, finding a hundred and ten dollars in gold eagles and a pocket knife. There was much leading Nathan to believe the man might have been a renegade. His clothes and boots were virtually new, and feeling less and less guilty, Nathan took them. The boots were a bit large, with pointed toes and undershot heels, but the coat, clothes and hat were almost a perfect fit. Nathan dragged the dead man off into the darkness, away from the fire. Only then did Cotton Blossom come near.

"Now," Nathan said, "we'll find this hombre's horse, saddlebags, and grub."

The horse proved to be a big black with a white blaze on his face. The saddle was double rigged, and the saddlebags proved the biggest treasure of all. There was half a side of bacon, a sack of dried beans, part of a sack of coffee beans, a change of clothes, and two hundred rounds of ammunition for the Colt. In the pocket of the extra shirt was an oilskin-wrapped packet of matches. Nathan shared some of the bacon with Cotton Blossom, broiled some for

himself, and finished the pot of beans that bubbled on the
fire. He then went to a nearby spring and scrubbed out the
pot. He took a handful of coffee beans, crushed them with
the butt of his newly acquired Colt, filled the pot with
water, and set it on the stone pyramid over the fire. When
the aroma told him the coffee was ready, he added some
cold water to settle the grounds. He waited until the brew
had cooled a little, and for the lack of a cup, drank it from
the pot.

"We got us an outfit, Cotton Blossom," he said, "but I'm
not proud of the way we got it."

When Nathan had finished the coffee, he washed the pot,
saddled the horse and led the animal well beyond the
spring. There they would spend the rest of the night. In the
morning he must find some means of burying the dead man.
Whoever or whatever the poor devil had been, he deserved
better than being left to predators and the elements.

With the dawn, Nathan had a good look at the black
horse. It appeared to be a fine animal. The brand on its
left hip was a forty-four connected. Badly as he needed a
horse, Nathan had his misgivings about this one, for it was
the kind that would be remembered. The dead man's riding
boots and double-rigged saddle suggested he was a Westerner. As the war had drawn to a close, Nathan had heard
of renegades from Missouri and Kansas being driven out,
forced to flee south to Indian Territory or north Texas. The
more he pondered his own situation, the more certain he
became that the man he had killed was likely wanted by
the law. The seven men Nathan Stone pursued were headed
west, leaving Nathan to ride a vengeance trail on a horse
that had belonged to an outlaw. The dead man's enemies
would become his own, and he knew not where he would
find them or how many there would be. He built a fire,
boiled coffee, and broiled some bacon, which he shared
with Cotton Blossom. He then undertook the disagreeable
task of burying the dead man. Since he had no tools for
digging, he found a deep gully where erosion had undercut
the banks, and these he caved in effectively covering the
body. He then mounted the black and rode south. Now
that he was mounted, he might reach Roanoke before dark.

Nathan found it a joy being in the saddle again after
being afoot for so long. The black horse fell easily into a
mile-eating gait and Cotton Blossom loped along behind.

In the early afternoon they reached a wagon road that veered in from the east and continued southwestward. Nathan slowed the horse to a walk. From a ridge he could see a farmhouse and a barn in the valley below. Warily he rode on, and when he reached the village he believed to be Roanoke, it was with an alarming suddeness. He rounded a bend in the road and found himself looking down the main street. While the town wasn't large, there was no evidence it had suffered during the war. At one time, most of the frame buildings had been painted, and there were board-walks along both sides of the street. A mule-drawn wagon clattered toward Nathan, and he nodded to the man on the box. Men stepped out of the various shops as Nathan rode past, watching him. He reined up before a weathered build-ing with a wide porch above which a crude sign proclaimed it "General Store." A hitch rail ran the length of the porch, with stone steps at both ends. A team of mules were tied to the hitch rail and in the wagon to which they were hitched was a wooden crate in which a trio of pigs grunted and squealed. Nathan dismounted, half-hitching the reins to the rail should he have to leave in a hurry. Cotton Blos-som sat down near the black horse as Nathan made his way into the store. He had no sooner closed the door be-hind him when Cotton Blossom began an ominous barking.

"He's in the store," a voice shouted from the outside. "Get him!"

There was an almost immediate thud of boots on the porch, and Nathan swept past the startled storekeeper, seeking a back door. He found it and hit the ground run-ning. He had but one chance, and that was to reach his horse. He reached one corner of the building, only to be spotted by two men who came after him with rifles. He ran to the opposite corner, only to face a third man coming after him with a scattergun. Nathan drew back, pulling his Colt, and as the startled man rounded the corner, Nathan seized the front of his shirt with his left hand and slugged him senseless with the muzzle of the Colt. By then the rifle-wielding pair had rounded the opposite corner of the building.

"By God," one of them bawled, "he's kilt Jake. Shoot the skunk."

Lead tore into the weathered wood of the store building, but Nathan was already around the corner, running for his

horse. As he rounded the end of the porch nearest his
horse, three men burst out the door. The mules and wagon
stood between them and Nathan's horse, but one man in
his eagerness leaped over the hitch rail. He screamed when
a snarling Cotton Blossom ripped out the seat of his trousers. Nathan was in the saddle and the black horse was on
the run when the other two men rounded the rear of the
wagon. The big black ran them down. Slugs burned the air
over Nathan's head like angry bees, but he was soon out
of range, riding back the way he had come. He slowed the
black, looking back, and there was Cotton Blossom trotting
along behind.

"Pardner," Nathan said, "you think fast and act faster.
That's what it takes to stay alive. I reckon the varmint that
owned his horse was through here. Whatever he done, he
got on the bad side of these folks. I don't think they aimed
for me to have a trial. Question is, how many other towns
has he passed through, where we're likely to get this same
unsociable treatment?"

Nathan circled wide, riding west, toward the mountains.
He kept to the terrain where tracking would be difficult,
should anybody be so inclined. When he was sure he was
well past the village, he again rode southwest. Another day
and he believed he could ride due west and cross into Kentucky. He and Cotton Blossom made camp beside a creek
and finished the bacon. There would be only coffee for
breakfast unless he took the time to boil some of the beans.
He sat hunched over a small fire, gloomily contemplating
his narrow escape. How was he to track down the seven
men he sought while in constant danger of being gunned
down for the misdeeds of the dead man whose horse he
rode? The obvious answer was to dispose of the horse, but
how? He had no bill of sale, and a man could be hanged
as readily for horse stealing as for murder. He could keep
the horse, facing the consequences as they arose, or he
could continue his journey afoot. It didn't take him long to
make his decision.

"Damn it," he said aloud, "this horse is mine. If the gent
that owned him ahead of me owed some shootin' debts,
then I reckon I'll have to pay 'em."

He let the fire burn low, with just enough coals to keep
the coffee hot. He then took the .44 caliber Army Colt and
began what would become a ritual. Time after time he drew

the weapon, "dry firing" it, getting the feel of it. He would perfect his skill until he could shoot accurately while falling, on his back, belly down, or on his feet. He had always been as adept with one hand as the other, and he border-shifted the weapon from one hand to the other for almost two hours. Weary, he rolled in his blankets and slept until first light. Having neither the time nor the taste for boiled beans, he made coffee and made do.

"Sorry, Cotton Blossom," he said to the hound. "Maybe we can lay our hands on some grub today without gettin' shot to doll rags."

Nathan made a decision. He would avoid the towns in southern Virginia and wait until he reached Kentucky before seeking to buy food. There was a chance that the former owner of the black horse had ridden in from the south, perhaps from Knoxville. That being the case, Nathan could ride west without fear of the horse being recognized, and without having to shoot his way out of hostile towns in which the dead outlaw had done God knew what. He saddled the black and rode southwest, keeping to the foothills. There was a cold wind out of the west, and riding it came an ominous mass of gray clouds. Three hours into the day, the snow began. At first it was fine and gritty, with a mix of sleet, but the flakes grew larger and the accumulation began. Nathan reined up and Cotton Blossom sat in the deepening snow, watching him.

"Pardner," Nathan said, "grub or not, we'll have to find us a place to hole up. It's gettin' colder by the minute, and come dark, it'll be downright uncomfortable."

Nathan rode on, heading west now, and with the snowfall becoming heavier, he almost didn't see the barn. Blowing snow had covered the shake roof and had whitened the log walls. If there were a barn, there should be a cabin, but through the blowing snow, he could see nothing. He lifted a wooden latch and opened the door enough to allow the black horse to enter. Cotton Blossom followed, and Nathan closed the door. He waited, allowing his eyes to become accustomed to the gloom, and then went looking for an empty stall for the black. There were other animals in the barn, for he could hear them. A cow lowed once. Finding an empty stall, he led the black in, closing the slatted gate behind the animal. Quickly he found the ladder to the hay-loft, and found the loft full of hay. His eyes were used to the gloom now, and finding a hay fork, he pitched some hay down into the black's manger. Cotton Blossom growled low.

"I'm up here, pardner," said Nathan. "Find yourself a soft place and keep watch."

Nathan dug into the soft hay, and out of the wind, was soon asleep. He was awakened by the ominous growling of Cotton Blossom, followed by a calm voice.

"Back off, feller. I ain't begrudgin' you shelter from the storm. And you up there in the loft, make yourself to home. Just one thing. Would you fork down some hay, so's I can milk this ornery old cow?"

"I'd be glad to," Nathan said, since he had no choice. "I'd have asked permission to take shelter in your barn, but it was snowing so hard, I had no idea where your house was." He forked hay into the manger in the cow's stall.

"You done the sensible thing," said the voice below. "It's likely to snow all night. We ain't had a bad one yet, and we're overdue. I'm thinking it'll be almighty cold by morning. When I'm done milking, you're welcome to come to the house for supper. I'm Isaac Wright. There's just me, my wife Jenny, and our grandaughter Daisy."

"I'd be obliged," Nathan said. "I'm half starved. I'm armed, but friendly, and I'm coming down. I'm Nathan Stone, and that's Cotton Blossom doing the growling."

"Come on down, then," said Wright. "I won't be long. My hands are already near froze."

When Wright had finished milking, Nathan followed his host through the swirling snow to the house. Cotton Blossom plodded along behind. Reaching the back porch, the men stomped the snow off their feet and Wright swung the door open. There was a delicious warmth, a smell of cooking food, and hot coffee.

"Jenny," Wright said, "we have company for supper. Nathan Stone and his dog, Cotton Blossom."

"Come on in," said Jenny. "Supper's ready. Cotton Blossom can sleep next to the stove, and there's a bed in the loft for Mr. Stone."

Nathan had trouble getting Cotton Blossom into the kitchen, but the food was more than he could resist and his belly led him on. Nathan breathed a sigh of relief. In the light from a coal oil lamp, he found Isaac and Jenny Wright as kindly a pair as he'd ever laid eyes on. The last of Cotton Blossom's suspicions vanished when Jenny set before him a bountiful bowl of food. Isaac allowed Nathan first use of the wash pan and towel, and when both men had taken their places at the table, Jenny began bringing in the food. There was ham, fried chicken, boiled potatoes, cornbread, and brown gravy. Isaac and Nathan sat on a bench on one side of the table, while Jenny sat on a bench on the opposite side.

"Daisy," Isaac shouted, "supper."

"Go ahead and eat, Mr. Stone," said Jenny. "She'll take her own sweet time gettin' here."

When Daisy took her place beside Jenny and was introduced to Nathan, she said nothing, but her eyes were on him throughout the rest of the meal. When Isaac and Jenny left the table, the girl spoke to Nathan for the first time.

"When you leave here," she said, "I'm going with you."

Chapter 2

Startled as he was by the girl's bold manner, Nathan continued eating, saying nothing. She eyed him boldly, without shame, and he forced himself to look at her. She was attractive enough, but not a day over fifteen, if he was any judge. As inviting as the bed in the loft sounded, Nathan decided that he didn't want to spend the night in that house. But before he had finished his supper, Isaac was offering to show him to the loft.

"Reckon you must be pretty well give out," said his host, "and there ain't nothin' to do 'cept set here and look at us, once you've et."

"You've fed me and my dog," Nathan said, "and that's all I have a right to expect. While I appreciate your generosity, I'd honestly feel better if I slept in the hay loft. I aim to get an early start in the morning."

"That won't bother us," said Jenny. "Isaac has to milk the cow, and he'll be up two hours before daylight. Besides, I won't have you taking the trail without a decent breakfast and somethin' to eat along the way."

There was no way out of accepting their hospitality, and as Nathan got up from the table, there was something akin to triumph in Daisy's dark eyes. Isaac led the way up the stairs, carrying the lamp. Nathan followed, Cotton Blossom padding along behind. When they reached the loft, there was room to stand only where the roof peaked. It wasn't all that warm, but comparing it to the barn, Nathan could appreciate the difference. The bunk was crude and home-made, but there were plenty of blankets.

"Won't be nobody up here but you and your dog," Isaac said. "Rest of us will be downstairs. When you're ready, just come on down. I'll be up with a breakfast fire goin'."

Even with all the blankets and the luxury of a roof over his head, Nathan removed only his boots, his hat, and his gun belt. The Colt he placed under his pillow. Cotton Blossom had curled up on the faded old handmade rug that covered the floor. There were no windows and no door. Nathan's bunk faced the open stairs. Tired as he was, he lay awake he knew not how long before he finally slept. It seemed only minutes until he was awakened by a low growl of warning from Cotton Blossom. Somebody was coming up the stairs. Nathan sat up, drawing the Colt from beneath his pillow. When Daisy appeared at the head of the stairs, a lighted candle in her hand, Nathan was struck dumb. The girl was stark naked, and even in the drafty loft by the light of a flickering candle, she left nothing to the imagination. She spoke softly.

"I want to go with you when you leave here, but I don't expect you to take me along for nothing. There's only this way that I can pay you."

"You don't have to pay me," Nathan said, "because you're not going with me. Now please get out of here. I want no trouble."

"Then take me with you, else I'll scream."

"Then scream, damn it," said Nathan angrily. "I haven't laid a hand on you, and I don't aim to."

"I'll tell the old man you had your way with me," the girl said exultantly. "You think he'll take your word over mine, with me standing here naked right in front of you?"

"I think he will," Isaac said, as he silently mounted the stairs in his bare feet. He took the candle from Daisy with his left hand, and in his right he held a razor strap by its metal hook. He swung the strap, swatting the girl across the bare behind. She screamed, fell to her knees, and tried to get under Nathan's bunk. Cotton Blossom snarled and she backed away. Isaac allowed her to get to her feet, and when she sought escape down the stairs, he busted her bare bottom again with the razor strap. It was an awkward time, and it was old Isaac who finally broke the silence.

"Jenny saw somethin' in her eyes, the way she looked at you durin' supper, and when you wanted to sleep in the barn, we knew she was up to somethin'. All I can say is, I'm sorry this happened."

"Forget it, Isaac," Nathan said, embarrassed. "No harm's been done."

"She's like her ma," said Isaac, as though he hadn't heard. "After our son died in the war, she lit out with a renegade, and we ain't seen her since. Daisy's our only grandchild, and we've done our damndest to do right by her, but there's too much of her mama in her. Tonight we lost her."

There was nothing Nathan could say. He eased the Colt off cock, again placing it beneath his pillow. Isaac sighed, and without another word, began descending the stairs. Nathan lay awake for a long time, half-expecting the wayward girl to return, but he wasn't disturbed. It was well past dawn when he awakened. He pulled on his boots, belted on his Colt, took his hat and descended the stairs. Jenny was at the kitchen table, but there was no sign of Isaac or Daisy.

"Sorry," Nathan said. "I'm not a man to lie abed."

"You needed the sleep," said Jenny. "Won't take a minute to hot up your breakfast. Your dog's hungry."

Cotton Blossom had followed Nathan down the stairs and stood there with his head canted toward the big stove with its odor of fried ham.

"Cotton Blossom's always hungry," Nathan said, "but I can't fault him. So am I. These are lean times."

"I've cooked enough so's you'll have something to take with you. Isaac is at the barn. I'll bring your breakfast. Yours too, Cotton Blossom."

When Isaac returned from the barn, he warmed his hands at the stove, then joined Nathan at the table. Jenny brought Isaac a cup of coffee, and he held the hot cup with both hands.

"I give your hoss a bait of grain," said Isaac. "Cold as it is, the snow won't be meltin' anytime soon. Graze may be hard to find."

"I'm obliged," Nathan said. "I'll be riding west. Can you tell me anything about what might lie ahead?"

"A day's ride will get you into Kentucky. First town I'm sure of is maybe three hundred and twenty-five miles, and that's Bowling Green."

"You don't know what's between here and there," said Jenny. "I've packed you enough grub for four days, so you won't starve."

"Ma'am," Nathan said, "that's more than I have any right to expect."

"Hush," said Jenny. "It's no more than we should do for

one another. Till you rode in, we ain't seen another human face since ..." She paused awkwardly.

"Since the man showed up that Daisy's ma run off with," Isaac finished.

Nathan still hadn't seen Daisy, but he could feel her dark eyes on him, and as much as he hated to leave Isaac and Jenny, he longed to be out of that cabin and on his way. On a peg in the wall hung Jenny's faded apron, and into its pocket Nathan managed to slip a gold double eagle without being observed. The sky was overcast and there was a cold wind from the north, but the snow had stopped shy of a depth that would have made traveling difficult. Nathan opened the barn door and the black horse nickered. Old Isaac hadn't spent all his time in the barn milking. Behind Nathan's saddle was a bag of grain for the black horse. Nathan saddled up, mounted, and with Cotton Blossom loping along behind, the trio again headed west.

Twice during the day they passed isolated cabins, the only sign of their habitation being the smoke trailing from the chimneys. Thanks to Jenny having supplied them with food, they might be able to reach Bowling Green without stopping at some settler's cabin where old hatreds from the war still burned bright. Before dark they reached a cave whose entrance was sufficient for Nathan to ride the horse into without difficulty. There was a supply of dry wood, evidence that the cave had sheltered others. A nearby creek had water aplenty, and thanks to old Isaac's thoughtfulness, Nathan had grain for the horse.

*   *   *

Bowling Green, Kentucky. February 1, 1866.

The snow melted and the weather became mild. Nathan took advantage of it, and riding warily, reached the little town of Bowling Green the day after he and Cotton Blossom had eaten the last of the food Jenny had prepared. The town seemed sleepy, peaceful, but recalling his near-disaster in Roanoke, Nathan took no chances. He rode down the single street, past the mercantile, to the other end of town. If somebody recognized his horse and men came out shooting, he didn't aim to be boxed in. Men on the boardwalk seemed to pay him no particular attention,

going on about their business. He rode back along the dirt
street to the mercantile and dismounted, taking his time in
slip-knotting the reins of his mount to the hitch rail. Still
there were no cries for the sheriff, no thump of booted
feet, and no roar of guns. Nathan made his way into the
store and the man behind the counter nodded to him.

Nathan looked around and found the store surprisingly
well stocked. A cedar beam extended from one side of the
store to the other, and hanging from it, slightly more than
head high, was an array of smoked hams and sides of
bacon. Cotton Blossom yipped in anticipation.

"Sorry about that," Nathan said. "You want me to take
him out?"

"Naw," the storekeeper grinned. "He can't get up there.
Anything I kin get fer ye, in p'ticular?"

"A ham and a side of bacon," said Nathan, "and I could
use some ammunition for my Colt, if there's any to be
had."

"Ain't none. But if there's any truth in what I'm hearin',
it won't make no difference. The Yanks has drummed up
a Reconstruction Act that says them that fought agin the
Union ain't allowed to have guns."

There was no flour or sugar, but Nathan managed to buy
a sack of coffee beans. His gold double eagle was accepted
without comment and he was given change. His purchases
were secured in a burlap bag that he evenly divided and
lashed behind his saddle. He then mounted and rode west,
unmolested, with Cotton Blossom trotting along behind.
Having food, Nathan bypassed the other towns and villages.
Paying his toll, he crossed the Mississippi on a ferry just
south of Sikeston, Missouri. He then followed the river
north to St. Louis.

*   *   *

St. Louis, Missouri. February 12, 1866.

Nathan reined up near the steamboat landing just as a
big sternwheeler was preparing to depart. A mighty blast of
the whistle frightened Nathan's horse and Cotton Blossom
behind him. Nathan rode on along the river, following a
winding, rutted street. There were warehouses, cafes, saloons, and bawdy houses. Just as Nathan rode past a dive

called the Emerald Dragon, a man was thrown bodily out the door. Somewhere ahead there was a shot, followed by loud cursing. Nathan took the first side street that led away from the river. He needed to find a hotel or boardinghouse and a livery for the horse, but he wanted to distance himself from the brawling, hell-raising riverfront. The streets were crowded with bearded mountain men with packs, ex-soldiers, fancy women, dogs, gamblers, hard-eyed men with tied-down guns, and a variety of others who did not seem to fit into a category. None of them gave Nathan a second look, and he felt all the more certain that the men he was seeking might linger here for a while. Perhaps some of them lived here.

Nathan didn't like being too far from his horse, so he sought a hotel with a livery nearby. He finally chose a boardinghouse. The sign said *Rooms by the Day, Week, or Month.* Behind the place, across an alley, was a livery. Nathan entered the boardinghouse, Cotton Blossom at his heels. A tall, thin old lady got up from a rocking chair. She wore wire-rimmed spectacles, had eyes like an eagle, and looked as though she had seen more of the world than she would have cared to.

"I need a room for a few nights," Nathan said. "You got anything against my dog?"

"Not yet," she snapped. "He makes a mess, you clean it up or pay to have it done. Dollar a night, five dollars a week, twenty dollars a month. You pay in advance."

"A week, then," said Nathan, handing her the money. "If I decide to stay longer, I'll pay well in advance."

"First room on the left, at the head of the stairs," she said. Her eyes seemed to soften a little as she handed him the key.

The room was nothing to get excited about, but it was clean. There was an iron bed with straw tick, clean sheets, a pillow, and a pair of blankets. There was an ancient dresser, and on the wall above it, a cracked mirror held in place with bent nails. There was a blue granite wash basin, a matching water pitcher, and a single chair. A coil of rope lay next to the only window, one end tied to the iron leg of the bed. The fire escape. Nathan placed his saddle in the corner, along with his bedroll.

"Make yourself at home, Cotton Blossom. I aim to rest my bones for a bit before I go out and have a look at this town. If this ain't the jumpin'-off place, it'll do till a better one comes along."

Nathan lay down across the bed and rested for an hour. By then it was nearly supper time, and he hadn't eaten since the morning of the day before.

"Come on, Cotton Blossom. Let's find some grub."

Nathan avoided the fancy places, choosing one that had no tablecloths and plain wooden benches instead of chairs. The place was virtually empty, and Nathan chose a table near the counter. Cotton Blossom sat on the floor beside him, and the cook in his greasy apron cast a dubious eye at the dog.

"We don't generally allow dogs in here."

"I reckon you don't generally have dogs that are paying customers, either," Nathan said.

"That's a fact," said the cook. "What'll he be havin'?"

"He's not particular," Nathan said. "Just be sure there's plenty of it."

Nathan ordered roast beef, fried potatoes, onions, apple pie, and coffee. Cotton Blossom got the trimmings from the beef haunch, and there was plenty.

"No charge for him," said the cook, as Cotton Blossom wolfed down the food. "He's got the trimmings from that beef haunch, and I'd just throw them out, anyhow. Never seen a hound in my life that didn't eat like he was two hours away from death by starvation."

Being only three or four blocks from his boarding house, Nathan was afoot, and after he and Cotton Blossom left the cafe, Nathan decided to walk another block or two along the street. A buckboard clattered past, going his way, and a young girl was driving. Half a block ahead, as the buckboard neared an alley, a man stepped out and seized the bridle of the horse. He ripped the reins from the girl's hands and led the horse into the shadows. The girl screamed, and Nathan was off and running. By the time Nathan reached the alley, the girl's antagonist had dragged her from the buckboard and had his hand over her mouth so she couldn't cry out again. Nathan drew and cocked his Colt.

"Let her go," said Nathan.

"I reckon not," the stranger said. "You drill me, and it'll be through her."

But the girl was resourceful and the odds changed in a

heartbeat. She went limp and slipped out of the man's grasp. His hand flew to the butt of his Colt, but before he cleared leather, Nathan shot him just below the Durham tag that trailed from the left pocket of his shirt. Nathan seized the girl from the ground and hoisted her onto the buckboard's seat. He vaulted to the seat in the driver's position, took the reins and backed the buckboard out into the rutted street. He trotted the horse as fast as he dared, lest they draw unwanted attention, taking the first side street. Only then did he speak to the girl.

"They'll be looking for us," he said. "Where can we hide ourselves, the horse and the buckboard?"

"Drive to my house," she said. "There's a barn."

He followed her directions and they were soon out of town. Although the house and barn seemed secluded, the trip took only minutes, and Nathan judged they were no more than two or three miles from town. The girl got down, opened the gate, and closed it behind them. She again got down when they reached the barn and opened the doors for Nathan to drive in. When she had closed the big doors, Nathan spoke.

"We left a dead man back there, ma'am. While I unhitch the horse and rub him down, maybe you'd better tell me what this is all about. You can start with your name. I'm Nathan Stone."

"I'm Molly Tremayne, and that was Frank Larkin. He's a brute, and he's been after me for months. Mama and Daddy took a boat to Memphis, and I drove them into town."

"They'd go to Memphis and leave you here alone?"

"Why not? I'm twenty-one years old, and I've lived here all my life."

"Well, you were screeching pretty fierce when the brute—old Frank—drug you out of the wagon. Should I have minded my own business and let him have his way with you?"

"Of course not," she snapped. "It's time he was taught a lesson. Daddy always liked Frank, and he'd just laugh when I'd tell him . . ."

"So old Frank felt like he had a claim on you," Nathan said.

"Yes, damn him. He'd waylay me every chance he got, and . . ."

"So I shot and killed a man who was about to violate you with your daddy's blessing," said Nathan.

"He was going to kill you," she shouted.

"Not until I interrupted his fun," Nathan said. "How do I know he hasn't had you before, and was just comin' back for seconds?"

Nathan caught the foot she drove at his crotch and threw her flat on her back, her long skirt swirling over her head. She directed some very unladylike language at him so hard his ears rang. Nathan caught her in a bear hug, pinning her arms, kissing her hard on the mouth. She fought furiously, but he didn't let up, and she began to respond. His arms went around her waist and hers around his neck. When they finally came up for air it was Molly who spoke.

"No man's ever had me," she said softly, "and none ever will. Not until I'm ready. Come on to the house."

Molly Tremayne was a beautiful woman, with dark shoulder-length hair and deep brown eyes that were almost black. Snow had begun falling, and as the night wore on, Nathan knew he would be there at the dawn. He forgot the dead man in the alley, the vengeance trail that he rode—everything—except that moment. In the lonely years to come, as he rode the long trails, he would not forget young Molly Tremayne, for she was about to leave him a legacy that would haunt him until the day he died.

*   *   *

Cotton Blossom had slept on the hearth, and Molly fed him his breakfast behind the kitchen stove. She then prepared breakfast for Nathan and herself. Little was said until they were finishing their coffee, and it was Molly who finally broke the silence.

"I'll drive you into town for your horse and saddle," she said.

Nathan had told her nothing about himself except that he had returned following four years with the Confederate army. He eyed the girl uneasily, aware that she was living in a dream that soon must become a nightmare. How was he going to leave her? Did he even want to? He had shared her bed last night, and in all probability, he would do so again tonight. She had given him all a woman had to give. Neither spoke as she drove him into town, allowing him time to think. He had gone to war before he'd been old enough to shave, and this was his first experience with a woman. Now he was beset with conflicting emotions, not knowing how he could ride away and leave her, yet knowing that he must. The hold she had on him was strong, but the oath he had taken on his father's grave was stronger. He directed her to the boardinghouse, and when she reined up before it, he stepped down from the buckboard. When she had driven away, he went to his room, retrieving his saddle and bedroll. Taking a loss on most of a week's rent, he crossed the alley and saddled the black horse. Before leaving town, he stopped and bought a copy of the *St. Louis Globe-Democrat*.

There was a piece on the front page of the paper about Frank Larkin's death. Before the police had discovered the body, it had been robbed. Even the dead man's boots had been taken, and robbery was the suspected motive. Nathan sighed. He had killed a man to save a woman's virtue, and had then taken her for himself. And now this woman believed—as she had every right to, after last night—that she had a commitment from Nathan Stone. But she did not know it was a commitment he could not honor without being haunted by the last words of his dying father. Nathan returned to the Tremayne house, rode to the barn, and unsaddled the black horse. Without a word, Molly let him into the house. He sat down at the kitchen table and proceeded to read the rest of the newspaper. When he had finished, he looked up and found her eyes on him. She spoke with some sarcasm.

"Are we just going to sit here and look at one another until it's time to go to bed?"

Nathan felt his face turning nine shades of red and his tongue seemed to have grown to the roof of his mouth. When he finally spoke, it was only to humiliate himself further.

"I .. uh ... was thinkin' of sleepin' in the barn tonight."

To his total surprise, she laughed until tears ran down her cheeks. She then got up, sat on his lap and put her arms around his neck. Embarrassed, unsure of himself, Nathan said nothing. Molly spoke softly.

"I was the ... first?"

"You were," he admitted. "Was it ... I ... that obvious?"

"No," she replied. "It's just that I've never seen a man blush before."

They laughed and Cotton Blossom trotted in from the kitchen to see what was going on. The rest of the day was pleasant, and their second night was spectacular. Lightning struck the next morning during breakfast.

"Now that the war's behind you, what sort of trade do you have in mind, Nathan?" Molly asked.

There it was. She had caught him with a cup of coffee halfway to his lips. Carefully he set the cup down on the table.

"Daddy has influence in town," she continued. "He could secure you a position . . ."

Her voice trailed off as she read the terrible truth in his eyes. Before he spoke, she knew.

"Molly," he said, the words choking him, "I can't stay here. Please, let me tell you what I must do."

She sat there in the stoney silence, and with every word he spoke, he could see her slipping farther and farther away from him. When he had finished, the very life seemed to go out of her, and when she finally spoke, her words were bitter.

"Killing these men will accomplish nothing, Nathan, except that in time you'll sink down to their level."

"Maybe," said Nathan. "but it was my father's dying request. That means something to me."

"And I don't? You can just ride away and forget what we have . . . ?"

"Damn it," he shouted desperately, "I didn't say I'm never comin' back. I will. I just don't . . . know when."

"Then I'll make it easy for you," she shouted. "If you can just ride away, after . . . after . . . this, then don't bother coming back at all. Now, damn you, get out of here, and if you're determined to go straight to hell, then be on your way."

Nathan heard her bolt the door behind him, and with heavy heart he walked to the barn, Cotton Blossom following. Returning to town, he left his horse at the livery. He still had his room at the boardinghouse, so he toted his saddle and bedroll up the stairs, dropped them on the floor, and lay down on the bed. Cotton Blossom lay down next to the saddle, watching him.

"Cotton Blossom," Nathan said, "leave the women

alone. They'll keep you walkin' a thin line between heaven and hell, and come the morning, you never know which side of the line you'll be on."

Having nothing better to do, Nathan went out, bought the latest edition of the *Globe-Democrat* and returned to his room. He stretched out across the bed and on the front page read an account of a bank robbery in Clay County, Missouri. On February 13 the James and Younger gangs had taken sixty thousand dollars from the bank at Liberty, killing one man. The outlaws had made their escape, a posse in pursuit. On page two there was a photograph—an engraving—of a man that brought Nathan to his feet. The accompanying story said the man's name was Bart Hankins, and that he had just returned home to Nevada, Missouri after serving with the Confederacy, and would become the vice president of his father's bank.

"By God," said Nathan aloud, "that's one of them. The damned albino."

There was a map on the wall at the railroad depot, and Nathan hunted for Nevada, finally finding it in western Missouri, almost on the Kansas line.

*   *   *

Four days after arriving in St. Louis, Nathan Stone rode out, again heading west. Having added to his supplies before leaving St. Louis, Nathan avoided towns, keeping to open country. He kept his cook fires small, dousing them before dark. Despite Nathan's precautions, the second day after leaving St. Louis, he discovered two riders on his back trail. Each time he topped a rise he watched for them, and they never gained. He was being followed and when the duo made no attempt to get ahead of him, he could draw but one conclusion. They intended to approach his camp after dark and murder him while he slept. Nathan considered an ambush of his own, but he had no long gun, and this was open country. He could get them within range of his Colt only by allowing them to approach his camp after dark, believing that he slept. With that in mind, he made camp before dark, in a cluster of rocks near a creek. He ate broiled ham, drank hot coffee, and fed Cotton Blossom. He then spread his bedroll, placing some stones under the blankets to give them body. The black horse he picketed near the creek. It was already dark, and he settled down a few yards away from his empty bedroll. He drew and cocked his Colt, his left hand restraining Cotton Blossom. While he appreciated the dog's vigilance, this was no time for a warning growl. Fearing the black horse would nicker a warning, his pursuers would have to approach on foot.

Nathan waited for what he judged to be an hour, and he knew they were coming long before he heard or saw them. Cotton Blossom began to bristle, and Nathan tightened his hold on the dog, lest he growl or bark. There was no moon, but the starlight would be sufficient, for Nathan had chosen his camp carefully. There was no cover. Nathan listened for the telltale snick of hammers being eared back, but heard nothing. The pair would be approaching with their weapons drawn and cocked. Nathan could barely see them in the dim starlight, but that didn't matter. The next move was theirs, and if it was what Nathan expected, it would be their last. Suddenly there was a roar of gunfire as the pair cut down on Nathan's empty bedroll. He fired four times. Once at each muzzle flash, and once to the right and left. Nathan heard what might have been the sound of a fallen pistol striking rock, and then nothing. But the tenseness had gone out of Cotton Blossom, all the assurance Nathan needed that the threat was no more. He took his bedroll, and with Cotton Blossom following, made his way to the creek where his horse was picketed. His pursuers wouldn't be going anywhere. He would view the grisly remains by the light of day.

*   *   *

St. Joseph, Missouri. February 18, 1866.

Less than a week after their successful robbery of the bank at Liberty, Missouri, the James and Younger gangs were about to strike again. But not all the outlaws favored what Jesse had planned.

"Damn it, Dingus," said Frank, "it's too soon. We stirred up a hornet's nest at Liberty. There'll be Pinkertons everywhere."

"Hell, there's *always* Pinkertons everywhere," Jesse said irritably. "Now I say we're goin' to take this bank at Nevada, Missouri. It's south of here maybe a hundred and

forty miles, and if there's a posse, we won't be that far
from Indian Territory."

"Jesse," said Cole Younger, "Frank's right about them
Pinkertons. We got sixty thousand at Liberty. Ain't that
enough to satisfy you?"

"There'll never be enough to satisfy me," said Jesse. "If
you ain't got the sand to ride with us, you can always go
home to your mama."

*   *   *

With the dawn, Nathan had a look at the two men he
had shot. They were well dressed, well armed, and were
carrying—between them—three hundred dollars in gold.
He took the gold and their Colts, and when he found their
picketed horses, discovered that a third horse was equipped
with a packsaddle. He loosened the diamond hitch, removed the tarp, and found a side of bacon, tins of con-
densed milk, coffee, sugar, and beans. On one of the
saddled horses there was a Henry rifle, and in the saddlebag
a considerable supply of ammunition for the weapon. Looping the reins about the saddle horns, Nathan slapped the
two saddled horses on their rumps. He spread the canvas
over the packsaddle and retied the hitch. Nathan felt no
guilt in the taking of the pack horse, guns, ammunition and
gold that had belonged to the pair of bushwhackers. Hadn't
they been about to rob and murder him? He saddled the
black and mounted. Then, with the packhorse on a lead
rope and Cotton Blossom trotting along behind, Nathan
rode west. To Nevada, Missouri.

Chapter 3

❖❖❖

Nevada, Missouri. February 22, 1866.

It was late afternoon when Nathan picketed the black horse behind a vacant store building and approached the town's main street afoot. For so small a town, the bank seemed elaborate. It was built of brick, with double glass doors and a plate-glass window across most of the front. There were four teller cages, and to the right and left of the lobby a series of closed doors that likely were offices. As vice president of the bank, Bart Hankins would surely occupy one of them. The bank's hours were painted on one of the glass doors. It opened at eight and closed at four, except for Saturday when it closed at noon. Closing time was now but a few minutes away. An enormous oak stood before the entrance to the building, and a white wooden bench had been built in circular fashion around the tree's trunk. As though weary, Nathan sank down on the bench. He tilted his hat over his eyes, studying the interior of the bank through the plate-glass window. He felt foolish, like he was casing the place with the intention of robbing it. But there were four closed doors at each end of the lobby, and Nathan expected Hankins to emerge from one of them. He had no idea where or how he would confront the man. At this point he had no plan beyond finding Hankins, and if all else failed, he needed to know in which of these offices he would find the man. Nathan was sure of just one thing. When the moment came for Hankins to die, it must be face to face. More than anything else, Nathan Stone wanted this man and his cowardly companions to know *why* they were dying.

Nathan watched as one of the tellers locked the front doors. Within a few minutes a heavy, silver-haired man emerged from one of the doors to the left of the lobby.

Using a key, he unlocked the front door, let himself out, and locked the door behind him. This, Nathan guessed, was the elder Hankins. He departed afoot, and that meant the family lived in town. When the fourth door to the right of the lobby opened, Nathan had his first look at one of the men he had sworn to kill. It had to be Bart Hankins, for he had a mane of white hair and the palid complexion of an albino. He fitted old Malachi's description perfectly. He too departed the bank afoot, and Nathan allowed him a good start before following. The Hankins residence was at the far end of the town's main street, and it stood out like a brahma bull in a sheep pen. It was a two-story, built of stone that had blackened to an ugly gray, and was surrounded by a heavy wrought-iron fence. The iron stanchions were inches apart, standing taller than a man's head, and the uppermost tips were pointed, like spear heads. Nathan watched Hankins unlock the gate and let himself in, to be met by a pair of long-legged hounds. Nathan was thankful that Cotton Blossom had learned to remain with the picketed horse.

Nathan was shocked. The house seemed more impregnable than the bank itself. Getting to Bart Hankins wasn't going to be easy. He must waylay the man before he reached the formidable house or after he departed it, or confront him within the bank itself. Nathan hadn't much time. The longer he remained in town, the more likely he would be remembered. He returned to the picketed black horse, and with Cotton Blossom following, rode out of town. He couldn't afford the luxury of a night in town. Any hotel desk clerk would remember a stranger. With the dawn, he would go as near the Hankins mansion as he dared and wait for the albino to leave. If for any reason he lost Hankins after he left the house in the morning, it would leave Nathan with but one dangerous option. He would have to confront Hankins within the bank itself.

*   *   *

Nevada, Missouri. February 23, 1866.

Nathan had camped far from town in a secluded draw where there was good water and graze. There he picketed the packhorse. He reached town before dawn, leaving his

horse and Cotton Blossom behind one of the saloons that
fronted the main street. The saloon wouldn't be open for
hours, and Nathan leaned against the corner of the building, looking down the street toward the Hankins mansion.
His heart leaped when the huge front door opened and
Bart Hankins stepped out. But the albino wasn't alone. The
older man who almost had to be the elder Hankins was
with him. That would have been bad enough, but the two
men were accompanied by a young girl. Locking the big
iron gate behind them, the trio headed down the main
street toward the bank. Cursing under his breath, Nathan
returned to the alley, mounted the black, and rode to the
farthest end of town. He circled around behind the bank,
and in a scrub oak thicket, left his horse.

"Stay, Cotton Blossom," he said.

Nathan waited until he was sure the Hankinses had entered the bank, and he allowed enough time for the four
tellers to become busy. He must enter the albino's office
unobserved. After the shooting, seconds would count. He
would have but a few seconds to make his escape. Nathan
entered the bank and walked rapidly past the first three
doors to the right of the lobby. When he reached the
fourth, he opened it, stepped inside, and closed the door
behind him. The surprise was total, and Hankins' reaction
was anger.

"It's customary to knock," he snapped.

"I didn't see the need for formalities," Nathan said
mildly. "I'm here to kill you."

*   *   *

As Nathan entered Hankins' office, six riders reined up
behind the bank. There was Frank and Jesse James, and
the four Younger brothers, Jim, John, Bob, and Cole.

"Frank," said Jesse, "you was in there yesterday. Let's
go over it all one more time."

"Four teller's cages," Frank said. "Bank officers behind
closed doors."

"Working from the left, then," said Jesse, "you take the
first teller, I'll take the second, and Bob, you and Cole take
the third and fourth. Just the big bills. Jim, you and John
hold the horses."

"Hell," growled Jim Younger, "I'd like to go inside. Why do I always have to hold the horses?"

"By God," Jesse snarled, "because I said so. Cole, you and Bob wait for me and Frank to get inside. Then you move fast. We'll hit all four tellers at once. Crack some heads if you have to, but no shooting."

*   *   *

"I've never seen you before in my life," said Bart Hankins. "I've done you no wrong."

"Think back to last November," said Nathan grimly. "Back to Charlottesville, Virginia. You were one of the seven scum who murdered my family and fired the house."

"You have no proof," Hankins said.

"I have an eyewitness," said Nathan.

"You'd shoot an unarmed man?"

"No," said Nathan, taking an extra Colt from his waistband. "I'll lay this Colt on the desk and you can go for it. It's more of a chance than you deserve. Stand up."

Hankins got to his feet, but his eyes were not on the Colt that lay on the desk. It was all that saved Nathan. Hankins had palmed the sleeve gun and the .41-caliber derringer's slug ripped a furrow in the desktop just as Nathan's slug tore into Hankins's belly. Hankins fell back down into his swivel chair. Nathan snatched the Colt from the desk and was out the door and running.

Frank and Jesse James and the Younger brothers had just approached the teller's cages, their Colts drawn, then the two shots ripped the early-morning stillness. After a moment of shocked hesitation, the four outlaws dropped their canvas sacks and broke for the door. Nathan Stone was already out of the bank and around the corner when Frank and Jesse hit the front door, the Youngers at their heels. Closed doors within the bank's lobby opened and Colts roared. The citizens of the little town had reacted swiftly, and from points along the main street, rifles began crashing. A hail of lead slammed into the wooden door frame and there was an explosion of shattered glass. Bob Younger dropped his Colt when a slug tore into his upper right arm. The four outlaws, reaching their horses, snatched the reins and mounted on the run. As the six rode away at a fast gallop, there was shouting behind them as the town mounted a posse.

Following the shooting of Hankins, it had taken Nathan Stone but a few seconds to escape the bank, but he was well aware that his action had foiled a bank robbery. Mounting the black horse, he rode west at a fast gallop, Cotton Blossom loping along beside him. A clatter of hoofbeats told him he was being pursued. There hadn't been enough time for a posse, so it had to be the outlaws. He looked back and there were six of them, the lead rider coming hard. They were already within pistol range, but a posse would be coming. They were going to ride him down. Nathan drew his Colt but thought better of it. Any gunfire would aid a posse that would quickly gun down Nathan Stone as one of the fleeing outlaws. The lead rider was gaining, and Nathan knew what was coming. He kicked free of his stirrups, and when the other man left his saddle, the two of them were flung to the ground in an ignominious tangle of arms and legs. Nathan fought free, rolled, and came up with his Colt. But so had his antagonist. It was a standoff, and they faced one another grimly.

"Go ahead," said Nathan, "but I'll take you with me."

The rest of the outlaws had reined up. "Jesse," Frank shouted, "leave it be. There's a posse coming. Mount up and let's ride."

"I been hit," Bob Younger cried, "and I'm bleedin' like a stuck hog."

"Hell, no," snarled Jesse James, "I ain't leavin' it be. This varmint got us the blame for a robbery and we ain't got a dollar to show for it."

"Well, this ain't no time to shoot him," Cole Younger said, "with a posse on our tail. Bob's hurt. Besides, since when has it bothered you what you was blamed for?"

"Since the damn Pinkertons started raisin' the price on my head," said Jesse. "Just like they'll be raisin' it on yours."

"Dingus," Frank said, "that posse will be mounted by now. A shot will bring them on the run. Now, damn it, you mount up and ride, or the rest of us will leave you standin' here."

Reluctantly, Jesse James holstered the Colt. He turned cold blue eyes on Nathan Stone and the look in them bordered on madness. When he spoke, his voice was almost inaudible, an evil hiss.

"You damn spoiler, if our trails ever cross again, I'll kill you, whatever it costs me. That ain't a threat, but a promise, and Jesse James keeps his promises."

The six of them mounted and rode away at a fast gallop to the southwest. Nathan mounted and rode due west, toward the Kansas line, where he had hidden the pack-horse. His one hope was that the posse wouldn't forsake the trail of the six outlaws to pursue him. While he had incurred the wrath of Jesse James, he decided it had been worth it. Unknowingly, the outlaws had drawn attention away from him, and the killing of Bart Hankins during the aborted robbery might become a mystery that would never be solved. Hankins, however, had known why he died.

Taking no chances, Nathan rode at a slow gallop, concealing his trail as best he could. He could hardly blame Jesse James for his fury. The outlaws had taken the blame while Nathan had taken his vengeance. But there was yet a debt unpaid. If Nathan Stone and Jesse James met again, one of them would die.

Indian Territory, from what Nathan had heard, was a desolate area where renegades on the dodge holed up. He doubted the James and Younger gangs would ride any farther into the territory than was necessary to lose the posse. Being from Missouri, they never strayed far from it. Nathan reined up and dismounted, resting his horse. There was no evidence of riders on his back trail.

"Cotton Blossom," said Nathan to the panting dog, "we have a decision to make. Hankins is dead, but where in tarnation are the rest of the varmints? Where do we go from here?"

While Nathan might be taken for an owlhoot in his own right, he had no fear of being recognized as a result of his brief association with the James and Younger gangs. The killers he sought wouldn't know they were being pursued, so there was little chance he'd find them hiding in Indian Territory.

"Those killers rode west," Nathan said, "and I'd bet a horse and saddle one or two of them are from Texas. Since we don't know for sure where this trail's taking us, Texas is a good place to start. Let's ride south, Cotton Blossom."

Nathan and Cotton Blossom passed the villages of Par-

sons and Coffeyville, Kansas without stopping, keeping out
of sight. The little towns were not too far from the Missouri
village where the killing had taken place. Nathan rode until
he was sure he was well into Indian Territory before stopping. There was a poorly painted sign nailed to the trunk
of a tree that told him he was approaching Muscogee.
While he doubted he would find the killers he sought in
Indian Territory, it would cost him nothing but a little time
and the price of a beer or two to visit some of the saloons.
He reined up before the Cherokee Saloon, half-hitching his
mount and the packhorse to the rail.

"Stay, Cotton Blossom," he said.

Four men sat at a back table, a bottle, glasses, and a
deck of cards before them. They eyed Nathan as he walked
to the bar and ordered a beer. He paid, took the brew, and
leaning his back against the bar, returned the stare of the
men at the table. They suddenly lost interest in him, and
one of them began shuffling the cards. Nathan finished his
beer, set the glass on the bar, and headed for the door. He
could sense the eyes of the barkeep and the four men at the
table on his back, wondering who he was. That he might be
on the dodge didn't concern them, but the possibility that
he might be a lawman—perhaps from Fort Smith—did. He
visited the other two saloons where the few patrons viewed
him with the same suspicion. Before he rode out of town,
Nathan stopped at the general store and bought a second
holster for his extra Colt. He now wore a tied-down Colt
on each hip, and after endless hours of practice, could draw
and fire with either hand. He rode on, pausing on a ridge
to be sure he wasn't followed.

Finding a spring, Nathan stopped and cooked his supper
well before dark. After watering his horses, he rode a mile
or more until he found a draw with ample graze. There he
picketed his horses and spread his blankets, secure from
the chill night wind. Cotton Blossom would warn him of
any intruders. But the night was peaceful enough, and he
returned to the spring for breakfast. The real danger in
Indian Territory, as he was well aware, was the possibility
of being murdered or robbed by renegades. But a change
had taken place that eased his mind considerably. No
longer content to just trot along behind the packhorse, Cotton Blossom had taken to ranging ahead and occasionally
falling behind. The hound seemed to sense Nathan's cau-

tion, and in the late afternoon, Cotton Blossom caught up, after scouting the back trail. He whined and trotted back a few yards the way he had come. Nathan reined up.

"Somebody on our back trail, Cotton Blossom?"

Cotton Blossom growled low in his throat. A few yards ahead was a mass of head-high boulders, and on a ridge almost a mile distant, a dense thicket. Nathan kicked his horse into a slow gallop. The animals must be picketed far enough ahead that they wouldn't nicker when the pursuers drew near. Quickly Nathan half-hitched the reins of his mount and those of the packhorse to a scrub oak, well within the thicket. Taking his Henry from the boot, he ran back down the slope to the distant pile of boulders, Cotton Blossom at his heels. They didn't have long to wait. There were three riders, and the first man Nathan thought he recognized from the poker table at the Cherokee Saloon. Nathan waited until the trio had ridden past and then stepped out behind them.

"That's far enough," Nathan said. "You're covered. Rein up."

He added emphasis to his words, cocking the Henry. "Now," said Nathan, "wheel your horses around to face me, and keep your hands away from your guns."

The three turned to face him, their hands shoulder high.

"I reckon," Nathan said grimly, "the three of you have some good reason for following me."

"This is free range," said the man Nathan remembered from the saloon. "We can ride where we damn please, and we don't owe you nothin'. Besides, we wasn't trailin' you."

"I don't believe you," Nathan said. "Using a thumb and finger, lift those guns and drop them. Then dismount."

Slowly they lowered their hands to the butts of their pistols, but the third man—the one farthest from Nathan—made a fatal mistake. He drew. Even as his finger tightened on the trigger of the Colt, a slug from Nathan's Henry ripped into his belly, tossing him over the rump of his horse to the ground. The remaining riders carefully lifted their pistols and dropped them. Then they dismounted.

"Now," said Nathan, "the two of you start walking. Back the way you came."

"Damn you," one of the men snarled, "it's a thirty-mile walk, an' we got no food or water."

"Then I'll just shoot the pair of you," Nathan said, "and solve all your problems." He cocked the Henry.

Without another word they lit out down the back trail in a shambling run. The only one of the trio who hadn't spoken paused, and looking back, made a final plea.

"Ain't you white enough to at least let us keep our guns? They's killer Injuns in these parts."

"Then you skunks should feel right at home among 'em," said Nathan. The Henry roared again, the slug kicking dust just inches from the man's boots. The pair stumbled on. Nathan gathered the two discarded weapons and the Colt from the hand of the dead man. All the weapons he placed in the saddlebags of one of the horses. Gathering the reins, he led the three horses up the rise to where his own mount and packhorse waited. He had another two hours of daylight. He would ride another twenty miles before making camp. In the morning he would dispose of the trio's weapons and turn their horses loose.

*   *   *

Red River. February 28, 1866.

Nathan rode shy of the little village of Durant, Indian Territory, and crossed the Red River into north Texas. While he knew little about the state, he believed he was far enough west that he could ride due south and reach Dallas or Fort Worth. By now he was certain the Federals had taken control of the state government. A mounted, armed stranger would be immediately suspect. Even more so one who led a packhorse. With the military in control, he dared not let it be known he was on a manhunt, riding a vengeance trail. If he rode through towns where soldiers were garrisoned, he would undoubtedly be questioned, forced to reveal his reason for being in Texas. On the other hand, if he avoided the towns and the soldiers, there was little likelihood he would ever find the killers he was seeking. One thing never changed, whoever had control of the reins of government. There would be saloons, thimblerig men, and slick-dealing gamblers.

"Cotton Blossom," Nathan said, "first big town we come to, I reckon I'll mosey through some of the saloons. I can slick deal when I have to. If we find the tinhorns at work in the saloons, then I reckon old Nathan Stone can become a gambler. At least in the eyes of the Federals."

It was a questionable profession at best, but more than one man made his living riding from town to town, spending his life hunched over a poker table in one saloon after another. Nathan still had most of the stake his father had left him, and all the gold he had taken from the outlaws and renegades he had been forced to shoot. He was well-enough heeled to put up a decent front for a while, and a good enough poker player that he could win more than he lost. Fort Worth had always been a Federal garrison, even before the war, and he suspected the fort might now be deploying Federal troops throughout north Texas. Why not ride immediately to Fort Worth, have them challenge his presence in Texas, and test his new identity as a knight of the green cloth? With that in mind, he rode on, more confident of the opportunity to continue his manhunt unmolested by the occupying Federals.

*   *   *

Fort Worth, Texas. March 2, 1866.

As a civilian in a state occupied by the military, Nathan was required to report to the commanding officer and state his business. When the young corporal who had escorted Nathan to Captain Ferguson's office had departed, the officer eyed Nathan critically, his gaze lingering on the pair of thonged-down Colts. He spoke before Nathan was allowed to introduce himself.

"The south is under Reconstruction," Ferguson said bluntly. "Men who fought against the Union are not permitted to bear arms."

"I'm from Kansas," Nathan lied. "I have no argument with the Union. I make my living, such as it is, at the card table."

For a long moment Ferguson said nothing, and Nathan suspected he had lost some ground with the captain. When he finally spoke, there was a coldness in his voice.

"While we don't encourage it, there is no law against professional gambling. You will, however, be limited to the saloon at the sutler's, and if you instigate trouble, you'll find yourself pulling time in the stockade."

"Captain," Nathan said, his eyes boring into Ferguson's, "I'm not a man to start trouble, but I've finished some in my time. When I'm prodded, I don't hang my tail between my legs and run. I stand my ground."

"Your choice," said Ferguson. "You've had your warning."

Nathan responded to that by letting himself out the door and closing it behind him. He had picketed his horses outside the fort, where the post's horses and mules grazed. There was no livery, and had there been, he doubted it would have been available to him and his animals. He unsaddled both his horses and the sentry allowed him to bring his saddle and packsaddle inside the gate. Other dogs wandered about the post, so Nathan allowed Cotton Blossom to follow. The hound had learned not to follow Nathan into a building without permission. Cotton Blossom trotted to one end of the long porch and lay down to wait. A post the size of Fort Worth required a large sutler's and an equally large saloon. There was a forty-foot bar of polished oak and a brass rail that ran the length of it. The floor was of oak, with an ample array of brass spittoons. There were two rows of hanging lamps, one running the length of the bar, and the other illuminating the string of tables that filled the other half of the saloon.

All the tables were occupied by men drinking, playing poker, or both. It was as good time and place as Nathan was likely to find, when it came to the launching of his new career. He wandered among the tables, listening to men talk. The names of six killers were branded forever into his mind, and when men drank and talked, there was always the chance he might hear one of those hated names. Finally, he paused at a table where the fourth chair was unoccupied. One of the players was a thin young man with spectacles who might have been a storekeeper or hotel desk clerk. The other two men might have been buffalo hunters, bullwhackers, or outlaws on the dodge. Each wore a Colt, a faceful of whiskers, and a hat tipped low over his eyes.

"Care if I sit in?" Nathan asked.

"You got money," said one of the bearded ones, "come on."

Nathan dropped five double eagles on the table and sat down. There was a five-dollar limit, and Nathan lost twenty dollars before he finally won a pot. The thin young man with the spectacles appeared to be the big loser, and soon dropped out.

"Hell," said one of the bearded men, "why don't we make this interestin'? Let's raise the limit to twenty dollars."

"Too rich for my blood, Driggers," said his companion. "I'm foldin'."

"What about you, stranger?" said Driggers. "I'm Jason Driggers, and I take my poker serious."

"So do I," Nathan said. "I'm Nathan Stone."

The pot quickly reached three hundred dollars, neither man willing to fold. Word quickly spread, and men drifted from other tables. The man who claimed this pot would need some hell of a poker hand and the nerve to back it. The showdown came when Nathan raised another twenty dollars, raising the pot to five hundred dollars. He had just been dealt a third king and thought he knew what was coming. Driggers was about to deal the cards when Nathan spoke.

"Lay the cards on the table, Driggers. I want somebody else to deal this hand. Somebody with no stake in the game."

"By God," shouted Driggers, kicking back his chair, "are you accusin' me of cheatin'?"

"I'm accusing you of nothing," Nathan said. "We'll let the next draw decide that. You," he said to the slender young man who dropped out of the game, "come deal this hand. But before he deals the cards, Driggers, you and me are going to have an understanding. I have three kings, and I'm pretty damn sure the next card on the top of that deck is the king of diamonds. I'm equally sure the card on the bottom of the deck is an ace. As you know, I have three kings, and the average gambler, drawing a fourth king, would raise. But I'm not the average gambler, Driggers. I believe you're holding three aces and that the card on the bottom of the deck is the fourth ace. I'm sure enough that I'll challenge you, if you have the guts to accept. If the top card isn't the fourth king and the bottom card isn't the fourth ace, then you have my apologies, and the pot's yours."

"Hell no," bawled Driggers. "I'll shoot any man layin' a hand on them cards."

But Driggers froze with his hand on the butt of his pistol.

Nobody had seen Nathan Stone draw, but suddenly in his right hand there was a Colt, cocked and rock steady.

"Morris," somebody shouted, "deal that last hand."

Morris—the thin young man with the spectacles—slid the card from the top of the deck and turned it face up. It was the fourth, the king of hearts. There was a shout from the onlookers, and Jason Driggers's face paled. He knew what was coming. Morris again took a card from the deck, this time, from the bottom. It was the ace of diamonds.

"Now," said Nathan, "show your hand, Driggers."

There was no way out. Driggers dropped his cards on the table, and three of them were aces. Desperately he turned to the angry, disgusted faces of the men who surrounded him and tried to bluff his way out.

"You can't prove a damn thing," he shouted. "You can't accuse me of bottom dealin'."

"No," somebody shouted, "but you sure as hell was plannin' to. I never seen a sweeter setup. You just played your last card here, you damn cheat. Won't none of us set in with you again. Now git up and git the hell out of here."

Driggers kicked back his chair and got to his feet, his face livid. He glared across the table at Nathan, and in his eyes was all the venom of a rattler about to strike. He spoke almost in a whisper.

"Someday, somewhere, I'll kill you."

"You can try," said Nathan, "but I'll be careful not to turn my back on you."

Then came the ultimate insult. The men who had witnessed Driggers's disgrace laughed. Driggers ran from the saloon.

"Belly up to the bar," Nathan said. "The drinks are on me."

Nathan endured the back-slapping and congratulations of the patrons in the saloon. He had established himself as a gambling man. It had been a slick piece of work, something men could appreciate, and the story would follow him. But the bartender had a word of caution.

"Driggers has had that comin' for a long time. He's killed men before, but he's a low-down, back-shootin' varmint, and there ain't been no evidence. He's got kin at Weatherford and Lexington, down in Lee County. Some of 'em are damn near as sorry as he is. You ride careful."

"Thanks," Nathan said. "I aim to do that."

After one night at Fort Worth, Nathan rode south, bound for Austin. He saw nobody, and after he had watered his horses at a spring, sought a coulee where he might safely spend the night. Cotton Blossom would awaken him if danger came close. But darkness was an hour away and the danger didn't wait. A distant rifle roared twice, and Nathan Stone slumped to the ground, blood welling from a head wound. Cotton Blossom whined, licking Nathan's face, but he lay unmoving ...

Chapter 4

It was well past dark when Nathan finally stirred. His head
hurt like seven kinds of hell. His left eye was swollen shut
and the left side of his face was crusted with dried blood.
Cotton Blossom trotted anxiously around him. Nathan was
but a few feet from the creek and he crawled there on
hands and knees. He slacked his burning thirst and then
buried his aching head in the cooling water. The shock of
it cleared his head and he was able to cleanse his wound.
The slug had struck him just above the left eye, ripping a
furrow along the left side of his head, just above his ear.
When he had washed away the dried blood, the wound
began bleeding again. Gripping a stirrup, he staggered to
his feet. He leaned against the horse, clinging to the saddle
horn while he gained strength in his legs. He had already
unpacked the packhorse before he'd been shot. Finally he
gained enough strength to remove the saddle from his
horse. He took an undershirt from his saddlebag, and returning to the creek, cleaned and bandaged his wound.
Then, without even removing his boots, he lay down, his
head on his saddle.

"Keep your eyes and ears open, Cotton Blossom. Tonight I have to rest, but come the morning, I have a debt
to pay."

*   *   *

Nathan awoke with an aching head and feet unsteady.
He got a small fire going, put the coffeepot on to boil,
and began broiling hunks of bacon for himself and Cotton
Blossom. He drank the strong coffee directly from the pot,
and again resting his head on his saddle, waited for the
hurt to subside. When he felt strong enough, he saddled
the black, and leaving the packhorse picketed, rode east. It

was from there the shots had come, and unless the bushwhacker had ridden all night, it was unlikely that he had
reached Fort Worth. Wherever he had ridden, he had left
a trail, and Nathan soon found it. It led northeast, and
Nathan suspected his man wasn't riding back to Fort
Worth, but to Dallas or some point beyond. Nathan rode
at slow trot. Cotton Blossom, sensing they were on a trail,
loped far ahead.

Dallas sheriff Eb Chasteen listened to Nathan's story
with little enthusiasm. "So you got yer skull creased," he
said. "You seen the hombre that done it?"

"No," said Nathan irritably, "but yesterday I exposed a
card cheat name of Jason Driggers in Fort Worth. He
promised to kill me, and he's the only bastard in Texas
with any reason to. I trailed him here, and when I find him,
there's goin' to be a reckoning. I just wanted to be sure
there'll be no misunderstanding between you and me after
I find Driggers."

"You got no proof this gent took a shot at you," Chasteen said. "Just your suspicions. Kill a man without provable cause, and you'll find yourself before a firing squad or
on the way to the gallows."

They stood on the boardwalk outside the sheriff's office,
and from an alley on the far side of the street, a rifle roared
once, twice, three times.

With the first shot, Nathan hit the boardwalk, drawing
his Colt as he went down. The sheriff was flung back
against the wall as a slug smashed into his shoulder. On his
belly, Nathan fired three times into the mouth of the alley,
but there was no return fire. Colt in his hand, Nathan
scrambled to his feet and in a zigzag run, lit out toward
the alley. There was no place for the gunman to hide between the store buildings. For the second time Driggers
had attempted a cowardly ambush, and Nathan doubted he
had the guts for a standup fight. His horse would be nearby
and he would run. Nathan caught up to him in the alley,
behind a saloon, already mounted. Driggers kicked the
horse into a fast gallop just as Nathan fired. The slug missed
Driggers but burned a gash along the horse's flank. The
animal screamed, began to pitch, and piled Driggers.

"Get up," said Nathan, holstering his Colt. "I'll give you
more of a chance than you deserve, you back-shootin'
skunk."

Nathan stood with his left thumb hooked in his pistol belt, for his left-hand Colt was fully loaded. Driggers got to his hands and knees, then to his feet. He knew what was coming, and sweat dripped off his chin.

"When you're ready," Nathan said.

Nathan waited, not making his move until Driggers slapped leather. Nathan drew left-handed, and two slugs tore into Driggers, while lead from his opponent's Colt kicked up dust at his feet. Driggers stumbled backward, fell, and moved no more.

The gunfire brought men on the run. One of them had heard of Driggers's disgrace in Fort Worth the day before. He told the story and it was repeated. It would spread across the frontier, and Nathan Stone would become respected as a gambling man and chain-lightning with a pistol, able to draw and fire a deadly Colt with either hand.

Ignoring the men who had gathered, Nathan reloaded both his Colts and took his time walking back to the sheriff's office. He found Chasteen stretched out on his desk, minus his shirt, a doctor dressing his wound.

"Driggers is up yonder behind a saloon," said Nathan. "Are you satisfied I had provable cause?"

"Yeah," said Chasteen grudgingly. "Now ride on."

Nathan rode out the way he had come, ignoring the questions of men who had gathered outside the sheriff's office. Let the sullen, appointed lawman do his own explaining. Nathan returned to the camp where he had left his packhorse. His head ached and he took the time to again cleanse and bind his wound. He then watered his horses and rode south, bound for Austin, wondering if his newly acquired reputation would be there waiting for him. There was no help for it. It was a thing with which he must live. Or die.

*   *   *

Waco, Texas. March 6, 1866.

Nathan found the Federals had not yet taken over the town of Waco. The sheriff was an amiable old fellow named Sid Hanks.

"I ain't got no prejudices ag'in gamblers," said Hanks. "If you end up shootin' somebody, or somebody blows out your light, then you'd best have the cash in your poke for a buryin'. We was broke 'fore the war, and we sure as hell ain't got no money now."

Nathan liked the looks of Waco. He tied both his horses to the rail before a saloon called the Lily Belle. Obviously the place had been named for the lady herself, for a full length painting of her—wearing only a smile—graced most of one wall. The barkeep said, "B'longs to old Sam Prater. Sam's grandpappy had money. Left Sam this place, along with a two-story house big enough to sleep half of Waco. Old Sam's three daughters takes in boarders when they's any to take in."

"Sheriff Hanks had no objection to gambling," said Nathan. "Do you have a regular game here?"

"Not any more. House dealer quit and left town by popular demand. You lookin' for work?"

"Maybe," Nathan said. "I can handle the cards, but I deal an honest game."

"Faro?"

"Yes," said Nathan, "but I don't have a box."

"We have that," the barkeep said. "Make yourself comfortable. Judge Prater will be along in a while, and you'll need to talk to him."

"Judge?"

"Old Sam's been judge as far back as I can remember," said the barkeep. "Hell, he's got enough kin in this county to keep him in office forever. By the way, I'm Ira Watkins."

"I'm Nathan Stone." He said no more. The barkeep's eyes dipped quickly to the pair of tied-down Colts and he just as quickly looked away.

"Is there a hotel in town?" Nathan asked, after the silence had dragged on for a while.

"No," said Watkins. "Don't need one. Not with the Prater house. Ain't a soul livin' there right now but the judge and his three daughters."

Nathan said nothing, but the question was so obvious, the talkative barkeep answered it anyway.

"Too many men went to war and not enough come back," said Watkins. "It's got to be worryin' the judge, what he's goin' to do with them three females. Eulie's thirty-five if she's a day, while Eunice and Eldora's right on her heels."

Nathan kept his silence. If the old Judge suddenly appeared, he would have no way of knowing that Nathan hadn't been asking these questions the talkative barkeep was so helpfully answering.

When Judge Sam Prater arrived, he looked every bit as stern and unbending as Nathan had expected. He stepped through the batwing doors and paused. He wore a frock coat, boiled shirt with string tie, dark trousers, a top hat, bushy sideburns, and a full white beard. His eyes rested on Nathan as though prepared to pronounce judgment for a crime of which only he was aware. He eventually cut his eyes to Ira Watkins and the barkup spoke nervously.

"His name's Nathan Stone," said Watkins. "I told him we was lookin' for a house dealer and he says he can handle the cards. I told him he'd have to talk to you."

"Room and board and ten percent of the take," said the judge, turning his hard old eyes on Nathan. "No drinking on the job. You'll come on at seven and be here until close. You're off Sundays because we're closed. I want an honest game, no slick dealing, and if you shoot anybody, I won't side you. It'll be strictly between you and the law. Any questions?"

"I have a horse, a packhorse, and a dog," Nathan said.

"There's a barn behind the house," said Prater, "and all three animals are welcome. I'll have the cook feed the dog table scraps. Come on. I'll take you to the house and then you can unsaddle your horses at the barn."

Cotton Blossom eyed the judge suspiciously, trotting along behind the packhorse at a distance greater than usual. To say the Prater house was magnificent wouldn't have done it justice. Nathan counted four chimneys. There were gables and windows everywhere, a full-length porch across the front of the second floor, and from each end of the peaked roof, gargoyles scowled at anybody who chose to look at them. Nathan half-hitched the reins of both horses to the rail and followed the judge to the front door. Cotton Blossom remained with the horses without a command. The hound had no intention of venturing into that house.

Nathan followed the judge into a foyer and there they paused.

"Eulie! Eunice! Eldora!" The judge bawled.

The three women came down the stairs from the second floor, taking their time. They all had shoulder length dark hair and appeared to have been eating too well too often;

from a distance, Nathan couldn't have identified one from another. The judge lined them up like soldiers, introducing them from left to right.

"Eulie's the oldest," said Prater, neglecting to say just *how* old, "and these are her sisters, Eunice and Eldora. Girls, this is Nathan Stone, the new house dealer at the Lily Belle."

Eulie actually smiled, while Eunice and Eldora only nodded.

"Stone," said the judge, "I won't have you toying with the affections of my daughters. If your intentions are anything less than honorable, then you will answer to me."

"Prater," Nathan said coldly, "I'm hiring on as a house dealer, nothing more. I don't take kindly to ultimatums or accusations before I've even had a chance to remove my hat."

Nathan expected the three women to hang their heads in embarrassment and shame, but they were furious.

Eldora spoke, and she was shouting. "Father, that was a perfectly horrid thing to say. Once again you've insulted a man before he's even had time to speak to us. We'll be taking our damned virtue to the grave with us, and we'll owe it all to you."

"Eulie," said the judge, ignoring the outburst, "take Mr. Stone to his room upstairs. Supper is at five, Stone, and I'll expect you at the Lily Belle at seven."

"I'll want my saddlebags," Nathan said.

"Find your room first," said the judge. "Then, when you've unsaddled your horses, you can bring in whatever you wish."

Nathan followed Eulie up the stairs, and while he didn't know if her walk was exaggerated or not, it was enough to get his attention. He didn't want the room at the very head of the stairs, and was relieved when she led him past it. The room they eventually entered was farther down the hall, and there was a window. The head of the iron bed was next to the window, and tied to the leg of the bed was a length of rope. The fire escape. There was an oak dresser with a framed mirror, an upholstered chair, and on one side of the bed, a stand with a pitcher and wash basin. Beneath the stand was a chamber pot. On the dresser was a kerosene lamp. For just a second, Nathan's eyes met Eulie's, and they had both been looking at the half-concealed chamber pot. Eulie winked and it was Nathan who blushed. She paused at the door.

"My room's right next to yours." She smiled. "If there's anything you need."

"Thanks," said Nathan, carefully avoiding her eyes.

She closed the door and Nathan sat down on the bed, fanning himself with his hat. Why was he sweating? He got up, pulled aside the curtain, and looked out. It couldn't be much past two o'clock in the afternoon. He stepped out into the hall and made his way downstairs to the front door. He saw nobody. He went out, leading his horses around the house and toward the barn, a good half a mile distant. Cotton Blossom followed. Reaching the barn, Nathan unsaddled both horses, hefting his saddle and packsaddle to a rail provided for that purpose. Cotton Blossom seemed to have the same feelings about the barn as the house, for he had remained outside. The sound was slight, but it was enough to drop Nathan to his belly, a cocked Colt in his right hand.

"You're a dangerous man," Eldora said, her eyes on the rock-steady Colt.

"Don't you ever again come up behind me without identifying yourself,' Nathan snapped. "What are you doing out here, anyhow?"

"I've lived in this house all my life," she said. "I can come to the barn for any reason or for no reason at all. Maybe I just wanted a better look at you, without my virtuous old daddy protecting my innocence."

Nathan laughed. "He does come on a mite strong." They walked back to the house together, and Nathan saw the curtains move at one of the upstairs windows.

"If you need anything," Eldora said, "my room's next to yours."

"I'd bet my horse and saddle," said Nathan, "that Eunice has a room just across the hall from mine. Or will she be sleeping *in* the hall, just outside my door?"

She laughed, but there was no humor on it. Nathan had no idea how long this shaky alliance in Waco might last. He knew only that he must avoid being lured into a compromising position with any of the predatory women. Returning to his room, he dragged off his boots, shucked his hat, and lay down across the bed. His first few nights at the saloon's table he would have to be careful. Both the players and the house would be testing him, and until he gained a reputation for fairness, his game must not be questioned. It was a dilemma facing every house dealer. He must win often enough to satisfy the house, but not so consistently that his honesty was questioned.

Nathan had begun his duties at the Lily Belle on Tuesday night, and by Thursday was mystified as to why the place needed or wanted a house dealer. For three nights, Nathan sat alone, shuffling the cards and dealing himself hands of solitaire. On Friday night there was a brief three-handed game of draw poker. On Saturday night there was a decent game of five-card stud that began early and lasted until closing time. Judge Prater came in an hour before closing and when the game ended, tallied the winnings.

"Not bad, Stone," Prater grunted. "You've earned twenty dollars."

"Decent for one night's work," said Nathan, "but spread over five nights, it's not all that impressive."

He half-expected Prater to explode, but the judge did not.

"Texans are broke," Prater said, "and you can't get blood out of a turnip. There'll be new blood when the soldiers and administrators from Washington arrive. The commander at Fort Worth tells me north Texas is still short two hundred soldiers."

When the soldiers arrived at Waco there were only six, one of whom was a Sergeant Dixon. Much to Nathan's relief, Judge Prater insisted on having the soldiers take rooms at the Prater house. While the soldiers were Yankees and half the ages of the Prater women, it made no difference.

Having found Nathan Stone close-mouthed, the barkeep was forever talking behind Judge Prater's back.

"Prater's a savvy old *paisano*," said Watkins, when he and Nathan had the saloon to themselves. "Notice how he's suckin' up to them blue bellies? He's had this county in his pocket 'fore they come, and he'll have it sewed up when they're gone. They'll owe him, and if there's any cash or goods comin' from Washington to Texas, old Sam will claim it all."

The presence of the soldiers made some difference, but not so far as Nathan was concerned. The youngest of the trio was more than a dozen years older than he, but that didn't stop them. In a way, Nathan enjoyed the constant attention of the three women, but he had a nagging premonition that all this was leading up to some kind of conclusion he wouldn't like. At some point, in passing their partially open doors, he was treated to views of them in various stages of undress. He didn't doubt that he could have enjoyed a full-blown affair with any one or perhaps all three of the Prater women, but Nathan Stone was no fool. Even while on his best behavior, there were all the elements of disaster, and it wasn't long in coming. While Eunice and Eldora didn't spare him their attention, he had the feeling Eulie was making plans that included him.

Disaster finally struck the first Sunday in July.

*   *   *

Waco, Texas. July 1, 1866.

It had been a big Sunday night at the Lily Belle, and Nathan had not been able to get away from the place until almost four o'clock in the morning. Nathan hadn't been asleep more than two hours when he was awakened by something. At first he thought he was dreaming, and, rolling over, tried to free his mind of the disturbance. But it refused to go away, and Nathan sat up. The sound was human, the persistent moaning of someone in pain. Nathan got up, and wearing only his Levi's, stepped into the hall. The door to Eulie's room stood partially open, but the curtains were drawn and he could see nothing in the darkened room. Without warning, something smashed into the back of Nathan's head. Stunned, he went to his knees, and then face down on the floor. The first conscious awareness came with the screaming of a woman. At first it seemed far away, coming closer as consciousness slowly returned. He opened his eyes and found it was Eulie—a stark-naked Eulie—doing the screaming. He lay on his back, and he no longer wore Levi's. Suddenly the room was full of people. There was Eunice and Eldora wearing dressing gowns, four of the soldiers wearing only blue trousers, and finally worst of all—there stood old Sam Prater in his nightshirt. Eulie was still screaming, and the judge exploded.

"Damn it, woman, shut your mouth and cover yourself!" Nathan sat up, looking around for his Levi's.

"Watch him, Sergeant," bellowed Judge Prater. "He's going to run for it."

"I doubt it," Sergeant Dixon said calmly. "He's not even wearing a pair of socks."

"As a matter of fact," said Nathan furiously, "I'm looking for the Levi's I was wearin' when I was lured in here."

Nathan felt something digging into his bare backside and found it was a piece of glass. Eulie had slugged him with a heavy glass vase. Finally the other two soldiers showed up, and the lot of them stood there as confused as a flock of geese viewing a dried-up pond. Nathan finally spotted his Levi's under the bed and reached for them. His action made Judge Prater aware that Eulie, still bare as a plucked chicken, was staring at Nathan while Sergeant Dixon and his men stared at Eulie. Without a word, Prater snatched a sheet off the bed and flung it over the girl's shoulders. One of the soldiers had helped Nathan to his feet, and although dizzy, he had managed to get into his Levi's.

"What do you want we should do with him, Judge?" Sergeant Dixon asked. "Lock him up in the jail?"

"No," Eulie cried. "He . . ."

"Shut up, woman!" Judge Prater shouted. "Just shut the hell up."

"If it's not asking too much," said Nathan, still furious, "I'd like to return to my room."

"Since it's Sunday," said Judge Prater, "you will be confined to your quarters until in the morning. Then the court will decide what to do with you. Sergeant Dixon, I'll want a man in the hall outside his room and another beneath his window. Search his room and confiscate his weapons."

"Nathan," Eulie began. "Nathan . . ."

Nathan looked at her just once, and the fury in his eyes silenced her. The soldiers followed Nathan to his room. They left him inside, Sergeant Dixon retaining Nathan's belt and holsters, and the twin Colts. He looked questioningly at Judge Prater.

"Leave his weapons with the guard in the hall," said Prater. "One man in the hall and one outside, the six of you can keep watch in eight-hour shifts."

"Judge Prater," said Sergeant Dixon, "I don't think . . ."

"Yes, Sergeant?"

"I don't think there'll be a problem," said the sergeant. He had been about to say this was not the kind of duty of which his superiors would have approved, but thought better of it. After all, it would last only until this poor bastard went before the court in the morning . . .

Still wearing only his Levi's, Nathan stretched out on the bed and tried to think. There was a bloody, egg-sized lump on the back of his head, and it hurt like hell. He silently cursed himself for a greenhorn, having allowed himself to be euchered into this ridiculous predicament. He recalled hearing his father speak of "the old days," when a man and a woman were caught in a compromising situation. A wedding generally followed, the sooner the better. Unless all this became a nightmare from which he suddenly awakened, Nathan thought he knew what lay ahead. Nathan Stone would marry Eulie Prater or go to jail, and one was as unappealing as the other. Did he prefer to have somebody bury a Bowie knife in his gut or shoot him through the head?

Despite his pain and nausea, he laughed. This was the kind of thing, if it continued to its obvious conclusion, that would be told and retold around camp fires until Judgment Day. There was a time to fight and a time to run, and a man stayed alive by knowing the difference. Come dark, Nathan Stone would recover his weapons, saddle his horses, and ride south.

Nathan slept, awoke, and slept again. Time dragged. For his escape to be successful, everybody had to be asleep except the two soldiers on guard, and it must be late enough for the edge of their subconscious to become dulled. Somewhere in the house a clock struck the hour, and Nathan waited impatiently until it struck twelve. He stood where he would be behind the door when it opened and began groaning softly. He must arouse the guard without awakening the rest of the house. He groaned louder.

"What's wrong in there?" the soldier asked softly.

"I . . . I'm sick," Nathan gasped, allowing his words to end in an even more agonized groan.

The door opened a little, but Nathan had blown out the lamp and the room was dark. The soldier took one more step and that was all Nathan needed. His left arm circled the man's throat, cutting off his wind, and he was quickly silenced with a powerful blow from Nathan's right fist. Nathan took his belt, holsters, and weapons from the hall, buckling the familiar rig around his middle. He then grabbed the guard's ladderback chair, securing it under the door knob. He spread-eagled the unfortunate soldier on the bed, and using part of a ripped up sheet, tied the man's arms and legs to the iron bed frame. He then stuffed a piece of the sheet into the unconscious man's mouth so he wouldn't be able to awaken the entire house with his shouts. Nathan secured his saddlebags to his belt. On second thought, he stuffed the rest of the sheet into his saddlebag. He still had to bind and gag another soldier.

Nathan eased back the curtain. He dared not simply slide down the rope intended for a fire escape. He would have to locate the soldier and drop on him from the open window. He could see nothing without raising the window, and he had to do that an inch at a time, expecting at any moment to have it creak and betray him. Slowly, ever so slowly, he raised the window enough to get his head and shoulders through. There was a moon, thank God, and he then understood why he hadn't been able to see the sentry. The man sat with his back against the wall, his head between his knees, probably asleep. Quietly Nathan got himself into position, sitting on the windowsill. He struck the ground on bended knees and walloped the sleeping soldier on the head with the muzzle of his Colt, assuring him an even deeper sleep. Using the rest of the sheet, Nathan bound the unconscious soldier hand and foot, and then tied a gag that would keep the man silent until somebody removed it. There was a slight sound, and Nathan crouched, his Colt cocked and ready. But it was old Cotton Blossom, and he followed as Nathan ran toward the barn.

Nathan led his horse and packhorse out into the moonlight, and in just a matter of minutes was ready to ride. He mounted and rode south, leading his packhorse, Cotton Blossom loping along beside him. Old Judge Sam Prater would be furious, but come the dawn, Nathan would be well out of old Prater's jurisdiction. The Federals, already shorthanded, wouldn't be sending out soldiers to trap a husband for one of Sam Prater's man-hungry daughters.

"I'll just have to be damn careful not to ride through Waco again, Cotton Blossom," Nathan said. "At least as long as old Sam Prater's alive."

It bothered Nathan that he had spent so much time in Prater's saloon but had learned nothing as to the whereabouts of the renegades on his death list. He rode a cold trail with little to guide him beyond the names old Malachi had managed to remember. But when a man rode west with the intention of leaving his past behind, he often took a new name. Still, Nathan thought grimly, these killers likely wouldn't expect pursuit. It was all the edge—all the hope—he had.

Chapter 5

Once he was safely outside Waco, Nathan took his time getting to Austin. The following day being July fourth, he found the town in a festive mood. It was the perfect holiday, right in the middle of the week. It allowed most of the populace several days prior to the event to get gloriously drunk, and the several days following in which to sober up. Nathan made the rounds of most of the saloons, listening to the talk, talking to barkeeps, learning nothing. Leaving town, he rode south until he reached a spring near which there was plenty of graze for his horses. He cooked and ate his supper early, dousing the fire well before dark. But he slept little, for he could hear exploding fireworks, and the distant rattle sounded almost like gunshots. Come first light, Nathan prepared breakfast, fed Cotton Blossom, and rode south, toward San Antonio.

*   *   *

Judge Sam Prater was the first to discover the two soldiers bound and gagged, and wasted no time in venting his wrath on the unfortunate Sergeant Dixon. But for once, Judge Sam Prater had met his match.

"Sir," said the sergeant, "you are not my commanding officer and I am not obliged to take orders from you. Yesterday you took advantage of me and my men, engaging us in a questionable activity of which my superiors would not have approved. As I see it, you detained, against his will, a man who had done no wrong. The military isn't here to assist you in your personal activities, and lest there be some further misunderstanding, I am immediately removing myself and my men from your residence."

Unaccustomed to what he considered insubordination, Sam Porter was reduced to a blubbering fury. By the time he could speak, Sergeant Dixon and his men were gone. Eulie Prater chose that moment to descend the stairs, and her outraged father turned his wrath on her.

"You brazen wench," he bawled, "throwing yourself shamelessly at some no-account gambler, stripping for him ..."

"Don't forget the soldiers," said Eulie calmly.

"Damn the soldiers," Prater shouted. "They allowed that four-flushing coyote to escape. You've disgraced us, damn you, and we've nothing to show for it."

"I'm not ashamed," said Eulie defiantly. "He's a man, and I wanted him. I still do. I just went about getting him the wrong way."

"Maybe it's time I taught you some shame," Prater snarled, removing his wide belt. He caught Eulie halfway up the stairs, and seizing the collar of her gown, ripped it from her body. He took her wrist, flinging her face-down on the stairs, beating her with the belt until his arm grew tired. Without a backward look he left her there, descending the stairs and leaving the house. Three nights later, with only the belongings she could carry behind her saddle, Eulie Prater left, never to return. She rode south, taking with her the two thousand dollars in gold from Judge Sam Prater's cash box.

*   *   *

San Antonio, Texas. July 6, 1866.

There were more soldiers in San Antonio than there had been in Austin, and the government-appointed sheriff eyed Nathan with suspicion. He had made camp south of town, leaving the packhorse and Cotton Blossom there. In postwar Texas, a man appearing too prosperous—leading a packhorse—might be shot in the back for his possessions. To justify his presence, Nathan spent several days playing five-card stud in the Alamo Saloon. He kept all his bets small, attracting no attention. He visited other saloons for brief periods without learning anything about the six men he sought. After four days, he rode south, toward Laredo.

He would follow the border south to Brownsville. If the killers he sought had ridden into Mexico, he believed the logical place for them to have crossed the border would have been the lonely stretch between Laredo and Browns-ville. If, after reaching Brownsville the trail was still cold, he could ride north to Corpus Christi, to Houston, or east-ward to New Orleans. So far he had nothing to show for his time in Texas except the killing of a pair of varmints intent on killing him. Nearing Laredo, Nathan didn't bother riding in. He needed time to think, to plan. He stopped north of town, unsaddled his horse, unloaded the pack-horse, and made camp near a creek.

"By God, Cotton Blossom," he said to the hound, "I'm sick of towns, sick of saloons, tired of shooting and being shot at. I'll spread my blankets and stretch out here by the creek. What could possibly go wrong out here?"

But something could and did. An hour before dark, Cot-ton Blossom growled and then barked, welcoming someone he recognized. And that was when Eulie Prater rode in.

"You showed me the goods and I wasn't interested," Nathan shouted. "Now why in hell are you following me?"

"Who says I'm following you?"

"I say you are," Nathan snapped. "Aren't you?"

"Of course I am," she said calmly. "My dear old daddy sent me."

"I'll just bet he did," Nathan said bitterly. "Did he re-member to send your dowry too?"

"Before I left, he gave me something to remember him by," she said, dismounting. She removed her shirt, dropped her Levi's to her ankles, and turned her back to him. From her shoulders to her knees, her body was a mass of ugly scars, and on top of them was the blue-black bruises of a recent beating.

"Great God Almighty," Nathan said. "You should have shot the heartless old varmint. Nobody would have faulted you."

"I did better than that," she replied. "I cleaned out his cash box and took his favorite horse."

"And just what the hell am I supposed to do with you?" he asked. "You know I'm not lookin' for a woman. You'll only be in the way."

"Do with me what you please," she said, "as long as you allow me to go with you. I can't blame you if you hate me. What I did was wrong, and I'm sorry. Take me on your terms, but take me. I can't go back. Ever."

"I wouldn't want you to," he said, "but I'm a gambler,

and I live in a hard world where it's shoot or be shot. I
have nothing to offer you."

"Oh, but you do," she said. "You're a man. You're every
inch a man, and to a woman, that's the most important
of all."

Nathan unsaddled her horse and Eulie cooked their supper. Eventually she must know of the vengeance trail that
he rode, and he vowed to tell her just as soon as the time
seemed right. She spread her bedroll next to his, beside the
creek. Sometime during the night he found her against him,
her arm flung across his chest. He didn't push her away . . .

*   *   *

In the light of dawn, Nathan had a better look at his new
companion. She saw him appraising her and spoke.

"I cut my hair short and dressed like a man. I thought
that would make it easier on us both."

"Smart thinking," said Nathan, "especially if your heart-
broken old daddy sends somebody looking for you."

"If he sends anybody looking for me," she said bitterly,
"it'll be to take back his gold and hang me for a horse
thief."

"I don't know how this is going to work out," Nathan
said. "I reckon this is goin' to play hell with my nerves,
you dressing and acting alike a man. I spend a lot of time
in saloons, because that's where the gambling is. There may
be drunks with their drawers down. There'll be swearing
and all manner of dirty talk. It's no place for a woman."

"I can't say it won't be a strain on me, remembering to
think, act, and talk like a man," she replied, "but it's the
only way. Besides, this is the frontier, and I can rope, ride,
and shoot. There's a .31-caliber Colt in my saddlebag.
Damn it, I'm not some prissy female with lace on her
drawers."

"I believe you," he said with a grin. "If you *wore* any
drawers, I'd not expect to find any lace on 'em."

They spent a few days and nights in Laredo, and not
once was there any trouble. Eulie played her part well,
and Nathan began breathing a bit easier. It was a strange
relationship that began to appeal to him, for after all they
had gone through at the Prater house, there were few secrets between them. The time Nathan spent in the saloons

was again wasted, for he learned nothing of the killers he was seeking. Leaving Laredo, they took their time riding along the border. When they reached Brownsville, Nathan wanted to cross the river into Old Mexico. Matamoros was just across the border.

*   *   *

Matamoros, Mexico. August 2, 1866.

Matamoros proved to be a squalid little hamlet where chickens wandered aimlessly along the dirt streets. A goat eyed them over a backyard fence. Suddenly gunfire erupted in a rundown shack a hundred yards up the street. A man in dark trousers, frock coat, and top hat backed out the door. His left arm, bloody, hung useless, while in his right hand a Colt roared. He backed into the street only to have a crackle of gunfire begin behind him from a shack on the other side of the street. The border was less than a hundred yards distant, but from the lone gunman's position, it might as well have been a hundred miles.

"Eulie," Nathan shouted, "take the pack horse and ride for the border. I'm going to try and snatch him away from those lobos."

Eulie rode for the border, watching fearfully over her shoulder. It was a fool thing to do, but Nathan galloped his horse down the narrow street, and the little man in the top hat saw him coming. Holstering his Colt, he used his good hand to grasp the one Nathan offered. The rescue was as unexpected as it was impossible, and it took the attackers totally by surprise. Nathan wheeled his horse, and even carrying double, the animal was soon out of range of the hostile guns. Eulie sat her mount on the Texas side of the river, Cotton Blossom beside her. Nathan reined up, allowing the man he had rescued to slide off the rump of the horse. The stranger wore a white silk shirt and a black string tie that matched his dark trousers and frock coat. He removed his top hat, running fingers through several bullet holes. Then he laughed, revealing white, even teeth beneath a flowing moustache.

"Friend," said the little man, "Ben Thompson owes you. Anything I own or ever hope to own, just ask, and it's yours."

"You seemed a mite outgunned," Nathan said. "I reckon your horse is still over there."

"He is," said Thompson, "and some no-account Mex will get a good mount at my expense. What kind of damn fool would pause for a poker hand in such a miserable place as that? They couldn't raise ten pesos if they sold every goat and chicken in the place."

Nathan laughed but Eulie did not. She didn't like this man. He had been shot, he was bleeding, and but for Nathan's heroic rescue, would have been dead. But he laughed, and in his eyes there was excitement, joy, madness.

Nathan Stone didn't know it at the time, but this would become a turning point in his life. He had just become the friend of the notorious Ben Thompson, one of the deadliest killers to ride through the pages of Western history.

As though seeing her for the first time, Thompson turned his eyes on Eulie, and cold chills crept up her spine. She felt as though he were stripping her, looking beyond what she appeared to be, seeing her for what she was. Beneath her male clothing, she felt all the more like a woman, and for one of the few times in her hard life, she was afraid . . .

Chapter 6

❖

Despite all the gunfire, Ben Thompson had suffered only a flesh wound to his left arm, above the elbow. The doctor who tended the wound said nothing. Brownsville was aware there had been shooting in the cantinas across the river, and normally nobody cared. It mattered not if the Mexes got drunk, if they fought, or if they eventually shot one another. But today was different. Two Americans had escaped in a hail of Mexican lead, one of them having ridden into the very teeth of the fight to rescue the other. When Thompson, Nathan, and Eulie left the doctor's office, men had gathered outside a saloon across the street.

"Friends of yours?" Nathan asked with a grin.

"I doubt it," said Thompson, without changing expression. "None of them offered any help when I had a pack of Mexes doing their damndest to ventilate me. I aim to find a livery, buy a horse, and be as far from this town as I can get before dark."

Thompson bought a bay gelding and the trio rode north, within sight of the Gulf of Mexico. Eulie neither trusted nor liked Ben Thompson, And there was little said until they made camp for the night. It wasn't the Western way to ask a man his intentions, so Nathan and Eulie had no notion as to Thompson's until the little man finally volunteered the information.

"I aim to ride north," said Thompson after supper. "Long as you folks are headed my direction, I'll ride with you. That is, if you don't mind."

"Come along," Nathan said, "and welcome. I've never seen the ocean. I aim to follow the coast to Corpus Christi, Galveston, and maybe Houston."

For two days, Ben Thompson spoke only when spoken to, and for the most part, kept his silence. When they rode three abreast, Eulie kept Nathan between herself and

Thompson. Cotton Blossom remained well behind, for he
had no liking for the silent Thompson. It was late in the
afternoon of the third day, when they were approaching
Corpus Christi, that finally Thompson spoke again.

"When I leave here, I'll be riding north. Until then, I
want some town-cooked grub and a hotel bed."

"We have our packhorse and all the comforts of home,"
said Nathan, "so I reckon we'll find us a fresh-water spring
or creek and pitch camp."

"After supper," Thompson said, "I'll be checking out the
saloons along the waterfront. Ride in and join me for some
poker, if you like."

"Thanks," said Nathan. "I'll keep that in mind. Good
luck."

Thompson rode on ahead without looking back. When
he was well beyond hearing, Eulie spoke.

"I know you're a gambler," she said, "but I hope you
don't go looking for him. Death rides with him."

"He's a strange one," Nathan said. "I don't believe I'd
like to face him across a poker table."

"My God," said Eulie, "he scares me to death. If it
hadn't been for you, he'd be lying dead in the street of the
dirty little Mexican town. As he stood there bleeding from
a gunshot, I couldn' believe what I saw in his eyes. It was
pure madness. There was the joy and excitement of a child
who has just taken part in a game. Thank God he's riding north."

"Well, it seems I'm a friend of his, whether I like it or
not," Nathan said. "Anyway, our trails may never cross
again."

But Nathan Stone had never been more wrong in his life.

*   *   *

Corpus Christi, Texas. August 5, 1866.

Corpus Christi was but a village, located on the left bank
of the lower Nueces River. There seemed to be no official
buildings, and many of the habitations were tents. As was
the case in most frontier towns, settlers had congregated
along the river, while a few had settled on the shores of
the bay that entended inland to the northeast. Fledgling
village though it was, two sailing ships were anchored off-

shore. Goods must be loaded or unloaded well beyond the breakwater after having been rowed to or from the ship by lighter.* Such a vessel, constructed of logs and heavy planks, lay alongside a dock on which freight from one of the anchored vessels were being unloaded. A dozen men wrasseled the barrels and crates to the lock. Finished, they released the lighter and took up oars, preparing to fight their way through the breakwater for another load. Nathan and Eulie had reined up on a bluff that was a good forty feet above sea level and the existing town. There was a cooling breeze from the Gulf, and the blue expanse of water seemed to stretch to infinity.

"I've never seen anything so magnificent," Eulie said. "Let's make our camp right here."

"It's a temptation," said Nathan, "but we'll need water, and I'd as soon the whole town not be able to keep an eye on us. I expect we'd better ride down and find us a place alongside the river or up yonder at the far end of the bay."

When they had descended the bluff, Corpus Christi seemed a little more impressive. There was a two-story hotel and a general store that had been built of lumber. Other buildings were of logs. There were four saloons. All of them were housed in tents, thanks to the mild climate. The dock had been built far enough from the village to allow for expansion, and what appeared to be a warehouse was under construction. Pilings that would become the four corners had been driven deep into the ground. Nathan and Eulie avoided the main street, riding along the upper bank of the Nueces until they found a fresh-water spring that was surrounded with sufficient graze for the horses.

"If there's no livery," Nathan said, "I hope the mercantile has grain. A horse can't live forever on grass."

Nathan unsaddled the two animals while Eulie began unloading the packhorse. Freed from their burdens, the three animals headed for the water. Their thirst quenched, they rolled, shook themselves, and began to graze.

"Nathan," said Eulie, "if I'm going to travel as a man, I'll need some things to complete my outfit. First thing, before we go anywhere else, I'll want to go to the store."

---

*A heavy barge, rowed to and from anchored vessels.

"We'll go to the mercantile first, then," Nathan said, "but you're a pretty believable gent, just like you are."

"Nathan," she sighed, "I have just three shirts, none larger than this one I'm wearing. See how tight it is across the front? How many men have you known who filled out their shirts like this?"

"Now that you mention it," he grinned, "you're the first."

"I'll want some shirts a size or two larger, and I have a few yards of muslin in my saddlebag. I'll use some of it to make myself a binder before we go to the mercantile."

"A binder?"

"A tight band of cloth that will flatten my chest and prevent movement that might cast some doubt on me being a man."

"Smart," said Nathan. "Without it, there's movement aplenty."

"I aim to buy a holster and belt for my Colt, too," she said. "I'd not be much of a man, riding unarmed."

"Pack an iron," Nathan said, "and you'll eventually have to use it."

"I *can* use it, and I'm damn sudden with it. I'm faster on the draw than most of the men who grew up around Waco. I owe that to my father. He wanted a son, and drove my mother to an early grave because all she could produce was daughters. He was hell-bent on me becoming the son he never had and would never have. He refused me a woman's underclothes, forced me to ride astraddle like a man, and saw to it that I spent two hours every day drawing and dry-firing a Colt. By the hour, he forced me to draw against him, both of us using empty Colts. God forgive me, how often I wished my pistol had been loaded."

This time it was Nathan who turned away, not allowing his eyes to meet hers. They were a mix of remembering, of bitterness, of hate, painting for him a picture more graphic than he wished to see. He now understood a disturbing fact that had escaped him when she had stripped, revealing the scars on her body. They hadn't been the result of a single beating, but were an accumulation of many years. Eulie started the supper fire and went about preparing the meal. Cotton Blossom had drifted off somewhere, exploring this new and unfamiliar territory. They were down to final cups of coffee when Nathan spoke.

"We'll ride into town in the morning. Go ahead and get a belt and holster for the Colt, along with whatever clothes you may need."

"I asked you earlier if you intended to gamble in the saloons. I had no right to ask that, and I'm sorry. Do as you wish, and don't mind me."

Nathan put down his tin cup and moved next to her. She knew virtually nothing about him, and Nathan had been intending that it remain so. But there was something about her—a kind of wistfulness and a totally lost look in her gray eyes—that changed his mind.

"I'm not needing money, Eulie," he said, "and while I can make a living at it, I'm not a gambler by trade or choice. That's not my reason for the nightly haunting of saloons. I think it's time you knew a little more about Nathan Stone."

"You don't owe me anything," she said. "My telling you a bit of my past in no way obligates you to speak of yours."

"What you've told me has nothing to do with what I am about to tell you. Just being near me, you could be shot dead through no fault of your own, and I won't have you riding with me, unaware of that danger."

She said nothing and he began talking. He began with his discovery of his family having been murdered and his vow of vengeance on his father's grave. He told her of killing Hankins in Missouri, and of his belief that some of the remaining renegades might have fled to Texas.

"So you're accounting for your always riding a different trail by seeming to be a gambler. With men like Ben Thompson at the tables, that's enough to get you killed."

"I know that," Nathan said, "but with Texas under Federal control, how many reasons can you come up with for an hombre like me to be prowling from one town to another?"

"I don't gamble. If the Federals get suspicious, how are you going to explain me riding with you? Or haven't you thought of that?"

"I have," he said gravely. "I can always deck you out in petticoats, bloomers, and a bonnet, and pass you off as my wife or sister."

"Like hell you can," she said. "I have all the parts in the right places, but I've never been allowed to be a female, so I don't know how. It's easier for me to pretend to be a man than to try and become the woman I've never been allowed to be. Besides, how far would we get, me pretending to be a fancy woman, with a loaded Colt belted around my middle?"

"You couldn't wear the Colt."

"The Colt stays," she said. "Along with the man's hat, boots, shirts, and britches. If a man ever needed somebody to watch his back, you do, and I can't do that without a gun."

"Hell's bells," he howled, "How would that look? A hardcase gambler with somebody to watch his back? And suppose somebody discovered you're a ... a ..."

"Female," she finished. "You'd be disgraced."

"You're damned right I would be," he said, "and so would you."

"Nobody but you and me has to know what's under these clothes," she said. "You aim to travel the frontier, killing men as it suits your fancy, and if you can't see how your story's going to end, then I'll tell you. Every snot-nosed, shirt-tail kid with the price of a Colt and a pocketful of shells will be gunning for you, just to prove he's faster than Nathan Stone."

"That being the case," Nathan said, "they can't prove anything by shooting me in the back."

"Once you've gained a reputation, there'll be some who will take you any way they can get you. Have you heard of Cullen Baker?"

"No," said Nathan.

"You will. He's maybe thirty-five, and his family moved from Tennessee to east Texas when Baker was a child. He killed his first man before he was twenty, and when it comes to drawing and firing a pistol, he's been called the fastest man alive. He's also being called 'The Swamp Fox of the Sulphur,' because he hides out in the brakes along the Sulphur River when the law gets too close."

"Well, hell," Nathan said, "he's an outlaw. He's fair game."

"That only provides an excuse for shooting him in the back legally. When a man gets a reputation as a fast gun, it doesn't matter which side of the law he's walking on. Glory seekers see him only as a target."

"And while I'm riding a vengeance trail, sitting in at poker tables, and establishing myself as a target, you're willing to risk your neck to help me avoid being ventilated by some skunk who fancies himself a fast gun. Why?"

"Why?" She laughed bitterly. "For God's sake, Nathan, why are men so ignorant in the ways of women? I'm thirty-four years old. I could almost be your mother. What choice did I have? Should I have hung around Waco until I died of old age or somebody shot me out of pity? How many women have you known who would lure a man into a bedroom, strip, and then screech long and loud enough to draw a crowd?"

"Not many," Nathan admitted, with a half grin. "There's a matter of pride."

"Pride, hell," she said venomously. "I had none, needed none. My pompous old daddy has enough for every living soul within a hundred miles of Waco. Pride? Damn the pride. I wanted a man, wanted to live like a woman, if only for a little while."

"I can understand your feelings," Nathan said, "but you call this 'living like a woman,' dressed like a man, drifting from town to town with a gambler who's a killer in disguise?"

"It's the closest I've been, so far. Beneath these clothes, you *know* I'm a woman. Since we seem to be laying all the cards on the table, and it was you who brought up the subject of pride, I have a question for you. From what you've told me, I think you come from a good family. I envy you, having had a father who meant so much, his dying words would have you riding this vengeance trail for God knows how many years. But what about *your* pride? Gambling isn't a proud profession, and having the name of a killer ought to be a few notches below that."

It got to him in a manner she had never expected. His face flamed red and he turned away from her. His eyes were on the distant Gulf, but empty, seeing nothing. She was immediately sorry. Genuinely so. She moved closer, her hand on his arm.

"I had no right to say that, Nathan. Actually, it's pride that's made you the kind of man you are, and the lack of it that's made me the woman I am. I have all the characteristics of a whore, lacking one thing. Pay me two dollars, and I will have gone full circle."

He took her by the shoulders and shook her until her teeth rattled. He then drew her to him in the gathering darkness, and the force of his words thrilled her as had nothing else in her lonely, dreary life.

"Damn it, Eulie Prater, you're no more a whore than I am a gambler. We may be sacrificing some pride, but by God, that's how life is. You have to trade one thing for another, and it's just a matter of deciding which is the most important. You've been truthful with me. You knew what you wanted, but you admitted you went about it the wrong way, luring me into your bedroom. Well, I'm not sure that was all wrong. It sure as hell got my attention, and I'm putting it behind me. As far as I'm concerned, you've proven yourself, and you're some kind of woman. There are times when courage stands taller than pride, and we *did* have a choice. God help the both of us, if we've made the wrong ones."

Far out in the gulf a light winked, disappeared, and winked again.

"It's on one of the sailing ships," Eulie said, "and it's been dark for more than an hour. What took them so long to make a light?"

"It's not on one of the anchored vessels. Too far out. I think it's one of the running lights on a third ship approaching the harbor. This has all the makings of a busy town. Why don't we walk down there and have us a look at the place? Cotton Blossom will stay with the horses, and they'll be safe enough. For the time being, I'll stay out of the saloons, using my role as a gambler only when I have to. Those sailing ships out there interest me. Not for what they are, but for what they represent. With Texas under Reconstruction, who's going to be able to afford this as a seaport, to import anything?"

"The Federals?"

"The Federals," said Nathan. "Texas is one hell of a big piece of territory, and I'm not sure the Federals haven't bitten off more than they can chew. Except for the Union Pacific, the frontier's years away from having railroads. I believe these sailing ships are evidence there's going to be a change in the government method of operation. I won't say there'll be no more wagon trains from the river towns such as St. Louis and Shreveport to points west ... I'm saying that these southern ports, such as Corpus Christi, Galveston, and New Orleans are going to be used more and more."

"If you're thinking of us maybe joining one of the freight outfits, I can drive a team. But suppose the Federals are doing their own freighting?"

"Perhaps they are," Nathan said, "but I doubt it. We got here early in the afternoon and there wasn't a blue coat in sight. If they don't have the men to garrison a few soldiers here, where are they going to get drivers and outriders for a freight outfit? Ever since I rode west, I've been hearing how undermanned the military is. And not just in Texas, either. Indians are raising hell on the frontier, and I think the Yanks have limped out of one war right into another. When those freight wagons show, I look for them to be civilian owned and driven. There'll be somebody here in this town who's responsible for all this incoming freight. With a third ship coming in, somebody will have to make a move pretty soon. Let's slope on down there and see what we can learn."

"If I'm to pass for a man," said Eulie, "I'll need a man's name. We'd best decide on that before we start meeting too many people."

"You're dead right about that. What's your middle name?"

"Eulie."

"Oh, hell," Nathan said. "Your first name, then."

"Elizabeth."

"That's even less useful," said Nathan. "Maybe we can use part of it. Suppose you become Eli Prater?"

"Appropriate," she said, "after what my father tried to do to me. I'm surprised he didn't think of that."

"You can be a quiet hombre," Nathan said, "speaking only when you have to. Thank God you don't have a high-pitched voice. You don't sound so much like a woman unless you get excited."

"Thanks, Nathan," said Eulie drily. "If some varmint gets me excited, instead of screaming, I'll just shoot him."

"That should solve all our problems," Nathan said, grinning in the darkness. "Strap on that binder. Then we'll walk down there and see what we can learn."

Once they neared the village of Corpus Christi, it seemed considerably more impressive. It was the tents housing the saloons that gave the place a temporary, sordid look. From a distance, even the permanent structures had seemed squat and inadequate, but a closer examination revealed glass windows, and next to the hotel, a less obvious building that turned out to be the town hall. Its name had been skillfully painted above double doors that boasted brass knobs.

"From the look of this," Eulie said, "you'd never know Texas has been involved in war. Some of it's new, but most of it's been here awhile."

"False prosperity," said Nathan. "Yankee money. While politicians in Washington have imposed military rule through Reconstruction, they still have to spend money to make it work. If they're using civilian labor and civilian bullwhackers, some money has to change hands. There must be a mercantile, with food and goods freighted in, if only to supply the administrators that Washington has sent or will send here. Their trade, along with that of the civilian laborers and freighters the military is forced to hire, makes it all look better than it probably is. I'd bet my saddle that all those saloons are backed by Yankee money."

False or not, even at night the town had an air of prosperity about it. Many of the structures—especially the tent saloons—had kerosene lamps aglow either beside or above the entrance. The Shore Hotel, by far the most grandiose building in town, had mounted a set of brass carriage lamps, one on each side of the wide front entrance. While less elegant, the double doors of the mercantile were similarly lighted. Despite the breeze from the Gulf, the doors were propped open.

"You might as well get your shirts, holster, and pistol belt," Nathan said. "Remember, the less said the better, and I'll speak for both of us if I can."

As Nathan had predicted, the mercantile was well stocked, including a good selection of arms and ammunition. Eulie chose a gun rig—a solid black holster and matching belt—with silver buckle and conchos. Whoever actually owned the store, there was a grizzled old Texan running it, and Nathan felt more at ease.

"You have a surprisingly good selection of weapons and ammunition," said Nathan, "considering."

"Considering the Comanches," the old man laughed. "One thing the Yanks learnt damn quick. You can't hire men to freight goods through Comanche country unarmed, Reconstruction or not. I got two dozen of the new seventeen-shot Winchesters. It's replacin' the Henry, you know."

"It won't be replacing mine," Nathan said. "If a man

can't shoot his way out with sixteen shots, one more won't make a damn bit of difference."

"Them's my sentiments exactly," the old man laughed, "but for them that's needful of a long gun, it's the best there is."

"My pardner here might want one," said Nathan. He looked at Eulie and she nodded.

"I'll git you one," said the storekeeper. "How many shells?"

"Two hundred rounds," Nathan said. "That won't be too many in Comanche country."

"Might not be enough."

"He can tell us something about the freighting business," Eulie whispered, when they were alone.

"Yes," Nathan said, "and we'll have to trust somebody not to get too nosey. I'll talk to him some before we leave."

The old-timer returned with the Winchester, and without warning, tossed the weapon to Eulie. She caught it expertly in her left hand, jacking it open with her right. The storekeeper broke the seal on the tin of shells, placed it on the counter, and watched approvingly as the new owner of the Winchester fully loaded it. The weapon was still coated with grease from the factory, and a greenhorn might have wiped his hands on the legs of his trousers. But Eulie stood at ease, the Winchester under her arm.

"Old-timer," said Nathan, "I'm Nathan Stone, and my pardner is Eli Prater. You spoke of freighting goods through Comanche country. When we rode in yesterday there were a pair of sailing ships anchored off shore, and we saw what looked like the lights of a third one a while ago. We reckoned there must be a lot of freight going somewhere, and wondered who's doing the hauling. If they're hirin', we could sure use the work, as outriders or teamsters."

"I'm Jed Hatcher," said the storekeeper, "and you could be in luck. That is, if you consider whackin' a freight wagon through Comanche country lucky. For the time being, the Federals are usin' a civilian freight outfit out of San Antone, run by a cantankerous old varmint named Roy Bean.*

---

*Roy Bean, born in Mason County, Kentucky about 1825, started a freighting business in San Antonio in 1866. He was destined to become a Western legend as "Judge" Roy Bean, "Law West of the Pecos."

He's never showed up with more'n three wagons, and he drives one of 'em himself. Dunno if he can't find more teamsters or if he just can't afford to hire 'em. He hauls to Austin and San Antone, and by the time he finishes one run, he generally has to turn right around and come back for another. He'll likely be in here sometime tomorrow. He'd better be, if he wants to keep his contract. The Federals is havin' to pay a man to keep watch over them goods out there on the dock until Bean's wagons shows up."

"No outriders, then," Nathan said.

"None," said Hatcher. "I sold him three Winchesters and a pile of shells for 'em. If the Comanches shows up, he depends on them Winchesters him and his men keep handy."

"We're obliged," Nathan said. "Maybe we'll hang around and talk some business with him."

"Good luck," Hatcher grinned. "I got plenty shells for that Henry, too."

"I'll keep that in mind," said Nathan. "I'll likely need them."

"Well," Eulie said, when they had left the store, "what do you think?"

"I think if Bean can get his hands on another pair of wagons, we'll get a chance to risk losing our hair to the Comanches. That is, if they ride this far south. I've heard that most of their hell-raising is confined to east Texas."

"Don't you believe it," said Eulie. "God, in 1842 the Comanches laid an ambush in Bandera Pass, just north of San Antonio. They waited until a party of Texas Rangers were in the gorge and then cut down on them. Five Rangers were killed and six were wounded. The survivors said mostly it was hand-to-hand fighting, both sides using Bowie knives."*

"It's unlikely the Comanches have changed their ways any since then," Nathan said, "so it's a serious threat. What do you think?"

---

*F. H. Bell, Creed Taylor, A. A. (Big Foot) Wallace, and Ben McCulloch were Rangers who survived the ambush at Bandera Pass and went on to become well known in Texas history. Prior to the Mexican-American War, McCulloch led an advance party of forty Rangers on a reconnaissance mission into Mexico.

"I think the Comanches will be an occasional threat, while working the gambling tables at the saloons could get you shot dead at any time. When I say that, I'm thinking of that cold-eyed devil, Ben Thompson. I can handle a team and a Winchester, and I'd feel safer taking our chances with the Comanches."

"Tomorrow, then," said Nathan, "we'll find out if old man Bean is able to rustle up two more freight wagons."

"We forgot the grain for the horses."

"I didn't forget it," Nathan said. "I can't see toting it up the hill afoot. We'll get it tomorrow."

Chapter 7

By first light, the ship's crew began unloading the packet that had dropped anchor during the night. To help pass the time, Nathan and Eulie saddled their horses and, returning to the mercantile, bought a sack of grain.

"We still haven't seen hide nor hair of Bean and his freight wagons," Nathan said.

"You ain't likely to," said Hatcher the storekeeper, "until near sundown. They'll get in late enough so's they can layover tonight an' maybe tomorrow night. It'll take some time to load the wagons."

"They'll have more freight than they can load into six wagons," Nathan replied. "What happens to the rest of it?"

"They'll take the oldest first," said Hatcher. "They're always behind an' the Federals is always raisin' hell. If Bean can afford the wagons an' teams, I ain't doubtin' he'll hire you."

Hatcher went on about his business. Nathan and Eulie left the store and returned to their camp near the spring. It was a good vantage point, offering a view of the town and the anchored ships, as well as the plains to the north, from whence Roy Bean's freight wagons were likely to come.

"Being behind with the freight," Eulie said, "I don't understand why they'd lay over here any longer than it takes to load the wagons."

"It's the way of bullwhackers," said Nathan. "They want some time in the saloons and the whorehouses."

Time dragged, and as Hatcher had predicted, it was late afternoon when the trio of ox-drawn wagons loomed on the horizon. They had to wend their way to the far end of the bench, circling back to the town and the docks below.

"Come on," Nathan said. "We'd best ride down there

and talk to Bean. Bullwhackers get a few slugs of red-eye under their belts, and they get damn unsociable."

Bean and his drivers had not backed the wagons up to the dock, a fair indication they had no intention of loading any time soon. Instead, the trio had lived up to Nathan's prediction and had reined up near one of the saloons. By the time the three drivers had stepped down, Nathan and Eulie had dismounted and were waiting for them. All three men carried Winchesters, and Nathan had no trouble identifying Bean, for his companions were Mexican. None of them had shaved recently, and Bean was only slightly better dressed than the Mexican drivers. While the Mexicans wore tight-legged trousers and dingy white shirts beneath dark jackets, Bean was dressed in baggy homespun trousers kept in place by wide red suspenders and a blue flannel shirt. His old flop hat appeared to have lost an ongoing battle with the elements, but the Mexican drivers wore wide-brimmed sombreros. The drivers were slender, but Bean had a pot belly. And curiously, none of them carried a sidearm. Bean looked maybe five-ten, and the pair of Mexicans not even that. The Mexicans paused, allowing Bean to confront Eulie and Nathan.

"I reckon you're Roy Bean," Nathan said.

"I reckon I am," Bean replied. "Just who the hell else would I be?"

His Mexican companions grinned, having been burned by similar sarcasm before, but the feisty Bean kept a straight face.

"If you're the owner of this rawhide freight line," Nathan said evenly, "I want to talk to you about me and my pardner hirin' on. If you're not, I purely don't give a damn who you are."

Bean laughed, slapping his dusty old hat against his leg. "By God, you got sand," he roared. "Come on. We'll git us a bottle an' talk. I'm dry as ten mile of Llano Estacado."

Nathan and Eulie followed Bean into the tent saloon. There were half a dozen tables, several benches, and assorted stools. There were a few chairs, no two of them alike. Bean chose a table that had chairs, took one for himself, and bawled an order at the bartender. Bean's Mexican drovers took a table of their own.

"Bottle an' glasses. None of that snakehead rotgut, damn it."

He said nothing to Nathan and Eulie, allowing them to stand or sit, as they chose. They each took a chair and sat down. When the bartender brought the whiskey and glasses, Bean seized the bottle and removed the cork with his teeth. He ignored the custom, filling his own glass and downing the contents in a single gulp.

"Well," said Ben, slamming down his glass, "you pilgrims too good to drink with me?"

Nathan said nothing. Taking the bottle, he poured three fingers of the stuff into his own glass and a lesser amount in Eulie's.

"Who told you I was hirin' whackers?" Bean demanded.

"Why would anybody have to tell us?" Nathan replied. "With the wagons you have, you'll need three trips just to move the freight that's piled up here. Only reason you wouldn't be hiring is that you're broke. Or maybe just too damn cheap."

The Mexicans laughed, the bartender suddenly got busy, and Eulie, seeking to hide behind the glass, got strangled on the whiskey. Bean glared at her, finally turning hard eyes on Nathan. He sighed and finally spoke.

"You're half right," he said. "I ain't exactly flush. You ever done any gov'ment haulin', you'd know the damn money don't never come on time. For the loads we're haul-in' now, we git paid month after next. That is, if we git lucky. I got no idee what Delmano and Renato finds so damn funny. The ugly varmints ain't been paid in near two months."

"You can't afford to hire us, then," Nathan said.

"I'm sayin' I can't afford to pay you till I get paid," Bean replied. "If you ain't hurtin' fer money, likely I kin figger a way to take you on."

"You'll need more wagons and teams," said Nathan. "If you're up to that, I reckon me and my pard can get in line behind Delmano and Renato for our pay."

"Times is hard," Bean said, "an' I'll have to take second-hand on the wagons, but I can get the oxen from the livery in San Antone. You get thirty a month an' two hunnert rounds of ammunition."

"My pardner's Eli Prater," said Nathan, "and I'm Nathan Stone."

"One thing I ain't told you," Bean said. "Them damn Comanches has been givin' us hell. We'll be haulin' to Aus-

tin an' sometimes Houston, an' them varmints likes to lay
out along the Colorado an' snipe at us. So I'm tellin' you
honest, there's considerable more to this than just handlin'
a team. You got to shoot quick an' straight. You'll be needin' long guns."

"We have them," Nathan said. "A Henry and a
Winchester."

"Get yer shells at the mercantile," said Bean, "an' tell
Hatcher I said put it on my tab. We'll load tomorrow an'
move out the day after. Less'n you be in a hurry to git to
San Antone, wait an' ride back with us."

"We'll do that" Nathan said, kicking back his chair.

"Whoa," said Bean. "You ain't finished your drinks.
Never let whiskey go to waste. That's the code of the
West."

As a rule, Nathan Stone shied clear of anything more
potent than a beer, but this time he made the best of it,
swallowing the stuff. He wondered what Eulie would do,
and to his surprise, she emptied the glass in a single motion,
without a tremor.

Nathan and Eulie left the saloon and not until they
reached their horses did Nathan speak.

"You put down that whiskey mighty slick. The stuff near
gagged me."

"Just a little thing I learned at my dear old daddy's
knee," Eulie said. "That was before he discovered I'd never
become the son he'd always wanted, and then you heard
him ranting at me because I was so unladylike. Well, hell,
I didn't know how. I was taught to do everything like a
man except to stand when I go to the bushes."

"You make a right convincin' hombre," said Nathan.
"Just one thing that we haven't counted on. Sooner or
later, you'll have to talk."

"I can talk slow," Eulie replied, "and lower my voice.
Like this."

She lowered her voice, speaking with an exaggerated
Texas drawl. Nathan laughed, and she raised her voice to
its normal pitch.

"You could fool me if I didn't know better," said Nathan. "I just hope you don't forget to lower your voice."

"I won't," Eulie replied. "I used to talk like that all the
time, just to please Daddy, until people started laughing
at me."

Nathan and Eulie were up at first light. Below them, one of the wagons had been backed up to the dock. Bean and his companions were already loading the freight.

"When the mercantile opens," Nathan said, "we might as well go after the shells Bean promised us."

"We have plenty," said Eulie. "We don't really need them."

"The hell we don't," Nathan said. "If we're goin' to fight Comanches for thirty dollars a month, the least he can do is pay for the shells."

It was early and Hatcher was alone in the mercantile. He brought two tins of shells for the Henry and two for the Winchester.

"There you are," Hatcher grinned. "Courtesy of Roy Bean. I ain't sure if I should congratulate you or pray for you."

*   *   *

August 11, 1866. North to San Antonio.

Bean led out, the other wagons lumbering along behind. To escape the swirling dust, Nathan and Eulie rode beside the lead wagon. They followed a river that emptied into Corpus Christi Bay, and when they stopped at noon to refresh themselves and rest the teams, Nathan asked about it.

"The Nueces," Bean said. "We'll be follerin' in about sixty mile, near halfway to San Antone. It's maybe 130 mile from Corpus Christi."

Eulie tested her low-pitched voice by asking Bean a question.

"Do you expect the Comanches to attack us on the way to San Antonio?"

"Won't be a damn bit surprised," said Bean. "They know we're loaded with grub, fancy goods, guns an' shells fer the soldiers' an' all manner of stuff. They may be heathens, but they ain't stupid. They know we got long guns an' they ain't about to risk bein' shot dead just fer scalps."

"Loaded," Nathan said, "you're lookin' at fourteen days from Corpus Christi to San Antone."

"That's if nothin' goes wrong," said Bean. "Empty, rollin' south, we sometimes make the run in ten days."

"Comanches will attack at night," Eulie said. "With so few drivers, how do you ever get any sleep?"

"We don't take off nothin' but our hats," said Bean. "Two of us sleeps while t'other keeps his eyes open an' his hands on his gun."

The day passed without incident and Bean reined up an hour before the sun would sink below the western horizon.

"We eat an' put out the fire before dark," Bean said. "After that, with the river handy, I aim to wash off some dust an' sweat."

Supper was prepared and hurriedly eaten, and the portly Bean began peeling off his dusty clothes. He looked questioningly at Nathan and Eulie.

"I don't think so," said Nathan. "We like to keep our britches on when there may be Comanches around. We'll keep our rifles handy."

Bean, Delmano, and Renato stripped and piled into the river, while Nathan and Eulie remained near the wagons. For the first time since early morning, Cotton Blossom joined them.

"I thought he had left us," Eulie said.

"He's been somewhere ahead of us," said Nathan. "Something about this he doesn't like. Delmano and Renato, maybe."

"I'm a little unsure of them myself," Eulie replied. "Fact is, I'm a mite nervous with all of them, Roy Bean included."

Nathan laughed. "Not near as nervous as they'd be if they knew they'd stripped before a woman. Is that what's making you nervous with them?"

"Oh, hell," she said in disgust, "it's not that kind of nervous. What I mean is that I doubt we can trust them."

"Why not?" Nathan insisted. "What are you seeing that I'm not?"

"I'm not seeing anything, damn it. It's ... just a bad feeling."

The sun had said goodnight to the prairie and purple shadows had crept in before the trio quit the river, shook some of the dust from their clothes and got dressed.

"Time we was splittin' up the watches fer the night," said Bean.

"I don't trust my hair to the eyes and ears of one man," Nathan said. "I have a better idea. The three of you take the first watch, and we'll take the second. We'll change at midnight."

"That ain't fair," Bean objected. "There's two of you an' three of us. If the varmints is comin' after us in the dark, they're most likely to show up in the stillest hours of the mornin'."

"That's why we want the second watch," said Nathan, "because there's also three of us. Cotton Blossom, my dog, will warn us if anybody tries to come close."

Delmano looked at Cotton Blossom and laughed. *"Feo perro,"* he said.*

Cotton Blossom growled low in his throat, his hackles rose, and he took a step toward the Mexican.

"Easy, Cotton Blossom," Nathan said, his eyes on Delmano.

"Damn you, Delmano," said Bean, "keep your mouth shut. You got no right to call anything or anybody ugly. Stone, that's a good idee. That dog knows a heathen when he sees one, an' I'll sleep better, him havin' his ears perked durin' them hours betwixt midnight an' dawn. You an' Eli git some shuteye. Me an' these ugly varmints will keep our eyes an' ears open."

Nathan and Eulie spread their bedrolls near where the horses grazed, for the animals would be quick to sense the approach of man or beast. Without a command, Cotton Blossom lay down at Nathan's feet.

"I'm glad he's there," Eulie said softly.

"So am I," said Nathan. "I'd miss him if he weren't."

"More than me?"

Nathan said nothing.

"Well?" she inquired.

"Don't rush me," Nathan said. "I'm thinking."

She laughed. "Damn you, Nathan Stone."

*   *   *

Five days north of Corpus Christi, the Comanches struck. Ten of them swept in from the east, offering no targets. Each clung to the offside of his pony, a leg hooked over its

---

*Ugly dog.

back, loosing arrows beneath the animal's neck. But their adversaries had an edge the Comanches hadn't counted on.

Snarling and yipping, Cotton Blossom pursued the attacking Indians. When he nipped at the hind legs of an Indian pony, the spooked animal broke stride and reared, dropping it rider to the dusty ground. The fallen warrior rose to meet a Winchester slug and sank down to move no more. Cotton Blossom went after a second pony and then a third, watching the horses pile their riders. Lethal Winchester fire cut down the two unhorsed Comanches and the others fled, vanishing as suddenly as they had appeared. Cotton Blossom trotted back to the wagons.

"By God," Bean shouted, piling off the wagon box, "I ain't never seen nothin' like it. That hound's worth his weight in gold coin."

Nathan and Eulie had dropped back behind the third wagon, using it for cover. They rode forward.

"Anybody hit?" Nathan asked.

"Couple oxen got nicked," said Bean. "Some sulfur salve to keep the blow flies away, an' they'll heal good as new."

*   *   *

August 25, 1866. San Antonio.

Roy Bean had no freight office, but operated out of a rundown house to the south of town. There was an enormous barn whose roof had begun to sag, and beyond that, a corral with a three-rail-high fence. The rest of the town seemed to have shied away from Bean's place, and he had used all the property to the fullest. There was a wagon box without wheels, extra bows leaning drunkenly against the barn, and a conglomeration of old wagon wheels with missing spokes or tires. Bean reined up his teams before the barn and stepped down.

"We'll unload this freight in the mornin'," said Bean. "We'll be layin' over here for a couple of days, givin' me time to round up some wagons an' ox teams. Stone, you an' yer pard are welcome to stall yer hosses in the barn an' there's room in the house fer yer saddles an' bedrolls. I'm a mite short of bunks, but there's plenty of floor."

"We're obliged," Nathan said. "We'll leave our saddles and rolls in the house and our horses in the barn, but I reckon we'll have us a couple of nights in a hotel bed and some town grub. This is Thursday. When are you aimin' to start for Corpus Christi?"

"Sunday at first light," said Bean. "Tomorrow to unload the wagons, an' Saturday fer me to dicker fer more wagons an' teams."

The business district was within easy walking distance of Bean's "office." Nathan and Eulie set out afoot with Cotton Blossom.

"I don't feel right about leaving everything we own back there," said Eulie.

"Not everything," said Nathan. "The horses are in the barn."

"Same difference," Eulie said. "We should have brought them with us and found a livery for them."

"You don't trust anybody, do you?"

"Why should I?" she replied. "I'm always disappointed."

"Have I disappointed you?"

"Not yet," she said.

"You expect me to, then."

"I don't know. I've only my father to compare you to. I'd take a crib in a whorehouse before I'd go back to Waco."

Nathan offered no response.

"Were you serious about taking a hotel room in town?" Eulie asked.

"Why not?" Nathan said. "We'll spend enough nights on the ground."

Cotton Blossom proved unwelcome at the fancier hotels, and they ended up with a room in a boardinghouse.

"Now," said Nathan, "we'll have to find an eatin' place where we can all get fed."

They found a dingy little cafe next to the Bull's Horn Saloon. There was a poorly lettered sign above the eatery that simply said "Grub." It was still early, not quite suppertime. The cook, wearing a dirty white apron, leaned across the counter and eyed Cotton Blossom with disapproval.

"There's nobody in here but us," Nathan said, "and he's a paying customer."

"Take that table in the back," the cook said, "and I'll set him a plate back there."

There would have been no trouble had not some of the patrons of the Bull's Horn Saloon decided it was time to eat. There were eight men, all in various stages of drunkenness, and with all the empty tables, they chose the one against the wall, behind that occupied by Nathan and Eulie. One of the drunkest of the party managed to tromp on Cotton Blossom's tail. The hound took his vengeance by sinking his teeth in the man's leg, just above the top of his boot. There was a curse, a cry of pain, and all hell broke loose. The table was upended, throwing Nathan and Eulie to the floor. There was a howl of pain and more cursing, as Cotton Blossom sank his teeth into yet another victim. Nathan struggled to his feet, only to be struck down with the muzzle of a Colt. Eulie lay face down, unmoving. Nathan blacked out when somebody kicked him in the head. Dimly he could hear shouting.

"Damn it, this is the law. Break it up!"

Finally the sheriff—whose name was Eb Dinkins—got them separated. Cotton Blossom crouched under a table, hackles up, daring anybody to come after him.

"Now," said the sheriff, when all the participants were on their feet, "what's this all about, and who started it?"

"That damn dog," one of the drunks scowled. "The varmint bit me."

"He bit me, too," another shouted.

"He's my dog," Nathan said coldly, "and I'm responsible for him. He bit nobody until one of these heavy-hoofed varmints stepped on him."

"That dog ain't got no business in here," snarled one of the men who had been bitten. "Let's drag the no-account skunk outside an' shoot him."

"You'll have to shoot me first," Nathan said.

"There'll be no shooting," said Sheriff Dinkins. "Any man touchin' his gun gets thirty days in the *juzgado*. Now get the hell out of here, all of you."

"Sheriff," Nathan said, "we came here to eat, and we'll leave when we've done so."

"He paid in advance, sheriff," said the cook, "and I don't refund nothin'."

"The hombres that have paid can stay," the sheriff said, "but I want the rest of you out of here. And that goes for the dog, too."

Seeing the humor in the situation, the cook laughed. "The dog's a payin' customer too," he said.

"Then, damn it," the sheriff sighed, "the dog can stay. But the rest of you get the hell out of here and sober up."

His face flushed from whiskey and anger, one of the men Cotton Blossom had bitten turned on Nathan. "You an' me will meet again. This ain't over."

"It is in this town," Sheriff Dinkins replied. "Now get out of here."

The eight of them departed, bestowing angry looks on the sheriff, Eulie, Nathan, and the cook.

"Hell," said the cook, when the drunken men were out the door, "the dog's got better manners than that bunch."

"Damn shame he ain't more careful who he bites," Sheriff Dinkins said. "That whole ugly bunch rides for old Kirk McClendon's brand, and them two who was bit is Morgan and Jethro, McClendon's sons. I hope you gents and the dog ain't plannin' to hang around these parts. Next time, I may not be around, and they'll ventilate you."

"They're welcome to try," said Nathan. "We won't start trouble, but we won't run from it, either."

Nathan, Eulie, and Cotton Blossom finished their meal undisturbed. When they were ready to leave, Nathan spoke to the genial cook. "We'll see you at breakfast. All of us."

"Perhaps we should return to our room and stay there," Eulie said, when they were again on the street.

"You can," said Nathan, "but I can't. The surest way for a man to run headlong into trouble is to try and hide from it. There's nothin' wrong with not wantin' to be gunned down in somebody else's fight, but as long as you're ridin' with me, you'll be takin' that risk."

"If I wasn't willing to take that risk," Eulie said, "I wouldn't be with you. I'll string along. There's eight of them, and I doubt you're quick enough with a gun to get them all."

"All the more reason not to try and avoid them," said Nathan. "Chances are, in an open fight, they won't gang up on me. If that pair of McClendon varmints have enough of a mad-on to come looking for us, then let there be witnesses. It would be a cowardly thing, all eight of them coming after us, and with old man McClendon being a power in this town, I doubt they'll do that."

"That makes sense in an odd sort of way," Eulie said. "So what do we do to avoid having them think we're dodging them?"

"I reckon we'll visit a few saloons," said Nathan, "and maybe I'll sit in on a poker game or two. I'll want you to take a table, order a beer, and keep a tight rein on Cotton Blossom."

"I will, but I'll also be watching your back."

Nathan and Eulie visited three saloons, Cotton Blossom accompanying them, without finding a poker game in progress. All the patrons were bellied up to the bar, except for one of the saloons that boasted a roulette wheel. Three men were gathered there placing halfhearted bets. The fourth saloon, the Tumbleweed, was larger and more pretentious than the rest, and it was there that a poker game was in progress. Nathan and Eulie took a table nearby, nursing their beers. Cotton Blossom sprawled unobtrusively at Nathan's feet. Two of the five men at the poker table were attired in town clothes and instead of boots, wore gaiters. Their fancy ties made them look like drummers. After losing three pots in a row they folded and withdrew from the game. Nathan dropped five double eagles on the table, took a chair, and sat in. He studied his companions. One looked to be a banker or lawyer, while the other two could have been cowboys. Nathan took a small pot, the affluent gambler took two, and the disenchanted cowboys kicked back their chairs and folded.

"Just you and me," Nathan said.

But even as he spoke, the saloon's batwing doors were flung back and the eight McClendon riders entered, led by Morgan and Jethro. They trooped to the bar, sipping their drinks until their eyes became accustomed to the dimly lit interior of the saloon. Almost immediately they spotted Nathan at the poker table, and to a man, they cut loose with a joyous shout.

"Well, damn my eyes," Jethro McClendon bawled, "If it ain't the yeller little varmint that has a dog to do his fightin'. What'n hell is he doin' in a man's game?"

"It looks a mite shorthanded," Morgan said. "Why don't we set in and make it interestin'? Come on, Jethro. You too, Pete."

Pete took a chair to Nathan's right, while Morgan and Jethro McClendon sat on the other side of the table.

"Dollar limit," said the man in the town suit.

"Dollar, hell," Jethro McClendon shouted. "I say we raise it to five. Anybody that ain't got the sand fer that, fold an' git out."

Nobody moved. Nathan lost seven consecutive pots, the McClendon riders taking six of them.

"By God," Morgan McClendon crowed, "that ain't bad, fer three *hombres* that's drunk as boiled owls. Where's yer dog, mister? Why don't you fold an' deal him in? He couldn't do no worse."

Nathan waited for the laughter to subside. Then, his eyes as cold as blue ice, he spoke directly to Morgan McClendon.

"Why don't you put your money where your mouth is, McClendon? Let's up the limit to twenty dollars. Those of you who don't have the sand or the money, fold and get out."

"I'm out," said the man in the town suit.

"Me too," Pete said.

"Stay, damn it," Jethro growled. "I'll stake you."

There was no more laughter, and the trio began to relax as they each won a pot. Then Nathan Stone took three pots in a row. The next hand, fifteen hundred dollars, lay on the table, and it was Nathan's turn to raise or fold. "I'll raise you five hundred dollars," he said.

Chapter 8

There was utter silence in the saloon. Finally Morgan McClendon spoke.

"I reckon this has gone far enough. Damn you, I'll match my hand agin anything you got."

"Lay them down, then," Nathan said.

Triumphantly, McClendon slapped down four aces. There were gasps and nervous laughter from his companions. McClendon was about to rake in the pot when Nathan Stone's cold voice stopped him.

"Hold it, McClendon. You haven't seen my hand."

"You poor damn fool," McClendon snarled, "they ain't no way in hell you can top four aces."

"One way," said Nathan, and he dropped five face-up cards. Four of them were jacks. The fifth was another ace, making it five aces in the deck.

Nathan Stone made no move until Morgan and Jethro McClendon had already cleared leather. He then drew his lefthand Colt and shot them both dead. On the heels of his shot there was a third. A Colt clattered to the floor and one of the McClendon bunch at the bar fell face down. Eulie stood with her back to the wall, the pistol cocked and steady in her hand. Cotton Blossom stood beside her, teeth bared.

"The rest of you McClendon riders stand pat," Nathan said. "Bartender, send somebody for the sheriff."

Sheriff Eb Dinkins arrived, and the grisly scene was an open book. The poker hands lay where they had fallen and spoke for themselves. So did the three bodies, for Nathan and Eulie still held their Colts cocked and ready.

Dinkins had but one question. "Who drew first?"

"The McClendons drew first, Sheriff," said the bartender. "The stranger at the table nailed them, and his pard shot

Tunstall, who was about to shoot the gamblin' man in the back.''

"Great God," the sheriff groaned. Nathan and Eulie holstered their Colts.

"What do you aim to do, Sheriff?" one of the McClendon bunch asked.

"Just one thing I can do," Dinkins said, and his next words were directed at Nathan Stone. "Mister, it's a clear case of self-defense, and I'm about to give you the best piece of advice you'll ever get. You and your pard get the hell out of here. Saddle up and ride. Tonight.''

"Why the hell should we?" Nathan asked. "It was more than a fair fight, and I'll argue that till hell freezes.''

"Then you'll be arguin' with Kirk McClendon," said Sheriff Dinkins. "You just gunned down both his sons, and your amigo killed Dub Tunstall, old Mac's longtime friend and segundo. You was justified in what you done, but you just try explainin' that to McClendon. I'm just one man, and I can't guarantee you protection. Now get out of here.''

Without a word, Nathan and Eulie left the saloon, followed by Cotton Blossom. There was angry shouting behind them, as Sheriff Dinkins held the McClendon riders at bay. But he couldn't hold them for long.

"McClendon sounds like the kind that will throw the whole damn outfit on our trail, and maybe hire some extra guns," Nathan said. "But I doubt they'll come after us before morning. Let's get back to our room and make some plans.''

But they never got that far. They met Roy Bean, bound for the Tumbleweed saloon, for there was nothing else on that dead-end street.

"I heard shootin'," said Bean. "Sounded like a Comanche attack.''

"We'd be better off if it had been," Nathan said, and told Bean what had happened.

"God," said Bean, "I reckon they built Texas around old McClendon, an' when he gits a mad on, he don't show no mercy.''

"Under the circumtsances," Nathan replied, "I think we'd better forget our bullwhacking deal with you. Something tells me that anybody close to us will be buzzard bait in McClendon's eyes.''

"You sure as hell got that dead-center," said Bean, "but

I ain't givin' up two new drivers that easy. You got till mornin'. Get back to my place, take yer rolls an' bed down in the barn. It's still early. I'll mosey down to the wagon yard an' dicker fer them wagons, an' then hustle to the livery an' see about the teams. If I can nail all that down, I'll work the hell out of Delmano an' Renato tomorrow, an' we'll get that freight unloaded. Then we can slope out a day early on our way to Corpus Christi."

"That's almighty generous of you," Nathan said, "but it's unfair of us to bring that bunch down on you over something we did."

"Nobody knows you rode in with me, 'cept Delmano an' Renato. McClendon damn near owns this town, an' he ain't goin' to expect you two to stay here. Now, do like I say, by God, an' lay low in my old barn. I know it rubs you the wrong way, but sometimes you just got to turn the cat around."

"You're a persuasive man, Bean," said Nathan. "We'll bed down with the horses until you're ready for that run to Corpus Christi."

"I been in court a time er two," Bean said, "an' I got me one of them law books. Back in Kaintuck, my daddy had ideas about me bein' a lawyer, but I just ain't that damn crooked. Mebbe when I can afford it, I'll buy me a stovepipe hat an' a swallow-tail coat an' be a judge."

He turned and left the way he had come, and they could hear him laughing as he vanished in the darkness.

"Just forget what I said about not trusting him," said Eulie. "Let's go back to that old barn."

But there was an uproar and a clatter of hooves behind them as Sheriff Dinkins had allowed the McClendon riders to leave. Quickly Nathan and Eulie diverted onto a side street and sought the shadows. Nathan silenced Cotton Blossom as the riders thundered past, and before the dust had settled, Nathan and Eulie were on their way back to Roy Bean's dilapidated barn.

*   *   *

The night dragged on. Nathan and Eulie saw nobody until first light, when Bean, Delmano, and Renato began harnessing the teams to the freight wagons.

"Yer in luck," said Bean. I got the wagons an' extry

teams. Didn't have the money, but times is hard. I got the whole damn shebang on credit."

"Bueno," Nathan said. "You still aim to leave in the morning?"

"That's what I said," Bean replied. "We'll unload this freight an' then bring the wagons back here. I'll have Delmano an' Renato hoof it to town, hitch up the other teams an' bring the other wagons here."

"There's a chance somebody's going to wonder why you suddenly need more teams and two more wagons," said Eulie.

"I reckon," Bean agreed. "You got any better idee?"

Bean returned to his wagon, mounted the box, and the trio of wagons set off for town to distribute the freight.

*   *   *

"Now I'm glad we didn't leave our horses at the livery in town," Eulie said. "Now nobody will know how we got here or how we left."

"I hope you're right," Nathan said. "Once we're away from here, we'll be maybe ten days getting to Corpus Christi. We'll lay over maybe two days, and we'll be fourteen days getting back to San Antonio. That's not even a month, not near enough time to water down old man McClendon's hate."

"So we'll spend all our time in San Antonio hiding here in the barn."

"No," said Nathan, "I refuse to do that. It destroys my reason for becoming part of Bean's outfit. It was that or continue haunting saloons, pretending to be a gambler, seeking the men I've sworn to kill."

"I thought that was a smart move," Eulie said. "Hiring on as a teamster would have allowed you to continue your manhunt without you having to gamble. Then last night, you threw all of that away on one damn poker game."

"We were legally in the right," Nathan said, more harshly than he had intended. "Damn it, this is a hard country. If you don't stand up for yourself, you get knocked down and walked on. There was no call for that bunch of drunks comin' down on us in that cafe. A man has his pride, Eulie. When he loses that, he ceases to be a man.''

"So that accounts for the poker game. That foolish scuffle in the cafe tainted your pride and you had to strike back. Now you have McClendons outfit ready to shoot you on sight if you show up here again. I can understand your need to avenge your family by stalking the killers. What I simply don't understand is where last night's shootout fits into your plans. When we come back to San Antonio, if we do, we'll face a ready-made lynch mob. That, or McClendon's bunch will ambush us and gun us down."

"Well, by God, I didn't ask you to team up with me," Nathan snarled. "Go on back to Waco and hide out in your old daddy's damn mansion."

That hurt her, and Nathan was immediately sorry for his outburst. But she was game, giving as good as she got. She didn't cry or scream at him. Instead, her voice became deadly soft, and she nailed him with an irrefutable truth.

"Nathan, we left three dead men in that saloon last night. If I hadn't been watching your back, one of those men would have been you."

"All right," said Nathan. "I have my faults, but refusing to admit being wrong isn't one of them. I didn't ask you to throw in with me, but ever since last night, I've been thanking God that you did. That's the last refuge of a prideful man, Eulie. He gets mad as hell when he has to swallow an ugly truth about himself. You should know that, and I'm sorry for what I said."

"I *do* know that," Eulied replied. "I should. My daddy's that way. He's never been wrong, and I've taken many a beating for disagreeing with him."

"Too damn much pride, then. Like me."

"Like you," she said. "He didn't care a damn about me leaving, but with his pride at stake, I'd not be surprised if there's a price on my head. Pride is a dangerous thing, if it's spread too thick."

"You're right," he said. "I never thanked you properly for last night, but I am now."

"I don't want thanks," said Eurlie. "I want your promise you'll put your pride on the shelf and back off when there's no good cause, and when you're surrounded by men who can and will shoot back."

"All right, damn it, all right," he said irritated. "I reckon after four years of war, comin' out on the losin' end, and then bein' kicked around by the Yankees in Libby Prison, I'm a mite touchy."*

"I don't care *what* your reasons are," she said, just as irritably. "I want to know if you've learned anything from last night."

"Yes," he growled. "I've already admitted you're dead right and I was wrong. What more do you want?"

"I want you to promise me you'll stay out of saloon poker games as long as you can," Eulie said, "and when you must sit in, don't be so damn quick to draw when you're outgunned eight to one."

"Yes, Mama."

"I'm not your mama," she snapped. "If I were, I'd get me a big switch and stripe your behind."

She lost him then, as a faraway look came into his eyes and in his mind he drifted beyond her reach, where she could not follow. Again he was seeing those lonely new-made graves in faraway Virginia, and finally the grave of old Malachi. From somewhere, sounding more distant and more lonely than ever, came the mournful howl of a dog. Suddenly he was jolted back to the present by the rumble of a wagon and the clatter of hooves.

"Somebody's coming," Eulie said. "We'd better get up in the hayloft."

They scrambled up the makeshift ladder, which consisted of slats nailed to the wall of a tack room. Through a wide crack they could see the front of the house, where two men had stepped down from a buckboard. They both were well dressed, and the older of the two stepped up on the porch and pounded on the door. There was an early-morning breeze, and being downwind from the strangers, Nathan and Eulie could hear their conversation.

"He's not here," the younger man said.

"I didn't expect him to be," said the portly one who had knocked, "but I wanted to be sure."

---

* Libby Prison, in Richmond, was an old converted warehouse the Confederacy used to imprison captured Union soldiers. Ironically, after Grant took Richmond, Libby became a Confederate prison, and many captured Rebs were held there until their eventual release.

"Leighton," said his companion, "he hasn't paid his rent in nine months. Why don't you just get the sheriff and have him thrown out?"

"Because he owes me two hundred and twenty-five dollars, Barnfield, and I don't intend for him to weasel his way out of paying it. If I kick the old fool out, I'll never see a dime. Let's have a look in the barn and see if he has any livestock worth the taking."

"Hell," Barnfield said, "you can't just take a man's property because he owes you money. You'll have to go to court and get a judgement against him."

"I know that," said Leighton, "but I don't know that he has anything more than his teams and wagons. Let's go look in the barn."

"Damn," Nathan growled under his breath, "they'll find our horses."

But the strangers never reached the barn. Cotton Blossom met them, his hackles up, growling ominously.

"Go back to the buckboard," Leighton said, "and get the whip."

"I'm goin' back to the buckboard," Barnfield replied, "but not for the whip. I'll wait for you there."

He retreated, but Cotton Blossom did not. The hound advanced, making it obvious he had no intention of backing off. The portly Leighton then made a big mistake. He turned for the buckboard. He almost made it. He was about to hoist himself to the buckboard's seat when Cotton Blossom sank his teeth into the seat of his pin-striped trousers and tore fabric.

"By the Eternal," Leighton bawled, as Barnfield drove away, "I'll sue!"

"I'd think about that," Barnfield replied. "We were trespassing."

In the barn loft, Nathan laughed until he cried, but Eulie wasn't so jubilant.

"I'd have paid good money to see that," said Nathan, wiping his eyes.

"I'm glad you enjoyed it," Eulie said, "because it could cost us more than money. If that pair does any talking, somebody could connect the dog to us. You heard what he said about Bean being nine months behind with his rent. They were trespassing, so that one Cotton Blossom went after can't complain about that. But he *can* go to court, get a judgement against Bean, and come back with the sheriff. They could take *our* horses and saddles, damn it, as part of Bean's property, to satisfy his debt."

"Like hell they can," Nathan said. "I never heard of such, taking a man's property for back rent."

"That doesn't mean it can't happen," Eulie replied. "Let's hope it can't be done quickly."

But as the day dragged on, they saw nobody, and eventually they joined Cotton Blossom in an empty stall near their horses. They drank water from their canteens and chewed on jerked beef from their provisions. Nathan fed Cotton Blossom hunks of jerky, and finally the three of them dozed in the heat of the afternoon. It was near sundown when they finally heard the rattle of wagons, announcing the arrival of Roy Bean and his Mexican teamsters. The wagons were drawn up near the barn. The oxen were unharnessed and turned into an adjoining corral, where Delmano and Renato forked hay down to them. Bean entered the barn, looking for Nathan and Eulie.

"Well," he said, finding them, "I reckon nobody come huntin' you."

"No," said Nathan, "but a pair of hombres was looking for you."

"Not really," Eulie corrected. "We heard them talking, and they had the notion to look around for something of yours they could take for back rent. Their names were Leighton and Barnfield, and it seemed like Leighton's idea. Cotton Blossom bit him on the behind and they left, with talk of a suit."

Bean laughed. "Lord A'mighty, Stone, I got to have me that dog. I'll give you fifty dollars fer him."

"Sorry," Nathan said, "I can't part with him. He's all the family I have left."

"Now as I look at 'im a mite closer," Bean said, "I reckon he does have yer eyes."

It was Eulie's turn to laugh, and Nathan joined in. Bean finally turned serious.

"I fin'lly collected some freightin' money that's been owin' me since spring. I went by an' give some to Leighton, to git the greedy varmint off'n my back."

"You caught your rent up, then," Eulie said.

"Some of it," said Bean. "Don't owe fer but five months now."*

"Since we can't go into town," Nathan said, "how are chances of us going to the house long enough for a decent meal? We'll bring our own grub."

"No need fer that," Bean said, "an' I'll feed the dog too. Come on. Delmano and Renato can eat after they bring them other teams an' wagons from town."

"Speaking of town," Eulie said, "have the McClendon riders been searching for us?"

"No," Bean replied, "an' you ain't got to worry about that. McClendon jist slapped a thousand-dollar bounty on each of yer heads, an' telegraphed the sheriffs in different towns, sendin' yer names an' descriptions."

"How in hell can he do that?" Nathan exploded. "He's not the law, and besides, we fired in self-defense."

"That's how powerful he is," said Bean. "He sent men all over town, an' they hunted till they found that boardin' house where you took a room. They got yer names from the register."

"Then we won't be safe wherever we go," Eulie said.

"That's spilt milk," said Bean.

They entered the house, and it was just as cluttered as the yard. The living room had no furniture. Instead, there was a pile of wagon canvas, old harness, a saddle, bridles, and four enormous wooden kegs that might have once—and perhaps still—contained whiskey. From there they went directly into the dining room. There was a heavy, handmade X-frame oak table that could easily seat twenty. There was a backless oak bench on each side, each one stretching the length of the table.

"Set," Bean commanded. "I know where ever'thing is."

Nathan and Eulie took their seats on one side of the table, watching Bean as he fired up an enormous wood stove that squatted in the adjoining kitchen. He made the coffee first, and when it was ready, cheerfully poured it into unmatched cups. He then set about preparing the meal. He brought knives and forks to the table, and then plates, none of which were alike. Finally he brought platters of ham,

---

* Bean was eventually evicted from the house for nonpayment of rent. That part of San Antonio is still known to some as "Bean Town."

eggs, and fried potatoes. He refilled the coffee cups, returned the pot to the stove, and took his seat on the other
side of the table. There was no talk until the meal was
finished. It was Nathan who finally spoke.

"You sure you want a pair of teamsters that's dodging
the law?"

"I ain't sure that'll be a problem," said Bean. "You know
Texas is under military law, an' that means most towns has
got a guv'ment-appointed sheriff. From what I seen in Austin an' Houston, lawmen that's been appointed by the Federals don't get excited long as it's Rebs agin Rebs. You
gun down a blue coat an' they'll set the whole damn army
after yer hide. I reckon when old McClendon hollers
froggy, San Antonio jumps, but that don't include the Federals. They're spread too thin, an' they're scared to death
of the Comanches."

"The soldiers control the telegraph, then," Nathan said.

"Damn right they do," said Bean. "McClendon raised
enough hell, I'd say, till they let him send his telegrams,
but they won't mean doodly, comin' from him. There's talk
the officer in charge in San Antone might get raked over
fer allowin' McClendon to use the telegraph. Jist be ready
to move out at first light."

*   *   *

August 27, 1866. Bound for Corpus Christi.

Bean's wagon led out at dawn. Delmano and Renato
followed, while Eulie and Nathan brought up the rear with
the fourth and fifth wagons. Both their horses and the packhorse trailed Nathan's wagon on lead ropes. Nathan had
made it his business to be last in line, knowing that Cotton
Blossom would follow the wagon. It would lessen the
chances of their being surprised from the rear, by Comanches or anyone else. The empty wagons made good time.
By Bean's estimate, fifteen miles.

"You'd do a hell of a lot better," Nathan observed,
around the supper fire, "if you took a load south from San
Antonio. Don't you ever haul anything *to* Corpus Christi?"

"Nothin' to haul," Bean replied. "Hell, after four years
of war, Texas ain't got nothin' to ship out. Ever'thing's got
to be brung in."

As Bean had predicted, the Comanches didn't molest the empty wagons. Sixty miles north of Corpus Christi, they had built their supper fire on the east bank of the Nueces, where the river began its southward journey toward the gulf. Suddenly, Cotton Blossom trotted a few yards downriver, his hackles rising.

"Somebody's coming," said Nathan.

"Indians, maybe," Eulie said.

"No," Nathan replied. "It's just one horse."

"Keep yer guns handy," said Bean. "In these times, you don't give no man the benefit of the doubt."

The stranger evidently shared Bean's skepticism, for he reined up well out of rifle range.

"Hello the camp," the rider shouted. "I'm friendly. Got three men down the river a ways, an' we've had Injun trouble."

"Ride on in," Bean responded, "but keep yer hands where we kin see 'em."

The stranger rode in, reins looped about the saddle horn, his hands shoulder high. His horse was a bay, and nothing seemed unusual about the man. His black Stetson had seen a lot of dust, wind, and rain, and his flannel shirt and Levi's pants were far from new. His Colt was tied down on his left hip, butt forward for a crosshand draw. He might have been a drifter or even a cowboy although Nathan noted that he sat a single-rigged saddle.

"Git down," Bean invited.

Warily the stranger dismounted, and Bean said nothing more. While the rider had already told them the nature of his trouble, it was still up to him to state what help he expected of Bean and his companions. He spoke, directing his appeal to Bean.

"There's four of us," he began, "two of 'em bad hurt. I'm Blevins. Me an' Springer wasn't hurt. Springer stayed with Coe an' Walker, while I come lookin' for help."

"Nearest town's sixty mile away," said Bean. "How'd you know we was here?"

"We're downwind from you," Blevins said. "I smelt smoke from your fire."

Bean nodded, for it was possible.

"Damn Comanches kilt three of our horses an' both pack mules," Blevins continued. "We got no way to get Coe an' Walker to a doc, an' no way to move our goods the mules was carryin'. If your wagons ain't too loaded to make room for us, we'd pay."

"Depends," said Bean, "on where yer headed. We got freight waitin' fer us in Corpus Christi. I reckon we could take you an' yer supplies there."

"We'd expect nothing more," Blevins replied. "Must be a doc there, an' we could buy horses an' pack mules."

"We'll take two wagons," said Bean. "One fer the wounded men an' one fer saddles, packsaddles, an' the load the mules was carryin'. I'll take my wagon, an' Eli, you drive yours. Stone, saddle your horse an' ride on ahead with Blevins. Delmano, you an' Renato stay here in camp."

It was a strange request, and for a fleeting moment, Nathan thought he caught some alarm in Blevins's eyes. Nathan saddled his horse, mounted, and followed Blevins downriver, and he believed his own thoughts were in line with Bean's. In leaving Nathan's wagon behind, they also were leaving two of the horses. Bean clearly wasn't sure of this situation, and wanted Nathan mounted and unencumbered by the heavy freight wagon. Nathan caught up to the other rider, for he had a question.

"Lucky for you, makin' it to the river," Nathan said. "Where did the Comanches attack?"

"Maybe two miles east of where we stood an' fought," said Blevins. "We knowed there was water ahead, for we could see some greenery."

"After woundin' two men and leavin' you afoot," Nathan said, "it's some mystery why they didn't take your scalps and your goods. You must have laid some of them low."

"Yeah," said Blevins. "There was eight of 'em, an' we gunned down four."

Nathan said nothing, but his sharp eyes noted the absence of a rifle on Blevins's saddle, nor was there a boot for one. While it was possible the four had fought off Comanches with revolvers, it didn't seem likely. Nathan wanted a look at the saddles belonging to the other riders. From the corner of his eye, he caught movement to his left—unbidden, Cotton Blossom followed.

Chapter 9

❖

It took only a few minutes for Nathan and Blevins to reach
the place near the river where the four men had stood off
the Comanches, and it took just a moment for Nathan to
discover that all had not been as Blevins had claimed. The
three horses *had* obviously died as the result of Comanche
arrows, but the pack mules had been shot through the head.

"All this wasn't Comanche work," Nathan said. "When
they attacked us, they had only bows and arrows. Those
mules were shot at close range. Hell, I can see the powder
burns from here."

"And just what would you of done?" Blevins demanded.
"They come down on us out of nowhere, an' there wasn't
no cover. Not even a mesquite bush. We needed a barricade an' we needed it quick. Better the mules than us."

"Where are the packsaddles and their loads?" Nathan
asked.

"Me an' Springer managed to tote ever'thing on to the
river," Blevins replied. "We knowed the Comanches would
come back for their dead, even if they done it after dark,
an' we didn't want 'em takin' all we had. Hell, we lost
enough."

When he and Blevins reached the camp near the river,
Nathan wasn't all that surprised to find that, while Coe and
Walker had been wounded, the wounds weren't nearly as
serious as Blevins had implied. He introduced his three
companions, and Nathan didn't like the looks of them. Coe
was minus his shirt and a dirty bandage covered most of
his left shoulder, while Walker's Levi's had been slit and
his right leg had been swathed in bandages above the knee.
Springer, Coe, and Walker—like Blevins—wore range
clothes, and each of them was armed with Colts. The butts
of the weapons were slick, Nathan noticed, from frequent
use. It was immediately apparent that the wounded men, if

they had been wounded at all, were in no danger. Nathan saw it as a ploy Blevins had used to influence Roy Bean's judgment. The four men, gunwise and otherwise, were a salty bunch. Obviously all they needed were horses to replace the mounts they'd lost and a means of transporting the heavy packsaddles. A quick look at the three men's saddles revealed that only two of them carried rifles. Nathan looked long and hard at the packsaddles, while the four men eyed him. Among them, the four could have carried necessary provisions in their saddlebags and bed rolls. Certainly the enormous canvas-wrapped loads the mules had borne were more than grub and personal belongings.

Nathan stood beside his horse, waiting for Bean and Eulie to arrive with the wagons. There was something wrong here, and since Bean had made a commitment to these men, it would be up to him to reach some decision. Bean reined up his teams and stepped down from the wagon box. Eulie remained where she was while Blevins again introduced his companions.

Roy Bean wasted no time in saying exactly what Nathan Stone had thought. "By God, Blevins," he said, "them mules was shot at close range, and yer pards ain't been more'n nicked, if that. I don't take kindly to havin' a man lie to me. You ain't got enough money to hire my wagons, an' I won't take you nowhere without some damn convincin' talk. Now talk."

Bean had his Winchester in the crook of his right arm, but the four men had their eyes on Nathan Stone. He stood with his thumbs hooked in his pistol belt near the butts of his Colts. Eulie had drawn her wagon up beside Bean's, and now leaned back against the seat, right hand resting near her Colt.

Blevins bowed to Bean's ultimatum. "All right, damn it," he said, "I wasn't levelin' with you. I only said what I had to. Like I told Stone, when the Comanches come down on us, we had no cover. We had to fort up quick, an' it was the mules or us. Now we're needin' a wagon—maybe two— so's we can get to the nearest town. We're on gover'ment business, an' you'll be paid."

"I got all the gover'ment business I can afford," Bean replied. "You lied to me once, Blevins, an' if you can't show some proof you're with the gover'ment, then the bunch of you can set here till you rot."

"I got proof," Blevins said. "In my shirt pocket."

"Use yer left hand," said Bean, "an' do it slow."

Slowly Blevins complied. He then tossed the object to Bean, who caught it in his left hand. It proved to be a silver star in a circle. The badge of a Texas Ranger.

"I reckon that covers you," Bean said, "but it ain't big enough to cover the rest of these hombres. They got somethin' like this, it's time to show it. You first, an' do it slow." He pointed the Winchester at Springer.

Slowly Springer removed another of the silver emblems from a pocket and Bean shifted the muzzle of the Winchester toward Coe, only to be shown a third Ranger symbol.

"I reckon you've seen enough," Blevins said, sarcasm touching his voice.

"You reckon wrong," said Bean. "One more." He swung the Winchester's deadly snout toward Walker.

There was no change in Bean's expression when Walker produced the badge. Again he turned to Blevins with a question.

"Jist where was you bound when the Comanches clipped yer wings? Fer sure you wasn't goin' to Corpus Christi, an' now yer ready to pay to go there."

"None of your damn business where we were bound," Blevins snarled. "You said you're going to Corpus Christi. We're going there because it's the nearest place we can buy horses and pack mules. Are you satisfied?"

"No," said Bean, "I ain't. I take you to Corpus Cristi, an' I'm makin' myself a party to whatever it is yer up to. I don't care a damn fer the *why* of it, but I'm sure as hell goin' to know where you're bound to end up."

"All right," said Blevins. "This and no more. We're on our way to the outpost at Laredo. When we get to Corpus Christi, why don't you telegraph the Laredo post commander?"

"Maybe I will," Bean replied. "Load yer saddles an' packs in the second wagon, an' them of ye needin' a ride, pile into mine."

Bean mounted the wagon box and waited until Springer, Coe, and Walker had clambered in through the open pucker of the wagon. Nathan thought the wounded men handled themselves well. Maybe a little too well. By the time the two wagons reached Bean's camp it was almost dark. Cotton Blossom was nowhere to be seen. It was significant that Bean said nothing to the new arrivals about taking a turn at watch. The saddles belonging to Springer, Coe, and Walker, along with the loaded, canvas-wrapped packsaddles, remained in Eulie's wagon, and the four men were never far away. The questionable quartet were within Bean's camp, but they were not part of it. They spread their blankets near Eulie's wagon, while Eulie and Nathan distanced themselves from the four. It was almost time for Nathan and Eulie to begin the second watch when Cotton Blossom finally appeared.

"He doesn't like them," Eulie whispered. "Rangers or not, I'm with him."

Nathan said nothing, waiting until they joined Bean, Delmano, and Renato. It would be the first opportunity they'd had to talk freely, and Nathan wasted no time.

Bean said nothing, listening. "Maybe you're satisfied," Nathan said grimly, "but I'm not. I've seen the varmints lookin' at our horses. They're needin' three horses and we have three. A damn shame we have oxen pullin' the wagons instead of mules."

"Ain't it, though," said Bean. "Them packsaddles is loaded almighty heavy with somethin', an' fer now they're needin' a wagon. I don't know where or how they got them Ranger stars. They're real enough, but something about this bunch jist don't wash. I'm thinkin' we'd best keep our guns handy."

"I'm thinkin' you, Delmano, and Renato had best spread your blankets near enough for us to keep close watch," Nathan said. "This bunch could kill all of you while you sleep, givin' 'em the edge over me and Eli."

"We'll do that," said Bean. "I don't trust this bunch as far as I could fling an ox by the tail."

"Neither do we," Nathan replied. "Just how long do you intend to trail with them without calling their hand?"

"Jist until first light," said Bean. "When we're done with breakfast, you an' Eli be ready. When Delmano, Renato, an' me go to our wagons, it'll be fer our Winchesters. Foller my lead an' we'll get the drop. Then one of us is goin' after them packsaddle loads. I reckon when we find out jist what these hombres is hidin', they'll either prove the truth of what they told us, or we'll see 'em fer what they *really* are."

With that, followed by Delmano and Renato, Bean faded into the darkness, leaving Nathan, Eulie, and Cotton Blossom alone. They stood beneath cottonwoods, watching as the trio became visible in the dim starlight. They were going to spread their blankets near Bean's wagon.

"We'll stay here," Nathan said quietly. "Blevins and his friends are down yonder behind your wagon, and we're downwind from them."

"None of this makes any sense," Eulie said. "I don't believe a word those four have spoken, but if they aren't what they seem, why are they going to Corpus Christi? Even if there are no soldiers, the government freight office will have the telegraph."

"If none of us reach Corpus Christi alive," said Nathan, "they won't be concerned with us using the telegraph. They could kill us somewhere north of town, and taking our horses, they'd all be mounted. One of them could ride on to Corpus Christi, buy a pair of pack animals, and the four of them could be on their way to the border with nobody the wiser."

"But suppose they *are* Rangers," Eulie said, "and when we force their hand, we kill some of them? God, we'll both go to Huntsville for life."

"If they're leveling with us," said Nathan, "I don't expect any shooting, and if it comes to gunplay over what's in those packs, then these pilgrims are no more Rangers than we are."

The dawn came and breakfast was eaten in silence. Bean, Delmano, and Renato did nothing to arouse suspicion. They caught up their teams, leading them to the wagons as though to be harnessed. But inside the wagon box, next to the seat, each man carried a Winchester, and when they turned with the weapons in their hands, the surprise was total. The cocking of the Winchesters was simultaneous.

"Nobody move," Bean said. "If yer what ye claim to be, then they won't be no harm done. Stone, you keep yer eye on Blevins. Delmano, Renato, and me will cover the others. Eli, git into that wagon an' tear into one of them packs. It's time we was knowin' what's so almighty valuable to these gents."

"Damn you," said Blevins, "you'll pay for this."

Bean said nothing. Nathan kept his eyes on the furious Blevins as Eulie climbed into the wagon. There was some commotion as she broke into one of the canvas-wrapped packs.

"Well?" Bean shouted.

"Gold," Eulie replied. "Double eagles, in canvas bags, with the mark of a Houston bank."

The very mention of gold was enough to distract a man, but Blevins and his companions knew what was coming, and the initial shock bought them a small advantage. It was all the edge they were going to get, and the four went for their guns. Blevins fired once, but the shot went wild as two slugs from Nathan's Colt tore into his belly. The three Winchesters roared almost as one. Springer, Coe, and Walker died without getting off a shot. It was all over in little more than a heartbeat. Eulie climbed down from the wagon and stood looking at the carnage.

"I reckon they told us what we needed to know," Bean said. "Somewhere betwixt here an' Houston, the buzzards is pickin' the bones of four Rangers. These varmints stole that gold an' was headin' fer the border, sure as hell."

"That's a safe bet," said Nathan, "and if it was taken from a bank, we're up against more than the Texas Rangers. I'd gamble the Federals are looking for it right now."

"Damn right they are," Bean agreed, "an' we're goin' to protect ourselves by takin' ever'thing these varmints has got in their pockets, includin' them Ranger stars. When we git to Corpus Christi, we're turnin' it all over to the gover'-ment. Stone, you search Blevins an' we'll get the others."

The search resulted in money, pocket knives, and pocket watches. Walker, Springer, and Coe each had two, a fair indication they had ambushed and robbed their pursuers.

"They's a shovel in ever' wagon," said Bean. "This bunch ain't deservin' of it, but we'd be skunks the equal of them if we didn't take time fer decent buryin'."

Nathan, Bean, Delmano, and Renato dug the graves, all within a few feet of one another. When the dead men had been buried and the graves filled, Bean stood at the head of the graves and removed his hat. Then, with a reverence Nathan would never have believed he possessed, he turned his face heavenward and spoke.

"Lord, we wasn't aimin' to gun down these thieves an' killers, but they wouldn't have it no other way. Resurrect the varmints or kick 'em on into hell, as you see fit. Amen."

The teams were quickly harnessed and Bean again led out in the first wagon, the others following. Blevins's horse had been tied behind the wagon Eulie drove, and Cotton

Blossom again foraged far ahead. It was he who warned them of approaching riders, this time from the south. By the time the six men rode into sight, their blue uniforms identified them. Union soldiers! Bean reined up, signal enough to the trailing wagons, and they reined up as well. Bean held up his hand and the soldiers drew up beside his wagon. One of them was a lieutenant, one a sergeant, and the remaining four were privates. The officer spoke.

"I'm Lieutenant Willingham and this is Sergeant Winkler. We've just been assigned to Corpus Christi, arriving there on a packet from New Orleans. We had a telegram waiting for us, ordering us to move out immediately. Four men robbed a bank in Houston, escaping with more than forty thousand in gold. They were pursued by five Texas Rangers. They managed to kill four of the Rangers in an ambush. The fifth Ranger escaped with his life, and he seemed to think the four men were going to cut between San Antonio and Corpus Christi, and make a run for the border. Have you seen them?"

"We have," Bean said. "After they kilt the Rangers, they was hit by the Comanches. Lost their pack mules an' three horses. Showed us them Ranger stars an' wanted a ride to Corpus Christi. I'm Roy Bean, and them's all my wagons an' drivers behind me. I offered 'em a ride, but even with them four Ranger stars, we didn't trust 'em. This mornin', we got the drop, an' one of my drivers busted into one of them packs. When we found the gold, them four went fer their guns. Wasn't nothin' we could do but cut 'em down. Planted 'em maybe five er six mile upriver."

"You have the gold, then," said Lieutenant Willingham.

"We got it," Bean said. "It's in the fourth wagon, an' we ain't laid a hand on it, 'cept the one sack we opened. We went through the pockets of the varmints, takin' ever'thing. Even the Ranger stars. The one horse they had is on a lead rope behind the wagon with the gold."

"You did exactly the right thing, sir," the Lieutenant said. "We were given execution warrants for those four, and you did no more than we would have been forced to do, had we caught up with them. Since you're going on to Corpus Christi, I would take it as a favor if the gold can remain where it is. I'll post a guard over it at night, until we can take it off your hands."

"Wagon's empty, 'cept fer the gold," said Bean. "Leave it there, an' welcome."

Nathan, Eulie, Delmano, and Renato had left their wagons and had moved close enough to hear the conversation between the officer and Bean.

"Two of those men had been wounded," Nathan said, "and not by Comanche arrows. They'd been shot."

"That fits in with what we were told," Lieutenant Willingham said. "The Ranger who managed to escape said he thought two of the robbers had been hit during the ambush."

Again Bean led out, and this time, a soldier rode on each side of Eulie's wagon. Two more followed Nathan's wagon, while Lieutenant Willingham and Sergeant Winkler rode beside Bean's wagon. Despite the delays, they made fifteen miles. The soldiers set up their own camp near Bean's, and from dusk until dawn, took turns—in pairs—standing watch near the wagon with the gold. The procedure continued for two more days and nights, until Bean reined up his wagon near the government warehouse. Eulie swung her wagon wide, and then backed it up, so that the gold might be conveniently unloaded.

Corpus Christi, Texas. September 7, 1866.

Enough freight had backed up to convince Bean they shouldn't lay over any longer than necessary, and the morning after their arrival, they began loading the wagons for the return to San Antonio. It was early September, but the Texas sun showed them no mercy. The bucket of water Bean had brought was good for less than an hour. Delmano and Renato occasionally poured a dipperful over their sweaty heads.

"Damn it," said Bean, after filling the bucket a second time, "take off long enough to dunk yerselves in the Gulf."

The wagon half-loaded, Nathan and Eulie paused to straighten up, resting their aching backs.

"It's been a while since I've sweated like this," Nathan groaned.

"Not me," Eulie replied. "Although I wasn't the manchild Daddy wanted, he worked me like one. Until the war killed the market for cotton, I reckon there wasn't a slave anywhere that worked harder than I did. Daddy had a quaint way of thinking. An unmarried woman living at home had to earn her keep, and he was the judge as to how much work she must do to earn it."

When Bean had designated what was to be loaded, he helped load the wagons, wrestling pieces heavy enough for two men. They worked steadily, and before sundown, the wagons were loaded with all the teams could pull.

"We'll get us a good feed of town grub, hit the blankets early, an' pull out at first light," Bean said.

He then headed for one of the saloons, followed by Delmano and Renato. Nathan and Eulie, leaving their horses and the packhorse at the hitch rail, entered a cafe, followed by Cotton Blossom. The place was far from full, and the few patrons eyed the newcomers, especially Cotton Blossom.

"Mister," said the cook, "the dog stays outside."

"He's a paying customer," Nathan replied. "We'll take a table near the back and I'll see that he doesn't bother anybody."

"Nathan," said Eulie, after they had taken a table and ordered their food, "There was a man who spent most of the day watching us load the wagons. I'd swear I've seen him somewhere."

"I saw him," said Nathan, "and I'm wondering if his interest in what we were doing didn't have something to do with those twenty cases of Winchesters and the cannisters of ammunition we were loading. In the hands of a Comanche, each of those rifles is worth its weight in gold."

"Outlaw whites might attack us and then deal with the Comanches?"

"Why not?" Nathan said. "It's happened before."

"This seemed like a good idea, at first, bullwhacking. Now, I'm not so sure. First the Comanches on the way to San Antonio, and then those thieves and killers when we started south. If we hadn't gotten the advantage, those men would have killed us."

"The white thieves are more dangerous than the Comanches," said Nathan, "because we'll be up against rifles instead of mostly bows and arrows. Men with rifles can hole up and cut us down from cover."

After they'd eaten and paid for their meal, they stepped out into the gathering darkness. To the right of the cafe entrance, new lumber had been stacked head high, and within the shadow of it, Nathan caught fleeting movement. Colt in his hand, he turned to face the danger, only to have lead slam into his right side, just above his belt. A second slug tore into his chest high on the left side. There were more shots, one of them sounding far away. On the ground, Nathan could see muzzle flashes only inches away. Eulie was on her knees, returning fire. It ended suddenly and Nathan heard Eulie's voice.

"I got him, Nathan. I got him."

The patrons in the cafe remained there. Men erupted from the nearby saloon, Bean, Delmano, and Renato in the lead. Cotton Blossom crouched over Nathan, his teeth bared, daring anyone to come close.

"Lord God," said Bean, when he and his Mexican teamsters arrived. Eulie had calmed Cotton Blossom and was on her knees, still clutching the Colt. Blood welled out of a wound just below her left knee. But it was Nathan Stone who looked dead.

"Delmano," Bean ordered, "git over yonder to that gover'ment warehouse an' tell them soldiers to git over here *pronto*, bringin' the doc with 'em. Eli, if you got any say with that dog, git him away 'fore the doc gets here. Lemme have that Colt, an' I'll see if you plugged the varmint that started all this."

Her eyes on Nathan, Eulie surrendered the Colt, and Bean moved cautiously toward the stacked lumber. It wasn't much cover, for it had been ricked in a loose manner so that the sun might dry it. In the shadow lay a man, belly-down, his right hand still clutching a revolver. Bean rolled the body over, so that a patch of light from the cafe window shone on the face. Immediately he recognized the man who had been watching them load the wagons. Even in the poor light, Bean could see the pair of bullet holes in the chest oozing blood, and barely visible from a shirt pocket, the corner of a piece of paper. Without knowing what it was, Bean took it.

Within minutes, Lieutenant Willingham, Sergeant Winkler, and two privates arrived. With them was a medic—Lieutenant Pilkington—who had just been assigned to the outpost at Corpus Christi. It was fortunate that Lieutenant Willingham recognized Nathan and Eulie as two of Bean's drivers, recalling their part in recovering the stolen gold.

Lieutenant Pilkington knelt beside Nathan, and failing to find a pulse, tried the big artery in the neck.

"He's alive," Pilkington said, getting to his feet. "Get him on the stretcher and down to quarters. Quickly."

The two privates who had brought the stretcher lifted Nathan onto it and set off toward the government warehouse where the soldiers were temporarily quartered. Sergeant Winkler helped Eulie to her feet; she leaned on him, and the two followed Lieutenant Pilkington. Lieutenant Willingham then turned to Roy Bean.

"What do you know about this?" the officer asked.

"Not much more'n you do," said Bean. "Stone an' Prater come here fer grub, while me an' my Mex drivers went to the saloon. Next thing we knowed, guns was blastin' away. We heard five shots, three of 'em quick. The last two, I'd say, was fired by Prater, and I reckon it was them that kilt the bushwhacker."

"He's dead, then," the officer said.

"Considerable," said Bean. "He's over yonder, betwixt the cafe an' that pile of lumber."

"If you'll witness it," Willingham said, "I'll search the body. Perhaps we can learn his identity and what his motive was."

At that moment the men within the cafe yielded to their curiosity and came out to see what had happened. Among them was the cook, with a lighted lantern. Bean borrowed the lantern and followed the officer into the shadows where the dead man lay. The search produced only a pocketknife, most of a plug of tobacco, and three double eagles.

"Strange," Lieutenant Willingham said, "the way this happened. You have no idea, I suppose, as to the reason behind it?"

"Nothin' fer sure," said Bean. "Now I got me a problem. Five loaded wagons an' three drivers, includin' me. If you got no objection, I reckon I ought to talk to the doc an' see what the verdict is. Prater took one in the leg, but Stone might have bought the farm. Looked almighty bad."

"Come along," Willingham said. "It might be too soon to learn anything, if Lieutenant Pilkington has to dig out the slugs."

Bunks had been set up in the back of the government warehouse, and on one of them lay Nathan Stone. His upper chest had already been bandaged, and the medic was cleansing the nasty wound in his side. Eulie sat on one of the bunks, anxiety in her eyes. One of the privates held a lamp close, providing as much light as possible for Lieutenant Pilkington. Bean and Willingham kept their silence until Pilkington had bandaged the second wound, and when the medic finally faced them, he answered their questions without being asked.

"If he never has another piece of luck, he's got no gripe coming," said Lieutenant Pilkington. "Shot clean through both times. If either slug had struck a bone, he'd be a dead man. He'll need a month of rest."

"I'm glad fer him," Bean said. "I was jist talkin' to the Lieutenant here, an' he reckons he kin put 'em up at the Shore Hotel till I git back from San Antone."

"We're obliged," Eulie said, "but we can pay."

"We're obliged to you and Stone for your help in recovering that stolen gold," said Lieutenant Willingham. "We'll stable your horses."

"I believe this man should remain here for the night," Lieutenant Pilkington said. "His worst enemy is infection, and I'll need to look in on him at regular intervals."

"I'll stay too, then," said Eulie.

Roy Bean left them there, returning to the loaded wagons where Delmano and Renato waited. Bean unfolded the paper he had removed from the dead man's pocket and lighted a match so that he could see. It was a bounty poster, and while there were no photographs, there was an accurate description of the pair Bean knew as Nathan Stone and Eli Prater. There was a bounty of a thousand dollars on each of their heads. Old McClendon was dead serious.

Chapter 10

◆◆◆

After Lieutenant Pilkington had heavily dosed Nathan with laudanum, he turned to Eulie.

"You're welcome to some of this," he said. "While your wound isn't all that serious, it may cause you some pain. This will help you sleep."

"Thanks," said Eulie, "but I aim to stay awake. You've done well, tending to Nathan's wounds, and we're obliged. Now about all that's to be done is see him through the fever. If you'll get me a bottle of whiskey, I'll do that."

"You're right," the officer said. "That's important, but you can pour whiskey down him as well as I can. He must sweat out the infection. I'll go get the whiskey."

While the medic was gone, Roy Bean returned. Having made certain that none of the military personnel was around, he took the bounty poster from his pocket and passed it to Eulie.

"I took this off'n the varmint that done the shootin'," he said, "an' I reckon it's clear enough why he done it. I told Lieutenant Willingham that I didn't know why ye was shot. It won't help none if word gets around."

Eulie sat up, leaning over enough to see by the light of the lamp next to Nathan's bunk. Quickly she read the death warrant for Nathan and herself.

"I jist thought you'd oughta know," said Bean. "Come mornin', get yerselves a room in that hotel an' lay low fer a while. Stay out of the saloons, an' when Stone can ride, git the hell outa Texas till this blows over."

"Thanks," Eulie said. "Now you have two wagons for which you have no drivers. But we hadn't counted on this."

"Hell," said Bean, "ye got no business goin' back to San Antone, even if ye was able. Delmano an' Renato met up with three Mexes that's needin' some reason fer bein' on this side of the border. I hired two of 'em to drive the extry wagons back to San Antone. If my credit's good fer another wagon an' teams, I'm hirin' the third one. Jist watch yer back, Eli, an' when yer pard's able, saddle up an' ride. Good luck."

On his way out, Bean passed Lieutenant Pilkington returning with a quart bottle of whiskey.

"If he gets too restless during the night," said Pilkington, "then don't hesitate to wake me."

"I doubt I'll be needin' to," Eulie said, "but thanks."

The rest of the bunks had been moved well away from Nathan and Eulie, and Eulie prepared for a long vigil. Some hours into the night she awoke, and feeling Nathan's brow, found he had a raging fever. It was time for the whiskey. She poured a third of the bottle down him, and not being much of a drinking man, he wheezed and coughed. For just a moment he opened his eyes, but there was no recognition in them. She eased him back down on the bunk. As the Lieutenant had promised, Eulie's wound began to ache, and she had no trouble keeping her eyes open for the rest of the night. When the windows began to gray with first light, Lieutenant Pilkington came to examine Nathan's wounds and to change the bandages.

"He could use another slug of that whiskey," Pilkington said. "I'd not be surprised if this fever stays with him all day, but it should break sometime tonight."

"I'll give him half of what's left," said Eulie. "This morning, if you will allow me the use of your stretcher and two of your men, I'll take us a room at the hotel."

"First, I'd better take a look at your own wound," Pilkington said. "How are you feeling?"

"You were right," said Eulie. "That leg hurts like hell, but I can stand on it."

"I don't recommend that for any longer than it takes to reach the hotel," Pilkington said. "Lie down and stretch out that leg."

The wound was clean and Pilkington grunted in satisfaction. He doused it with more disinfectant and bound it with a clean bandage.

"It should heal clean," said Pilkington. "Here's a day's dose of laudanum. Now one of us can help you to the hotel, if you like."

"Thanks," Eulie said, "but it's not that far. While you're

gone for the stretcher, I'll pour some more whiskey down Nathan."

Eulie paid for two weeks in advance at the Shore Hotel, and since it was still early, Nathan was moved there without attracting undue attention. For the time and place, the Shore was fancy. There were braided rugs on the floors and the rooms were large. Extra blankets had been provided for Nathan so that he might sweat out the fever. The room's single window was curtained and the furniture was made of heavy oak.

"His temperature's down," said Lieutenant Pilkington, when he came by in the afternoon to check on Nathan. "By tomorrow, he'll be out of danger, I think. I'll leave you enough laudanum to get him through the night, and by this time tomorrow, he should be awake and ready for some food. I'll see you in the morning."

By late afternoon, Nathan's fever had broken, and near suppertime, he opened his eyes.

"God," he groaned.

"Do your wounds hurt?" Eulie asked.

"No," he croaked, "but my head does. Feel like I've been on a three-day drunk. My mouth and throat feel like a desert. Water."

Eulie fished a tin cup out of a saddlebag and filled it with water for Nathan to drink.

"Thanks," he said. "What'n hell have you been pouring down me?"

"Whiskey," Eulie replied. "You've been burning up with fever."

"How long ... have I ..."

"Since early last night," Eulie said. "The army doctor dug two bullets out of you, and you're supposed to rest."

"Rest, hell. Reach me that chamber pot. Then I want to know who cut down on us, where I am ..."

"All right, damn it, I'll tell you," she said. And she did. Nathan had closed his eyes and she thought he had dropped off to sleep, but when she stopped talking, he was looking straight at her.

"This whole thing just makes me mad as hell," he growled.

Eulie said nothing, but he could see exasperation in her eyes.

"That bushwhacking varmint put two slugs in me before

I could pull my iron," he said. "I came off like a damn greenhorn, and I reckon I got just what I deserved."

"Well, by God," Eulie said, "I'd hoped, after that shooting in San Antone, I wouldn't have to tangle with the Nathan Stone pride again, but I reckon I was wrong. What's bothering you is that you got gunned down in an ambush and a female pistoleer saved your bacon."

That silenced him. The truth was, he felt inadequate. This woman—Eulie Prater—had come to his rescue for the second time in a matter of days, and while he didn't wish to seem ungrateful, it rankled his hide, made him feel less a man. He sighed. She knew him too well.

"If the damn shoe fits, you got to wear it," he said. "I got no call to look down on you. With two slugs in me, I was in no condition to fight back. I'm beholden to you, because if you hadn't plugged him, the varmint that cut me down would have escaped. I'm a prideful man, and there's times when old pride jumps on me and digs in the spurs before I know he has control of me."

"You *were* being a little selfish, wantin' to gun the varmint down," said Eulie. "Hell, he was trying to kill me too. I had as much right to him as you did."

*   *   *

The following morning Lieutenant Pilkington came by and was amazed to find Nathan Stone sitting on the edge of the bed eating breakfast.

"You should be in that bed," said Pilkington. "Do you want to start those wounds bleeding again?"

"I wouldn't be sitting here," Nathan said, "if I wasn't up to it. It's a testimony as to how well you patched me up. I'm obliged."

"I can't take all the credit," said Pilkington. "You were damned lucky. Either of those shots could have killed you if they'd struck bone. When you feel strong enough, Lieutenant Willingham will be wanting to question you. He must file a report on the incident."

Nathan nodded and the medic departed.

"That's all we need," Eulie said, when Pilkington had gone, "is to have our names on file with the military. Somebody's just liable to put two and two together and tie us to that shooting in San Antonio."

"Let them," said Nathan. "They can't prove we've gunned down anybody that wasn't trying to kill us."

"Roy Bean said we should leave Texas as soon as you're able to ride, and do it before they find out we're fugitives."

"By God," Nathan said, "it puts a crimp in my tail, bein' run out when I've done no wrong. Besides, I believe the killers I'm lookin' for are here somewhere."

"Oh, damn," said Eulie wearily, "Nathan Stone's iron-clad pride rears its ugly head again. And don't use your manhunt for an excuse, because you don't have so much as a thread of evidence that a single one of those six men is anywhere in Texas."

It was irrefutable logic, and Nathan grinned despite himself. He then stretched out on the bed, weaker than he had been willing to admit.

"I reckon we'll go," he said.

*   *   *

Corpus Christi, Texas. September 25, 1866.

Two weeks after the shooting, a ship arrived from New Orleans. There was much excitement, for the packet had brought a bundle of newspapers only a few days old. Eulie bought one and the news-starved outpost snatched the rest of them in less than an hour. The paper was a Sunday edition in two sections, so Eulie took one and Nathan the other. Nathan read only a little of the front page when he came off the bed with a shout. Eulie looked at him as though he had lost his mind.

"By God," Nathan said, "They're there! In New Orleans!"

"Who's in New Orleans?" Eulie asked.

"Tobe Snider and Virg Dillard," said Nathan. "But for the one I found in Missouri, I'd lost track of the murdering varmints I'm lookin' for. Now I know there's two of them in New Orleans. Here, read this."

Eulie took the newspaper and found the brief story that had excited Nathan. Snider and Dillard were identified as a pair of killers who had been linked to French Stumberg, the man behind a New Orleans gambling empire. The killers, as the newspaper referred to them, had been freed by the courts through the influence of Stumberg. There was no more, but that was enough.

"We ride out at first light tomorrow," Nathan said.

"Like hell we do," Eulie replied. "Lieutenant Pilkington said you should have a month to recover from your wounds. You've had just half that."

"It's my damn carcass," said Nathan, "and I reckon I know when it's able to ride. I've been all the way across Texas without accomplishing anything except bein' hogtied by you and gettin' myself shot. Now I know where two of those murdering sidewinders are, and by God, I'm going after them."

But Lieutenant Pilkington warned him about opening his wounds by riding before they had properly healed, and Nathan grudgingly agreed to wait another week.

*   *   *

On October first, Nathan and Eulie rode out of Corpus Christi. Cotton Blossom ranged ahead, and with Nathan leading the packhorse, they rode northeastward, following the shoreline.

"Do you aim to stop along the way?" Eulie asked. "There's Houston."

"I don't aim to stop anywhere in Texas," said Nathan. "Like Bean told us, it's time to ride on, and now I have a damn good reason."

Nathan and Eulie passed to the north of Houston, spending their nights on the plains of east Texas beside spring or creek. There was an excitement in Nathan that he found hard to contain, but he was often sobered by something in Eulie's eyes—a despondency—that got to him. She would be with him but a few more months, and when she was gone, that haunting look in her eyes would follow Nathan Stone down every lonely trail he would ride ...

*   *   *

Nathan and Eulie crossed the Mississippi twenty-five miles south of Natchez.

"When we reach New Orleans," Eulie said, "we should find us a boardinghouse, with a stable for the horses."

"I aim to," said Nathan. "Since these two skunks I'm after seem to be under the wing of a big-time gambler, it may take me a while just reaching the varmints."

Chapter 11

❖❖❖

New Orleans. October 16, 1866.

Nathan and Eulie had followed the Mississippi, and their first sight of New Orleans was the western outskirts, which soon would become known as the Garden District. There were no shops, saloons, or hotels, for much of it was residential, with stately two-story dwellings shaded by live oak and magnolia trees. The first identifiable street they reached was St. Charles. They rode for what seemed half a mile before reaching a cross street, which a faded sign said was seventh.

"Damn," Nathan grumbled, "we should have stayed with the river. This is too highfalutin' for boardinghouses and hotels."

"I think we should shy away from the river," said Eulie. "I don't know how it is here, but I talked to a drummer once who had come from St. Louis. He said every drunk, thief, and killer in town always hangs out near the river."

"My kind of people," Nathan said. "We'll ride on for another mile or two, and if we don't soon see a boardin'-house or hotel, we'll ride south, back toward the river."

St. Charles looked like a boulevard into what seemed more and more of a residential area. Virtually all the homes were two story, many of them taking refuge behind what appeared to be stately marble columns, the whole surrounded by well-kept grounds and spreading oaks. Graceful palms hung their heads over the wide street, offering shade from the October sun. A buckboard, drawn by an aging gray horse, approached and passed them. A fashionably dressed woman held the reins in her left hand, an open parasol in her right, and seemed not to notice the pair of dusty riders and their packhorse. Cotton Blossom took offense, trotting after the buckboard, barking.

"Cotton Blossom," Nathan said, "stop that. Come here."

The hound obeyed, not in the least repentant, and gave Nathan a curious look. Eulie laughed.

"I reckon he's never seen anything the equal of that," she said.

"My God," said Nathan, "neither have I. I can't imagine anybody gettin' all frocked up like that. This ain't Sunday, is it?"

"No," Eulie replied. "It's Thursday, I think. Tarnation, if they dress like that in the middle of the week, what *do* they wear on Sunday?"

"I don't know," said Nathan. "If we dig in here for a while and get all civilized, I reckon that's what you'll be wearing. Just promise me you won't tote a parasol when it ain't even rainin'. That looks foolish as hell."

"If I thought you was serious," she said, "I'd shoot you. That's just about the way my daddy thought a woman should get herself up, if she ever had any hope of snaring a man. Me, I always reckoned that if a man had to fight his way past four petticoats and pantaloons, he'd just say the hell with it."

Nathan laughed. "You don't want to be a lady, then."

"I tried not to be for thirty years, but I reckon I would rather be a woman. In private, anyhow."

"The next decent-looking cross street we come to," Nathan said, "I think it's time we cut back toward the river. If we don't find the kind of place we're lookin' for, there should be somebody we can ask. In this fancy neck of the woods, we're likely to be shot, just on general principles."

They rode south on Eutarpe, and nine blocks later, found themselves within sight of the Mississippi. As Nathan had expected, there were warehouses, eateries, saloons, and bawdy houses strung out along the river as far as he could see. Far ahead, where the Mississippi fed into the Gulf, the masts of sailing ships were visible.

"I doubt we'll find decent quarters by asking directions at a saloon or whorehouse," said Nathan. "Let's try one of these warehouses. Where there's wagons backed up, there'll be bullwhackers."

Finding a wagon that had just been loaded, they approached the grizzled old man who was preparing to mount the box.

"Pardner," Nathan said, "we're lookin' to be here a spell.

With three horses and a dog, we're needin' a decent board-inghouse instead of a hotel. Can you point us in the right direction?"

"You're lookin' fer the McQueen place, out on Bayou Road," the teamster said. "Barnaby stables hosses fer town folks. He raises hosses, trains 'em, an' races 'em. Bess, his wife, keeps a boardin' house mostly fer hoss folks that's here fer the races. Ride east fer maybe a mile, takin' a left on Iberville. Take a right after six blocks, follerin' Rampart two mile. Look fer a sign that'll say Bayou Road. There's a sign pointin' to McQueen's, and you kin see the hoss barn from the road."

"We're obliged," Nathan said.

Nathan and Eulie rode on, receiving curious looks from people they met along the way. Eventually they crossed a wide boulevard, and there were two faded signs nailed to a post at the corner. Eulie rode closer to read them.

"This is Orleans," she said. "The other must be French. *Vieux Carré.*"*

They were less than a mile west of Bayou Road, and once they were on it, the town quickly fell away. They passed beneath mighty oaks from which the leaves had fallen, leaving only wraiths of Spanish moss trailing from barren limbs. Dry leaves crunched under the hooves of the horses. Nathan's horse shied as a cottontail sprang up, running for its life with Cotton Blossom in hot pursuit.

"It's so peaceful," said Eulie. "I like it."

"It reminds me of the old South, before the war," Nathan said.

"I can't see that the war even touched it," said Eulie. "Did it?"

"Louisiana seceded in 1861," Nathan said. "Farragut moved Federals into Vicksburg, Natchez, Baton Rouge, and New Orleans in 1862. The Rebs never got this far, from what I've heard. We didn't get deep enough into town. I'd bet my saddle there's soldiers here somewhere."

Despite the seclusion of the McQueen place, it wasn't that far from town, and they soon were able to see the outbuildings to their right. The road led them down a tree-lined lane and a message burned into a slab of oak wel-

---

* An exclusive district in the eastern part of New Orleans.

comed them to McQueen's. Three hounds loped to meet
them, baying as they came, and Cotton Blossom rose to
the challenge.

"They'll eat him alive," said Eulie.

Just when it seemed the prophecy was about to be ful-
filled, the trio was halted in their tracks by a booming voice.

"Come here, you dogs."

The hounds turned and loped away. Cotton Blossom,
aware that he'd had nothing to do with their retreat, wisely
gave up pursuit. Nathan and Eulie reined up, waiting, as
the man who had called off the dogs approached. The enormous structure from which he had emerged looked to be
three hundred yards in length, with adjoining corrals at either end. To the south of it, there were other outbuildings
that looked like conventional barns. There was no house
in sight. Nathan and Eulie turned their attention to the big
man who was about to greet them.

"I'm Barnabas McQueen," he said. He was maybe six
and a half feet tall, somewhere past fifty, and weighed a
good two hundred, none of it fat. He had gray hair, friendly
blue eyes, and he dressed like a Westerner. His riding boots
were jet black and newly polished, while his brown Levi's
and red-checked flannel shirt were clean. His gray Stetson
looked new.

"I'm Nathan Stone and my partner's Eli Prater. We aim
to be in these parts for a while. As you can see, we have
three horses and a dog. When we asked a teamster about
a decent place to board for a spell, he sent us to you."

"You need to talk to Bess," said McQueen. "We don't
actually have a boardinghouse. They're just cabins with
bunks. Sleeping quarters where you can stash your saddles
and belongings. There's a cookhouse, with a full-time cook.
We feed three times a day. But you're a mite early. The
next race is set for December twenty-ninth, the first Saturday after Christmas."

"You cater mostly to folks here for the horse races,
then," Nathan said.

"Usually," said McQueen, "but we don't turn away
teamsters, drummers, or anybody else that don't hanker to
stay in town. Sleepin' quarters and meals is a dollar a day,
or twenty dollars a month. Same for each of the horses."

"My God," Nathan exclaimed, "that's high for stablin'
a horse."

McQueen laughed. "That includes grain, my friend. You must remember there's been a war going on. We haven't had a decent crop of *anything* since 1860. The grain comes from St. Louis by steamboat. Why don't you ride around and compare? I'm sure you can beat our prices, but I must warn you, during the week or so before the race, the others all double their prices. We don't."

"Nathan," Eulie said. "I like it here."

"So do I," said Nathan. "We'll stay a spell."

"Ride on to the house, then," McQueen said. "It's over yonder beyond the barns. You can stable your horses in the second one."

He watched them ride away, and Eulie waited until they were well out of his hearing before she spoke.

"You're always forgetting that I have two thousand dollars. This would be worth twice what he's asking. At least we didn't have to come up with a story as to why we're here. You don't look all that innocent with a Colt on each hip."

"None of his damn business," said Nathan irritably. "He took it upon himself, assumin' we're here for a horse race. Hell, that's ten weeks off."

"No matter," Eulie replied. "We're going to that race. At least, I am. In the old days, before the war, Daddy owned some thoroughbreds. I've ridden in a race or two myself. That's why I took Daddy's horse. I trained him."

"Damn," said Nathan, with a straight face, "havin' seen you naked as a skint coyote, I reckoned there wasn't any secrets left. Now you tell me you train and ride thoroughbreds. You find that easier than ropin' and brandin' men?"

"I do," Eulie said, with an equally straight face, "and a hell of lot more satisfying. Horses are smarter, they learn faster, and unless they're mistreated, they don't get ornery and bite at you."

Nathan laughed, slapping his thigh with his hat. By then, they were almost to the house. Built of logs, it was squat and sprawling, with two chimneys. A few yards from the main house was another log structure that looked like the cookhouse McQueen had mentioned. Beside it was stacked three head-high ricks of stove-length wood. Smoke spiraled from the chimney and the air was rich with the tantalizing odor of cooking food. Well beyond the house, there was a line of lesser log structures that had to be the cabins where

the boarders slept. Eulie and Nathan dismounted, and by
the time they reached the long porch, the front door had
been opened by a woman who seemed a fitting companion
for Barnabas McQueen.

"Welcome," she said. "I'm Bess." She was tall and still
slender, and the years had been kind to her. While there
was gray in her hair, there was youth in her eyes. Nathan
answered her greeting.

"I'm Nathan Stone, ma'am, and my partner's Eli Prater.
We'll be needin' room and board for a while. We spoke to
Barnabas on the way in. There'll be us, our three horses,
and my dog, Cotton Blossom. Here's a hundred dollars for
us and the horses for a month. Barnabas didn't say how
much for the dog."

"And he'd better not," Bess said. "There's no charge for
him. Already I'm feeding that pack of four-legged gluttons
that Barnabas keeps, and not a one of them worth the
shells it'd take to blow their heads off. Take your pick of
the sleeping quarters. Right now, they're all empty. Stable
your horses in the nearest barn. We'll have supper in an
hour."

While the cabins were small, they were spacious, with a
comfortable bed, dresser with mirror, water pitcher and
basin, and a pair of cane-bottomed, ladder-back chairs.
There was a coal oil lamp on the dresser and curtains on
each of the two windows. The back door opened to reveal
an outhouse. A large braided oval rug covered most of
the floor.

"I can't imagine there being a better place in all of New
Orleans," said Eulie.

"I'm glad you like it," Nathan replied, "but I'm not likely
to learn anything out here. I'm after two killers, and I look
to find them somewhere in town, in the gambling houses
or the saloons."

After taking the packsaddle and their provisions into the
cabin, Nathan led their horses to the barn and unsaddled
them. He rubbed the animals down, found stalls for them,
and returned to the cabin. There, he and Eulie found themselves waiting until suppertime.

"After supper," said Eulie, "Let's ask McQueen if we
can go to the stables where he keeps his thoroughbreds.
I'd like to see them."

The bell that announced supper looked as though it had

once been part of a locomotive. When Nathan and Eulie answered its call, they found their hosts taking their meal in the cookhouse. Bess McQueen introduced the cook—a graying little man in a chef's hat—as simply Pierre.

"Pierre speaks English tolerably well," said McQueen, "but when he gets steamed, he cusses entirely in French. I reckon that's why Bess hired him."

"That," said Bess, unperturbed, "and he's an excellent cook."

Following a superb meal, after final cups of coffee, Eulie spoke.

"Mr. McQueen, do you mind if we go to the stable? I enjoy horses, and I'd like to look at your thoroughbreds."

"I don't mind at all," McQueen said. "It won't take long, since I have only three. Bess, are you coming with us?"

"No," said Bess.

Through the cool of the evening, with sundown just minutes away, they walked to the distant stables. It still being daylight outside did nothing to diminish the gloom within the stable, and McQueen took a lantern from a peg beside the door. Even in the poor light from the lantern, it became obvious why the building was so enormous, for an oval horse track dominated the center of it.

"Being so near the Gulf," said McQueen, "there are times when we have three or four straight days of rain. Weather's not fit for man or beast."

The stable consisted of many stalls, all of them arranged around the oval that was the track. One horse nickered while another began blowing and stomping about.

"That's Diablo making all the noise," McQueen said. "I don't know what I'm going to do with him. Thoroughbreds can be high strung, temperamental, and nervous, but Diablo goes beyond that."

"He's never been raced, then," said Eulie.

"Not that I know of," McQueen replied.

The stalls had Dutch doors, allowing only the top half to be opened. Thus one could see into a stall without being kicked or trampled by a nervous or frightened horse. McQueen opened the Dutch doors to one of the stalls, and the horse—a gray—stood there quietly looking at them.

"This is Prince," said McQueen. "He's won considerable money for me."

McQueen opened the Dutch doors to the next stall, re-

vealing a chestnut, and while he didn't seem as calm as
Prince, neither was he frightened.

"This is Duke," McQueen said. "He's the youngest of
the three, and I'm working with him now."

"All geldings, I reckon," Nathan said.

"All geldings," said McQueen. "Otherwise they couldn't
keep their minds on the race, with mares around."

Finally they reached the stall where the third horse still
snorted and kicked the walls.

"Better stand back," McQueen said. "He can't get out,
but when I open the upper halves of these doors, he may
try to bite your ears off."

A big black with a white star on his forehead, Diablo
didn't lunge at them, but he flattened his ears and bared his
teeth. While Nathan stood behind McQueen, Eulie hadn't
backed away. Suddenly she spoke softly, and while the
words sounded strange and meaningless to Nathan and
McQueen, the big black horse seemed to understand. The
ears perked up and the terrible teeth were no longer bared.
Without a word, Barnabas McQueen stepped aside as Eulie
continued the strange one-sided conversation. The horse
came a step closer and nickered, but not in fear or anger.
Eulie went no closer and Diablo remained where he was,
seeming to understand every word spoken. It all ended as
suddenly as it had begun, when Eulie stepped back.
McQueen closed and latched the doors, and almost immediately Diablo began pawing and nickering.

"I've never seen anything like that," McQueen said.
"What did you say, and how in thunder did he . . ."

"Something I learned years ago, in south Texas," said
Eulie. "From an old Indian horse gentler. He was a Lipan
Apache, and I spoke just as he did, in the Apache tongue."

"No wonder I didn't understand," McQueen said. "What
did you say? What is the secret?"

"No secret," said Eulie. "I just told him he's a handsome
horse, that I want to become his compañero. Perhaps it is
the music of the words."

"Gentle him, train him," McQueen said. "Get him ready
for this next race, and I'll pay you five hundred dollars."

"No," said Eulie. "I won't take your money. Diablo was
honest with me, and I'll be honest with him. Should we
become friends, it will be only because the two of us desire

it. I will become his friend, and perhaps later on, should you conduct yourself properly, he'll become your friend."

Barnabas McQueen had been profoundly impressed, and the conversation ended with Eulie agreeing to gentle the black horse and ready him for the coming race. Nathan said nothing until he and Eulie reached their cabin, and when he finally spoke, it struck her the wrong way.

"Sometimes," he said, "I forget you're not a man."

"I can believe that," she snapped. "You haven't laid a hand on me since Corpus Christi, before you were shot. Don't I have everything in all the right places?"

"Yes," he said, "you're everything you should be. It's ... I ... damn it, I don't *know* what's wrong with me. For a while, with you, there in south Texas, I ... I just forgot I was trailin' a bunch of killers. Now I know that a pair of them are here ... in New Orleans ... and they're heavy on my mind. I ... damn it ... I have trouble thinking of anything else."

"How well I know," Eulie said with a sigh. "I had you for a while, and you were Nathan Stone, the man. Now you're riding the vengeance trail again, and you're Nathan Stone, the killer."

"The truth hurts," said Nathan. "What do you aim to do?"

"I can't go back to Waco," Eulie said. "I'll stick with you, help you if I can, bury you if I must. But if you ever again turn to me, I want it to be you wanting me, not because I've tried to force you into it. Go on back to the saloons and gambling halls. I'll gentle McQueen's horse, if I can."

"I never knew you felt that strong about horses."

"I've never been hurt or disappointed by a horse," said Eulie.

Nathan could think of no suitable response to that, and when he shucked his boots and hat, Eulie blew out the lamp.

*   *   *

In the house, the McQueens were very much awake. And talking.

"I tell you, Bess," McQueen said, "I never saw anything like it. Why, the confounded horse would have taken off my head if I'd been close enough, but this Prater spoke some gibberish, some Apache tongue . . ."

"And wouldn't take your money," said Bess.

"That's the damn mystery of it," McQueen agreed. "A down-at-the-heels rider, with nothing but a horse and saddle."

"No mystery, Barnabas. This Prater is a Texan. So was my father. He'd work for nothing, if he believed the cause worthy, and if he felt it unworthy, there wasn't enough gold in the world to buy him. Besides, these riders—especially Stone—are here for some reason other than a horse race."

"I reckon you're right about Prater bein' a Texan," McQueen agreed, "but I ain't sure about Stone."

"I am," said Bess. "He walks, talks and rides like a Westerner, but I have the feeling he's a Southerner who went West after the war. You know, they didn't actually tell us they're here for the race. We just assumed they were. While I don't know who Stone is, I doubt he carries those two tied-down pistols for show."

"You reckon he's running from the law?"

"If he isn't, he will be," Bess said. "You know the Federals are using the Reconstruction law to take away the guns of Southerners."

"Unless they happen to be part of a gambling empire owned by a Yankee scoundrel like French Stumberg," said McQueen.

"That kind of talk can get you killed," Bess warned, "and even if you had proof, there's nothing to be done."

"Stumberg should have stayed with his fancy gambling halls and steamboats," said McQueen. "Now he's got himself some fast horses and reckons he can steal our races like he steals everything else. The first sign of anything crooked, and somehow, I'm going after him."

Chapter 12

❖

Nathan and Eulie were awake well before first light, with time on their hands. For a while they sat on the edge of the bed in silence, and it was Nathan who finally spoke.

"You got reason enough for bein' here, but what can I say about me?"

"Tell them you're a gambler," Eulie replied. "How else can you account for spending all your time in town?"

"Damn it," said Nathan, "I was just trying to be considerate. Once they learn I'm a saloon gambler and house dealer, they'll likely kick us out."

Eulie laughed. "Hell, Nathan, saloon gambling and house dealing sounds downright respectable, compared to what you're *really* after. Suppose you just tell them the truth, that your only goal in life is to track down and kill six men?"

"Maybe I'll just do that," he snarled.

He saddled his horse and rode out, uncertain as to what his next move would be. Remembering the saloons near the river, he made his way there first. But it was early—not quite ten o'clock—and most of the places were empty, except for a bored bartender. Nathan tried the Baltimore, the Amsterdam, Mother Burke's Den, and the Emerald Dragon.

"Where is everybody?" Nathan inquired of the Dragon's barman.

"How the hell should I know?" the man answered sourly. "Sleepin' it off, I reckon. It's too early. Onliest reason I'm here, I got to mop up all the vomit and spilt beer from last night."

Nathan left in disgust, and without any destination in mind, rode north. Eventually he found himself on St. Charles, and before him was the largest and fanciest hotel he had ever seen. It was three stories, and it seemed to be

a local watering hole, with a good portion of the first floor
devoted to a thriving restaurant. Nathan dodged buckboards and men afoot, riding all the way around the great
hotel. There were entrance and exit doors on all four sides,
with little room at any of the hitching rails. Many of the
horses and mules were harnessed to buckboards and wagons, and among the many saddled horses, a few carried
side saddles. A well-dressed man slumped on the seat of
one of the buckboards, apparently waiting for someone.
Nathan spoke to him.

"Pardner, what kind of place *is* this? What's going on
in there?"

The man laughed. "It's dinnertime, and the St. Charles
is the best place in New Orleans to eat."

Eventually Nathan found a place at one of the hitching
rails for his horse and made his way into the restaurant.
He had to wait until an all-in-black waiter showed him to
a table. The menu looked as big as a wagon tailgate, and
Nathan ignored it. Eventually the waiter returned, raising
his eyebrows.

"Bring me a steak," Nathan said. "Rare. Besides that, I
want potatoes, fried onions, and coffee."

When the food arrived, Nathan tried to pay, and was
given a handwritten bill. He looked at it, then at the waiter,
and the man backed away.

"God Almighty," said Nathan. "Seventy-five cents? Why,
I rode all over Texas and I never paid more than a dime."

"Then perhaps you should take all your meals there, sir,"
the waiter said. "This *is* the St. Charles, in New Orleans.
You may pay as you depart."

He turned his back before Nathan had a chance to glare
at him. At the next table, a man laughed over the top of
the newspaper he had been reading, and before Nathan
could redirect his anger, the stranger spoke.

"Relax, friend. This is the fanciest diggings between here
and Frisco.* They treat us all like we're not quite good
enough to belly up to their bar or pay six times what their
grub's worth. I'm Byron Silver, not long out of Texas
myself."

---

* The St. Charles Hotel dining room was highly popular in Old New
Orleans.

Nathan found himself facing a man no older than himself. Silver had gray eyes and hair as black as a crow's wing, and looked to have some Indian or Cajun in him. His gray pin-striped suit was well tailored, and he made no attempt to conceal the pistol belt beneath the coat. A black, flat-crowned Stetson with silver band lay on a chair next to him. Nathan spoke.

"I'm Nathan Stone, and I don't take kindly to having highfalutin' varmints talking down to me. With the South on the losing end of the war, how in tarnation can all these folks afford to come here?"

"You're here," said Silver, "and I'm here, so obviously we aren't broke. We're paying for the privilege of rubbing elbows with the gentry, the elite of New Orleans. Some of us always have money, Stone. Even with the country going to hell, we've made even more money, while some damn fools were getting their heads blown off at Shiloh and Gettysburg."

"I was one of those damn fools," Nathan said coldly. "I reckon I was just lucky some of the Yanks were shootin' a mite low."

"Too bad," said Silver, "but as I see it, I speak the truth, and I don't apologize for that."

Silver folded his paper, donned his hat, got to his feet, and made his way toward an exit. His meal unfinished, Nathan decided he'd had enough of the St. Charles. By the time he had paid his check, Byron Silver was already out the door. Nathan watched as two men hurriedly rose from a table, and he had a strong suspicion the duo had been waiting for Silver to leave. Clearly this was none of Nathan Stone's affair, but he had found himself liking the outspoken Silver. On impulse, he waited for the suspicious pair to reach the street, and as they followed Silver, they were in turn followed by Nathan. He wondered what mischief they had in mind, since it was broad daylight, but he realized he didn't know the city. The men trailing Silver might know where he was bound, and somewhere along the way there might be ample opportunity to waylay him.

Since Silver and the questionable pair trailing him were all afoot, Nathan had left his horse outside the St. Charles. Reaching a cross street, Silver turned south, toward the river. When his two pursuers followed, Nathan wasn't surprised. Obviously they were up to no good, and even in daylight, there were numerous alleys, warehouses, and lonely stretches along the river where they might make their play and disappear without being discovered. However, Nathan thought grimly, that might work against them if the hunted had an ace in the hole. But Byron Silver was no short horn. Reaching the end of what appeared to be a deserted warehouse, he ducked between it and an adjoining building. His pursuers halted just shy of the aperture where Silver had vanished, and when they tried to advance, a slug screamed off the brick wall just inches above their heads. Stooping low, one of them threw himself half a dozen feet, into the protection of the next building. Drawing his pistol, he ran along the front of the warehouse. His intentions were obvious. He would make his way down the opposite side of the building, and between the two of them, Silver would be boxed. It seemed to Nathan that the backs of these warehouses were likely against the backs of similar ones on the next street, but he couldn't be sure. While there might be a crawl space allowing Silver's pursuers to box him, there might be no way he could escape to the next street. Unless someone was attracted by the shooting, the pair could advance on Silver from two directions, and apparently that's what they had counted on. But it didn't work out that way. The gunman who had remained near his original position had drawn his pistol. Twenty yards behind him, his thumbs hooked in his pistol belt, Nathan spoke.

"Drop the gun and turn around."

Instead, the startled gunman threw himself away from the wall, twisting as he fell. But the jolt spoiled his aim and the shot went over Nathan's head. Nathan allowed him to get to his knees, but before he could fire a second time, Nathan drew his left-hand Colt and shot him dead-center.

"Silver," Nathan shouted, "It's Nathan Stone. Run for it."

Silver did, for Nathan could hear the pound of boots. But the second man who had tried to box Silver appeared at the farthest corner of the warehouse, his pistol blazing. One slug went wide, striking the brick wall to Nathan's left, while a second one snatched off his hat. Nathan drew and fired just once, and the gunman's knees buckled. He tried to raise the pistol for a third shot, but was dead on his feet.

He dropped the pistol, fell on his back, and didn't move. Silver appeared, a cocked Colt in his right fist.

"I hope you know this place better than I do," said Nathan. "All this shooting won't go unnoticed."

"Back the way you came," Silver said. "I'm not all that familiar with this warehouse district along the river. I suspected I was being followed, and I hoped to reach the saloons and cafes, but they wouldn't have allowed that. You helped me out of a nasty situation, my friend, and should word of it reach certain people, your life won't be worth a plugged peso."

Reaching the corner of the warehouse, they turned north along the street that led back to St. Charles.

"Damn it," said Nathan, "I'm not used to so much walking. Don't you own a horse?"

"No," Silver replied. "My, ah . . . line of work doesn't require one. I'm registered at the St. Charles. It's where I live when I'm in New Orleans."

"By God," said Nathan, "you're a caution. Two killers trailing you, and you light out for the river. That pair of varmints wouldn't have shot you at the hotel, among all those people."

"No," Silver agreed, "but they'd have hounded the hell out of me, waiting for a time and place."

"So you aimed to pick the time and place, salting them down before they got you," said Nathan.

"Exactly," Silver said. "I have—or I should say my employer has—friends at most of the saloons. They collect handsome rewards for providing sailors to sailing ships bound for ports around the world."

"Then you had no intention of shooting these coyotes who were hell-bent on shooting you."

Silver laughed. "Of course not. That's a messy solution, involving the law. Mind you, I'm not diminishing your skill with the pistols, but there may yet be a problem resolving the killings. I regret that I was unable to lure them into a position where they could have been shanghaied and sent to sea."

"I doubt we were seen after the shooting," said Nathan.

"So do I," Silver said, "but you're a stranger in town, and somebody may recall seeing the dead men leave the St. Charles with you trailing them."

"Where are we going now?" Nathan asked.

"Back to the St. Charles Hotel," said Silver. "I have a room there and I suppose your horse is somewhere near there."

"When you refer to the law, are you referring to an elected sheriff or the Union soldiers?"

"Neither," Silver said. "As long as you don't shoot a soldier or make a questionable move against the Union, the Federals won't bother you. As for an elected sheriff, there is none. The town—or parish—has a mounted police force, overseen by a commissioner name of Quay Becker. He's entrenched to the extent a keg of black powder wouldn't move him, and he's the bastard who'll take your gunplay personal."

"I reckon he's got some reason," said Nathan. "Do you aim to tell me what it is?"

"Yes," Silver said. "You've earned the right to know. The truth, Stone, is that New Orleans is a gambling town, and as such, it's pretty well divided into two camps. Most of the saloons and halls within the city where high-stakes gambling is allowed are controlled by Hargis Gavin, brother-in-law to Commissioner Becker."

"Slick dealing with kickbacks, then," said Nathan.

"Yes," Silver said, "but you're getting ahead of me. There are a dozen gambling houses over which Gavin has no control, and these have become quite a thorn in Gavin's side. These legitimate halls are situated in the country, and patrons are taken there by coach, and by invitation only."

"So the hombres gunning for you were Gavin's men," said Nathan, "so that puts you on the other side. Who's the tall dog in the brass collar?"

"French Stumberg," Silver replied. "He moved in during the war, taking one hell of a bite out of Gavin's business. He owns a steamboat, a big sidewheeler called the *Queen of Diamonds*. The *Queen* makes a run to St. Louis and back every week. High rollers coming to New Orleans with gambling on their minds get a free ride both ways, with grub and sleeping quarters."

"Before Gavin can get his hands on them, they've been sucked dry," said Nathan. "Where do you fit into all this?"

"I'm in charge of security for the steamboat," Silver replied, "and that consists mostly of seeing that nothing happens to it while it's docked here. One dark night a couple of Gavin's men took a dinghy into the river beyond the

Queen. They had a keg of black powder, but something went wrong and they were blown to hell and gone. Gavin's had it in for me ever since."

"So I've earned myself a place right alongside you," said Nathan.

"I wouldn't be surprised," Silver said. "That is, if you expect to remain in New Orleans."

"I'm almighty damn tired of being told where I can and can't go," said Nathan. "I'm paid up for a month out at McQueen's, and I aim to be there for the race the Saturday after Christmas."

"The track's at Gretna," Silver said, "and so far, McQueen's managed to keep Gavin out, but he won't be so lucky with Stumberg. French owns horses, and he aims to enter them."

"You're telling me, in your own roundabout way," said Nathan, "that the McQueens won't take kindly to me saving your hide."

"Barnabas won't," Silver replied, "but that's the least of your worries. What concerns me is Gavin, and he's the reason I go to such lengths to avoid shooting the skunks he sends after me. He has the local law in the palm of his hand, and he can trump up enough charges to chuck you in the *juzgado*. He can't hold you for more than a day or so, but that's long enough to have you gunned down while trying to escape."

"Nobody saw the shooting," said Nathan.

"Nobody had to," Silver replied. "You saw the two men follow me when I left the St. Charles, but you don't know that they were the only men Gavin had watching me. If another of Gavin's men saw you trailing the pair that you shot, then you won't be safe anywhere in New Orleans. Even if Gavin did not hate McQueen's guts, he'd have you trailed there. Then he'd torch every building on the place and gun you down when you tried to escape."

"Damn it," Nathan said, "you're boxing me in. Either I run like a yellow dog or risk being shot in the back."

"I'm just calling it the way I see it," Silver said, "because I've seen it happen before. You got in neck deep saving my bacon, and I owe you. I don't aim to tell you what to do, because from what I've seen, you're plenty man enough to stomp your own snakes. I'm going to talk to French

Stumberg about you. He can use a man of your caliber, if you're interested."

"Don't do me any favors," said Nathan. "What the hell makes Stumberg any better than Gavin?"

"Stumberg won't have you shot in the back," Silver said. "When you've learned a little more about Gavin's game, talk to me. I'm in room 301, near the head of the stairs."

They parted company, Silver entering the hotel, Nathan seeking his horse. He looked carefully around, but nobody seemed interested in him. The sun told him it was no later than three o'clock, but it seemed much later. He mounted and started back to McQueen's, pondering what Silver had told him. If Dillard and Snider *were* part of Stumberg's empire, going after the two killers would undoubtedly bring Stumberg's wrath down on Nathan Stone, trapping him in a deadly cross fire between the two factions. Just then, the roar of a Winchester seemed loud in the evening stillness, and lead ripped across Nathan's ribs, beneath his right arm. He rolled out of the saddle, taking his long gun with him, knowing he had no cover. He was on the very outskirts of town, and with the bushwhacker behind him, there were many points from which the shot could have come. There were no more shots, and Nathan rose cautiously to his feet. He dismissed any thought of pursuit, for he would be riding back into town, an open invitation to another shot. That, and the firing, might have attracted the unwelcome attention of the Gavin-controlled law. His wound paining him and blood soaking his shirt, he mounted and rode on toward McQueen's.

The more Nathan thought of it, the more Silver's proposal made sense, but not for Silver's reason. If he had no reason for remaining in the city, he could simply ride on, removing himself from Gavin's reach. But his reason—actually two of them—would not let him ride away. If the killers Nathan sought had sold their guns to Stumberg, what better way to find them than just hiring out to Stumberg, as Silver had proposed? Shying clear of Stumberg, he would again be searching one saloon or gambling house after another, all the while risking being shot in the back by one of Gavin's killers. Nathan cursed under his breath. It seemed like the law became whatever a man with wealth and power chose to call it. Now he must leave McQueen's place, or risk dragging Barnabas and Bess into conflict with Gavin or

Stumberg, or possibly both. Granted that he gunned down Dillard and Snider, Stumberg's gunmen would come after him like hell wouldn't have it, but then he would be free to leave New Orleans. But until then, what of Eulie? She must remain at McQueen's, and he would leave Cotton Blossom with her. Eulie would welcome that part of his decision, but she would surely raise hell at the prospect of his becoming part of Stumberg's gambling empire.

Reaching the McQueen place, Nathan rode to the barn without being seen by anyone, and he wondered where McQueen's hounds were. Supper wouldn't be for another hour, so he expected McQueen and Eulie to be at the horse barn. Reaching the cabin he and Eulie shared, he found it deserted. Cotton Blossom would be with Eulie, or running with McQueen's hounds. Nathan removed his gunbelt and stripped off his shirt. Filling a basin with water from a big wooden bucket, Nathan set about cleansing his wound. From his saddlebag he took a bottle of disinfectant, and from Eulie's saddlebag a roll of white cotton muslin. Soaking a pad with disinfectant, he bound it tight against the painful gash, gritting his teeth. The medicine caused him more discomfort than the wound. That done, Nathan removed his boots and stretched out on the bed. He dozed, awakening when Eulie arrived.

"Well," he said, "are you and Diablo getting along?"

"We're friends," said Eulie, her eyes on the bandage girding Nathan's middle. "Did you accomplish anything in town, besides getting yourself hurt?"

"Yes," he said, ignoring her sarcasm. "I shot a pair of varmints trying to ventilate me. Turns out they were hired by a big-time gambler who owns the local law. Somebody tried to bushwack me on the way from town."

"My God," cried Eulie, "you're cursed. So now you have the choice of riding on or staying here to shoot or be shot."

"No," said Nathan, "I can't ride away, and you know why. But I won't be staying here. Hargis Gavin, the varmint that's down on me, hate's McQueen's guts. He'd likely jump at the chance to give McQueen hell, while comin' after me. That pair of killers I salted down were after Byron Silver, a Stumberg man. I saved his hide, and he believes Stumberg will be interested in me. It's the best chance I have to find Dillard and Snider, without having Gavin's bunch bushwhack me. It won't affect you in any way. You'll be able to remain here and train McQueen's horse."

"I intend to," Eulie said. "It's something I want to do. Besides, you don't need me, unless it's to bury you."

"You have no obligation to do that," said Nathan, "and I'm not asking for your approval. I just believe you should know what I aim to do, and I reckon I'll have to tell McQueen."

The bell called them to supper, and despite Nathan's determination, he didn't relish telling Barnabas McQueen of his decision. Not after Silver had told him of Stumberg's plan to force his thoroughbreds into the coming race. Again Barnabas and Bess joined them for supper, and Nathan delayed his revelation as long as he could. Finally he swallowed hard and waded in.

"I reckon I'll be staying in town," he said. "Just take what I've paid toward room and board against what Eli will be paying. I'll need to leave Cotton Blossom here too."

"We'll be sorry to lose you," said Bess.

"You won't be," Nathan said, "when I tell you why I'm going."

He told them of the events of the day, not sparing himself. What he did not tell them was that this possible alliance with French Stumberg would be his way of finding Dillard and Snider, two more of the brutal killers he had trailed from Virginia.

"I can understand how you got involved," said Barnabas, "and I have to agree with your friend Silver on several counts. He's dead right about Hargis Gavin. He'd have his men burn this place to the ground, shooting us all as we ran out. Regarding my fight with Stumberg, Silver told it straight. Frankly, if I had to chose between Gavin and Stumberg, Stumberg is the more ethical of the two. But that doesn't diminish the fact that he's using his thoroughbreds to force us to recognize professional gambling at the track."

"Haven't you had betting at the track before?" Eulie asked.

"Yes," said McQueen, "but nothing of the magnitude Stumberg has in mind. He'll bring gamblers all the way from St. Louis, and like all professionals, he'll find some means of fixing the races. Big-time gambling took over the track at Natchez, and now it's about finished. There was a big stink when word got out that jockeys were being paid to throw the races."

"I've heard of that," Nathan said, "and I'm against it. I've done my time as a house dealer, and I refuse to slick deal."

"I don't hold it against a man for doing what he feels he must," said McQueen. "Since you were accidentally caught up in this shootout with Gavin's men, nobody could fault you for just riding on. When Gavin learns you're with Stumberg, that'll be all the more reason for Gavin having you gunned down."

"I've considered that," Nathan said, "but I have my reasons for staying in New Orleans. One of them is that I resent being pushed around, when all I have done is defend myself. Besides, there may be a way I can help you keep big-time gambling away from your track."

"I'll be everlastingly grateful if you can," said McQueen, "but don't underestimate Stumberg. While I consider him slightly more ethical than Gavin, I have no doubt that death will be swift and sure if he so much as suspects you're about to cross him. Be damn careful, and if the lead gets too hot and heavy, run for it. We can hide you for a while."

It was more than Nathan had expected. Eulie could remain at the McQueen place, and, thanks to McQueen's tolerance, in a hostile town where he needed one the most, Nathan had a friend.

"I'm obliged, Mr. McQueen," said Nathan. "I'll be riding back to town tomorrow morning, before Gavin's bunch makes any lasting ties between me and you. But before I go, tell me as much as you can about the Gavin and Stumberg organizations."

"It won't be a lot," McQueen said, "and some of it's only rumor. Gavin pretty well controls the inner city, while Stumberg's gambling houses are all in outlying areas. He sends carriages into town every night, offering free transportation to and from his places. I'm told there's a carriage at the St. Charles Hotel every night at seven, and when the steamboat is here, sometimes it takes half a dozen carriages or more, transporting the gamblers to and from Stumberg's places. On the surface, that doesn't sound too bad, but that's where the rumors come in. There's talk that Stumberg's involved in white slavery, taking young women to Mexico and selling them."

"My God," said Nathan, "that's serious. It should be a Federal crime."

"It is," McQueen replied, "and that's how the rumors— if they *are* that—got started. Stumberg came here five years ago, and during the war, he had nobody watching him except Hargis Gavin. But now the Federals are in the saddle, and they're under considerable pressure from the folks back East. Too many women have come to New Orleans never to be seen again."

"You're telling me that if I throw in with Stumberg, I may be up against more than the possibility that Hargis Gavin will have me shot dead."

"Your words," said McQueen, "not mine. While what I've just told you is only rumor, there *are* some cold, hard facts that can't be ignored. Stumberg has picked up on a trend that first caught on in San Francisco, which involves staffing all his gambling houses with those young women wearing ... well, very little. 'Pretty Girls Saloons' is what they're called in California."

"The saloons and gambling houses could be stepping-stones to Old Mexico and white slavery, then," Nathan said.

"Precisely," said McQueen. "That would account for the many young women missing without a trace. I'm telling you this, rumors included, so that you may decide how far you want to go with Stumberg."

"I'm obliged," Nathan said, "and I'll keep it strong on my mind. It kind of makes Gavin sound like small potatoes, by comparison."

"Which he is not, by any means," said McQueen. "Gavin is the power behind every sleazy New Orleans honky-tonk.* He supplies one or more house dealers, depending on the size of the place, and collects anywhere from fifty to eighty percent of the gambling take. Some owners get nothing, their only profit being from the sale of drinks."

"I reckon that backs up Silver's story," Nathan said. "He told me that Gavin has the law in the palm of his hand, forcing the local saloons to work with him, or else."

"That's it," McQueen agreed. "A few saloon owners

---

* The term "honky-tonk" is Southern, attributed to the post-Civil War Negro.

tried to buck Gavin, only to learn they had two choices. They could fall in line, taking what Gavin offered, or close their doors. If they balked, Gavin sent some men to their place and a fight broke out. When they were done, the place would be a shambles of busted chairs and tables and broken bottles. If that failed, the Gavin-controlled law could declare the place a public nuisance and close it."

"Gavin and Stumberg," said Nathan. "By God, Shakespeare was right. There *is* small choice in rotten apples."

Chapter 13

After breakfast, having said goodbye to the McQueens, Nathan followed Eulie back to the cabin they had shared only twice and perhaps never again. There was little to be said, and while Nathan wanted to be on his way, he was reluctant to go.

"I might as well ride in and talk to Silver," he said.

"Before you do," Eulie said, "come inside for a minute."

He did so, and without a word, she threw her arms around him. It was the kind of farewell he had dreaded and had hoped to avoid, but there were no tears. Eulie backed away, and when she spoke, her voice was steady.

"Nathan, keep your temper, and don't shoot unless you have to."

Not trusting himself to speak, he nodded and stepped out the door. When he set out for the barn, to saddle his horse, Cotton Blossom followed.

"Not this time, Cotton Blossom," said Nathan. "Stay."

Before riding out of sight beyond the McQueen house, Nathan looked back. Eulie stood before the cabin, Cotton Blossom beside her, and Nathan had a chilling premotion that he might be seeing them for the last time. But he swallowed hard, tugged his hat down over his eyes, and rode on. After the attempted ambush he rode warily, and reached town without incident. The St. Charles dining room served breakfast until half-past ten, so Nathan again had trouble finding room at one of the hitching rails for his horse. Entering the dining room and failing to find Silver there, he went on through the restaurant to the hotel lobby. The St. Charles was plush beyond belief, with banks of windows reaching from the floor almost to the high ceiling. Gold velvet drapes matched the thick carpet, which continued up the stairs and down the halls. Nathan looked around the lobby and then quickly mounted the stairs. Reaching the third floor, he looked down the hall, and finding it deserted, knocked on the door to 301.

"Identify yourself," said a voice from within.

"Nathan Stone."

There came the sound of a deadbolt being drawn, and the door opened just enough for Nathan to enter. He did so. Silver, fully dressed except for his hat and boots, held a cocked Colt in his right fist. He thumbed down the hammer before he spoke.

"I don't mean to seem inhospitable, but I don't have many visitors."

"And among them," Nathan said, "few friends."

Silver's laugh was brittle, without humor. "Among them, no friends. Present company excepted, of course."

"I'll come right to the point," said Nathan. "As I rode back to McQueen's yesterday, somebody cut down on me with a rifle."

"I don't see any holes in you," Silver observed. "It must have been a warning shot. Hargis Gavin has officially invited you to either become the guest of honor at a funeral or leave New Orleans. Have you come to say goodbye?"

"One thing I don't like about you, Silver, is your damned untimely sense of humor. What do *you* think?"

"I think I'd better introduce you to French Stumberg. You have the kind of sand he likes in a man, and you don't run just because you're up against a skunk who has you outgunned and wants your head on a platter. Have you had breakfast?"

"Yes," Nathan replied.

"I haven't," said Silver. "You can drink coffee while I eat."

Nathan said nothing, waiting while Silver tugged on his boots and found his hat. They stepped into the hall and Silver locked the door behind them. After making sure nobody observed him, Silver took from his coat pocket a spool of fine thread. He unwound and snapped off a length of it, tying one end to the knob of the door. The other end he looped over the head of a slightly protruding nail in the door frame, beneath the knob. In the dimness of the hall, the slender thread was invisible.

"I can't figure you," Nathan said. "You have gunslingers after your hide, yet you're camped out on the third floor of the fanciest place in town."

"I have my reasons," said Silver. "They *know* where to find me, but as you pointed out yesterday, I'm not likely to be gunned down here in the hotel. At least not in a crowd. Gavin has the law in his pocket, but there's still some limits. Besides, Stumberg likes having me here. It's a slap in the face, a way to rankle Gavin. Stumberg picks up the tab for the room and grub."

Silver said no more, for they were descending the stairs to the lobby. Most of the breakfast crowd had cleared out of the dining room. Silver, when a waiter approached, pointed to an isolated table from which the entire room could be seen. There were two chairs next to the wall. Silver took one and Nathan took the other. The waiter brought a tray with a fancy porcelain pot full of coffee and two fancy porcelain cups. Silver ordered breakfast and sipped his coffee.

"Well, damn it," Nathan said impatiently, "tell me something about French Stumberg."

"No," Silver replied. "I prefer to wait and let you draw your own conclusions. I may have said too much already. He'll be in town sometime tonight."

"Here at the hotel?"

"No," said Silver. "He never comes here. He'll be coming in from St. Louis. The *Queen of Diamonds* will be docking just before sundown. There'll be a carriage arriving at the hotel at seven o'clock. It will take us to the Old Canal House, on Old Canal, north of here."

Nathan said no more, drinking his coffee while Silver dug into his food. Not until he had finished his breakfast did Silver finally speak.

"You're welcome to spend the rest of the day in my room. I wouldn't recommend wandering about town, after that near miss yesterday afternoon."

"I'll accept that invite," Nathan said, "but first I have to find a livery and stable my horse."

"There's one within sight of the hotel," said Silver, "but it's not the cheapest in town."

"I didn't reckon it would be," Nathan said. "I have money."

"I'll go with you," said Silver. "If you hire on with Stumberg, you'll likely have to sell your horse and saddle."

"I'll be damned if I do," Nathan replied. "Nobody, Stumberg included, will ever own me that completely."

The livery was but a short distance away, and Nathan made arrangements to leave his horse and store his saddle. His saddlebags and bedroll he took with him. On their way through the lobby, Silver stopped at the desk and bought two newspapers, something Nathan had neglected to do. One of them was an eight-page local weekly, while the other was a recent issue of the *St. Louis Globe-Democrat.* Reaching the door to 301, Silver found the slender thread unbroken. He removed it, unlocked the door, and they entered. Silver shot the deadbolt, sat down on the bed, and removed his boots. Nathan was studying the newspapers.

"I don't know why I bother with those," said Silver, "except they're a way to kill time."

"With you in charge of security of the *Queen of Diamonds,*" Nathan said, "I'd reckon you'd be stayin' with it most of the time."

"I spend all my time with it while it's docked here," said Silver, "but when Stumberg goes to St. Louis, I have time on my hands."

"That's kind of obvious," said Nathan. "You ever wonder why he goes to St. Louis and you're always left here?"

"I try not to wonder out loud about anything that could get me shot dead," Silver replied. "Unless you have some kind of death wish, let me give you some strong advice. If Stumberg takes to you, keep your mouth shut, your eyes open, and your pistol handy."

His eyes met Nathan's and there wasn't a hint of a smile.

As the day dragged on, Nathan read both newspapers, starting with the *Globe-Democrat.* From it he learned that the James and Younger gangs were still robbing banks in Missouri, and that the crazed Cullen Baker was loose somewhere in Arkansas. Not until he began reading the local weekly did Nathan find anything of real interest.

"God," Nathan said aloud, "what a crazy damn fool."

Silver had been stretched out on the bed, half asleep. He opened one eye and spoke.

"Are you referring to me or to yourself?"

"Neither," said Nathan, rising from his chair. "Ben Thompson."

"The little varmint that's sudden death with a pistol," Silver said. "Do you know him?"

"I met him in south Texas," Nathan replied. "Last I saw of him, he was riding north toward San Antone."

"He's the kind that wears out his welcome pretty quick," Silver said. "I didn't know he was here. What's he done now?"

"Picked a fight with somebody in one of the saloons," said Nathan, "and they settled in with knives. Had themselves locked in an icehouse, with no light. Thompson was cut pretty bad, but managed to walk away. The paper's a little shy on details. By the time they got word, it was too late to talk to Thompson. He found a doc, got himself patched up, and rode away."

"I've heard that Ben's younger brother Billy is even worse than Ben," Silver said. "Either of them is sidewinder-mean, but the two of 'em together, I hear, is a keg of powder with a short fuse."*

"Then I hope I never get involved with them both at the same time," said Nathan. "I manage to scare up all the trouble I can handle, without help."

Nathan and Silver took an early supper, going to the hotel dining room shortly past four o'clock. Again Silver tied the tiny thread after locking the door, and was careful to see that it was unbroken upon their return. They had whiled away a little more than an hour in the dining room and still had the better part of two hours until the seven o'clock departure for Stumberg's gambling house.

"I reckon," Nathan said by way of conversation, "you're sure Stumberg will be at this gambling house. Me, I'd first be sure the boat's at the landing."

"You don't know Stumberg," said Silver. "If the *Queen* isn't there come sundown, then the damn thing's sunk somewhere between here and St. Louis."

There seemed nothing more to say, and Nathan leaned his chair back against the wall, dozing. After what seemed only a few minutes. Silver spoke.

"Time to go. By the time we get down there, the coach will be waiting."

Again, after locking the door, Silver tied the thread in place, and they made their way down the stairs. The stage *was* waiting, and it proved to be a red and green Concord, drawn by four matched bays. The stage itself bore no mark-

---

* The Thompsons were born in Knottingley, England, Ben in 1842 and Billy in 1845.

ings, nothing to indicate who it belonged to or where it was bound. Byron Silver confidently mounted the step and took one of the three remaining seats. Nathan followed. All the other passengers were men, well dressed, apparently affluent. They paid little attention to Silver, but eyed Nathan Stone with some interest, thanks to his pair of tied-down Colts. It was already dark, and Nathan knew only that they traveled west along St. Charles. When the coach finally slowed, it took a right on what Nathan guessed was Old Canal, for the lights of town faded quickly and the coach jounced over a not-too-well-kept dirt road. They rattled across a wooden bridge and drew up before a rambling two-story house. A long front porch stretched the length of it and carriage lamps flickered on either side of the wide double doors. The other passengers left the coach and Silver fell back so that he could speak to Nathan without being overheard.

"Everybody goes into the parlor," he said. "Actually, there are two parlors. The others will go into the second. You'll wait in the first until I talk to Stumberg. Stay there. Don't go wandering around."

Apparently having been there before, the other guests went immediately into the second of the two parlors. Nathan remained in the first, watching as Silver continued through the second and up an elegant spiral staircase. The two parlors seemed identical in furnishings, with elegant rose drapes matching a gray, rose-patterened carpet. Nathan had never seen anything like it, and he remained standing, reluctant to sit on the elegant mahogany furniture. He eyed the wide, white-railed spiral stairway at the end of the second parlor and so got his first look at one of Stumberg's "pretty girls."

She didn't look a day over eighteen. She came down the spiral stairs, obviously to escort the newly arrived patrons. Her blonde hair was tied with a red ribbon, her slippers were a matching red, and her waist-length jacket was red, embroidered with gold. The jacket was open down the front, and she wore absolutely nothing else. Barnabas McQueen hadn't exaggerated.*

The practically naked girl beckoned to the goggle-eyed

---

* By 1869, the "pretty girl" concept had moved west to San Francisco.

men, and they all followed her eagerly up the stairs. Nathan suspected her motions—and whatever might take place later—had been devised to take a man's mind off his gambling, along with the heavy losses he was likely to suffer. Nathan had grown tired of waiting when Silver returned.

"Come on," said Silver. "I built you up as much as I could. He knows you're on Gavin's list for having sided me. It's up to you to convince him he needs you."

Nathan followed Silver through the second parlor and up the long spiral stairs. Silver paused before a door and knocked.

"All right," said a voice from within.

"You're on your own," Silver said. "I'll be downstairs."

Not knowing what to expect, Nathan turned the knob, opened the door, and stepped into the room. Its furnishings were as elegant as any of those in the downstairs parlors. Stumberg sat behind a mahogany desk the length of a Conestoga wagon, chewing an unlit cigar. He had lost some hair in the front, and what remained was graying. In the glow from hanging, brass-shaded lamps, diamonds glittered from rings on both his beefy hands. His frock coat was black, and beneath it he wore a boiled white shirt with ruffles at the front and at the cuffs. His black string tie lay on the desk. He had jowls that reminded Nathan of a hog, and his deep brown eyes were hard, unblinking. While both his hands were on the desktop, he looked like the kind who would have a derringer up his sleeve or a Colt in his lap. There were no chairs before the desk, but several to either side, along the walls. A visitor was not permitted to face Stumberg head-on.

"There's chairs," Stumberg growled. "Set."

"Nobody tells me when to sit, or where," said Nathan. He positioned himself directly before Stumberg, his cold blue eyes boring into the gambler's.

Stumberg laughed. "Ex-Reb, mean as hell, bowed but unbeaten. Are you as quick with a pistol as you are with your tongue?"

Stumberg never saw Nathan's right hand move. In less than a heartbeat the gambler found himself looking into the cold, deadly bore of a cocked Colt revolver. Stumberg thought of the derringer up his right sleeve, and a chill swept over him. Nathan Stone could have shot him dead three times before he could have gotten the sleeve gun into play. Having made his point, Nathan returned the Colt to its holster. Hooking his thumbs in his pistol belt, he remained where he was, his eyes on Stumberg. In a totally different tone of voice the gambler spoke.

"Silver has told me some interesting things about you, Stone. He seems to think you might fit into my ... ah ... organization. What do *you* think?"

"I think I'd like to know more about your ... ah ... organization," Nathan said, "and then *I* will decide whether or not I fit into it."

Again Stumberg laughed, an unpleasant sound. From a coat pocket he withdrew a match, popped it aflame with his thumbnail, and lighted the cigar. Through a cloud of smoke, he fixed his hard eyes on Nathan for a moment before he said anything.

"I'm a gambler, Stone. As much a gambler as any of the suckers who can't wait to get to my tables. The difference is, I gamble on men. When I place my bets on you—if I do—then I don't expect to lose. My games are honest, and any man caught slick dealing will regret it. Can you deal faro?"

"Yes."

"Good," said Stumberg. "As Silver told you, the *Queen of Diamonds* makes a weekly run from here to St. Louis. She leaves on Sunday afternoon, lays over a night in St. Louis, and returns here the following Saturday. I want you aboard, starting this Sunday. That's tomorrow. That is, if you find the proposition agreeable. You will be paid two hundred dollars a month, and when you're in town, your room and board will be provided. Have you any questions as to what I'm expecting of you?"

"Yes," Nathan said. "I get the feeling you're expecting more of me than just dealing faro on a steamboat. Why don't you tell me the rest of it?"

"I need a man who thinks on his feet, is quick with a gun, and who isn't afraid to use it when he must. You will deal some faro on the way to St. Louis, provided that some of my homebound guests still have money. But on the return run to New Orleans, you will prowl the decks, heading off trouble. Once a month, I'll be going to St. Louis with you, and while we are at the landing there, you are not to leave the *Queen* at any time, for any reason. Other times, the night and the town are yours. Send Silver back up here, and you wait for him downstairs."

Nathan stepped into the hall, closing the door behind him. He found Silver in the second parlor, standing at the foot of the stairs.

"He wants you up there," said Nathan. "I passed muster."

Silver was gone only a few minutes, and when he returned, Nathan looked at him questioningly.

"When you're in town," Silver said, "you'll be bunking with me at the St. Charles. There's room enough for the hotel to set up another bed, and I'll get you a key. There won't be a coach to town until eleven, so we'll be here awhile. Do you want to visit the gaming rooms and look at Stumberg's pretty girls?"

"I've seen one," said Nathan. "Are the others that much different?"

"Not that I could see," Silver said. "The cook's already gone, but there'll be food and coffee in the kitchen. Let's go there."

Like the rest of Stumberg's place, the kitchen was more than adequate. The stove was still hot, and two large blue granite coffeepots sat directly over the firebox. The coffee was black and steaming. There was a large pot of boiled potatoes and a pan with half a haunch of roast beef. A serving tray on the table held three loaves of sliced bread.

"Let's eat," said Silver. "It's been five hours since supper."

They helped themselves to coffee, roast beef, and potatoes, taking chairs at the table.

"What did he tell you?" Nathan asked. "Or am I not supposed to know?"

"Not a damn thing," said Silver, "except that I'm to get you a room key and have the hotel set up a bed for you. I reckon anything you tell me will be at your own risk, since he obviously doesn't want me to know."

"Oh, hell," Nathan said, "How can you *not* know, with us sharing a room? He wants a man who can think on his feet, is quick with a gun, and isn't afraid to use it. I'm to deal faro on the *Queen* as she takes the gamblers home to St. Louis. That is, if they have any money left. On the return runs to New Orleans I'm to prowl the decks, heading off trouble."

"By God," said Silver, "that's been *my* job, except when Stumberg goes to St. Louis. On those runs I've never been allowed to go."

"I hate telling you this," Nathan said, "but I'll be going on those runs, but I'm not allowed to go ashore at any time the *Queen*'s at the landing in St. Louis."

"And I'll be cooling my heels here at the hotel," said Silver bitterly. "I'm not sure I really want to know, but how much is he paying you?"

"Two hundred," Nathan said. "You know what he's doing, don't you?"

"Except for the money, he's playing one of us against the other," said Silver. "It's his quaint way of telling us he doesn't trust either of us completely. When Stumberg makes the run to St. Louis, I'm not allowed on the boat. You're allowed to go, but you're not allowed ashore."

"Something's taking place in St. Louis that can't stand the light of day," Nathan said. "I'll bet my month's pay against yours that it involves those naked women Stumberg is using in these gambling houses."

"No bet," said Silver, "and if that kind of talk gets back to Stumberg, you may be gambling more than a month's pay, my friend."

Chapter 14

❖❖❖

By the time Sunday arrived, Nathan had his own bed and room key, but was thoroughly sick of the St. Charles hotel and the inactivity. There had been no word from Stumberg, and Silver prepared for the run to St. Louis as usual.

"Until Stumberg says different," Silver said, "I'll be making the run to St. Louis with you. Except for Stumberg's once-a-month runs, of course."

Despite the fact that the *Queen of Diamonds* wouldn't back away from the landing until three o'clock, Nathan and Silver arrived a little after one. A man on the main deck lowered the gangplank, raising it immediately after Nathan and Silver were aboard.

"There's two bunks in my usual cabin," said Silver. "Unless somebody has other ideas, you can bunk there."

After storing their meager belongings, Silver took Nathan on a tour of the sternwheeler. It was much larger than Nathan had expected, for he'd never been on a steamboat. The main deck looked like a large open shed, and in the center of it—forward—was the housing for the boilers and mighty engines. Below deck, secured by hatches, was another deck that Silver avoided.

"Most of the lower deck's closed off," he said by way of explanation. "The rest of it's taken up with a couple dozen cords of firewood used to feed the fireboxes under the boilers."*

The second deck, above the fireboxes and boilers, boasted the steamboat's fanciest accommodations. There was a long, central lounge and saloon, three-quarters surrounded by state rooms. The rearmost fourth of this deck, separated from the forepart by folding doors, was the

---

* Average consumption was a cord of wood an hour.

kitchen. The enormous lounge was not only a saloon, complete with gaming tables and a roulette wheel, but a dining room as well. A third deck—the roof of the cabin deck—was the hurricane deck, so named because it had no covering, except in the central part forward. Here was the "Texas," which included cabins for the ship's officers, the pilots, and the many waiters needed to staff the dining room. Atop the Texas was the pilothouse, with many windows, from which the pilot could see in every direction. Just in front of the Texas, a pair of lofty flaring crowned stacks spewed columns of woodsmoke heavenward.*

"God," said Nathan, "how many men does it take to operate this thing?"

"Twenty-seven, I believe," Silver replied, "including the captain. Two pilots take turns at the wheel and there are eight different firemen who work in shifts of four. There's the cook and his helper, a dozen waiters who serve the meals, and of course, two girls who cater to the gamblers."

"That's a lot of waiters." said Nathan. "Why so many?"

"There are times," Silver replied, "when there's not enough. You saw the lounge and saloon. It's empty now, but it's usually full when we pull out of St. Louis. Like I said, the girls devote their time to the gamblers. The waiters who serve the meals also serve drinks. Damn convenient for everybody, since the lounge and saloon is also the dining room."

"A floating saloon and gambling hall," said Nathan. "It cost a pile, I reckon."

"A specially built steamboat can cost anywhere from twenty thousand up to a quarter of a million," said Silver. "Just another means of showing all the peons how powerful Señor Stumberg really is."

"This is nothing like an ordinary steamboat, then."

"The upper deck and the lower deck are almost entirely different," Silver said. "A conventional boat of this size would have the upper deck divided into fourths. There would be a lounge for men, another for women, a small saloon with poker tables, and a kitchen. During meals, partitions would be removed, converting the lounges into a

---

* The "Texas" was named for the State of Texas. Nobody knows exactly why.

single dining room. A regular steamboat makes good use of the lower deck. The part beyond what's needed for the boilers, fireboxes, and firewood is devoted to wagons, mules, horses, cows, or people needing passage who can't afford anything better. They sleep in their wagons or on the deck. But this one, being a custom-built steamboat, has part of that lower deck closed off. There's a series of cabins, all of them fitted with special locks."

"That's curious," said Nathan. "With the officers, pilots, and waiters having quarters on the hurricane deck, why is there a need for more cabins on the lower deck? and why the special locks?"

"In either case," Silver replied, "I have no idea, and since I'm a hell of a lot smarter than I look, I'm not about to ask."

Nathan said no more, but he was becoming increasingly certain that Byron Silver knew or suspected more than he was willing to divulge. Half an hour before the *Queen of Diamonds* was scheduled to depart, three Concords, each with teams of matched bays, drew up at the landing. The same crewman who had lowered the gangplank for Nathan and Silver now lowered it for the occupants from the coaches. There were eighteen passengers in all, two of which were women. They, of course, were the "pretty girls" who would entertain the men.

"Tarnation," said Nathan, "that many men come from St. Louis to lose their money at Stumberg's tables?"

"That's a light turnout," Silver said. "Usually there's three times as many. Besides, a pair of those—Stevens and Harkness—are Stumberg's housemen."

"If this is a light turnout," said Nathan, "then three times this many is more than forty. Two housemen to accommodate forty gamblers on the ride back to New Orleans?"

"Either man can deal anything from faro to stud poker," Silver said, "and either of the girls can operate the roulette wheel, if need be. You can, as Stumberg said, deal faro on the run to St. Louis. As for gambling on the boat, it's more a diversion than anything else. Stumberg likes to divide his passengers among all his gambling houses, and he doesn't like for them to be broke when they arrive. It's bad for morale."

"I reckon it helps morale considerable," said Nathan, "making good use of this time on the river. The house losing some pesos to the visiting gamblers fattens them up for the kill, once they reach New Orleans."

"If I were you," Silver replied quietly, "I'd not spend too much of my time speculating on Stumberg's motives. At least, not out loud."

Nathan said nothing for a moment, and when he spoke again, he changed the subject.

"How far is it to St. Louis, and how long will we be on the river?"

"Near seven hundred miles," said Silver. "We'll arrive sometime late Wednesday afternoon, lay over one night and return to New Orleans. We'll take on wood at Vicksburg, Memphis, and Cairo, Illinois."

With two shrill blasts from her whistle and woodsmoke boiling from twin stacks, the *Queen of Diamonds* departed on schedule. Nathan and Silver stood at the rail as the *Queen* swung away from the landing.

"Nobody out here but us," Nathan said. "Where is all that bunch?"

"The gamblers are in their cabins licking their wounds," said Silver. "The gambling—if there is any—won't get under way until after supper. The cook and his helper are French, and you can't understand a damn thing they say, but they flat know how to turn out the grub."

"Do we eat with the crew or with the passengers?"

"With the passengers," Silver said. "They have to get used to us."

Supper was announced at five bells, and the passengers who had visited Stumberg's gambling houses were a morose and unenthusiastic bunch. They all looked, Nathan thought, as though they had learned the truth of the old adage that the odds always favor the house. The two house dealers ate alone, while the women chose not to eat at all.

"I'd say there won't be much gambling between here and St. Louis," said Nathan. "They're all too busy licking their wounds."

"That's usually the way of it after a week at the gambling tables," Silver replied. "We'll get plenty of shut-eye."

"We don't know that some of them won't be in here after some hair of the dog that bit them," said Nathan. "We can't just hibernate in our cabin, can we?"

"Stevens and Harkness will be here in the lounge," Silver

said, "and they can probably provide any needed action. If it becomes heavy enough, they'll pound on our door."

"No women, either, I reckon," said Nathan.

"Not usually," Silver said. "Trinity and Shekela are two of Stumberg's most dependable girls, and they're along mostly to excite the new crop of gamblers on their way to New Orleans."

"They're the most dependable," said Nathan, "meaning there are some who might jump ship if they got the chance."

"You said that," Silver replied. "I didn't."

Nathan said nothing, drawing his own conclusions. As Silver had predicted, Trinity and Shekela were absent from the lounge, as were all the gamblers on their way back to St. Louis. House gamblers Stevens and Harkness sat with hats tipped over their eyes, apparently resolved to a long evening of doing absolutely nothing. Nathan and Silver returned to their cabin.

"At first," said Nathan, "it seemed like two hundred a month was too much to pay a man for settin' on his hunkers and doing nothing. Now, damn it, I'm startin' to wonder if it's enough."

Silver laughed. "It's always dull on the way to St. Louis, but you'll see some action when we pick up a new crop of gamblers and head south to New Orleans."

For the lack of anything better to do, Nathan and Silver shed their boots and hats and tried to sleep. But for Nathan Stone, sleep was long in coming. It seemed the throb of the engines and the throbbing of his head were one and the same. His was a long, restless night, and he was thankful when at last he could see the graying of the dawn through the single porthole. The call to breakfast came at seven bells, and Nathan thought the despondent gamblers looked as washed out as he felt. There was one difference, though. When he and Silver chose a table, they were joined by the house gamblers, Stevens and Harkness, and eventually, by the saloon girls, Shekela and Trinity. The latter was discreetly dressed, smiling, and a far cry from the nearly naked girl Nathan had seen at Stumberg's gambling house. Stevens and Harkness were dressed in almost identical pinstriped suits, and looked exactly like what they were. Silver spoke to the four with easy familiarity, introducing Nathan. It was to Nathan that Harkness spoke.

"Maybe we can get up a friendly four-handed game," Harkness said.

"Yeah," Stevens agreed. "Trinity and Shekela won't play with us."

"You're always wanting us to play strip poker," said Trinity. "We don't get paid to strip for you."

"A woman that strips for money shouldn't be so damn particular," Stevens said.

"That's *all* we do for money," said Trinity, and she didn't smile.

With that, Shekela and Trinity left the table and returned to their cabin, ignoring the laughter of the leering gamblers. Nathan and Silver said nothing, and conversation lagged. It suited Nathan when nothing more was said about a "friendly" game. The day dragged on. Surprisingly, after supper, three of the gamblers who had visited Stumberg's place gathered around the roulette wheel. Stevens, representing the house, took charge of the contraption. For a while, Nathan and Silver watched, but the bets were small and they soon lost interest. They returned to their quarters and stretched out on their bunks.

"God," said Nathan, "we've been on this damn boat just a day and a night, and I can't rightly remember when I wasn't here."

"Get used to it," Silver said. "This is only Monday night. It'll be near sundown on Wednesday before we dock in St. Louis."

Nathan lay awake in his bunk for what seemed like hours, until he ached all over. Finally he got up, and when Silver's snores continued, he slipped out the door. He was in his sock feet, but it didn't matter. Reaching the lounge, Nathan wasn't surprised to find it empty, and continued on until he reached the open deck. For a while he stood near the rail before the stern, watching the big paddlewheel churn the muddy water to silver in the pale moonlight. He started back the way he had come, and when he reached an open hatch to the lower deck, he paused. Yielding to temptation, he climbed down the steel rungs that formed a ladder. When he reached the lower deck, he was well past the forward portion of the deck where firemen fed the greedy fireboxes beneath the boilers. Ahead there were but two bracket lamps along the corridor. Nathan could see the doors to sixteen cabins—eight on either side—and again he recalled Silver's obvious reluctance to discuss them. They were probably locked, just as Silver had said, but Nathan was determined to see for himself. The first seven doors were locked securely, but Nathan's heart leaped when he tried the eighth. The knob turned easily, and in the flickering light of the single bracket lamp, Nathan Stone found himself looking through heavy iron bars! French Stumberg was indeed involved in white slavery!

The bars were a second door—the door of a jail or dungeon—and it was locked securely. But the bars didn't prevent Nathan from looking into the cell. Against the wall, one above the other, were two narrow bunks. Near the barred door there were two sets of chains, one end of which had been bolted securely to the floor. The other end of each set had sprung manacles, waiting to encircle the legs of the pair of unfortunates who were cast into the tiny cell. Above the throb of the engines, Nathan's danger-sensitive ears heard the snick of a hammer being eared back. Never without his Colts, he tensed.

"Don't try it," said Byron Silver quietly.

Nathan relaxed, moving his hands carefully away from the butts of his twin Colts. Just as carefully, Silver eased down the hammer of his Colt and then holstered the weapon. Only then did he speak.

"Curiosity killed the cat, my friend. You don't take advice well, do you?"

"Stumberg told me to prowl the boat, and this is part of it. I believe I'm entitled to know how these cells with leg irons fit into Stumberg's plans."

"I'm sorry you feel that way," Silver said. "I was beginning to like you."

"And now you don't?"

"I don't have much feeling, one way or another, for a dead man," Silver replied, "but I owe you something. I'm going to give you one more piece of advice. Don't trust anybody in Stumberg's pay."

"Even you?"

"Even me," said Silver.

Without another word, he walked away. Nathan closed the door on the cold iron bars and followed ...

St. Louis. October 25, 1866.

During the rest of the trip, Byron Silver said nothing to Nathan about the incident on the lower deck involving the chains and barred doors. Nathan was left to draw his own conclusions, and they were by no means pretty. The *Queen of Diamonds* docked at the landing a few minutes before sundown, while the weary—and probably broke—visitors to Stumberg's gambling houses could hardly wait for the gang plank to be lowered. It would be a while, Nathan thought, before any of the lot again undertook so foolish a journey. Captain Elias Lambert, a man shaped rather like a rum keg, had positioned himself so that he could observe those departing.

Nathan was quick to notice that none of the crew did. "None of Stumberg's bunch is going ashore," Nathan said. "Do we have to ask permission from the captain?"

"No," said Silver. "We can go now. The captain will remain aboard, of course, to secure the boat, and several firemen will be needed to keep up steam. We'll be leaving at eight o'clock in the morning."

"Then we don't have much time," Nathan said. "I believe I'll just pass up supper. How do we get back aboard tonight?"

"Be here before ten o'clock," Silver replied. "That's when old Lambert puts everything to bed. After that, he wouldn't lower the plank for Stumberg himself. I reckon I'll go with you. Do you have any destination in mind, or do you just aim to look around?"

"I've only been through here once," said Nathan, "and I don't know the town. There's some ex-Rebs I promised my Daddy I'd look up, and I've heard that St. Louis is a kind of crossroads where, sooner or later, everybody shows up. Do you know of a particular place that might cater to varmints that's pretty much rough around the edges?"

"Hell," Silver said, "that could apply to half the joints in town. But if I had to choose just one, I'd pick the Red Rooster Tavern."

The Red Rooster was within walking distance of the steamboat landing, one of many such establishments along the river. Not only was it a saloon of considerable proportions, it also boasted a lunch counter. There were sandwiches of several kinds, including ham, steak, or bacon and

egg. There was cornbread and beans, Polish sausage with
sauerkraut, chicken and dumplings, fried fish and roasted
sweet potatoes. After the limited fare on the steamboat, it
was a veritable feast. There was even fresh butter and
plenty of hot coffee.

"It's suppertime," said Nathan. "Before we do anything
else, let's eat."

The bar was virtually deserted, with two bartenders pol-
ishing glasses, while men were lined up at the lunch counter
awaiting tables. Nathan and Silver had a table against the
wall where they could see the door. The two men who
took the table next to Nathan and Silver had the look of
frontiersmen; their Colts were thonged down and their
range garb was rough and worn. Suddenly Nathan paused,
set down his coffee cup, and listened to the conversation.

". . . already a five-hundred-dollar reward for this Cullen
Baker," one of the pair was saying.*

"There's a scar-faced bastard ridin' with him," his companion replied. "A gent name of Tobe Snider. I hear he's
as snake-mean as Baker. Ought to be some bounty on
him."

It was enough for Nathan. He slid back in his chair and
stood up, and for the lack of a better approach, he leaned
on the back of a chair and spoke to the strangers.

"I wasn't meanin' to listen in, but I heard you gents
talking about Tobe Snider. I'm looking for a gent name of
Virg Dillard, and he once rode with Snider. I promised my
pa I'd look up Virg. Have you heard of him?"

The pair laughed, and the one who had mentioned
Snider spoke.

"Your daddy ought to be more careful who he socializes
with. A man that's a friend to Baker *or* Snider is askin' for
a bad name. And no, we ain't heard of Virg Dillard."

"I didn't say he was my pa's friend or mine," Nathan
replied, irritated. "I owe him something. Do you have any
idea where Cullen Baker is?"

"Hell," said the second man, "we don't know *where* he
is, else we'd track the varmint down and collect the bounty.
He's wore out his welcome in Texas again, and the Federals
have chased him back into Arkansas."

---

* Cullen Baker was born in Weakley County, Tennessee, in 1835.

Nathan took his seat at the table and continued eating, but his mind was wrestling with what he had just heard. He now had reason enough to believe Tobe Snider had left New Orleans, but had Virg Dillard gone with him? When there was nobody seated within hearing distance of their table, Silver spoke.

"So that's your game. The vengeance trail. Is this Dillard the only one, or just next on the list?"

"I don't consider that any of your business," Nathan said.

Silver smiled, but it didn't reach his eyes. "You're right. According to frontier custom, I have no right to know any more about you than you want to tell me. Just as you have no right to question me."

Neither man spoke again. A waiter brought a pot of steaming coffee and refilled their cups. Only then did Silver speak.

"For what it's worth, you'd best hang around New Orleans for a while. I seem to recall that when Cullen Baker gets in trouble in Arkansas, he crosses the line into Louisiana until he can sneak back into Texas."

Nathan nodded, saying nothing. It was as close as Silver would get to an apology for his breach of Western etiquette.

"I'm not much of a drinking man," said Nathan. "What are you of a mind to do, short of going back to the *Queen of Diamonds?*"

"I'd like to get my back to the wall and play some poker."

Nathan laughed. "You're a caution. All the way from New Orleans, Stevens and Harkness tried to lure you into a friendly game."

"Where I come from," Silver said, "there are no *friendly* games. There's only win or lose. For reasons you can likely figure out for yourself, it's not healthy knowing too much about the habits of Stumberg's house men."

There were plenty of poker tables in the Red Rooster, most of them fully occupied. When two men folded, Nathan and Silver took their places at a table with three big men who looked like bullwhackers. Their names were Keller, Zondo, and Thigpen. The three were well oiled, and their skill with the cards—if they had any—had suffered mightily. It was table stakes. Nathan took two pots and Silver took the next two.

"You varmints is winnin' jist too damn often to suit me," said Thigpen, loud enough for the entire saloon to hear.

"I don't play to suit you," said Silver coldly.

"You know, Silver," Nathan said, "Thigpen is almighty close to Pigpen."

"By God," said Silver, "you're right. I been wondering what that smell was."

Thigpen's two companions had already folded. They roared with laughter, along with everybody else who had heard the exchange.

"Damn you," Thigpen shouted, "cut the palaver an' play poker. I raise you ten."

"I'll see that," said Silver, "and I raise you twenty."

"I'm out," Nathan said.

"My deal," said Thigpen with a triumphant smirk.

"One card," Silver said.

Thigpen dealt the single card, and before he could deal for himself, Silver's cold voice stopped him.

"This time, take the card off the top."

Thigpen seemed about to strangle on his fury as he carefully slid a card off the top of the deck. It was time to put up or shut up, and Thigpen came up lacking. The best he could do was three aces. When Silver showed his hand, he had four kings.

"You bastard," Thigpen snarled. "I should of—"

"Drawn a fourth ace," said Silver. "It's on the bottom of the deck."

With a heave, Thigpen upended the table. He heaved a whiskey bottle, but Silver ducked and the bottle struck somebody else. Another bullwhacker had drawn back a Colt to slug Silver, but a slug from Nathan's left-hand weapon sent the Colt spinning. Some of the bullwhackers were so drunk they began slugging one another, while others drew their guns and began shooting. The affair had gotten out of hand and quickly became a knock-down saloon brawl. On hands and knees, Nathan and Silver began crawling toward what they hoped was a back door. Finally out of the fray, they got to their feet and escaped out the back door into an alley.

"We'd best find another place and get off the street," Silver panted.

"Yeah," Nathan agreed. "They'll pull the Red Rooster's

tail feathers plumb out, and it'll cost a pile to put the place back together."

They reached another saloon whose back door stood open, with lamplight leaking out into the alley.

"We'd best ease around and go in through the front door," said Silver. "If the law comes nosin' around, the bartenders will remember any likely pair that snuck in from the alley."

They ducked between two buildings and found themselves on a boardwalk between a saloon and an eatery.

"To hell with the saloon," Nathan said. "Let's get some coffee and maybe some pie. That'll give us a chance to catch our wind and find out if anybody's lookin' for us."

They walked into the little cafe, and since it was early evening, found it crowded. There were no available tables, so Nathan and Silver took stools at the counter. The coffee was hot and black, and they sipped their way through a first cup before starting on the pie. By the time their cups had been refilled, it seemed unlikely that they had been pursued as a result of the ruckus in the Red Rooster.

"Well," Silver said, "I know a place where the women are young and not too hard to look at. Not free, of course, but reasonable."

"I don't think so," said Nathan. "I hate to say it, but that bunk on the *Queen of Diamonds* is looking better by the minute."

Silver laughed. "I wouldn't have thought one saloon fight would leave you runnin' for cover."

"Well, by God," Nathan said, "I didn't see *you* hanging around for the finish. I've been in enough saloon brawls to learn that they usually end with somebody gettin' shot and the law comin' at a fast gallop. Last time I tangled horns with a slick dealer, him and his pard drew on me. I had to shoot the varmints to save my own hide, and *still* had to shuck out of there without the pot I'd fought for. A man ought to have better sense than to sit in on those small-stakes games with saloon riffraff. You lay with dogs, you end up with fleas."

"After tonight," Silver said, serious for a change, "I'd have to agree with you. When you pulled iron, I thought you were going to drill somebody. That was one damn good shot. By all rights, that hombre should have been a dead man."

"I'd never kill a man in a saloon brawl," said Nathan, "unless there was no other way. Dead men—even those in the wrong—have friends, and if they don't come after you, they'll send the law."

"We'd as well mosey on back to the *Queen of Diamonds*," Silver said. "If we wander into another saloon, we're just likely to run into those varmints from the Red Rooster, ready to continue the fight."

Reaching the landing, Nathan and Silver could see the dim hulk of the steamboat. Near the gangplank sat one of the crew in a deck chair. Quietly he got up and lowered the plank. Nathan recognized the man as one of the waiters. He immediately raised the gang plank, once Nathan and Silver were aboard. They were past the lounge and saloon, nearing their cabin, when they were frozen in their tracks by a scream. Drawing their Colts as they ran, Nathan and Silver headed for the lounge, only to find it empty. They shoved through the swinging doors and into the kitchen. There they found the gambler, Harkness, standing over the body of Shekela. The girl had been stripped to the waist. Nathan had the shaken Harkness covered, his Colt cocked, while Silver knelt beside the girl.

"She's dead," said Silver grimly.

"It was an accident," Harkness whined. "I ... I ... she fell ..."

Chapter 15

❖

"You can tell it to the captain, Harkness," Silver said. "Stone, keep him covered while I go for Captain Lambert."

"That won't be necessary," Lambert growled, shoving through the swinging doors and into the kitchen. Behind him was the crewman who had lowered the plank for Nathan and Silver to come aboard. Lambert, in a fury, turned on the cowering Harkness.

"Speak up, damn you," Lambert bawled.

"She ... she agreed to ... to meet me here," Harkness stammered, "but she ... she ... tried to back out ..."

"And you strangled her," said Silver. "Her neck's broken."

"No," Harkness cried, "no. She ... she fell ..."

Captain Lambert took from his pocket a key, which he handed to Byron Silver. "Take him to the lower deck," Lambert said, "and lock him in one of the cabins. He is to remain there until we reach New Orleans. He will then be turned over to Mr. Stumberg."

"No," Harkness begged. "Please." His face was pasty white, and he sank to his knees before Captain lambert.

"Get him away from me," Lambert snarled in disgust. "You," he said, his hard eyes on Nathan, "take the girl's body to the first deck, and when Silver has disposed of this ... vermin, he will unlock another of the cabins. Leave the girl there until I determine what we are to do with her."

The trembling Harkness stumbled ahead of Silver and practically fell down the hatch to the lower deck. Nathan wasn't so fortunate. He finally had to take the dead girl by the wrists and, easing her as near the lower deck as he could, drop her the rest of the way. He swallowed hard, sick to his stomach. Reaching the first deck, he shouldered the body of the hapless girl and made his way along the dimly lit corridor, following Silver.

"That's far enough," said Silver. Taking the key Lambert had given him, he unlocked the sixth door on the right, and finally, the barred door. "Now, he said, "get in there."

Harkness stumbled in and fell to the floor, sobbing. Silver slammed the barred door, locking it, and then locking the outside door. Without a word, he unlocked both doors to the fifth cabin and swung them back. Nathan took Shekela inside and eased her down on the lower bunk. For just a moment, he thought Silver was going to slam and lock the barred door. It would have been a treacherous thing to do, and Nathan couldn't understand why the possibility of it had crossed his mind. Quickly he stepped into the dim corridor, and Silver locked both the doors. Only then did Silver speak.

"This is one hell of a mess. Stumberg will have Harkness skinned alive, and maybe us with him, just on general principles."

"I don't take kindly to bein' gunned down in another man's fight," said Nathan. "We had nothing to do with this."

"Try talking sense to Stumberg when he's killing mad," Silver replied. "My God, it can't get any worse than this."

But it could, and did. Nathan and Silver reached the second deck to find Captain Lambert bellowing like a fresh-cut bull, while the entire crew—even the pilots—thundered down the gangplank to the landing. Lambert, red-faced, so angry he couldn't speak, glared at Nathan and Silver.

"Now what's happened?" Silver asked, as mildly as he could.

"The damn fool I had manning the plank left his post," Lambert shouted, "and the other girl—Trinity—jumped ship. The two of you get the hell out there and look for her."

Again Nathan and Silver left the steamboat, joining the mystified crew in what seemed like a fruitless search. There wouldn't be a moon until later, and the only light was the little that leaked through the doors and windows of the saloons and eateries, several hundred yards distant.

"Captain or not," said Nathan, "he's not playing with a full deck. Hell, the man left his post to tell Lambert something was wrong. With this old fool, you're damned if you do and damned if you don't."

"I wouldn't be too harsh on the captain," Silver replied.

"He's afraid. Afraid of Stumberg, and like a mortally wounded rattler, he's striking out at anything and anybody within reach."

The desperate crewmen searched until almost midnight, going into every eatery and saloon along the river. Nathan and Silver searched streets leading away from the landing, toward town, to no avail. Wearily they started back to the landing, and found most of the crew waiting there, like dejected, lost sheep.

"Damn it," said one of the men, "she ain't to be found. I say we go on back and tell the old grizzly, and be done with it."

"God," Stevens groaned, "we're in for it."

It was worse than they had expected. Captain Elias Lambert stormed up and down the deck, cursing every man and his ancestors back three generations. Finally his shoulders slumped and the life seemed to go out of him. Quietly he turned to Silver.

"What would you have us do?"

"Call off the search, sir," said Silver. "All the commotion around the landing is starting to attract attention in the saloons and cafes. It won't take much for somebody to call the law to investigate."

"Everybody aboard," Lambert said. "Hennessy, you raise the plank. The firemen to your posts. The rest of you to your quarters. We depart in the morning at eight bells."

Nathan and Silver, back at their bunks, could not sleep. It was Silver who finally spoke.

"I reckon Harkness deserves whatever Stumberg chooses to do with him, but I can't help sympathizing with the poor bastard. He's there in the pitch dark, without even a light."

"You still have the key," said Nathan. "If we slipped down there and lit a lamp for him, would Lambert have us drawn and quartered?"

"Only if he finds out about it," Silver said. He got up, opened the door and looked down the corridor. "Come on. It's clear."

They stepped into the corridor and Nathan closed the door behind them. Even if Lambert caught them, they might survive his fury as long as they were on the main deck, but they couldn't remain there. In their sock feet, they practically slid through the hatch and down the steel-runged ladder to the dimly lit first deck. There was nobody

to observe them except the two firemen who fed the fireboxes at the forwardmost end of the deck. It took but a
moment for Silver to slip the key in the lock and swing
back the first door, and that was as far as they needed to
go. There had been no light, but Harkness hadn't needed
any, nor would he ever again. Around the gambler's head
was a halo of blood, while the dead fingers of his right
hand gripped a .41-caliber sleeve gun. Harkness had shot
himself in the temple.

"God," said Silver, closing and locking the door.

"Are you going to tell the captain?"

"Hell, no," Silver hissed. "We're not supposed to be
away from quarters. This can wait until morning. Harkness
won't be going anywhere."

"Had he been with Stumberg very long?"

"Long enough to know what lay ahead of him" Silver
replied. "Let's get back to our quarters, if we can."

Luck was with them, and Nathan sighed with relief when
at last they let themselves into their cabin and quietly
closed the door.

"Why do you suppose Trinity ran away?" Nathan asked.

"I have no idea," said Silver, "but I can guess. I'd say
she was homesick. I don't know for sure, but I suspect
these girls are mostly runaways, and after a few weeks of
walking around in a gambling house mostly naked, they
only want to go home."

"And Stumberg would never allow that."

Silver said nothing, for in the darkness, his hands were
busy. From his pocket he had taken the key to the mysterious cells on the first deck and was doing a curious thing.
In his hands he warmed a small cube of wax, and when it
was soft enough, he pressed the key into it, creating an
impression . . .

*   *   *

Breakfast was at seven bells, and many of the gamblers
bound for New Orleans were already aboard. The very first
thing Silver did was seek out Captain Lambert and return
the key to the cabins with barred doors on the first deck.
Silver then made himself scarce before Lambert realized
Harkness must be taken breakfast. One of the waiters was
soon assigned the task, and when he returned, he was terri-

fied, almost incoherent. Lambert dragged him through the swinging doors and into the kitchen, before he could alarm the newly arrived gamblers who were having breakfast. When Lambert left the kitchen, he headed straight for the table where Nathan and Silver were eating.

"Here he comes," said Silver. "Be ready for anything."

But Captain Lambert never raised his voice. "Mr. Silver, I am told that the party you took to the first deck last night is dead. I wish you to confirm this immediately, bringing me all the pertinent facts." He passed Silver the key.

Without a word, Silver left the dining room. Lambert stood there a moment as though he wanted to speak to Nathan, but did not. He turned away, returning to the kitchen. Silver returned quickly, and Nathan pointed toward the kitchen. Silver was in there for a very short time, and then returned to his breakfast.

"Well?" Nathan asked quietly.

"Well, what?"

"What did he say?"

"Hell," said Silver, "what *could* he say? I told him Harkness was dead, had shot himself with a derringer, and that it was in his hand. He didn't say anything, and I hauled it out of there before he could *think* of anything."

"Two dead bodies," Nathan said, "and we won't reach New Orleans until Saturday. They'll be almighty ripe by then."

"Not my problem," Silver replied. "Lambert's got enough witnesses, so I'm pretty sure he won't have to prove the deaths by delivering the dead bodies to Stumberg. If you want to offer any advice, go ahead. Me, I got nothing to say unless I'm asked, and then I'm sayin' damn little."

"You take a lot for granted," said Nathan, "and there's times when it purely irritates the hell out of me. I know Stumberg won't be interested in seeing the dead bodies, but I'm equally sure the law *will* be."

Silver laughed, but there was not a hint of humor in it. "Let me see if I'm gettin' the straight of this," he said. "Are you suggesting that these dead bodies be turned over to Hargis Gavin and his personal police force? This could trigger a scandal that would rock New Orleans and blow French Stumberg higher than a keg of black powder."

It was Nathan's turn to be amused. "Thanks," he said. "I just wanted to be sure I'm on the right track. I think we'll be disposing of the bodies between here and New Orleans. I also believe this will strengthen our position with Stumberg. We'll know where the bodies are buried. Our silence ought to be worth something."

"Perhaps," Silver agreed, "but if it becomes too expensive, Stumberg can always lighten the load by having us shot dead."

*   *   *

Nathan had ample opportunities to deal faro. His was an honest game, and the "house" contributed much to the confidence of the New Orleans-bound gamblers. Nathan had no doubt that the little they won aboard the *Queen of Diamonds* would be quickly lost once they reached Stumberg's gambling houses.

The first day of the return journey was uneventful. Nathan spent much of his time in the combined lounge and saloon, dealing faro and poker. The other house man, Stevens, had nothing to say to Nathan, and he had rarely seen Byron Silver all day. Everybody seemed ready for a break from the gaming tables at five bells, when the call came for supper. While Stevens made it a point to eat alone, Silver joined Nathan.

"I've been wondering about you," Nathan said. "I reckoned maybe you'd jumped ship."

"It's a temptation," said Silver, "the more I think about it."

Nathan wanted to ask about the bodies on the first deck, but changed his mind. While he genuinely liked Silver, he had no idea which way the calf was going to jump once they reached New Orleans. Disposing of the bodies would be Captain Lambert's problem. Nathan found himself hoping Lambert wouldn't involve Silver. Silver left the table and Nathan continued dealing faro. Mercifully, the gamblers began thinning out around ten o'clock, and Captain Lambert declared the saloon closed for the night.

"I see you lucked out," said Silver, when Nathan entered the cabin. "I have seen die-hard gamblers hang over those tables until well past midnight."

"Captain Lambert closed the saloon at ten o'clock," Nathan said.

It was the perfect opportunity for Silver to suggest the

very thing that Nathan was thinking: that Captain Lambert had devious plans, and sought to clear the decks of possible witnesses. But Silver said nothing. Nathan drew off his boots, hung his hat over them, and stretched out on his bunk. For a change, he was tired enough to appreciate it, and was soon asleep.

*   *   *

It was the small hours of the morning, when the stars had begun to recede, that Captain Lambert made his move. Quietly, with four trusted crewmen, he made his way along the dim corridor of the first deck. Since he did not know in which of the cabins were the bodies, he went all the way to the eighth cubicle and worked his way back to the sixth.

"He's in there," Lambert said softly.

Two of the crewmen entered the cabin and swiftly rolled the dead Harkness into a square of canvas, binding it with rope. Captain Lambert swung open the doors to the fifth cabin and the second pair of crewmen quickly wrapped and bound Shekela's body. When the dead had been moved into the corridor, Lambert closed and locked the cabin doors. He then moved swiftly. The four crewmen followed, each pair bearing a canvas-wrapped burden. To avoid being seen by the firemen on duty, Lambert had the bodies hoisted through the hatch to the second deck. From there, they were carried forward to the rail. When hoisted over the side, they must have time to sink before the wash from the big paddle wheel caught up to them. Lambert had two lengths of heavy pipe ready, and one was tied securely to each of the body bags. The captain made sure the deck was clear and then he gave the order.

"Over the side, and drop them as far from the vessel as you can."

He watched as the canvas-wrapped bodies sank out of sight and then gave his men a final order.

"You will go to your quarters immediately and you will forget what you have done this night."

When they were gone, he leaned against the rail and buried his face in his hands. There had been no means of communicating with French Stumberg, so he had done what he must, but disposing of the bodies was the least of his problems. Stumberg couldn't abide failure, and Elias Lambert had failed. He had no idea what his punishment would be, but his long association with the evil little man told him Stumberg would think of something ...

*   *   *

Barnabas McQueen could scarcely believe his eyes. The slight cowboy that he knew as Eli Prater had spent almost a week just getting a calming hand on the big black, Diablo. Now Prater approached the horse with a saddle blanket. Diablo shied, ears laid back, and again Prater began talking. Slowly Diablo relaxed, his ears went up, and he sniffed the horse blanket. Once he was sure the blanket was harmless, he snaked his head around and watched as his friend draped it across his broad back. There was more "horse talk" that McQueen didn't understand, but Diablo seemed to relish every word. He didn't flinch when Prater reached both arms across him, arms resting on the saddle blanket. The arms bore down, applying pressure, and still Diablo remained calm. This being acceptable, the mysterious cowboy lifted both feet off the ground, with all the body weight resting on the horse. Prater let up, feet on the ground, and then repeated the procedure. Diablo looked around, curious, but remained calm. Prater removed the blanket, flung an arm around Diablo's neck, and the animal nickered.

"Good boy," said Prater. "That's enough for today."

Diablo followed Prater into the stable without even a halter. When the rider stepped out into the warm October sun, McQueen was waiting.

"I've never seen the like," McQueen said. "He's ready for a saddle."

"No," said Prater. "No saddle. Tomorrow I'll ride him with only the saddle blanket. Don't ever burden him with more than that, if you aim to win races."

"Damn it," Mcqueen said, "nobody's goin' to ride a bareback race. A man needs a saddle."

"This one doesn't."

"I reckon this is a good time to speak my mind," said McQueen. "I don't have a rider for this comin' race. Will you ride Diablo?"

"Yes. I was counting on it."

"Bueno," McQueen said. "Bueno. That takes a load off my mind."

Eulie Prater returned to the little cabin to await the call to supper. Cotton Blossom lay beneath an oak that shaded the cabin. He got up, walked a few paces toward the McQueen house, looking expectantly toward the road beyond.

Eulie sighed. "Not today, Cotton Blossom." Maybe not ever ..

*   *   *

Nathan was awakened by a seven-bells call to breakfast. Silver had not left the cabin, apparently, for he seemed as though he'd just awakened from a sound sleep. It now seemed probable that Captain Lambert would not depend on Silver for the disposition of the bodies. Whatever was done with them, it would have to be done soon. Unless, Nathan conceded, it had been done during the night. He said nothing to Silver as they prepared for breakfast.

"You looked like you'd been rode hard and hung out to dry when you turned in last night," Silver observed. "I reckon you got a workout at the tables."

"I got all I wanted and some to spare," said Nathan. "I won't really care if this bunch plays on the run back to St. Louis or not. It's been a while since I worked as a house dealer, and I'd forgotten just how damn boring it can get."

"I wouldn't give too much thought to the ride back to St. Louis until we test the water in New Orleans. When Stumberg gets a report on what happened in St. Louis, we could end up emptying spittoons at some of his gambling houses."

"Or worse," Nathan said. "He made it a point to tell me that when he's laid his money down, he expects to win. I'd say he lost big time. We didn't shuffles the cards, but we were there. If I understand him, then he won't be satisfied without a dog to kick."

"You understand him perfectly," said Silver. "I reckon we'll have to do some tall talking if we're to go on bein' part of his string."

"That'll be my decision," Nathan replied. "Not his."

"You'd best make up your mind," said Silver. "Far as Hargis Gavin's concerned, you're in Stumberg's camp. If

you decide that ain't where you want to be, the next hunk
of lead won't ventilate your hat. They'll be shootin' a
mite lower."

Nathan said nothing. One of the things he thoroughly
disliked about Byron Silver was the man's virtual certainty
that Nathan Stone was a dead man without the protection
of French Stumberg. What *was* Silver's game? Despite the
unusually good pay and a life of comparative ease, Nathan
couldn't escape the feeling there was some underlying motive for Silver's remaining with Stumberg. By the time he
and Silver reached the dining room, everybody else was
already there except Captain Lambert. Nathan hadn't seen
the captain since their last night in St. Louis. The days and
nights wore on, and eventually the on-board gambling all
but ceased. Stumberg's "guests" were saving it all for the
big time.

*   *   *

New Orleans. October 27, 1866.

The *Queen of Diamonds* docked on schedule, and only
then did Captain Lambert appear. The gamblers would remain on the steamboat until the coaches arrived later in
the evening. Then they would be taken to Stumberg's
various gambling houses. Nathan and Silver reached the
St. Charles late in the afternoon, taking supper there.
After the meal, reaching the third floor, they paused before the door to 301.

"Damn it," said Silver, "somebody's been in there."

"Maybe the maid," Nathan said.

"I've told them to stay out of there, except on Sundays,
when I'm here."

Silver drew his Colt, and with the key in his left hand,
unlocked the door and kicked it open. The room apparently
was empty and the beds had been neatly made. Unsatisfied,
Silver stood to one side of the closet, turning the knob,
easing the door open. Again his suspicions were unfounded.
Except for the few clothes left hanging there, the closet
was empty. Nathan and Silver waited in uncomfortable silence until the scheduled arrival of the Concord coach. It
arrived on time, carrying four of the gamblers from the

Queen of Diamonds. They nodded politely as Nathan and Silver took their seats.

Nathan wondered if Captain Lambert was, as that very minute, telling Stumberg what had happened in St. Louis. To Nathan, it seemed the worst kind of intimidation, pitting one man's word against that of another, but it was unquestionably effective. By the time Nathan and Silver faced Stumberg, the man would likely be in a towering rage. Even if the gambler accepted the deaths of Shekela and Harkness as unavoidable, how could he possibly accept Trinity's escape? It was conclusive proof, whatever Stumberg said to the contrary, that his "pretty girls" were virtual prisoners. But it went beyond that. What Barnabas McQueen had said about Stumberg being involved in white slavery fitted in perfectly with the shackles, chains, and barred doors on the lower deck of French Stumberg's *Queen of Diamonds ...*

When the coach drew up before the Old Canal House, another Concord was just leaving. Nathan and Silver stepped down, but allowed the quartet of guests to enter the house ahead of them. By the time Nathan and Silver went into the first parlor, one of the near-naked "pretty girls" was leading the visitors up the spiral stairs. Silver flashed Nathan a weak grin and spoke softly.

"Step into my parlor, said the spider to the fly."

Nathan had no response to that, and almost immediately his and Silver's attention was drawn to the head of the stairs, where Captain Lambert stood. He descended slowly, holding to the rail as though fearful he might fall. He somehow seemed smaller, less barrel chested, his demeanor exhausted. He spoke just four words.

"He's waiting for you."

Silver nodded to Nathan and they mounted the stairs. Silver knocked on Stumberg's door.

"All right," said the voice from within.

Silver entered and Nathan followed, closing the door behind him. Stumberg sat hunched behind the big desk as though he hadn't moved since Nathan had last seen him. He glared at them through cigar smoke, as though he hadn't quite decided their fate. Finally he stubbed out his cigar in a porcelain cup and spoke.

"In the morning, I want both of you checked out of the

St. Charles. You are to ride immediately to the Mayfair House, at McDonoughville."*

Looking from Silver to Nathan, he found no change in the expression of either man. He continued, more arrogantly than before.

"There is a stable and an exercise track behind Mayfair. There are two thoroughbreds in the stable. You are to feed, water, exercise, and rub them down daily. You will take your meals at Mayfair. There are bunks in the stable. Now get out."

For a long moment, Nathan and Silver stood before the gambler, unmoving. While they said nothing, their eyes spoke volumes.

"By God," Stumberg roared, *"I said get out!"*

Almost imperceptibly, Nathan nodded to Silver, and slowly they started backing toward the door. It was the ultimate insult, a show of contempt, the frontier way of showing French Stumberg they didn't trust their backs to him. Silver reached the door first, and with his left hand behind him, opened it. He backed into the hall and Nathan followed. Still facing Stumberg, Nathan closed the door. Neither man spoke, and when they reached the first parlor, Captain Lambert was there, looking even more dejected. Nathan and Silver sat down, for they, like Lambert, must wait for the eleven o'clock coach to town.

"Damn it," Silver said, "it's goin' to be a long night."

"You think you got troubles," Lambert growled, some of his old spirit returning, "but you're a young man. I'm sixty years old, with forty years on the river, and by God, I've been fired. Fired!"

"If it's any consolation," said Silver, "so were we. Hell, while we're waiting for the coach, let's go to the kitchen and eat."

"Thanks," said Lambert, "but I'm not hungry." The Captain remained in the parlor, seemingly deep in his own bitter thoughts. Nathan and Silver went to the kitchen they had visited before, and with hot coffee and food to be had, they took their time. After an hour in the kitchen, Nathan and Silver returned to the parlor to find Captain Lambert gone.

---

* McDonoughville existed until 1913, when it merged with Gretna.

"Where in tarnation did he go?" Silver wondered. "It's nowhere near time for the coach to town."

"Maybe he's outside," said Nathan.

"I don't think so," Silver said, "and I don't like the feel of this. We won't step out that door until the coach arrives. Even then, we'll be perfect targets for a bushwhacker with a rifle."

Nathan Stone shared the eerie, uneasy feeling. He couldn't dismiss the premonition that something had happened to the old captain, and with that in mind, he examined the chair in which Lambert had been sitting. There, on the chair's oval mahogany back, he discovered what appeared to be a single drop of blood. Using a corner of his handkerchief, Nathan allowed the white fabric to absorb the stain. Without a word, he passed it to Silver.

"By God," said Silver softly, "if I'm any judge, that's blood."

"I've seen enough blood that I don't have any doubts," Nathan said. "It looks like somebody found the old man here alone—somebody he knew, or they couldn't have gotten that close—and drove in a knife where it would do the most damage. It wasn't enough just to fire him. He knew too much."

"Hell," said Silver, "except for disposing of the bodies, we know as much as he did."

"That's why we're the highest-paid horse handlers on the face of the earth," Nathan said. "What better way to dispose of us than to send us to some godforsaken place and have us shot dead?"

"Enough, damn it," said Silver. "Keep a lid on it until we're out of here."

It was good thinking, and Nathan nodded. There was little they could discuss, and time lagged. They each sat in chairs next to the wall, so that they could see not only the front door, but the spiral stairs to the second floor and the doorway from the first parlor that led down a hallway to the kitchen. A grandfather clock stood just inside the second parlor, and the ticking seemed inordinately loud. They listened as it struck ten times, and waited impatiently until it chimed once on the half hour. Finally there was a clatter of hooves and the rattle of the Concord as it crossed the wooden bridge below the Old Canal House.

"He's early," Silver said. "Let's get aboard."

They did so, knowing that the coach must wait until the appointed hour before leaving. Finally the front door opened and the other passengers got into the coach. Oddly enough, the same four gamblers who had ridden with Nathan and Silver to the gambling house were returning to town. They, as did all of Stumberg's guests, had the option of spending the night on Stumberg's *Queen of Diamonds* or taking rooms at the hotel. The ride back to the hotel was a silent one, and Nathan had the feeling that the visiting gamblers had been sobered by their first night at Stumberg's tables. There would be other coaches at three o'clock in the morning, returning to town those persistent— or perhaps more foolish—men who had chosen to remain at the tables just a little longer. Nathan and Silver got out at the St. Charles and quickly made their way into the lobby. A clerk dozed at the desk, but nobody else was in sight. They ascended the stairs, and reaching the door to 301, Silver found the slender thread unbroken. He quickly unlocked the door, they entered, and he locked and bolted the door behind them. Silver was the first to speak.

"I'll be glad to get away from here. The first thing I'm doing in the morning is buying myself a saddle and a good horse. There's something that's unnatural, a Texan bunking in a fancy diggings like this."

"You'd better get yourself a Winchester too," Nathan said, "and a saddlebag full of shells."

"You could just ride out in the morning and keep going," said Silver.

"So could you," Nathan replied, "but you won't."

Silver laughed. "I ain't that smart. I've always regretted that I wasn't around for the fight at the Alamo. I'd've fitted right in. Hell, a Texan would go after a cougar with a cottonwood switch. That's my excuse, Stone. I'm a Texan, born and bred."

"So how do you know I'm not?" Nathan asked.

"You don't have the lingo," said Silver. "I'd give you another five years, if you live that long. You're an unreconstructed Southerner. I'd say you've dodged some Yankee lead, and somebody that's roosted in your family tree had some education."

"I'm a year out of Virginia," Nathan said, "and all the Yankee lead didn't miss. My mother was a schoolteacher before the war, and the little I know, I learned from her."

It was the most he had revealed of his background to anybody except Eulie Prater, and he said no more. Silver didn't press him, nor did he volunteer any information about himself. Silver tugged off his boots, evidence enough that he was calling it a night. Nathan followed his example, and Silver blew out the lamp. Nathan lay awake with his thoughts, and he suspected Silver was doing the same, for there was no snoring. It would be a long night ...

Chapter 16

McDonoughville. October 28, 1866.

Nathan and Silver arose well before first light and had their final meal in the St. Charles dining room. Checking out was a matter of gathering their few belongings and turning in their keys. They went immediately to the livery, and while Nathan paid his bill, Silver went from stall to stall, looking for a horse that appealed to him. Eventually he selected a grulla, a gray so dark it was almost black. He then bought a second-hand double-rigged Texas saddle, with saddle blankets included.

"God," Silver growled, "a hundred for the horse and fifty for the saddle. Time I'm fixed with a Winchester, saddlebags, and a bedroll, I'll be busted."

"You could have bought a center-fire rig for ten dollars less," Nathan observed.*

"Well, hell," said Silver, "I could have saved *fifty* dollars if I'd just bought a long-eared jack. You ain't even a Texan, and I don't see *you* settin' a center-fire saddle."

"Oh, shut up," Nathan said. "A man drawin' two hundred a month can afford expensive fixings and fancy horses."

When they reached the mercantile, Silver bought bacon, beans, coffee, and salt. To that he added a bedroll, saddlebags, a Winchester, and three tins of shells. Immediately he loaded the Winchester, the mark of a cautious man, for he knew not what lay ahead. It was a turbulent time, and a man who aimed to stay alive planned accordingly.

"I reckon," said Nathan as they mounted, "you know the way to McDonoughville."

---

* A "center-fire rig" is a saddle with a single cinch in the center.

"I've never been there," Silver replied, "but it ain't the kind of place you're likely to get lost. We follow the river east and just before it forks, there's a ferry. We'll cross there, and it ain't more'n two miles to Gretna. A little ways past Gretna is what they call McDonoughville. A wide place in the trail, I reckon."

"I've heard some talk about the track at Gretna," said Nathan. "That's where the races are held. Damned convenient for Stumberg, having his Mayfair House in McDonoughville. Who do we report to?"

"One of the house gamblers," Silver said. "A surly varmint name of Drew Shanklin. He rode shotgun on the *Queen of Diamonds* on her runs to St. Louis, until Stumberg replaced him with me."

"When you show up," said Nathan, "I reckon it's safe to say he won't be breakin' out the good whiskey and renewin' old friendships."

Silver laughed. "I'd be flattering myself if I said he hates my guts. I'd say I'm a hell of a lot lower than that on his totem pole. And don't look for him to take a fancy to you, when you ride in with me."

"It wouldn't matter if he'd never seen either of us in his life," Nathan observed. "I'd be downright disappointed if Stumberg didn't send him word last night. If we go astray, somebody's got to spank us."

"Stone," said Silver with admiration, "I purely like your way of gettin' a handle on a situation pronto. The time's a-comin', if you don't get shot dead, when you can call yourself a Texan and nobody will disagree."

Reaching the ferry crossing, they found the vessel on the south bank of the river and had to await its return. They each paid a dollar, led their horses aboard, and were taken across. The south bank of the river was lined with willows, and when they rode away from the ferry landing, they couldn't see more than a few feet in any direction.

"Prime place for an ambush," Nathan said. He shucked out his Winchester and jacked a shell into the chamber.

"God, but you're a doubting hombre," said Silver, "and so am I." Drawing his own Winchester from its saddle boot, he cocked it.

But they heard nothing and saw nobody. The undergrowth and willows diminished until they could see the roofs of a few buildings ahead.

"That's Gretna, I reckon," said Silver. "Let's ride through there until we reach the south fork of the river. We can follow it to McDonoughville."

Gretna, strangely enough, was strung out on both sides of the river's south fork, connected by a crude wooden bridge. There was a mercantile, a livery, a single-story hotel, a pair of saloons, and half a dozen residences. Nathan and Silver rode south without drawing any attention.

"There's the horse track," Silver said.

The track—if that's what it was—ran for a quarter of a mile along the river and was visible only to the extent that the underbrush and bushes had been cleared away. There were clumps of broom sedge and weeds that reached a horse's belly. To the west of the track, maybe a hundred yards, was a long, low horse barn. There was a series of slatted stalls, each of which opened into a common corral. Behind the barn, overhanging it, was a line of trees. Between the grown-up track and the river were more trees, so dense that the river was no longer visible.

"I don't like the looks of this damn track," Nathan said.

"Neither do I, for the same reason you don't," said Silver. "Too much cover, too close."

Nathan and Silver rode on, and not more than a mile after the track played out, they reached what had to be McDonoughville. There was only a mercantile, surrounded by a few residences. A few hundred yards beyond, on the west bank of the river, sat an imposing two-story house. It was white with green shutters, at the end of a winding lane lined with stately oaks.

"I reckon that's Mayfair House," Nathan said.

"I reckon it is," Silver agreed. "Who else but Stumberg would want all that fancy trappings at the tag-end of nowhere?"

"He can ride that steamboat right up to the front door," said Nathan, "If the south fork of the river's deep enough."

"It is," Silver said. "That's something you'd best keep in mind."

There was a rise behind Mayfair House, and beyond it was the stable Stumberg had mentioned. There would be room for a dozen horses, Nathan guessed, and behind the stable was a cleared stretch a dozen yards wide and several hundred yards long.

"We ought to unsaddle and stable the horses," said Nathan. "The question is, do we do it before or after we announce our arrival?"

"Before," Silver said cheerfully. "Whatever we do, he'll welcome us like a pair of bastards at a family reunion, so why bother?"

Nathan and Silver bypassed the house, dismounting before the stable. A horse nickered from within, and Silver's mount answered. There were a dozen stalls within the stable, four of them occupied. Nathan and Silver unsaddled, securing their saddles, bedrolls, and saddlebags in a tack room. Then, using old saddle blankets, they rubbed down their mounts and led each of them into an empty stall. Nathan forked down some hay for them.

"Only two of them are thoroughbreds," said Nathan from the loft. "Are we to exercise all of them, or just the two for the race?"

"Unless we get specific orders to the contrary," Silver said, "just the two thoroughbreds. I figure the others belong to the house gamblers, one of them Shanklin."

The bunks Stumberg had spoken of were in the tack room. There were two, against opposite walls, and they consisted of wood frames latticed with two-inch-wide strips of rawhide. Nathan took one bunk and Silver the other. When they had spread their bedrolls, they stretched out. Silver tipped his hat over his eyes.

"I reckon you're in no hurry to renew old friendships," Nathan said.

"You reckon right," said Silver. "Besides, it's not even ten o'clock, and that bunch at the house is still gettin' their beauty sleep. You wouldn't deny 'em that, would you?"

But Silver had figured wrong. They had relaxed for only a few minutes when they were roused by a bellow that would have awakened the dead.

"Get the hell out of those bunks. You *peladoes* think this is some kind of rest home?"

Silver eased back his hat and opened one eye. Suddenly he leaped to his feet—acting as if he were in fear of his life, he snapped to attention.

"My God," he hissed at Nathan in mock terror, "it's him. It's *him*."

Nathan emulated Silver's performance, falling from his bunk and getting hastily to his feet. It had the desired effect on Shanklin. His pale face flamed red, and when he opened

his mouth, speech failed him. Nathan's first impression of
the man verified Silver's negative description. Shanklin was
dressed like a dandy, with black pin-striped trousers, black
silk vest, and white shirt with ruffles. He was hatless, his
dark hair slicked back. A wide black leather belt with silver
concho buckle circled his ample middle, and from it, in a
cutout holster on his right hip, rode a pearl handled pistol.
Shanklin looked angry enough to draw the weapon and
begin firing. Eventually, after a mighty struggle, he recovered enough of his dignity to speak.

"I have been instructed to see that you men attend to
Mr. Stumberg's thoroughbreds," he said haughtily, "and
you are to begin immediately."

"Yes, massah," Silver replied with maddening sarcasm.
"When do we eat, suh? We ain't had a bite in nigh two
hours, suh."

Nathan could see it coming, but it was Silver's play, and
Nathan let him handle it. Shanklin was painfully, impossibly
slow. Before he even had a hand on his pistol, he was
staring into the muzzle of Silver's cocked Colt. Shanklin's
hand fell away from his gun and the breath went out of
him.

"Supper is at five," he hissed through clenched teeth.
"The two of you will take your meals in the kitchen. The
rest of the house is strictly off limits to you."

Silver's contemptuous laughter spoke volumes and it silenced Shanklin. Without another word he stalked out. Silver eased down on the hammer and returned his Colt to
its holster.

"You purely know how to get under a man's hide," Nathan said. "He ain't very sudden with his iron, but if he
back-shoots you, speed don't make a hell of a lot of
difference."

"When a man turns his back on a sidewinder," said Silver, "he deserves gettin' bit. Let's take a look at Stumberg's
thoroughbreds."

One of the horses was a bay, the other a chestnut. The
slatted fronts of the stalls were only head high, allowing
the horses to see anyone approaching. Silver came face to
face with the chestnut and the horse snorted, laying back
his ears.

"You're a handsome critter," Silver said, leaning over
the gate, "but I reckon you've been led about by some

hombre that was scared of you. Well, old hoss, I'm not afraid. Pick up them ears and let's be friends."

Silver extended his hand as though to touch the horse, and the chestnut snorted and reared, but he didn't back away, though there was room to do so. Silver's extended hand never wavered and the horse moved closer. Slowly the hand moved, stroking the animal's muzzle, and the chestnut relaxed, unafraid of this man who didn't fear him. Silver watched as Nathan Stone went through a similar routine with the bay. Within minutes they were able to open the stall gates and lead the horses out into the corridor of the barn. Both the animals submitted readily to a halter and were led out to the exercise track. The horses were thoroughbreds in every sense of the word. Their coats were thin and silky, their long, graceful necks running into well-defined withers and long, sloping shoulders. Their eyes were big and alert, their nostrils large, their heads clean cut and very fine. Each of them stood sixteen hands or more.

"We'll give them an hour to start," Silver said, "and increase it some as they get used to it."

They began by walking the horses, progressing to a trot, and, finally, to a slow gallop. Finally they dropped back to a walk.

"God," Nathan panted, "I never spent so much time afoot since the Yankees shot my horse from under me."

"I reckon we'll get ourselves in shape along with the horses," Silver replied. "At least it's comin' on winter. In summer, I suspect some of that Texas heat bleeds over into these parts."

While the sky was overcast, an hour of activity had both men and horses in a sweat. Nathan and Silver used old blankets and rubbed both animals down before returning them to their stalls. Besides a plentiful supply of hay in the loft, there were several hundred-pound bags of oats in the tack room.

"Well," said Nathan, "our day's work is done. Unless Stumberg's expectin' us to work out the horses more than once a day."

"Once a day's enough," Silver replied. "If he demands more than that, it's not for the benefit of the horses, but to harass us."

The afternoon dragged on. By five o'clock, Nathan and Silver were ready for supper. They walked up to the house, crossed a wide back porch, and went in through the back door. Following the odor of baking bread, they found the kitchen at the end of a short hall. Beyond it was a sumptuous dining room. A chandelier of six lighted lamps hung above a long table covered by a crisp white cloth. Within the kitchen was a plain oak table with four hard-bottom chairs, obviously for the cooks and servants. An enormous fat man in chef's hat and dirty white apron stared at Silver. Finally, when it seemed he wasn't going to speak, he did.

"Well, by God, Silver, I ain't seen you since I was at Old Canal House. I was told just this mornin' you'd be up here lookin' fer grub. I reckoned I was just bein' hoorawed, but damn, here you are, an' you dragged some poor soul down with you." He lowered his voice almost to a whisper. "What you done, sunk the steamboat?"

"Nothin' I can talk about, Antoine," Silver said. "This hombre is Nathan Stone. Are we allowed to sit down decent and eat off plates, or will you just heave some scraps out the back door?"

"You can eat here in the kitchen till somebody tells me different," the cook said. "I didn't know you was a horse handler."

"Neither did I," Silver said, "until last night."

*   *   *

Nathan and Silver got through the first week without difficulty, mostly because they saw nothing more of Drew Shanklin. But on the eighth day, as they walked the thoroughbreds, things changed. There was the distant crack of a rifle, and a slug whipped through the crown of Silver's hat. Before the echo of the shot had died, Nathan and Silver were belly down, Colts cocked and ready. But there were no more shots. The horses had pranced away.

"That one wasn't serious," Silver said. "He wasn't that far away, and he could have cut me down, dead center."

"I reckon we'd better go back to the barn and get our Winchesters," said Nathan, "and from now on, take them with us."

"*Si, bueno*," Silver agreed.

From then on, when leaving the barn for any reason, Nathan and Silver always carried their Winchesters. But there were no more shots, and the first time they took their rifles to the house, Antoine noticed. He said nothing at the time, but waited until the next morning. When Nathan and Silver showed up for breakfast—when it was likely that Shanklin and the rest of Mayfair House still slept—Antoine spread part of a New Orleans newspaper on the kitchen table.

"If anybody know you see this," Antoine whispered, "I don' know nothin' about it."

"Thanks, Antoine," said Silver. "Nobody will hear anything from us."

Quickly Nathan and Silver read the short article, then read it again:

Gunmen identified in recent killings, the headline read. *It has come to this editor's attention by anonymous letter that Nathan Stone and Byron Silver are responsible for the deaths of two men who were gunned down in a secluded area near the river. Our informant claims Stone and Silver are employed by gambling czar French Stumberg, while the dead men were representing Stumberg's rival, Hargis Gavin. Neither gambling kingpin could be reached for comment.*

"I reckon we know who the anonymous informer is," Nathan said. "Just one thing I don't understand. Why didn't the varmint go one step farther and tell Gavin's killers where they could find us?"

"That might have been a little obvious," said Silver drily. "Stumberg has an even dozen gambling houses, and if Gavin's even half smart, he could have found us in a couple of days."

"If Gavin's bunch is planning to gun us down," Nathan said, "they've had plenty of chances. Hell, they're shootin' from cover."

"We're supposed to *believe* it's Gavin's killers after us," Silver replied, "but I doubt it, for reasons you've just pointed out."

"I ain't wantin' to hear this," Antoine said. "There's ham, eggs, bread, potatoes, an' coffee on the stove." With that, he went to the far end of the kitchen and took a chair.

Nathan and Silver refilled their coffee cups and then heaped their own plates from the food on the stove. For Antoine's sake, they finished their breakfast and left the house before discussing their perilous situation any further. Reaching the tack room, they sat on Silver's bunk so they could talk softly.

"That means we're bein' saved for somethin' that Stumberg reckons he'll be able to use to his benefit," Nathan observed. "Any ideas?"

"Nothing I'd swear to," said Silver, "but if I had to guess, I'd say he aims to use us in some way to give himself an edge in that horse race."

"That's been botherin' me some," Nathan replied. "Back before the war—before our way of life was taken from us—we had our share of races. There was one horse, a thoroughbred, that comes to mind. There was some big money ridin' on him, but he came in almost dead last on a quarter-mile track. When the race was done, that horse was just hittin' his stride. If that race had been two miles, that horse would have run the legs off the rest of them, but he wasn't worth a damn in a short run."

"I've never seen thoroughbreds run," Silver said. "These animals have had plenty of exercise. Why don't we get them up to racing speed for a trial run, and see how fast they are? We're a mite heavy, I reckon, but we should be able to make up for that by not using saddles."

They led the thoroughbreds along the track for a while, walking and trotting, and then at a slow gallop. Then, without even saddle blankets, they mounted; Silver on the chestnut and Nathan on the bay. Simultaneously they kicked the horses into a fast gallop, wheeling them at the end of the short track and galloping back to the barn. They rubbed the animals down and returned them to their stalls.

"That's damn disappointing," said Silver. "Just looking at the critters, you'd believe they could fly if they had wings. But by God, I believe my old roan could beat both of them from a standing start, without working up a good sweat."

"I think so too," Nathan said, "on a quarter-mile track. But make it a two-mile race, and your roan would be eatin' their dust."

"But the track at Gretna is a quarter mile," said Silver. "That likely means Stumberg's about to lose a bundle unless he has an edge."

"Count on it," Nathan said, "but I believe he aims to *have* that edge. I only wish I knew how we figure into it."

Chapter 17

Three weeks after Nathan and Silver arrived at Mayfair House, they were again the targets of hidden riflemen. They had been to the house for breakfast and were returning to the barn when the concealed rifles cut loose. But this time, Silver and Nathan had their Winchesters, and, dropping to the ground, they returned fire. Three more slugs kicked up dirt, searching for them, and then the firing ceased.

"Close," Nathan said, holding a handkerchief to his left ear. "One of the first two came within a whisker of taking my head off."

"Looks like they mean business," said Silver, "and that pretty well kicks our theory about the race hell west and crooked."

"Maybe not," Nathan said. "They had us pinned down on the lee side of this rise, and there was two of them. They could have stayed with it until they got the range and cut us to ribbons. They're still playing with us."

"Maybe you're right," said Silver. "Look up yonder."

Drew Shanklin was standing on the back steps looking toward the distant trees from whence the shots had come. Seeing Nathan and Silver watching him, he turned and went back to the house.

"He can always testify that somebody—probably Hargis Gavin's killers—were gunning for us," Nathan said. "That would draw suspicion from Stumberg, point the finger at Gavin, and get rid of us, all with two Winchester slugs."

"But not until the day of the race," said Silver. "I don't know how it figures in, but damn it, you've seen Stumberg's nags run, and they don't have a prayer in a quarter-mile race."

* * *

At Barnabas McQueen's breakfast table, a somber mood prevailed. McQueen had opened the New Orleans paper to the damning story blaming Byron Silver and Nathan Stone with the killing of two of Hargis Gavin's men. The rider McQueen knew as Eli Prater had read the story and now turned troubled eyes on McQueen and his sympathetic wife, Bess.

"They're only guessing," Eulie fumed. "Why would a newspaper print something like this, when it's only rumor? Don't they know they're signing the death warrants of two men?"

"The newspapers can argue what they've done is in the public interest," said McQueen. "On the face of it, one gambling faction is gunning for the other, and nobody really gives a damn."

"It was a shameful thing to do," Bess said. "They've told everything except where those poor souls can be found, leaving them at the mercy of Hargis Gavin's killers."

"Oh, they've left no doubt as to where Stone and Silver can be found," said McQueen. "The paper says they're employed by French Stumberg, and that means they're in or near one of Stumberg's gambling dens. It'll be a matter of time until Gavin finds them, if he's so inclined."

"It seems like he *wants* them dead," Eulie said bitterly. "Nathan threw in with Stumberg to escape Gavin's guns, and now it looks like Stumberg's thrown him to the wolves."

"It does, for a fact," McQueen agreed. "I'd bet the farm that this damn unknown informer was Stumberg or somebody close to him. Who else could have known the names of the pair that shot it out with Gavin's men?"

"I can't speak for this Silver," said Eulie, "but Nathan Stone ain't the kind to set on his hunkers and wait for somebody to shoot him. I don't know where he is, but I know this: If somebody's gunning for him, he'll know it, and he'll take a lot of killing."

"I don't know how or if this fits in," McQueen said, "but I have it from a good source that Stumberg's thoroughbreds are at McDonoughville, near his Mayfair House. That's no more than a stone's throw south of the horse track at Gretna. I'm thinking of riding down there. If Stumberg's smart, there'll be somebody working those horses, and I'd like a look at them."

"I'm going with you," said Eulie. "I have a stake in this race."

"We'll ride at first light tomorrow," McQueen said. "Stumberg's barn will be somewhere near Mayfield House, I reckon, and that bunch will be up most of the night. We ought to be able to get close enough to see the barn and the horses without anybody seeing us."

* * *

The morning following the attempted ambush, Nathan and Silver took their time getting to the house for breakfast. Taking chairs at the kitchen table, they watched Antoine fuss around the stove, doing his best to seem uninterested in them.

"That shooting yesterday makes no sense," Nathan said. "Why didn't they gun us down from behind, instead of waiting for us to leave the house?"

"Damn it," Silver growled, "I thought we had decided this whole thing is to establish a reason for us bein' gunned down at a time suitable to Stumberg, and maybe shifting the blame to Hargis Gavin."

"I reckon we agree on that," Nathan replied, "but why all this show? The story in the paper was enough to throw the blame in Gavin's lap."

"We're in no position to make any moves," said Silver. "Stumberg has a reason for keeping us alive, and I don't aim to jump the traces as long as he's stacking the deck."

Antoine brought them steaming cups of coffee, and while they sipped that, he heaped their plates. Conversation lagged as Nathan and Silver began eating. Antoine brought the coffeepot, refilling their cups. Finally he poured himself some coffee and took a chair at the table, acting as though he had something to say.

"Damn it, Antoine," Silver said, "speak up before you bust a gut."

"Stumberg will be here tomorrow," said Antoine.

"Any idea as to why?" Silver asked.

"No," the cook replied. "Shanklin's got a burr under his tail. Come in here an' told me to wear a clean apron an' hat, like I ain't got the sense to do it without him tellin' me."

Nathan and Silver said nothing more while they were in

the kitchen, but it was something to think about. On the way back to the barn, Silver said what they were both thinking.

"I reckon he aims to see what we have to say about bein' shot at."

"He won't hear a damn thing out of me," Nathan said.

"Nor from me," said Silver. "Our hole card's likely a deuce, but we'll not let him know that."

Their usual routine was to spend at least an hour exercising the horses as soon as they returned from breakfast, and they did so this morning, for big gray clouds hung low and there was a promise of rain.

*   *   *

Eulie Prater and Barnabas McQueen took the ferry across the river, and with McQueen knowing the way, they bypassed Gretna, coming in to the west of Stumberg's Mayfair House. Cotton Blossom trotted along somewhere to the rear, and wasn't with them when they reined up among the trees several hundred yards west of Stumberg's barn. Nathan and Silver were walking the horses.

"There! With the bay," Eulie cried. "That's Nathan!"

But she wasn't the first to make the discovery. With a glad yip, Cotton Blossom went tearing through the brush.

"Cotton Blossom!" Eulie cried. "No."

"Let him go," said McQueen. "Maybe we can talk to Stone. There'll be less chance of us bein' seen if he comes to us."

Cotton Blossom danced around Nathan and almost spooked the bay. Nathan had to calm him before he could welcome the dog.

"This is Cotton Blossom," Nathan said by way of introduction. "I reckon there's friends of mine up there in the woods. Hold the bay. I'm goin' up there."

"It may be risky," said Silver. "Stumberg may be arriving any time."

"It's a chance I'll have to take," Nathan replied.

Silver took the bay's halter rope and Nathan, with Cotton Blossom ahead, set out for the stand of trees. But soon he was well into the woods and out of sight of the house.

"Well, by God," Nathan said, when he reached McQueen and Eulie. "How did you know I was here?"

"We didn't," said McQueen. "I learned that Stumberg's horses were down here and we hoped to get a look at them. What *are* you doing here?"

"There was trouble aboard the steamboat in St. Louis," Nathan replied. "Stumberg kicked me and Silver off the boat and sent us here. We'll be here until the race at Gretna."

"We saw the piece in the paper," Eulie said. "Has there been trouble because of that?"

"There's been some shooting," Nathan said, "but we believe it's Stumberg's doing. We're supposed to think, along with everybody else, that Gavin's gun-toters are after us. We're figurin' we're being set up to draw suspicion from Stumberg. We look for some gunplay during the race, because we can't see Stumberg's thoroughbreds winning on a quarter-mile track."

"Neither can I," said McQueen. "There'll be only twelve horses entered, including Stumberg's, and I'm convinced Diablo can beat the lot of them."

"Who's riding him?" Nathan asked.

"I am," said Eulie.

"Then do this," Nathan said. "Keep your head down, on the horse's neck. McQueen, bring your Winchester and ride your fastest horse. Stay near the finish line. There's cover on both sides of the track, so be prepared to shoot to either side. I have a feeling that Stumberg aims to position me and Silver on our horses somewhere along the track, and we'll draw some of the fire, but perhaps not all of it. Stumberg needs an edge in this race, and I believe he deliberately planted that newspaper story to blame any gunfire on Hargis Gavin."

"So he might dispose of you and Silver," said McQueen, "and if necessary, shoot any horse or rider that might cost him the race. He could then blame the shooting on Gavin, denying any responsibility."

"That's how I see it," Nathan said. "We've been fired on twice, and we could have been shot dead both times. Since we weren't, this has to be a setup for what's to come."

"I believe you," said McQueen. "When you think about it, Hargis Gavin would be a damn fool to go gunning for you and Silver. If either of you were gunned down, Gavin would get the blame. Do you want me to bring more men who will shoot if need be?"

"No," Nathan said. "Three of us can handle it. Too many armed men might arouse suspicion and get some of them killed needlessly. Be ready to ride out quickly. I believe Silver and me will have to run for it, and I'd like for us to lay over at your place for the night, if you'll risk it. We'll arrange not to ride in until after dark."

"Come on," said McQueen.

"I'd better be gettin' back," Nathan said, Stumberg may show up at any time." He shook McQueen's hand and then Eulie's, and saw the worry in her eyes.

Eulie held Cotton Blossom to prevent him following Nathan, while he hurried back to the stable as quickly as he could.

"I don't believe you were seen," said Silver, as Nathan stepped into the corridor of the barn.

Nathan explained McQueen's and Eulie's circumstances to Silver without unnecessary detail, and Silver asked no troublesome questions. He was quick to voice the same fear that Nathan had left unspoken.

"That hombre ridin' Diablo may be in more danger than we are," Silver said. "Those skunks with rifles could pretend to be Gavin's men, shooting at us, when they're really firing at McQueen's horse or the rider."

"I'm afraid of that," said Nathan, "the more I think about it. I believe Stumberg aims to win this race, that he's using us to justify enough gunfire to give his horses an edge, and then send gunmen after us. That's when we'll be rattlin' our hocks for McQueen's place, once the race is done."

Stumberg arrived in the afternoon, after the rain had begun. Nathan and Silver saw him coming down the rise, swallowed up in a yellow slicker. He left it hanging on a wooden peg near the barn door.

"How are the horses comin' along?" he asked.

"We're walking, trotting, and slow-galloping them for an hour or more every day," Silver said. Nathan said nothing.

"Good," said Stumberg. "Had any trouble?"

"Nothing we couldn't handle," Silver replied.

"Good," said Stumberg smoothly. "I was a bit concerned. Somehow that old fool at the newspaper connected the two of you with those Gavin gunmen who jumped you near the river."

Silver kept his silence and so did Nathan. It would have been a perfect opportunity to have told Stumberg about the hidden riflemen, and when they did not, Stumberg donned his slicker. Before leaving, he spoke once more.

"Keep the horses in shape."

Silver nodded, while Nathan didn't even afford him that. Stumberg was almost to the house before Silver spoke.

"He wasn't here to see about the horses. What he *really* wanted to know was, are we fools enough to believe Gavin's bunch was throwin' lead at us."

"That being the case," Nathan said, "the cards are on the table. Now he knows that *we* know this foolishness about Gavin coming after us is just a cover for something else. I think we just increased our chances of gettin' shot dead before that race ends."

At supper, Antoine wore a spotless chef's hat and apron, obviously in compliance with Drew Shanklin's order.

"God, I'm glad Stumberg's gone," the cook said. "Something must have happened. I heard a little of what was said to Shanklin. Stumberg won't be here for the race, 'cause he's goin' to be in St. Louis an' won't be back until Sunday."

"That's December thirtieth," said Silver. "What do you think happened?"

"I dunno," Antoine said, "but the steamboat ain't goin' back to St. Louis until that last week in December, when he goes with it. There was some talk about the dark of the moon and a sailin' ship. I didn't hear no more."

Antoine had nothing further to say and Silver didn't press him. When Nathan and Silver left the house, they found it had been raining hard. The rumble of thunder and a rising wind brought the promise of a stormy night. There being little else to do, Nathan and Silver dragged off their boots and stretched out on their bunks. Weary of the silence, Nathan spoke.

"What do you make of Stumberg giving up his gambling shuttle to and from St. Louis?"

"I reckon what happened in St. Louis shook him," Silver said. "That, and he no longer has a captain. He'll back off for a while, likely until after the first of the year."

"If we're to believe what Antoine told us," said Nathan, "Stumberg will be in St. Louis the week of the horse race, returning on Sunday. Why?"

"Your guess is as good as mine," Silver said. "I expect hell will bust loose sometime durin' that race, and Stumberg wants to be as far removed from it as possible."

Nathan had the same feeling—a premonition—and it had sunk its spurs into his mind. It had rankled him since he'd learned Eulie would be riding Diablo. But he knew Eulie Prater well enough to understand the futility of trying to change her mind.

*   *   *

New Orleans. December 16, 1866.

In his upstairs office at Old Canal House, French Stumberg chewed on an unlit cigar and studied the quartet of men before him. He knew them well, knew their capabilities, for they were killers Stumberg had successfully dealt with on more than one occasion. The four—Ringo, Jarvis, Sloan, and Brodie—killed without remorse, shooting from ambush. As usual, Stumberg had been careful to have them arrive after dark. Should their mission fail in any way, he dared not risk their implicating him. Finally he spoke.

"December twenty-ninth, I want the four of you near the track at Gretna. Ringo, I want you on one side of the track and Jarvis on the other, within rifle range. Your targets will be the horse handlers you've been harassing at McDonoughville. They will be mounted, and I want you to hold your fire until the race is well under way. Then I want them cut down."

"You got it," Ringo said. "Five hundred each."

"Sloan," said Stumberg, "I want you and Brodie to ride to McDonoughville. I want you to slip in behind Mayfair House and observe my two horses as they are being exercised. It's damned important that you *know* them, because you are going to give them an edge in that race. You are to shoot the riders of any two or three horses that are threatening mine. But above everything else, keep this in mind: You are *not* to fire at any riders until Ringo and Jarvis have dropped their men."

"So *that's* why you've had Ringo an' me throwin' lead at them hombres that's workin' with your hosses," Jarvis said. "We're supposed to be gunnin' for them, and a stray slug or two just happens to blow some riders out of the race. Them that's threatin' yours. That'll look fishy as hell, I think."

"By God," Stumberg shouted, "I'm not paying you to think, and I'll not have you questioning or second-guessing my motives. Is that clear?"

"Yeah," Jarvis growled, his hard eyes meeting those of Stumberg's. "It's your funeral. We won't be stickin' around to defend your good name."

"Wait a damn minute," Sloan bawled. "There's one thing that ain't clear. Me an' Brodie gits five hunnert a man, just like Ringo an' Jarvis. Now you're wantin' us to shoot maybe three riders if they're threatenin' to cost your hosses the race. We plug an extry rider, that's an extry five hunnert. Is *that* clear?"

"I don't know that a third rider will figure into it," said Stumberg. "I'm only saying that it's possible, that if the situation arises, you are to act in my best interests. If you and Brodie account for more than two riders, you will be paid accordingly. I am as good as my word."

Sloan's laugh was nasty, without humor. "In our line of work, mister, we don't take nobody's word. Not even yours. We always done whatever you paid us to do, an' you paid in advance. It ain't gonna be no different this time."

"Very well," Stumberg said, striving to control his temper. "Ringo will take an extra five hundred. If there *is* a third rider, Ringo will see that the man who earns the extra money receives it. Ringo, there is twenty-five hundred dollars in this envelope. Take it, count it, and then get the hell out of here."

Ringo took the envelope from the desk. Counting it, he found there were twenty-five one-hundred-dollar greenbacks. He nodded to Stumberg, opened the door, and stepped into the hall. Without a word, Jarvis, Sloan, and Brodie followed.

French Stumberg sighed. They were scum. It rankled him, having to come to terms with the likes of them. But this would be the last time, he promised himself. If everything went as planned, he would take his millions and retire to a life of ease in Mexico or South America.

*   *   *

After leaving Nathan Stone, McQueen and Eulie rode in silence. When McQueen eventually spoke, it was about what Eulie had expected.

"You don't *have* to ride Diablo in the race," McQueen said. "I believe you will be in some danger, and in good conscience, I can't hold you to such a promise."

"You're not holding me to it," said Eulie. "I'm holding myself to it. It's something I want to do. Do you realize how little would ever be done if we all just set on our hunkers and shied away from everything that was just the least bit dangerous?"

McQueen laughed. "You have a point, and I'd have to agree. But despite what Nathan said, there's a precaution I intend to take. I aim to have some other horse owners on hand with Winchesters. If Stumberg's people start anything, maybe we can finish it."

*   *   *

McDonoughville. December 16, 1866.

"Tomorrow," Byron Silver said, "I have business in New Orleans. Before first light, I'll lead my horse into those woods where you met with your friends. After breakfast, I'll ride out."

"I reckon you wouldn't be going without a good reason," said Nathan. "I can stay out of sight, and unless Shanklin actually comes down here, you'll have a chance to go and return without him knowing."

"Thanks," Silver said. "All I can tell you is that I'm about to play my hole card. If anything happens to me, it could involve you. If it does, you won't be alone. When the time comes, you'll know all I can tell you."

Nathan and Silver went to breakfast as usual and saw nobody except Antoine. When they returned to the barn, Silver waited awhile. Finally he got up, stomped into his boots, and tipped his hat over his eyes. Nathan said nothing. The burden was all on Silver, and he spoke.

"I should be back by noon. If I don't make it, you'd do well to ride out and keep going. Adios."

Silver rode far enough west that he would not be observed as he passed Gretna. He reached the south bank of the Mississippi a mile west of the ferry landing and rode along the river until he reached the crossing. He shouted and waved his hat until he got the attention of the ferrymen on the New Orleans side of the river. If anybody cared enough to ask, the ferrymen would have no trouble remembering him. He paid his dollar, and, reaching the farthest bank, rode north. His first stop in New Orleans was at a mercantile that carried a wide variety of tools. It was still early and a bored clerk stood behind the counter.

"I need a key made," Silver said. "Can you do it?"

"Yeah," said the clerk, "but I'll need another key or a pattern."

"I have a wax impression," Silver said. From his pocket he took a red bandanna, and from its folds a small beeswax cube.

"That should be satisfactory," the clerk said, examining the impression in wax. "It'll take me a little while."

"I have other business," Silver said. "Where is the telegraph office?"

"On St. Charles, two blocks west of the hotel."

Silver rode west along a less-traveled side street until he was sure he was past the hotel. He had lived there almost three months, and he couldn't risk being recognized. He found the telegraph office, and using the desk provided, wrote a brief message. There was nobody in the office except the operator, and he studied Silver's message.

"This don't make no sense to me," he said, looking over his glasses.

"No matter," said Silver. "It's not addressed to you."

"Eighty-five cents. You expectin' it to be answered?"

"No," said Silver. He pocketed his change and left the office. Returning to the mercantile, he found his key was ready.

"Fifty cents," the clerk said. "If it don't work, or if it's just hard to turn, bring it back and I'll hone 'er some more. No charge."

"Thanks," Silver said, with a grim chuckle. If he ever had need of the key, it had to work on the first try. There would be no time or need for another . . .

*   *   *

Dismounting, Silver led his horse into the corridor of the barn. He had been gone a little more than three hours.

"I'll take care of him for you," Nathan said.

"Thanks," Silver replied. He sat down on his bunk, tugged off his boots and dropped his hat over them.

"I've seen nobody since you rode out," said Nathan from the corridor, while he unsaddled the sweating horse.

Silver said nothing. On the inside of his right boot, just below the mule-eared top, there was an all but invisible slit in the leather. Into this concealed place Silver slipped the newly made key. Now he could only wait for the fateful race, barely two weeks away. During this time he needed to talk to Nathan Stone. Doing so would greatly endanger Stone's life, but Silver could not trust anyone else. For that matter, how far could he trust Nathan Stone? It was a crucial, perhaps fatal, decision. He would delay it as long as he could . . .

Chapter 18

❖

McDonoughville. December 22, 1866.

It was exactly one week before the race when Stumberg returned to Mayfair House. At breakfast, Antoine had whispered a warning to Silver, so that he and Nathan were not caught off guard when the boss arrived. Contrary to his usual nature, Stumberg seemed jovial.

"Bring out the horses," he said, "and let me have a look at them."

Nathan led the bay and Silver the chestnut. They walked the animals to and fro while Stumberg nodded approvingly. Finally he beckoned them to him and then he spoke.

"Red and Jake Prinz will be riding for me. The race will begin at two o'clock next Saturday afternoon. Drew Shanklin will be representing me, and I want you to take the horses to him at the track no later than half-past twelve. Silver, when the race begins, I want you mounted and two thirds of the way toward the finish line. You will be on the west side of the track. Stone, I want you mounted and in a similar position on the opposite side of the track. Have your rifles ready, for Hargis Gavin may be seeking vengeance. I expect him to attempt it in a manner that will endanger you, embarrass me, and cost me the race. Mind you, I can't be sure, but be prepared. This information has been sent to me anonymously."

"Likely by the same varmint that had our names printed in the newspaper," Nathan said.

The implication was clear enough, and though Stumberg kept his silence, the hard eyes that bored into Nathan spoke volumes. The gambler walked away and up the hill toward Mayfair House.

"Never kick sleeping dogs when you don't have to, and

don't stomp a sidewinder that ain't strikin' at you," said Silver.

"Hell," Nathan said angrily, "I don't feel the need for stayin' on the good side of a varmint layin' plans to have me shot dead."

When Nathan had unsaddled and rubbed down Silver's horse, he led it into a stall and returned to the tack room. He sat down on his bunk, dragged off his boots, and hung his hat over them. He eyed Silver, but Silver said nothing. Finally Nathan spoke.

"I'll say one thing for Stumberg. The varmint's got more brass than a whorehouse bed. He as good as told us we're goin' to be bushwhacked durin' that race. How can he be so sure we won't just ride and say to hell with it?"

"He has an edge, an ace in the hole," Silver said. "Like you said, he's as good as told us we'll likely be caught in a crossfire. He figures between that and kicking us off the *Queen of Diamonds,* we'll be mad as hell and of a mind to get even."

"He's right about that part of it," said Nathan, "but I have a stronger reason. My pard will be ridin' Barnabas McQueen's Diablo, and McQueen thinks the black can walk away from all the others. Especially those thoroughbreds of Stumbergs. I think so too."

"If that's true," Silver said, "you'd have been wise to figure some way of keeping your friend out of that race."

"To this particular friend," said Nathan, "riding McQueen's Diablo next Saturday is worth the risk. We're talking about a south Texas rider who has more feeling for horses than anybody I've ever known."

"So that's part of your reason for playing out your string," Silver said. "To try and save your friend from being shot out of the saddle."

"A big part of it," Nathan replied.

"I suppose yours is a more noble cause than mine," said Silver, "but I am committed, and when I've given my word, I'll stick till hell freezes."

"I admire you for that," Nathan said. "At the finish, after we shoot our way past the ambush, we'll be finished with Stumberg. I have the promise of a bunk at McQueen's place out on Bayou Road. I can't see that he'll be in any more danger with both of us than he'll risk with just me."

"I'll ride with you," Silver replied. "I'll need a place to

hole up until Sunday, when the *Queen of Diamonds* returns from St. Louis. I have a hole card to play, and when the dust settles, I doubt McQueen will be bothered for having taken us in. Once we've drawn fire from those bushwhackers, we can raise some hell of our own."

"We have to face the possibility that one or both of us won't come out of this alive," said Nathan. "Those varmints will be shootin' to kill this time. Damn it, this could be the end of the trail."

"I've considered that," Silver said. "I don't know you any better than you know me, but I feel like we've been over the mountain together. If I make it and you don't, is there anything I can do for you, besides evening the score?"

"All my kin are dead," said Nathan, "so I reckon that'll be enough. I'd say you're a bueno hombre, Silver. If I live and you cash in, I'll gun down those bushwhackers if I have to follow them to hell. Besides that, is there anything else I can do?"

"Just one thing," Silver said. "If I live, I'm bound to silence, but if I die, all bets are off. Inside my right boot there's a slit in the leather. Behind the lining you'll find written instructions that must be followed to the letter. There is a telegram that must be sent. The message will be just two words: 'Twenty-one.' It is not be be signed. After that, you follow the instructions. That's all I'm permitted to tell you. If you'd just done the sensible thing and got the hell out of here, I'd not be revealing this much."

Nathan laughed. "If I escape the ambush, you're givin' Stumberg's bunch another chance at me."

"Wrong," Silver said. "If I don't make it, I'm placing in your hands the power to destroy French Stumberg. But unless I'm shot all to hell, you or nobody else is going to deny me that privilege."

"There *is* one thing you can do," said Nathan. "If we both live through this, I'd like to know why you're so willing to risk your neck. God, I knew fire-breathing Rebs who wouldn't have taken the risks you're taking."

"Let's just say that something lit a fire under me," Silver said. "If you side me through this and we both live to talk about it, I reckon you'll have earned the right to know where I'm coming from."

This talk with Silver forced Nathan to question his own

motives. While he rode a perilous vengeance trail, committed to gun down seven killers, it had been his own choice.
So had been his decision to gain the confidence of French
Stumberg as a means of getting to Dillard and Snider, a
pair of the killers he sought. Now it appeared that Snider—
and possibly Dillard—had fled New Orleans. Nathan's vengeance trail had taken a new turn and he now knew enough
about Stumberg's unsavory activities to consider just riding
on, but he could not. He had committed himself to a cause,
an unlikely alliance with the enigmatic Byron Silver that
could destroy them both. But, he had to admit, his motivation went beyond his word to Silver, and Nathan Stone had
to face a truth he had been avoiding. Eulie Prater had
become a part of his life, and with her determination to ride
Diablo into what promised to become a deadly ambush, he
couldn't forsake her. The vengeance trail would have to
wait until he either saved Eulie's life or until they both
died in the same hail of bushwhacker lead. Damn it, he
would keep his word to Silver and save Eulie if he could,
but when the smoke cleared—if he were alive—he would
again ride the vengeance trail, and all the devils from hell
wouldn't stop him ...

The rain began on December twenty-third and continued
through Christmas Day. It was a tiresome, dreary time with
little to do but wait. One morning, Nathan kicked off his
blankets and sat up in his bunk.

Silver grinned at him. "Merry Christmas," said the
Texan.

"Yeah," Nathan grunted. "The same to you."

"I reckon we won't be swappin' gifts," said Silver with
a straight face.

"On, we can do it in spirit," Nathan replied sourly. "I
won't swear at you if you'll dig a hole and drop your
damned good humor into it. I reckon there's nothin' that
gets on a man's nerves more than trying to be mad as hell
and havin' some grinnin' varmint trying to be funny."

*   *   *

Gretna. December 29, 1866.

Three days of sun had done wonders for the track, and
by eleven o'clock, a substantial crowd had gathered in an-

ticipation of the race. A dozen fires crackled under as many coffeepots and a rich aroma filled the air. Most of the horse owners and their riders were there, Bess McQueen and Eulie in a buckboard and McQueen on his horse. McQueen had spoken to a dozen men who shared his hatred of French Stumberg, and these staunch friends had arrived with Winchesters in their saddle boots. If Nathan Stone's suspicions were well founded, McQueen was determined that none of Stumberg's killers was going to escape.

"Here they come!" somebody shouted.

Nathan Stone and Byron Silver rode from the south, each of them leading one of Stumberg's thoroughbreds. Drew Shanklin waited, accompanied by Red and Jake Prinz. Nathan and Silver reined up, passing the lead ropes of the horses to Shanklin. Then, without a word to the trio, Nathan and Silver rode back beyond the starting line, where McQueen stood beside his horse and Bess and Eulie waited in the buckboard. Nathan performed the introductions, and Silver swept off his hat. Cotton Blossom regarded Silver with undisguised suspicion.

"When this is all over," Nathan said quietly, "I'm bringing Silver with me. He needs a place to hole up for a night or so."

"Right," said McQueen.

"Lots of hombres driftin' around with Winchesters," Nathan said. "Do you know anything about that?"

"Not a thing," McQueen said innocently.

As the start of the race drew near, the crowd became restless. Few wished to remain at the starting line, and began arranging themselves at intervals along the track. While they wanted to see the finish, they didn't want to risk missing what might happen prior to it. The finish line was marked with a wide red ribbon stretched across the track, and on either side of it stood one of the judges. Each horse was numbered according to its position at the starting line. Stumberg's horses were numbers two and twelve, while Diablo had drawn fourteen. That put Eulie on the outside, nearest the river, and Nathan took some comfort in that, for he would be riding nearest her. Unless he and Silver had figured everything totally wrong, they would be the first to draw fire, allowing them to go after the bushwhackers before Eulie and the other riders were in danger. It all depended on who took the lead in the race, and Nathan knew Eulie Prater would never hold back, if it meant her life . . .

There was a shot signaling the start of the race and the horses were off and running. A big roan took an early lead, with Diablo running a close second. The rest of the horses were bunched. Eulie leaned forward and seemed to speak to the horse, and Diablo responded. Clearly, unless something went wrong, he would soon take the lead. Nathan rode well to the rear, Winchester ready. Uncertain as to what was expected of him, Cotton Blossom trailed behind. Then without warning, several of the bunched horses tried to break free. Shouldering into others, they sparked a neighing, biting ruckus. It allowed Stumberg's bay and chestnut to gallop ahead. They seemed to be getting into the spirit of the race, for they surged into the final stretch running third and fourth. Nathan tensed. If there were going to be trouble, now was the time.

Suddenly there were two rapid shots, the second sounding like an echo of the first. Lead burned across Nathan's right arm, just above the elbow. As rapidly as he could jack in the shells, he fired three times into a thicket, just below a rising puff of smoke. There were more shots, but from different positions. Firing while mounted posed some difficulty, and Nathan rolled out of the saddle. He hit the ground running, zigzagging toward the river with Cotton Blossom right behind him, but there were no more shots. Nathan moved cautiously into the brush and found a dead man. Nathan doubled back, caught up his horse and rode toward the finish line. It seemed everybody had congregated there, and Nathan soon learned why. The shooting had ceased and an ominous quiet reigned. The big roan's rider sat on the ground, the left shoulder of his shirt bloody. Bess McQueen was doing her best to calm the riderless Diablo, but everyone else seemed in shock.

On the ground, on their backs, lay Byron Silver and Eulie Prater. Cotton Blossom had taken a position beside Eulie. Lifting his lean muzzle toward the heavens, he howled mournfully. Blood soaked the entire left side of Eulie's shirt. A slug had torn into Silver's right side, just above the butt of his Colt. Silently Nathan knelt beside Eulie and took her wrist, seeking a pulse. It was there, but one look at her pale face told him it no longer mattered, for on her lips was a red froth. Sick to the depths of his soul, tears blinding his eyes, Nathan knelt there, never wanting to rise. Then he remembered Silver lying there, perhaps dying, and taking a limp wrist, sought a pulse. It too was detectable, but weak. Sleeving his eyes dry, Nathan forced himself to look at Silver's face. There was no telltale froth on Silver's lips.

"Nathan ..."

Her voice was no more than a whisper, but Nathan heard. Eulie's eyes were dull with pain, but they were open, desperately seeking his. Others had crowded around, but Nathan ignored them. On his knees he leaned close.

"Diablo ... won ..." she whispered. "He ... won .."

Those were her last words. Nathan got blindly to his feet and through tear-dimmed eyes, found himself face to face with Drew Shanklin.

"Damn it," Shanklin snarled, "you and Silver are responsible for this. It was you they were after ..."

Nathan brought up a bone-crushing right all the way from his knees, behind it all the anguish and fury that engulfed his soul. It smashed into Shanklin's jaw, lifted him off the ground, and dropped him into an unconscious heap under the hooves of Silver's grulla. Blind with fury, Nathan jacked a shell into the chamber of his Winchester. He paused only when he felt a hand on his arm.

"Barnabas's gone for a doctor," said Bess McQueen. "I'll have some of the men wrap Eulie in some blankets and take her to the buckboard."

"You ... you knew about her," Nathan said wonderingly.

"A woman always knows," said Bess. "She had a home with us, and I don't believe she would ever have left. Now she'll be with us always."

"Thank you," Nathan said brokenly. "She wanted ... very little, and God knows, that's all she ever got ... from me .."

Cotton Blossom stood over Eulie and growled. Nathan had to restrain him so that Eulie could be taken away. When her body was placed in McQueen's buckboard, Cotton Blossom stationed himself beneath it and resumed his mournful howling. McQueen soon returned with a doctor whose name was never mentioned. The doctor only looked at the rider with the bloody shoulder and went immediately to Byron Silver. Kneeling, he raised Silver enough to probe his back. The doctor spoke.

"The slug went on through. Unless it damaged his vitals, he has a chance. But he's lost a lot of blood. Where will you be taking him?"

"To my place," McQueen said. "We have a buckboard."

"I'll dress his wound, then, and you can take some laudanum with you. I can have another look at him in the morning. Wrap him in blankets, keep him warm, and when he become feverish, pour whiskey down him."

Quickly he cut away Silver's shirt, doused the ugly wound with disinfectant, and bound it securely. He then turned to the other wounded man, leaving McQueen, Nathan, and several of McQueen's friends to carry the blanket-wrapped Silver to McQueen's buckboard. McQueen drew a sharp breath when he saw the other blanket-shrouded body already in the buckboard. When they got Silver stretched out, McQueen turned away, cursing bitterly under his breath.

"Barnabas," said one of his friends, "two of the sidewinders tried to run. We gunned 'em down."

"How many were there?" McQueen asked.

"Four," said Nathan, answering the question. "I got one of them, and I reckon Silver got one."

"Nathan," McQueen said, "I'm a damned old fool who ought to be gut-shot for allowing her to ride that horse."

"Barnabas," said Nathan, "if she could have been stopped, I'd have stopped her. It was her life, her way, and she died a winner."

Bess drove the buckboard while McQueen rode his horse and led Diablo. Nathan followed with Silver's grulla. When they reached McQueen's place, Nathan and McQueen lifted Silver from the buckboard and carried him into the McQueen house. Bess had insisted on it, and turned down the covers to make the wounded Silver comfortable. Nathan removed Silver's boots and it was then that he remembered his promise to Silver. But that would have to wait. He had no intention of leaving Eulie in the buckboard, nor did Bess McQueen.

"Bring Eulie inside," Bess said. "She's been staying here at the house with us. She can spend this last night in her own bed."

Nathan and McQueen brought Eulie in and placed her on the bed in a back room that Bess had fixed up especially for her. Cotton Blossom trotted in and lay down beside the bed.

"I'd better put him out," said Nathan.

"No," Bess said. "Let him stay. His loss is as great as yours."

Bess prepared supper, and after all that had happened, Nathan found he still had an appetite. As he ate, he told the McQueens the little he knew about Byron Silver and of his promise to Silver.

"I believe whatever he had planned to do depended on his getting forces together before Stumberg's *Queen of Diamonds* returns to New Orleans From St. Louis," said Nathan. "I think it's time I had a look at whatever is hidden in Silver's boot."

McQueen, being nearest the room where Silver lay, brought the boot and handed it to Nathan. Without difficulty he found the slit in the leather, and the first item he brought forth was the key Silver had stolen by wax impression. Besides the key, Nathan found only a thin strip of paper. When he had unfolded it, there were just two printed lines. They read: *Office of the Attorney General, Washington, D.C.*

"God Almighty," said McQueen, "a government man."

"Yes," Nathan said, "and now I know why he didn't talk about himself or why he worked for Stumberg."

"That little piece of paper could have become his death warrant," said McQueen, "and I wonder why he carried it at all? He could have remembered the address."

"I don't know," Nathan said, "unless he feared a situation such as this, where he had to depend on somebody else to make contact for him."

"Contacting the attorney general's office could get you killed," said McQueen. "Any message you send will likely fall into Stumberg's hands. From what I hear, he pays handsomely for information from any source."

"This one won't matter," Nathan replied. "It's a code, and there's only two words. Silver told me that and I'm to send it by telegraph, without a signature. The hell of it is, I don't know what to do after that."

"I'd say you're to wait at the telegraph office," said McQueen. "Those code words are to tell Silver's people where he is. Or in this case, where *you* are. There are Union soldiers in town, and they have a private telegraph."

"That's sensible," Nathan said, "and I reckon I'd better ride in and do it tonight. I can't believe Stumberg would

leave everything in the hands of those bushwhackers. I'd
be plumb disappointed in him if he didn't leave orders for
Silver and me to be shot on sight, in case either of us
survived the bushwhacking."

"If you start now, you'll have all night for Washington
to contact you. There must be a powerful reason for everything coming together at this particular time."

"There is," Nathan said, "and this key plays a strong
part. It gives me an idea as to what Silver reckoned is about
to happen tomorrow night. Whatever happens tonight, I'll
be here in the morning to ... to say goodbye to Eulie."

Nathan rode carefully, reaching town without incident.
He remembered where the telegraph office was—he and
Eulie had passed it on St. Charles that first day they had
ridden into New Orleans. Entering the office, Nathan
quickly wrote the Washington address on the form provided, following it with his two-word message. For a moment the little man in wire-rimmed spectacles studied it.

"Why, that's the same ..." His voice trailed off.

"The same what?" Nathan demanded.

"Nothin'," the operator said. "I meant to say you ain't
signed it."

"I don't aim to," Nathan said. "Send it like it is. How
much?"

"Eighty-five cents."

Nathan paid, waited until the message was sent, and left
the office. He would wait outside. While the telegraph man
had cut himself short, Nathan believed he knew what might
have been said. Prior to Nathan's message, the man had
seen a similar one. Silver had never told Nathan why he'd
been in town for three hours. Might he not have copied
the key and telegraphed Washington? The little man in the
telegraph office had been entirely too curious, hadn't he?
Stumberg would no doubt know of one or both telegraph
messages. Barring quick response by powerfully placed
friends of Byron Silver, Silver's and Nathan's remaining
hours in New Orleans were few. The contact came fifteen
minutes later. A man in town clothes and heavy topcoat
approached the telegraph office. He was smoking a cigar
and he barely paused before the telegraph office. He
spoke softly.

"Twenty-one?"

"Yes," Nathan replied.

"Wait until the clock strikes eight. Then come to room 200 at the St. Charles. Knock three times, pause, and knock again."

He walked on, allowing Nathan no time to speak. But Nathan had no desire to ask any questions until he was off the street. He mounted his horse and rode east along St. Charles. He was more than half an hour from knowing what this was all about, and he chafed at the delay. He considered going into one of the saloons for a beer, but that was asking for trouble. Finally he tied his horse to a hitch rail outside the St. Charles and walked across the street to a wooden bench before a darkened store. There he would sit until time to enter the hotel. At least he had the storefront to his back, and could see anyone who approached from across the street or from either direction along St. Charles. Finally the big clock struck the hour, and as the eighth tone died away, Nathan crossed the street to the hotel. He allowed his eyes to sweep across the lobby before mounting the stairs, and once in the hall, he looked both directions before approaching the door to room 200. Quickly he knocked three times, paused, and knocked again.

"Identify yourself," said a voice within.

"Nathan Stone, friend of Byron Silver."

Slowly the door opened and Nathan was virtually certain someone was back of it, probably with a gun. He stepped into the room and the door was closed. The man with the gun slipped it under his coat. His companion, who sat on the bed, was the same man who had contacted Nathan outside the telegraph office, and it was he who spoke.

"Who are you, and why did you send that telegram?"

"I'm the friend of a man who uses the name Byron Silver," Nathan said, "and I did only what I promised him I'd do. I'm not saying another damned thing until I know who *you* are."

"I'm Powers," said the man on the bed, "and he's Grago. We are officers in the Union army. We are civilian dressed for obvious reasons. You say you are a friend of Mr. Silver. What do you know of his activities, and where is he now?"

"I know nothing of his activities," Nathan said, "except that he asked me to contact you if something happened to him. The two of us worked together for a while as gunmen for French Stumberg, until we got on the bad side of him.

Today we were caught in an ambush that we believe Stumberg planned. Silver's hard hit. He's been seen by a doctor and is being cared for in a place of safety."

"Mr. Silver obviously trusted you, Stone," said Powers, "and you have justified that trust by acting on his behalf when he was shot. We need a man like you, and we need him now, or all Silver's work will have been in vain. Just how far are you willing to go in bringing Silver's mission to a successful conclusion?"

"In that same house where Silver lies wounded," Nathan said, "lies the body of the best friend I ever had. A friend who died in Stumberg's ambush. Does that answer your question?"

"Then I don't have to warn you that French Stumberg is utterly ruthless," said Powers. "You said Silver told you little, but you must know *something* of Stumberg's activities, or he wouldn't be after you. Are you aware of his reason for being in St. Louis and of what is about to take place tomorrow night?"

"Only what I've guessed," Nathan said. "Silver and I traveled only once to St. Louis aboard the *Queen of Diamonds*. There was trouble aboard while we were in St. Louis. Two of Stumberg's people died and one of the saloon girls escaped. Until now, that was the last time the *Queen of Diamonds* traveled to St. Louis. We never knew why."

"I suppose you're in deep enough for me to tell you," said Powers. "The girl who escaped—Trinity—is one of us. With her testimony alone, we have a case strong enough to hang French Stumberg a dozen times. Through contacts in St. Louis, we know he is about to deliver cargo—human cargo—into the hands of Mexican slave traders tomorrow night. White slavery. Are you familiar with the term?"

"Yes," Nathan said. "I saw the cabins, with barred doors on the first deck of the *Queen of Diamonds*."

"That's a problem," said Grago, speaking for the first time. "Somehow we must stop him short of international waters, but in a showdown, count on him to use the young women as hostages. What is your answer to that?"

"Exactly what Silver's would have been," Nathan said, taking the key from his pocket. "Thanks to him, we have a key to those barred doors."

"Great God," said Powers, "we have a means of freeing the hostages!"

"Only if one of us can get aboard that vessel," Grago said.

"I'm going aboard," Nathan said, "but only if I'm allowed to do it my way. By God, it's my neck, and I give the orders."

Chapter 19

❖❖❖

"Perhaps you'd better tell us what you have in mind," said Powers. "This endeavor represents almost two years of undercover work, and we are in no position to relinquish control of it to an outsider."

"I'm not an outsider, Powers," Nathan said. "I have a stake in this that is stronger than yours. For starters, we'll need a steamboat."

"We thought of that," said Powers. "We have a government-owned packet. Go on."

"We'll approach the *Queen of Diamonds* after dark," Nathan said. "When I have freed the women from the lower deck, I'll send them over the side. You will pick them up. Then you will issue a challenge to Stumberg and crew to surrender."

"Your plan is acceptable so far," said Powers. "Without hostages, they will be forced to surrender."

"No," Nathan replied. "I believe Stumberg's playing for high stakes. I expect him to have enough firepower aboard to blow you and your government packet out of the water. I said you will *challenge* them to surrender. I did not say they're going to."

"If they do not," said Grago, "I presume you have some alternative in mind."

"I do," Nathan said, "and aside from getting me close enough to board the *Queen of Diamonds,* I need only one thing more of you. I want a canister of black powder with a five-minute fuse."

"My God," Powers cried, "you're going to destroy the craft!"

"Do you have a better idea?" Nathan asked.

"Yes," said Powers. "When they reach the landing here ..."

"They'll keep on going," Nathan said. "Whatever Stumberg is, he's not a fool. Once you challenge him to surrender, he'll know he's reached the end of his string. I'm telling you, he'll head for international waters and safely in Mexico. I can stop him. You can't, unless you aim to ram his steamboat."

"That's out of the question," said Powers. "Our packet's half the size of his craft. But my God, man, do you realize the risk you'll be taking? If you're successful in freeing those unfortunate women on the lower deck, every man on board will be looking for you."

"Not if you're keeping them busy," Nathan replied. "Once you challenge them to surrender and Stumberg discovers his hostages are gone, I want you to have enough armed men on deck to keep their minds off looking for me. I want enough time to plant the powder, light the fuse, and hit the water. For that reason, I want your packet as close behind them as you can get. I figure, by the time I light that fuse and get over the side, I'll have maybe three minutes before she blows. Will that be time enough for you to gather me aboard and for Stumberg's boat to leave us behind?"

"God, no," said Grago. "You're cutting it too fine. If this is the only way, then double the length of the fuse. I'd want them at least half a mile ahead of us."

"Well?" Nathan asked.

"By God, it's daring enough," said Powers. "Stumberg deserves to hang, but if he won't surrender, then your plan is fully justified."

"I agree," said Grago.

"We don't know when Stumberg's boat will be arriving," Nathan said, "and we can't approach them until after dark. Is there any way—maybe by wire—that you can learn when they left St. Louis?"

"We already know that," said Powers. "We don't expect them here until after midnight tomorrow. "But if you're right and they refuse to surrender, we must intercept them long before they reach New Orleans. An explosion of such a magnitude will scatter debris for a mile. They should reach Natchez well after dark tomorrow. We'll pursue them from there, making our move when we're well past the town. Does that meet with your approval, Mr. Stone?"

"Yes," Nathan said, "but I'll need a little time in the morning. I have some buryin' to do."

"Give me time to get a horse from the livery," said Grago, "and I'll ride with you. I'll need to check on Mr. Silver and make arrangements for his care until he can be moved. How much do these friends of your know . . . about this?"

"They've known all along Stumberg was into more than just gambling. I'd trust Barnabas and Bess McQueen with my life. It was Barnabas who warned me about Stumberg's involvement in white slavery before I got involved with him."

"If we all live through this," said Powers, "I'd be interested in hearing how you got involved with Stumberg."

"We shouldn't be seen leaving the hotel together," said Grago. "Give me ten minutes, and then meet me at the livery."

Nathan waited, and by the time he mounted his horse and reached the livery, Grago was waiting. They rode a block north, to a less-traveled street, and from there rode east. Neither spoke until they turned north on Bayou Road.

"You could have saved yourself a trip," Nathan said. "Silver's in good hands."

"I'm not doubting your word," said Grago. "I have to make an in-depth report on Silver."

"Is he related to you?" Nathan asked.

"Hell," said Grago, "it's worse than that. Remember the little girl who jumped ship in St. Louis? Well, Trinity's my sister. She volunteered for this Stumberg assignment, and she has more than a passing interest in our Mr. Silver, if you know what I mean."

"I reckon I know what you mean," Nathan said, "and was I you, I'd do my damnedest to get the both of 'em into some other kind of work."

When they rode into McQueen's place, he greeted them from the darkness, a Winchester in his hands. Once they were in the house, Nathan introduced Grago only as an army officer involved in the Stumberg investigation. When it was all over, before Nathan left New Orleans, he would tell them the whole story. They had earned the right to know. Grago told the McQueens exactly what he had told Nathan, and he was allowed to go into the room where Silver snored noisily. Bess turned back the cover enough to test Silver's forehead.

"He's building up to a fever," said Bess. "The doctor

said we should pour whiskey down him. Barnabas has a gallon of it."

"He's never been much of a drinking man," Grago said. "The hangover may hurt him more than the wound. We're in your debt for taking him in."

"You're welcome to stay the night, Mr. Grago," said Barnabas. "We have the room."

"Thanks," Grago said, "but I ought to get back to headquarters. I have to send a telegram to a certain young lady and tell her Silver's alive. Be at the hotel in the morning at nine, Stone. Wait in the lobby, if you like. One of us will meet you there."

He rode out and Nathan sat down in a rocking chair. Suddenly he was very tired, and the events of the day seemed like a bad dream.

"About time you was turnin' in," McQueen said. "We'll need to roll out early in the morning. Bess and me will look in on Mr. Silver and load him up with whiskey when he's in need of it."

Bess led Nathan to a bedroom adjoining the one where Eulie lay. When she had closed the door, Nathan removed his hat, gunbelt, and boots. He stretched out, and, despite the fact his mind was in turmoil, he slept.

*   *   *

Nathan rose before first light, and when he reached the kitchen, Bess already had breakfast under way. McQueen sat at the table drinking coffee.

"Nathan," said McQueen, "unless you have another place in mind, I think we should make a place for Eulie at the north end of the horse barn, under the oaks."

"I can't think of a better place," Nathan said. "There'll always be horses near. She would like that."

After breakfast, when the eastern sky had begun to gray, Nathan and McQueen dug Eulie's grave. When they were ready, Nathan and McQueen carried the blanket-wrapped body while Bess brought the family Bible. Saturday night, working by lantern light, McQueen had built a rough wooden coffin. Now they placed Eulie in it and McQueen tightened the lid. Using ropes, they lowered it into the grave. McQueen took the Bible and read passages from it. When he had finished, he said a prayer. Cotton Blossom had remained silent until Nathan and McQueen began shoveling dirt into the grave, and then the finality of it seemed to strike him. He howled long and mournfully.

"God, Cotton Blossom," Nathan shouted, wiping his eyes, "stop it!"

Cotton Blossom paused, but not for long. Finally, when the grave had been filled, there was nothing to do except return to the house. At first, it seemed Cotton Blossom would follow Nathan, but he changed his mind. He trotted back to the new-made grave and resumed his mournful howling.

"He's takin' it mighty hard," said McQueen.

"Since we came to New Orleans, he spent more time with her than with me," Nathan said. "I'm not sure when I'll be returning here. Maybe when I come back . . ."

"We'll see that he don't starve," said McQueen. "Just give him time."

"I forgot all about Silver," Nathan said. "How is he?"

"As well as can be expected," said Bess. "I began giving him whiskey at three o'clock this morning, and I'll continue giving it to him until his fever breaks. That's all anybody can do."

A few minutes past eight, Nathan rode to town and left his horse at the livery near the St. Charles. Reaching the hotel lobby well before the appointed time, he took a chair and waited. When Grago entered the lobby, Nathan remained seated. Grago took his time, and without a sign of recognition, left the hotel lobby by another door. Only then did Nathan rise and follow. He didn't hurry, and he allowed Grago to stay a few yards ahead until they were around a corner and out of sight of the St. Charles. Only then did he catch up, as they walked toward the river.

"How is Silver this morning?" Grago asked by way of greeting.

"Feverish and full of whiskey," said Nathan. "He's in good hands."

"The packet should be ready, with steam up," Grago said. "Powers should have the canister of powder and the length of fuse. He's also having a small dinghy brought aboard. Once it's dark, that will float you down alongside Stumberg's craft. You'll have oars, and it'll be up to you to stay out of the backwash from the paddlewheel."

"I don't aim to chase Stumberg's steamboat in a dinghy

with oars," said Nathan. "Since it will be dark when they reach Natchez, and since they'll be taking on wood, that's where I aim to go aboard. After that, I'll need time to open those cells on the lower deck and get those women over the side. Since I can't signal you, I'll want you and Powers to keep your eyes on the water nearest the south bank. Once the women are over the side and you've picked them up, the next move is yours. When you've laid down your challenge, then I'll take it from there."

"You should be confirming all this with Captain Powers," Grago said. "He's the ranking officer, and it's he who will be in the pilot house, directing the pilot."

"I aim to talk to him," said Nathan, "just as I'm talking to you. Time is important, once that fuse is lit, and I can't stop the clock's ticking."

As they neared the river, Grago veered away from the landing. A hundred yards downriver was a trio of lesser docks that were seldom used, and it was at one of them the government packet had drawn up. It was a nondescript vessel, devoid of markings, and, compared to the *Queen of Diamonds,* pathetically small. There was no gangplank. A removable ladder provided entry. Once aboard, it seemed even smaller. There were but two decks, and the lower was devoted to a boiler, a firebox, and the storage of firewood. Its single stack puffed smoke. The pilot house was circular, with glass all around. There seemed barely room for Powers and the pilot. Powers beckoned to Nathan and he managed to get into the cramped glass cubicle.

"I wouldn't want to be stuck in here facing a good man with a Winchester," Nathan said.

"Neither would I," said Powers. "This is Captain Tolliver, and we want you to explain to us, one step at a time, what's to take place."

Again Nathan went through the routine he had already covered with Grago. When he was done, Captain Tolliver whistled long and low. Nathan took that as a negative response and his temper rose.

"Damn it," Nathan said, "I'm the one risking my neck. If you can't do this, don't wait till I'm aboard Stumberg's boat with a lighted keg of powder to tell me."

"At ease," said Powers. "Captain Tolliver's a bit awed by what you are about to do. That doesn't mean we won't be with you every step of the way."

"Just keep two things in mind," Nathan said. "Once I send those women over the side, their lives are in your hands. Then, when you have them safely aboard, you are to challenge Stumberg. Once he discovers he has no hostages, he'll ignore your challenge, and here's the second thing that had better be strong on your mind. I'll be lighting the fuse to that canister of powder, and by the time I'm over the side, we're maybe seven minutes away from hellfire and brimstone. When I hit the water, I want you watching for me."

"Count on it," said Powers.

They were soon under way. With no private quarters and no bunks, it was a tiresome voyage at best. Nathan sat with his back against the pilot house and dozed. Besides Grago, Powers, and Captain Tolliver, there were just four more men aboard, and all of them were on the lower deck. If by some miracle Stumberg heeded the challenge and surrendered, this bunch would play hell boarding and capturing the *Queen of Diamonds*.

"This is typical army," Grago said, hunkering beside Nathan. "You wait, and wait, and then wait some more."

"Answer me a question," said Nathan. "I want Stumberg's hide, so goin' after him this way is my kind of justice. But you said, with testimony from Trinity, you could hang Stumberg. Hell, the army's got jurisdiction everywhere. Why didn't you just arrest the varmint in St. Louis?"

"I favored that," Grago said, "but I was outranked. My superiors want him nailed with the goods, but they've underestimated him. Captain Tolliver, Captain Powers, and myself are armed with Winchesters, and so are the men on the lower deck, but can you imagine us commandeering Stumberg's craft, should he actually heed our command to surrender?"

"No," said Nathan. "I've never even considered that, because Stumberg's never going to surrender. We'll have to blow the damn boat with him aboard, or allow him to escape to Mexico."

"Why are you so certain he's going to Mexico?"

"Some of Stumberg's conversation was overheard and passed on to Silver and me. There was talk about the dark of the moon and international waters. Before you ever talked to me, you people knew there would be women aboard, bound for Mexico, didn't you?"

"Perhaps," said Grago cautiously.

"Perhaps, hell," Nathan said. "You've been watching Stumberg's activities in St. Louis, and you know he's not taking his usual load of high rollers back to New Orleans."

"Proving exactly what?" Grago demanded.

"Proving that you *knew* Stumberg was about to run for it, that you knew or suspected this would be your last chance to get your hands on him. What I don't understand is how you aimed to stop him, with all those women locked in cabins on the first deck."

"That," said Grago, "is something you will never know. I can tell you this and no more. We knew, after receiving Silver's telegram, that the *Queen of Diamonds* was returning to St. Louis after a long absence. It wasn't all that difficult to learn, from Stumberg's actions, what he probably planned to do. There was an alternate plan that may or may not have involved Silver, but we scuttled that, after talking to you."

"I'm flattered," Nathan said.

"Don't be," said Grago, "and don't waste your time meditating on all the things I haven't told you."

"Maybe I'll just back out," Nathan said, "and let you resurrect your alternate plan."

"I don't believe you will," said Grago. "There would be some very serious consequences."

"You're right," Nathan said. "I won't back off, but not because I care a damn for your consequences."

That ended their conversation. The officer walked away and Nathan tipped his hat over his eyes, not caring if Grago shared their conversation with his superior, Captain Powers. Time dragged. Nathan could almost measure their progress by the westering sun warming him through the glass of the pilot house. He seemed to be dozing when Powers spoke.

"There's food below, if you're hungry."

"Thanks," said Nathan, but he wasn't hungry. Occasionally he rose to dip a tin cup of water from the water keg beside the pilot house. Satisfying his thirst, he again settled down, apparently to doze. But his mind was unable to rest, for it drifted back to Barnabas McQueen's place, to a lonely grave beneath the oaks ...

*   *   *

With a blast from her whistle, the *Queen of Diamonds* had just backed away from the landing at Vicksburg, pausing only long enough to take on more wood. French Stumberg reclined in his cabin, his mind racing ahead to his final and most profitable transaction. Within a matter of hours he would rid himself of his human cargo and be on his way to a life of luxury in Mexico. For a moment he regretted leaving his empire behind, but the Federals had the war behind them and were turning their attention to other matters, and French Stumberg had been high on their list of priorities. Of course, they would seize all his gambling emporiums, but they would find little. Stumberg had drained off all but a few hundred dollars to keep the doors open, and in the safe next to his bunk was more than a quarter of a million dollars in gold. Aboard were a dozen trusted men, all heavily armed. Stumberg had hated leaving Drew Shanklin behind, but there was no help for it. Sacrifices had been necessary to create the illusion that French Stumberg was in New Orleans to stay. Even his apparent interest in horse racing had been contrived. Now he wondered where and how his departure would be challenged, for there had been a telegram waiting for him in St. Louis from his contact in Washington. He knew they had been watching him, but he didn't believe they could stop him before the *Queen* could reach international waters. The vessel was worth a fortune, but there he must abandon her, for there was no other way . . .

*   *   *

It was still daylight when the government packet reached Natchez, and it was time to take on wood. The craft must keep up steam, for it must be ready for pursuit. While the *Queen of Diamonds* would stop for fuel, that wouldn't delay her very long. Captain Powers hunkered down beside Nathan, and finally he spoke.

"How are you feeling, Stone?"

"Sick," Nathan replied. "Sick of this damn boat."

Powers laughed. "That makes two of us. The most difficult part of any maneuver is the waiting."

"There's somethin' I've been overlooking," said Nathan. "I'm dead sure Stumberg plans to make a run for Mexico, but where's he goin' to get wood for the steamboat?"

"He'll take on enough wood here at Natchez to reach international water," Powers said. "There's a sailing ship— a craft flying Mexican colors—waiting for him. His partner in white slavery, we think."

"Well, by God," said Nathan, "you've known this all along, and you've left me to piece it together as best I could."

"I saw no reason to involve you to that degree," Powers said. "If your plan works, it won't matter if the entire Mexican fleet's out there."

"From talkin' to Grago," said Nathan, "I get the feeling your whole damn operation depended on Byron Silver, and that you're taking me as a poor second."

"If your pride is suffering, put it to rest," Powers said. "As I am sure Mr. Grago told you, what we *might* have done is of no consequence. The fact is, your tactics are much like Silver's. This plan of yours is daring enough and dangerous enough to have been conceived by him. Are you sure it wasn't?"

"Silver told me almost nothing," Nathan replied. "Now that I'm neck-deep in this, I wish he *had* told me what he had in mind."

"When this is over," Powers said, "assuming that you survive, you will have earned the right to *ask* him what he might have done. For the next few hours, however, I'd suggest you free your mind of everything except what lies ahead."

The packet had drawn up several hundred yards above the Natchez landing, near a series of warehouses. It would appear as a dark hulk by the time the *Queen of Diamonds* arrived, for there would be no moon. Somewhere in the nearby town—probably in a courthouse tower on the square—was a clock, and a light breeze carried the sound of it each time it struck the hour. When it struck ten, Grago, Powers, and Tolliver joined Nathan for a final briefing.

"The *Queen* will head in to the landing to take on wood," Nathan said, "and while she's at rest, I'm going aboard. Once they've passed us, let down the dinghy. While they're on the move, the undertow from that paddlewheel could swallow me like the whale took Jonah. When they leave Natchez, stay far enough behind so they can't see you, but close enough for you to see me. Once I free those

women and get them over the side, don't waste any time
in getting them aboard. I can't make my move until you
challenge Stumberg, and if I'm discovered before your challenge, the varmint will escape and I'll be dead. Now is there
anything we've forgotten?"

"Maybe," said Captain Tolliver. "Suppose some of those
captive women you'll be shoving over the side can't swim?"

"My God," Nathan said, "I don't know. Suppose I roped
the dinghy to the *Queen*'s rail, and let the captives down
into it?"

"For one thing," said Grago, "if there's more than a
dozen, there won't be room. But what choice do we have?"

"None," Powers said. "Stone, you'll have to secure the
dinghy and assist those women in getting aboard it. It's
going to double your risk, because it will require some time.
We can't challenge the vessel until those hostages are clear
of it, and we don't know for sure how many there'll be."

"There's sixteen cabins," Nathan said, "and there could
be two women in each of them. Damn it, Powers, your
people had Stumberg watched while he and the *Queen* were
in St. Louis. Why don't you *know* how many women are
aboard?"

"Because these women were taken aboard against their
will," said Powers, "and they were loaded somewhere south
of St. Louis. Stumberg hired attractive women to entertain
men in his gambling houses, and these voluntarily left St.
Louise aboard the *Queen of Diamonds*. Those who were
victims of the white slavery trade were never taken aboard
at the same place, and that's why it's been damn near impossible to catch Stumberg with the goods. Are you
satisfied?"

"No," Nathan said, "but there's nothin' I can do about
it. See that I've got plenty of rope to secure the dinghy
once I'm aboard the *Queen,* and I want forty feet of the
heaviest line you have. If these poor souls have to climb
down a rope, make it heavy enough for them to get a grip
on it. I'll do my best to get them over the side and into the
dinghy, if possible. From there on, it's up to you hombres. I
may not hear you after you've challenged the *Queen of
Diamonds.* When Stumberg defies your challenge, fire one
shot from a Winchester. That will signal me to light the
fuse to the powder and get the hell out of there. Are we
together on that?"

"Yes," Powers said. "I will issue the challenge, and Mr. Grago, you will fire the warning shot."

They seemed capable enough. Nathan felt he should have more confidence in them than he did, but jagged slivers of doubt flickered like lightning on the distant horizons of his mind. Mentally he tried to picture the lower deck of the *Queen of Diamonds* and the distance from the captive cabins to the trailing dinghy. Would he have a flock of hysterical females on his hands as he sought to elude discovery by the men feeding the fireboxes on the forward deck? His train of thought was derailed by the excited voice of Captain Tolliver.

"Yonder she comes!"

With a blast of her whistle, running lights aglow, the *Queen of Diamonds* swept in to the landing.

"The dinghy's in the water," Captain Powers announced. "When you are ready, Stone, we'll let you down and lower the canister of powder."

"I'm ready," Nathan said. "Let's go."

Backwash from the larger craft lapped water against the hull of the packet as Nathan let himself down toward the bobbing dinghy below. He clung to the rope until he gained his balance in the dinghy. Powers then dropped the heavy rope that Nathan had used in his descent, and Nathan coiled it. Next came the canister of powder. The long fuse had been coiled and tied. When Nathan had the canister safely in the dinghy, Powers spoke softly.

"You have heavy rope, powder canister, and fuse. Do you have matches?"

"Yes," Nathan replied, "and I'm ready with the oars. Release the dinghy."

The little craft was caught up and pulled away into the darkness . . .

Chapter 20

✦✦✦

Weary of the confines of the *Queen of Diamonds,* Stumberg's men wasted no time in reaching the main deck as the vessel neared the Natchez landing. It was a fuel stop, but still it offered a half-hour respite from the incessant pitching of the craft and the throb of the engines. Stumberg himself stood at the rail, watching as cord after cord of wood was loaded to feed the greedy fireboxes. Late as it was, the arrival of a steamboat was still sufficient to attract some townspeople, and that was Stumberg's reason for being forward, near the rail. His eyes missed nothing and he was suspicious even of the men who brought the wood aboard. But he saw nothing to suggest there was anything amiss, and that made him wonder all the more. Was it possible he might face a blockade farther south, near New Orleans? So be it, he thought grimly. He had the utmost confidence in his men armed with Winchesters, but he was prone to stack the deck in his own favor when possible. Mounted on the forward deck, under wraps, was a well-oiled, fully loaded Gatling gun, and at least four of Stumberg's men were trained in the use of the formidable weapon.*

Nathan had to fight the current so that he didn't drift past the *Queen of Diamonds.* He wanted to board her as near the big paddlewheel as possible, keeping him well within the shadows and well beyond the activity on the landing. Having been to and from St. Louis on the vessel, Nathan had some idea as to how long it would take the crews to load the necessary fuel. There was a chance he might free the captives from the cabins on the first deck and get them over the side before the steamboat left the

---

* First demonstrated by its inventor, Richard J. Gatling, in 1862.

landing. The sooner they were out of danger the better were Nathan's chances of escape without discovery. Eventually, by skillful use of the oars, he managed to get the dinghy on a line with the shadowy stern of the *Queen of Diamonds*. Once he secured the dinghy, it must be far enough from the big paddlewheel that it would not be caught in the undertow when the *Queen of Diamonds* departed. There was a small chance that Nathan might free the captives and cut the dinghy loose during the fuel stop, but he couldn't count on that. He had the line ready and when the dinghy bumped into the hull of the *Queen,* he cast a loop at an iron stanchion that secured the rail of the lower deck. When his loop was secure, he took up the slack until the dinghy was snug against the side of the *Queen.* Using the heavy rope, Nathan cast and secured a second loop. This line he would use to reach the lower deck. Hopefully, the freed captives would use this same line to descend into the water or the dinghy. To the loose end of the heavy line he secured the canister of powder. This he would hoist to the lower deck when he was aboard. He tested the heavy line, found it secure, and began his ascent.

Reaching the first deck, Nathan drew up the heavy line, released the canister of powder, and dropped the end of the line back into the dinghy. The canister of powder he shoved into a shadowy alcove along a catwalk that led behind the enormous wheel. From there Nathan hurried toward the point where he would enter the closed portion of the deck, his only access to the series of locked cabins. Nathan could hear the crackle of flames and the clatter of wood being chunked into the fireboxes. He noted with satisfaction that the space on either side of the fireboxes had been stacked high with wood, meaning that the firemen had no ready access to the rearmost part of the deck. There was virtually no chance of his being seen by the firemen or the crew loading the wood. Discovery, if it came, would be from the upper deck. The critical moment was at hand. Would Silver's key fit? Nathan ran to the far end of the corridor and began with the first door on the right. At first the key seemed not to fit, but slowly it turned. The latch yielded to pressure and Nathan swung the door open. A terrified girl with blonde hair sprang off the lower bunk.

"Don't you dare scream," Nathan warned. "I'm here to free you."

"Thank God," the girl sobbed.

"I'll need help," Nathan said. "Do you know how many others are locked in these cabins?"

"I . . . I . . . let me think . . ."

"Make it quick," said Nathan. "We don't have much time."

"There was fifteen of us to start," she said in a quavering voice, "but there were stops. I . . . don't know if there . ."

"We'll find out," said Nathan. "Help me calm the others. We don't have time for tears."

Nathan led her into the corridor and began unlocking doors. Fortunately some of the women were quick to realize they were being freed and were helping to quiet the others. The garments of some were in tatters, some were stripped to the waist, and from their cuts and bruises, all appeared to have been in some way abused. Once they were on the open deck, there must be no delays. Nathan spoke rapidly and the urgency in his voice got their attention.

"All of you are going to have to climb down a rope into a small boat," he said. "It'll be crowded. When I cut you loose, take the oars and push your boat away from the steamboat until the current pulls you downstream. A government boat is waiting to take you aboard. Now let's go."

Minutes counted. Nathan dared not tell them that should the *Queen of Diamonds* back away from the landing before the current carried the dinghy away, the little boat would be sucked under and demolished by the huge paddlewheel. While some of the fearful women had bare feet, most of them wore slippers, and it seemed to Nathan the clatter must surely be heard on the upper deck. Nathan began to breathe again when they reached the point on the open deck where the heavy rope led to the dinghy below. Its shape was barely visible in the dark and some of the newly freed captives were looking fearfully toward the dark water that seemed farther away than it was.

"You can see the boat down there," Nathan said quietly. "Who wants to go first?"

"I will," said the girl who had been freed first.

Nathan helped her over the rail, gripping her shoulders until she was able to take hold of the heavy rope. She went down the rope too quickly and her feet struck with such force she almost capsized the dinghy. It righted itself, and Nathan could see her pale face below.

"She made it," Nathan said, "and so can the rest of you."

They loaded the dinghy surprisingly well, with Nathan keeping one eye on the forward deck. When the last of the captives had joined the others in the boat, Nathan pulled the slipknot, gratified to see them using the oars to propel the dinghy away from the hull of the *Queen of Diamonds*. Slowly, the eddying current pulled the dinghy toward open water. Close to the farthest bank, the packet lurked without running lights and was all but invisible. The blast of the steamboat's whistle rent the night. The *Queen* was about to depart. By now, Nathan hoped the small government vessel had taken aboard the women occupants of the drifting dinghy. Nathan now had but one task remaining. Taking the canister of powder, he crept along the narrow catwalk until he was directly behind the huge paddlewheel. He was outside the deck rail, and he hoisted the cannister of powder up onto the deck, next to an iron upright that supported the rail. With a length of rope that he'd brought for that purpose, he bound the canister to the iron upright. That put the charge where, if it did nothing else, it would permanently disable the craft. Nathan made his way back along the catwalk, trailing the fuse until it ran out. He was but a few steps from the open side of the lower deck, and here he would remain until he'd lit the fuse.

Nathan thrilled to the sound of three shrill blasts from the packet's whistle. It seemed Captain Powers was about to get Stumberg's attention. Almost before the echo of the whistle had died, there was a babble of voices on the main deck almost above Nathan's head, then French Stumberg's angry voice.

"Get your rifles ready. When they're close enough, fire."

But Captain Tolliver had expected that. He remained just far enough behind to make shooting uncertain but near enough for Captain Powers to issue his challenge through a megaphone.

"This is Captain Powers, representing the attorney general's office of the United States of America. We have a Federal arrest warrent for French Stumberg and Federal John Doe arrest warrents for every man on board. If you refuse to submit to arrest, we'll sink you."

"We have hostages aboard," Stumberg shouted. "A hostile move from you, and they die."

"You have no hostages," Powers responded. "This is your last chance."

"Danvers, Odom, Dawson," Stumberg bawled, "bring me three of the women, and do it fast."

From the deck of the trailing packet, Grago cocked a Winchester and fired a single shot. Nathan waited only to hear Stumberg's reaction when he was told his hostages were gone. He was in a position where he couldn't be seen unless they came looking for him, but the three men Stumberg had sent to the lower deck didn't think of that. They hastened to report the shocking news.

"Gone!" Stumberg bawled. "Gone! Damn it, Frazier, you and Watkins get the wraps off the Gatling gun and be prepared to fire. They won't come to us, then by God, I'll turn this boat around and we'll go after them."

Nathan heard no more. He had no idea how swiftly the *Queen of Diamonds* could reverse her course, but if she were close enough, the blast might take the government packet with it. As swiftly as he could, Nathan again crept along the catwalk until he reached the end of the trailing fuse. Stumberg's Gatling gun on the main deck had tilted the odds and they no longer *had* ten minutes. With his knife, Nathan cut away a third of the fuse and lighted the rest. It greatly reduced his escape time, and his life was in the hands of Captain Tolliver. Reaching the open deck, he leaped the rail and plummeted into the cold, dark water. Slowly the stern of the *Queen* began to turn to the farthest bank, as Stumberg made good his threat. But again old Captain Tolliver was ready, and the packet, too, had changed course. She glided as near the far bank as possible, neatly escaping Stumberg's cumbersome craft. Nathan ceased fighting the current and drifted with it. He wished to be as far downstream as possible when the explosion came. He tried to estimate how much time had elapsed. While Captain Tolliver wouldn't know of Stumberg's intention to use a Gatling gun, there was no mistaking the intended pursuit. And Tolliver *was* aware of the coming explosion, perhaps only seconds away. He should be fleeing downriver, seeking to distance his craft from the *Queen,* nearing Nathan's position. *And there she was!* Still without running lights, she came near enough for Nathan to see

Grago throwing him a line. Nathan caught it, thankful for the harness, for his arms were numb with cold and exhaustion. They hauled him aboard, gasping for breath, trying to speak through chattering teeth.

"Ease up," Grago said. "The worst is over."

"No . . . time," Nathan gasped. "No . . . time. I shortened the . . . fuse . . ."

"My God," said Grago, "they're comin' after us. Captain Tolliver, give it hell. He shortened the fuse and she could blow any second."

"He has a . . . Gatling gun on the . . . main deck," Nathan said. "Something I didn't . . . know . . ."

But turning the big vessel had taken some time, and for the *Queen*, time had run out. When the explosion came—though she was half a mile distant—the force of it shook the government packet, shattering some of the glass in the pilot house. Upriver, flames leaped toward the moonless heavens, stretching ghastly, dancing reflections along the surface of the dark water. Every soul aboard the little vessel huddled on the main deck, awed by the enormity of what they were witnessing.

"Great God Almighty," Captain Tolliver breathed, "I've never seen the like of this, and I hope I never do so again."

"Captain Powers," Grago asked, "will there be a search for survivors?"

"No," said Powers, "I see no need. We will report no survivors."

New Orleans. December 31, 1866.

Nathan promised to meet with Powers and Grago before leaving New Orleans. He then took his horse from the livery and for what might be the last time, rode to Barnabas McQueen's place. He took some satisfaction in having Cotton Blossom come running to meet him. McQueen and Bess stood on the porch, watching him ride in.

"Well," McQueen said, "we're glad to see you, for several reasons. This friend of yours has been hard as hell to keep abed, even with a bullet hole through him. I swear, he's worried about you like he's your old granny."

"I reckon I needed somebody to worry about me," said Nathan. "There's a lot to tell, so let's all get together so I don't have to tell it but once."

Silver sat up in bed, looking every bit as fidgety and out-of-sorts as McQueen had implied.

"If I ever step into your boots again," Nathan said, "I aim to know more about your commitments."

Silver laughed. "Sorry. They swore me to silence. Tell me what you did and how you did it. Maybe I can learn something."

"I doubt that," said Nathan, "but I'll tell you what I did. God only knows *how* I did it."

He began with the sending of the coded telegram and ended with the destruction of the *Queen of Diamonds*.

"God," Silver said, "that took sand. With Powers, Grago, and me behind you, you could name your own price with the Federals."

"I reckon not," said Nathan. "Why don't you saddle up and ride with me?"

"It's a temptation," Silver said, "but this easy living is gettin' to me. Bein' from Texas, cowboying and bein' shot at is all I know. Cowboying, after you've been throwed and stomped a few times, kind of loses its appeal."

"I'll be riding out tomorrow," said Nathan, "and it may be a long trail. With my Daddy's dying breath, he asked me to pay a blood debt, and I swore on his grave I would. If it's the last thing I *ever* do, I'll do it."

*   *   *

Nathan stayed the night, treasuring the short time he would remain with the McQueens. Early the next morning, the first day of 1867, Powers and Grago arrived in a buckboard. Nathan and McQueen greeted them from the front porch.

"I suppose you've come for Silver," said McQueen. "He's almost bearable, once you get used to him."

"He does take some getting used to," Powers said. "We don't dare leave him here too long, sleeping late and taking his meals in bed. He'd take it for a habit, and God knows, we'd never break him of it."

Powers and Grago stayed for breakfast, and it became a time Nathan Stone would long remember. When Powers and Grago declared it was time to return to town, Nathan decided to ride with them. While they helped Silver to a pallet of blankets in the buckboard, Nathan said his good-byes to the McQueens.

"Nathan," said McQueen, "if you're ever again in New Orleans, remember that you have friends here."

"I will," Nathan promised. "It's been my pleasure and privilege, and I just wish ... it could be ending ... another way."

"I'll tend Eulie's grave," said Bess, taking his big hand in hers. "Do ride carefully, Nathan, and you're always welcome here."

Nathan followed the buckboard, Cotton Blossom trotting behind the pack horse. Nathan had given McQueen Eulie's horse and saddle. Reaching the big horse barn, Nathan paused at Eulie's grave. Cotton Blossom regarded Nathan with mournful eyes, and if dogs could have wept, Nathan believed the hound would have done so. Nathan removed his hat, wiping his eyes on the sleeve of his shirt.

"He paid, Eulie," Nathan said softly, "but not nearly enough. He could have died a thousand times without being worthy of you .."

Nathan rode away, Cotton Blossom following, and they soon caught up to the buckboard. Nathan followed as far as the St. Charles Hotel, where Silver would recover. Nathan would have ridden away, but Silver stopped him.

"I've asked Powers and Grago to present you with something to help you to remember us," said Silver, "and as you ride into new territory, it could be of some help to you."

Captain Powers handed Nathan a small white box, and inside it was a gold watch and chain.

"Raise the lid," Silver said.

Nathan did so, and inside the lid was the Great Seal of the United States. Inscribed beneath the seal was a series of numbers.

"Wherever you go," said Silver, "if you find yourself needing a friend, present this to any Union officer. There's only two of these in existence. I have the other. If you need me, wire Washington, using the code. I'll find you. Vaya con Dios."

Nathan nodded, unable to speak. He shook hands with the three men and rode west along St. Charles. Nathan could have reached Baton Rouge before sundown, but wishing to be alone, he made camp a few miles shy of town. He prepared a meager supper for himself and Cotton

Blossom. Perhaps in the morning they could pass through
Baton Rouge and have breakfast there. Dousing his fire
well before dark, he rolled in his blankets. Not to sleep,
but to think. All the way from New Orleans, he had tried
to drive Eulie from his mind, but found he could not. Now
he invited her in, aware that it was the only way he could
live with her memory. Compared to Molly Tremayne, Eulie
had been a plain woman, but it was she who dominated
Nathan's thoughts. He tried comparing her to Molly Tremayne, but Molly kept slipping away. Molly had wanted
him, but on her own terms. But Eulie? Without question,
Eulie had ridden the vengeance trail with him, becoming a
wanderer, accepting him for what he was. Suddenly he
knew, beyond a shadow of a doubt, that had Eulie lived,
she would be with him, not in New Orleans with the
McQueens. Eulie had been humble and unselfish, becoming
his woman the only way she could. Denied the feast, she
had accepted the crumbs. Then, like a divine revelation, it
struck him. Despite what he was, knowing what he could
never be, Eulie Prater had loved him. Now Eulie would
never know that *he* understood, and he wept and cursed
himself by turns.

Nathan slept fitfully, awakening often, and the dawn
seemed long in coming. He saddled his black, loaded the
packhorse, and he and Cotton Blossom set out for Baton
Rouge. Following breakfast in a secluded cafe, Nathan went
to a mercantile and bought St. Louis and Memphis newspapers. North of town, beside the river, Nathan dismounted.
Allowing the horses to graze, he sat with his back to a pine
and went through the newspapers. The Memphis paper
yielded more information than he had expected, for it reported another killing in Arkansas, laying it to Cullen
Baker. There was a pair of drawings, one of Baker and the
other of Tobe Snider. Snider, the paper said, was a deserter
from the Union army, and was said to be a member of
Baker's renegades. Nathan studied Snider's scarred face,
committing it to memory. He opened one of his saddlebags,
intending to save the newspaper. There was a heavy leather
bag, closed with a drawstring. Emptying the contents on
the grass, Nathan counted a hundred and twelve double
eagles. $2,240! There was also a brief note:

*Nathan, Eulie gave me this the night before the race. She
said if anything happened to her, you were to have it.*

It was signed simply *Bess.* His last night there, while he slept, she had slipped it into his saddlebag. With the gold of his own, his stake had risen to more than three thousand dollars. Eulie had feared that his saloon gambling would be the death of him, and if she could speak to him now, he knew what she would say:

Stay out of the saloons, Nathan. You have money . . .

A little more than sixty miles north of Baton Rouge, Nathan reached a fork in the river where the Red joined the Mississippi.

"We'll have to cross the Mississippi, Cotton Blossom," Nathan said. "We can then follow the Red into western Arkansas."

But the Mississippi was deep and wide. Horses, rider, and dog had to swim, and it seemed they would never touch the sandy bottom, allowing them to wade out on the west bank. Two days later, Nathan passed near Shreveport, and on the third day, followed the Red into southwestern Arkansas.*

After three days of having seen nobody, Nathan gave up and rode north toward Fort Smith. It had been founded in 1817 as a military post and had become an important supply point during the California gold rush. The town was located near the joining of the Arkansas and Poteau Rivers and had become a "jumping-off place" insofar as western migration was concerned. If Baker and his gang were anywhere in Arkansas, the authorities at Fort Smith should know. Nathan had made his camp a day south of Fort Smith and had just started his supper fire when a rider hailed his camp. The man rode a grulla and led a black. A man's body was tied across the saddle of the led horse.

"Ride in," Nathan said, "but keep your hands where I can see them."

The rider reined up a dozen yards away. His grulla's head was down and the animal seemed near exhaustion. The rider was poorly dressed. His Levi's were faded and ripped and his once-blue flannel shirt was faded white in places, while his hat brim drooped like the wings of a sickly

---

* Near present-day town of Texarkana, which is on the state line between Arkansas and Texas. Texarkana was founded January 15, 1874.

bird. But pinned to the left pocket of his shirt was a law-man's star. A Colt rode on his right hip.

"Step down," said Nathan. "I was about to have supper. You're welcome to join me."

"I'd be obliged," the newcomer said, dismounting. "My hoss is ready to drop. Run out of grub two days ago, in Injun Territory. I'm Deputy U.S. Marshal Russ Lambert, from Fort Smith."

"I'm Nathan Stone. While I get the grub ready, unsaddle your horses. When they've rested and watered, I have some grain in my pack."

"Much obliged," said Lambert. "They can use it."

Nathan already had the iron spider spraddled over the fire and the coffee was beginning to boil. He began slicing thick rashers of bacon into a fire-blackened frying pan. Lambert unsaddled the grulla, and when the animal had rolled, it was almost too weak to get to its feet. When Lambert had removed the body from the black, he unsaddled it. When the horse had rolled, it got to its feet and began grazing with the grulla. Cotton Blossom had been away from camp when Lambert had ridden in. He now regarded the lawman suspiciously.

"That's Cotton Blossom," Nathan said. "He's not very trusting at first."

"Neither am I," said Lambert. "You live longer. Seein' as how I rode in with a dead man, I reckon you got a right to know why, and who he is."

"I admit to bein' a mite curious," Nathan said, "but I believe a man who wears a badge has a right to hold back whatever he wants."

Lambert laughed. "You're a generous man. The Yeager brothers—Jabbo and Jake—took to thinkin' of themselves as another Frank and Jesse, and when they robbed a bank near Fort Smith, they went too far. They killed a man. I tracked the varmints into Injun Territory. When they laid for me, I drilled Jabbo. That's him over there on the ground."

"Couldn't you just leave him for the buzzards and coy-otes, instead of totin' him back to Fort Smith?"

"I could," said Lambert, "but I need the bounty. A U.S. deputy marshal earns fifty dollars a month. With that, he's got to feed himself and his hoss, and buy ammunition."

"I reckon the other Yeager rode for his life, then," Nathan said.

"No," said Lambert. "He's been trailing me, waiting for a chance to get even. I ain't slept for two nights."

"You'll sleep tonight," Nathan said. "Cotton Blossom will warn us if anybody comes near. Tomorrow we'll ride on to Fort Smith."

The food was ready. They ate warmed-over beans, fried bacon, hard biscuits, and hot coffee.

"I'd near forgot how good warmed-over beans and bacon is," said Lambert, "and Lord, there ain't nothin' to beat hot coffee."

"You're pretty well used up," Nathan said. "Turn in when you're ready. I'll stay up for a while."

Head on his saddle, Nathan lay awake listening to the horses cropping grass. Cotton Blossom drowsed. Suddenly the hound got to his feet, growling deep in his throat. Nathan lay still, and moving only his right hand, eased his Colt from its holster. The fire had long since gone out, and Lambert lay in deep shadow.

Finally Cotton Blossom lay down and Nathan holstered the Colt. The gunman—if there had been one—had contented himself with scouting their camp. Come first light, Nathan was hunkered starting a breakfast fire when Lambert awoke. The lawman had been so exhausted he had removed only his hat.

"God," he said, getting to his feet, "I was dead for sleep. I .."

The shot seemed loud in the morning stillness, and Lambert was driven to his knees when the slug struck him. A second slug barely missed Nathan and screamed off a rock. Nathan rolled to his feet, his right-hand Colt spitting lead. With his left hand he grabbed his Winchester, and in a winding run, headed for a thicket where there were still traces of powder smoke. Two more shots sang over Nathan's head. Holstering the Colt, he fired the Winchester as rapidly as he could lever shells into the chamber.

Chapter 21

✦⋄⋄⋄✦

The bushwhacker had been forced to leave his horse some distance away, lest the animal nicker and reveal his presence. Now, forced to flee the withering fire from Nathan's Winchester, the man's headlong flight through brush and dead leaves allowed Nathan to follow at a comfortable trot. When Nathan emerged from the thicket, he spotted his quarry with a boot in the stirrup, preparing to mount a blue roan. Nathan fired twice, the second shot snatching away the rider's hat.

"Step into that saddle," Nathan shouted, "and I'll shoot you out of it."

There was no more bluff in Nathan Stone's voice than there had been in his shooting. The surly bushwhacker backed away from the horse, his hands shoulder high. He was dressed like a cowboy, from flop hat to runover boots. There was a rifle in his saddle boot and a Colt on his right hip.

"With your thumb and finger, pull that pistol and drop it," Nathan said.

That order was obeyed and Nathan advanced until he was behind the horse.

"Now," said Nathan, "you walk back the way you just come, and you do it slow. I don't usually shoot a man in the back, but I make exceptions for bushwhacking varmints like you."

Slowly they made their way back to camp. Lambert had his shirt off, but had been unable to deal with the wound. The lead had struck him in the arm, just below his left shoulder. He eyed Nathan's captive grimly before he spoke.

"You should have kept running, Jake. There's a rope waiting for you in Fort Smith."

"Fer bank robbery?" Jake bawled. "Wasn't me shot that bank clerk."

"You'll have to convince the judge of that," said Lambert.

"He's got a horse over yonder beyond that thicket," Nathan said. "I'll go after it when this skunk's been hogtied and I've seen to your wound."

While Lambert kept his Colt handy, Nathan took strong rope and, standing Jake Yeager next to a pine, bound his wrists securely behind the tree.

"Ain't you gonna tie my feet too?" Yeager asked.

"One more word from you," said Nathan, "and I'll do better than that. I'll stuff a horse apple in your mouth."

Finished with the outlaw, Nathan used the coffeepot to heat water, and when it was ready, he cleansed Lambert's wound. Then, using part of an old shirt, he bound it as best he could.

"I don't have any whiskey," Nathan said. "You'll need something to kill the infection, but we should reach Fort Smith before it becomes a problem."

"I'm obliged," said Lambert. "If you want to go ahead with that coffee, I can go fetch Jake's horse."

Nathan had built up the fire and had the coffee boiling when the lawman returned with Jake Yeager's dun. Lambert had also recovered the outlaw's Colt and had slipped it under his belt. Nathan fried bacon, and that, with hard biscuits and hot coffee, was their breakfast. Nathan fed Cotton Blossom what was left of the bacon.

"You'd feed a damn dog," Yeager said bitterly, "an' let me go without."

"Jake," said Lambert, "this dog—or any other—stands considerably taller than you."

In deference to Lambert's wound, Nathan saddled the horses. When he had his packhorse loaded, he then loaded the dead Jabbo on his horse and bound him to his saddle. Calming the horse was difficult, for the animal had no liking for its burden. Nathan then untied Jake Yeager and forced him to mount the dun. He bound Yeager's hands behind him and tied a lead rope to the man's saddle horn. They then rode north, Nathan leading out, with Jake Yeager's mount following on a lead rope. Lambert came behind Jake, leading the horse bearing Jabbo Yeager's body. They stopped every hour or so to rest the horses, untying Jake long enough for the surly gunman to walk about and stretch his cramped arms. Big gray clouds swept in from the southwest, and shortly after midday a cold, drizzling rain began. The last time they stopped to rest the horses, Lambert took the opportunity to speak to Nathan.

"I'd appreciate you goin' with me when I take Jake in. He'll try and weasel his way out of killin' that bank teller, but I aim to see that he gets charged with tryin' to gun us down from ambush. I want the court to take your testimony. Besides, you won't be doin' it for nothin'. You got a five-hundred-dollar bounty comin' for capturing Jake."

"I'll testify," Nathan said, "but I don't want the bounty. Jake's your prisoner."

They rode on, and when the wind rose, the rain seemed even colder. It was dark when they finally reached Fort Smith. The marshal's office and the jail were in the courthouse basement. Nathan helped Jake Yeager to dismount, and with Lambert guiding him inside, Nathan loosened the bonds that secured the dead Jabbo to his saddle. He then shouldered the sodden, stinking corpse and followed Russ Lambert into the marshal's office. An angry old man of maybe sixty leaned across a desk glaring at Deputy U.S. Marshal Lambert, and when Nathan appeared with the dead outlaw, the old-timer began shouting.

"Damn it, Lambert, you come sloppin' in here knowin' ever'body's gone fer the day, bringing' two outlaws, one of 'em dead and a-stinking. Jist what in hell am I s'posed to do with 'em till mornin'? S'pose they . . . he escapes durin' the night?"

"Not my problem, Simpkins," said Lambert. "You're in charge here for the night, and all I want from you is a receipt for this pair, showin' that I brought 'em in. I'm sopping wet, exhausted, cold, hungry, and I've been shot, so my patience is wearin' damn thin. You write me that receipt, and you do it now."

Simpkins took a receipt book from a desk drawer and began to write. For lack of a better place, Nathan dropped the body of Jabbo Yeager on the floor directly before Simpkins' desk. Finished, he passed the receipt to Lambert and fixed his horrified eyes on the dead outlaw before him.

"You're not leaving him . . . there?"

"Why not?" Nathan said. "I've been totin' the varmint around all day. It's your turn."

Lambert laughed when he had closed the door behind them. "That grouchy old scutter gets twenty dollars a month for settin' in there where it's warm and dry. When he finally has to get off his hunkers and do something, he's bawlin' like a fresh-cut calf."

"You'd best find a doc and have that wound tended to," said Nathan. "Me, I want grub, plenty of hot coffee, and a warm bed. Where can I find a bunk and grub that Cotton Blossom's welcome?"

"Ma Dollar's boardin' house," Lambert said, "and she owns the cafe next door too. There's a livery across the street. I always take a room at Ma's place when I'm in town. Doc Avery lives there too, and he'll patch me up. It's too early for him to be drunk. Let's take the horses to the livery, and then we'll go to Ma's."

"You go on and let the doc look at that wound," said Nathan. "Tell the lady of the house I'll want a room for me and my dog. I'll be there when I've seen to the horses. What about the horses the Yeagers were riding?"

"Take them too," Lambert said. "I reckon the court will confiscate them."

Nathan led his two horses, Lambert's, and the two that had belonged to the Yeagers into the welcome shelter of the livery. A boy of maybe fifteen sat on a stool beneath a lighted lantern that hung on the livery's log wall.

"It's worth fifty cents apiece to me to have these horses all rubbed down, watered, and grained," Nathan said. "Would you be willing to do it?"

"Yes, sir," the boy replied eagerly.

"Bueno," said Nathan. "I'll pay you now, because I'm pretty well give out. When you're done, stall them for the night and we'll settle up tomorrow. Do you have a safe place for the saddles and my packsaddle?"

"Tack room," the boy said. "I'll see to them."

Nathan took his saddlebags, and with Cotton Blossom following, made his way to the boardinghouse across the street. Cotton Blossom didn't much like boardinghouses, but trusting Nathan, he went in. Ma Dollar proved to be in her sixties, probably. She greeted Nathan warmly and spoke to Cotton Blossom.

"We'll likely be here a few days, ma'am," Nathan said.

"It's a dollar a night," said Ma, "or five dollars for seven days."

"I'll pay for a week, then," Nathan said. "This is my dog, Cotton Blossom. It's all right if he stays with me?"

"Long as he don't bark or make a mess, he's welcome. You're right next to Deputy Lambert. Room three, down the hall."

The door to Lambert's room was open and the lawman was struggling into a clean shirt. The doctor was preparing to leave.

"Soon as I change into dry clothes, I'll be ready to try that cafe grub," said Nathan. When he had changed, he took his saddlebags with him, for they contained the leather sack with the gold Eulie had left him.

"Tomorrow morning," Lambert said, as they walked next door to the cafe, "we'll talk to the judge and he can hear your testimony. He may want it in writing, unless you plan to be around for a while."

"I haven't made up my mind as to how long I'll be here," said Nathan.

"If you've got nothin' better to do and you'll work cheap, I can get you a deputy marshal's badge," Lambert said. "Couple of weeks back, Cullen Baker and his bunch had to skeedaddle out of Texas, and they rode into our territory. Would you believe we was so damn short-handed the court didn't have nobody to send? Time we had a man that could ride south, the varmints was gone again."

"I've heard of them," Nathan said, careful not to betray his excitement. "Do they bother you often?"

"Often enough," said Lambert. "Two or three times a year, anyhow. All depends on what Baker's done in Texas. If he's killed somebody, then he'll ride across the line and hole up somewhere to the south of here. It takes a while before he can ride back to Texas."

"I've never been a peace officer before," Nathan said. "Maybe I'll try it, if the court will have me."

"Long as you didn't desert the Union army and you ain't wanted by the law," said Lambert, "you got yourself a job."

The rain had become more intense and the cafe had few customers. Nathan and Lambert entered, and before they took a table, Nathan spoke to the cook about Cotton Blossom.

"Just keep him near you," the genial cook said. "With both of you as payin' customers, the dog eats for free, if he don't mind beef scraps."

Nathan laughed. "He never complains. Muchas gracias."

After a meal of roast beef, potatoes, onions, biscuits,

apple pie, and hot coffee, Nathan and Lambert returned to Ma Dollar's boardinghouse. The rain hadn't let up, and Nathan was thankful for a roof over his head. He blew out the lamp, and with Cotton Blossom on the rug beside the bed, the two of them were soon asleep.

*   *   *

Fort Smith, Arkansas. January 8, 1867.

Nathan was pulling on his boots when Russ Lambert knocked on the door.

"I'm goin' to breakfast," Lambert said. "I thought you might be up and about. The courthouse opens at nine."

"After a bit of grub and some hot coffee, there's a small chance I'd feel human," said Nathan. "Let's go eat."

Nathan waited until they were down to final cups of coffee before speaking what was on his mind.

"When there are outlaws or killers on the run, who decides which lawman goes after them? Why did the court choose you to go after the Yeagers?"

"The court had no choice," Lambert said, "and neither did I. Like I told you, we're shorthanded, and I was the only deputy in town. If the need arose for a lawman and there was two of us here, one of us would have the chance to volunteer. If neither of us did, the court would send the man who had been inactive the longest."

"I reckon it ain't often you have help on a chase, then," said Nathan.

"Often, hell," Lambert scoffed. "I been behind this badge three years come April, and I never had any help. Anyway, not till you come along," he added hastily.

By the time they reached the courthouse, the clouds had broken up and a mild sun peeked through.

"By now," said Lambert, "Judge Corbin will have read Simpkins's report. The judge will want to talk to you, but let me talk to him first."

Nathan waited, thinking of the decision he had made. From what Lambert had told him, it seemed just a matter of time until Cullen Baker's nefarious activities in Texas would force him and his gang back into Arkansas. On his own, Nathan had no idea *where* he might find Baker and the scar-faced man, Tobe Snider, but as a lawman, Nathan would have an edge. With the law having free access to the telegraph, Baker's activities and whereabouts could be reported within minutes. At that moment, Lambert left Judge Corbin's office and beckoned to Nathan.

"Go on in," said Lambert. "Room 112. I'll wait in the lobby."

Judge Corbin proved to be a tall, graying man, probably in his fifties. He arose behind his desk and extended his hand.

"I'm Elliott Corbin."

"My pleasure," Nathan said. "I'm Nathan Stone."

"Take a chair, Nathan," said Corbin. "First, I want to thank you for coming to the aid of Deputy U.S. Marshal Lambert. It's a rare act of courage, taking a man alive when he's doing his best to kill you."

"I take no pleasure in killing a man," Nathan said, "unless he won't have it any other way." Nathan felt a twinge of guilt, for that was no longer true. He had begun to change with the death of French Stumberg.

"Mr. Lambert tells me you're considering applying for a position as a deputy U.S. marshal. I suppose he has told you what it involves and the legal stipulations."

"He has," said Nathan. "I've never deserted from the army and I'm not wanted by the law. To be honest, I've been making my living as a house dealer. A man gets almighty tired sleeping days and spending his nights in saloons."

"I can appreciate that," Corbin said. "Based on what you've told me, I am prepared to swear you in as a Deputy United States Marshal."

Nathan placed his hand on the Bible and repeated the short oath as the judge spoke the words. When it was over, Corbin took a silver badge from a desk drawer and handed it to Nathan. He again extended his hand and Nathan took it.

"There are no assignments at the moment," said Corbin, "but that's subject to change at any time. Your time is your own as long as you're available when you're needed."

"I have a room at Ma Dollar's," Nathan said.

Russ Lambert was waiting, and Nathan grinned, flashing the star that he held in his hand.

"Pin it on," said Lambert, "so's the owlhoots have somethin' to shoot at."

*   *   *

Weeks passed, and five times Nathan Stone rode after thieves and killers. Only one escaped, fleeing into Indian Territory. Eight men were returned to Fort Smith, six of them alive. Nathan earned almost a thousand dollars in bounties, but that wasn't what he sought. Not until the first of June was his patience rewarded. He was at Ma Dollar's, awaiting orders, when Judge Corbin sent for him.

"Nathan," Corbin said, "we just got word by telegraph that Cullen Baker's killed a man in Cass County, Texas. As usual, he's expected to ride across the Red and hole up in Arkansas. You have an admirable record as an officer of the law, but don't take any chances. While I don't encourage killing, I'm arming you with execution warrants for Baker and Snider. As for any others, you'll have to use your own judgment. Good luck."

Nathan rode out within the hour, leading his packhorse, Cotton Blossom loping on ahead. They were perhaps a hundred and fifty miles north of where the Red crossed the line from Texas into Arkansas. From a map in the judge's office, Nathan had discovered that Baker wasn't more than a day's ride from his crossing of the Red, while Nathan must ride hard to reach the same point in two days. Nathan had ridden through that part of the country when he had first come to Fort Smith, and there were brakes along the Red that would conceal a tribe of Indians. Taking the advice of Russ Lambert, Nathan had removed his badge, carrying it in his pocket. It was a sensible precaution for a lawman seeking wanted men, lest he be gunned down on sight. Nathan rode until long after dark, stretching the first day as much as he could. The next morning, after a hurried breakfast, he rode out at first light.

"Cotton Blossom," Nathan said, "you run on ahead and keep your nose to the ground. I can't afford any surprises."

While the hound didn't understand Nathan's specific words, he possessed an inherent distrust of strangers. If he saw or heard other riders, he would consider them enemies until Nathan had passed judgment. Nathan's second day on the trail would be short, as he had planned, and as he neared the Red, he slowed the gait of his horse. From what he had learned about Cullen Baker, the renegade wouldn't ride far north of the river. He was likely to hole up under an overhang where he couldn't easily be found, with an eye to defense. Nathan' best—and perhaps only—possibility lay in cutting Baker's trail. With that in mind, he found a shallow place and crossed to the south bank of the Red. There was one thing of which he wasn't sure, an element that didn't set easy on his mind. He didn't know exactly *where* Baker would cross the Red. Nathan estimated he was at least a dozen miles east of the Texas–Arkansas line, and one thing in his favor had been the recent rain, for it would be all but impossible for a rider to conceal the trail left by his horse. Unfortunately, clouds sweeping in from the west promised more rain, and unless Nathan found the trail he was seeking before dark, it would be rained out before the dawn.

Nathan rode west along the Red, all too aware of his own trail. Suppose he had miscalculated? Suppose Baker and his friends reached the river at some point *behind* Nathan? Being on the run, Baker would be immediately suspicious of fresh tracks, and the hunted would become the hunters. Nathan reined up, his unease, the premonition of impending disaster, was growing stronger by the minute. If the outlaws were trailing *him*, he dared not backtrack. Instead, he must take cover and gain whatever advantage he could. But there *was* no adequate cover, except possibly along the river, for the banks were high. He would have to lead his horses down. But there was no time. A horse nickered and his own answered. Nathan rolled out of the saddle, taking his Winchester with him, only to have a slug kick dirt in his face.

"You're covered, pilgrim," said a cold voice. "Leave that rifle on the ground an' git up. Don't use the hoss fer cover, neither."

Nathan considered his options. He was a dozen yards from the river bank. If they killed the horse, its body would offer him little protection, for one of the killers could quickly flank him. Vainly he tried to see his foes, for until he could, he had no target. His chances were small, at best, and unless he coaxed the outlaws into the open, none. Leaving his Winchester on the ground, he got to his knees, then to his feet.

"Smart hombre," said the unseen gunman. "Now step out from behind that hoss."

"Why should I?" Nathan countered. "When I do, how do I know you won't shoot me?"

"You don't," said the voice. "You'll just have to trust me."

There was laughter, and Nathan learned there were at least three men. He might have a small chance, even against such odds, but not without being able to see them. He tried one last desperate ruse.

"You have the guns," Nathan said. "I'll move when you step out where I'm able to see you. It don't take much of a man to hide in the brush and shoot from cover."

"By God," said the first voice, "I don't need no cover. Nobody says I'm less of a man an' goes on living."

"Damn it, Baker,' said a second voice, "he's got law wrote all over him, and he's just jawin' to save his hide."

"All the more reason fer me killin' the scutter," said Baker. "Curry, you an' Snider just hunker down here in the bushes, so's you don't git hurt."

Nathan's heart sank. If Curry and Snider remained out of sight, then he hadn't a chance. Baker was fast. Almighty fast, and even if Nathan outdrew him, Baker's companions could shoot Nathan from cover. Somehow he had to get them all where he could see them.

"That's right, Baker" Nathan taunted. "Let them hide there in the brush. After I gun you down, they'll be that much closer when they run for their horses."

"You mouthy varmint," said Snider, "even if you're good enough to take Baker, I'll kill you."

"Nobody's faster than me," Baker snarled. "Side me if you got the sand, but if either of you pulls iron ahead of me, I'll kill him and pistol-whip you."

Despite Baker's arrogance, Snider and Curry had been shamed out of hiding. When Baker stepped out, they were with him. Baker was to Nathan's extreme right, Snider to his left, and Curry facing him. They had fanned out so that there was no possible way Nathan could take them all. By some miracle, he might get two of them, but the third man would surely kill him. There was no point in sacrificing the faithful black horse, so Nathan stepped clear of the animal. But Nathan had an edge. A snarling, clawing Cotton Blossom darted out of the brush, and the very moment Baker's hand touched the butt of his revolver, the hound sank his teeth into the outlaw's left leg. Baker's shot tore into the ground and he began beating Cotton Blossom with the revolver.

Snider and Curry were taken by surprise, but they recovered quickly. Snider had his gun clear of leather when Nathan put two slugs through his belly. Curry got off a shot and the lead tore through Nathan's right thigh, just above the knee. Nathan stumbled backward and went down, allowing Curry's second slug to go over his head. From flat on his back, Nathan shot the outlaw once in the chest. Despite Cullen Baker's reputation and big talk, the deal had gone sour. Baker was running toward the brush and his waiting horse. Nathan fired twice, but Baker was hunched over, zigzagging. The wound in Nathan's thigh was bleeding badly, and only by seizing the stirrup leather of the black horse was he able to get to his feet. His first concern was for Cotton Blossom. He hadn't actually seen Baker's reaction to the dog's attack, and he feared the shot from Baker's revolver had struck Cotton Blossom. With difficulty he got down on his knees. The dog's head was bloody, but on closer examination, Nathan found he had been knocked senseless by the heavy muzzle of Baker's revolver. Nathan had begun carrying a quart of whiskey in his saddlebag for just such a need as this. He removed it, along with some yard-long lengths of muslin. Some of these would cleanse and bind his own wound, but first he soaked some of the cloth with whiskey and cleaned the nasty gash on Cotton Blossom's head. The dog's eyes were open, but he lay still, aware that Nathan was trying to help him. When the blood had been wiped away, Nathan poured whiskey into the open wound.

"Sorry, old pard," said Nathan. "It burns like hell, but it's all I have for either of us. It'll have to do till we get back to Fort Smith."

There was a chance Baker might return, but Nathan thought it was more likely the outlaw would ride a few miles and then lay in ambush. By morning, Nathan wouldn't be able to stand on his wounded leg, and the whiskey might not stave off infection. Baker had escaped, but Nathan didn't feel like risking the loss of a leg by pursuing the outlaw. He was satisfied, having accounted for Tobe Snider, one of the seven men he sought. He was a hundred and fifty miles south of Fort Smith, in a cold, drizzling rain. If he rode all night, stopping only to rest the horses, he would be there by early afternoon of the next day. Nathan found the horses belonging to Snider and Curry, took time to unsaddle the animals, and then set them free. He then went through the pockets of the dead outlaws, but found only a few gold coins, no identification.

"Hombres," said Nathan to the dead men, "I'm goin' to do as much for you as you'd have done for me. Good luck with the buzzards and coyotes."

Cotton Blossom was on his feet, but he was weak, and there was no prowling ahead. He loped along beside the packhorse as Nathan began the long ride to Fort Smith.

*   *   *

Fort Smith. June 15, 1867.

Upon returning to Fort Smith, Nathan had given up his badge. After ten days of rest, his wound healed, he was at the livery, loading his pack horse. The rest had restored Cotton Blossom's enthusiasm, and he too seemed ready for the trail.

"Sorry to see you go, Nathan," Russ Lambert said. "That means the rest of us will have to work harder for the same money."

"I have a hankering to ride back to Texas," said Nathan. "Maybe I'll meet Cullen Baker again, if somebody else don't get him first."

"I expect you'll have to stand in line," Lambert said. "The man just don't make friends easy."

*   *   *

Taking his time, Nathan rode south. He crossed the Red about seventy miles north of Dallas, and spent more than a week in the town, frequenting all the saloons. He neither drank nor gambled, but listened to the conversations of gamblers, bullwhackers, soldiers, cowboys, and farmers. Saloon women did their best to lure him upstairs, but to no avail. He bought them watered-down drinks so that he might question them, but when he rode out of Dallas, he had learned nothing regarding the whereabouts of the five killers he sought.

He considered riding to Waco and telling old Judge

Prater of Eulie's fate, but thought better of it. The old varmint would just blame Nathan, and might have him shot on general principles. He shied away from Waco and rode on. Somewhere north of Austin he began seeing crudely lettered signs announcing a horse race in Lee County on July fourth.

"Cotton Blossom," Nathan said, "I've endured half the damn saloons in east Texas, and all for nothing. A horse race ought to draw folks from all over. I reckon we'll just slope on down there and see who shows up."

Two hours before sundown, he rode into the little town of Lexington, Texas.*

---

* Oldest settlement in Lee County. James Shaw and Titus Mundine (early settlers) gave the townsite in the early 1850's, naming the new town for Lexington, Massachusetts.

Chapter 22

❖❖❖

Lexington, Texas. July 3, 1867.

In Texas, it was a time in which the affluence of a town was judged by the number of saloons it boasted, and Lexington had three. There was a hotel of sorts, a mercantile, a livery, and two cafes. Food could be had at all the saloons, if a man wasn't too picky. There was no courthouse, no jail, and apparently, no sheriff. A small sign nailed to an oak announced to anybody who cared that the population was a hundred and fifty-two.*

"A room for tonight and tomorrow night," Nathan told the hotel desk clerk. "You got any objections if my dog stays with me?"

"Not if he don't cause a ruckus or bite nobody," the man replied. "Two dollars, in advance."

"Where will the race be run?" Nathan asked, handing him the money.

"Right down main street, quarter mile." He was short, gray, with mild blue eyes, and he fixed them on Nathan's twin Colts.

He looked as though he wanted to say something more, but allowed his better judgment to prevail. Nathan took his room key and returned to his horses. Although the hotel was a single-story affair, he didn't wish to take his loaded packsaddle to his room. Instead, he rode on to the livery, making arrangements for his horses and requesting that his saddle, packsaddle, and bedroll be secured in the tack room. His saddlebags he chose not to leave in anybody's

---

* Lee County was officially created in 1874 and named for Robert E. Lee. Giddings, thirty-five miles south of Lexington, became the county seat.

hands but his own. It was still early on a Wednesday afternoon and there were few horses tied to any of the saloon hitch rails. It seemed the Tumbleweed had the fewest patrons, and Nathan elbowed his way through its batwing doors. He needed a talkative bartender. Two men sat at a back table, while the bartender leaned on the bar. He was an elderly Negro, bald except for a gray fringe above his ears. He reminded Nathan of old Malachi, resting in an unmarked grave in Virginia.

"What'll it be, suh?"

"A beer," said Nathan, "and maybe you can tell me somethin' about the race tomorrow."

"They don' be a lot to tell. Ain't but two hosses runnin'. One of 'em's a black, name of *Shadow*. T'other is a *Todillo*."*

One of the men at the table slid back his chair, got up, and headed for the bar. When he spoke, it was to the bartender.

"Simon, why don't you tell him the truth of it."

"Ah can't take no sides, suh," Simon replied.

"Why don't you leave Simon out of it and tell me yourself," said Nathan.

"Why not? I'm Johnson McKowen. If you aim to take part in tomorrow's race, there's two sides. Put your money on the black and you're lined up with the cattlemen. If you're fool enough to go with the other nag, you're in bed with Negroes and sodbusters."

"I don't take kindly to having somebody make my bed and then tell me I have to lie in it," Nathan said.

"Ah don' want no trouble in here, gentlemens," said Simon.

"Come on, Driggers," McKowen said.

The second man at the back table got up and brought the bottle, and the two of them shouldered their way through the batwings and onto the boardwalk.

"Somebody needs to beat his ears down around his boot tops," said Nathan.

"Amens, suh," Simon said, "but he do his fightin' with a pistol. He bad, but his friend be worser."

---

*Iron gray.

"I reckon his pard has horns, hooves, and a spike tail, then," said Nathan.

"Close, suh," Simon replied. "You evah hear of Wil' Bill Longley?"

"Yes," said Nathan, "but nothing good. Are he and this McKowen varmint involved in the race tomorrow?"

"I afraid so, suh, an' it wasn't none of our doin'. There be cattlemens here, an' there be farmers, an' whilst we ain't always love one another, we always git along."

"But Longley and McKowen have changed all that, I reckon," Nathan said.

"They do, suh," said Simon. He kept his eyes on the front door, lest he be overheard. Satisfied, he continued. "My people, they come here as slaves, back when Texas be owned by Mexico. They come from Alabama, Miss'ssipi, Georgia, an' Kaintuck. White folks what bring us here, they be farmers. My people be farmers too, for they work the land. Cattlemens they come, but we still git along. We been have this hoss race ever' July fourth, back far as I remember. Now it become a war, cattlemens agin the rest of us."

"They're laying their money on *Shadow* to win the race, then," Nathan said, "and are using hatred and distrust to scare the rest of you into losing."

"They do that, suh," said Simon. "Odds agin *Todillo* be twenty to one."

"I like that kind of odds," Nathan said. "Where do I place my bet?"

"The mercantile. Mr. Hicks take all bets. Lawd bless you, suh."

When Nathan reached the mercantile, he wasn't surprised to find McKowen and Driggers there. Hicks proved to be a grim-faced man who looked as though he hadn't smiled in his life. He said nothing, his arms folded, waiting for Nathan to speak.

"I'm here to place a bet in tomorrow's race," said Nathan.

"Cattlemen or sodbusters?"

"Neither," Nathan said grimly. "I'm betting on the gray. The *Todillo*."

"Haw, haw," McKowen scoffed, "don't bet no more'n you can afford to lose."

"I'll take my loss," said Nathan "if it's honest." From his pocket he took a handful of double eagles. He dribbled

them out on the counter one at a time until there were
twenty-five.

"Five hundred dollars!" Hicks exclaimed. "I ... I'm not
sure we can cover a bet that large. The odds ..."

"According to the odds, you'll owe me ten thousand
dollars," said Nathan. "Now write me a receipt, and be
sure you include the odds."

Hicks looked helplessly at McKowen and Driggers, but
found no support there. Reluctantly he wrote out the receipt, signed it, and gave it to Nathan. Without a word,
Nathan left the store. Cotton Blossom was waiting, and
since it was nearing suppertime, Nathan decided to try the
cafe nearest the hotel. The sign in front had faded, leaving
nothing legible except "Cafe." It was still early, so the place
was virtually empty, and that's how Nathan liked it. The
graying old fellow behind the counter looked and walked
like a stove-up cowboy.

"I'm paying for the dog's supper too," Nathan said, "if
you have no objection to him coming in."

"He's welcome. I allus thought a man should own one
good doog an' one good hoss 'fore he dies."

Nathan had just begun to eat when the girl entered the
cafe. She had dark hair and green eyes, and was probably
not more than a year or two past her teens. The other
diners had left, and she headed straight for Nathan's table.
He pushed back his chair and stood as she approached.

"I'm Viola Hayden," she said. "You just bet five hundred dollars on the horse I'm riding in the race tomorrow."

"I did," Nathan said. "I'm a gambler and I like the odds.
Anything wrong with that?"

"No ... yes ... I ... I'm not sure," she said. "When I
heard you had bet so much on *Daybreak,* I just wondered
why. There's ... something I think you ought to know.
Most everybody's afraid ..."

"Of Wild Bill Longley and his amigos," said Nathan.

"Yes," she replied. "My father and most of the other
farmers settled here in the thirties when this area was part
of a Mexican land grant arranged by Stephen Austin. After
Lincoln's proclaimation freed the slaves, some of the
ranchers resented us. Bill Longley, Johnson McKowen, and
a few others have taken to fanning the flames, claiming the
ranchers are on one side, while the farmers and the Negroes are on the other. Our annual Fourth of July race is

a countywide event. Now it's being used to set neighbor against neighbor. I believe you should know that if Daybreak wins, the cattlemen are promising trouble. You may never collect your winnings."

"That's part of the risk in gambling," Nathan said. "I get the feeling that the cattlemen—sided by Longley and his bunch—don't intend to lose that race."

"That's what Daddy says, and he's threatening to withdraw Daybreak from the race, because he fears for me to ride him."

"It wouldn't be a bad idea," said Nathan. "If your horse is withdrawn there won't be a race."

"We can't withdraw," the girl said. "Things have gone too far. Somehow we must make people in this county understand they are being used by Longley and his kind. Do you know he's known as the 'Negro Killer'?"

"No," Nathan said. "I've never seen the man."

"He's killed before. Mostly Negroes, and he's always managed to bribe or buy his way out. He's promised trouble tomorrow, if Daybreak wins."

"I haven't seen either horse and nobody's told me anything about them," said Nathan, "except that one represents the farmers and the other the cattlemen. Being fair, if nobody interferes, which do you think has the best chance?"

"Daybreak," she said. "I raised him from a Colt and I can ride him bareback. Nate Rankin is the rancher who owns Shadow, and he's a fine horse, but Rankin's son will be riding him. Hugh outweighs me by at least sixty pounds."

"That might make the difference, then," Nathan replied. "Has anything been done to prevent Longley and his bunch from interfering with the race?"

"Daddy's taking some precautions, I think. Would you like to ride out to our place and see Daybreak? Besides, with so much of your money riding on our horse, I'd like Daddy to talk to you. I think you should know of trouble that might arise tomorrow."

Nathan liked this girl and her forthright manner. "I'll go with you," he said.

Viola Hayden rode south, Nathan beside her and Cotton Blossom following. Long before they reached the house and outbuildings, there were fields of young cotton that seemed to go on forever. The girl noticed him eyeing the fields and spoke.

"This will be our first decent crop since before the war. God knows how we'll ever get it to market, and if we do, it may not be worth enough to pay for the hauling. For five years, we've grown only fruits and vegetables. What we couldn't use, Daddy gave to our neighbors. Mostly the ones who have turned against us," she added bitterly.

Grasshoppers fled before the hooves of their horses and a breeze rustled the leaves of the red oaks that lined the dirt road. Before they reached the house, Nathan could see that the place was well cared for. At a time when a man seldom could afford to paint his house, the Hayden barn had been painted brick red.

"First painted barn I've seen in a coon's age," Nathan said.

"Daddy saw the war coming and managed to plan ahead. During the war, we had only what we were able to grow. I hated the war. It brought out the best in some, but the worst in others."

"Such as Longley and his bunch," said Nathan.

"Yes," she said. "Them and others like them. The men who went to war and lived to talk about it are sadder but wiser. Those who were just boys—too young to fight—are bitter, wanting to hurt others to ease their own hurt."

When they dismounted before the house, darkness was only minutes away, and lamps glowed behind curtained windows. Jesse Hayden met them on the porch. Viola introduced Nathan, explaining how she had heard of his bet, and how, on impulse she had gone to talk to him.

"I'm beholden to you for seein' Viola home," Hayden said. "I was startin' to worry. Supper's on the table."

"I've had supper," said Nathan, "but I wouldn't refuse some hot coffee."

When they were seated at the table, an elderly Negro woman poured their coffee. Nathan nodded to her.

"This is Lizzie," said Hayden. "We couldn't get along without her. She stayed on when the others left, although we could offer her nothing more than food and a roof over her head."

"I thankful," Lizzie said. "With the damn Yankees all aroun', we lucky to have that."

Despite himself, Nathan laughed. As so often was the

case, the liberated Negroes thought of themselves as Southerners and resented the intrusion of carpetbaggers, scala-
wags, and Union soldiers.

"I wanted Mr. Stone to talk to you, Daddy," said Viola.
"He stands to lose a lot of money if Daybreak loses the
race tomorrow. Since he's already laid his money down, I
suppose there's nothing he can do, but I think he has the
right to know what we're up against."

"I agree," said Hayden. "We got no sheriff here, but I've
contacted the Texas Rangers in Austin. They've promised
to send help. Besides that, I aim to have a dozen armed
men handy."

"That's precaution enough," Nathan said. "Where will
the race be run?"

"Right down the main street of town," said Hayden.
"Come on to the barn and have a look at the horse your
money's on."

Hayden lighted a lantern and the three of them walked
to the big red barn. Viola went in first, and there was a
nickering welcome. She led the horse out of his stall, and
Nathan was impressed with the big gray. He stood a good
fourteen hands, a stocky, deep-muscled, and sturdy-legged
animal. His chest was deep, his withers low, his hindquarters powerful. His neck was thick while his head was broad
and short.

"I like the looks of him," said Nathan. "He'll be hard to
beat in a quarter-mile run, if I'm any judge. I believe one of
us should stay here with him tonight, and I'm volunteering.
Cotton Blossom will warn me if anybody comes near."

*   *   *

There was no trouble during the night. Nathan slept in
the hayloft and Cotton Blossom in the stall next to Daybreak. When Viola Hayden came to milk the cow, Nathan
and Cotton Blossom returned with her to the house. In the
kitchen, next to the stove, Lizzie fed Cotton Blossom, while
Nathan sat down to breakfast with the Haydens.

"I've been hearing about this Wild Bill Longley ever
since I got here," Nathan said, "and I have yet to see him.
Where is he?"

"Laying low," said Hayden. "He's had run-ins with the
law before, and he's become cautious. The Rangers were

looking for him last year, and I'd say he's looking for them to return. But even if he don't show, he's got a passel of friends like Driggers and McKowen who are hell-raisers in their own right."

After breakfast, Jesse Hayden rode out to call on some friends, having them arm themselves to prevent trouble in town. Nathan would ride in with Viola.

"The race doesn't start until three o'clock," said Viola, "but I'd like to be in town by noon. There'll be friends I haven't seen since this time last summer, and I want some time to visit. After the race, there'll be a street dance. It's a custom the Negroes began, back in the slave days, and they don't object when some of the rest of us take part. There'll be someone blowing a mouth harp, another with a fiddle or banjo, or maybe a guitar. Would you like to stay for that?"

"I don't think so," Nathan said. "Remember, I have a five-hundred-dollar bet with twenty-to-one odds. If you win that race, somebody's going to owe me ten thousand dollars. They might find it easier just to shoot me."

"Please don't joke about such things," she cried. Impulsively she leaned across the table and took his hands in hers, and he was touched by the concern in her green eyes. The pleasant interlude ended when the grandfather clock in the parlor struck eleven.

"My stars," Viola laughed, "we've been sitting here three hours. Please saddle the horses. I'll be ready by then." She went through the kitchen and out the back door.

"She gone to the outhouse," Lizzie chuckled.

"That must be an almighty big coffee pot, Lizzie," said Nathan.

"It don' be that big," Lizzie said from the kitchen. "I refill it t'ree times."

*   *   *

When Nathan and Viola reached town, every hitch rail was occupied by saddle horses or mules, and there were countless buckboards and wagons, some of which had brought entire families for the event. Many had brought basket lunches, while others crowded into the cafes and saloons.

"God," said Nathan, "everybody in the county must be here."

"Close to it," Viola agreed, "and some from other counties as well."

Room had been made at one of the hitch rails for the horses entered in the race. Jesse Hayden was already there, and he took charge of Daybreak. Viola hurried away to talk to friends, while Nathan wanted to talk to Hayden.

"I got eight men lined up," said Hayden with satisfaction, "so with you an' me, there'll be ten of us. Better yet, there's a Ranger here. Captain Jennings just rode up from Austin. I've talked to him, and he doesn't think Longley will have the nerve to try anything."

"I'd like to talk to this Captain Jennings," Nathan said. Every Texas Ranger carried a black book of wanted men. It was often referred to as "Bible Two," second in importance to the Holy Bible. If any of the five killers that Nathan was seeking were wanted in Texas, the Rangers would know. Even if he must reveal his oath of vengeance to gain the cooperation of these vigilant Texas lawmen, he would do so. Some families had spread their lunches beneath giant oaks, and it was there that Nathan found the Texas Ranger, Captain Sage Jennings. The familiar star in a circle was pinned to his vest and a Colt revolver was tied low on his right hip. He was taking advantage of an invitation to share some fried chicken.

"Captain," Nathan said, "when you're done with that chicken, I'd like to talk to you. I'm Nathan Stone."

"I believe I've heard of you," said Jennings. "These are the Swensons, friends of mine. There appears to be plenty of chicken, if you'd care to join us." The Swensons nodded in polite agreement.

"Thanks," Nathan replied, "but I'm not that far from breakfast."

Nathan leaned against an oak, waiting. He wondered if Jennings had heard of him as a result of that ill-fated shootout in San Antone. While it seemed unlikely, one never knew when the past would deal a busted flush. Jennings got up, dusted off the seat of his Levi's, and headed for Nathan. He opened the conversation with a question.

"Are you the hombre who shot it out with the Baker gang a month or so ago?"

"Yes," Nathan replied, "but I did a poor job of it. I

managed to salt down a pair of varmints sidin' him, but he escaped. One of his pards managed to get some lead in me, so I wasn't any condition to trail Baker.''

"Hell's bells," said Jennings, "you've accomplished more than the Rangers, the Union army, and half the sheriffs in north Texas combined. We got a wire from Fort Smith, but not in time for us to take Baker's trail."

"I'm not surprised," said Nathan. "I rode most of the way back to Fort Smith in the rain."

"We can use men like you in the Rangers," Jennings said.

"I've heard the Rangers are having trouble with the Reconstructionist governor," Nathan said.

"He won't officially recognize us," said Jennings, "but he won't stop us. The truth is, the Union army is spread too thin. They're trying to build a string of forts in Wyoming Territory, while Quanah Parker and his Comanches are raising hell with every fort and soldier outpost in West Texas. Renegades are as bad or worse than the Comanches, looting and killing south of the Red, then running like coyotes into Indian Territory. That's how Texas inherited that varmint, Tobe Snider. Him and another Reb deserter, Virg Dillard . . ."

"Virg Dillard?"

That's the handle he's ridin' under," Jennings said. "Do you know him?"

"I've heard of him," said Nathan, "and none of it good."

"Snider and Dillard had cozied up to a renegade outfit from Kansas," Jennings said, "and the lot of 'em were holed up in Indian Territory. Next thing we knew, Snider was with Cullen Baker. We've heard nothing more about Dillard, but that bunch of renegade varmints is still ridin' across the Red, looting and killing."

"And as far as you know, this bunch of renegades—including Dillard—is holed up in Indian Territory."

"Yes," Jennings said. "From your obvious interest in Dillard, would I be close if I suspected you have a reason for tracking him down?"

"You would," said Nathan, "and that's why I can't afford to join your ranks as a Ranger. Even if your badge had jurisdiction in Indian Territory, it could get me shot dead as a Christmas goose."

"It likely would do that," Jennings agreed. "All I can do

is wish you luck and tell you the little we know about Dillard. He carries his revolver on his right hip, butt forward. Only gun-thrower I ever heard of with a cross-hand draw that pulls it with his left."

"It's uncommon all right," said Nathan. "Uncommon enough to be remembered. I'm obliged."

"I'll be here the rest of the day," Jennings said, "but I don't look for any trouble out of Longley. He prefers picking on people who can't or won't fight back."

A quarter of an hour before the race, Shadow and Daybreak were led to the starting line. While Nathan was partial to Daybreak, Nate Rankin's horse had good points too. Shadow, however, as Viola had pointed out, must carry more weight than Daybreak. Son Hugh, Nathan observed, had spent entirely too much time at the dinner table. Jesse Hayden and Captain Jennings had joined eight other armed men strung out along the course of the race, lest the elusive Wild Bill Longley and his bunch showed up. Suddenly there was a single shot and the horses were off and running. Viola's Daybreak took an immediate lead. Hugh Rankin wasted no time in using his quirt, but it gained him nothing. It quickly became obvious that Viola had an even greater edge than her opponent's added weight. There was an affinity between the girl and the big gray horse, and Daybreak needed no quirting. The horse was running for the sheer joy of it, and the wild cry of his rider only added to his momentum. Within a few yards, he was a length ahead, then two, and finally a distance the black couldn't possibly regain. Nathan spotted McKowen and Driggers on the flat roof of a saloon, but they did nothing to arouse suspicion. When the big gray had swept past the last of the town and was in the clear, Nathan and the rest of the protective riders rode on to the finish line. When Hugh Rankin dismounted, he made no move to congratulate Viola. Instead, using the quirt, he began raining blows on the tender muzzle of the black horse.

There was a moment of shocked silence, and before anyone else could make a move, Viola caught Rankin's arm on the backswing. Off balance, Rankin lit on his back in a cloud of dust. Furious, he got to his feet and came after Viola with the quirt. Standing her ground, she planted the toe of her right boot in young Rankin's groin. With a groan, he folded like an empty sack. Nate Rankin came stomping through the crowd, his hand on the butt of his Colt.

"What the hell's been done to him" Rankin bawled.

"He went after the girl with a quirt," said Captain Jennings, "and she gave him a boot so's it got his attention. You'd better get him away from here before somebody shoots him on general principles. Might do it myself."

"By God," Rankin shouted, "you ain't heard the last of this."

"You'd better hope we have," said Jennings. "If there's trouble, I'll come looking for you."

Leading the black, Rankin stalked away, leaving Hugh to follow as best he could. Nathan made his way through the circle of friends crowding around Viola and Daybreak.

"A grand ride," Nathan said. "Nobody on any other horse could have even come close."

To Nathan's surprise, Viola threw her arms around him and the onlookers all roared their approval. Amid all the merriment, Jesse Hayden became serious.

"I reckon we'd best take Daybreak and ride to the house," he said.

"But we'll miss the street dance," Viola protested.

"Best if we do," said Hayden. "Captain Jennings is ridin' back to Austin. With nothing happenin' during the race, I'd not be surprised if there ain't trouble tonight."

"That's sound thinking," Nathan said. "I'll collect my bet, load my packhorse, and go with you."

"You'd best take some of us with you to collect that bet," said Hayden.

"I'll manage," Nathan said. "It's something I aim to enjoy."

When Nathan reached the mercantile, he wasn't in the least surprised to find McKowen and Driggers standing on the porch. They said nothing as he entered, and as he had half-suspected would be the case, Nate Rankin was with Hicks.

"Count it out," said Nathan. "In gold."

"Pilgrim," Rankin said, "we don't take kindly to strangers comin' here and interferin' in local affairs."

"I don't care a damn for your local affairs," said Nathan. "I came here, placed a bet, and I won. You took my money, and I'm here for some of yours. Now pay up. Put it in a sack, Hicks."

"Go ahead," Rankin said sullenly. "He's got it comin'."

Nathan said nothing. He suspected he would have even more coming before he rode out of Lee County. Hicks piled the double eagles on the counter and was preparing to sweep them into a gunny sack when Nathan stopped him.

"Not yet," said Nathan. "Count them in stacks of five hundred."

It was an obvious, intentional insult, and Hicks's face flushed. Rankin looked as though he might explode. Nathan had turned sideways, prepared should the door open suddenly, yet keeping his watchful eyes on Hicks and Rankin. When Hicks presented it, he took the heavy sack in his left hand and with his eyes on the pair behind the counter, he backed toward the door. When he stepped out, McKowen and Driggers had gone. Jesse and Viola Hayden were waiting.

"I'll get my packhorse from the livery," Nathan said, "and we'll ride."

The packhorse loaded, Nathan rode by the hotel and left his key.

"You're paid through tonight," the clerk said.

"Forget it," Nathan replied. "I have business elsewhere."

Leading his packhorse, Nathan followed the Haydens. Cotton Blossom ran on ahead. There was no conversation until they reached the Hayden barn.

"I reckon I'd better sleep in the barn again tonight," Nathan said. "I have a feeling they're not finished with us."

"The same feeling I have," said Hayden, "but you can't sleep in our barn forever, can you?"

"No," Nathan replied, "but I don't want them coming down on you because of what I've done. If they aim to get at me through you, I look for them to try it tonight. You saw what Rankin's kid did to the black. They might try to shoot or hamstring your gray, just to get even."

"If they hurt Daybreak or act like they want to," Viola said angrily, "I'll kill them. I swear to God, I will."

Nathan won out in his bid to remain in the barn with Daybreak. While there was a chance that Rankin and his friends might seek revenge by trying to harm the horse, Nathan didn't really think so. What he most feared was the parting with Viola. He had known the girl for twenty-four hours, and if her actions meant anything, he would have one hell of a time convincing her it was in her best interests if he moved on. What he expected from old man Rankin was some attempt to recover the money Nathan had won. If that were the case, he believed he could direct Rankin's hostilities toward himself, leaving Jesse and Viola Hayden free to mend their fences after Nathan had departed. Suddenly his thoughts were disrupted by the clatter of a horse's hooves. It had the sound of urgency and Nathan took the ladder from the hay loft three rungs at a time. Before he reached the house, he could hear the frightened voice of the Negro barkeep he knew only as Simon.

"Mistah Jesse, suh, Wil' Bill Longley an' his frien' McKowen, they done shot up the street dance. Some us done been kilt."

"Get down, Simon," Jesse Hayden said, "and tell it from the beginning."

Simon practically fell from the mule he'd ridden. He sat on the edge of the porch and clasped his hands, trying to control their trembling. Finally he steadied himself enough to tell the story.

"Antler Joe an' Fat Jack be dead," said Simon, "an' Joe's woman be hurt bad. Five others be shot in arms an' laigs. I send rider to Tanglewood to fetch Doc Trotter."

"You did exactly right, Simon," Hayden said. "Are you *sure* it was Wild Bill Longley and McKowen who did the shooting?"

"I see 'em, suh," said Simon. "I swear before God it be them. Wil' Bill, before he shoot, he holler at us. He not be satisfied, he say, until we uns all be dead er run out'n Lee County."

"That sounds like him," Hayden said grimly. "When they rode out, which way did they go?"

"North, suh."

"Bound for Indian Territory," Hayden said. "About all we can do is send a rider to the Ranger outpost in Austin, or to the Union army's commanding officer there. The telegraph might head them off at Waco, Dallas, or Fort Worth."

"If I was running from the law, bound for Indian Territory," said Nathan, "I'd shy away from any towns between here and there."

"I know," Hayden sighed, "and so will Longley and McKowen."

"My God," Viola cried, "they can't be allowed to escape. The Rangers will send a man after them."

"The Rangers have no jurisdiction in Indian Territory," said Nathan, "and from what I've heard, all the Union outposts are shorthanded. But you're right. The law should have a record of this. I'll ride to Austin tonight and report it. How far is Austin?"

"Forty-five miles," Hayden said, "but this is not your responsibility."

"As much mine as anybody's," said Nathan. "Besides, I have reasons for riding out tonight. Reasons of my own."

"You'll be coming back, won't you?" Viola asked anxiously.

"I hope so," said Nathan. He hated lies and half-truths, and he knew if he rode to Austin tonight, he would take the coward's way out and not return.

"Then saddle Daybreak," Viola said, "and I'll ride with you."

Nathan sighed. She wasn't going to make it easy for him. Now she must know what he hadn't intended telling her.

"Viola," said Nathan, "I told you I have reasons of my own for riding out tonight, and now you're forcing me to spell out those reasons. When I ride out, I'll be followed, and when the showdown comes, I don't want you in the line of fire."

"Nate Rankin, then," said Jesse Hayden.

"Rankin and maybe some hired guns," Nathan said. "If I can draw him away from here and pull his fangs, he shouldn't trouble you again. If he wants to carry a grudge, then let it be against me."

"No," said Viola, "I won't let you do it. Return his money. Nobody has to know."

"He'll know," Nathan said. "It's more than just the money. He's got his share of pride. It's time somebody poked some holes in him and let it out. It's time for me to ride. There'll be a moon later."

"Nathan," said Jesse, "I don't like this. It's a job for the law."

"Wrong," Nathan said. "The killings in Lexington are a job for the law. The law won't care a damn what I *think* Rankin's about to do. They'll be concerned only after I'm shot dead, provided there's enough proof to go after the varmints that did it. They won't be expecting me to ride out tonight and that gives me an edge. Whatever happens after I leave here, you're to know nothing about it. Understand?''

"I understand," said Hayden. "You're welcome here anytime. Simon, come in the house and Viola will make some coffee. Come on, Viola.''

Bit Viola was not easily discouraged. Suddenly Nathan found her face uncomfortably close to his, and in the lamplight from the front door, there was no mistaking the tears on her cheeks.

"I know what you're doing and why you're doing it," she said softly. "Just tell me that you won't forget me, that I'll see you again."

"I won't forget you," he said, "and if I live, somehow—somewhere—I'll see you again." Despite the presence of her father and old Simon, he kissed her long and hard. Without another word, he turned away.

"Vaya con Dios," she cried.

Nathan wasted no time. When he reached the barn, he led the black out of his stall and saddled the animal in the darkness. It took him longer to load the packhorse, for he dared not light a lantern. He led the horses out of the barn, pausing a moment. There was a light breeze out of the southwest, and it brought the fragrant odor of tobacco smoke. At least one of them had a lot to learn about stalking a man. Nathan mounted and rode south, leading the packhorse. Cotton Blossom loped on ahead.

Five hundred yards west of the Hayden barn, Hugh Rankin waited. With him were Driggers and Gadner, a pair of gunmen Nate Rankin had hired.

"Damn it, Junior,' Driggers said, "I told you to stomp out that smoke. You might as well of fired a couple of shots so he'd know we're out here."

"I told you to stop callin' me Junior," Hugh snarled, "and I don't take orders from you. Daddy put me in charge of this."

"Shut up, the both of you," Gadner said. "I thought I heard something."

"He's ridin' out," said Hugh. "Let's go after him."

"Go ahead," Driggers said sarcastically, "and get your ears shot off."

"By God," said Hugh, "if we lose him, I ain't takin' the blame."

"Perish the thought," Driggers said, with an ugly laugh. "I reckon your daddy would spank you, an' I hear he's got a heavy hand."

"Come on," said Gadner. "We'll ride a couple of miles behind him until he beds down for the night or until moonrise, whichever comes first."

"Daddy wants him dead," said Hugh. "Just don't neither of you forget what you got to do."

"Oh, we ain't about to forget," Gadner said. "Are we, Driggers?"

"Naw," said Driggers. "We got it planned out perfect."

The pair had been paid five hundred dollars apiece for the killing of Nathan Stone, but their ambition went beyond that. It was no secret that the gambler they were trailing had ridden away with ten thousand dollars of old man Rankin's gold. When the gambler was dead, who was to stop Gadner and Driggers from claiming the gold as their own? Certainly not the snot-nosed Rankin kid ...

Chapter 23

❖

Nathan rode for an hour, rested the horses, and rode on. He waited until the pale quarter moon added its glow to that of the twinkling stars. He then began seeking a suitable spot to spread his blankets for the night. He rode into a hollow and reined up beside a fast-running creek. On the farthest bank was an upthrust of waist-high boulders. Nathan led his horses a few yards up the creek. There he unsaddled the black and removed the packsaddle from his packhorse. It must appear that he had indeed made camp for the night. He spread his blankets near the creek, directly across from the stone barricade on the farthest bank. With some brush, dry leaves, and stones, he arranged his blankets so that from a distance the intruders couldn't tell he wasn't in them. While it was an old trick, it was still the best defense a man had while being stalked at night. After they cut down on his empty blankets, they wouldn't know whether he was alive or dead until he made some move. Before he fired, he must know how many men he faced, for his own muzzle flash would reveal his position. He crossed the creek, and with Cotton Blossom beside him, settled down behind his stone abutment to wait. His pursuers, when they came, must be afoot, lest their horses nicker and reveal their presence. He had a definite edge, for the night wind was out of the northwest. Cotton Blossom heard them first, for his hackles began to rise. Nathan tightened his grip on the hound. He drew and cocked his right-hand Colt. Nathan's eyes were used to the gloom beneath the trees that lined the creek and he could see them when they paused to study the mound of blankets beside the creek. Suddenly two Colts roared, then roared again. Nathan held his fire. After a long silence, a voice spoke.

"That finished him, Driggers. There's his saddle an' saddlebags. Let's have a look."

"Like hell, Gadner," said a young voice. "Daddy told me to take charge of those saddlebags. I'll get them." He stepped forward.

"You're about to get more than you bargained for, kid," said Gadner. He cocked his Colt and shot Hugh Rankin in the back.

Nathan's shot sounded like an echo of Gadner's, and the slug slammed the gunman backwards into the brush. Driggers got off one quick shot, sufficient to mark his position with a muzzle flash, and Nathan shot him. Nathan waited, lest one of the three be playing possum, but there was no sign of life. Nathan crossed the creek, gathered up his blankets, saddle, and saddlebags, and made his way to his grazing horses. Quickly he saddled the black, loaded his pack horse, and rode south.

* * *

Austin Texas. July 5, 1867.

Nathan found Ranger headquarters, and Captain Jennings was one of the two Rangers on duty. Quickly Nathan reported the killings by Longley and McKowen.

"I'll have word sent north to every outpost with the telegraph," Jennings said, "but I doubt it'll do much good. They'll expect that. One of these days, unless somebody shoots him first, Longley will get his neck stretched."

"Any more word on Virg Dillard?" Nathan asked.

"No," said Jennings, "but that bunch of renegades he's been running with is still raising hell in north Texas. You'll find them somewhere in Indian Territory or likely southern Kansas. Or worse, they'll find you. I hope this Virg Dillard is worth what it's likely to cost you, finding him. Ride careful, my friend."

* * *

Indian Territory. July 10, 1867.

Nathan rode across the Red, and with sundown just minutes away, began looking for a spring or creek where he might spend the night. Cotton Blossom was somewhere ahead, exploring these new surroundings. Nathan rode eastward along the river until he found a stream that emptied into it. The stream was the runoff from a spring, and there were numerous remains of old fires. There were bits of paper, rusted tins, and a faded paper tag from a sack of Durham. White men. Beyond the spring, half buried in leaves, a white object caught Nathan's eye. It was a human skull, its sightless eye sockets fixed grimly on the darkening sky. Had it belonged to one of the renegades who had come to a predictably bad end, or to one of their hapless victims? Nathan gathered dry wood, and using a stump hole for a fire pit, cooked supper for himself and Cotton Blossom.

"Cotton Blossom," Nathan said, "I'm counting on your ears. I'm turning in for the night."

Nathan lay awake listening to the horses cropping grass. He wasn't sure how long he'd been asleep when he suddenly awakened, uncertain as to what had roused him. There wasn't a sound. And then it hit him. The horses no longer cropped grass! Nathan rolled to his left, coming up with his right-hand Colt cocked and ready. The night erupted with gunfire, lead slapping into the blankets where Nathan had slept only seconds before. Nathan's Colt roared once, twice, three times, as he fired at muzzle flashes. A horse nickered, Cotton Blossom snarled, and there was an agonized scream. Cotton Blossom had made his presence felt. Then it ended. Again there was the reassuring sound of the horses cropping grass. The attack, for whatever purpose, hadn't succeeded. Nathan began searching in the direction from which the shots had come. He hadn't expected his hurried return fire to have found a target, but in the dim starlight he could see a body lying face down. He dared not strike a light, for there had been two bushwhackers. Had it not been for Cotton Blossom's timely attack, Nathan might have been caught in a deadly cross fire. There was a slight sound and he turned, his Colt ready, but it was only Cotton Blossom returning.

"Thanks, pard," Nathan said, fondling the dog's ears. "Without you, I'd be a dead man."

The suddeness of the attempted ambush had shaken him, and Nathan slept poorly. With the first gray light of dawn he was on his feet. The dead man was maybe thirty years old and dressed like a cowboy. His pistol lay beside him, while his holster was tied down on his right hip for a cross-

hand draw. A left-hand cross-hand draw! In the man's
pocket there was a knife and two double eagles. Fifty yards
distant, Nathan found where Cotton Blossom had surprised
the second of the two bushwhackers. On a rock out-
cropping there were brown stains, evidence that Cotton
Blossom had drawn blood. Almost a mile away, Nathan
found where the horses had been tied. The survivor had
ridden away, leading the dead man's horse, leaving a trail
that Nathan could follow at a fast gallop. After a hurried
breakfast, with Cotton Blossom trotting ahead, Nathan
rode in pursuit. He reined up after crossing a small creek.
Here his quarry had paused to cleanse his wound, leaving
behind a bloodied bandanna. Nathan rode on, stopping occasionally to rest the horses. He had ridden not more than
ten miles when Cotton Blossom came loping back to meet
him. Now *this* was an unusual occurrence. Cotton Blossom
rarely doubled back, unless summoned. He hadn't even returned when Nathan had stopped to rest the horses, for the
pause had clearly been temporary. His return made it clear
Nathan should not continue following the obvious trail. Nathan tied the packhorse's lead rope to a low-hanging pine
branch. He then rode away at a right angle, east, for a
few hundred yards. Then he resumed a northerly direction,
Cotton Blossom bounding ahead of him. Far ahead, Nathan
could see a rock- and tree-studded rise.

"If this varmint aims to hole up, Cotton Blossom, that's
a likely place," Nathan said.

He dismounted, tied his horse to a shrub, and continued
on foot. He dared not ride any closer, lest his horse nicker
and betray his presence. Cotton Blossom had gone on
ahead. Now he looked back, assured himself that Nathan
was following, and trotted on. He would know where the
bushwhacker was hiding, and experience had taught him
not to take the obvious approach. Nathan watched Cotton
Blossom, taking his direction from the dog. It soon became
obvious he was being led around the rocky, brush-shrouded
ridge. Reaching the far side, still following Cotton Blossom,
he cautiously made his way through concealing brush until
he could see two picketed horses. That should put him
somewhere behind the bushwhacker, he concluded, and he
silently thanked the ever-observant Cotton Blossom. The
bushwhacker's position was an elevated one, and he could
have fired straight ahead or to either side with ease, had

Nathan not ridden beyond his field of vision. Nathan crept on until he could see the black crown of a hat beyond some brush. He drew his left-hand Colt and shot off a branch just above the hat.

"Come out of there with your hands over your head," he shouted, "or the next shot will be a mite lower."

Slowly a head appeared above the brush, and finally, two hands.

"Come on," Nathan said impatiently, "move."

The rider wasn't much over five feet, if that. Above the left knee, the leg of his Levi's was in tatters, revealing a once-white, now bloody, bandage.

"I'm tired of skunk-striped bushwhackers," said Nathan angrily. "I ought to stomp hell out of you and then hang you upside down over a slow fire."

"Then come on, damn you, if you're man enough."

"I'm man enough," Nathan said. He strode forward, seizing the front of the faded shirt. In the resulting struggle, his adversary's hat was flung aside, and Nathan froze. This renegade was not a man, but a hard-eyed, long-haired, hellcat of a female!

While she lacked the strength of a man, she had the element of surprise, and she used it to her advantage. She threw a hard right that caught Nathan full on the nose. A bloody, blinding blow, that for a few seconds clouded his vision. Anticipating her next move, he grabbed the front of her shirt, hauling her up short just in time to save himself from a boot in the groin. But she was quick, using their proximity to one another to snatch his left-hand Colt from its holster. Nathan caught her right wrist in his left hand, forcing her to drop the revolver, and again she drove a boot toward his groin. He caught her right foot with his right hand, and with a firm grip on wrist and foot, he swept her off the ground, slamming her down flat on her back. Her head struck hard and she went limp. Nathan rolled her over, and using his bandanna, tied her hands behind her back. She now had a bloody gash on the back of her head where it had struck the edge of a stone. Retrieving his dropped Colt, Nathan spoke.

"Now, by God, what in tarnation am I goin' to do with you?"

"Turn me over," came the muffled reply. "I can't breathe."

"I'm tempted to leave you on your belly," Nathan growled, wiping his still-bleeding nose on his shirtsleeve. "Anything to water down your snake-mean disposition."

Finally, after much wriggling, he took pity on her, rolled her over and allowed her to lean against a stunted oak.

"Why don't you drag off my Levis' and tie my ankles?" she shouted. "You won't ever get a chance like this again."

"You have the body of a woman," said Nathan grimly, "but you got slickered out of everything that goes with it."

Nathan endured a round of swearing that would have put a bullwhacker to shame. Behind her, avoiding her booted feet, he took hold of her shoulders and helped her to stand. For all her hostility, she would have fallen without his support.

"Your wounds need tending," Nathan said, "but I'll need water. I'll help you to your horse and then I'll get my packhorse. I have medicine."

"It was your damn dog near chewed my leg off," she said accusingly.

"You're lucky he didn't chew on you some more, while you were kicking and clawing at me," said Nathan. "He don't take kindly to me bein' gunned down by some low-down, no-account bushwhacker."

"That wasn't my idea," she said, refusing to look at him.

"Maybe not," said Nathan, "but you were all set to help cut me down in a crossfire if Cotton Blossom hadn't changed your mind."

She had nothing more to say. When they reached her two picketed horses, Nathan examined them critically. One was a roan, the other a bay.

"We don't need two horses," Nathan said. "Which do you want?"

"The bay. He's mine."

Nathan unsaddled the roan, and the animal looked questioningly at him. After helping the girl mount the bay, he led the horse toward the place he had left his black. There was a nicker, and when he looked back, the roan was following.

"Loose my hands," the girl begged.

"I would," Nathan replied, "but for some reason, I don't

trust you. When we reach water and I've seen to your wounds, then I'll turn you loose."

Nathan mounted his black, and leading the bay, rode back and reclaimed his packhorse. With Cotton Blossom ranging ahead, and Nathan with two horses on lead ropes, they rounded the hill and headed north. The water, when they reached it, was a spring concealed by willows. It was better than Nathan had expected, for the dense foliage would dissipate smoke, lessening the danger of a fire. After helping the girl to dismount, Nathan unsaddled all three horses, allowing them to roll.

"Now," said Nathan to the still-bound girl, "if I turn you loose, can you resist clawing out my eyes while I see to your wounds?"

"I won't fight you," she said. "My leg hurts like hell."

"You could lose it," said Nathan, "if it gets infected."

Nathan untied her hands and she meekly did as he told her, stretching out on her back, her head on her saddle. Nathan started a small fire and put some water on to boil. From his pack he took yard-long lengths of white muslin for bandages, a quart of whiskey, and bottles of laudanum and disinfectant. These he spread on a folded blanket, and when the water began to boil, he brought the pot.

"I'll have to cut away the leg of your Levi's," he said.

"No," she said. "These are all I have. I'll take them down."

"If that's what you want, go ahead."

Raising herself on her elbows, she unbuttoned the Levi's and slid them down well below the wound. Nathan devoted his attention to her wound. While it wasn't deep, the skin had been torn. It should have been tended hours ago. Nathan doused it with disinfectant and was about to bind it with muslin when he recalled something his father had once told him. Puncture wounds—animal bites—must drain, and should not be bound, for the healing must begin inside.

"This wound should be left uncovered until it starts to heal," Nathan said. "It'll have to drain some."

"Meanin' I have to lay here until then, with my britches down?"

"No," Nathan said. "The bite wasn't that deep. After a day or two of keeping it clean and applying this disinfectant, it'll start to heal. If you have fever, that's a warning sign of infection, and you have to sweat it out before you begin to heal. That's what the whiskey's for. This is a good camp, and since there's a fire going, we might as well eat. Are you hungry?"

"Near starved. It's been three . . . four days . . ."

Having a closer look at her, he realized how thin she was. Her eyes were blue and her hair was red, and when she smiled—if she ever did—she would have dimples. He made coffee first, and when it was ready, he brought her a steaming cup. Recalling something he had overlooked, he took two extra blankets from his pack.

"Move over some," he told the girl. "I forgot your bare backside was on the ground."

She moved to one side and he doubled the blanket. When she was again in place, her head on her saddle, there was a heavy wool blanket beneath her. Nathan then removed the damaged Levi's, covering her with the second blanket.

"You may sweat some," he said, "but that's a good sign. Now I'll start us some grub."

Cotton Blossom had remained in camp, studying this person who had only hours ago been the enemy. Finally he trotted away into the surrounding brush, where he would remain until the food was ready. The girl's eyes followed Nathan as he prepared the meal. When Nathan took her a tin plate of beans, bacon, and hard biscuits, she had emptied her tin cup, and Nathan refilled it. He watched her eat, and when the tin plate was empty, he replenished it. She finished the second helping and drank the rest of her coffee. Then she sighed and studied Nathan for a moment before she spoke.

"Why are you doing this? If it hadn't been for your dog, I'd have done my best to kill you."

"I'm not sure," said Nathan, "unless you're more than you seemed at first. When we got past all the cussing, clawing, and kicking, I wondered if maybe you would respond to some kindness. I've heard talk about man-hating, outlaw horses, but I don't believe a horse can hate unless he's given a reason. I wonder if people, like horses, don't learn to hate because they've never known anything else?"

He had no idea how she might respond, and was amazed when a single tear rolled down her dirty cheek. Then there was a flood of them, as her slender shoulders shook with heart-wrenching sobs. Nathan made no move, for it was something of which she must purge herself. Finally, when she looked at him, he felt like he was seeing a rainbow after the storm.

"I'm eighteen years old," she said, "and I've never done . . . that . . . since I was very young."

"I reckon it's time for introductions,' said Nathan. "I'm Nathan Stone."

"I'm Lacy Mayfield," said the girl. "I'm from Springfield, Missouri."

"I'm from Virginia," Nathan said. "I was with the Confederacy, and when the war was over, I had nothing left. So I rode West."

"I'm ashamed to tell you why I'm here," she said.

"You don't have to tell me anything," said Nathan. "I don't want to know more than you're comfortable telling me."

"But I need to talk," Lacy said. "I didn't understand that about myself until . . . until you started talking to me . . . about hate. The man I was with last night, I . . . I didn't even like, but I . . . I ran away with him."

"Trouble at home, I reckon," said Nathan.

"Oh, God, yes. Pa died when I was young, and Ma married a preacher. He was evil, and I was afraid of him. He wanted me . . . took me . . . in ways that I knew were wrong. When I went to Ma, she didn't believe me. The day after I became eighteen, I . . . I left with him. Virg Dillard."

"Virg Dillard?"

The third of seven men whose acts had determined the course of Nathan's life. Dead, Dillard could not be used to obtain information as to the whereabouts of the others. Nathan felt cheated.

"Did you know Virg Dillard?" Lacy asked.

"No," said Nathan, offering the truth and no more. "I heard about him while I was in south Texas. The Rangers believed he was part of a band of renegades holed up here in Indian Territory."

"He was," said Lacy, "but he was on the outs with them. He said they owed him money. He came back to Springfield, and that's when I . . . I met him. He seemed to . . . care about me, and he talked of going to Colorado."

"But he brought you to Indian Territory," Nathan said.

"Yes. He hated the bunch he'd been riding with. He was gonna get even with 'em. But when we caught up to them, some of Quantrill's bunch had joined the band, and there was twenty or more men."

"So old Virg didn't have that much sand," said Nathan.

"No, and then we ran out of food. He said before we rode to Colorado, we must have food."

"So he aimed to ambush me and take mine," Nathan said.

"Yes. He said you were just one man, and this being Indian Territory, nobody would ever know."

"I'd have shared my grub with the both of you," said Nathan.

"I know," she said, swallowing hard. "I listened to him because I ... I didn't know what else to do. I just knew I ... I couldn't ever ... go back."

For a while, Nathan said nothing, digesting what she had told him. It had a ring of truth, and when her arrogance and hostility had been stripped away, there remained only a frightened, homeless girl. She was his only link to Virg Dillard and Dillard was dead.

"Did Dillard tell you why y'all were going to Colorado?"

"Friends of his were there," she said. "They were in the army together. There was talk of a silver mine. We were going to Denver."

While it wasn't much of a lead, it was all Nathan had. Those "friends" might well be the very renegades he was looking for.

"I've never been to Colorado," Nathan said. "It might be a good place to spend some time until the hard times that followed the war have eased up."

"I have no right to ask this," she said, "but will you take me with you? I have only the clothes I am ... was ... wearing, and my horse and saddle. Since I have no money, there's just one thing I can offer, and it ... that's been used."

"Your disposition has improved considerable," said Nathan. "All I'd want from you is the promise you won't gun me down some dark night."

"Please don't remind me of last night," she pleaded. "If it's any help, I've never fired a gun in my life. Virg told me to ... to get your attention, to just fire in the air."

"Count your blessings," Nathan said. "If you'd fired first, I'd have shot you, which would have given him time to shoot me. He was counting on that. Let's put that behind us. If we're riding to Colorado, let's talk about something more pleasant. Deal?"

"Deal," she said, and she almost smiled.

"We'll stay here the rest of the day and tonight," said Nathan. "If you don't have fever by tonight, you should be able to ride by tomorrow."

Eventually she slept, awaking as Nathan was starting supper. Feeling her eyes on him, he turned.

"The coffee woke me," she said.

"It's ready," Nathan replied. "I'll get you some."

Filling a tin cup, he took it to her. He placed the flat of his hand on her forehead. It was slightly moist.

"I feel all right," she said. "The food and coffee was what I needed."

"Maybe so," said Nathan. "You don't have any fever. After supper, I'll see to that gash on your head and pour some more disinfectant into the wound on your leg."

                    *   *   *

Nathan had a breakfast fire going when Lacy awoke. When the coffee was ready, he filled a tin cup and took it to her. Feeling her forehead, there still was no sign of fever.

"I'm all right," she said, "but I need to wash. I've been sweating under this blanket."

"After breakfast," Nathan said, "I'll boil some water. I have soap, too."

While the water was boiling, Nathan took from his pack some soap, a pair of his Levi's, and a shirt.

"The shirt and Levi's are too big for you," he said, "but you need something to wear until we reach a town. Then we'll buy some that fit."

"Thank you," she said.

"I'll leave you alone for a while," said Nathan. "I'll load the packhorse and saddle our horses."

Nathan led out, and with Lacy following, they rode northwest. Cotton Blossom ran on ahead. Nathan, mindful of that large band of outlaws with whom Virg Dillard had ridden, was thankful for the dog's vigilance. An hour or more before sundown, they came upon a swift-flowing creek. Following it a ways, they reached a secluded hollow.

"We'll camp here," Nathan said. "There's about enough time to cook some grub and put out the fire before dark."

The night passed without incident. Come first light, Nathan was about to saddle the horses when Cotton Blossom growled a warning. The packhorse nickered and there came a distant answer.

"Trouble," said Nathan. "Stand fast and try not to look scared."

Three Indians rode in from the northeast. They were gaunt and their mounts even more so. They reined up a few yards away, their eyes on Nathan's packsaddle. The spokesman for the trio grunted and then spoke.

"Much hungry. Want eat."

Nathan nodded, pointing to the still-smouldering fire. They soon had the fire going. Nathan filled the coffee pot, suspending it over the fire from an iron spider. From the pack he removed a pot with what remained of yesterday's beans, along with most of a side of bacon. He pointed to the food, telling them in sign language they were to do their own cooking. They looked at the cold beans and laughed uproariously. With their knives they hacked off rashers of bacon and wolfed it down raw. Finished, they wiped greasy hands on buckskin leggings and went after the coffee. One of them removed the lid and they took turns drinking from the pot. Cotton Blossom regarded the trio with hostility, growling when one of the Indians took a step toward him.

"Much grub," the Indian shouted, pointing at Cotton Blossom. His hand was on the haft of the Bowie knife that rode under the waistband of his buckskins.

"No," Nathan said, his hands near the butts of his Colts. Nathan hoped that would be the end of it, that the three would mount and ride away, but they didn't. The one who had been first to speak spoke again.

"Tabac," he said. "Want tabac."

"No tabac," said Nathan. He pointed to himself, shaking his head. They may or may not have understood that he had no tobacco because he didn't use it. They mounted their horses and rode south.

"My God," said Lacy, "would they eat a dog?"

"They would," Nathan said. "From what I've heard, some tribes fatten them for that purpose. Let's saddle up and ride."

Each time they stopped to rest the horses, Nathan studied the back trail. While there was no sign of the three, Nathan was uneasy. They had shown too much interest in

Nathan's pack. While they had been armed with only bows, arrows, and knives, they were in their element, and that was a definite edge. But nothing disturbed the quiet. They were passing through a stand of large oaks and suddenly an arrow tore through Nathan's arm, above his left elbow. With perfect timing, an Indian dropped from a branch overhead. He came down behind Nathan, driving a Bowie toward his throat, but instead it plunged in deep, just below Nathan's left collar bone.

The two tumbled to the ground, the Indian on top. He raised his arm for another thrust with the Bowie, only to have Cotton Blossom leap on him like an avenging terror. Nathan was free, but only for a moment. The other two Indians had taken advantage of their comrade's diversion, and now they rushed Nathan, their Bowies drawn. Nathan drew his right-hand Colt and shot one of them, but the other slammed into him and they went down. Nathan tried to hump the Indian off, and the blade thrust at his belly was driven deep into his right thigh. Suddenly there was a shot, and Nathan's assailant was flung flat on his back. Lacy hadn't been armed, but she had taken the Winchester from Nathan's saddle. The remaining Indian had lost his Bowie and was fighting for his life, as Cotton Blossom went for his throat. But the dog was bleeding from many cuts, and when Nathan had a clear shot, he killed the Indian. Cotton Blossom sank down, panting. Lacy dropped the Winchester and ran to Nathan.

"I got your rifle as quick as I could," she said. "You're bad hurt."

"Yeah," said Nathan. "I'm losing blood. Take my bandanna and knot it tight, just above the thigh wound. The others will have to wait. Bring me my horse. We must find water, make camp."

Somehow Nathan mounted his horse, and with Lacy leading the packhorse, they rode on. Cotton Blossom followed, leaving a trail of blood. The water, when they reached it, was a spring. Nathan was dizzy and all but fell out of the saddle. Lacy unsaddled the horses and managed to remove the packsaddle from the packhorse. She spread Nathan's blankets, brought his saddle for a pillow, and helped him to lie down.

"I'll get a fire going," Lacy said, "and boil some water.

I've never done anything like this before. You'll have to
help me."

Nathan said nothing. Unlike gunshot wounds, which for
a while were numb, knife and arrow wounds wasted no
time. They hurt like hell immediately. Lacy learned quickly,
and despite her inexperience, she kept her nerve at the
sight of blood. With steady hands, she cleansed the wounds
with the hot water. The arrow had cut through the flesh of
the upper arm, and when the shaft had been broken, the
deadly missive was easily removed. The knife wounds were
far more serious. The blade had gone deep, and cleansing
them did little to stop the bleeding.

"Bring some mud from the spring," Nathan said. "Lay
it on thick over the knife wounds. If we can't stop the
bleeding, I'm done."

Lacy brought the mud and halted the bleeding. She applied disinfectant—fiery alcohol—to the less serious arrow
wound and bound it with muslin. She then covered Nathan
with one of the blankets. Little more could be done until
they were sure the bleeding had stopped.

"Cotton Blossom's cut near as bad as you," said Lacy.
"While we wait for your bleeding to stop, I'll see to him,
if he'll let me."

"If he's hurtin' half as bad as me, he'll let you," Nathan said.

Timid at first, Lacy approached Cotton Blossom with the
pot of hot water and some of the clean muslin.

"I won't hurt you any worse than you're hurtin' already,
Cotton Blossom," said the girl. "Just rest easy and let me
work on you."

Cotton Blossom didn't flinch as she washed the blood
from his many cuts. Some of them needed an application
of mud to stop the bleeding, while others could be cleansed
with hot water and disinfectant.

"You can't bandage him," Nathan said. "When you've
cleaned the wounds and applied disinfectant, use a coat of
sulfur salve. There's a tin of it in my saddlebag."*

By the time Lacy went to the saddlebag for the sulfur
salve, Nathan was snoring. She found the tin of salve, but

---

*A common remedy used on open wounds of cattle, horses, and
humans.

in so doing, discovered the canvas bag that contained ten thousand dollars in double eagles. It all but took her breath away, for she had never seen more than a handful of the coins in her life. How could one man honestly accumulate such riches? Had she rid herself of one outlaw only to tie in with another? The more she considered the possibility, the less likely it seemed. She had conspired with Virg Dillard to murder Nathan Stone while he slept. Nathan had, on the other hand, treated her only with kindness, never once even suggesting that she sleep with him. Now he was hurt and needed her, but she had a horse and a sackful of gold for the taking. She fought down the temptation, ashamed of having considered it. She carefully replaced the canvas sack in the saddlebag, fastening the buckle afterward. She smeared Cotton Blossom's wounds with the salve and he watched her every move.

"Now, don't you lick that off," she said reprovingly.

It was time to look at Nathan's knife wounds again, to see if the thick coat of mud had stopped the bleeding. He awoke when she turned back the two blankets.

"The pain's eased up some," said Nathan. "The mud's doing more good than the medicine."

"I think we'd better go with the medicine," Lacy said, "unless there's still some bleeding."

But when she removed the mud packs from the wounds, the bleeding had stopped. After again cleansing the wounds with warm water, she applied plenty of disinfectant.

"Damn," said Nathan, "that alcohol must be a hundred and fifty proof. It's more painful than the wounds."

"When you're able," she said, "I want you to teach me to fire a gun."

"You did right well a while ago," he replied.

"But if I'd had a gun of my own and had known how to use it, you wouldn't have been cut so bad."

"That's behind us," said Nathan, "but this being the frontier, you ought to be able to defend yourself. I'll teach you to shoot."

Lacy cooked supper and doused the fire well before dark. She gave Nathan some laudanum to help him sleep, and by midnight he had a raging fever. She gave him whiskey. He was still feverish at dawn and she forced him to take more whiskey. Cotton Blossom remained in camp and it appeared he hadn't licked the wounds she had doctored with the salve. Nathan slept all day, and when he awoke near suppertime, he was sweating.

"Lord," he said, "get these blankets off me. I feel like I've been spitted over a slow fire, and all I can taste is that God-awful whiskey. I need water and plenty of it."

Chapter 24

It took two weeks for Nathan to heal enough to resume the journey to Colorado. He spent much of the time instructing Lacy in the use of a Colt revolver. She practiced "dry firing," lest the actual shots be heard by unwelcome visitors, and by the time Nathan was again able to ride, she had become adept at drawing and cocking the Colt.

"Once we reach a store with guns for sale," Nathan said, "I'll get you a Colt pocket pistol. It's deadly as either of mine, but it's a .31 caliber, not quite so heavy, and with a shorter barrel."

After Nathan had been wounded, Lacy had taken to spreading her blankets close to his, until one night, they overlapped.

"Lacy," he said, "I ... I'm not ready for anything to ... happen."

"I'm old enough to know my own mind," she snapped. "Whatever happens, I'm not expecting anything from you."

"I believe you," said Nathan, "but a man's responsible for what he does. If he compromises a woman with no intention of standing by her, then he's less of a man. All you know about me is that I'm from Virginia, that I rode West after the war. I'm riding a vengeance trail, Lacy, and there's no place for a woman."

"A woman can make a place for herself," Lacy said. "Why do you think I'm learning to fire a gun? You were so interested in Virg Dillard, I felt like it was him—or one like him—that you're after."

"Lacy, Dillard was the third of seven men I've sworn to kill."

"Then I don't feel so bad about you killing him," she said. "He must have done somethin' awful."

"He did," said Nathan. "Him and six riding with him."

She deserved to know the truth, and without sparing himself, he told her. She listened in silence, and it was a while after he finished before she spoke. When she did, her reaction was much like Eulie's had been.

"Why couldn't I have had a family that meant as much to me as yours did to you?" she asked. "You made a promise, and I understand your need to keep it. It's the last thing you'll ever be able to do for your Pa. Let me ride with you as far as I can, as far as you want me. I've never had much, Nathan, and I'm taking what I can get, while I can get it. You don't hold that against me, do you?"

"No," Nathan said. "We all have to play out each hand as the cards are dealt to us. I don't spend all my time shooting no-account skunks. I'm a gambling man, and I'm not broke. When we come to a town, I'll stake you to some finery."

"I've never had finery," she said, "and I don't know that I'd want any. But I would like to have more than one shirt and one pair of Levi's, and the Colt pistol. I've been afraid most of my life, and I don't want to live the rest of it that way."

Nathan reined up his horse near a creek. There he saw the very thing he had been dreading. All the animals had been shod. The tracks led in from the east and fanned out toward the northwest, the same direction he and Lacy were riding. Nathan counted the tracks of at least twenty horses as he rode. While there were some Union forts in Indian Territory, it was doubtful any of them could muster a patrol large enough to account for so many horses. A more sinister possibility was that these riders were renegades.

"There were so many horses," said Lacy, "these must have been the outlaws Virg rode with."

"I have no doubt they are," Nathan said. "Twenty horses or more, and they're somewhere ahead of us, maybe just a few hours. But if they're bound for a raid, it'll have to be in Kansas. Texas is the other way."

*   *   *

The next morning, after they had first seen the tracks, Nathan was loading the packhorse when he heard the distant rattle of gunfire. It was loud enough for Lacy to hear it too, for the wind was out of the northwest.

"Mount up," said Nathan. "I've been expecting us to

catch up to that bunch. They've got one hell of a fight going with somebody. Whoever it is, I expect they're needin' all the help they can get."

"But there's just one of you," Lacy protested. "I haven't actually fired a Colt, and I don't have a rifle. Nathan, that's not our fight."

"It will be," said Nathan grimly, "and I'm of a mind to pitch in while I've got some help. How long do you think we can ride the back trail of that many outlaws without them turning on us?"

"I was hoping we might stay far enough behind them . . ."

"Lacy," Nathan said, "when you hide in the brush to avoid a fight, you always lose, because you're always at the mercy of your enemy, whatever move he chooses to make. That hard experience and two hunks of lead is all I have to show for my years with Mr. Lee's army. I want you to stay put and hold the horses. Nothing more. In a strategic position, one man with a Winchester can make a hell of a difference in anybody's fight. Now let's ride."

She mounted, keeping her silence, but Nathan sensed she wasn't pleased with his decision. So be it. Men did what they must, anticipating victory, without agonizing over the consequences of possible defeat. As they drew near the conflict, Nathan reined up. There was a tree-lined ridge ahead, and the conflict was such that powder smoke rose from the brush.

"Lacy," said Nathan, "I want you to remain here, out of sight. Tie the packhorse and your own mount. I aim to flank this fight and see just who's shooting at who."

He rode west until he was past the line of skirmishers on the ridge. He then rode north until he reached the crest of the same ridge, and from there he could see the powder smoke rising from the opposite ridge. The men under fire, whoever they were, had been trapped in a thicket that partially concealed a shallow arroyo where the foot of one ridge joined that of the other. The slopes of the ridges didn't have enough cover to conceal a cottontail. The defenders were caught in a withering crossfire, and as Nathan watched, one of them was hit. He staggered from cover and was hit again. He wore the blue of a Union soldier. Nathan rode along the ridge until he reached the first man's position. Saving his Winchester, he drew his Colt and cut down the outlaw. He rode on, taking out a second man.

The roar of his Colt was lost in the fire from the long guns, and while the concealed men ahead of him were unaware of his presence, their comrades on the next ridge had spotted him. They began shooting at Nathan instead of the men in blue, but he was out of range. He continued along the ridge, and as he eliminated the riflemen, their confederates began to notice the diminishing fire from their line. The last three or four backed away from the crest of the ridge and stood up, and what they saw sent them running for their horses. Nathan holstered his Colt and cut loose with the Winchester. He knocked down one of the fleeing men while the others escaped into the brush along the upper end of the ridge. Nathan heard a slight noise and found Cotton Blossom approaching from the rear. The dog had bowed out, for there had been too many guns and too many men. The firing from the opposite ridge had ceased, and as a result, there was no more firing from the besieged men below.

"You men in the arroyo," Nathan shouted, "I'm friendly. Come on out."

"Who are you?" came a shouted inquiry.

"Nathan Stone," Nathan replied. "Who are you?"

"Lieutenant Lanford," came the response. "I'm officer in charge of a patrol from Camp Supply, just north of here. I have one man dead and two wounded. Can you help us?"

There still was no activity on the far ridge, so Nathan trotted his horse down the slope. The lieutenant and six men were unhurt. One of the wounded men had been hit in the side, the other in the shoulder, high up.

"What happened to your horses?" Nathan asked.

"After they'd trapped us here," said Lanford, "they threw enough lead to spook our mounts. Last we saw of them, they were galloping down this arroyo."

"My horse won't be of much help to you," said Nathan. "I'll ride down yonder a ways and see if I can catch your mounts."

Fortunately, the outlaws hadn't known whether Nathan was one man or ten, so they had made no effort to gather or further stampede the soldiers' horses. Nathan caught them without difficulty and led them back to the grateful soldiers.

"I have a packhorse beyond that ridge," Nathan said, "and there's medicine, if you want to see to your wounded men."

"We're obliged," said Lieutenant Lanford. "We'll need water, and there's a spring maybe two miles north of here. Get your pack horse; we'll wait."

Nathan rode out as they were tying the dead soldier across his saddle. Lacy's relief was obvious when she saw that Nathan was unharmed, and as they rode to where the soldiers waited, he explained the situation to her. Even the lieutenant was speechless when Nathan introduced Lacy, but they all recovered quickly, removing their hats. As they rode on toward the spring, Lieutenant Lanford explained what had happened.

"There were twenty or more of them. We were outnumbered at least two to one, and they must have had an advance rider. They knew we were coming, and they had plenty of time to let us ride into a trap. I feel like a damn fool, begging your pardon, ma'am."

"At least eight of them are dead," said Nathan. "When you file your report, you don't have to say who shot them. That ought to help some."

"Yes," Lanford said, "it will help if we can report at least some of the thieves and killers have paid for their crimes. We received telegraphed word from Fort Worth that this bunch had been looting and killing in Texas. There seems to be some method to their madness, and that suggested to us that while the law's looking for them in Texas, they might strike somewhere in southern Kansas. Trouble is, nobody told us there was so many of them."

"From what I've heard," Nathan said, "they've added to their number, and they might have done that since they were in Texas."

"I can believe that," said the officer. "The last report we had, there was perhaps a dozen men."

"Well," Nathan said, "you can report that they're *back* to a dozen. In the information you've received, has there been any mention of names? I'm looking for four varmints, and this bunch you tangled with seems like just the kind of sidewinders they'd throw in with."

"No names," said Lieutenant Lanford. "It seems they're a mixture of deserters, thieves, and killers, with different men coming and going."

"While you're caring for your wounded," Nathan said, "I aim to ride back to that ridge and see if I can identify any of the dead. Besides, they likely had horses picketed that should be turned loose. Will you be spending the night here?"

"No," said Lanford. "We're no more than thirty miles south of Camp Supply. Your medicine will help, and we're obliged, but there's a medic on post, and I want him to tend these wounded men. They'll be less able to ride tomorrow than they are today."

"I respect your judgement, Lieutenant," Nathan said. "We'll ride on with you and spend the night at your fort, if we may."

"Do," Lanford said, "and welcome."

"Lacy," said Nathan, when they reached the spring, "I'll be back as soon as I can." He mounted and rode back the way they had come, meeting Cotton Blossom. Wary of the soldiers, he had been lagging behind.

Nathan found where the renegades had tied their horses. He found little of interest in their saddlebags except a change of clothes, hard biscuits, and jerked beef. He turned the horses loose, tying the reins around the saddle horns. He then began the most disagreeable part of his task—going through the pockets of the dead men. The results were disappointing, for he found no identification. Several of the men had more than a hundred dollars in double eagles, and that he took, for it would be of no use to them. He mounted and rode back to the spring, finding Lieutenant Lanford and his men had already built a fire and heated water.

"Nobody had any identification," Nathan said, dismounting.

"That's not surprising," said Lieutenant Lanford. "It's doubtful that any of them are using their real names. We'll be ready to move out in half an hour."

Lieutenant Lanford called for frequent rests for the sake of the wounded soldiers, and it was early afternoon when they reached a wide, deep river.

"This is the North Canadian," the officer said, for Nathan's benefit. "The fort's maybe ten miles from here, on the north bank."

Lieutenant Lanford led the column to a shallow crossing, and they rode northwest along the north bank. In less than an hour they were able to see the log palisades of Camp Supply. Soldiers walked the parapets, but the log gates remained closed until Lieutenant Lanford hailed one of the sentries. The gates were then opened. The soldiers on duty eyed Lacy, then Nathan, and finally, the body of the soldier roped to his saddle.

"Nathan Stone wishes to speak to the post commander," said Lieutenant Lanford.

"Sergeant of the guard," one of the sentries shouted.

"The post commander is Captain Chanute," Lieutenant Lanford told Nathan. "Protocol demands that you meet with him, stating your purpose for being in Indian Territory. What you choose to tell him regarding your ... ah ... encounter with the renegades is entirely up to you."

"I never volunteer information," said Nathan. "Prepare your report as you see fit."

"You're a generous man, Stone. There may be some bounty on those dead men, and I can't claim it."

"And I don't want it," Nathan replied. "Leave me out of your report."

The sergeant of the guard arrived and saluted.

"At ease, Sergeant," said Lieutenant Lanford. "This is Nathan Stone and the lady is Lacy Mayfield. Please escort them to Captain Chanute's office. This," he said, speaking to Nathan, "is Sergeant Wilson. I'll talk to you again before you leave the post."

Sergeant Wilson saluted and had his salute returned; then he nodded to Nathan and Lacy. As he led them to meet the commanding officer, Nathan noticed the rundown, dilapidated state of Camp Supply. There was an overall appearance of seediness and decay. Entire log sections—especially those nearest the ground—were rotting away. Much of the mud chinking had fallen from the log walls, and if Camp Supply ever became a permanent military installation, the entire post would have to be torn down and rebuilt. The sergeant knocked on a door, opening it when a voice granted entry. Captain Chanute stood up behind a battered desk, returning the sergeant's salute. "At ease, Sergeant," he said.

"Sir," said Sergeant Wilson, "this is Nathan Stone and Lacy Mayfield. They rode in with Lieutenant Lanford and his patrol. They request a meeting with you."

Nathan looked around. The captain's desk had seen a hard life, as had his swivel chair, but at least the office had a crude wooden floor.

"You are excused, Sergeant," said Captain Chanute, and

when the sergeant had departed, he spoke to Nathan and Lacy. "Welcome to Camp Supply. As you can see, we have little to offer in the way of convenience and comfort. What do you wish of me?"

"We're on our way to Colorado Territory," Nathan said, "and we understand it's the proper thing to do, telling you our reason for being here."

"It is," said Chanute, "for your sake and ours. It seems we're being overrun by renegades and outlaws who have become unwelcome elsewhere."

"We're somewhat familiar with them, Captain," Nathan said. "We had the good fortune of joining Lieutenant Lanford's patrol, following a fight. We will be riding out in the morning. Exactly where are we?"

"By noon tomorrow," said Chanute, "you'll be in Kansas. Just before you leave Indian Territory, you'll cross the Cimarron River. From there, you'll be maybe twenty-five miles from Fort Dodge."*

"With your permission," Nathan said, "we'd like to visit the sutler's store. We're shy a few things."

"You have my permission," said Chanute, "but don't get your hopes too high. This is not as well-provisioned a post as those nearer civilization. Everything must be freighted in, from Leavenworth or Santa Fe, and thieves are as numerous as buzzards. Quanah Parker and the Comanches are rampant in west Texas and eastern New Mexico, murdering teamsters and soldier escorts, and, in general, robbing us blind. Here in Indian Territory and southern Kansas, it's white renegades and bands of Kiowa."

In the sutler's store, Nathan and Lacy found many things in short supply and others lacking entirely. There was no sugar, no coffee, no flour, no guns or ammunition. Nathan bought Lacy a new pair of boots, two shirts, and two pair of Levi's. While they were there, Lieutenant Lanford came in.

"You're welcome to take your meals with us," the lieutenant said, "and there are cabins you can use for the night. But I must warn you, unless it's raining or snowing, I spread my blankets outside, because I don't much like spiders and other things dropping on me during the night."

"I'll be sleeping outside," Lacy said.

---

*Dodge City was founded in 1872, eight miles west of the fort.

"I reckon I will be too," said Nathan.

Nathan brought the horses inside the stockade, and since graze was out of the question, each of the animals was given a measure of grain. Watering troughs were plentiful. There being nothing else to do, Nathan and Lacy lay down next to the stockade wall, heads on their saddles.

"I reckon the worst of Indian Territory's behind us," Nathan said. "When we reach Fort Dodge, we'll look for your Colt there."

It was near suppertime, and when the bugler blew mess call, Nathan and Lacy waited until the soldiers had entered the mess shack. Surprisingly, the strength of the post numbered only thirty-one men, including Captain Chanute. Nathan and Lacy took tin plates, tin cups, and eating tools. There was hot coffee, beans, and fried steak. Almighty tough steak. They were about to take seats at one of the rough tables when Nathan remembered Cotton Blossom. The dog had followed him inside, but, unsure of his status, he waited beside the door. But the soldiers had seen Cotton Blossom, and before Nathan could make a move, a corporal shouted.

"Looky here, boys! I knowed if we waited long enough, somethin' would come along with teeth enough to eat cookie's steak."

Everybody laughed except the disgruntled cook, and more than one soldier beckoned to Cotton Blossom. They offered him hunks of steak, and with his belly overriding his distrust, he wasted no time in accepting the food. The men whooped and hollered, for this was a rare diversion. When Cotton Blossom had accepted each offering, he trotted back to the door and sat down.

"I swear," said the cook, "the dog's got better manners than the lot o' ye scutters."

*   *   *

As Nathan and Lacy departed Camp Supply the following morning, a burial detail dug a grave for the soldier who had been killed the day before.

"I'm sorry about yesterday," Lacy said. "You were right. There were so few soldiers, they wouldn't have had a chance without your rifle."

"We owe them our lives," said Nathan. "I made a difference because those renegades split their forces and because I had the element of surprise. When you have to fight, take the offensive and do it on your own terms."

Nathan and Lacy reached the Cimarron, rode across and entered Kansas. The sun was barely noon-high. They rode on, and after resting the horses, allowed them to drink sparingly when water was available.

"We'll reach Fort Dodge before dark," Nathan predicted.

Following Lieutenant Lanford's directions, they rode on across the muddy Arkansas, following it westward. The fort, when they first saw it, was all that Camp Supply hadn't been. The stockade had a look of permanence, and beside the river, Union soldiers marched in close-order drill. Sentries walked in parapets high above the walls, and Nathan heard one of them shout to someone below. Nathan and Lacy had been seen, and as they approached the huge gates, they were swung open. A sentry stood before him, his rifle at port arms.

"Identify yourselves and state your business," the soldier ordered.

"I'm Nathan Stone," Nathan replied, "and the lady is Lacy Mayfield. We are civilians, bound for Colorado Territory."

*   *   *

Fort Dodge, Kansas. August 5, 1867.

Again Nathan and Lacy met with the post commander. This time it was Major Hennessy, and Nathan told him nothing except that they were on their way to Colorado. Again they visited the sutler's store, and it seemed to have just about everything, including a saloon. Nathan had no trouble finding the Colt pocket pistol, so he bought one, along with four hundred loads for it. The men in the adjoining saloon were all eyes, despite Lacy's shirt and Levi's. Most of them were bearded, and from their dress, buffalo hunters. There was one, however, who had the look of a professional gambler or gunman. He was dressed in a dark suit, flowing red tie, flat-crowned hat, and polished black boots. A Colt was tied low on his right hip. He sauntered out of the saloon and into the store. Removing his hat, he bowed before Lacy.

"Dalton Gibbons, ma'am, and I'd be pleased to make your acquaintance."

"The lady's with me," Nathan said grimly, "and she won't be making your acquaintance."

"Oh?" said Gibbons. "And who are you? Her daddy?"

"Close enough," Nathan replied, and his right fist against Gibbons's chin had the solid sound of an axe thunking into a log. Gibbons crashed into a wall, bringing down a shelf of lamp globes. They smashed in a crescendo of tinkling glass, bringing everybody from the store and the saloon on the run. One of those drawn to the scene happened to be a United States marshall who had been assigned to the territory. It was he who confronted Nathan.

"I'm Marshal Jed Summerfield," he said. "I suppose you had a good reason for that."

"I'm Nathan Stone," Nathan replied. "He was molesting the lady who is with me."

A big man, six-and-a-half feet tall and weighing near three hundred pounds stalked up to Nathan. He was dressed in striped trousers, white boiled shirt, and sleeve garters. He ignored the marshal, speaking to Nathan.

"I don't care a damn *what* your reason was, pilgrim. You owe me money. Pay up, and then get the hell out of here."

Gibbons had gotten groggily to his feet and was approaching Nathan, fire in his eye and blood oozing from the corners of his mouth. The marshal hauled him up short, leaving Nathan to face the big man from the store. There seemed only one way out.

"I'll pay for the globes," said Nathan. "How much?"

"A dozen of them at a dollar apiece. Ever' damn globe I had in stock."

It was more than they were worth, but Nathan paid. He then took Lacy's arm and guided her out of the store. Throughout the ordeal, she had spoken not a word, and when she finally spoke, it did nothing to improve Nathan's mood.

"I'm sorry you had to fight because of me."

"There was nothing else I could do," Nathan said. "He came after you like you were a saloon whore. I don't like that damn marshal, either. Come on. We're riding to Colorado."

They rode west, following the Arkansas River, Cotton Blossom running on ahead. They weren't more than a dozen miles from Fort Dodge when Nathan reined up.

"Why are we stopping?" Lacy asked. "There's another hour of daylight."

"I have some unfinished business to attend to," said Nathan, dismounting. "Get down."

She dismounted. Nathan unsaddled her horse and his own, and then unloaded the packhorse. By then, the dust along their back trail was obvious, even to Lacy.

"He's following us," Lacy said. "What are you going to do?"

"I reckon that'll be up to him," said Nathan. "I'll shoot the varmint if he won't have it any other way."

She took notice of the grim set of his jaw and wisely said no more. As she had begun to learn, life on the frontier was one absolute after another. The only middle ground was that where the weak and indecisive were buried. Dalton Gibbons reined up a hundred yards away and shouted his challenge.

"You surprise me, Stone. You didn't strike me as being the kind who would run, denying me satisfaction." He dismounted, his hand near the butt of his Colt.

"There's no satisfaction in dying," Nathan replied, beginning his walk. "I don't believe in killing a man for his first mistake. You're about to make your second and last. It's your play, when you're ready."

Speechless, Lacy Mayfield looked on in horror. Trying to watch them both, she found she could not, for her eyes were drawn to Nathan. His hands swung at his sides, as though drawing a pistol was the farthest thing from his mind. The distance lessened until only eighty yards remained. Seventy. Sixty. Forty.

Gibbons drew first. Lacy caught the movement from the corner of her eye, and while he seemed incredibly fast, Nathan's Colt was already spitting lead. Gibbons' arm sagged, and his single shot slammed into the dirt at his feet. He seemed to stumble, and when he fell flat on his back, a gust of wind took his hat, cartwheeling it toward the river. Not looking back, Nathan slid his Colt into the holster and headed for the grazing horses.

"We'll ride a ways yet, before we make camp," he said.

*   *   *

Colorado Territory. September 10, 1867.

Nathan and Lacy took their time, following the Arkansas River until they were out of Kansas. Gradually the land changed. Far to the west, snow had silvered the peaks of a mighty mountain range.*

Eventually they came upon a large boulder, across the face of which some untalented soul had scrawled "Colorado Terr."

"To what part of it are we going?" Lacy asked.

"Denver," said Nathan. "Virg Dillard told you he had friends there, that they were interested in a silver mine. These hombres could be the very bunch of varmints I'm after, and if I have to ride through a lot of mining towns, I'd as soon start with the biggest one. One thing I forgot. We should have bought coats, gloves, and more blankets."

"I've never seen it so cold, so early in the fall," said Lacy. "We'd be lots warmer if we ..."

"Slept together," Nathan finished.

"Yes," she said, not looking at him.

"Tonight, then," Nathan said, "unless you change your mind."

She didn't.

*   *   *

Nathan broke ice so the horses could drink and for the making of breakfast coffee.

"Soon as we reach a town with a mercantile," he said, "we'll outfit ourselves with warm clothes. Some long handles, if we can find them."

"Long handles?"

"Wool underwear," Nathan said. "They cover you all over, from your neck to your feet."

"They sound nice," she said, "but how do you ..."

"There's a flap in the seat," said Nathan. "It unbuttons."

---

*The Rockies.

They continued riding northwest, and after two days, had come upon no town or settlement.

"Good cattle country," Nathan observed, "but it'll be hell in winter, when the snow's neck deep."

Chapter 25

There were many mercantiles in Denver. Choosing one of the largest, Nathan and Lacy found an enormous selection of clothing. They each chose a sheepskin-lined, waist-length coat, sheepskin-lined gloves, and a dozen pair of wool socks.

"Now," said Nathan to the bespectacled clerk, "we want some heavy wool long handles."

"We . . . ah . . . don't have them for ladies, sir," the man said, embarrassed.

"I kind of expected that," said Nathan. "Is there any law against a lady wearing a man's long handles?"

"Ah . . . not that I know of, sir."

"Then we'll take six pairs of them," Nathan said. "Three to fit her, and three to fit me."

After considerable inquiring, Nathan learned of a boarding place to the south of town known as Cherry Creek Manor. There was a livery, and the owners—Ezra and Josephine Grimes—reminded Nathan of his friends, Barnaby and Bess McQueen. Nathan only told them Lacy's first name.

"Dollar a day for you and the wife," said Josephine, "or twenty dollars a month. That's with meals. The livery's Ezra's business. He'll take care of your horses."

"Dollar a day, per horse," Ezra said, "or twenty dollars a month. That's with grain."

"Here's a hundred dollars for all of us, for a month," Nathan said. "Do you object to Cotton Blossom, my dog?"

"Not as long as he behaves himself," said Josephine. "I'll feed him for free, long as he ain't too picky."

"He's easy satisfied," Nathan said. "He'll eat anything

that don't bite him first, and all he expects is that there be plenty of it."

"Bring him with you to the dining room," said Josephine, "and he can eat in the kitchen. Breakfast is at seven, dinner's at noon, with supper at five. You're welcome to use the parlor from seven in the morning until ten at night. We have a pretty respectable library, too. Ezra used to teach school."

The "manor" consisted of a series of cabins, each with two large rooms. They were built of logs and were well sealed, and although they shared a chimney, each had its own fireplace. Nathan unlocked the door to their side, and they found it adequate and comfortable. The bed, made of cedar, had a feather tick. There was a dresser with an attached mirror, two ladderback chairs, a white porcelain pitcher with matching basin, and a chamber pot. There were curtains on each of the two windows and a heavy oval rug on the wooden floor.

"They think I'm your missus," Lacy said, "and you didn't tell them any different."

"Why bother?" said Nathan. "You're playing the game, so you might as well have the name."

They were two hours away from supper, and Lacy donned a pair of the long handles. Nathan watched her fall on the bed, burying herself in the feather tick.

"We have plenty of time," she said. "Why don't you join me?"

"With or without your long handles?"

"Without," she said.

*   *   *

Supper proved to be an interesting affair, for most of the "boarders" who gathered at the table were professional people. Ames Tilden interested Nathan, for he was president of Denver Bank and Trust, one of the first banks in the Territory. He and Eva Barton took control of the conversation, and everybody else listened. Eva, as Nathan and Lacy learned, was an actress, performing nightly at Denver's Palace Theatre.

"There's a new melodrama coming to the Palace," said Eva excitedly. "It's *Under the Gaslight,* and was first presented to New York audiences this past August. Our open-

ing night is December sixth. All of you simply must
attend."*

It was an interesting interlude. Nathan and Lacy remained
after the meal, joining some of the other residents in the
parlor. Lacy quickly gained the friendship of the actress by
asking numerous questions, and when Nathan and Lacy returned to their quarters, Lacy had the promise of passes to
the opening performance of the new melodrama.

"I didn't know you were interested in the theatre," Nathan said.

"I didn't know it myself, until tonight," said Lacy. "Listening to Eva, talking to her, it all came back to me. When
Pa died and Ma remarried—when I was so unhappy—I
pretended that I lived in St. Louis, that I rode in fancy
carriages, that I was somebody. It became real to me, and
I . . . I believed it."

"Maybe you should talk to Eva about getting into the
theatre," Nathan said. "I've never been to the theatre, but
I've heard you can learn the trade by becoming an understudy. I reckon you have to work for nothing until you
learn what to do and when to do it."

"God," said Lacy, "I could never do anything as glamor-
ous as that. I'm just a coward. I escaped into my dreams
because I hated my life like it was."

But the more Lacy saw of Eva Barton, the more she
changed. At first, she and Nathan attended the theatre, but
Nathan grew tired of the repetition. So there were nights
when Lacy went with Eva, remaining backstage.

Nathan spent his days learning the town and visiting various saloons. There were many, such as the Albany, the
Windsor, the Silver Dollar, the Brown Palace, and the Denver Bagnio, owned by Laura Evans. Competition was fierce,
and some saloons employed barbers. It was a convenient
means for more timid patrons to sneak a few drinks before
or after a haircut or shave.

But all Nathan's time wasn't spent in saloons. He developed a friendship with the banker, Ames Tilden, and taking
Tilden's advice, deposited most of his money in the bank.
He had gained the banker's confidence by expressing an
interest in mining. By doing so, it entitled him to ask ques-

---

Under the Gaslight was written by rising playwright Augustin Daly.

tions about mines in Colorado Territory. He pursued the lead he had gotten from Lacy regarding the possibility that Clint Foster and Milo Jenks were in Colorado because of a silver mine. But Ames Tilden quickly dashed all his hopes.

"There have been traces of silver to the south of here," said Tilden, "but it's all been low grade ore. Nobody's going to kill himself digging for a pittance in silver, when there's gold to be had."

"I reckon not," Nathan said. "How far south is gold being mined?"

"The most prominent mines," said Tilden," are Gregory Diggings, Idaho Springs, California Gulch, and Fairplay. They're all within a day's ride, and along the plains, before you get into the foothills approaching the divide. There are some lesser diggings farther south, but most have played out. One such place that's still being worked—on the Rio Grande, not more than a dozen miles this side of New Mexico Territory—has a town built around the diggings. It's called Ciudad de Oro."*

"But you don't think it's worth considering."

"Probably not. There are far more promising mines—gold and silver—in Nevada and southern Arizona. In Nevada, there's Virginia City, Gold Hill, Wellington, Aurora, Rawhide, Tonopah, Goldfield, Pioche, and Callville. In south central Arizona, there's the Tip Top and the Vulture. Southwest from there is the Texas Hill, the Ajo, the Cooper, and the Tubec. There are others, I'm sure. There are government maps available, if you're interested."

"Get me those maps," Nathan said, "and I'll pay for them. What I'm looking for may not be in Colorado."

Denver. December 4, 1867.

Nathan rode to several of the mines nearest Denver, but found not a trace of either of the men he sought. He wasn't surprised, as he could not imagine killers involving themselves in anything even close to honest labor. Nathan returned in the early afternoon to Cherry Creek Manor to find Ezra, Josephine, Lacy, Eva Barton, and a local doctor gathered around a sheet-covered utility table in the

---

*City of Gold. In 1878, this became the site of Alamosa, Colorado.

Grimes's kitchen. Cotton Blossom lay on his left side. His right hind leg and most of his hindquarters oozed blood.

"Nathan," Lacy cried, tears streaking her cheeks, "he's been shot."

"Who did it?"

"We have no idea," Ezra said. "He'd dragged himself as far as the road, and I found him as I was returning from town. This is Doc Embry. I rode back to town for him, and he's promised to do what he can."

"This is completely beyond any training I've had," said the doctor. "He's been hit with buckshot. I've managed to stop the bleeding. Now it'll all depend on how deep the lead is, and whether or not it's damaged any vital organs. For a certainty the lead will have to be removed."

"Do what you can, doc," Nathan said. "If there's anything you need, any medicine . . ."

"What I have with me will be sufficient," said Embry. "All I can do is remove the lead and disinfect the wound. After that, he'll be up against the same danger as a man with a gunshot wound. The infection could kill him."

"God," Nathan groaned, "how do you get whiskey down a dog?"

"You don't," said the doctor, "and it wouldn't matter if you could. A dog doesn't sweat. Right now, he's more dead than alive, and all I can tell you to do is wrap him in blankets, get him before a roaring fire, and try to raise his body temperature. He can't sweat, but he can pant. See that he at least does that. In the morning, if he's still alive, remove the bandage and douse the wound with more disinfectant. Keep him warm until he dies or shows some signs of healing."

With that, Doc Embry began the tedious job of probing for the buckshot, and not even Nathan could stomach that. He turned away, recalling the miles he and Cotton Blossom had traveled together, wondering if this trail would be the last one. Josephine left the room for a few minutes and returned with an armload of blankets.

"These have been retired until there was a need for them," she said.

Doctor Embry worked for almost an hour removing all the lead pellets. He doused the wound with disinfectant and bandaged it as best he could. He cleaned his instruments, returned them to his satchel, and then he spoke.

"He's more fortunate than I at first thought. He didn't

take a full load, but enough to cost him a lot of blood. Keep him warm, or better yet, hot. If he makes it through tomorrow, he'll be all right."

"I'm obliged, Doc," said Nathan, insisting that the doctor accept a double eagle.

When Doctor Embry had gone, Nathan and Ezra carefully wrapped Cotton Blossom in all the blankets, until only his nose was visible.

"I'll build a fire at our place," Nathan said. "You folks have done more than enough, and I'll stay up with him tonight."

"You'll need hot coffee," said Josephine. "Build up the fire here in the parlor, and lay him before it. We'll stay up and keep you company."

And that's the way it was. Nathan kept adding wood to the fire, and he sweated far into the night. Each time he touched Cotton Blossom's nose, it felt warm. Before dawn he was exhausted, and Ezra took over adding wood to the fire. Nathan slept an hour, and when he awoke, he thought his eyes were deceiving him, for the bundle of blankets was moving! Dropping to his knees, he drew the blankets away from Cotton Blossom's head, to find the dog looking at him.

"By God," Nathan shouted, "he's gonna make it!"

Ezra Grimes knelt beside him, feeling Cotton Blossom's nose.

"He's better," said Ezra, "but he ain't gonna be lopin' around for quite a spell."

"I expect he thinks we're trying to roast him alive," Josephine said. "Ezra, fix up a wide wooden box for him. With that mess of blankets, he ought to be plenty warm in the kitchen, next to the stove. He's welcome to sleep there until he heals."

Cotton Blossom improved and began to eat. Often. It would be a while before he could walk, however. Josephine seemed to enjoy his company.

"She should have had a houseful of young'uns," Ezra confided. "We had a son, and he died young."

*   *   *

Denver. December 6, 1867.

It was still early, hours before Nathan would escort Lacy to the Palace Theatre for the first performance of *Under the Gaslight.* With Cotton Blossom on the mend and time on his hands, Nathan's mind turned again to the elusive Clinton Foster and Milo Jenks. Damn it, if he failed to find them in Colorado, where would he go from here? Frustrated, he rode into town, determined to visit every saloon there at least one more time. Some of them wouldn't open until noon. In the first two, he encountered bleary-eyed barkeeps who told him nothing. The third saloon—the Denver Bagnio—had a whorehouse upstairs and a single patron in the saloon. Nathan ordered a beer, and when the barkeep brought it, he posed the same question that had gone unanswered many, many times.

"I'm looking for a pair of hombres name of Clinton Foster and Milo Jenks. Ever hear of them?"

"Friend," said the barkeep, "I don't remember names worth a damn. Keeps me out of trouble."

Nathan finished his beer and was about to go, when the Bagnio's lone patron caught his eye. Dressed in miner's garb, he hoisted the bottle, and Nathan thought he was being offered a drink. Out of courtesy, he spoke.

"Thanks, pardner, but it's too early for that."

"Hell, that wasn't what I was meanin'. Bring *me* a bottle, and I'll tell you about them varmints you was askin' about. They friends of yours?"

"No," Nathan said. "Barkeep, bring this gent another bottle of whatever he's drinking. I'm buying."

"Now," said Nathan, taking a chair, "what do you have to say that's worth a bottle of whiskey?"

"Depends," he said, "on how much you want to know about Foster an' Jenks. I can tell you where they was two weeks ago, an' what they was doin'."

"Then tell me."

The stranger said nothing, waiting until the barkeep brought the bottle. He pulled the cork with his teeth, filled his glass and emptied it. Only then did he speak.

"Virginia City, Nevada. Foster an' Jenks is part of a bunch of thieves that's robbin' miners of their gold. Kind of like the Plummer gang, back in Virginia City, Montana Territory, in sixty-three an' -four. These two-legged varmints wait till you got enough gold in your poke to make it worth their while, an' then they bushwhack you. Me an' two other hombres snuck out in the middle of the night an' escaped 'em. They purely ain't no law, an' these sidewinders hang around the saloons an' play cards, waitin' for some fool to wind up his diggings an' try to leave with his gold. This Foster an' Jenks, besides bein' thieves an' killers, is just poison mean. I seen 'em provoke a man into a fight an' then beat him to death."

"You're sure about the names, then," Nathan said.

"Hell, yes, I'm sure. They claim to be from Missouri, an' they talk like it. They look like some of the trash that might of deserted durin' the war. Are you the law?"

"No," said Nathan, kicking back his chair. He got up and left before any more questions could be directed at him. He didn't know the man's name, but that wasn't important, for his story had a ring of truth. Nathan rode back to Cherry Creek Manor. Despite his strong lead, he wanted those maps Ames Tilden had promised, even if he had to wait for them.

Under the Gaslight opened to capacity crowds. It was a major production, with musicians in the orchestra pit. Nathan was impressed. Later, when he and Lacy were alone in their quarters, she made an announcement that didn't surprise Nathan.

"Monday, I'm reading for a part in *Under the Gaslight*. If I'm good enough, I'll become Eva's understudy. Do you think I can do it?"

"Yes," said Nathan, "I believe you have the feeling for it. I've learned that Foster and Jenks, two of the men I'm after, are holed up in a Nevada mining town. Will you look after Cotton Blossom while I'm gone?"

"If he *needs* looking after," said Lacy. "Josephine's spoiling that dog. Why don't you wait until after Christmas before you go? We may never spend another Christmas together."

"Maybe I will," Nathan said, knowing he must wait for the maps that Ames Tilden had promised him. "Before I go, I need to talk to Ames Tilden. I aim to leave you a thousand dollars. I've deposited most of the rest of it in the bank, and if I don't return within a year, Tilden will see that you get it."

*   *   *

Despite his desire to take up the vengeance trail, Nathan didn't regret his decision to wait until after Christmas, for in mid-December a blizzard swept in from the west, filling the mountain passes with impossibly high drifts of snow. The temperature didn't rise, and there was more snow. Three days before Christmas, Nathan stopped by the bank and picked up the government maps Ames Tilden had secured for him. But the bad weather continued, and Nathan could only wait. Not until the second day of January was there a warming trend and relief from snow and freezing temperatures. Nathan decided to travel light, and arranged to leave the pack horse with Ezra. While Ezra and Josephine knew nothing of his purpose in riding away, with Lacy remaining in Denver, they had no reason to question his return. He rode into town and bought enough supplies to last a month, and while there, he bought a newspaper. One item interested him. In October, Ben Thompson had been involved in a near shooting in Austin, Texas. As noted by the press, it was one of the rare occasions when Thompson had acted on the other side of the law. He had drawn his pistol and driven away five thugs who had been attacking a local judge.

*   *   *

Virginia City, Nevada. January 28, 1868.

Encountering more snow along the way, Nathan had been forced to hole up and wait out several storms. The very first thing that caught his attention as he rode into the mining town was a prominent sign that read "Sheriff." His informant had said there was no law. Nathan dismounted and entered the office. The sheriff was a big man, none of it fat. He carried a tied-down Colt on his left hip, and a Winchester leaned against the wall. Nathan introduced himself.

"Sheriff Ab Dupree. What can I do for you?"

"I'm lookin' for a pair of hombres," said Nathan. "Jenks and Foster by name."

"Friends of yours?" Dupree asked. His eyes had turned cold.

"No," said Nathan. "I aim to kill them both."

"I wish you luck," Dupree said, relaxing. "We strung up nine of the no-account coyotes just before Christmas. Thieves and killers, every one, and my one regret is that Jenks and Foster—if that's their names—escaped."

Discouraged, Nathan rode out, bound for Gold Hill.

* * *

Gold Hill, Nevada. February 2, 1868.

"Them varmints wouldn't of stopped here," Nathan was told. "Try Tonopah, Callville, or Pioche. They're new camps, an' likely no law."

Callville, Nevada. March 10, 1868.

Nathan rode to Tonopah and Pioche, but learned nothing of Jenks and Foster until he reached Callville, far to the south, on the bank of the Colorado. It was a small camp, all but played out, and Nathan found the miners angry.

"Hell, yes, they was here," Nathan was told. "They hung around the cafe and the saloon, learnin' what they could. Three miners was dry gulched in two days, losin' their gold and their lives."

"Which way did they go when they left here?" Nathan asked.

"The bastards crossed the river an' rode into Arizona," a miner said. "We got up a posse an' went after 'em, but they lost us."

Nathan studied the map of Arizona Ames Tilden had supplied. While there were many mines marked on the map, Tilden had cautioned that some of them had probably played out. Wearly, Nathan mounted and rode across the Colorado.

* * *

Tombstone, Arizona. April 15, 1868.

Wearily, Nathan dismounted before the sheriff's office. He had ridden into almost two dozen mining camps without finding a trace of the men he was seeking. Not surprising, he thought, for most of the camps were small pickings, not wealthy enough to attract the murderous Jenks and Foster.

"They were here," said Sheriff Lon Hankins. "We ain't a mining town, but we got a strong bank, and we've learned to recognize bank robbers before they clean us out. We met these varmints with a dose of lead, and if they hadn't hit us at closin' time, we'd have run 'em down. We got some lead in 'em, but nothin' serious enough to stop 'em. They hung on until dark, and that's when we lost 'em. They rode north."

There had been no rain, and Nathan managed to pick up the northbound trail of two horsemen. While he had no assurance the riders he was trailing were the elusive Jenks and Foster, he had no other leads. Near the ashes of a recent fire, he found a bloody bandanna, proof enough that at least one of the men had been wounded. Nathan's spirits rose. While the pair had eluded him so far, they were on the run. They had avoided villages and isolated ranches, and seemed to have some destination in mind. Nathan studied his map of Arizona, and from landmarks, decided the fugitives had crossed into northwestern New Mexico Territory. His heart leaped. Could they be bound for Denver? But that didn't seem possible. The trail continued almost due east, and when it reached a river, Nathan reined up, searching his memory. While studying a map of the southwest, he had noticed that the famed Rio Grande—which became the border between Texas and Mexico—had its beginning in southern Colorado. Could this be the Rio Grande? The trail Nathan was following turned due north, following the river.

"By God," said Nathan aloud, "they're headed straight for that little town in southern Colorado, Ciudad de Oro."

*   *   *

Denver, Colorado Territory. April 1, 1868.

Lacy Mayfield and Eva Barton had just left the Palace Theatre, having made arrangements for Lacy's debut on stage the next Friday.

"God," Lacy said, "I'm scared to death. I wish Nathan was here for this."

"Perhaps it's better that he isn't," said Eva. "When he returns, you'll have a surprise for him."

While Nathan was gone, Lacy had been sharing a room with Eva, and from time to time, Cotton Blossom joined them. It had taken him a month to gain the use of his hindquarters. Now he often sat near the barn, waiting, for he knew that when Nathan returned, he would be riding the black horse. Sometimes, Ezra or Josephine would lure

Cotton Blossom into the kitchen, feed him, and he would spend the night beside the stove. Lacy had begun reading the local newspaper, for it carried accounts of Indian raids, such as those by Quanah Parker and his Comanches in West Texas, of doings at the various forts, of new diggings in Montana and Nevada Territories, and of outlaws who had been killed or captured. Ezra found her at the table in the kitchen, with a cup of coffee and the newspaper.

"Anything good happening?" Ezra asked.

"If there is," said Lacy, "I haven't found it. In January, in California, a man named John Morco was beating his wife. Four men came to her rescue, and this Morco murdered them all. In March, the James and Younger gangs robbed the Southern Bank of Kentucky, in Russellville."

She folded the newspaper and put it aside. She always read it with the hope there might be some word of Nathan Stone, yet fearing that if there was, it would chronicle his death.

*   *   *

Ciudad de Oro, Colorado Territory. May 3, 1868.

Ignoring the rest of the town, Nathan reined up before the Oro Peso Saloon. On the glass window, lettered in fancy red and gold script, Nathan read: "Law Offices and Court Room—Judge Elijah Tewksbury." Dismounting, he looped the reins of his horse over the hitch rail and stepped through the swinging doors into the saloon. Nathan counted six men, one of them the barkeep. He stood with his hands on the bar, while the five men gathered at an oval table forgot their poker hands. Nathan stepped to his left, away from the bar, away from the swinging doors, his back to the wall. Then he spoke.

"I'm looking for Clinton Foster and Milo Jenks."

The silence became deadly, the only sound being the distant clang of a blacksmith's hammer. One of the men facing Nathan backed his chair away from the table, leading several of the others to do the same. The barkeep might have a sawed-off shotgun beneath the bar, lethal at close range, and it was a risk Nathan Stone couldn't afford to take. He spoke again.

"I want Foster and Jenks, nobody else. But I'll kill any man backing their play."

Slowly the first man who had backed away from the table stood up, and when none of his comrades moved, Nathan knew he had a chance. He waited for the other man to draw, and when he did, Nathan shot him, slamming him into his chair and tipping it over backwards. Nobody moved, and Nathan kept the Colt steady. Suddenly a door at the far end of the bar opened, and a man who had to be Judge Elijah Tewksbury stepped into the room. His dress consisted of a long swallowtail coat, dark trousers, black polished boots, and a white boiled shirt behind a black string tie.

"I am Judge Elijah Tewksbury," he said in a bullfrog voice. "This is a peaceful town. Who are you, and what is the meaning of this?"

"I came here looking for Clinton Foster and Milo Jenks," said Nathan. "They're a pair of killers. One of them just drew on me and I shot him. Now who is the varmint I just shot, and where's the other one?"

"The man you just shot is Clinton Foster," Tewksbury said. "At least, that's how we knew him. We know nothing of his past. Milo Jenks rode out a week ago. He was asked to leave, and I have no idea where he went. Do any of you know?"

"When they come here," said one of the men, "they rode in from the south. I remember Jenks talkin' about a woman he knowed in Austin, Texas. Kept sayin' he aimed to go there."

"I am asking you to leave," Tewksbury said. "Immediately."

Nathan said nothing. Keeping his Colt cocked and ready, he moved to his right and backed toward the doors. Knowing the risk, he backed out of the saloon. Once he was clear of the swinging doors, he whirled with his back to the wall. Immediately there was the clamor of voices and the thump of boots, and Nathan fired once beneath the swinging doors. The lead slammed into the saloon floor and the activity ceased. His Colt ready and his eyes on the door, he seized the reins and mounted his horse. He sidestepped the black away from the door and kicked it into a fast gallop, riding south.

*   *   *

Milo Jenks hadn't shared Clinton Foster's liking for the seclusion of the Ciudad de Oro, and when Jenks had fought with another of Tewksbury's men, he had willfully allowed himself to be driven out. From there he had ridden to Fort Dodge, taking with him two thousand dollars in gold, his share of the money he and Foster had accumulated from various robberies. Let Foster lay around Tewksbury's saloon and drink himself broke. While Jenks didn't know exactly what he was looking for, he quickly decided Fort Dodge wasn't it. It was no better than Ciudad de Oro, and possessed the added disadvantage of an eagle-eyed marshal who viewed strangers with suspicion. Jenks rode west, bound for Denver. There he made the acquaintance of Laura Evans, owner of the Bagnio Saloon, and after two weeks of sharing her bed, invested his two thousand dollars. A man could do worse than owning part of a saloon in a boom town, especially when there was a thriving whorehouse upstairs ...

*   *   *

Riding far enough south to be sure he wasn't being followed, Nathan reined up to rest the black and to consider what he had learned. Should he ride on to Austin, with no word to Lacy? Already two days out of Denver, if he returned here, it would cost him another two days. Besides, Lacy couldn't go with him. Tomorrow she would be reading for a part in *Under the Gaslight*, and the wounded Cotton Blossom might be unable to travel for a month. As he recalled, his last words to Lacy had cautioned that he could be gone for as long as a year. With that possibility in mind, he had left her money enough for just such an absence. He rode south, bound for Austin.

*   *   *

Santa Fe, New Mexico Territory. May 5, 1868.

Nathan rode into Santa Fe, New Mexico Territory at sundown, two days south of Ciudad de Oro. After stabling his horse, he found a restaurant and ordered a platter of ham and eggs. Finishing that, he ordered a second one. His hunger satisfied, he got himself a hotel room and slept soundly until first light. Arising, he returned to the restaurant and had breakfast. Next to his hotel, the Santa Fe Saloon did a thriving business around the clock. It offered drinks of all kinds—domestic and imported—and there was a trio of billiard tables. Early as it was, there was a poker game in progress, with four men pitting their skills against those of a house dealer. Despite Eulie's warning, Nathan still thrilled to a fast-moving saloon game, the captivating flutter of the shuffled cards, the clink of glasses. Mostly to justify his being there, he sidled over and questioned the barkeep.

"I'm looking for an hombre name of Milo Jenks. Have you maybe seen or heard of him?"

"No. Not much goin' on during my shift. Talk to the night men."

Nathan returned to his room for his saddlebags. With Jenks riding to Austin, Nathan thought it unlikely that he would remain in any town for more than a night, and just as unlikely that he would be remembered. However, it required only a little time to inquire along the way, and Nathan did exactly that in each town or village through which he passed.

When Nathan reached the point in the Rio Grande where the river veered due south, he rode southeast, knowing this would eventually put him in Texas. If his sense of direction hadn't failed him entirely, somewhere in southwest Texas he would come up on the Rio Colorado. He could then follow it the rest of the way, for the river flowed through Austin on its way to the Gulf of Mexico. Three days after leaving the Rio Grande, Nathan reached what he believed must be the Rio Colorado.* It was sluggish and shallow, but it reached a width and depth worthy of its name as it progressed. Nathan rode all that day and the next, uncertain as to exactly where he was, but sure of his direction. He moved away from the river at night, carefully dousing his fire, lest it draw the unwelcome attention of

---

*The Rio Colorado rises in intermittent draws in northeast Dawson County, Texas, flowing six hundred miles across the state, crossing or touching twenty-eight Texas counties on its way to Matagorda Bay and the Gulf of Mexico.

marauding Comanches. This being Nathan's first time through west Texas, it seemed sparsely populated, if at all.

At the end of his second day on the Colorado, he was about to unsaddle his horse when there came the unmistakable sound of gunfire somewhere to the south. While it wasn't his fight, there was the possibility that some poor soul was pinned down by Indians, and a man with a Winchester might make a difference. There were no more shots, and Nathan reined up when he heard cursing. Drawing his Winchester from the boot, he cocked it and trotted his horse ahead until he came upon seven men dressed in Union blue. One of them—a private—was using a doubled lariat to beat a half-naked man who lay face down on the ground.

"That's enough," Nathan said. "You're exceeding the limits of military discipline."

"I am Captain Derrick," the one man in officer's uniform said, "and this is none of your business. Ride on, or you'll be placed under military arrest and taken to the guard house at Fort Concho. Carry on, Private."

The private drew back for another blow with the lariat only to have a slug from Nathan's Winchester rip through the flesh of his upraised arm. But the impromptu act cost Nathan, for one of the soldiers shot him out of the saddle. His Winchester was torn from his hand, and his entire shoulder and right arm was numb. He had been hit high up, beneath the collar bone.

"Get up," Captain Derrick ordered. "Sergeant Webber, relieve this man of his weapons and assist him in mounting. Privates Emmons and Taylor, lash the deserter across his saddle."

Webber took Nathan's Winchester and his cartridge belt with its twin Colts. Nathan watched as Emmons and Taylor hoisted the beaten man across his saddle. All the blood hadn't come from the beating. The poor devil had been shot at least twice. In the back. Captain Derrick regarded Nathan with hard, cruel eyes. Finally he spoke.

"You, sir, are under military arrest. You will be taken to Fort Concho, given medical attention and held there until I decide your punishment."

Chapter 26

❖

Fort Concho, Texas. May 11, 1868.

The column rode south, the horses of both captives on lead ropes. Nathan couldn't believe this was happening, couldn't believe the cruelty he had witnessed, couldn't believe these men were Union soldiers. None of the Unionists he had known—even the Yankee guards at Libby Prison—had been insensitive and cruel. The more certain he became that these men were imposters, the more determined he became to undo their scheme and destroy them. But first he must have his wound tended, for the shock had worn off and the pain swept through him in waves. The fort, when they reached it, looked newly constructed, and was on the bank of a river. On the farthest bank, downstream from the fort, was a cluster of log buildings that looked like the beginning of a town.*

Once inside the gates, they proceeded to a log hut that was used as a dispensary.

"Dismount," Captain Derrick said, his eyes on Nathan. He then turned to his men. "Emmons, you and Taylor take the deserter inside and have him seen to."

"Hell," said one of the privates, "he looks dead."

"That'll be for the doc to say," Captain Derrick said. "Now, by God, take him inside."

---

*At this time, San Angelo was "San Angela." The town's history began with the location of Fort Concho (1867) at the junction of the north and main Concho Rivers. Bart DeWitt established a trading post across the river on the nearest available site. The town was eventually named San Angela, honoring Mrs. DeWitt's sister, a Mexican nun. But the name had to be changed when the Federal government—prior to issuing a bank charter and establishing a post office—objected to the masculine "San" and the feminine "Angela."

"Now," said Derrick, turning back to Nathan, "who are you and where were you going?"

"I'm Nathan Stone and I'm bound for Austin. I'm going there to join the Rangers."

"You're lying."

"You asked," Nathan said, "and I told you. Captain Jennings is expecting me."

"I can telegraph Austin and find out."

"Do that," said Nathan. "Captain Jennings knows me well."

Derrick looked undecided and Nathan pressed his advantage by not saying another word. Finally Derrick flung open the door to the dispensary.

"Get in there," he said. "I'll deal with you later."

Nathan stepped into the room, Derrick behind him. Privates Emmons and Taylor leaned against the wall. The man accused of desertion lay face down on a bunk. The man working over him wore only an undershirt and Union blue trousers. He had the look of a soldier and the dexterity of a doctor.

"Here's another for you, sawbones," Derrick said.

The doctor said nothing. Derrick stalked around to the other side of the bunk until he was facing the medic.

"I'm talking to you, by God," Derrick shouted.

"Yes, sir. I heard you, sir," said the doctor coldly. He saluted crudely with his bloody left hand.

Privates Emmons and Taylor were grinning widely until Derrick turned to them, changing their expressions entirely.

"Get the hell out of here," Derrick said. "Unsaddle my horse and the mounts of the two prisoners."

"You," he said, pointing to Nathan, "will remain here until your wound has been treated. Then you will be taken to the guardhouse. There will be an armed guard outside the door and all sentries have been instructed to shoot to kill." He left, closing the door behind him.

"I'll get to you as soon as I can," said the medic, looking at Nathan for the first time. "This man is near death."

"I know," Nathan said. "They were beating him with a doubled lariat when I stopped them."

"Your mistake," said the doctor. "He's not going to make it, and you're trapped here with the rest of us."

"I think I've earned the right to know what the hell's

going on here," Nathan said. "As much as you can tell me, anyhow. I'm Nathan Stone."

"I'm Lieutenant Calloway," said the doctor, "and this post has been overrun by outlaws. Renegades. The only reason I'm not in the guardhouse with the others is because I'm needed here in the dispensary. They captured the fort a week ago, and the man I'm working on now is the third they've shot. The other two—a corporal and a private—are dead."

"God Almighty," Nathan said, "every man on the post is locked up?"

"Eighteen soldiers," said the doctor. "The civilians needed for various duties are free, but they're living in fear of their lives. Sutton, here, is the blacksmith. They have made an example of him."

"I can't believe they were allowed to just ride in and take over."

"If any of us live through this," Lieutenant Calloway said, "I expect we will all be cashiered out of the service. That is, if we're not laughed out. Derrick and his bunch rode in a week ago yesterday. They all were in Union blue, and that got them through the gate. They moved quickly, taking our post commander, Colonel O'Neal, prisoner. They then threatened to kill him unless the rest of us surrendered our weapons."

"What in tarnation do they have in mind?"

"None of them has talked," said Lieutenant Calloway, "but I have my own ideas. The last week in June, some of the brass from Washington will come to Fort Worth. During July, they'll be conducting post inspections here, at San Antonio and at Houston. They'll be traveling with the same military escort that brings our payroll. The difference is, this will be the payroll for all three outposts. They'll be coming here first. That's why I believe they've taken over this post. The payroll for any one fort might not be worth the risk, but the payroll for three of them should be more than ten thousand."

"By God," Nathan said, "that has to be what they have in mind, but hell, there's time to turn this around."

"When you figure it out," said Lieutenant Calloway, "I'm sure every man on this post will be eternally grateful. Now take off your shirt and stretch out on the other bunk.

Maybe I'll have better luck with you. Come sundown, Mr. Sutton will no longer be with us."

Lieutenant Calloway didn't have to probe for the lead, for it had gone on through. He applied disinfectant and bound Nathan's wound.

"No bones broken," Calloway said. "I'm going to ask Derrick to allow you to remain here until tomorrow. There'll likely be some fever and you'll need to sweat out the infection. I have most of a quart of whiskey."

"Captain Derrick didn't strike me as a man known for his compassion," said Nathan.

"Compassion-wise," Lieutenant Calloway said, "he's just a few notches below a rattlesnake. That is, of course, unless he has some reason for wanting you kept alive."

"He just might have such a reason," said Nathan. "Do you have the telegraph here, and a man who can operate it?"

"We have it," Lieutenant Calloway replied, "and Corporal Drago knows the code. They brought him out of the guardhouse once to answer a telegram sent to Colonel O'Neal."

"Wound or not," said Nathan, "I need to get into that guardhouse just as soon as I can. I can get us out of this, but I must talk to Corporal Drago and figure some way for us to use that telegraph."

Lieutenant Calloway almost smiled, but something in Nathan's Stone's ice-blue eyes changed his mind. He spoke.

"I don't really know you. I don't know what influence you have, but I believe you're serious. God knows, we need a miracle, and maybe you're it. If there's anything I can do, I'll side you till hell freezes."

Nathan was lying on the bunk when Captain Derrick returned. He ignored Nathan, turning his attention to Lieutenant Calloway.

"Sutton won't last out the day," Calloway said. "The other man should remain here at least until in the morning. There may be infection that could kill him."

"Keep him here, then," said Derrick, and he left.

"You do have something going for you," Lieutenant Calloway said.

Nathan said nothing. Calloway had given him some laudanum and he slept.

Lieutenant Calloway looked in on Nathan between midnight and dawn. The fever was there, but slight, and Nathan forced down a third of the whiskey Calloway had saved for just such a purpose. Nathan arose at dawn, so stiff and sore he could hardly move. He went with Lieutenant Calloway to the mess hall, where he had breakfast. The renegade, Captain Derrick was there and he wasted no time approaching Nathan. With him was one of his men, dressed as a private and armed with a Winchester. They took Nathan at riflepoint to the guardhouse. It was a sturdy structure, built of logs, with a wooden outer door and an inside door of steel bars. Behind Nathan they locked the doors.

Some of the captive soldiers sat on hard wooden bunks, while the others sat on the floor, their backs to the wall. The only light came in through a trio of small windows, and they too were barred. The men said nothing, but their anxious eyes were on Nathan. He spoke.

"I'm Nathan Stone," he said. "Yesterday, I stopped some varmints wearin' soldier blue from beating a man they'd shot. One of them shot me, and I spent last night in your dispensary. Lieutenant Calloway told me how these outlaws captured your post. Do you have any plans for busting out of here?"

"I am Colonel O'Neal," said a graying man with a scabbed wound over his eye. "It's a disgrace the way they rode in here and took us without firing a shot, and I'm sorry to say that we've been in here for a week without devising any sensible plan of escape. Sutton tried to escape, to bring help."

"Sutton died yesterday, in the dispensary," Nathan said.

"I was afraid of that," said O'Neal.

"Calloway believes these men have taken over the post with the intention of stealing a military payroll due here sometime next month," Nathan said. "Do you agree with his thinking?"

"Yes," said O'Neal. "I haven't spoken to him since the takeover, but we have had plenty of time to consider their motivation. How the hell did they *know* of this payroll, of this post inspection? Damn it, they rode in here less than a week after I had received word of it myself. There will be officials from Washington, so the escort will number perhaps a dozen soldiers, but that won't be nearly enough. There are twenty-two of these renegades, and their uniforms will give them all the edge they'll need."

"If we can't break out of here," Nathan said, "then we'll have to send for help. We'll use the telegraph."

"I'd like to know how you aim to do that," said a corporal.

"Do any of these renegades know how to operate the telegraph?" Nathan asked.

"We don't think so," said Colonel O'Neal. "Corporal Drago is our post telegrapher, and he's had to answer several telegrams directed to me. If they had a man who knows the code, they wouldn't need Drago."

"That makes sense," Nathan said. "Which of you is Drago?"

"I am," said the corporal who had questioned Nathan's intention to use the telegraph to send for help.

"Drago," Nathan said, "if none of them understands the code, why couldn't you add a second message immediately after the reply they forced you to send?"

"I . . . didn't think of that," said Drago sheepishly.

"Even if they don't read the code," Colonel O'Neal said, "they ought to have some concept as to how long it would take to send their message."

"Not if the second message is short," said Nathan. "Drago, the next time you're forced to respond to a message in Colonel O'Neal's name, can you bury a short second message immediately after the first?"

"I can try," Drago said. "How short?"

"Seven words," said Nathan.

"I can do it if I memorize the message," Drago said. "If I break rhythm, they're likely to catch me."

"He won't get the chance," said O'Neal, "unless we receive another telegram that requires an answer. That may not happen again for weeks."

"You'd better hope it happens sooner than that," Nathan said, "because it'll take time for help to reach us after word goes out. Do any of you have paper and pencil?"

"I do," said Drago. "Write out the message and I'll memorize it."

Nathan took the stub of pencil and a page torn from Drago's notebook and started to write. The soldiers crowded close and read:

Attorney General Washington Concho seized Twenty one

"Who *are* you?" Colonel O'Neal demanded.

"I told you my name. I'm Nathan Stone."

"Hell," said one of the privates, "that's just a jumble of words, and it don't make sense."

"It makes good sense to me," Corporal Drago said. "All but the last two words. But that's some kind of code."

"Unless," said O'Neal, "they question the message and wire back to have it confirmed."

"It won't be questioned," Nathan said. "Just pray that somebody sends you a telegram requiring an answer."

To Nathan's surprise, he was taken from the guardhouse right after the evening meal. Two privates with Winchesters marched him back to the dispensary. One of them opened the door, and when Nathan entered, the door was closed. Nathan had no doubt that when he was ready to leave, the armed men would be waiting for him.

"I reminded Captain Derrick you needed your wound disinfected and the bandage changed," said Lieutenant Calloway. "I'm surprised he agreed."

"So am I," Nathan said. "Thanks. Colonel O'Neal has reached the same conclusion as you. He believes the outlaws are after that military payroll."

"That has to be what they have in mind," said Calloway. "Does the colonel have any plans for escape?"

"None that I know of," Nathan said. While he didn't question Calloway's loyalty, the less the doctor knew, the better. Despite Calloway's—or any man's—loyalty, he could be tortured and made to tell anything he knew.

After his wound had been tended to, Nathan stepped out the door, found his guards waiting for him, and was marched back to the guardhouse.

"That was unusual," said Colonel O'Neal, "these hellions being concerned about your wound. Did you have a chance to speak to Lieutenant Calloway?"

"Yes," Nathan replied, "but I told him nothing of our plans. Like you said, there's something strange about me being sent back to the dispensary. Now let's just hope the good doc has a high tolerance for pain."

"By God," said O'Neal, "they *would* torture a man, wouldn't they?"

Nathan was not taken to the dispensary again. After two weeks, there seemed to have been no call for Corporal Drago's services as a telegrapher. The call finally came on June tenth, and according to Colonel O'Neal, less than two weeks before the delegation from Washington and the payroll was scheduled to arrive. Corporal Drago was gone only a few minutes, but to Nathan and the desperate soldiers, it seemed much longer. After Drago was returned to captivity, he waited a few moments before he spoke.

"Telegram for you, sir," he told Colonel O'Neal. "The team of inspectors will depart Fort Worth on June twenty-first, arriving here on June twenty-fifth. You were asked to verify accommodations."

"Damn," said O'Neal, "that's a two-word response."

"Yes, sir," Drago said with a grin, "but these owlhoots don't know that. I took a chance and sent our message first, and there was no question, no request for a repeat. The line kind of went dead for a minute, and I told them their message didn't go through, that I'd have to repeat it. That's when I sent the verification in your name."

"Well done, corporal," said O'Neal, "but are you *sure* the code message went through to Washington?"

"I can't swear to it, sir," Drago said, "but the key was live and I was given permission to send."

"Colonel," said Nathan, "the nature of the message should have alerted those receiving it of trouble here at the fort. We can only trust that somebody is sharp enough to understand we don't have free access to the telegraph."

*   *   *

In Washington, the strange telegram had stirred an immediate interest. An aide to Ira McCormick, assistant to the attorney general, had just delivered the message to his superior.

"This just came in, sir," said the aide.

McCormick studied the few words. Three of them hit him hard. One was Concho, the other two, Byron Silver's code. Clearly this was a plea for help, but perhaps it was more than that. In just a matter of days, military personnel from Washington would be visiting outposts in Texas, and Fort Concho would be one of them. An inspection team of high-ranking officers would be traveling with a military escort bearing a substantial payroll. McCormick was well aware of the coming inspection, for hadn't he prepared Byron Silver's orders, sending him as an advance guard to Fort Worth? He *knew* Silver was there, yet his code—intended as an alert—had been used in this telegram from

Fort Concho. Something was definitely wrong at Fort
Concho. McCormick composed a message, addressing it to
Byron Silver at Fort Worth.

"Here," said McCormick to an aide, "have the telegrapher send this at once."

McCormick waited, and in less than an hour, he had his
reply from Fort Worth. The message was brief: *Riding to
Concho.* It was signed simply *Silver*.

*   *   *

Of necessity, Byron Silver had requested a meeting with
Captain Ferguson, the post commander at Fort Worth.

"Captain," Silver said, "I was sent here to spearhead this
planned inspection tour, but I may not be able to. My orders have been changed, and I'm to ride to Fort Concho.
How do I find it?"

"The fort's on the Concho River, maybe a hundred and
seventy miles northwest of Austin. Or from here, southwest, it's something over two hundred miles. Is something
wrong at Concho?"

"Nothing to concern you," Silver said. "Washington
wants me to check out the post, since it's first in line for
inspection."

While saddling his horse, Silver allowed his mind to re-
view what he had learned from McCormick's telegram. The
use of his code told him two important facts. First, the call
for help must have come from Nathan Stone, and two, the
situation must be truly desperate. The brevity of the message told Silver that it had been sent under circumstances
that would have made further details impossible. Fort
Concho had been taken, and that meant its defenders were
dead or had been taken captive. Silver rode south, to Austin. It would be out of his way and would virtually double
the miles to Fort Concho, but he was needful of much that
Captain Ferguson and the military might be unable to supply. While he was employed by the Federals, he was forever
a Texan. He had aided the Texas Rangers when he could,
and stood by them even when the Reconstructionist governor of Texas didn't officially recognize them. Now he had
to call on them for service that might go unrecognized, and
if it failed, might meet the reprimand of the president himself. While this was a military matter, he thought grimly,

there was not a soul within military ranks equal to what lay ahead. This called for a man with unquestionable courage and dedication, a man with the stealth and resourcefulness of a Comanche.

*   *   *

Austin, Texas. June 17, 1868.

While Byron Silver was known among the Rangers, Captain Sage Jennings had been his lifelong friend, and it was to Jennings that he turned now.

"Yes," said Jennings, "I know Colonel O'Neal, and Nathan Stone as well. I once tried to recruit him for the Rangers."

"Then I'd like you to ride with me to Fort Concho," Silver said. "I don't know why Stone's there, but he is, and somehow he got word to Washington. We must get inside that stockade, and it wouldn't be unusual, would it, for a Ranger to visit the fort?"

"I reckon not," said Jennings. "I can get us in, and I can request a meeting with the post commander, who, if I'm following you, won't be Colonel O'Neal."

"No," Silver said. "I look to find Colonel O'Neal, his entire command, and probably Nathan Stone in the guardhouse."

"Good God," said Jennings. "How much time do we have before this spit-and-polish bunch shows up from Washington?"

"They're arriving in Fort Worth on June twenty-first," Silver said. "I must report the status of Fort Concho before the brass will be cleared to leave Fort Worth. We have, at most, four days."

"We'd better saddle up and ride," said Jennings. "We're two days from Fort Concho."

*   *   *

Time dragged for the men locked in the guardhouse at Fort Concho. Most of them had stripped down to their trousers, for it was stifling hot. Nathan had removed the sweaty bandage, for his wound was well on its way to healing.

"Drago," somebody asked, "what day is it?"

"June seventeen, by my reckonin'," said Drago.

"Damn," Sergeant Watts growled, "time's runnin' out. After that bunch grabs the payroll, they'll likely shoot all of us."

"There won't be any payroll for them to grab," said Nathan, "Until Washington investigates that telegram we sent. It'll take some time to get help to us from anywhere, and some smart heads to learn what's happened to us."

"God," Drago groaned, "if a company of soldiers rides in here, we're goners."

"If our message got to the right man," said Nathan, "there'll be no soldiers."

*   *   *

"We're maybe ten miles from the fort," said Captain Jennings, when he and Silver had stopped to rest their horses. "It'll be dark when we get there."

"So you're just going to ride up and demand a meeting with the post commander, then," Silver said. "You're a Ranger, but how do you aim to account for me?"

"You'll be a Ranger too," Jennings replied, handing Silver a silver star-in-a-circle. "There's no guarantee we won't be shot dead before we leave, but we'll get in. To refuse us would arouse suspicion, and if the situation is what we suspect, they won't dare run that risk."

Reaching the fort, they rode boldly up to the gate.

"Halt!" a sentry commanded. "Identify yourselves."

"Texas Rangers," Jennings replied. "Request permission to meet with the post commander."

When the gate finally opened, Silver and Jennings found themselves facing three men. Two of them held Winchesters at port arms, while the third carried a lantern. He wore the stripes of a sergeant, and it was he who spoke.

"How do we know you're Rangers?"

"We're wearing the shields," said Jennings. "Rangers are commissioned by the State of Texas, and we cooperate fully with all military outposts. Take us to your post commander."

"Privates," the sergeant growled, "take their hosses and picket them outside the gate."

Unwilling the soldiers stepped aside, allowing Jennings

and Silver to pass through the gate. They followed the sergeant toward a log building where light glowed dimly through the single window. The sergeant pounded on the door.

"Who's there?" growled a voice from inside.

"Sergeant Webber. There's some Rangers here, wantin' to see you."

"Let 'em in," said the voice.

Jennings went in first, followed by Silver. Webber came in behind them, closing the door. Lightning quick, Jennings drew, and Captain Derrick found himself looking into the deadly muzzle of Captain Jennings' Colt. The move drew Sergeant Webber's attention, allowing Silver to club him unconscious with the muzzle of his Colt.

"The key to the guardhouse, Captain," said Jennings coldly.

"I . . . don't have it," Derrick muttered.

"The key, damn it," Jennings gritted, shoving the cold muzzle of the Colt under Derrick's nose.

"Webber has it," said Derrick sullenly.

Silver knelt beside the unconscious man, turning his pockets inside out. He found a ring with two keys. Taking Webber's Colt, he shoved it under his waistband. Jennings passed to Silver the Colt he had taken from Derrick, and Silver quickly searched the room, taking every available weapon, including a pair of Winchesters. Besides his own, he had six Colts, and he looped his bandanna through the trigger guards, knotting it. He then began looking for a way out of the room besides the door, for the sentries would be watching that. But there was no other door, and the two windows were too small.

"Is there another way out of here?" Jennings demanded, again prodding Derrick with the muzzle of the colt.

"No," said Derrick.

Silver dragged the desk to one side, and rolling back an oval rug, found a trap door. Taking hold of an iron ring, he lifted the door, revealing steps leading downward.

"Wherever it leads," Silver said, "it's better than the front door. But I need some light."

He rummaged through a supply cabinet and found some candles. One of these he lighted. Then, taking up the Colts by the looped bandanna, and with the Winchesters under his arm, he started down the steps.

"Luck," said Captain Jennings.

At the bottom of the wooden steps, Silver found himself on a dirt floor. But there was no door, no window, nothing . . .

Chapter 27

"Nothing down there but a hole in the ground," Silver said, returning to the post commander's office. "Looks like a last-ditch refuge from Indian attacks. I'll have to go out the door."

"Then we'll both go," said Jennings. "The good captain will guide us."

"Like hell I will," Derrick snarled.

"You're through making decisions," said Jennings. "I don't often shoot a man in the back, but I make exceptions when there's a need. Now open that door and step out, slow and easy."

"They'll see the guns when the door opens," Silver said. "I'll put out the lamp."

They went down the steps and had gone only a few yards toward the guardhouse when one of the sentries grew suspicious.

"Captain Derrick," he shouted.

"It's a trap!" Derrick bawled.

He tried to throw himself to the ground, but Jennings caught his belt and knocked him senseless with the muzzle of his Colt. Already there was lead singing. Jennings fired at muzzle flashes in the dark.

"Run," said Jennings. "I'll hold them off."

Silver was already off and running, drawing some of the fire away from Jennings. The Ranger knelt behind the unconscious Derrick and one of the searching slugs ripped into the outlaw's body, and it became a burden. While Jennings had accounted for one man at the gate, the remaining sentries were laying down a withering fire. Jennings could hear rifles roaring from other positions, ominous evidence that other outlaws had jumped into the fight. Jennings let go of Derrick and lit out toward the guard house.

As Silver tried the first key, a slug slammed into the door

of the guardhouse. The key wouldn't fit the lock. Silver
tried the second. With a grunt of relief he swung the first
door back, only to be confronted with a second with iron
bars.

"We're out of time," Jennings panted. "What's wrong
with the door?"

"Two of them," said Silver. "Both locked, just one more
key . . ."

But the key slipped into the lock and Silver swung the
barred door open. Alerted by the shooting, the imprisoned
men had been waiting. Nathan was the first to emerge, but
lead had begun to rip into the log guardhouse, and one of
the soldiers was hit. Starlight made for difficult shooting,
but two of the renegade sentries had Winchesters and they
almost had the range.

"Here," said Silver, shoving a Winchester at Nathan.
"We have enough guns for eight of you."

"Silver," Nathan said, "you didn't bring near enough
guns. There's twenty-two damn outlaws, and they're aiming
to steal an army payroll."

"Sorry," Silver growled. "Next time, I'll hitch up a
wagon."

"Silver, Stone," said Jennings, "come with me. We're
going to go after those varmints at the gate. You men without weapons, stay out of the line of fire. The rest of you
keep shooting."

Jennings moved far to his left, within the shadow of the
high log walls of the stockade. Silver and Nathan followed.
It was a flanking movement that would make shooting difficult for the men at the gate, especially if they were concealed behind the parapets above. Reaching the corner of
the stockade, they turned, keeping within the shadow of
the front wall through which the gate opened to the outside. Nearing the gate, they stepped over the body of one
of the outlaws. Intermittent firing told them there were two
others atop the wall, firing from the parapets in response
to soldier fire near the guardhouse. Jennings backed away
from the wall, but still within its shadow, and his companions followed his example. When next the rifles roared from
atop the wall, Nathan, and Silver, and Jennings fired at the
muzzle flashes. There was a dull thump and then a second,
sounding like an echo of the first. The pair on the wall had
dropped their Winchesters.

"They'll have Colts, probably," said Jennings, "and we need them." He started for the ladder.

"Back off, Captain," Nathan said. "They could be playing possum. I'll go up there. It's time I took some of the risk."

"Then you don't need a Winchester," said Jennings. "Here, take this Colt that belonged to the dead owlhoot back yonder."

Nathan shoved the Colt under his waistband and climbed up to the narrow catwalk atop the walls. Both the men lay face down, and Nathan was forced to roll them to unbuckle their pistol belts. When Nathan rejoined his comrades, the soldiers were there.

"Let us have any extra weapons," O'Neal said. "You men have already done more than your share. We know this post, and we'll get the rest of them, dead or alive. Just see that none of them try to escape through the gate."

"With lariats they could scale the walls," said Nathan.

"They could," Corporal Drago said, "but they ain't likely to. The hosses is all brought in at night, and nothin' but a damn fool would risk bein' on foot in Comanche country."

Nathan kept the Colt and gave up the Winchester. With the two Winchesters and two Colts taken from the dead man at the gate, O'Neal and eleven of his soldiers were now armed. For the first time, Nathan, Silver and Jennings were able to talk about this bizarre situation that might have gotten them all shot dead. Nathan explained how he had become involved, giving much of the credit for their rescue to Corporal Drago.

"The corporal deserves some recognition for getting that telegram on the wire with a gun to his head," said Silver. "I've never encountered anything like this, having outlaws overrun a fort. Why the hell can't they just go on robbing government supply trains? We have procedure for that."

"It's far from being finished," Captain Jennings said. "Somewhere within your military chain of command, you have a Judas. How did this bunch learn of the coming inspection, to be integrated with the delivery of military payrolls? And how in tarnation did they manage to outfit themselves in twenty-two Union army uniforms, all with proper brass and insignia?"

"God," said Silver with a sigh, "there'll be one hell of an investigation, but some good will come of it. Under the circumstances, Washington can't very well fault Colonel O'Neal and his command for falling into a trap so well set. They'll likely make regulations that will prevent this happening again. Someday I'll have to explain how this varmint, Nathan Stone, was able to use my distress code."

"I reckon that'll be easier than explaining the loss of three military payrolls and some dead, high-ranking army brass," said Nathan. "You had to already be in Texas to have reached us in time, and that tells me you were an outrider for this military inspection."

Silver laughed.

"I wouldn't dare say this on the street," said Captain Jennings, "but if we Rebs had laid our plans a little better, these soldiers would be wearing Confederate gray. We had—and still have—the strategists."

"I take my life in my hands, just thinking such things," Byron Silver replied, "but I must agree with you. From now on, we're one nation under God, but by God, Texas will always be *our* nation."

*   *   *

Austin, Texas. June 19, 1868.

Byron Silver had to ride directly to Fort Worth to prepare for military inspectors from Washington. Captain Jennings and Nathan returned to Austin, and on the way Nathan mentioned his need to find Milo Jenks.

"South Texas has always been a hangout for owlhoots, suspected and genuine," said the Ranger, "but I never heard of Milo Jenks. Generally, when they leave here on the run, somebody else has to gun them down or hang them. They don't often return."

"I reckon it helps, havin' a Ranger outpost in town," Nathan said.

"Hell," said Jennings, "since you were here last, Ben Thompson actually did something decent. Old Judge Schuetze's never been too popular, and five gents with knives had him cornered. Ben pulled his pistol and they all lit out. Ben rode out and we haven't seen him since."

"Maybe he rode to Matamoros," Nathan said. "He has a following there. They followed us both, once, throwin' lead as they came."

Jennings laughed. "He's got kin here, but he'll come back. He's already past due for some time in the *juzgado*."

While the Ranger had said it in jest, it was a prophecy the deadly Ben Thompson would soon fulfill.

* * *

While the outlaws who had overrun Fort Concho had taken Nathan's gold, he had recovered it. After a prolonged stay in Fort Concho's guardhouse, Nathan wasn't ready for the long ride to Colorado. He took a room at the Capitol Hotel, stabling his black at a nearby livery. There being little else to do, he made the rounds of the saloons. There might, he thought, be some talk. If not of Milo Jenks, then perhaps of Ringo Tull or Dade Withers. He went from the Bullwhacker Saloon to the Star, The Keno, the De Oro, without any word of the men he sought. When he reached the Texas, however, he made a discovery that took his breath away.

Her back was to him and she wore the dress of a Mexican señorita, but when she faced him, she paled. Nathan recovered first, got an arm around her slender waist and led her to a table. The months hadn't been kind to Viola Hayden. While barely out of her teens, she looked thirty.

"For God's sake," Nathan said, "what are you doing in here?"

Her laugh was bitter. "It was this or a whorehouse."

"Jesse ..."

"Dead," she said dully. "He was ambushed a month after you left. Close range, with a shotgun."

"Your place," said Nathan. "Your horse ..."

"All gone." Silent tears crept down her cheeks. "I sold everything ... for what I could get ..."

Nathan's rage all but choked him. He had turned Nate Rankin's ambush around, gunning down Driggers and Gadner after they had shot young Hugh Rankin. Now Rankin had gotten his revenge, taking it out on Viola.

"By God," Nathan gritted, "Rankin won't get away with this."

"He already has," said Viola softly. "I accused him to his face, and he laughed in mine. There's nothing you can do. Please don't get yourself in trouble over something that ... can't be changed."

Nathan said no more. He waited, drinking an occasional beer to justify his presence, until the Texas closed for the night. He left the saloon with her, not even concerned with where she lived, guiding her toward his hotel.

"I have a room at a boardinghouse," she said.

"I have one at the Capitol Hotel," said Nathan.

She didn't object. She seemed not to care about anything or anybody. He unlocked the door, and when they had entered, locked it behind them. Viola kicked off her sandals and skinned the long dress off over her head. She wore nothing else, and stretching out on the bed, stared vacantly at the ceiling.

"Damn it," Nathan said, "this is all my fault."

But she said nothing, refusing to condemn him. Her eyes were empty, seeing nothing, as though her body existed while the soul within had departed. Nathan was consumed with guilt. He had lived by the gun, shooting his way out of each deadly situation, unmindful of the consequences. Now the chickens had come home to roost, and someone else—Viola Hayden—was paying for Nathan Stone's dedication to the gun. Not knowing what to say or do, he sat down beside her. Suddenly she threw her arms around him and wept with an intensity that shook him to his very soul. She clawed him, tore at his clothes, until he was caught up in the frenzy of her passion, and it resulted in the very last thing he had wanted or expected. He got up, his Levi's around his ankles, and drew off his boots. He removed his shirt, which no longer had buttons, blew out the lamp and lay down beside her. She slept as though she were exhausted, while Nathan lay awake far into the night.

                    *   *   *

Nathan awoke to the sun streaming in through the window, fervently hoping that what was still strong on his mind had been only a nightmare. But she was there beside him, naked, leaning on one elbow, looking at him.

"I'm sorry ... about last night," he said.

"Don't be," she replied. "I'm not. Better you than some stranger. I ... it's ... been hell. Did you know that when the hurt goes deep enough, there's just ... not enough tears to drown it? It ... takes something ... more."

"I can believe that," said Nathan, "and I owe you ..."

"You don't owe me a damn thing. The last thing in the world I want is a man who feels obligated to me. I took what I wanted, and you're free to hike up your britches and ride wherever the hell you want."

There were no more tears. The fury in her eyes bordered on madness.

He stood.

"What's wrong?" she taunted. "I was good enough last night. Why not this morning?"

"You're not the Viola I knew," he said. "I feel responsible for what ... you've become. I don't like you this way. For what it's worth, I don't sleep with a woman I don't even like. Last night, there was no giving. Only taking. No more, Viola. No more."

Nathan took a shirt from his saddlebag, pulled on his Levi's, and stomped into his boots. He then belted on his Colts, took his hat, and without looking back, stepped out the door. He still felt some guilt for having left Viola to face Nate Rankin's revenge, but her don't-give-a-damn attitude had left him less remorseful than he might have been. The question was, what was he to do now? Certainly he wanted no more nights like the one he had just endured, but he couldn't just ride away and put her out of his mind. He had no idea what—if anything—could be done for Viola Hayden. He sought out Captain Jennings and asked the Ranger's advice.

"I feel as helpless as you," said Jennings. "She came to me with her suspicions, I turned her down, and now she hates my guts. Hell, if I went after people on suspicion, I'd have to build a fence around Texas."

"It's killing Viola."

"Viola is killing Viola," Jennings said. "I just thank God I'm not the county sheriff. She's been locked up for being drunk and disorderly so many times, I've lost count, and her reputation's such that she'd give a whore a bad name. There's only one thing she hasn't done, and that's get a gun and go after Nate Rankin."

Nathan spent the day and much of the night making the rounds of other saloons, carefully avoiding the Texas. It was late when he finally returned to his room. He had failed to lock the door when he had left, and it was still unlocked. As quietly as he could, he eased the door open, and in the moonlight through the window, he could see someone in his bed. There was a loud snore. He closed the door and lighted the lamp. His first thought was that she had never left the room, and then he saw the empty bottle on the floor beside the bed. Her dress lay in a heap on the floor and she was just literally, hopelessly, dog-drunk. He rolled her naked body to the other side of the bed, making room to sit and remove his boots. Unbuckling his pistol belt, he placed his Colts on the floor beside the bed, his hat on top of them. He then stretched out on the bed, trying to ignore her snoring. Eventually he slept, and when he awoke, the snoring had stopped. He turned over and found her staring at him. Finally she laughed. It was ugly, bawdy.

"First man ever slept with me an' kept his britches on," she cackled.

"Viola," he said, "if I took you away from here—far away—could you put this life behind you and forget everything that's happened?"

"No," she said. "I'll never forget. Never."

To Nathan's surprise and relief, she got up, dressed, and left without a word. Nathan bought a newspaper in the hotel lobby and went from there to a restaurant. During breakfast, he read the newspaper. All he found of interest was that Austin was about to have its own Cattleman's Emporium, a private club for drinking, gambling and hell raising. It was set to open on August thirty, and one of its charter members—having paid a thousand dollars—was Nate Rankin. Another was Ben Thompson! There was more, including a stud poker competition, with a five hundred-dollar first prize. The affair was more than two months away, but it promised to be well attended. There would be gamblers from all over Texas. It would be an excuse for Nathan to remain in Austin for a while. As though he needed one. He had to admit to himself that he was unwilling to desert Viola Hayden, despite her obvious desire to go to hell by the fastest possible means. The next time he encountered Captain Jennings, he asked the Ranger about the Cattleman's Emporium.

"I don't consider it an asset," Jennings said, "and I'm opposed to anything that brings Ben Thompson to town. There'll be sleeping rooms upstairs for the high rollers, after they're too drunk to buck the tiger, and I won't be surprised if there's some high-class whores available on the house, to the big spenders. Do you aim to stick around for it?"

"I'd kind of like to see Ben Thompson play poker," said Nathan. "I've been around after the game, when he was bein' shot at, but I've never seen him play."

"Watch," Jennings said, "but stay out of the line of fire. If ever you buy into another man's fight, be damn sure he's worthy of the risk. That eliminates Ben Thompson."

Nathan occasionally visited the Texas Saloon, but Viola either ignored him or stared at him as though he were a total stranger. Mostly, Nathan frequented other saloons, where there was nearly always a poker game in progress. He preferred five-card stud, but played draw poker, and on occasion, the less popular seven-card stud. Some days he lost. On others, he won as consistently as he had lost the day before. He still had more than three hundred dollars in gold, for he was living off his winnings. He took the time to write a lengthy letter to Lacy Mayfield, in care of Cherry Creek Manor, in Denver. He would be returning to Denver some time in September or October. However, he warned her not to despair if he did not.

*   *   *

Austin, Texas. August 29, 1868.

Ben Thompson arrived on Saturday, the day before the grand opening of the Cattlemen's Emporium. Nathan found him in De Oro Saloon, downing scotch and watching a poker game in progress.

"The next one's on me," Nathan said.

Thompson nodded. He wasn't one for frivolous conversation. How talkative he was on any occasion depended on his mood, which was subject to change on short notice. He tossed off the rest of his scotch and finally spoke.

"Big doings at the Cattleman's tomorrow night. I can get you in as my guest, if you're of a mind to go."

"I'm obliged," said Nathan.

Nathan hadn't seen Viola in almost two weeks, and when he looked for her at the Texas, she wasn't there. He questioned one of the bartenders.

"Quit," the bartender said. "I hear she's hired on as one of them fancy girls, over to the Emporium."

That brought to mind what Captain Jennings had said, about the Cattleman's Emporium supplying whores to the big spenders. Surely she wouldn't resort to that, he thought. He wanted to talk to her, but realized he had no idea where she lived, for he had always been able to find her at the Texas. He made the rounds of the other saloons, coming back to the Texas, without a sign of her. It was possible, he decided, that she was sleeping off a drunk or embarking on one. Tomorrow, perhaps, he could talk to her at the Cattleman's Emporium.

* * *

For sheer elegance, the Cattleman's Emporium rivaled anything Nathan had ever seen. There were two floors, and the staircase leading to the second was a dozen feet wide. The carpet, including the stairs, was deep red. The walls were of cedar, while the sixty-foot bar and all the furniture were of polished walnut. A mirror ran the full length of the bar, and there were pyramids of bottled whiskey from one end to the other. Four kegs of beer were on line and there were five bartenders in white coats. At the far end of the room, behind swinging doors, was the kitchen. Suspended from cedar beams were sixteen chandeliers, each the size of a Conestoga wagon wheel, each with pyramided tiers of lighted lamps. Opposite the bar, fancy tables lined the wall, each with a red-and-white-checked cloth. Each chair had a padded back and seat upholstered in red, to match the carpet. There was no sign of gambling on the first floor, reminding Nathan of the Stumberg houses in New Orleans. How well-heeled must a man be to climb those stairs? Windows had been opened and cool night air guttered some of the flames in the many-tiered chandeliers. Nathan allowed his eyes to roam the length of the first floor, and he finally sighted Viola at a table with three men, one of whom was Nate Rankin! Before Nathan could make a move, Ben Thompson spoke from behind him.

"The gambling's upstairs. Join me?"

"Yes," said Nathan. "I'm obliged."

Nathan suspected these were high-stakes games and that if he didn't go with Thompson, he might not be allowed to enter. He followed the dapper little gambler up the stairs, and Thompson seemed to know where he was going. Without knocking, he opened the first door on the left, and when he entered, Nathan followed. There were more chandeliers, more fancy carpet, and another bar. There was table after table, with every possible game of chance in progress, and there was the distinctive whirr of a roulette wheel. Each poker table had chairs for a house dealer and five gamblers. Thompson chose a table with two empty chairs. He took one and Nathan the other. Thompson, attired in solid black with a black top hat, looked as though he had just preached a funeral, or was about to. Nathan, in flannel shirt and Levi's, drew a doubtful look from the house dealer. Thompson caught the house man's eye and he hastily began shuffling the cards. When he spoke, he didn't look at Nathan or Thompson.

"Five-card stud. Ten dollars a throw."

While it was Nathan's favorite game, a few losses played hell with a man's roll. Covering all bets, he could lose as much as forty dollars in a single game. On the first draw, Nathan received a face-down hole card and a face-up jack. He put his ten dollars in the pot, noticing that Thompson had drawn a face-up ten. On the second draw, Nathan drew a face-up seven, while Thompson got a second ten. Each of them added another ten dollars to the pot. On the third draw, Nathan drew another jack, while Thompson got a third ten. Each man cast another ten dollars in the pot and received a fourth face-up card. Nathan drew another face-up seven, while Thompson drew a fourth ten. Come showdown, Nathan's hole card proved to be a third jack, while Thompson's was a fourth ten. But another gambler took the pot with four kings. Nathan lost two pots before winning one, and after that, he took two more. He lost another, and dropped out, breaking even. Ben Thompson had lost two hundred and forty dollars, not having won a single pot. He dropped out of the game when Nathan did, and while he seemed calm enough, Nathan could see a storm building in his eyes. Thompson paused at the head of the stairs.

"If you're of a mind to sample the grub," Nathan said, "I'm buying."

"Another time," said Thompson. Turning, he walked farther down the hall and disappeared through another door.

Nathan went on down the stairs to the first floor. Viola and Rankin were no longer at the table. The other two men were lingering over drinks, and Nathan took the bull by the horns and approached their table.

"There was a lady with you gents a while ago," Nathan said, "and I wanted to talk to her. Do you know if she's still here?"

"Oh, she's here," one of them said, "but I reckon she's busy. Old man Rankin took her upstairs, and they wasn't goin' to play poker."

"Rankin wasn't, anyhow," the second man added, and they both laughed.

Nathan turned away, furious. How did you defend a woman's honor when she had none, when she had willingly become a whore?

Nathan had started up the stairs, uncertain as to what he should do, when somewhere ahead of him there was a shot. He took the steps two at a time and when he reached the upper hall, doors were open and men looked questioningly at one another. When a second shot rang out, Nathan was better able to place it. He started down the row of doors on the other side of the hall. When he tried the first two, he found them locked, but the third opened easily. Nathan stepped into the room, aware that others were behind him. A lamp burned beside the bed, and on it lay Nate Rankin and Viola Hayden. Wearing only his socks, Rankin clutched his bloody belly.

"She ... shot me," he groaned. "She ... gut-shot ... me ..."

Beside him lay the naked body of Viola Hayden, a Colt in her limp hand and the side of her head a bloody mess. Nathan backed away, sick to his very soul. Others had seen the gory sight, and there were shouts of confusion.

"Rankin's still alive," a man bawled. "Somebody get the doc."

But Viola Hayden had known what she was doing, and by the time the doctor arrived, Rankin had joined her in death. Nathan walked slowly down the hall, toward the stairs, recalling the last words he had heard her speak.

I'll never forget. Never.

"Neither will I, Viola," he said aloud. "Neither will I ..."

Chapter 28

❖

Nathan had no idea where Jesse Hayden was buried, but he was feeling a burden to lay Viola to rest beside her father. It was still early—not more than an hour after Viola's terrible act of vengeance—when Nathan went looking for Captain Jennings.

"Yes," Jennings said, "I know where Jesse's buried. There's a little graveyard not far from where they lived. In the morning we'll rent a buckboard and take her home."

*   *   *

On Monday, August thirty-first, Nathan and Jennings claimed Viola's body from a local undertaker. They split the cost of having her laid out, and of a decent coffin. With Nathan driving the buckboard and Jennings riding alongside, they were about to leave when Ben Thompson rode up.

"I didn't know the lady," he said, "but I've heard she had cause, and I admire her for playing out her hand. I'm riding along to pay my respects."

Captain Jennings said nothing. Nathan, knowing the Ranger's opinion of Thompson, spoke.

"Come along, then," said Nathan.

Thompson rode on one side of the buckboard and Jennings on the other. It was still early and Austin had not yet come alive. They reached the little church with its adjoining burying ground shortly past noon. It came as a pleasant surprise to Nathan to find many people gathered before the church. One of them was a black-robed preacher.

"They were neighbors to the Haydens," Captain Jennings said. "I sent a rider out last night, believing they all would want to know. The grave should be ready."

It was, and the lifelong friends of the Haydens had not

forgotten. They wept, heaping wildflowers on the new-made grave beside that of Jesse Hayden.

Austin, Texas. September 2, 1868.

Nathan had heard of Ben Thompson's younger brother, Billy. In some ways, it was said, Billy was the complete opposite of Ben, while in other ways they were disturbingly alike. Like Ben, Billy had a short fuse, was moody and quick to take offense, and was lightning fast with a Colt. Ben had a room at the Capitol Hotel, and it was there—in the lobby—that Nathan met Billy for the first time.

"Let's go eat," Billy suggested, "and then find us a poker game."

After supper they went to De Oro saloon, where Ben and Billy bought into a game of five-card stud. Recalling the fury in Ben's eyes after his loss at the Cattleman's Emporium, Nathan backed off. When it came to gambling, one Thompson at a time was plenty. But Billy lasted for only a few hands. He began sharing a bottle with William Burke, an army sergeant, and Burke wanted to leave.

"I'm goin' to a whorehouse 'fore I git too drunk," said Burke. "Any of you man enough to go with me?"

"Hell," Billy said, "anything you can do, I can do better, and twice as often."

But as it turned out, both Burke and Thompson were too drunk, for when they reached the whorehouse, three other soldiers—friends of Burke—were outside. An argument ensued and Billy Thompson left, cursing the soldiers. He returned to De Oro Saloon as Ben and Nathan were leaving. But Sergeant Burke had followed Billy.

"Damn you," Burke shouted, "I'll kill you."

Billy Thompson turned, drew, and fired once. There were many witnesses to the shooting besides Nathan and Ben, two of whom were soldiers who knew Burke. To everybody's surprise, including Billy Thompson, Sergeant William Burke was unarmed. There was ugly talk directed at Billy Thompson, and the military was about to become involved, for the soldiers had quickly mounted and had ridden away. None of this was lost on Ben Thompson.

"Billy," said Ben, "get your horse and let's ride."

They rode out without so much as speaking to Nathan. It was still early, but he returned to his room at the hotel.

Tomorrow he would ride out, bound for Colorado. While he had a good friend in Captain Jennings and a certain liking for fiery Ben Thompson, he felt the need to leave Austin, for strong on his mind was the tragic loss of Viola Hayden.

*   *   *

Nathan had checked out of his hotel and taken his horse from the livery, and was having breakfast when Captain Jennings joined him.

"I saw you when you came in," Jennings said, "and you looked like a man about to take to the trail."

"I'm bound for Colorado," said Nathan. "I left my dog with friends there and I'm afraid he'll forget who I am."

"Our friend Ben Thompson's in jail," Jennings said. "The Federals are considering filing charges against him for helping Billy escape last night. He could have beaten that, but Ben's never been one to leave well enough alone. Five years back, he had a shooting scrape with James Moore. Last night, after helping Billy escape, Ben ran into Moore again, in a saloon. They had words and Ben shot and wounded Moore. Ben went before a magistrate a while ago. Would you believe he cussed the man and threatened to kill him, once he got his gun?"

"God," said Nathan, "what's going to happen to him now?"

"He'll do some time," Jennings said. "Just watch the newspapers."

Nathan considered visiting Ben Thompson before riding out, but what good would it do? The little gambler would be in a vile mood, and Nathan's mind was burdened enough. He rode northwest, following the Rio Colorado. Despite the Comanche raids in northwest Texas, Nathan left the Colorado when it made its westward turn, riding in a more northerly direction. Before reaching the Red, he crossed another river whose name he didn't know.*

Reaching the Red, Nathan found tracks of unshod horses, but they were many days old. Searching his memory, he tried to recall the other rivers that lay ahead. After the Red, there was the Canadian, the North Canadian, the

---

*The White River, flowing southeast out of New Mexico.

Cimarron, and finally, after he was into Colorado, the Arkansas. Nathan never heard the shot, for the slug struck
him above the left ear and flung him out of the saddle. The
black horse stopped, looking back at its fallen rider, but
Nathan Stone didn't move. Suddenly a bearded apparition
appeared. His hair long and bushy, he wore no hat, while
animal hide covered his thin body and his feet. Under his
arm was a .50-caliber Sharps. The black horse was about to
spook when the strange man spoke. The black perked up its
ears and allowed the stranger to take the reins. He led the
horse to where Nathan lay. Kneeling, he felt for a pulse.

"The varmint's alive," he said aloud, "an' he don't look
like no damn Yankee."

He lay down the Sharps long enough to hoist Nathan
across his saddle. He then led the black north, toward the
distant Canadian River. Reaching the river, he followed it
west until its channel became deeper and its banks rose
higher and higher as he progressed. Finally there was nowhere to walk, shy of the water, and he stepped into it,
leading the horse along the shallows. He eventually reached
a dry shelf that was the start of a break in the river's high
north bank. The entrance to the cave was such that it was
invisible unless one waded the river westward. The stranger
led the black horse inside, and after easing the still-
unconscious Nathan to the cave's stone floor, he unbuckled
the pistol belt, removing Nathan's twin Colts. He then unsaddled the black horse. Finally he stirred up the coals from
an earlier fire, and filling a blackened pot from the river,
put some water on to heat. Suddenly Nathan groaned and
stirred, lifting a hand to his bloodied head.

"Git yer hand away from there, boy. I'll fix it when the
water's hot."

Slowly Nathan sat up, shaking his head. Finally he was
able to focus his eyes on the bearded old man before him.

"Where . . . am I? Who . . . am I?"

"Yer in my cave, an' yer my only son, Jed Whittaker.
Who else would ye be?"

"I . . . don't know," Nathan said. "How did I . . . get
here?"

"I brung ye here. Me, Jeremiah Whittaker, yer pa. Found
ye upriver a ways, after some Yankee shot ye out of yer
saddle. They's a bad wound upside yer head. Lay back on
yer good side an' I'll see to yer hurt."

From a small brass-bound trunk he took a woman's petticoat and ripped a strip from it. This he soaked in the hot water and cleansed Nathan's wound. He then took a tin of salve from the trunk and applied some of the ointment to Nathan's wound. Another wide, folded strip from the petticoat provided a bandage. He then stood back to admire his handiwork.

"Be good as new in a week," Whittaker said. "I knowed ye wasn't kilt in the war, like they said. Takes more'n damn Yankees to kill a Whittaker. I knowed ye'd come ridin' back. Damn it, why couldn't yer ma of lived to see it? That's Lillie's things back yonder in the trunk."

"I don't know anything about any war," said Nathan, "and I don't remember you or anyone named Lillie."

"Ye been addled by that gash on yer head," Whittaker said. "Rest up a spell an' it'll all come back."

"Tell me about the war, about the past," said Nathan. "Maybe that will help me to remember."

"We had us a place up in Kansas, along the Cimarron," Whittaker said, "an' yer ma throwed a fit when ye joined the Rebs. Then come that day in sixty-three, when we got word ye was dead. Lillie took sick an' she never was well again. She died, an' when the Reb deserters an' renegades took to raidin' us, they was worse than the damn Yankees. I loaded as much as our mule, old Mose, could tote, an' I lit out down here. The blamed wolves got old Mose last winter."

"The war ... what about the war ..."

"The war ain't never gonna end, Jed. That's why I'm so glad to see ye come a-ridin' home. It's a mite late in the year now, an' the first snow's a-comin' soon. But come spring, son, with ye sidin' me, we're takin' back our place on the Cimarron. Rebs or Yanks, we'll kill all the varmints."

The snow came and they lived on deer and elk downed by Jeremiah and his Sharps. Nathan's wound healed but his memory continued to fail him. Try as he might, he could remember nothing prior to the time he came to his senses in Jeremiah's cave. Gradually he learned a little more about his surroundings. The black horse had to be taken beyond the confines of the cave and the river banks for grazing, and for a lack of grain, the animal grew gaunt. Despite Nathan's lack of memory, something stood between him and Jeremiah Whittaker, and he could never think of the old man as his father. Occasionally he wore the twin Colts, and as he handled them, his mind tried vainly to reach back into his past, to grasp some long-forgotten experience.

*   *   *

Denver, Colorado Territory. January 15, 1869.

Despite the letter received from Nathan the past fall, Lacy Mayfield had begun to fear the worst. Nathan well knew of the terrible winters on the high plains, and she couldn't imagine him delaying his return this long, unless he was waiting for spring. While Lacy's success on the stage was exciting, and her future in Denver seemed assured, that wasn't enough. Her mentor, Eva Barton, had been accepted by a professional troupe and was only seldom in Denver. It was bitter cold outside, with snow drifted high and the promise of more. Lacy went into the Grimes kitchen and from the ever-present pot, poured herself some coffee. Ezra Grimes sat at the table, snow melting off his boots, nursing his hot cup of coffee. Beside the kitchen stove, where he spent more and more of the cold winter days and nights, lay Cotton Blossom.

"I brought the paper from town," Ezra said.

"Thank you," Lacy said. "At least we can read about places where there's something going on besides a snowstorm."

"That's because news takes so long to get out here," said Ezra. "Some of what you'll read about likely happened last fall."

"Here's one," Lacy said. "Ben Thompson was involved in a shooting in Austin, Texas last September. He's serving two years in the state prison. His brother Billy killed a soldier the same day, but escaped."

"I've heard a lot about the Thompson brothers," said Ezra, "and none of it's been good."

"Lord," Lacy said, "here's something that happened in Arkansas not even two weeks ago, on January sixth. The killer, Cullen Baker, was poisoned by his own father-in-law."

"Josephine came into the kitchen and stirred up the fire in the stove. Cotton Blossom stood up, watching her expectantly. Ezra laughed, winking at Lacy.

"Josephine's done ruint Nathan's dog," he said. "Every time you throw a chunk of wood on the fire, Cotton Blossom thinks the cooking's about to start."

"I'll say one thing for him," said Josephine, "since he showed up, I've never had to throw anything out."

*   *   *

Milo Jenks's relationship with Laura Evans was short lived, for Jenks was a womanizer and a dandy who used his shared proprietorship in the Bagnio Saloon as a means of expanding his conquests. Evans soon found it in her best interests to dispose of him, and did so by paying him five thousand dollars for his share of the Bagnio. That suited Jenks, for his original investment had more than doubled, enabling him, as he saw it, to advance to a higher level in Denver's business and social order. He changed his name to Monte Juno, bought a struggling saloon and renamed it Monte's Hacienda. With the exception of beer, he limited his drinks to rye and bourbon, catering to patrons with an "educated thirst." Contrary to prevailing custom, he eliminated the upstairs whorehouse and installed a gambling casino.

Jenks—now Juno—began dressing more elegantly than ever, attending the theatre, and tipping his hat to the ladies. Especially the pretty, unescorted ones. He would conduct himself like a gentleman, setting his ambition higher than the saloon girls and whores who had always been part of his checkered life. Once he had adopted this new standard, he began eyeing women boldly, and some who never knew Milo Jenks existed began showing some interest in this Monte Juno. But the girl who caught and held his eye appeared nightly on the stage of the Palace Theatre. He began his pursuit of Lacy Mayfield in mid-January and it was the last day in April before she finally agreed to see him.

*   *   *

North Texas, on the Canadian River.* May 15, 1869.

Nathan often spent his days staring into the murky waters of the river, his tangled mind a confusion of names, places, and almost-remembered events. He no longer lis-

---

*Twenty miles northwest of present-day city of Amarillo.

tened to old Jeremiah Whittaker and his recounting of a
past that meant nothing. While he didn't know how he
came to be in the old man's company, he had a feeling—
and that feeling was growing stronger—that he was in no
way related to Whittaker. He had gone through his bedroll
and his saddlebags, sharing his provisions with Whittaker
until they were gone. His hope of finding some means of
identifying himself was short lived. There was the account—from an Austin newspaper—of a pair of outlaws
suspected of a series of robberies, but there were no
names. Was *he* one of those hunted outlaws? Then there
was the watch. Was he in some way affiliated with the
United States government? He had more than three hundred dollars in double eagles. Had he earned the money
or stolen it?

Whittaker had become sullen as a result of Nathan's continued indifference and obvious inability to recall anything.
There were times when the two of them looked at one
another across the fire, one as hostile as the other. Whittaker did all the hunting, traveling afoot, refusing to ride the
black horse. Nathan had grown thin, the result of a continu-
ous diet of nothing but elk, venison, or an occasional wild
turkey. Finally the day came when the old man didn't return from the hunt. Despite the lack of rapport between
them, Nathan felt lost, and he slept little. He waited until
almost noon of the following day before making a decision.
He saddled the black, buckled on his Colts, took his bedroll
and saddlebags and rode out to look for Whittaker. He
rode east, following the river, and when he found Whittaker, the old man lay face down, his back bristling with
arrows. His Sharps and ammunition were gone.

There were tracks of many unshod horses that led in
from the north. The tracks continued eastward along the
river. Whittaker had talked some about the Indians—the
Comanches—and despite having been at odds with Whittaker most of the time, he found himself furious at the cowardly manner in which the old man had been killed. He
slid the Winchester from the saddle boot with intentions of
seeking vengeance, a question troubling his mind. Had he
ever shot a man? In seeking his identity, he had practiced
drawing the twin Colts, and his dexterity with the weapons
now came to his defense. At some time in his life he had
been forced to defend himself. If he must again use these

weapons against men, was he not justified? He rode around a bend in the river and immediately it began to widen. He soon discovered he was riding along the north bank of what had become a substantial lake.*

Nathan reined up. The tracks of the Indian horses had been crossed and recrossed by other animals coming to water, meaning that the Indians might be as much as a day ahead. The wind had risen, coming out of the northwest, and the sun had been swallowed by a mass of clouds rolling in from the west. He might have time to bury old Whittaker, for there was a spade back at the cave beside the river. But Nathan never reached Whittaker's body or the cave. He heard the thump of hooves and the excited shouts of the men who straddled the horses. They were riding from the north, seeking to head Nathan off. While they weren't quite within range, those who were nearest were already loosing arrows. He counted at least a dozen, and shoving the Winchester back into the boot, he rode for his life. Seeing that he was trying to outride them, the Indians turned their mounts west, paralleling the river. The storm was all that saved Nathan. Thunder rumbled and the rain was whipped in on the wind in blinding gray sheets. Rounding the bend in the river, the black horse continued straight ahead, thundering into a stand of trees. It was dark as night and Nathan never saw the low-hanging limb. It swept him from the saddle and he was thrown flat on his back on stoney ground. Minus his rider, the black horse stopped, waiting patiently. When Nathan finally came to his senses, the rain had stopped and night was upon him. His head hurt like fury, and when he put his hand to the gash, he could feel the blood on his fingers. Dark as it was, he could see the black horse standing near, waiting.

"Black horse," he said aloud, "what'n hell happened and where are we? For sure, it ain't Colorado. It's almighty warm for September, too."

Leading the black, Nathan got out into the open where he could see the stars in a clearing sky. He was still wet from the rain, the wind was cold, and he felt like he hadn't eaten in days. He dug around in his saddlebags seeking food—perhaps jerked beef—and found nothing.

---

*Lake Meredith

"By God," he grumbled, "somebody's cleaned me out, but what damn fool would take food and leave double eagles?"

He mounted the black, and following the stars, rode north. He knew not where he was, his last recollection being of the Canadian river, in northwest Texas. He knew only that he needed food, and occasionally resting the black, he rode until dawn. The sun came up in a sky so intensely blue it hurt his eyes. Finally, when the chill was out of his bones, he lay down and slept for what he judged was two hours. He sat up, watching the black graze.

"God Almighty, feller, what's happened to you? You was grained every day in Austin. Now you're a rack of bones."

For that matter, so was he. Saddling the black, he rode on. Before noon he crossed a river that he decided must be the North Canadian, and he was sure of it when he reached another in just a few minutes. This, he was virtually certain, was the Cimarron. The crossing of it would take him into southern Kansas, and if he continued due north, he judged he was not more than half a day's ride from Fort Dodge. But Fort Dodge was a military installation not catering to civilian needs, and he doubted it had changed since he and Lacy were there. He needed grain for his horse and food and rest for himself, and after crossing the Cimarron, he rode eastward along the river. He was hopeful of finding a village where he might at least stay the night. The wind was out of the west, caressing him with moist fingers, promising more rain. Finally he reached the bend in the Cimarron where it flowed southeast into Indian Territory.

"Damn," he said aloud, "I might ride plumb to Missouri before finding grub and a bed."

He was sorely tempted to just ride north and take his chances at Fort Dodge when he came upon a clearly defined wagon road from the northwest. The ruts told him there had been more than one wagon and the direction that they had been going to or from Fort Dodge. The trail led east as far as he could see, and he rode on. He reached a stand of willows, and from the runoff, he realized there was a substantial spring. He rode around, still following the trail, and came upon a sprawling, false-fronted building built of logs.* There was a crudely lettered sign hanging from a pole that read: *Trade goods, grub, whiskey, rooms.* There wasn't another building anywhere in sight. Along the front ran a hitch rail and tied to it, heads drooping, stood three horses. It was the most unlikely place in the world for a trading post until one considered the proximity of Indian Territory. This opportunist, whoever he was, had gone after the owlhoot trade, catering to men who dared not venture any closer to civilization. The prices would be outrageous. With that in mind, Nathan tied the black alongside the other horses and entered the building. He wasn't too surprised that one side of it had been devoted to a saloon. There were just four tables and the three men who sat at one of them eyed him suspiciously. Two of them had skewed their chairs around so that they all faced the door. Nathan didn't even look at them, going straight to the part of the building that was devoted to goods of all kinds. But the patrons of this isolated post were not permitted to walk freely among the counters piled with goods. A whiskered, barrel-chested man wearing run-over boots, grimy Levi's, and an undershirt approached. His sweaty, florid face suggested that he had drunk too much of his own whiskey.

"What are you needin', pilgrim?" There are no friendliness in his eyes.

"Grain for my horse," Nathan said, "and grub for me. Enough coffee, hard tack, bacon, and jerked beef to last a week. Do you have airtights?"

"Peaches an' tomatoes. Dollar apiece."

"Half a dozen of each," said Nathan. "Twenty-five pounds of grain, in burlap."

"Forty dollars for the lot," said the storekeeper, with a straight face.

It was four times too much, but Nathan paid. As he was about to leave, a calendar caught his eye. Pages had been turned forward to May 1869.

---

*In 1873, this village would become the town of Medicine Lodge, Kansas. Near here, in 1867, the U.S. government and the five tribes of plains Indians—the Apache, Arapaho, Cheyenne, Comanche, and Kiowa—met and agreed upon what became known as the Medicine Lodge Treaty. It was a dismal failure, and was the government's last attempt to make peace with the Indians. It was in Medicine Lodge (1899) that Carrie Nation began her antisaloon crusade.

"That calendar says May 1869," Nathan said. "That can't be."

"Sorry it don't meet with your approval, bucko, but this is the eighteenth day of May. Last year was 1868. You got some reason for believin' otherwise?"

Nathan turned away, saying nothing. The storekeeper had spoken so loud the three men at the saloon table had heard and Nathan could hear them laughing. They all watched with amusement as he made his way to the door, but his mind was occupied with the startling thing he had just learned. There was more than eight months of his life for which he was unable to account. What had happened to him? He loaded his food into the saddlebags and divided the burlap sack of grain behind his saddle. He hadn't liked the looks of the trio in the saloon. He rode back the way he had come, determined to put as much distance between himself and this owlhoot paradise as he could. The bed and town grub would have to wait. He could still reach the Arkansas before dark, and might be fortunate enough to find shelter from the coming storm.

But the rain found him two hours from sundown. There was no lightning, and for that he was thankful. He rode on, following the wagon ruts that had led him to the trading post, virtually certain if he continued following them northwest, they would lead him to Fort Dodge. He didn't reach the fort until after dark, and the rain hadn't let up. The sentry refused to open the gate, and called the sergeant of the guard.

"I'm Sergeant Helms," the soldier said. "We do not admit civilians after dark. If you're needing food and quarters, there's a tent city eight miles upriver, on the west bank."

"Tent city?"

"Yes," Helms said. "There's plans for a town. The railroad's coming."

Nathan rode on. He had heard talk of a railroad, but he had also heard the Union Pacific had priority. But the tents were there. One was stocked as a mercantile, the second had been set up as a cafe, while the third was serving as a hotel. A cot and blankets for the night cost two dollars, and Nathan paid. Sleeping dry would be worth it. He lugged his saddle, bedroll, and saddlebags into the tent. He then rubbed down the black, despite the drizzling rain, and then fed the animal a good bait of rye. He then went to the makeshift cafe. There were X-frame tables and benches, and a dozen men were eating and talking. The menu consisted of thick beef stew, cornbread, and black coffee. Nathan paid for two orders. While he ate, he listened to the talk, and by the time he was finishing his coffee, most of the men had departed. Nathan directed a question at the two that remained.

"Is it true there's goin' to be a town here?"

"Damn right," said one of the men. "It's already been surveyed, and lots are going for two hundred and fifty dollars."

"Seems a mite soon for building a town," Nathan said. "The railroad won't be here for a while, I hear."

"They're sayin' two years," the second man replied. "Folks with money is buying up all they can. Once the railroad gets here, these lots will go for a thousand dollars and more."*

Nathan returned to the tent where he had rented a cot. Removing his gunbelt, his boots, and his damp clothes, he stretched out under the blankets, listening to the patter of rain on the canvas above. He fell asleep pondering those months of his life for which he could not account.

---

*The fledgling town became Dodge City in 1872, when the railroad arrived.

Chapter 29

Denver, Colorado Territory. May 29, 1869.

Nathan took his time, following the Arkansas west, spending the night in several villages where there was some kind of hotel. As soon as he was sure he was in Colorado, he rode northwest. He reached Cherry Creek Manor in the early afternoon and found Ezra Grimes at the barn, Cotton Blossom with him. The dog raced madly around Nathan, circling the horse, and when he dismounted there was a glad reunion. When Nathan finally freed himself from the excited Cotton Blossom, he walked to meet Ezra, who was grinning.

"I didn't want to get between you and him," Ezra said. "I reckoned I'd wait my turn."

"He looks some better than when I last saw him," said Nathan. "Thanks."

"Thank Josephine. She fed him about six times a day, soon as he got so he'd eat, and he's had plenty of rest. You go on to the house, and I'll rub down your horse."

"I'm obliged," Nathan said. "God, it seems like I've been gone forever. Is Lacy home?"

"No," Ezra said. "Tell Josephine to put the coffee on. I'll join you in a few minutes."

Nathan walked on toward the house, wondering what had happened while he had been gone. When Nathan had mentioned Lacy, Ezra's lips had tightened and all the joviality had gone out of him. Cotton Blossom trotted beside Nathan as though fearful he might disappear again. Josephine heard him when he hit the first step and met him on the porch with a hug. The moment the door was opened, Cotton Blossom bolted into the kitchen.

"Cotton Blossom," said Nathan, "mind your manners. Out."

"Oh, let him stay," Josephine said. "He slept by the stove while he was hurt, and by the time he had healed, he just kind of made a place for himself beside the stove. My land, I'm glad to see you. We expected you last September. October at the latest. We were afraid something had happened to you."

"Something did happen to me," said Nathan, "and I'm not sure what. Why don't we wait for Ezra and I won't have to tell it but once."

"But there's Lacy . . ."

She caught herself, but Nathan was quick to note that same look of consternation he had seen in Ezra's face.

"While we're waiting for Ezra," he said, "why don't you tell me all about Lacy? I reckon she's made a name for herself on the stage."

"That she has," Josephine said, "but that's not what concerns you, is it?"

"No, ma'am," said Nathan. "She's making a name for herself in other ways?"

"Ezra's told me to mind my own business," Josephine said doubtfully. "I'd not want to cause trouble . . ."

"If there's somethin' I need to know," said Nathan, "I'd take it as a favor if you told me. I won't fault you if it's bad news. You have my word."

"I told Ezra you should know" she replied, "and that it would be better coming from one of us. She's the gossip of the town."

"Then tell me," Nathan said. "I had no hold on her. As long as I've been away, I can't blame her for making a life for herself."

"Nor could anyone else," said Josephine, "if she hadn't done it with that no-account Monte Juno."

"Who is he?"

"He owns a saloon and gambling casino called Monte's Hacienda. He's taken to showin' up here in the evenings with a buckboard, driving Lacy to the theatre, and he doesn't always bring her back. She started seeing him the last week in April, and I've lost count of the times she's been out all night. He came for her last night, and we haven't seen her since."

"I can't fault a man for owning a saloon," Nathan said. "There's been times when I've worked as a house dealer. I won't say it's fair, but when a woman gets a bad name, it's usually blamed on her conduct, not the hombre she runs with."

"I understand," said Josephine, "but this Monte Juno has a reputation in town that goes beyond his owning this saloon and gambling place. He dresses well and has the ways of a gentleman, and Lacy sees only that."

"I reckon I'll just have to wait and see what she has to say for herself," Nathan said. "I'm obliged for you having told me."

At that point, Ezra came in, wiping his hands on the legs of his Levi's.

"Now," he said, looking at Josephine, "I reckon you've heard all the bad news I told Josey to keep to herself. What can you tell us about your travels?"

Nathan told them much of what he had experienced, but not of the tragic vengeance of Viola Hayden. Instead, he concentrated on the months that had passed for which he couldn't account.

"Sounds like amnesia," Ezra said. "A heavy blow to the head can shuck your memory, leaving you with no recollection of who you are, where you're from, or where you're going. Another blow can bring it all back to you."

"Maybe that's what happened to me," said Nathan. "I came to my senses in a stand of trees, right after a storm, with a nasty cut on the back of my head."

"If there was lightning," Ezra said, "it might have spooked your horse. A good, strong tree limb can unhorse a man almighty fast in the dark."

There was the sound of footsteps on the back porch. Lacy Mayfield stood in the doorway, her eyes wide and her face pale with shock.

"Hello, Lacy," said Nathan.

"After all these months," she snapped, "is that all you have to say?"

"I doubt anything I have to say will interest you," said Nathan. "I reckon what you have to tell me will be more interesting."

"Ezra," Josephine said, "let's you and me set on the front porch awhile."

Lacy said no more until Ezra and Josephine were well out of hearing. It took her only a few seconds to find her tongue, and what she had to say came as a shock even to Nathan.

"So they told you. I don't give a damn what they think, or what anybody thinks. I'm moving to town. I just came back for my things."

"It's your life," said Nathan mildly. He refused her the satisfaction of knowing that he was disappointed in her, that he cared what she did, and that further infuriated her.

"Damn you," she screamed, "you *don't* care, do you?"

"Would it matter if I did?"

She then resorted to tears, but they were tears of anger and frustration. He said nothing, watching her. Finally she stomped off into another part of the house, to the room that she had been occupying. Nathan got up and went out the back door, Cotton Blossom following. Between the house and the barn there was a buckboard, a pair of matched bays hitched to it, and on the seat, a man about Nathan's age. He was dressed all in black, including his hat. Taking his time, Nathan approached, and when the man turned to face him, his hand was near the butt of his Colt. His eyes hard and cold, Nathan spoke.

"When a man greets me with his hand on his pistol, I get the feeling he's been up to something that won't stand the light of day."

"I've heard of you," he said, with a contemptuous half-smile. "You're Nathan Stone, the man-killer. Well, I'm Monte Juno, and you don't look so damn tall to me."

"I look taller when you're on your back in the dirt," said Nathan, "but I won't kill a man without cause. I can laugh at you and pity her, and that's all either of you are worth. But if I ever have cause to kill you, then you'd best be wearing your buryin' clothes."

Before Juno could respond—if he had intended to—Lacy walked stiffly past Nathan without speaking. Juno reached down for her carpetbag and then gave her a hand up to the buckboard seat. He clucked to the horses and wheeled the buckboard, and Nathan watched them as they rounded the house and were soon out of sight on the road toward town. With a sigh he walked back to the house, but instead of going into the kitchen, he continued on around to the front porch. Ezra and Josephine sat on the top step and Nathan hunkered on the ground.

"I brought her here," Nathan said. "If she left owing you, I'll pay."

"She's paid through the end of the month," said Josephine, "and that's two more days. Anyway, we wouldn't expect that of you."

"I'll pay for another month for me, the black, and my packhorse," Nathan said. "I need some rest and I reckon the black does too."

Despite the trouble with Lacy, Nathan welcomed Josephine's bountiful supper. Banker Ames Tilden arrived late, and he seemed genuinely glad to see Nathan.

"After supper," said Tilden, "we need to talk."

When the meal was over, Nathan followed the banker out to the front porch. Tilden leaned on the rail and Nathan leaned there beside him.

"We had an agreement," Tilton said, "that in the event of your death, Lacy Mayfield was to receive your estate. I believe you should know that she has gone to great lengths to have you declared legally dead so that all your funds—including interest—could be turned over to her."

"I'm not a damned bit surprised," said Nathan. "She didn't succeed?"

"She did not," Tilden replied. "There's a legal procedure involved, and just last fall she seemed excited at having received a letter from you. Since you had to be alive to write that letter, I persuaded her legal counsel they were wasting their time."

"I'm obliged," said Nathan.

*   *   *

For two weeks Nathan made the rounds of various saloons, vainly seeking some clue to the remaining three men on his death list. One night, while at the bar in the Silver Dollar, Nathan heard that Wild Bill Hickok was in the house. He found Hickok observing a poker game. Hickok wore his hair down to his shoulders. His black pin-striped trousers were stuffed into the tops of stove-pipe boots. His stiff, white shirt had ruffles down the front and hung open at the throat. His unbuttoned black vest partially covered the forward-turned butts of his pearl-handled revolvers. An expensive pinch-creased black Stetson was tilted back on his head. Two of the five men dropped out of the game and Hickok took an empty chair, his back to the wall. Nathan took the other chair, and the two of them played for an hour without winning a single pot.

"Gentlemen," Hickok said, "Lady Luck is a faithless wench who appears to have forsaken me. I bid you adieu."

"I'd have to amen that," said Nathan, getting to his feet. "Belly up to the bar," he told Hickok, "and I'll buy. At least we'll get something for our money there."

Hickok laughed, appreciating the humor. It was still early and Nathan had grown tired of saloons. It soon should be suppertime at Cherry Creek Manor, and unless Nathan intended to eat in town, it was time he rode out. Having made Hickok's acquaintance, he found himself reluctant to leave.

"It's near suppertime," Nathan said. "Will you join me?"

"Why not?" said Hickok. "There's something to be said for a bad night at the games of chance. It frees a man to seek decent nourishment, instead of hunkering over a poker table all night, grazing off the saloon free lunch."

Nathan found himself liking Hickok immediately, for he was an amiable man with a sense of humor and apparently, some degree of education. However, there was much that Nathan had yet to learn. When sober, Hickok had a way with women, an undefinable charm that in no way seemed affected. On the other hand, he possessed a violent temper that often manifested itself when he was drunk. Hickok chose one of the more fashionable restaurants, and in the lobby was a placard announcing the opening of a comedy, *My American Cousin,* at the Palace Theatre. Nathan swallowed hard, for Lacy Mayfield's name was prominently displayed. When Nathan and Hickok were about to leave the restaurant, Hickok paused before the placard.

"I've never seen a mining town that didn't have some kind of theatre," Hickok said, "and I've never attended this one. Tonight would be a good time to go. Will you join me?"

"I reckon I'll go," said Nathan. "A man can't spend all his time in the saloons." The truth of it was, Nathan had been doing exactly that, allowing it to serve a twofold purpose. While he sought some information on the three men on his death list, he was using the activity as a means of ridding his mind of Lacy Mayfield. With her in mind, the very last place he wanted to go was the Palace, where her memory would be personified for a painful two hours. However, he told himself, it wasn't his nature to run and hide from anything or anybody. He would attend her damn play, taking a seat as near the stage as he could. Nathan and Hickok arrived early, and despite it being an opening night, they were able to get seats near the front row, at center stage.

For a while Nathan was uncomfortable watching Lacy perform. However, the stage was well lighted, and after the intermission, the girl discovered Nathan in the audience. Where her earlier performance had been flawless, she now began to stumble over her lines.

"She keeps looking this way," Nathan said to Hickok. "I think she's got her eye on you."

"I'd not be surprised," said Hickok, dead serious.

When the play was over, many of the patrons gathered near the stage in hopes of speaking to some of the cast, but Lacy Mayfield didn't appear. But Monte Juno did. He wasted no time in confronting Nathan.

"Damn you, he said, "you made her nervous."

"Is that a fact?" said Nathan. "Why, this is the first time I've ever seen her on stage. I'm so taken with her, I might just be here every night for the run of the play."

Juno was so furious his mouth worked, but no words came out. He stomped away and Nathan laughed.

"Ah," Hickok said, seeing the light. "The plot thickens."

"She gave me the boot for him," said Nathan, "and you can see why. I've never looked worth a damn in a clawhammer coat and top hat."

"It's a hardship," Hickok replied, biting his upper lip and jiggling his flowing mustache. "He looks like the kind who'd live off a lady's wages."

"Oh, he has a place of his own," said Nathan. "Saloon and gambling house called Monte's Hacienda. I've been meaning to drop in for a neighborly visit and try a few hands at his tables. I hear he serves only rye and bourbon, catering to gents with an educated thirst."

"By the saints," Hickok thundered. "Let us not delay this visit any longer. I have been known to down good rye until the sun rises or until I can't."

Hickok was becoming well known on the frontier, and certainly in its many saloons. Monte's Hacienda was no different. He was met at the door by Monte Juno himself, and while he welcomed Hickok, he cast dark looks at Nathan, who grinned at him. Hickok looked around, saw no gambling tables, and headed for the stairs. Nathan followed. The second floor was devoted entirely to gambling, although there was a bar along one wall. Hickok paused at the bar.

"Bottle of rye," he thundered.

The bartender produced the bottle and a glass.

"Another glass," Hickok bawled. "What do you reckon my pard's gonna drink out of? His hat?"

There was a burst of laughter and the bartender hurriedly brought another glass. Hickok snatched the glasses in one hand and the bottle in the other and went looking for a table. One of the poker games had dwindled down to two participants and the house man. Hickok took a chair, his back to the wall, and Nathan took one across the table from him. Hickok belted down two shots of rye, while Nathan drank nothing. He hung his vest on the back of an empty chair and got down to some serious five-card stud. The house man was nervous, his eyes on the forward butts of Hickok's Navy Colts. The fickle Lady Luck who had scorned Nathan and Hickok earlier now smiled on them abundantly, as Hickok took the first and second pots, while the third and fourth went to Nathan. The other two gamblers eyed the house dealer suspiciously, as Hickok took the fifth pot and Nathan the sixth. It was time for Juno to appear, and he did.

"Gentlemen," he said, "this game is over."

"Like hell it is," shouted one of the losing gamblers. "I want a chance to git my money back."

"Some other time," said Juno. His eyes shifted from the empty whiskey bottle to Hickok, who was now gloriously drunk.

"Well, hell," Hickok muttered, "we got to make our own fun."

With dazzling swiftness he drew the Navy Colts, firing first one and then the other. Four seperate pyramids of bottled whiskey exploded, while the long mirror behind the bar came down in a tinkling crash. Three men piled on Hickok while a fourth swung a Colt at Nathan's head. He caught the arm, slammed the man's face into the surface of the table, and buffaloed him with the muzzle of one of his own Colts. He tried to go to Hickok's aid, but as was the case with most saloon brawls, men leaped into the fray for the sheer hell of it. Bottles flew, chairs smashed into walls, tables broke, and Colts roared. A slug struck a hanging lamp, showering men with burning oil. Nathan went down under an avalanche of bodies and somebody drove a knife into his left arm, just below the shoulder. A Colt roared close by, and one of the men pinning him down screamed.

"Enough, damn it," a bull voice roared. "This is the law."

It ended as abruptly as it had begun. Men got to their feet nursing bloody noses, spitting blood from smashed mouths, rubbing throbbing heads. Blood dripped off Nathan's fingers from the knife wound in his upper arm, but Hickok had been shot three times. Once in the left side, and once in each upper thigh. The sheriff was dressed in a town suit, gray Stetson, and black polished boots, but the shotgun he carried was all business.

"You varmints got some walking to do," he said. "Is anybody unable?"

Hickok, gripping the edge of a table, managed to get to his feet.

"Damn it, Sheriff," a man complained, "I didn't have nothin' to do with all this."

"I expect none of you jaspers had anything to do with it," said the lawman, "so I aim to be fair. I'm lockin' all of you up, and you can tell it to the judge in the morning."

"I'm hurt," a man complained.

"I'll send the doc around to patch up them of you that's needful of it," said the sheriff. "Now get movin', all of you."

They moved, Hickok limping, as were some of the others. There were twelve men. Hickok and Nathan were locked in one cell, while the others were divided two or three to a cell.

"You got the worst of it," Nathan said. "That doc's taking his own sweet time gettin' here."

"It's painful," said Hickok, "but I've been hurt worse. What about you?"'

"Knife wound," Nathan said. "I reckon old Juno's hurtin' the most. He won't soon find another bar mirror to replace what he had. When he does, I reckon he'll be payin' for it with our money."

"Lord" Bill said, "wasn't that the sweetest sound you ever heard in all your born days, that glass rainin' off the wall?"

The doctor eventually arrived, and disinfected and bandaged their wounds. Everybody had been fortunate, for no lead had to be dug out and no bones had been broken. The bunks in the cells were about as comfortable as stone slabs, and nobody slept much. The sheriff showed up early with a proposition.

"Unless some of you varmints is mule headed enough to want to argue with the judge, Juno's agreed to let you loose with payment of damages. He figured six hundred dollars, and that's fifty dollars apiece. Now if there's anybody that ain't satisfied with that, tell it to the judge. He'll fine you fifty dollars, add ten dollars for court costs, and lock you up until you pay."

Nobody argued with that. They were turned loose, some of the others casting baleful looks at Nathan and Hickok.

"I can bring your horse," said Nathan. "Where is he?"

"At the livery, near the Albany Saloon," Hickok replied. "Just leave him there. I have a room at the Tremont House, and I can make it that far."

He did, painful as it must have been.

"I'll come back tomorrow morning," said Nathan, "and if you're feeling up to it, I'll buy your breakfast. Do you want me to bring you a bottle of whiskey, in case there's infection?"

"I want a bottle of whiskey whether there's infection or not," Hickok said with a grin, "but there's a bar in the hotel lobby."

*   *   *

Nathan went on his way, taking his horse from the livery and riding back to Cherry Creek Manor. Cotton Blossom came bounding out the kitchen door to greet him, and he was thankful for the friendship of Ezra and Josephine and for their affection for the faithful hound. He stepped into the kitchen, aware of a painful purple bruise beneath his left eye and the ripped, bloody sleeve of his shirt. He found Ezra and Josephine at the kitchen table.

"I saved you breakfast, if you want it," said Josephine.

"I want it more than anything," Nathan replied. "All I got in jail was a hard bunk, and I paid fifty dollars for it."

Ezra laughed, and Nathan told them of meeting Hickok, and of the brawl that had erupted as a result of Hickok's pistol work in Monte's Hacienda.

"From what I've seen of Mr. Juno," said Josephine, "it must have been almost worth fifty dollars."

"It almost was," Nathan agreed. "Hickok's laid up at the Tremont House, with three bullet wounds. He could have been killed, and all for nothing."

"You should have brought him with you," said Ezra. "I'd like to meet him. We could always send Josephine into the parlor."

"You could try," Josephine sniffed. "If someone as well known as he is shows up here, I want to hear everything he has to say. Besides, from what I have read, he can be a perfect gentleman."

"He can be," said Nathan, "and he is, while he's sober. He was roaring drunk when he shot up Juno's place."

"He's still welcome here, if he needs a place to stay," Josephine said.

"I'm riding in to have breakfast with him tomorrow, if he's able," said Nathan. "I'll tell him what you said."

Nathan spent the day resting and went to bed early. He was awake before first light and on his way into town by sunup. He found Hickok stretched out on his bed, dressed except for boots and hat.

"You look ready for breakfast," Nathan said.

"Hungry as a grizzly just out of hibernation," said Hickok, "and aimin' to go, if I have to crawl on hands and knees."

Nathan could only marvel at the man's endurance and rapid recovery. He still limped, but if his wounds pained him, he gave no sign. A restaurant adjoining the Tremont House provided the nourishment Bill so desired.

"I've about had enough of Colorado for a while," Hickok said. "Another week—mid-July—and I aim to ride back to Hays."

"Hays?"

"Hays City, Kansas," said Hickok. "They're holdin' an election for county sheriff in August. I might just have a go at it."

"I might just ride with you," Nathan said, "if that sets well with you."

"Come on, and welcome," said Hickok. "It's a comfort, having a gent sidin' you that's set with you at the poker table, had his head cracked in your saloon fight, and shared a cell with you in the *calabozo.*"

Nathan laughed. He had never known a man like Wild Bill Hickok. After leaving Hickok, he visited some of the shops in Denver, purchasing some new Levi's, shirts, and socks. It was too early for most of the saloons to be open, and there were still a few Nathan had not visited. These were often more of a whorehouse than a saloon. Nathan had heard of Laura Evans's Bagnio, but had never been there. Despite the early hour, the place was open, and it seemed that Laura herself was behind the bar. Nathan thought she must have been an attractive woman once, but the years and her profession had taken their toll. Three men leaned on the bar, apparently regulars, for all were laughing at some private joke. Nathan finished a beer and was about to leave, when something one of the men said gained his undivided attention.

". . . glad you got rid of that bastard, Milo Jenks."

"Pardner," Nathan said, "I'm not one to butt into a private conversation, but I heard you mention Milo Jenks. I've been looking for him."

The man laughed. "Ask Laura. She knows him well."

But Laura Evans didn't think it was funny. "If you're a friend of his," she said, "get the hell out of here. You're not welcome."

"Ma'am," said Nathan, "I'm no friend. He'll wish he'd never laid eyes on me."

"In that case," Laura said, "try Monte's Hacienda. The two-faced, two-timing skunk that's calling himself Monte Juno is Milo Jenks. At least that was his name when he first showed up here."

"I'm obliged," said Nathan. He tipped his hat and left hurriedly.

The three men at the bar watched Nathan out the door, and the one who had mentioned Jenks spoke.

"I'd say Mr. Jenks has a past, and that some of it's about to make some big changes in his future."

"Praise be," Laura Evans said. "Gut-shooting's too good for him."

Milo Jenks, now known as Monte Juno, wasn't to be found at the saloon, for the place wasn't open. There was the sound of hammering from somewhere inside, and Nathan guessed the upstairs was being cleaned up and repaired. He waited across the street, but Jenks didn't show. He was probably out with Lacy, Nathan thought with disgust. He grew tired of waiting and returned to the Tremont House, thinking he would spend the afternoon with Hickok, but he got no answer when he knocked on the door to Hickok's room. Nathan had his supper in the restaurant adjoining the Tremont House, and when it was near time for the play to begin at the Palace Theatre, he went there. Others were waiting near the stage door, probably for Lacy's arrival, and Nathan joined them. When Jenks drove up in the buckboard, Lacy stepped down. Nathan must wait until she was out of the line of fire, and as she approached the theatre, he started toward the buckboard. Then he shouted his challenge.

"You in the buckboard, Milo Jenks. Get down. I'm going to give you more of a chance than you gave my family, back in Virginia."

"You got the wrong man," Jenks shouted.

"No," said Nathan. "Get off that seat and face me like a man, or I'll kill you where you set."

"No," Lacy Mayfield screamed. She ran toward Nathan, about to throw herself at him, when Jenks fired. Once, twice he fired, and the slugs stopped Lacy in her tracks. She stumbled forward and fell face down at Nathan's feet. Jenks fired a third time, but the slug went over Nathan's head. He drew his right-hand Colt and shot Milo Jenks twice, through the chest. The outlaw stumbled back against the buckboard team, spooking them. They bolted, leaving the dying outlaw lying in the dust. Women screamed and men cursed, but Nathan Stone was oblivious to it all. His heart was heavy, recalling the days past when young Lacy Mayfield only wanted to be somebody ...

Chapter 30

◆◆◆

Every witness swore that Milo Jenks had fired first, that his slugs had struck Lacy, and that only then had Nathan shot Jenks. Lacy's funeral was a nightmare that Nathan Stone wanted only to forget. Wild Bill Hickok was there, and when Lacy had been laid to rest, Hickok approached Nathan.

"I reckon this is a bad time to talk," Wild Bill said.

"There won't be any good times for a while," Nathan replied.

"I'm ridin' out for Hays in the mornin'," said Hickok.

"I'll be riding with you," Nathan said.

Ezra and Josephine Grimes approached, and Nathan found it necessary to introduce them to Hickok. It was a good time to tell them he was riding out the next morning, and he did so.

"We'll hate to see you go," Josephine said. "Why don't you and Mr. Hickok take supper with us tonight? The both of you can spend your last night with us."

"I'd consider it a pleasure, ma'am," said Hickok, tipping his hat.

"Then just ride back with us," Ezra said. "It's quite a while until supper, but we can put on a pot of coffee, and there's fresh apple pie."

Nathan was glad to get away from the town, for he had become a curiosity, as people sought to discover his motive for hunting down Milo Jenks. Nathan and Hickok rode their horses alongside the Grimes's buckboard. Trotting along behind was Cotton Blossom, for he had refused to be left behind. However, the enormous crowd had intimidated him, and keeping him out of the church hadn't been a problem. Despite the plainsman's overtures, Cotton Blossom was still wary of Hickok. While the day had gotten off to a terrible start, Hickok was at his charming best and cold sober, and by suppertime, even Nathan smiled at some of Wild Bill's tales. Following Nathan's instructions, Ames Tilden had brought Nathan a thousand dollars from his account.

"Invest the balance," Nathan said, "and if you go as long as five years without hearing from me, see that it goes to Ezra and Josephine."

"You can count on me," said the banker. "If you're needing money fast, send me a telegram. I can arrange for you to get your money from any other bank. Except those in states under Reconstruction, of course."

"I understand," Nathan said, "and I'm obliged."

*   *   *

Hays, Kansas. August 2, 1869.

Fort Hays was but a mile south of the town of Hays. From Fort Hays, the government freighted all supplies to Fort Larned, Fort Dodge, Camp Supply, Fort Sill, and other small forts. There were more than a thousand civilian clerks and "whackers" employed in the different departments at Fort Hays. Meanwhile, with the arrival of the tracks of the Kansas–Pacific Railway, the village of Hays had been elevated to the status of boomtown. Every building necessary for the making of a railroad town was located just east of the Schwaller Lumber Yard. There was the Othero and Sellars Warehouse, which did considerable freighting. North and South Main Streets ran along either side of the track from Chestnut to a little west of Fort Street. On North Main, east to west from Chestnut, was the Capless and Ryan Outfitting Store; the Leavenworth Restaurant; Hound Saloon and Faro House; Hound Kelly's Saloon; the office of M.E. Joyce, justice of the peace; Ed Godard's Saloon and Dance Hall; Tommy Drum's Saloon; Evans' Grocery Store and Post Office; Cohen's Clothing; Paddy Welshes' Saloon and Gambling House; the Perry Hotel; and Treat's Candy and Peanut Stand—and that was only the beginning. Fort Street was built on the same order from Normal Avenue as far north as the courthouse square. In addition to the railroad, Hays was the stomping grounds of the buffalo hunters, skinners, and hide hunters.

"Tarnation," said Nathan, as he and Wild Bill rode down North Front, "I've never seen the like."

"Most of it follows the railroad," Hickok said. "Give it a few weeks and it'll move on, to end-of-track."

Nathan and Hickok took a room at Root's Railroad Rest, a boardinghouse catering to railroad men. Each room had two bunks, and Cotton Blossom slept on the floor between them. The town had twenty-three saloons, and during his first two weeks in Hays, Nathan visited most of them, usually in the company of Hickok. Wild Bill's reputation resulted in an almost immediate following, and he was often drunk or nearly so, as well-wishers bought him drinks. The town—and Ellis County—was without a sheriff and the governor had declared that Hays must wait until November to elect a new one. But the Ellis County Commission took drastic action and set a special election for August twenty-three.

"I was here on my way West," said Hickok, "and they was having a big fuss with the governor then, petitioning for an election in August."

"God," said Nathan, "you must enjoy bein' shot or shot at, wantin' to be a lawman here. Soldiers and civilians combined, there must be near fifteen hundred men at the fort, and a good five hundred railroaders, when you consider the grading and track-laying crews."

Hickok laughed. "Don't forget the gamblers, pimps, and whores," he said.

Wild Bill won the election handily, and those who previously hadn't taken him seriously now looked upon him with respect. Hickok wasted no time taking advantage, trading his plains garb for a Prince Albert coat, expensive pin-stripe trousers, white shirt with ruffles, and flowing, black string tie. He was often hatless, displaying his long hair. Men who had joked about his passion for cleanliness now followed his example and visited the bathhouses daily. But for all his vanity, Hickok took his duties as sheriff seriously, seldom drawing his pistols except as clubs to subdue unruly drunks. But one such drunk refused to submit to arrest, and Hickok shot him. He was John Mulrey, a cavalryman; mortally wounded, he died the next day. Newspapers, recalling Wild Bill's days as a scout for the Union army, were critical of the shooting.

"Damn it," Nathan said, "when we came here, they were

giving the soldiers hell for wrecking the saloons and fighting with civilians."

"My friend," said Hickok, "a man elected to public office is cursed with the responsibility of performing his duties without offending anybody. Even those who opposed him and hate his guts."

Nathan found some advantages to life in an end-of-track boomtown, for there were regular newspapers from Kansas City and St. Louis. While he felt some urgency for seeking out the remaining two men on his death list, he had not a clue as to where he might find them. He was spending less and less time with Wild Bill, for Hickok had become a marked man. There had been attempts on the sheriff's life; men had fired at him from the darkness, his only clue the sound of running feet. Wild Bill became cautious, avoiding strong light, dark alleys, and sidewalks. He stalked down the center of Main Street, his eyes darting right and left. Reaching a saloon that seemed unduly noisy, he turned sharply, and shoving the doors back against the wall, advanced into the room. His back to a wall, he spoke his piece and got out. Hickok made no exceptions for what he perceived as his duty.

Nathan's trouble with Wild Bill arose over an incident with a drunken soldier in the Drum Saloon. Nathan was having a decent night at poker. Next to him sat a soldier who had lost as consistently as Nathan had won. The man got up, slapped his losing hand on the table, and deliberately kicked Cotton Blossom, who wasn't in his way. Cotton Blossom responded in a predictable manner, sinking his teeth into the soldier's leg. The man shouted in pain, reaching for his sidearm, only to find himself looking into the muzzle of Nathan's Colt.

"You owe him an apology," said Nathan. "His name's Cotton Blossom. Mr. Cotton Blossom to you."

"By God, I ain't apologizin' to nobody's dog. I'm damned if I will."

"You'll be damned if you don't," Nathan said coldly.

Cotton Blossom had backed away, growling ominously. At that moment, another soldier kicked over the table and a brawl ensued which didn't cease until Hickok fired a shot into the ceiling. When Wild Bill had been told the cause of the fight, he turned to Nathan.

"You'll have to keep the dog out of the saloons," he said.

"The dog wasn't at fault," Nathan replied.

"I said you'll have to keep the dog out of the saloons," Hickok repeated.

"I'll do that, Sheriff," said Nathan coldly.

Nathan returned to the room he'd been sharing with Hickok. Taking his bedroll and saddlebags, he went to the livery, where he saddled his black and loaded his pack-horse. He then rode east, following the rails, toward Abilene.

*   *   *

Abilene, Kansas. October 15, 1869.

Abilene had seen its day as a railroad boomtown, and Nathan found it far less rowdy than Hays had been. But its day as a cattletown had just begun, and Nathan was awed by the numerous cattle-holding pens with loading ramps that stretched along the tracks. It was late in the season for Texas herds, so most of the residents were store-keepers or the owners of various other kinds of businesses. Especially saloons. A bank, stores, and saloons stretched along both sides of the tracks. There were more saloons and stores along Texas Street, while to the north, a collection of shacks housed whorehouses and a few dance halls. As Nathan would learn, Abilene was a town virtually built by Joseph McCoy, an Illinois businessman. It had been McCoy who had finally persuaded the governor of Kansas to lift the long-standing quarantine against Texas cattle, permitting the herds to reach the rails at Abilene. The law had been passed by the Kansas legislature in 1855 to protect local cattle from "Texas" or tick fever, carried by Texas longhorns. Abilene's most prominent establishment was its three-story hotel, the Drover's Cottage. It featured a bar, a restaurant and a nearby livery, and it was the only place that had charged extra for Cotton Blossom. In fact, the clerk had been reluctant to allow the dog in the hotel at all.

"Highfalutin damn diggings," Nathan growled.

"You are fortunate, sir," the desk clerk said. "These are winter rates. They are considerably higher in spring and summer."

"I'll keep that in mind," Nathan said. At least there was

no shortage of rooms and theirs was on the first floor. He had to admit it was probably worth what he was paying, for there was deep-piled tan carpet on the floor and heavy drapes on windows that reached from the floor almost to the ceiling. The bed frame was of heavy oak, with thick mattress and strong springs beneath it, while the sheets and blankets looked new. There was a matching oak dresser with a high-standing mirror, a stool, and two chairs of oak, with padded seats and backs. A white porcelain water pitcher, matching basin, and chamber pot completed the ensemble.

"We'll stay here a week or two, Cotton Blossom," Nathan said.

There were current newspapers from Kansas City and St. Louis in the hotel lobby, thanks to regular westbound trains. Nathan found the local saloons lifeless, and spent little time there. They, like the whorehouses and dance halls, were just marking time until spring, when Texas cowboys came up the trail with their longhorn cows and their wages. After two weeks, without knowing why but lacking a better destination, Nathan rode east, toward Kansas City.

*   *   *

Kansas City, Missouri. November 4, 1869.

Long before reaching the town, Nathan could hear the shriek of steamboat whistles, for the mighty Missouri River flowed through Kansas City on its way to rendezvous with the Mississippi just north of St. Louis. The lonesome wail of the whistles brought a flood of memories that swept over Nathan's mind like fallen autumn leaves. He thought of faraway New Orleans, of his friends the McQueens, of the lonely grave where Eulie slept. Her image faded, only to be replaced by that of Viola Hayden, to whom vengeance had meant more than life. Finally, like a recurring nightmare, he saw Lacy Mayfield come into the line of fire, saw Milo Jenks draw his Colt ...

"My God," he said aloud. "My God ..."

Nathan found a boardinghouse just north of Kansas City, near the river. It was far less pretentious than the Drover's Cottage had been, and Cotton Blossom was welcomed. A widowed lady, Eppie Bolivar, owned the place, and it had the kind of informality and family meals that Nathan appreciated. There was a view of the river from the front porch, and Nathan could see the big boats bound for Omaha and points north, while others steamed south to Kansas City, St. Louis, and beyond. Nathan made the rounds of all the saloons, many of them along the riverfront, without hearing a word about the men he sought. He rode to town three times a week for newspapers, including those from St. Louis, and it wasn't until December eighth that his persistence paid off. The big black headline of the *St. Louis Globe-Democrat* read: "James Gang robs, kills." The Kansas City paper had a similar headline, and the facts in both papers were the same. Frank and Jesse James had entered the small bank at Gallatin, Missouri, pretending to have business with proprietor John W. Sheets. One of the outlaws—thought to be Jesse—had shot Sheets through the head and heart. A clerk, although wounded, had run outside, sounding the alarm and shouting that Sheets had been killed. The outlaws had reached their horses with a small amount of money, when one of them had lost a stirrup while mounting. He had been dragged some distance before freeing himself, and one of his comrades had returned for him. The pair had then escaped on one horse, stealing another from a farmer outside town.

There had been witnesses, and one witness had mentioned a third outlaw who had held the horses. The Kansas City paper had printed a reward dodger being circulated by the Pinkertons in their unrelenting determination to capture the James gang. There were no photographs, just the names; below the names of Frank and Jesse was a third name: Ringo Tull! Long ago, in Virginia, that had been one of seven names burned indelibly into Nathan's Stone's mind. Somewhere there might be another man who bore that name, but Nathan didn't think so. Only one of the seven had changed his name, and that had been to escape the unsavory reputation he had acquired in Denver. Outlaws—at least on the frontier—had their own kind of vanity that led them to use their own names. There was Ben Thompson, Wild Bill Longley, John Wesley Hardin, Clay Allison, Frank and Jesse James, and the list went on. It was the first lead Nathan had encountered in months. He rode back and said good-bye to Mrs. Bolivar, saddled the black, loaded his packhorse, and set out for Gallatin, Mis-

souri. Cotton Blossom loped ahead, and they reached Gallatin an hour before noon. The bank was closed, and
Nathan soon discovered the reason. Up one of the shaded
streets Nathan could see a church steeple and he heard the
moan of an organ. On Thursday afternoon it could scarcely
be anything but a funeral. Nathan rode slowly toward the
church. It was a poor time to ask questions, but he needed
to know in which direction the James gang had ridden after
the robbery. The black hearse with its teams of matched
blacks waited outside the church. The black-garbed man
beside it had to be the undertaker, and it was to him Nathan spoke.

"Pardner, is this ... Mr. Sheets, from the bank?"

"It is, and if you're from some newspaper ..."

"I'm not," said Nathan. "I have an interest in capturing
the James gang, and I had hoped I might talk to some of
the witnesses."

"Sheriff Kilmer's inside. Wait and talk to him."

"Thanks," Nathan said. "I'll do that."

Nathan waited across the wide street, well out of the
way, until the grim proceeding was over the pallbearers
brought out the coffin. When the hearse rolled away, most
of the mourners followed, some mounted, some afoot. Nathan left his horses and walked across the street, approaching a tall, thin man with a star pinned to his
cowhide vest.

"You're Sheriff Kilmer, I reckon," said Nathan.

"I reckon I am. I've already talked to the Pinkertons.
You a bounty hunter?"

"No," Nathan said. "This is a personal thing. One of the
James gang had a hand in murdering my family. Just to get
him, I'll turn the whole bunch in, if I can. The reward has
nothing to do with it."

"They ain't much to tell," said the sheriff. "I got up a
posse, pronto. We trailed the varmints north to the Des
Moines river, and that's where we lost 'em. Just tee-total
lost 'em."

"How many riders?"

"Three," the sheriff said. "I know the damn newspapers
didn't mention a third man, but we tracked three horses.
Trouble is, that's farm country, and there's wagon roads
crossin' that river at every shallows. All them varmints had
to do was keep their horses in the water till they got to the

first wagon crossin'. There they could of got out, mixin' tracks of their horses in with God knows how many others. Pinkertons lost 'em, just like we did."

"The papers said one of them lost his horse and that they stole another."

"That they did," said the sheriff. "Took old Dan Smoot's bay, and he's been givin' me hell ever since."

"What became of the stray horse, the one that belonged to the outlaws?"

"Why . . . I dunno," the sheriff said. "We had three riders to foller, and we all lit out after 'em, hell for leather. It was dark when we got back to town."

"Thanks," Nathan said. "It won't bother you if I try my luck?"

"None whatsoever," said the sheriff.

Nathan mounted his horse, and leading the packhorse, set out down the street toward the bank. It suited his purpose perfectly that all or most of the town had followed the unfortunate banker's body to the cemetery. There had been no rain, nothing to destroy the sign, and he quickly found where the outlaw had been dragged. It was equally easy to find where he had managed to free himself from the stirrup, and from there the tracks of the freed horse led west. Most western men—outlaws included—had a favorite horse, and if set loose, that horse would return to the nearest corral it considered home. With that in mind, Nathan set out to trail the horse. He soon discovered part of the calk on the left rear shoe was missing, and he sighed with satisfaction. With that kind of edge, he could trail the animal over any wagon road, through innumerable other tracks. It all depended on how long the outlaw had owned the horse, how long the James gang had been holed up at some particular place, and whether or not they felt safe in returning to that place, following the Gallatin bank robbery. The gang had gone to great lengths to lose the sheriff's posse and the Pinkertons, and that argued favorably toward their return to a favored hideout. Nathan had to ride carefully, for he had no idea where the trail would lead, but with the outlaws riding their horses in the water, they must ride north or south until they struck off along a well-traveled wagon road. If his thinking was running true, this horse he was following must, at one of these wagon crossings, turn east or west. Slowly but surely, the trail he followed veered northeast, toward the Des Moines river. When the horse had reached the river, the animal hadn't crossed, but had traveled south. Nathan followed, feeling he was safe until the trail turned east or west, along one of the numerous wagon crossings. Nathan estimated they had traveled at least ten miles to the south, crossing many wagon roads, when the horse he was trailing suddenly veered west. He had indeed taken one of the wagon crossings, and his tracks were mixed with those of many other horses. Nathan was all the more thankful for the broken calk, for he could follow the trail easily. But when the horse left the wagon road, he must ride with caution, for he had no idea where the outlaw stronghold might be.

He rode for almost an hour, and by the time the trail left the wagon road, sundown was near. Nathan dismounted, looping the reins of the black and the lead rope of the packhorse over a pine limb. On foot, he continued to the top of a ridge. In the valley below was a farmhouse. A few hundred yards to the east of the house was a barn, and in an adjoining corral, Nathan counted five horses. He had heard Frank and Jesse James had friends all over Missouri, otherwise respectable people who harbored the outlaws. If this were the case here, he might have trouble rooting them out. He returned to his horses. When it was dark enough, he would then approach the house, hoping to prove or disprove his suspicions. If there were dogs involved, his reaching the house would be difficult, with or without Cotton Blossom. While he could command the dog to remain with the horses, that left him open to the very real possibility that he might stumble into one or more dogs without warning. But there was another thing to consider, if Cotton Blossom accompanied him and had the misfortune to encounter other dogs. Nothing drew attention quicker than a stomp-down good dogfight.

Nathan was perhaps a mile west of the ridge from which he had observed the farmhouse. Here he must leave his horses. As he and Cotton Blossom chewed on jerked beef, he listened for any sound, especially of barking dogs. Fearing discovery, he had been unable to follow the trail any farther in daylight, so he didn't know for certain the isolated farmhouse concealed the outlaws. But all evidence led him to that conclusion. Nathan had heard and read enough about Frank and Jesse James to know that they sometimes escaped a sheriff's posse by using relays of horses. Leaving their tired horses and mounting fresh ones, they could ride a hundred miles, if necessary. When he judged it was dark enough, Nathan set out for the point where the trail he had been following led across the ridge. In the house far below there was a tiny pinpoint of light.

Nathan started down the ridge toward the light, Cotton Blossom following. He heartily wished he could communicate to the dog a need for caution, but as they progressed, he realized Cotton Blossom had learned certain things, as evidenced by his conduct. When Nathan rode the black horse, Cotton Blossom could trail ahead, but when Nathan was afoot, it meant he didn't wish to be discovered. The dog remained slightly behind Nathan, and but for his shadow in the dim starlight, he might not have existed. Nathan circled far to the east of the house, coming in behind the barn. A horse in the adjoining corral stomped its foot and snorted. Nathan would have liked to examine the hooves of the animals, verifying the broken calk, but that was too risky. Any kind of disturbance among the horses would bring wanted men on the run, their guns blazing. Nathan approached the house from the dark side, working his way around to the lighted window. Fortunately the house had been built on the side of a slope, and the kitchen end—where the lighted window was—sat virtually on the ground.

A lighted lamp sat on a dining room table, and while its glow was feeble, there was light enough to get a man killed, should be fool enough to stand directly before the window. Nathan kept to the side, peering in from the darkness. There were four men at the table while a woman was bringing in food from what obviously was the kitchen. Only one man had his back to the window, and Nathan guessed that man was probably the host. Two of the men—Frank and Jesse James—sat on the far side of the table, facing the window. The third man sat on Jesse's left, at the end of the table, and Nathan studied him. His eyes were cruel, his mouth turned down at the corners in a perpetual frown, and the hat tipped back on his head was that of a Union officer. Nathan had seen enough. He slipped away, thinking. He might have shot the third man on suspicion alone, but not without exposing himself to murderous fire from both Frank and Jesse James, and had he not killed his man with the first shot, there would be no chance for another. Nor had he ever forgotten that day when the cold eyes of Jesse James had bored into him and the outlaw had promised to kill him. What bothered him most was that these outlaws were slick as calf slobber when it came to escaping. One failed shot on his part could cost him an opportunity that might never come his way again. This situation called for a posse, enough men to surround the house at dawn. Then he remembered the funeral in Gallatin, the hordes of mourners following the coffin of a man the outlaws had gunned down in the bank. Where else was he likely to find a sheriff and a posse willing and eager to ride out in the small hours of the night on the word of a stranger?

Returning to his horses, Nathan rode back to Gallatin, taking note of various landmarks along the way. He found nobody at the small jail, but it was still early and there were lights in many windows. He had no trouble finding the little house where Sheriff Kilmer lived. He was a small-town lawman, but he was no fool. The light went out, and Kilmer spoke from behind the front door.

"Who is it, and what do you want?"

"I spoke to you this afternoon, after the funeral," Nathan said, "and I want a sheriff and a posse. I've found the owlhoots who killed your banker."

"Open the door and come in," said Kilmer. "You're covered."

Nathan turned the knob and stepped into the living room. Light from another room bled in through an open door. Kilmer was fully dressed except for his boots and hat. Nathan closed the door and lifted his hands shoulder high. Only then did Kilmer ease down the hammer of his Colt and holster the weapon.

"Set," said the sheriff, "and talk."

Nathan did, and Kilmer listened, chuckling with appreciation as Nathan told of trailing the riderless horse to the isolated farm, swearing when he learned of the presence of Frank and Jesse James in the farmhouse.

"By God, that's Sim Hinkel's place," Kilmer said. "Him and Emily's been here forty years and more. How in hell can they shelter outlaws and killers?"

"There's no accounting for the hombres men choose for their friends," said Nathan. "I'm telling you what I saw. You'll have to take my word until you see for yourself.

Like I told you, I don't care a damn about any reward or recognition. All I want is a clean shot at Ringo Tull."

"I can't promise you that," Sheriff Kilmer said. "I'll be in charge of the posse and there'll be no shooting unless they start it. We'll surround the house and they'll be ordered to surrender."

"Sheriff," said Nathan, "you can't drown a man that was born to be hung. Jesse James will never be taken alive. I understand your position, and while I don't aim to try and tell you how to do your job, I'd like to offer you some advice, based on hard-won experience. When you organize your posse, be sure every man can and will shoot. I'll follow your rules, because I want to ride with you. I believe I've earned that right."

"Beyond a doubt," Sheriff Kilmer said. "I want you to come with me while I organize the posse. There's a small stable behind the house, room enough for your packhorse. Why don't you leave him there?"

Chapter 31

◆◆◆

Sheriff Kilmer quickly found ten men eager to take part in the capture of the notorious Frank and Jesse James. Nathan led them to the farmhouse and was satisfied with the manner in which the sheriff deployed his men in the surrounding of the house. He believed, however, that the lawman was underestimating the ruthlessness and resourcefulness of Frank and Jesse James, and his doubts were justified when Sheriff Kilmer issued his challenge. It came an hour before the dawn.

"You in the house," Kilmer shouted. "Frank and Jesse James. This is the law, and you're under arrest. Come out with your hands up. We have the house surrounded."

"We're comin' out," came the reply from within the house, "but Sim and Emily are comin' with us. They'll see us safe to our horses, and if you cut down on us, they'll die. Now back off."

Nathan slipped away and ran for the barn. He didn't intend for all his work to be for nothing, and this might be his last chance at Ringo Tull. He ducked between the rails of the corral fence, and with his back to the barn wall, concealed himself in the shadows. There was more shouting near the house, and Nathan doubted the posse would fire at any of the outlaws if they emerged in a group, with the Hinkels before them. Once they reached the corral, however, they must separate to mount their horses. Nathan heard Emily Hinkel sobbing before he saw their dim shapes in the starlight. One of the outlaws dropped three rails from the corral, and they moved toward the horses. But the animals were wary of so much activity in the predawn darkness, and moved toward the far side of the corral.

"Come here, you damn jughead," somebody mumbled.

Saddles were out of the question, and they were having trouble mounting the skittish horses bareback. Nathan recognized Ringo Tull, for he wore the broad-brimmed hat of a cavalry officer. The other two men were hatless, and it was they who mounted first. They kicked their horses into a gallop, leaving Sim and Emily Hinkel lying in the corral dust. Tull had managed to mount, but before he could gallop away, Nathan put two slugs beneath the hooves of the already skittish horse. The animal reared, throwing Tull to the ground.

"Get up," Nathan ordered, "and be careful what you do with your hands."

Tull got to his feet and lifted his hands shoulder high.

"In the fall of 1865," said Nathan, "seven no-account varmints murdered my family. You were one of them."

"You got the wrong hombre," Tull said. "I never been in Virginia in my life."

"I didn't say you had," said Nathan, "but you've just given me all the proof I need." He holstered his Colt. "Now go for your gun."

It was almost Nathan's undoing. Tull's Colt was on his left hip, butt forward, but his right hand didn't move. His left hand came down slowly and he had the sleeve gun palmed before Nathan drew. The derringer roared once, the slug plowing into the dust of the corral, for Nathan had shot Ringo Tull just above his belt buckle.

The sheriff and some of the posse were close enough to have witnessed the shooting.

"Damn," said one of the sheriff's men, "you were close enough to plug Frank or Jesse, and you shot this varmint."

"It was this varmint I wanted," Nathan replied. "I'm leaving Frank and Jesse to you and your amigos."

He left them standing there. Returning to where the horses were tied, he mounted the black. With Cotton Blossom following, he rode back to Gallatin, to Sheriff Kilmer's stable, and got his packhorse. From there he rode south to Kansas City, reclaiming his room at Eppie Bolivar's boardinghouse. When he had rubbed down his horses, then watered and grained them, he returned to the house seeking breakfast.

"You're late," said Eppie. "Cotton Blossom's already finished."

"Cotton Blossom's never finished," Nathan said. "He just likes to catch some shuteye until it's time to eat again."

*   *   *

Two days later, Nathan found a short paragraph in the Kansas City paper about Sheriff Kilmer and his posse flushing Frank and Jesse James from a farmhouse south of Gallatin, Missouri. While it stated that Ringo Tull, a member of the James gang, had been killed during the escape, Nathan's name was not mentioned.

Nathan decided to remain in Kansas City for a while, mostly because he enjoyed the nearness of the river and the quiet living at Eppie Bolivar's boardinghouse. Cotton Blossom always made friends with whoever did the cooking, and Eppie had fallen victim to his charm. It was convenient for Nathan when Cotton Blossom was satisfied to remain behind, for the dog was never at his best in saloons and gambling houses. Nathan continued riding into town three days a week, occasionally visiting the saloons, listening to the talk of bullwhackers, roustabouts, bartenders, and gamblers. There were newspapers from Omaha, St. Louis, Memphis, and New Orleans, as well as the local *Kansas City Star*. It was in the Kansas City paper that he read of the most recent episode in the lives of Frank and Jesse James. Despite their clash with the law, they had holed up at yet another farmhouse in Clay County, not far from Kansas City.*

Four members of a sheriff's posse had been about to close in on Frank and Jesse as they hid out in a barn on the Samuels farm. Warned by a Negro who was employed by Samuels, Frank and Jesse had spurred their horses out of the barn when the posse had begun to close in. There had been a wild exchange of gunfire that had killed Deputy Sheriff John Thomason's horse. The notorious James brothers had again escaped.

*   *   *

The first week in January 1870, there was a story in the Kansas City newspaper that intrigued Nathan. It concerned trouble along the right-of-way of the Kansas–Pacific Rail-

---

*Near the present-day town of Liberty, the seat of Clay County.

road between Kansas City and Hays, some three hundred miles west. It was a twofold problem, both of vital concern to the government, and it threatened the very existence of the railroad. Telegraph poles and lines were being pulled down by Indians—the Cheyennes—who hated and feared the "talking wire" and sought to destroy it. Fort Hays—a mile south of the town—had become a major government supply point for forts in all of western Kansas and part of Indian Territory. Disruption of telegraph service between Kansas City and Fort Hays had incensed the military. But that wasn't all. Military payrolls went by rail as far as end-of-track, tempting outlaws to rob the trains, stopping them by destroying part of the track.

The Kansas–Pacific was fighting back, offering pay of a hundred dollars a month to plainsmen—men who could and would shoot—to ride along the Kansas–Pacific track from Kansas City to Hays, and back again. Four such men were to be hired. Nathan went to the Kansas–Pacific office and asked for Joel Netherton, the man responsible for hiring. Netherton proved to be a slender young man with glasses who looked like a schoolteacher. He regarded Nathan with interest, his eyes lingering on the twin Colts.

"Do you own a repeating rifle?" he asked.

"I do," said Nathan.

"Sit down," Netherton said.

Nathan took the only available chair except for the swivel chair behind Netherton's desk in which he sat. The office was only a cubicle whose walls extended only a little above a man's head, allowing all the dirt, smoke, and noise of the railroad yard to descend like a fog. Somewhere a telegraph key chattered frantically, became silent, and then chattered again. The shrill blast of a locomotive whistle seemed to vibrate the very walls. Netherton shrugged his shoulders, waiting until the train had departed before he spoke again.

"Can you read and write?"

"I can," Nathan replied.

"Do you by any chance know Morse code?"

"No," said Nathan.

"We can teach you that," Netherton said. "The railroad decided it would be easier to teach an Indian fighter the code than to teach a telegrapher to shoot Indians."

"I'm not too sure about that," said Nathan. "That set talks almighty fast."

"You must know the code," Netherton said. "You'll have a portable set with you. There will be times when you'll have to repair and test a line, and if there's damage to the track, you'll have to warn us so we can delay or stop the next train."

"I like the sound of it," said Nathan. "When do I start?"

"Eight o'clock in the morning," Netherton replied. "I'll need you to complete and sign this form before you leave. Place it here on my desk."

He went out, leaving Nathan with a single sheet of paper and a pencil. He grinned. All the Kansas–Pacific required of him was his signature. That absolved them of all responsibility in the event he was killed by Indians or outlaws, struck by lightning, run over by a locomotive, if his horse threw him or fell on him, if he shot himself ... and the list rambled on. He signed it, leaving it and the pencil on Netherton's desk. He believed he could learn Morse code and believed it was knowledge he could use to his advantage on the frontier. Besides, his duties would take him across three hundred miles of frontier every five days. When he reached Hays on Friday, he had the weekend there. The next Monday he would ride out for Kansas City, spending the next weekend there at Eppie's.

*   *   *

Nathan spent three days laboring over the code, attempting to memorize the combinations of dots and dashes that formed different letters of the alphabet. Finally, at the end of the third exhausting day, Netherton felt he was ready for the test. The morning of the fourth day, he was allowed to try his hand at "receiving" a message. It came slowly, and to his everlasting surprise, he found himself able to take it down on paper. As he mastered the code, the transmissions were speeded up. When he was allowed to "send," he quickly became adept, for he knew the code.

"Congratulations," said Netherton. "You leave for Hays next Monday."

Nathan had made arrangements to leave his packhorse at Eppie's place, for he would pass through Abilene, as well as several other villages that had sprung up along the

Kansas–Pacific tracks. If he were chased by Indians or outlaws, a packhorse might hinder him when he should be riding for his life. Worse, the horse and its pack might prove an added temptation to the Cheyennes. He could survive from his saddlebags, taking up the slack when there was town grub to be had. He had no idea what situation might confront him as he rode from Kansas City to Hays and back again, but the railroad led west, and it might bring him the one remaining killer who had yet to die ...

Abilene was only seventy-five miles west of Kansas City, a day's ride for a man on a good horse, and for that reason, most of the trouble with Indians and outlaws was taking place between Abilene and Hays, for the telegraph could relay messages quickly to Kansas City. A locomotive with tender and a freight car could be dispatched within the hour, bringing soldiers or a posse with horses, but only if the telegraph line was intact and there was somebody who knew the code to send the message. Every train crew included at least one qualified telegrapher, but Indians and outlaws had rendered them useless, for they had taken to pulling down or cutting telegraph lines ten to fifteen miles east of where they had torn up the track. That left a train crew with a dead telegraph line back to Kansas City and the soldiers at Fort Hays more than two hundred miles ahead. The outlaws, seeking military payrolls, were a hazard only to westbound trains. The Indians, however, intent on the destruction of the telegraph and the railroad, might strike anywhere along the line. So far they had concentrated on the lonely stretch of track between Abiline and Hays.

January 10, 1870, Nathan Stone rode west, following the Kansas–Pacific tracks. He knew the train schedule. For the time being, thanks to destruction of the track by Indians and outlaws, trains ran only during daylight hours. A train leaving Kansas City one morning remained at Hays overnight and returned to Kansas City the next day. Roundhouse facilities were always at end-of-track. From what Nathan had been told, a second line rider would leave Kansas City on Wednesday, scheduled to reach Hays on Sunday. Another pair of riders would follow a similar schedule, riding east to Kansas City, and, following a two-day layover, returning to Hays. Maybe a hundred and fifty miles west of Kansas City, Nathan should meet the eastbound line rider from Hays. By the time Nathan reached Hays on Friday, a second rider from there should be leaving for Kansas City. While these four outriders couldn't possibly cover the entire line, they would make it more difficult for those who wrought destruction on telegraph lines and Kansas–Pacific tracks.

Nathan felt he had an edge, Cotton Blossom being with him, and the hound ranged far ahead. He distanced himself from the track, however, when a train bound for end-of-track rumbled past. There were three flat cars loaded with rails and ties, two boxcars, and a caboose. The engineer and fireman waved, for they knew of the outriders hired by the railroad. There had been some criticism of the railroad for including a baggage car on any train carrying a government payroll, and Nathan could understand what the critics were getting at. Why make it obvious a train carried a government payroll by transporting it in a "money coach?" Why not just bolt a safe or strongbox to the floor of a caboose? Nathan reached Abilene before sundown and took a room at the Drover's Cottage. There would be two or three nights each week when he must roll in his blankets wherever darkness found him, but he wouldn't turn down a bed and hot grub when it could be had.

By first light he was riding west, and two hours out of Abilene he found where Indians had sabotaged a section of track. Lacking tools for wrecking the track by dislodging the rails, they had devised a means of having the weight of the locomotive do it for them. Beneath coupling joints— where one rail met the next—they had dug away the ballast, leaving ties and rails suspended over a hole four feet deep and a dozen feet long. Not only would the rails buckle under the initial weight of the locomotive, the iron monster would topple from the track and possibly be destroyed. The train had already left Hays and end-of-track, and would be two hours or more into its return journey to Kansas City. Nathan had no tools to repair the roadbed, nor was it his job. It was his duty, however, to warn the crew of the oncoming train.

From his saddlebag he took a lineman's belt and his portable telegraph key. Telegraph poles had spikes for hand- and footholds driven in on two sides at alternating levels. Nathan climbed a pole, tied his instrument into the line, and tried a preliminary code. There was no response. Using a similar code, he tried to reach an operator at Hays and again there was no response.

"Damn Indians," he growled aloud.

He climbed down, returned the telegraph key and lineman's belt to his saddlebag, and rode on westward. Somewhere between where he was and Kansas City, the telegraph line was down, just as it was down ahead of him. While he must eventually repair both breaks, his most urgent duty was to warn the oncoming train, stopping it short of the ruined track. The crew might or might not be able to repair the roadbed to the extent that the train could proceed. Nathan would be forced to backtrack until he found where the telegraph line was down, repair the break, and report the situation to the Kansas–Pacific dispatcher at Kansas City. That done, he must try to make up for lost time as he rode toward Hays looking for a second break in the telegraph line. Suddenly he reined up. Why was he riding to intercept the train, when all the engineer needed was enough distance to brake the locomotive to a stop before it reached the damaged road bed? Every unnecessary mile he rode toward Hays would be a mile he must backtrack, seeking the downed line that must be repaired before he could telegraph Kansas City. He rode on, dismounting when he reached a stream that flowed through a culvert under the railroad track.

"We might as well eat, Cotton Blossom. This is as good a place as any to wait for the train."

He shared jerked beef with Cotton Blossom and they drank cold water from the stream. Nathan opened the cover on his watch and found it was almost two o'clock. He judged he was at least a hundred miles west of Kansas City. The train from Hays was six hours into its journey, and within the hour there had to be some sign of its coming. He got down on his knees, put his ear to a rail and heard a distant humming. The train was coming! One thing to be said for the Kansas plains, he thought. If there was anything in the sky for ten miles—be it circling buzzards or smoke from a locomotive—a man with good eyes had no trouble seeing it. There was virtually no wind, and he soon could see a dirty gray smudge against the unrelenting blue of the western sky. He tied his horse well away from the track, beside the stream. He then took his position on the track. It stretched straight ahead as far as he could see.

There was no excuse for the engineer not seeing him. He was able to discern the rising column of smoke long before he could see the train. Growing larger by the second, it came on. Nathan removed his hat, waving it high over his head. Suppose the engineer failed to see him or just ignored him, and the train went thundering on to destruction? But that didn't happen, for outlaws had no reason to rob east bound trains. There was a screech of the big locomotive's brakes, and Nathan could see the engineer hanging out the big window of the cab. Nathan walked back so that he could be heard without shouting over the chuffing and hissing of the locomotive.

"Indians dug out the roadbed half a dozen miles up the track," Nathan said. "Telegraph line's down, east and west."

"Damn," the engineer growled. "We'll be settin' here till dark, waitin' on a section crew."

"I won't mind that," said the fireman, who had climbed down to the ground. "I'm just thankin' God you found the sabotaged track. That's hard as hell to see from a moving train. Even if we'd seen it, we likely couldn't have got this ol' iron horse stopped before she buckled them rails and rolled over with us. I'm glad you was out here, mister."

"So am I," Nathan said. "Now I have to ride back toward Abilene and find where they've broken the line. I'll telegraph Kansas City for a section crew."

Mounting his horse, he saw the brakeman step down from the caboose, on his way to learn what had stopped the train. Nathan rode almost to Abilene before finding the broken line. Their method had been simple enough. Roping the top of the pole and dragging it down had snapped the slender wire. Nathan made no effort to raise the pole, leaving that for the section crew. Using pliers the railroad had provided, he managed to twist the broken ends of the wire together after releasing one of them from the glass insulator attached to the fallen pole. He then tied his instrument into the wire and got immediate response from the operator in Kansas City. Following instructions, Nathan sent, as nearly as he could, the location of the downed pole and broken wire, and then the location of the sabotaged section of track. When Kansas City had confirmed, he returned the key to his saddlebags and again rode west. When he reached the undermined track, he found that the engineer had brought the train to within a few hundred yards. Nathan paused on his way west and spoke to the engineer and fireman.

"I patched the broken line and telegraphed Kansas City. They know where you are and why."

"Thanks," said the engineer.

Nathan continued west, following the track, and found the second break in the telegraph line some twenty miles distant. He then telegraphed Hays and again contacted Kansas City to report the location of the second break. The section crew was going to be busy for a while. Come sundown, he unsaddled the black and shared a meager supper with Cotton Blossom. He believed he was at least a hundred and twenty-five miles west of Kansas City, and he felt some satisfaction in his accomplishments. He had saved a train being derailed, found and repaired two widely separated breaks in the telegraph line, and successfully sent and received messages using Morse code. There was considerable satisfaction in having stepped into this new role and performed successfully. He again rode west at first light, and an hour later met his counterpart, a rider bound for Kansas City.

"Howdy," said Nathan. "I'm Nathan Stone, riding for the Kansas–Pacific from Kansas City to Hays."

"Benton Valentine," the other rider said, offering his hand. "Nothing's happened at my end. How about yours?"

Nathan told him of the events of the day before, and they parted. Nathan reached Hays on Friday morning, meeting with Otto Donaldson, the Kansas–Pacific dispatcher there. Donaldson welcomed him with a grin.

"I've been hearing nothing but good about you, Stone. If the other three perform as well as you, there may be hope for the Kansas–Pacific yet."

Nathan returned to the boardinghouse where he had shared a room with Wild Bill. He had three nights in Hays before returning to Kansas City, and he paid in advance for a room through Sunday. He and Cotton Blossom found a cafe where they had eaten before and had an early supper. Donaldson, the local dispatcher, had told of Nathan's achievements on behalf of the railroad, and the editor of the local newspaper found him in the cafe.

"I'm Emmet Plato," the young man said. "I'm editor of

the newspaper here. Donaldson said look for a two-gun man with a dog. You're Nathan Stone?"

"I am," Nathan replied. "Donaldson has a big mouth."

"That he does," said Plato cheerfully, "and I'm glad he does. He's one of the few sources of news. You have no idea how difficult it is, publishing a weekly paper in Hays. If you have the time, will you tell me what it's like being an outrider—a troubleshooter—for the railroad?"

"I'll be here till Monday morning," Nathan said. "I seem to have plenty of time."

He related all the details of his ride from Kansas City, including the discovery of the damaged roadbed, stopping the train, repairing the telegraph line, and the sending of messages to Kansas City and Hays. Plato scribbled it all down, and his gratitude was boundless. He was easy to talk to, and the conversation quickly centered on the boomtown violence that prevailed in Hays.

"When I left here last October," said Nathan, "Hickok was county sheriff, and there was some question as to whether his election was legal or not. Was it?"

"It was not," Plato sighed. "Governor Harvey and the State of Kansas refused to validate the Ellis County election for sheriff, held last August. A new election was held on November second, and Pete Lanihan beat Wild Bill. He was allowed to remain in office until the first of the year. He certainly wasn't afraid of drunken soldiers and bullwhackers. I'm afraid that can't be said of Lanihan."

*   *   *

Nathan continued to perform his duties with distinction, and when he reached Hays on Friday, July fifteenth, he was surprised to find Wild Bill Hickok in town. Nathan and Cotton Blossom were in their usual cafe having supper. Hickok came in, and, as though they had parted only hours before, dragged out a chair and sat down across the table from Nathan.

"I hear you've become the Kansas–Pacific's righthand man," said Hickok with a grin. "There was a story on you in the Denver paper."

"I could put in a word for you with the railroad," Nathan said, returning the grin. "It pays a hundred dollars a month, and all you have to do is stay alive. They'll teach you Morse code, too."

"I'd jump at it, if it wasn't for that Morse," said Hickok. "I never was much good at sums, and I reckon those dots and doodles would hurt my eyes."

Somewhere, in one of the newspapers he was constantly reading, Nathan had seen a report that Wild Bill was losing his sight. At the time he had doubted the truth of it, but now he wasn't sure. On Sunday morning, Nathan joined Hickok for breakfast.

"Since you're ridin' out in the morning," said Wild Bill, "let's have us a night on the town."

"I reckon not," Nathan replied. "I aim to get an early start."

But Wild Bill Hickok wasn't a man to take no for an answer, and again he caught Nathan in the cafe having supper. Hickok seemed to have no friends in Hays, and Nathan finally agreed to visit a saloon or two for a few hands of poker. Drum's was one of the more popular places and it was there they went. The poker didn't bother Nathan nearly as much as Wild Bill's drinking, for he had seen Hickok drunk before. The saloon was full of soldiers from the Seventh Cavalry at Fort Hays, and five of them had congregated at a huge round table playing poker. The only civilian was the house dealer. There was just one empty chair and Hickok took it, his back to the wall. Nathan stood out of the way, content to observe. Already the soldiers were loud and rowdy. Cotton Blossom had retreated to a corner, wary of everybody.

"Hey," somebody at the bar shouted, "yonder's old duckbill, the sheriff that got throwed out."

There was laughter, but Wild Bill wasn't quite drunk enough, and he kept his calm. However, he had a full bottle of rye whiskey, and Nathan started looking for a break in the game in which he might lure Hickok outside. Any saloon in Hays would be better than this, for the soldiers at the table were already drunk, or nearly so. They had become careless in their play, and as a result, Hickok was winning consistently. Intentionally or otherwise, the soldier to Bill's right knocked the half full bottle of whiskey off the table, upside down in Hickok's lap. He stood up, the front of his trousers soaked, and men roared with laughter. Hickok seized the whiskey bottle and broke it over the head of the soldier who had upended it. Wild Bill's chair toppled backward when a soldier lunged across the table at him. Nathan drew a Colt and buffaloed a soldier about to smash a chair over Hickok's head, only to have another soldier slug him with the butt of a revolver. Dazed, Nathan fell to his knees and his assailant hit him again. The soldiers had begun kicking Hickok, when Wild Bill drew his revolver and started shooting. Two soldiers were hit, and the others backed hastily away. Hickok got to his feet, the pistol in his hand. His back already to the wall, he followed it to the door, the revolver cocked and unwavering in his hand. Reaching the saloon door, he backed out. Seconds later, there was the pound of hooves as Hickok rode away.

Sheriff Lanihan came, accompanied by a doctor, and the two badly wounded soldiers were taken away. Nathan's had his badly cut scalp tended to by the doctor. With Cotton Blossom following, Nathan left the saloon, returning to his room at the boardinghouse and to bed. He rose early with a sore head and after breakfast went to the Kansas–Pacific dispatcher's office to tell Donaldson he was leaving.

"Some hell of a brawl at Drum's last night," Donaldson said.

"So I heard," Nathan replied. "Anybody bad hurt?"

"You could say that," said Donaldson. "Private Kile's dead. Lanigan may not make it. Hickok's done it this time."

Chapter 32

❖

The last week in November 1870, Nathan Stone surprised everybody who knew him. He resigned from the Kansas–Pacific. He had friends in Kansas City, Abilene, and Hays, none of whom wanted him to leave. He had found a home, if he had wanted it, but he had not wanted it. He told himself the unfulfilled promise to his dead father lay heavy on his mind, but he didn't really believe that. In the old South, vengeance had seemed a noble calling. Now it seemed more and more like he was using his vendetta as a crutch, leaning on it, without a life of his own and wanting none. Somehow, somewhere, he must find and kill Dade Withers, the last man on his death list. In a few days it would be four years since he had taken an oath on his father's grave, and he had not a single clue as to the direction he should take in satisfying that oath. He had found Clinton Foster in the wilds of Indian Territory, and from what he had heard and read, it was still a haven for renegades, deserters, and comancheros. Leading his packhorse, with Cotton Blossom following, he headed there, via Wichita.

*   *   *

Wichita, Kansas. December 2, 1870.

The last of the Texas herd had come up the trail until the next spring, and there was little activity in Wichita. Nathan knew it wasn't wise to enter Indian Territory without a packhorse. He could carry only a little food in his saddlebags, and certainly none of the utensils necessary for cooking. His wages from the railroad and the twelve hundred he had brought with him from Colorado left him with more than two thousand dollars. It was more than enough to cost him his life anywhere on the frontier, living among outlaws. But the man he sought was an outlaw who might remain on the outer reaches of civilization indefinitely. To find that man, the time had come when Nathan Stone must become—or appear to become—an outlaw himself. He bought enough supplies to last six months. While he wasn't a drinking man and didn't use tobacco, he took along four quarts of whiskey, a supply of plug, and a dozen sacks of Durham. If he survived the outlaws and renegades, he still might have to contend with the Indians.

*   *   *

Indian Territory. December 5, 1870.

Nathan followed Chisholm's wagon road* for two days before riding west, deeper into Indian Territory. The first evidence of human habitation came with the distant crack of a rifle. The lead tore into a pine close enough to spook the black, and the horse reared. Nathan calmed the animal and reined up. It was a warning shot, and he waited for a challenge. It wasn't long in coming.

"Who are you, and what do you want?"

"My name is Stone," Nathan shouted, "and I'm lookin' for a quiet place where I ain't likely to be bothered, if you know what I mean."

"I reckon I know what you mean," the voice said, and there was a some sly laughter. "Ride on the way you're headed. Just don't do anything funny with your hands."

Nathan rode on. He came to a spring, and beyond it, through the pines, he could see the shake roof of a shack. As he neared the shack, he was aware that the rifleman who had challenged him was now behind him. The man spoke.

"That's far enough."

Nathan reined up, waiting. A man emerged from the shack, and he was armed as though he had just fought a war or was about to start one. There was a pistol in a tied-down holster on each hip, a third such weapon shoved under the waistband of his dark trousers, and a Winchester

---

*The Chisholm Trail.

in the crook of his right arm. A bandolier of Winchester shells was slung over his left shoulder. His dress was that of a Mexican, including a high-crowned sombrero. A black vest embroidered in red partially hid a sweat-stained ruffled shirt that had once been white.

"I am El Gato, segundo of Cocodrilo Rancho," he said.*

"I am Silver," Nathan replied. "What do you expect of me?"

"I will ask the questions, señor, and you will answer them. How do you know of this place?"

"Your pet coon took a shot at me and brought me here with a Winchester at my back," said Nathan grimly. "Now what do you expect of me?"

"One hundred American dollars for each month you remain here, in advance. For this you have a place to sleep and you are under my protection. You will supply your own food."

"That's almighty high for a place to sleep," Nathan said, "and I don't care a damn for your protection."

"Oh, but you should, señor," said El Gato, jacking a shell into the Winchester's chamber. "Without it, you are dead."

It was as slick a shakedown as Nathan had ever seen. He would be forced to remain until they picked him clean. Then he might or might not escape with his life, but he couldn't count on that. For the time being, he must play along. He dug into his pocket, taking a handful of double eagles, counting out five. He took a step forward.

"Stay where you are," El Gato commanded. "Breed?"

The unshaven man who had challenged Nathan stepped up from behind and took the gold. Only then did El Gato's manner change slightly. From a vest pocket he took a thin cigar, stuck it between his teeth, and spoke around it.

"You are welcome here, Señor Silver, until you betray my trust. Then I kill you. Breed, you will guide him to the bunk house."

Behind El Gato, the door of the cabin opened. A dark-haired girl stood there, barefooted and in rags. She was American, and didn't look more than sixteen, if that. Breed's greedy eyes were on her, and she hurriedly closed the door. Breed turned his attention back to Nathan, point-

*Crocodile Ranch

ing northwest with the muzzle of the Winchester. Nathan
set out in that direction, leading his horses. Cotton Blossom
slunk out of the brush where he had taken refuge, for he
had developed an immediate dislike for Breed and El Gato.
The bunkhouse was almost half a mile beyond El Gato's
cabin. Long and low, it was built of logs, with a shake roof.
At each end was a chimney and a heavy oak door. At
intervals, below the eaves, were cutouts for rifle barrels, a
last line of defense against Indian attacks. Smoke curled
from one of the chimneys. To the left of the bunkhouse
was a corral, and Nathan counted fifteen horses.

"Unsaddle your hoss an' unload the pack hoss," said
Breed.

Nathan unsaddled the black and unloaded the packhorse.
Breed led the animals to the corral and turned them loose
with the rest of the stock. For the lack of anything better
to do, Nathan shouldered his saddle and started toward the
bunkhouse. He was puzzled. El Gato was treating him as
though he were a prisoner, yet he had been allowed to
keep his weapons. Nathan could only play along until he
learned what they had in store for him.

He stepped into the bunkhouse unannounced, and within
a split second every man had his hand on the butt of his
Colt. There was no light except that from the open door
and the fire that blazed in the fireplace. Nathan counted
eleven men when he was finally able to see into the gloom.
While there were many bunks, everybody had congregated
in one end of the bunkhouse, probably so they only had to
feed one fire. Most of the men simply reclined on their
bunks, some of them smoking quirlys. One, however, sat
on a three-legged stool running chords and fingering soft
notes from a guitar. The bunks were two-tiered along both
walls. Each consisted of a heavy cedar frame with latticed—
crisscrossed—strips of cowhide as wide as a man's hand.
Nathan chose a lower bunk, leaving his saddle on it, while
he went out for the packsaddle. He found Breed lifting the
edge of the canvas that covered his pack. Nathan paused,
saying nothing, his thumbs hooked in his pistol belt. Breed
stood up, his eyes lighted with anticipation. But Nathan
didn't follow through, and Breed backed away. Near the
corral, Nathan saw Cotton Blossom. As long as he remained at Cocodrilo Rancho, he would have to feed the
dog outside. Cotton Blossom, Nathan thought wryly, used

better judgement in choosing his companions than did Nathan himself. When Nathan entered the bunkhouse with the packsaddle, he found the bunk he had chosen had been claimed by another, and his saddle lay on the rough floor.

"Gents," he said mildly, lowering the packsaddle to the floor, "I aim to have one of these bunks. If any man of you wants a different one, he'd best claim it now. The next one I choose, I aim to keep."

Nobody said anything, and he chose yet another lower bunk. A big man got up off the lower bunk whose head was near the foot of the one Nathan had taken. He was two or three inches taller than Nathan, outweighed him by thirty pounds, and his doubled fists looked as big as hams. If a bullfrog could have spoken, its voice would have matched his.

"My name's Yokum," he said, "an' when I turn in, I pile my boots an' hat on that bunk. I reckon you'll find it a mite crowded."

"I don't think so," Nathan replied. "Your hat and boots won't be there."

Nathan backed away from Yokum's first punch and threw one of his own. His right connected with Yokum's chin, and it was like slugging an oak. The big man staggered but didn't go down. He tried to trap Nathan in a bear hug and Nathan backed away. The man with the guitar retreated to the far end of the bunkhouse, while others sought the security of upper bunks. Nathan was more agile than his opponent, but when Nathan stumbled over his saddle, he fell back against the frame of an upper bunk and Yokum took advantage. He wrapped his big arms around Nathan and began to squeeze. While it was dirty fighting and left him wide open for retaliation, Nathan drove his right knee into Yokum's groin. Yokum groaned, involuntarily loosing his grip, and Nathan was free. He needed to catch his breath, but there wasn't time. Again he threw a right, connecting with Yokum's chin, and had the satisfaction of seeing Yokum stagger, but the big man didn't go down.

Yokum's next move took Nathan completely by surprise. The big man just threw himself at Nathan like a pouncing cougar, and they went down. Nathan's head struck the heavy cedar frame of a lower bunk, and it was a struggle to remain conscious. He tried to kick free, but Yokum had

caught his legs and was working his way up Nathan's struggling body. Nathan swung blindly, and more by luck than
anything else, smashed Yokum's nose. The pain was such
that he loosed his grip on Nathan, and using his elbows on
the floor, Nathan was able to grasshopper himself backward. He then drove his right foot as hard as he could, and
the boot heel slammed into Yokum's chin. Yokum lay there
belly down, breathing hard. Nathan got to his feet, sucking
air into his starved lungs. Finally he sat down on the lower
bunk he had chosen. Yokum sat up, wiping his still-bleeding
nose on his shirtsleeve. He spoke in his bullfrog voice.

"I reckon I'll just leave my boots an' hat on the floor,
under my bunk."

While Nathan didn't have to prove himself again, he still
was an outsider. After the fight, Yokum spoke pleasantly
to him, as did Kalpana, the Spaniard who played the guitar.
The others—Breed, Kirkham, Vanado, Tarno, Wolf, York,
Peyton, Fortner, and Hickman—remained distant. When
Nathan had been there two weeks, he began to understand
his position. El Gato rode out early one morning, taking
all the men with him except Nathan, Breed, and Kirkham.
Neither of the pair remaining with Nathan talked to him,
and he began to have a better understanding of his status.
El Gato and these other men were actually one of the renegade bands holed up in Indian Territory. Nathan had been
allowed to keep his weapons because he was suspected of
being an outlaw. In time, he would be expected to prove
himself worthy of becoming a member of the renegade
bunch. If he failed to measure up, then his death would be
swift and sure.

The second day El Gato and the bunch were absent,
Nathan managed to get away from the bunkhouse and the
watchful eyes of Breed and Kirkham. As long as he didn't
go near the corral, where the horses were, his watchful
companions seemed unconcerned with him. The first time he
and Cotton Blossom walked to the spring, Breed followed,
seeming satisfied when they drank from the runoff. In the
afternoon, Nathan and Cotton Blossom again went to the
spring, and this time, they weren't followed. El Gato's cabin
stood between the bunkhouse and the spring, and it was
Nathan's hope that he might again see the young girl he
had seen briefly his first day there. But not until the third
day of El Gato's absence did he see her again. She stood

in the door looking at him, but when he lifted his hand in greeting, she quickly closed the door. Before he saw her again, before he could talk to her, El Gato and his men returned. They had been gone six days, and, at least by their standards, the raid had been successful. They drove before them nine horses, three of them with heavy packs. Some of the men had burlap sacks behind their saddles.

Nathan was expecting some ultimatum from El Gato and he wondered how long he must wait for a confrontation. He got his answer to that the second day following the return of the renegades, when the outlaw leader sent Breed to fetch him. This time, Nathan was ushered into the small cabin. El Gato sat in a big rocking chair, with his boots off and without the bandolier of shells draped over his shoulder. He nodded to a straight-backed chair, and Nathan sat down. He allowed his eyes to roam around the room. There was very little furniture. Instead, there were two saddles, most of a hundred-pound sack of grain, bridles, and various other horse gear. Other items seemed so out of place, Nathan felt certain they had been stolen. The door to the next room wasn't a door at all, but a blanket hung over the opening.

"Señor Silver, for the next week, during daylight hours, you will take your turn at sentry duty. Three weeks from today, we have some ... ah ... business to attend to. You shall ride with the others, and we shall see whether you are worthy of becoming one of us."

Nathan said nothing. While he had no intention of becoming a member of El Gato's band of thieves and killers, any objection at this time would only assure him of a fatal dose of lead poisoning. He must devise some means of escape, and it wasn't going to be easy. He began his sentry duty, stationing himself behind an upthrust of stone, half a mile beyond the spring. When he became drowsy and boredom overtook him, he walked back to the spring for a drink. The weather was unseasonably warm for December. Cotton Blossom spent most of the first day with him on sentry duty and then took to roaming the woods. None of the outlaws bothered Nathan, for his saddle was in the bunkhouse and both his horses in the corral. One afternoon, after he had become particularly weary of sentry duty, he started back to the spring for water. While Cotton Blossom had begun the day with him, the dog had quickly satisfied his own boredom by wandering away. As Nathan neared the spring, he heard a voice. A soft female voice. He crept closer and found the girl from El Gato's cabin carrying on a one-sided conversation with Cotton Blossom. While Nathan was unable to understand the words, he could hear the sorrow and misery in her voice. Her arms were around Cotton Blossom and he sat there patiently, as though aware of her distress. At Nathan's approach, Cotton Blossom barked once. The girl sprang to her feet, but before she could run, Nathan spoke.

"That's my dog, ma'am, and I won't hurt you. Please stay and talk."

"If I'm caught, he'll beat me," she said, "and he'll kill you."

"Then we'll both have to take some risk," Nathan replied. "Who are you, and why are you here in Indian Territory with outlaws?"

"I'm Mary Holden," she said timidly, "and I'm here because they brought me here. They burned our place in Kansas and shot my ma and pa." Her face paled but she didn't cry, and that said a lot for her.

"How old are you, Mary, and how long have you been here?"

"I just turned seventeen," she said, "and I've been here almost a year. Are you ... one of them?"

"No," said Nathan, "and I'm counting on you to keep my secret. Somehow I aim to escape, and I'll take you with me. Will you trust me?"

"Oh, God, yes," she cried, hope brimming in her eyes. "When?"

"I don't know," said Nathan. "They're riding out again in a few days, and I must ride with them. I may have to wait until we're far from here, free myself of them, and ride back for you. Have you been harmed ... in any way?"

"No," she said, "but he ... the pig ... makes me take off my clothes and ... he ... just looks at me. He tells the others he will take me to Mexico and ... sell me."

"Put that out of your mind," said Nathan, "because it's not going to be that way. I can't come looking for you, so you'll have to find me. I can get to the spring without being followed. Watch for me. I'll be here at least two or three days before I ride out with them. Does he always leave men here when they ride out?"

"Yes," she said. "At least two. He wouldn't dare leave me alone."

"I can handle two of them," said Nathan, "but not the whole pack. Just remember, next time they ride out, I'll be going with them. But I'll be back for you. I don't know just when, because it'll depend on how soon I'm able to break away. Just don't say or do anything to arouse suspicion."

"I won't," she said. "I don't talk to him, and he won't let the others come near me. I'd best be going back."

With a final tug on Cotton Blossom's ears, she started back. Nathan felt his temper rising. While he might rescue Mary Holden, how long would it take El Gato to replace her with another unfortunate girl? He drank from the cool water of the spring and started back to his post, Cotton Blossom following.

*   *   *

Indian Territory. January 24, 1871.

Three more times Nathan was able to speak to Mary Holden, the third time the day before El Gato's band was to ride out. That same afternoon, El Gato sent for Nathan, and this time he came immediately to the point.

"We are withdrawing some money from the bank at Wichita," he said. "I will take three men into the bank with me. You will be one of the three. We ride in the morning at dawn."

*   *   *

When they rode out, only Breed and Kirkham were left behind. Every man carried enough rations in his saddlebags for four days. Nathan had brought enough jerked beef to share with Cotton Blossom. While the dog disliked all the outlaws, he would follow Nathan, probably at some distance. The weather had turned bitter cold right after the first of the year, and there had been a continual threat of snow. Nathan wanted it, needed it, if he were to escape from the outlaws. He must break away and return to Cocodrilo Rancho before El Gato discovered what he had in mind. His packsaddle and packhorse were still there, of course, but so were Breed and Kirkham. The big unanswerable question was whether or not El Gato would delay his raid in Wichita to pursue Nathan Stone. The nearer they were to Wichita when Nathan broke loose, the greater a possibility the renegades would let Nathan go and continue without him. Or so Nathan hoped.

Come dawn of their second day on the trail, the snow started. At first it was fine, mixed with sleet that rattled off their hat brims and stung their faces as it was whipped on a rising wind. Finally the snow took on all the porportions of a blizzard, making it difficult for a rider to see the man and horse ahead of him. Eventually El Gato led them to the lee side of a ridge, clothed with a thick stand of pines. It was all the shelter they were likely to find. Already the snow was deep enough to supply them with water. There was no sun, but a quick look at his watch told Nathan they were less than two hours away from nightfall. There were many fallen pines, some resinous, so the outlaws built a roaring fire. El Gato seemed especially pleased. They weren't far south of Wichita, and it might well snow all night. What better time to rob the bank than during a blinding snowstorm? There was hot coffee, and the ridge offered some protection from the howling wind. Nathan found Cotton Blossom near the picketed horses, and fed the dog some jerked beef.

"Yokum, Vanado, and Hickman, you will stay awake and feed the fire until midnight. Fortner, Peyton, and York, you will take over at midnight and feed the fire until dawn."

It was the sensible thing to do, for when the wind howled across the plains and the snow lay deep, even marauding Indians sought shelter. Most of the renegades spread their blankets as near the roaring fire as possible, and Nathan allowed them to take all the available space. It suited his purpose to remain on the outer fringes, for he intended to ride away at the first opportunity. There was a possibility, with Yokum, Vanado, and Hickman well away from the fire gathering more wood, that Nathan might reach his horse unseen. Once in the saddle, he could give the black its head, for the horse had been at Cocodrilo Rancho long enough to consider the corral home. There was even a chance, Nathan thought, that he might escape and not be missed until the next morning.

The snow continued, and there being nothing else to do,

the outlaws had rolled in their blankets. Nathan followed
their example, waiting for the trio of fire tenders to drag
in more dead pines. As soon as they were so engaged, he
quickly rolled his blankets and made his way to where the
horses were tied. His hands were numb with cold before
he managed to get the black saddled. He led the animal
for half a mile before climbing into the saddle. Cotton Blossom was a dark shadow against the white of the snow,
loping along beside him. He gave the black its head, bowing
his own, for the wind still whipped the snow in from the
west. That and the intuition of the faithful black horse was
all that told him he was riding south. At times he reined
up to listen, but heard only the lonely shriek of the wind.
He rode on, not knowing where he was or how far he had
ridden, for time stood still. Somewhere a pine limb snapped
under its burden of snow. The forest through which he rode
assured him he was back in Indian Territory and offered
some welcome protection from wind and snow. Despite the
bone-chilling cold and the deepening snow, he was compelled to stop at intervals and rest the black. He walked
about, stomping his feet in a vain attempt to restore circula-
tion. He removed his gloves, thrusting his hands into his
pockets. He was tempted to find a place to hole up for the
night, but without a fire he could freeze to death in his
sleep. Besides, El Gato and the renegades might be pursuing him. The old varmint just might be vindictive enough
to mount a search for him, snowstorm or not. So he rode
on. When the dawn came, it was almost unnoticable, for
the sky lightened only a little. Reaching a stream, Nathan
reined up and dismounted. After the black had rested, Nathan took a sack of rye from behind his saddle and poured
his hat a third full. He held the hat while the black horse
hungrily devoured the contents. He then watered the animal, shared what was left of the jerked beef with Cotton
Blossom, and rode on.
    Try as he might, Nathan was unable to recognize any
landmarks, for the snow had changed everything. He realized they had reached Cocodrilo Rancho only when he
reached the spring, a few hundred yards south of El Gato's
cabin. Nathan dismounted, leading the black. He would
leave the horse at the cabin and proceed on foot to the
bunkhouse. But by the time he reached the cabin, the girl
had the door open.

"You came back!" she cried joyously. "You came back for me."

"Yes," he said, "but I'll have to silence the two men at the bunkhouse. If you have any coffee, put some on to boil. I'll be back."

He started for the bunkhouse, thankful it had no windows. He would be discovered only if Breed or Kirkham opened the door before he was able to get the drop. He had no intention of killing them, unless they forced him to. In the pocket of his sheepskin coat was strong twine that he had brought for the occasion. He drew his right-hand Colt, cocked it, and slammed open the bunkhouse door. Breed and Kirkham sat up on their bunks, grabbing frantically for their weapons. Nathan fired once, the lead ripping into the floor between the two men. It had the desired effect. They froze.

"Belly down on the floor," Nathan ordered. "I only want what's mine, and I reckon you gents won't interfere if you're tied good and tight."

"Damn you," Kirkham snarled, "we'll freeze."

"That's a chance you have to take," said Nathan, "unless you'd prefer I just shoot you."

Given the alternative, they sprawled face down on the floor. Nathan had only begun to tie Kirkham's hands behind his back when Breed made his play. He rolled over, but got no farther, for Nathan slugged him just above the eyes with the muzzle of his Colt. Breed lay still.

"Get up," Nathan told Kirkham, loosing his bonds. "Stretch out on your bunk. I'll give you a break."

Kirkham did so, and Nathan lashed each of his ankles to the foot of the bunk and each of his wrists to the head. He then dumped Breed on his bunk and lashed him down as he had Kirkham. It was more consideration than they deserved, but they might be many hours away from discovery, and he was leaving them in positions not all that torturous. He took their Colts, opened the door, and flung them far out into the snow. He then shouldered the packsaddle and stepped out the door. Cotton Blossom was already near the corral, and Nathan quickly caught up and loaded the packhorse. He led the animal back to the cabin where Mary Holden waited, and knocked on the door. She let him in, and he smelled the coffee.

"I heard a shot," she said, "and I was afraid ..."

"Nobody's hurt," said Nathan. "Breed and Kirkham are tied to their bunks. They'll be a mite stiff, but they'll get over it. Can you ride?"

"Yes," Mary said, "but not like this . . . I . . ."

"I'll take one of these saddles," said Nathan, "and saddle you a horse. But you can't travel the way you are. Until we can do better, can't you wear some of El Gato's duds? Take a warm shirt, Levi's, and a coat. Find a pair of boots, shoes, something to protect your feet, even if they're too large. I can get you something decent once we're away from here, but it's almighty cold out there."

"I'll try to find something," she said dubiously. "The coffee's ready."

Nathan found a tin cup and drank most of the coffee. By then, Mary had returned with an assortment of things, including a pair of boots.

"You can change out here by the fire," said Nathan. "I'll go to the corral and catch you a horse. Which of these saddles do you prefer?"

"The one nearest the door," she said. "That's mine. They took my horse, too. He's dark gray, a grulla."

Nathan took the saddle and headed for the corral. There were three more horses, one of them a grulla, and Nathan caught him without difficulty. He led the horse back to the cabin and knocked on the door.

"Come in," she said.

He almost laughed, for she looked like a scarecrow. The sleeves of the blue flannel shirt came well over her hands, and the legs of the Levi's were a foot too long. They were far too large in the waist, too, for when she bent down to roll up the legs, the Levi's slid down around her ankles.

"Oh, damn," she cried, "I can't do it."

"You'll have to," said Nathan, "until we can do better. He must have an extra belt somewhere."

Nathan managed to find one, and with his knife, cut some extra holes. The boots were too large, but with three pair of socks, she made them fit. Then, wearing a coat that swallowed her small frame, Nathan hoisted her into the saddle. They rode southeast, the snow covering the tracks of the horses . . .

Chapter 33

While the snow had changed the landscape, the Chisholm wagon road had been in use for three years as a cattle trail, and would be well defined. It would lead them south to Red River, and crossing that, they would be less than an hour from Dallas or Fort Worth. Mary Holden rode well, trotting her grulla easily alongside his black.

"Where are we going?" she asked.

"Fort Worth, Texas," said Nathan. "I need some sleep and some hot food, and you need some clothes and boots that fit. Time enough to get you back to Kansas, after El Gato and his bunch have returned to Indian Territory."

"I'm not going back to Kansas," she said.

"You have kin somewhere else, I reckon," said Nathan.

"None that I claim," she replied. "Ma and Pa married against the wishes of her family and his. Now they're all dead. Them that's left—aunts, uncles, cousins—I don't know them. I don't know where they are, and I don't want to know."

"Then you have nowhere to go?"

"Nowhere," she said, "unless I go with you."

"You can't go with me," said Nathan. "It wouldn't be . . . proper. I'm older than you."

"Pa was ten years older than my Ma."

"I'm not looking for a wife," Nathan said firmly.

"I'm not offering you one," she replied. "Just tell people we're married. When you get tired of me, I'll go away."

"I'm no-account," said Nathan, "but I'm more of a man than that. Let's just say I have my reason—an almighty good reason—for not wanting a woman riding with me. Can't we let it go at that?"

She said no more, but he had the feeling this wasn't over. He suspected that when her hair was cut and she was dressed decently, Mary Holden was going to be an almighty pretty girl, more temptation than he could resist on a regular basis.

*   *   *

Fort Worth, Texas. January 28, 1871.

The snow ceased before they reached the Red, and by the time Nathan and Mary rode into Fort Worth, there were patches of bare ground everywhere.

"First we must report to the post commander," Nathan said. "Then we'll find you some clothes that fit. Then we're going to find someplace where there's a roof over our heads, and I aim to sleep for two days."

Nathan asked to speak to the post commander, and found Captain Ferguson was still there. He recognized Nathan, and seemed somewhat amused at his poorly clothed companion.

"We've ridden across Indian Territory," said Nathan, "and we're needing quarters for several nights. I realize this is a military post, Captain, but I'd be glad to pay."

"It's not our custom to rent quarters," Ferguson said, "but in deference to your wife ..."

"She's ... this is ..." Nathan was caught off guard, and Mary cut in.

"Mary," said the girl glibly, "and we're most obliged, Captain. You are a gentlemen."

Ferguson grinned like a mule eating briars, turning them over to a waiting corporal, and he led them to a small cabin that customarily housed a pair of officers at the post's bachelor officer's quarters. The corporal let them in and closed the door, leaving them alone. The room was small, and there was just one bed.

"Damn," Nathan said, glaring at her.

She laughed. "You wouldn't have gotten this cabin if it weren't for me," she said.

"You can have the bed," he told her. "I'll spread my blankets on the floor."

"You're right," she said. "You don't need a wife."

"Come on," said Nathan wearily. "We'll go to the sutler's and get you some clothes that fit."

Mary Holden was small, and it was difficult to fit her in men's clothes. The man who tried to assist them was at first amused, but he became irritated as the task consumed more and more time. Finally he came up with a suggestion that was too much.

"Sir," he said to Nathan, "have you considered allowing her to wear ... ah ... more ladylike apparel? Perhaps a floor-length skirt?"

"Pardner," Nathan said, "have you ever seen a lady hike her leg over a saddle, wearin' a skirt? Would you want your missus doin' that?"

Others had heard the exchange, and men roared with laughter, but one of those who had overheard came to Nathan's aid.

"I'm Lieutenant Masters," he said, "and my wife's a seamstress. Just buy as close as you can to what you need, and it won't cost that much to have everything altered to fit."

"That's most kind of you," said Mary, again jumping in ahead of Nathan. "Tell me where I can find her."

"Here," Masters said, "I'll write it down for you."

He did so, and the embarrassed clerk managed to select shirts and Levi's of a size near enough to Mary's that they could be altered. To Nathan's everlasting relief, the store had wool socks and boots that fit well enough, and while the sleeves on the sheepskin coat were a little long, it would do. They returned to the cabin Ferguson had assigned them, and no sooner had Nathan closed the door than Mary began removing the too-large clothing of El Gato.

"What the hell are you doing?" Nathan demanded.

"Taking off his clothes," she said. "I want out of them."

"But yours have to be altered," Nathan protested.

"When I go to have them altered, I'll wear them," she said. "You say you need sleep, and I don't feel safe walking around this place alone. I'll wait until you can go with me."

She had already removed the shirt, and when she loosened the belt, the Levi's fell down to her ankles. Despite all his resolutions, Nathan stared at her, and she laughed.

"Don't just stand there," she said. "Take these boots off." She sat down on the bed, extending her feet, and he dragged El Gato's boots off. She discarded the Levi's and stretched out on the bed.

"Nice bed," she observed. "More comfortable than the floor."

Nathan had left the horses and the packsaddle at the post livery and his saddlebags were under the bed. Finally it occurred to him he had forgotten Cotton Blossom. He opened the door a little, wary of Mary Holden stretched out on the bed. Cotton Blossom poked his head around the corner of the cabin, and started reluctantly for the door. He paused, looked around, decided that the cabin was the lesser of many evils and came inside. Mary called to him, and he seemed more confident. Nathan removed his hat, his gunbelt, and then his boots. He stretched out on his back on the other side of the bed, which didn't offer all that much room.

When Mary Holden was sure Nathan was asleep, she got up. The clothing to be altered was much nearer her size than that of El Gato's. She sat on the room's only chair and pulled on a pair of the wool socks, and when she looked up, Nathan was looking directly at her.

"I . . . I thought you were asleep," she stammered.

"I'm a light sleeper," he said. "It keeps me alive. Just where the hell do you think you're going?"

"I was going to have the clothes fixed . . ."

"That can wait," said Nathan. "If you don't aim to sleep, then be quiet so I can."

"Would you prefer that I sit here, or may I lie on the bed?"

"If you aim to get up and down, stay where you are," Nathan said.

Nathan was snoring when she again lay down beside him. She wore one of the new shirts and new Levi's.

"You forgot the boots," Nathan said, not bothering to open his eyes.

She got up, stomped into the new boots, and lay down again. Nathan said nothing, continuing to snore, but he had a hard time suppressing a grin.

He had no idea how long he had slept, but when he awakened, the girl's exhaustion had caught up with her, for she slept soundly. Cotton Blossom sat beside the door. Nathan got up and let him out. The sky had cleared and the sun was low on the western horizon. Nathan sat down on the chair, watching Mary Holden sleep. Had she planned to take her clothes to the seamstress, or had she been about

to run out on him? He decided she had not, for it made
no sense. She had no money and her clothes didn't fit. She
seemed impulsive, restless, and more than a little put out
that he hadn't yielded to temptation and taken her when
he had the chance. By her own admission she had nowhere
to go, nowhere she wanted to go, and that fueled the fires
of Nathan's suspicion. Nathan had told her he wasn't seeking a wife and she had denied wishing to become one, but
no honest man could take a woman and not feel some
obligation to her. He had a strong suspicion she had been
counting on that. While he had told her nothing about himself, she was no fool. When he had returned for her, he
could have taken her there in El Gato's cabin, making that
a condition for his rescue, but he had not. He was well
armed, owned not only horse and saddle, but a packhorse
as well. He had readily paid for her new clothes, so she
was aware that he wasn't poor. He shook his head. Women
were a paradox, all too often giving themselves to men who
in no way suited their dreams, but could offer some small
measure of security. On the other hand, a man—or woman,
for that matter—who seemed indifferent and unattainable
became all the more desirable. Nathan resolved to help
Mary Holden in any way that he could, but on his terms,
not hers. If, somewhere within her, lived a woman whose
feelings were genuine and whose affection was not for sale
or trade, then he would be ready and willing to reconsider.

A knock on the door brought him out of his chair. It
was the young corporal who had guided them to the cabin.

"Captain Ferguson says you and the missus are welcome
to eat at officer's mess. It's the long, low building directly
behind the orderly room."

"We're obliged, Corporal," Nathan said. He closed the
door.

"I'm starved," said Mary, sitting up and showing none
of her earlier irritation. "Where's Cotton Blossom?"

"Outside," Nathan replied. "You'd better roll up the legs
of those Levi's so's you can walk."

She did, and within a few minutes, the bugler blew
mess call.

"We'll wait a few minutes," said Nathan, "and let the
soldiers go first. They're doing us a good turn, and I'm not
one to take unfair advantage of a man's hospitality."

When Nathan and Mary reached officer's mess, Cotton

Blossom was already there. A large pan of roast beef trimmings had been left outside the door, and Cotton Blossom had wasted no time in partaking of them. Captain Ferguson sat at a table near the door and nodded to them as they entered. When Nathan and Mary had their trays filled, Nathan spoke to the cook.

"I'm obliged to you for feeding my dog. Neither of us has been eating very well lately."

"My pleasure," the cook said.

Nathan and Mary took seats at an empty table near where Captain Ferguson sat talking with two other officers. It soon became apparent that one of the officers was the post doctor and that he and Ferguson were discussing the illness of their telegrapher. Nathan waited for a pause in the conversation, and then spoke to Ferguson.

"Captain Ferguson, I couldn't help overhearing your conversation. I was with the Kansas–Pacific Railroad for a while, and I know the code. If you're in need of a telegrapher, I'd be glad to fill in until you can make some other arrangements."

"Stone," said Ferguson, getting to his feet, "you're the answer to a prayer. Sergeant DeWitt, our telegrapher, is deathly ill, out of his head with a fever. We're authorized two telegraphers, but the post is undermanned. The instrument's been clattering all day. By now, Washington probably thinks we've been overrun by Quanah Parker's Comanches. When you've finished eating, please come to my office. The first thing I want you to do is inform Washington that you're a civilian, filling in for the one telegrapher they've sent me in the four years I've been post commander here."

Ferguson and the other officers left, and Mary paused.

"That must have been interesting," she said, "working for the railroad."

"It was for a while," said Nathan. He continued eating.

"You don't talk much about yourself, do you?"

"No," Nathan said. "I've never thought of myself as a conversation piece. I'm a jack of all trades and master of none. I've been a soldier, a gambler, a railroad man, and a deputy U.S. marshal. I've killed some hombres that was needful of it, and unless somebody salts me down first, I aim to kill a few more. I'm not a drinking man, and I don't use tobacco or visit whorehouses. I do sleep with women

occasionally, but I'm considering giving that up, because
the last three are dead, because of what I did or failed to
do. Will that be enough for now?"

"Yes," she said, in a small voice. The rest of the meal
was eaten in silence. They had returned to their cabin before Nathan spoke again.

"Gather up the rest of your clothes," he said. "I'll leave
you with Mrs. Masters. Have her take up at least one shirt
and one pair of Levi's, so's you have something to wear.
Leave the others, and she can take them up when she gets
to them."

The lieutenant's seamstress wife did sewing in the cabin
where she lived, and after leaving Mary there, Nathan went
to Captain Ferguson's office. Even then, the telegraph was
chattering, demanding attention.

"Thank God," Ferguson groaned. "Find out what that
thing wants. It's been driving me to distraction."

Nathan sat down at the table with pencil and paper. Most
of the messages were followups to earlier messages, seeking
to learn the reason for the lack of response from Fort
Worth. Nathan quickly sent a lengthy response from Captain Ferguson detailing the problem. Ferguson had given
Nathan credit for aiding him in his emergency. When
Washington acknowledged, there was a five-word message
for Nathan: *Silver sends regards to Stone.*

Nathan's apparent recognition in Washington didn't go
unnoticed by Captain Ferguson. When he had read the
message, he spoke.

"So it was you who alerted Washington to the ... ah ...
difficulty some months ago at Fort Concho. Silver ...
Byron Silver ..."

"A friend of mine," Nathan said. "I hope your operation
that began at Fort Concho worked out to everybody's
satisfaction."

"Very much so," said Captain Ferguson. "If it won't in-
convenience you, I would consider it a personal favor if
you will act as post telegrapher until I can make other
arrangements."

"I'd be glad to," Nathan replied.

By the time Nathan returned to the Masters's cabin, Mrs.
Masters had a pair of Levi's and one of the shirts altered
to fit Mary.

"If you can leave the rest with me," said Mrs. Masters, "I can have them ready in the morning."

Nathan and Mary returned to their cabin, for it was getting dark. Cotton Blossom waited at the door.

"I may be here several more days," Nathan said. "I promised the Captain I'd remain here as telegrapher until he makes other arrangements. We'll have our meals and a place to sleep."

Nathan removed his gun belt, his hat, and his boots, and lay down on the bed.

"Do you always sleep in your clothes?" Mary asked.

"When you travel a lot and you don't often have a bed, it helps keep you warm," said Nathan.

"There's something unnatural about a man who never takes his clothes off," she said, looking at him critically. "There's not ... some of you ... missing, is there?"

It caught him off guard, and when he realized she was serious, he laughed until he cried. Angrily she grabbed the chair and sat down facing the door, her back to him. When he began to snore, she got up and kicked the chair up against the bed. He opened one eye.

"You ... you're impossible," she shouted. "You sleep with your clothes on, you won't talk to me, you won't listen to me. Damn it, I might as well have stayed with El Gato. At least, he ... he made me feel like a ... a woman."

Nathan got up and lighted the lamp, for it was dark in the room. He then took her bodily and threw her on the bed, and taking her boots by the heels, jerked them off her feet. She tried to get up and he shoved her back down. Unbuttoning her Levi's, he dragged them off. By the time he got to her shirt, he had to fight her to remove that, but he managed it. He got up, leaving her lying there. When he caught his breath, he spoke.

"If that's your idea of being treated like a woman—being stripped and having a man salivate—then so be it. I've seen naked women before. When you have something more to offer me than what El Gato could have taken, then maybe you and me will have somethin' to talk about. Meanwhile, you just lie there and feel like a woman."

He sat down in the chair, leaned its hind legs against the wall and just looked at her. He alternated between feeling sorry for her and wishing he'd never laid eyes on her. Finally she rolled over, buried her face in a pillow and began sobbing. Even as he was feeling guilty and snake-mean, he wondered if she weren't just putting on another act for his benefit. He got up, opened the door, and then closed it, as though he had gone out. But her wailing continued, becoming louder, until he feared others would think he was beating her. He rolled her over, but her eyes were closed, and she kept them closed. He kissed her gently on the lips, just once. She almost strangled as she choked off a sob. When she opened her eyes, the anger had been replaced by wonder.

"Mary," he said, "if you can't get a man's attention without taking off your clothes, then there's something wrong with you. Or with him. You're an almighty pretty girl, but that's not enough. You've been trying to prove something—maybe to me, maybe to yourself—I don't know. Starting right now, I want you to just be you. Understand?"

"I . . . I understand," she said, "and I'll try."

He got up, blew out the lamp, got undressed, and lay down beside her. She remained where she was, unmoving. She was silent for so long, he breathed a sigh, thinking she was sleeping.

"Nathan, are you asleep?"

"Yes," he said, "and it's not easy, with you talking to me."

She laughed, poking him in the ribs with a finger. "Aren't you afraid you'll freeze?"

"There are times when I like to live dangerously," he said.

*   *   *

Sergeant DeWitt, after a long bout with fever, died from causes unknown. Captain Ferguson telegraphed Washington, and was informed that it might be as long as a month before a qualified telegrapher could be assigned to the post.

"This is embarrassing," Captain Ferguson said, after Nathan had given him the telegram from Washington. "Is there a chance you can remain here until I get this new man assigned? I don't expect your services for nothing. I can authorize payment of a dollar a day, retroactive to the day you began."

"I can stay," said Nathan, "and the pay isn't necessary.

You're providing me with food and quarters. That's enough."

Nathan was enjoying his temporary duty, for the telegrapher at Fort Worth was liaison between Washington and the state of Texas, as well as parts of Indian Territory. Much information came his way. Despite the Reconstructionist governor of Texas refusing to recognize the Texas Rangers, the Rangers had survived and were now stronger than ever. The Union army had developed a healthy respect for these men who had led the fight in the war with Mexico. Much of the information that came over the wire concerned outlaws of concern to Texas lawmen, and there were names of Rangers Nathan recognized. The last week in January, a report came in involving John Wesley Hardin. The gunman, in custody of two state lawmen, along with two other prisoners, was being transferred from the little town of Marshall, Texas to Waco. While one of the guards had gone to buy grain for the horses, Hardin produced a hideout gun and shot the remaining guard. Hardin and the other prisoners had fled on horseback. One of the other prisoners, captured with Hardin, had been Dade Withers!

Nathan swore under his breath, for he was committed to fill in as post telegrapher for at least three more weeks, and maybe longer. His position now seemed a blessing and a curse. A blessing, because he might have ridden for months, searching saloons and reading newspapers before learning this bit of information that had fallen into his hands. However, he was cursed by being committed indefinitely to the very instrument that had served him so well, for he was unable to look for Hardin and Withers. But he had one thing in his favor. With access to the telegraph, he could watch for reports on Withers and Hardin's whereabouts. Withers might not alone command the attention Hardin would, so it was to Nathan's advantage if Withers kept with Hardin.

At last Captain Ferguson received word that three newly assigned soldiers would be arriving on February twenty-first. One of them was the long-awaited telegrapher. The next report on Hardin came from south Texas, from Gonzales County. Hardin and some other riders had stopped at a Mexican camp, and after taking part in a game of monte, quarreled with the dealer. Hardin slugged the man with his gun barrel and when two other Mexicans drew knives, Hardin shot and wounded them. There was no mention of names other than Hardin's.

On February fifteenth, word came that buffalo hunters had brought a wounded man to Fort Griffin. The men claimed they had been attacked by four riders, one of whom was believed to have been John Wesley Hardin. Identify had been unconfirmed. Nathan went to the huge map of the United States in Captain Ferguson's office. Fort Griffin was in northwest Texas. That could mean Hardin and his friends were bound for Indian Territory to hole up until it was safe to return to Texas, or it could mean they were going all the way to Kansas.

"Where are we going when we leave here?" Mary Holden wanted to know.

"North," said Nathan. "Maybe to Indian Territory, maybe to Kansas."

"Am I allowed to know why?"

"I reckon," said Nathan. "If you aim to ride with me, you might as well know what you're up against. I'm going to kill a man. He was one of seven who murdered my family."

"Where are the others?"

"Dead," Nathan replied. "Now you know all there is to know about Nathan Stone. Are you satisfied?"

"No. What will you do after you've killed this last man?"

"I don't have the faintest idea," said Nathan.

On February 21, Nathan gave up his temporary position as telegrapher, and Captain Ferguson thanked him profusely.

"If you're ever in trouble and need the army," Ferguson said, "call on us. However, we're always undermanned, so I can't promise there'll be enough of us to save you. Of course, you can always telegraph Washington."

"I can't count on that, either," said Nathan. "Silver's the kind who'd go out and get himself shot just when I'm needin' him the most."

*   *   *

Fort Griffin, Texas. February 25, 1871.

Nathan had a letter—enclosed in oilskin—from Captain Ferguson informing any and all concerned that Nathan

Stone had, on more than one occasion, rendered service to the army of the United States of America. Ferguson had requested that Nathan be shown every consideration by other military installations, including food, lodging, and use of the telegraph. It quickly got Nathan and Mary into the office of Fort Griffin's post commander, Colonel Lowell.

"Sorry," Lowell said, after Nathan's inquiry, "but the man you're seeking was released from our dispensary more than a week ago. His wound wasn't all that serious. The report we have of the shooting is sketchy, because none of the buffalo hunters had ever seen Hardin. Therefore, we don't know if it was him or not. It well could have been, because that's how most of these Texas killers operate. When the law gets after them in Texas, they go somewhere else. By the time they're in trouble there, things have usually cooled down enough for them to return here. We're never entirely rid of them till they're hung or shot."

Nathan and Mary were offered lodging and meals, so they spent one night at Fort Griffin. After breakfast they rode north. Nathan had no doubt that he would be shot on sight if they rode anywhere close to El Gato's stronghold. Mary hadn't said anything, but he could see the fear in her eyes at the very mention of Indian Territory. Finally, when they stopped to rest and water the horses, he decided to ease her mind.

"We're not going anywhere near El Gato's place," he said. "It's a good hundred and fifty miles east of here. I think we'll just ride on to Fort Dodge. From there, I can telegraph Captain Ferguson and see if there's been any more hell-raising by Hardin anywhere in Texas."

"I'm glad we're not going anywhere close to those outlaws," she said. "I don't even like to think of what he ... El Gato would do to me if he ever got his hands on me again."

"No more than he'd do to me," said Nathan. "That's practically the first thing he said to me, that he'd kill me if I ever betrayed his trust."

"I wonder what happened after you left them? Did they go ahead and rob the bank at Wichita?"

"I don't know," Nathan said. "I haven't read a newspaper since leaving Kansas. In a way, I hope Hardin and his bunch are in Kansas. I have friends there, and it's a hell of a lot more civilized than Indian Territory."

They crossed Indian Territory's panhandle and rode on toward Fort Dodge.

Chapter 34

John Wesley Hardin was bound for Kansas. However, he and his friends did not take the most direct route, and as a result, didn't arrive until early June. Following the shooting in Gonzales County, Hardin rode to Cuero Creek, where a rancher he knew was about to take a herd up the Chisholm Trail to Wichita.* In between scrapes with the law, Hardin often hired on as a cowboy, and he did so this time, taking two other men with him. The drive eventually crossed the Red into Indian Territory at the same point Nathan and Mary had left it, after their escape from El Gato's band. Hardin managed to stay out of trouble until the trail drive was out of Texas. However, for no apparent reason, in Indian Territory, he shot and killed an Indian. Fearing retribution, the cowboys helped Hardin conceal the body. The incident went unrecorded until much later.

*   *   *

Fort Dodge, Kansas. March 1, 1871.

Nathan and Mary were well received at Fort Dodge, but a telegraphed inquiry to Captain Ferguson at Fort Worth proved unrewarding, for there was no further word as to the whereabouts of John Wesley Hardin. After spending a night at the fort, Nathan and Mary rode upriver to the tent city. Many of the tents were gone, and in their places, wood-framed buildings now stood. The mercantile was one such building and was quite impressive. It was larger than many Nathan had seen in larger, already-established towns.

"Are we going in?" Mary asked.

---

*In 1873, the town of Cuero, Texas, was founded on Cuero Creek.

"I reckon," said Nathan.

One display especially intrigued Nathan, for it was a new blasting method, a vast improvement over the bothersome, unpredictable black powder.

"It's called dynamite," a clerk told him. "You just cap it and light the fuse, using as many sticks as you need. It's been available back East for several years. Because of the recent war, we're just now getting it."

"We can reach Hays before dark," Nathan said, when they had left the store. "I know the Kansas–Pacific dispatcher there, as well as the editor of the newspaper. I may learn something from them."

So they rode north. Nathan took a room in the same boardinghouse where he had once shared a room with Wild Bill Hickok. Cotton Blossom followed willingly only when they went out for meals, for he didn't like Hays. It was late when they reached Hays, and Nathan decided he would talk to Donaldson, the dispatcher, and Plato, the newspaper editor, the next day. However, he had been away from the saloons for months. Perhaps it was time to inquire there again.

"I'm going to visit a few of the saloons and see what I can learn," he told Mary. "I want you to stay here and keep Cotton Blossom with you."

He visited Drum's Saloon first, finding it crowded, but subdued. Others were much the same, and after less than two hours, Nathan was finished with them, having learned exactly nothing. He was afoot, and by the time he was in sight of the boardinghouse, he knew something had happened. Men wandered around in front of the place, and he could hear shouting. Pete Lanihan, the county sheriff, was there.

When Nathan reached the outer fringes of the crowd, he discovered what the commotion was all about. Mary Holden knelt with her arms around a growling, bloodied Cotton Blossom. The buttons had been ripped off Mary's shirt. A pair of soldiers—privates—stood within the circle of spectators. The trousers of one of them had been ripped from the knee down.

"That's my dog," Nathan shouted, raising his voice above the uproar, "and I want to know what's happened here."

Nathan shoved his way through, coming face to face with

Sheriff Lanihan. Lanihan didn't show any friendliness, and the first thing he said rubbed Nathan the wrong way.

"So it's your dog," Lanihan growled. "You're prepared to pay—"

"Nothing," Nathan finished. "I'm prepared to call on the post commander at Fort Hays and demand that these men be court martialed. Look at the front of the girl's shirt."

"Cotton Blossom bit him only after he did this," said Mary, standing to allow the shirt to hang open. "They beat him with a gun barrel."

An ugly murmur arose from the crowd that had gathered, for most of them were civilians. Sheriff Lanihan realized what must be done and did it quickly, raising his voice so he could be heard.

"That's enough. All of you clear out. I'm taking these men to jail and notifying the post commander. This will be handled in an orderly manner."

"Now," he said, turning to Nathan, "I'll want both of you at the courthouse in the morning at nine o'clock. I'll need your names to file my report."

Nathan told him, and he left afoot, leading his horse, the pair of crestfallen soldiers plodding ahead of him. Nathan and Mary returned to their room, Cotton Blossom trotting beside them. Inside, Nathan removed a bottle of strong disinfectant from his pack. With a clean strip of cloth, he cleaned Cotton Blossom's wound and doused it with the fiery medicine. Finally Mary spoke.

"I shouldn't have gone out," she said, "but I was only a short way from the door. It was like . . . they were looking for someone."

"Likely they were," said Nathan. "There are few women in this town, or in any other town on the frontier."

"What's going to happen to the soldiers?"

"They'll do some time at hard labor," Nathan said. "The post commander can't allow them to go unpunished."

"But they didn't hurt me. It's Cotton Blossom that was hurt."

"He'll live," said Nathan. "He did what he thought was right."

*   *   *

The next morning, Nathan and Mary went to the courthouse. They did not see the two soldiers who had been charged. Mary left a deposition with the clerk, with the assurance it would be used at the hearing.

"I've never cared much for this town," Nathan said. "I'll talk to the Kansas–Pacific dispatcher and the newspaper editor, and we'll move on."

"Hey," said Donaldson, his eyes on Mary, "you've come up in the world since leaving the old KP."

"I'm surprised you've been able to keep any trains on the track without me out there," Nathan said.

"It ain't been easy, son," said Donaldson. "I never knowed there was so many Indians with nothin' to do 'cept worry other folks."

But Donaldson had little to report, except that Wild Bill Hickok was in Colorado. Nathan had never visited Emmet Plato's newspaper office, so he and Mary had to search for it. When they walked in, Plato virtually ignored them, fixing his eyes on Cotton Blossom, who clearly would have preferred to be somewhere else.

"Ah," Plato exclaimed, "so this is the savage beast that singlehandedly undermined the credibility of the United States Army."

"He bit a soldier who wasn't minding his manners," said Nathan.

"God," Plato said, rolling his eyes heavenward, "if he's here come next election, he could be the new sheriff."

"I hear Hickok's in Colorado," said Nathan. "What happened after he shot those two soldiers last July?"

"One of the men died and the other recovered," Plato said. "There was talk about charging Wild Bill with murder, but there was some more trouble involving the military, and a civilian was killed. When it all came back to Hickok, he got out of it. The judge decided it was a Mexican standoff, bein' as much the fault of the soldiers as Hickok's. They were all drunk, and it wasn't Hickok that started the fight. If I had any say, I'd not build a fort anywhere close to a town, or a town anywhere close to a fort."

Plato had no other information of use to Nathan, so he and Mary rode out of Hays, bound for Abilene. They were following the Kansas–Pacific track, and not more than fifty miles east of Hays, they came upon the body of a Kansas–Pacific outrider, Denton Valentine. He had been shot in the back. Twice.

"Outlaws," Nathan said. "There must be a train coming carrying an army payroll."

"What are you going to do?" Mary asked.

"See if I can find Denton's horse," said Nathan. "He'll have a telegraph instrument in his saddlebag. Maybe I can stop the train."

They followed the tracks of the riderless horse, eventually finding the animal grazing beside a spring runoff. The telegraph instrument was in the saddlebag, but it was of no use. The telegraph line had been cut somewhere to the east. The line to Hays was open, and Nathan quickly sent a message to Hays, to Donaldson. Quickly he placed the telegraph key in his own saddlebag and mounted his horse.

"We have some riding to do," he told Mary. "They've cut the telegraph line somewhere between here and Kansas City. I have to stop that train, if I can."

"Suppose we run into the robbers before we reach the train?"

"There'll be hell to pay," Nathan said. "I look for them to try and stop the train somewhere between here and Abilene. We may not have time."

He kicked his horse into a slow gallop, Mary following. Cotton Blossom loped along behind. They had stopped to rest the horses for the third time when Nathan put his ear to the rail.

"The train's coming," he said. "Stay far behind me. Somewhere just ahead, the outlaws will be waiting, likely to blow up the track."

"Please be careful," she said.

Nathan mounted and rode on, Cotton Blossom following. Soon he could see the locomotive's smoke against the sky. Far down the track, tiny figures were scurrying about. Nathan unshucked his Winchester, jacking in a shell, but he was too late to save the track. There was an explosion that seemed to shake the earth, as twisted rails were flung heavenward, amid a rain of ballast and ties. If he could get *past* the outlaws, Nathan still might be able to warn the trainmen. But the outlaws had seen him. They lost all interest in the train, for it was theirs unless the engineer was warned in time to stop. Lead sang all around Nathan. He held his fire, for shooting from a fast-moving horse was a waste of ammunition. A slug tore into his left side, the force of it almost driving him from the saddle. Grimly he hung on, as more lead hit him high in the chest. Ahead, through dimming vision, he could see the train, and it seemed to be slowing. Suddenly the valiant black horse staggered and broke stride. Nathan quit the saddle, rolling with the fall. He tried to turn on his belly, to bring the Winchester into firing position, but his body refused. Dimly he thought he heard gunshots. Somebody was firing from the train. Finally, he saw Mary's face. But just for a fleeting moment. Then he knew no more.

What Nathan hadn't known was that while he had drawn the outlaws' fire, Mary Holden had ridden as near as she dared, desperately waving her sheepskin coat. The engineer had been able to stop the train, and thanks to a new railroad policy, half a dozen armed men had begun riding every train that carried an army payroll. Heavy fire from the train drove the outlaws away, and now the railroad men concerned themselves with the fate of Nathan Stone.

"I know him," the engineer said. "He used to work for the KP."

"Please," Mary cried, "we must get him to a doctor."

"We can't take him to Hays," said the engineer, "but we can reverse this train and take him back to Abilene. Some of you men let down a ramp and load the lady's horse and packhorse into a boxcar. Remove his saddle and saddlebags from the dead horse, too."

They rolled Nathan in his own blankets and placed him in the same boxcar into which they had loaded the horses and Nathan's saddle.

"I'll ride with him," Mary said. "Come on, Cotton Blossom."

Cotton Blossom would have refused if he'd had any choice. The locomotive lurched into reverse, and Cotton Blossom fell, skidding up against the end of the car. No sooner had he gotten to his feet when the train lurched a second time, and again he was thrown up against the end of the car. Finally he crept into a corner and huddled there until the train reached Abilene. The Kansas–Pacific had built a depot of sorts, and when the telegrapher tested the line to Kansas City, he found it intact.

"Contact Joel Netherton," said the engineer. "Tell him Nathan Stone just saved him a train and an army payroll, not to mention our lives. There's a three-day job for a section crew maybe seventy-five miles west of here."

The doctor brought his buckboard to the depot, and with the help of the engineer, lifted Nathan from the boxcar into the buckboard.

"I'm going with him," Mary Holden said, "wherever you're taking him."

"To my house," said the doctor. "We don't yet have a hospital."

"Joel Netherton of the Kansas–Pacific will be in touch with you," the engineer told Mary. "One of you men ride with the doc, to help him unload. We're going to be here awhile. I expect we'll be returning to Kansas City."

The doctor's name was Webber. Gerald Webber. His wife Madelyn, a thin, efficient woman, was his nurse.

"Ma'am," said Doctor Webber.

"Mary."

"Mary, then," the doctor said. "He's in serious condition. Neither of the slugs exited, which means I'll have to dig them out. He's already lost a lot of blood. Maybe too much. It's not going to be easy to watch. Perhaps you'd better wait in the parlor."

"No," Mary said, "I'll stay with him, whatever happens."

Cotton Blossom sat outside in the doctor's yard. The railroad men, while they waited for orders from the dispatcher in Kansas City, led Mary's horse and Nathan's packhorse to the livery. Their saddles and the packsaddle was taken inside the Kansas–Pacific depot. For two hours, Doctor Webber worked over Nathan. Finally he rinsed away the blood and disinfected and bandaged the wounds.

"I can't do more than give him a fighting chance," said Webber. "He lost a lot of blood before I got to him, and he lost more while I was probing for the lead. Neither slug struck any vital organs or bones, and that's in his favor, but it's been a severe shock. If he's alive this time tomorrow, I'd say he'll make it. He'll need to remain here tonight, and possibly tomorrow night. The rest of the way, he'll be fighting infection."

"I'm staying with him, then," Mary said, "no matter how long."

"Then I'll have Madelyn set up a cot for you in here. I'll be looking in on him several times during the night."

*   *   *

Four days later, the doctor declared Nathan out of danger. He was then taken to the hotel, and it was there that Joel Netherton, of the Kansas–Pacific, came to see him.

"I'm pleased to see you again," said Netherton, "although I'd like the circumstances to be different."

"So would I," Nathan replied.

"I have good news for you," the railroad man said. "The Kansas–Pacific has authorized me to pay you a reward of a thousand dollars and to pay all your medical expenses, your lodging here at the hotel, until you're back on your feet."

"That's mighty generous," said Nathan. "I'm obliged."

"We're in your debt," Netherton replied. "All we're out is the repair of a piece of track. But for you, we might have lost a train, its crew, and an army payroll."

"You're having considerable trouble with train robbers, then."

"Yes," said Netherton. "We believe these robbers you intercepted are the same ones who have dogged us for months. A sheriff's posse once picked up their trail just south of here, but lost it when they escaped into Indian Territory."

"Ten or eleven riders?"

"Eleven, as a matter of fact," Netherton said. "How did you know?"

"I think I know who they are and where they are," Nathan said.

The frown on Mary Holden's face and the worry in her eyes told him her thinking was running neck and neck with his own.

"Great Scott," said Netherton, "when you're feeling up to it, will you share that information with railroad authorities?"

"I reckon," Nathan said, "but it'll be a fight to the death."

When Netherton had excused himself, Mary looked at Nathan long and hard. Finally she spoke.

"You're not thinking of leading a posse into Indian Territory, are you?"

"I haven't thought about it, one way or the other," said Nathan, "but don't you think the world would be a better place without that bunch of gun-totin' varmints?"

"Yes," she said, "but why does it have to be you who

rids the world of them? I want you alive. Doesn't it matter to you what I want?"

"You know it does," he said, "but you also know the kind of hombre I am, that I won't cash in my chips settin' in a rocker before the fire, with you holding my hand."

"Yes," she said, "you'll go out in a hail of bullets, doing your damndest to take as many with you as you can. I just want to put it off as long as possible."

"So do I," he replied.

*   *   *

The wounds had taken more out of Nathan than he had believed, for it was the first week in June before he began to feel himself. The doctor advised another month of rest, and the next time he saw Netherton, the railroad man encouraged it.

"We're having a big celebration July fourth," said Netherton, "and I want you and Mary there. There'll be brass from Washington, railroad officials, all the beer you can drink, speeches . . ."

"Oh, no, you don't," Nathan said. "Shooting outlaws, si, speeches, no."

"Whoa," said Netherton, "you unjustly accuse me."

"I've heard of these hog killings where a bunch of hombres talk, with nobody carin' a damn what they say. I'll be there on one condition, that I can leave when I'm good and ready."

"That's how it'll be, then," said Netherton.

*   *   *

Kansas City, Missouri. June 20, 1871.

The Kansas–Pacific offered transportation from Abilene to Kansas City, but Nathan wanted to ride. It was a good time to buy horses in Abilene, for many a cattleman sold his remuda at trail's end. Nathan still mourned the loss of his faithful black, and made up his mind never to own another black, for it would be a constant reminder of one that could never truly be replaced. He finally settled for a grulla, almost the exact shade of gray as Mary's. They reached Kansas City and when Nathan presented Mary to

Eppie Bolivar, she welcomed the girl without question. They settled in at Eppie's boardinghouse and Nathan resumed his habit of reading newspapers from other towns, forever seeking a name that was never there. What had become of John Wesley Hardin and the men who rode with him?

A week before the affair on July fourth, Netherton's wife took Mary into town and outfitted her in what was considered proper dress for the time. The fun began when she returned, and spent an hour getting herself up for Nathan's approval. It was a ballroom dress that almost swept the floor, with what seemed a never-ending array of petticoats. Her slippers were a matching light blue. She came out, almost falling over the numerous petticoats, and Nathan laughed.

"What's so funny?" she demanded. "Would you rather I wore a flannel shirt and Levi's?"

"There'd be less chance of you falling and breaking your neck," said Nathan. "I'm wearing what I always wear, or I don't go."

But Nathan yielded to pressure, some of it from Mary, and eventually bought new black pin-striped trousers, white ruffled shirt, string tie, black boots, and a new, high-crowned gray hat.

"Damn it," he complained, "a man walks around dressed for burying, he's likely to be shot, just on general principles."

But the affair was deemed a huge success, and Nathan Stone enjoyed it far more than he expected to or would later admit. Byron Silver was there, and while much of his and Nathan's joint efforts could not be discussed, they had their moments.

"I reckon we'd best enjoy this blowout," Silver said. "It's the first time we've even been together for any length of time that one or both of us wasn't bein' shot at."

"Yeah," said Nathan. "I miss it, don't you?"

Silver remained in Kansas City two more days before returning to Washington. Finally, on July eighth, Nathan hit paydirt with his newspapers. On July sixth, in Abilene, Charles Cougar had been shot dead after a quarrel with John Wesley Hardin. Another piece charged Hardin with killing Juan Bideno, a Mexican, in the tiny village of Bluff City, Kansas. There was no mention of the men who had supposedly left Texas with Hardin. The writer of one of the articles had suggested that Hardin had come up the trail with a Texas herd to Wichita, but that was unconfirmed. The trail-drive story made sense to Nathan, accounting for the time it had taken Hardin to reach Kansas.

"I'm riding to Wichita," Nathan told Mary. "You can stay here, if you want. There's a chance the man I'm after came up the trail from Texas with a Texas herd."

"And if he didn't," said Mary, "you'll be off on another trail, and I may never see you again. I'll go with you."

*　　*　　*

Wichita, Kansas. July 11, 1871.

Nathan made the rounds of all the saloons without learning anything that was helpful to him, until a bartender suggested he ask at the hotels and the boardinghouses.

"Most gents just off the trail usually stay at least one night," said the helpful bartender.

"Do you really think these men are going to use their own names?" Mary asked.

"There's a good chance they will," said Nathan. "This would have been their first night here. I reckon Hardin won't be usin' his own name now that he's shot some hombres, but he might have, that first night off the trail."

"I'm sorry," the desk clerk at the Drover's Cottage said, "but we do not reveal information about our guests."

"Damn uppity place," said Nathan, as he and Mary went out the door.

But Nathan's luck turned completely around when he reached a less-than-elegant hotel called the Texas.

"I've been looking for some hombres to get here for three months," said Nathan to the clerk. "They were comin' up the trail with a herd, and I'd say if they got here, it was on maybe the fourth or the fifth."

"Have a look at the register, if you want," the clerk said.

Nathan started on July third, and on the next page, found what he was seeking. The scrawled signature read: *J. W. Hardin,* and on the line below it, *D. Withers.*

"They may not be in Wichita," Nathan said exultantly, "but they're somewhere in Kansas."

"You can't be sure of that," said Mary. "It's not more

than forty miles from here to Indian Territory." Immediately, she bit her tongue, for Indian Territory was the last place she wished to go, or have Nathan go. But to her surprise and relief, he had other ideas.

"After Hardin left here, he went to Bluff City," Nathan said, "and from there, he had to ride to Abilene. What I need to know is whether or not Dade Withers is with him. If Withers is on his own, then the hell with Hardin. I've been trailing him because he's been my only contact with Withers."

*   *   *

Abilene, Kansas. July 12, 1871.

Nathan found no record of John Wesley Hardin at any of the hotels, and when he was about to admit defeat, he found Withers's scrawled signature on an out-of-the-way hotel register. The date was July ninth.

"By God," Nathan said, "that's what I've been looking for. Withers was still in Abilene two days after Hardin killed the second man. That means that Withers is no longer riding with Hardin."

"Is that going to make him any easier to find?" Mary asked.

"Yes. I ... hell, I don't know," said Nathan. "It means Withers has kept his nose clean enough to sign his own name. I'm going to at least ask at the livery. His horse may have a Texas brand."

"Jist one Texas brand I seen lately," the liveryman grinned. "XIT."

Nathan turned away without even thanking him.

"That's no help?" Mary asked.

"My God, no," said Nathan, looking at her pityingly. "The XIT is likely the biggest damn spread in the world. It covers ten counties. That's what XIT means: Ten in Texas. I doubt there's a cowboy west of the Mississippi who hasn't ridden for XIT."

"You don't have to talk to me like I'm a dumb cow," she said. "I've never been anywhere until I met you."

"Sorry," said Nathan. "I keep forgetting that."

"You know Withers isn't here," Mary said, "because the

date on that hotel register was July ninth. Unless he stayed somewhere else for a longer time."

"That makes no sense," said Nathan. "If I stay at a hotel for one night, why the hell wouldn't I stay there till I was ready to leave town?"

"I don't know," Mary said. "We're talking about Dade Withers, not you."

"You're right," said Nathan grudgingly. "It makes no sense, but I can't ride on without knowing for sure."

Nathan studied as many hotel registers as he was permitted to see, and didn't find Withers' signature again.

"Now where are we going?"

"He could have ridden to Hays, Dodge, or even Denver," Nathan said. "We'll try Dodge first, and then Hays. If I don't find him in either place, then I reckon we'll ride farther north."

"If you find no further trace of him in Kansas," said Mary, "how do you know he didn't just ride back to Texas?"

Speechless, Nathan leaned on his saddle and rubbed his eyes. Why did a woman always have to be so right?

Chapter 35

◈

In Texas, riding with John Wesley Hardin, Dade Withers had taken part in several robberies. While nobody had been killed, Withers had welcomed Hardin's decision to join the trail drive bound for Wichita. Withers had been drawn to the Texas outlaw because of Hardin's lightning-fast draw and his devil-may-care attitude, but while crossing Indian Territory with the trail drive, Hardin had shot and killed an Indian without cause. Withers realized that Hardin had a hell of a temper, and he killed for any reason, or for no reason at all. Withers had thus reached the sobering conclusion that just riding with such a man could get him gunned down or hanged on the same limb as Hardin. When he had reached Kansas, Withers had just begun to breathe a little easier when, in the space of just two days, Hardin had killed two more men. Hardin had been forced to leave town in a hurry, so it hadn't been difficult for Dade Withers to sever his ties with the outlaw.

Now Withers was riding southwest, for he had heard of the lawless tent city on the bank of the Arkansas, soon to become Dodge City. Withers didn't bother stopping at Fort Dodge, but rode eight miles west, where he paid for a cot in the tent that was soon to become a hotel. Withers then spent the rest of the day sizing up various businesses. Most of them, except for the mercantile, still occupied tents. He quickly decided the mercantile was his best bet for some fast money, for thanks to the soldiers and civilians at Fort Dodge, it did a landslide business. While in Wichita, Withers had seen a map of the state, and he judged that, on a fast horse, he was less than an hour from Indian Territory. He could be well on his way before the marshal took the trail, if he even bothered.

But Dade Withers would have hurriedly scrapped his plan to rob the store, had he known that others were of the same mind. Breed and Vanardo had already spent half a day in the tent city, and even as Withers settled down on his cot for the night, the two renegades rode south, bound for Indian Territory. Their report would bring El Gato and his outlaw band to the tent city the next evening, just after dark. The new mercantile had prospered and the vultures had begun to gather ...

*   *   *

Unsure as to where he should ride next, Nathan had chosen Fort Dodge, in hopes he could avoid Hays. Mary had been quiet since leaving Abilene, and to break the lengthy silence, Nathan spoke.

"If these forts ever come up to strength, I reckon we'll end up sleeping on the ground. No more vacant officer's quarters."

"Maybe by then you won't be riding all over the frontier," Mary said. "What would it take to get you to settle down in one place?"

"I don't know," said Nathan. "Do you *want* me settled down in one place?"

"It would be nice," she said, "when you have a son or daughter."

"What?" he said, reining up. "Are you ... ?"

She laughed at the expression on his face. "Not yet. But how would you feel ... if I were?"

"I reckon I'd be proud," he said. "God knows, I've done little else in which I can take pride."

*   *   *

Fort Dodge, Kansas. July 15, 1871.

Dade Withers waited until suppertime before entering the mercantile, for when one clerk went to eat, the other would be alone in the store. Withers entered the mercantile, browsing until the first clerk had gone, then waiting impatiently until the last customer departed. Only then did he approach the counter. When the clerk looked up, he found himself facing a masked man with a cocked Colt revolver.

"Put the money in this sack," Withers said, "and you won't be hurt."

Quickly the clerk complied, and while there were many bills, it seemed to Withers they were mostly of small denomination.

"The rest of it," Withers growled. "The gold too."

It was Monday, following a busy weekend, and the nervous clerk had hoped to get off as easily as he could by sacking only the paper money. But now he began piling handfuls of double eagles into the sack. Finally he held up his hands.

"That's all," he said. "I swear that's all."

Withers grabbed the sack, and holding the Colt steady on the clerk, began backing toward the door. Already the sun had slid below the western horizon, with purple shadows announcing the coming of darkness. Withers was no sooner out the door when it was shattered by a shotgun blast. Before the angry clerk could cut loose again, Withers was mounted and galloping away. He removed his bandanna from his face. He felt like shouting, for he had pulled it off without firing a shot, and he didn't have to share it with anyone else. At least that's what he thought, but circumstances changed quickly. Comfortable with the shielding darkness, he slowed his horse to a walk, only to find himself surrounded by horsemen. Even in starlight there was no mistaking the muzzles of revolvers, and Withers groaned inwardly. They could kill him ten times over. Finally a figure in a Mexican sombrero spoke.

"I admire an ambitious man, señor, but not when his ambition robs me of what is mine. You will come with me as my guest and we shall discuss your ... future."

"Damn you," Withers snarled. "I don't take orders from you."

"It is that, señor, or I kill you. The choice is yours."

"I'm ridin' with you," Withers said, swallowing hard.

*   *   *

Nathan and Mary went directly to Fort Dodge, arriving the day after Dade Withers had robbed the store. The post commander, Lieutenant-Colonel Hatton, knew Captain Ferguson well, and Hatton had been impressed with Ferguson's letter of recommendation. He was cordial as Nathan and Mary were shown into his office. Without going into detail, Nathan told Hatton of his search for the outlaw, John Wesley Hardin, and of the trail that had played out after Hardin's gunplay at Abilene.

"I don't know if this fits in or not," Hatton said, "but yesterday at dark, a lone gunman robbed the mercantile at tent city. Marshal Summerfield investigated last night. Tell him I've authorized the release of information he may have, and you may want to talk to the men at the store."

"I'm obliged, sir," said Nathan. "May we impose on your hospitality for the night?"

"You may, and welcome," Hatton said. "The corporal will show you to your quarters. See me again before you leave the post."

Nathan left Mary and Cotton Blossom in the cabin that Hatton had assigned them and went looking for U. S. Marshal Jed Summerfield. Nathan didn't like the man, but he had jurisdiction over all of western Kansas and went out of his way to see that nobody forgot.

"One man, masked, entered the store just at dark," said Summerfield, "and escaped with a large amount of gold and paper currency. That's all I can tell you."

"The robber must have left a trail," Nathan said. "Which way did he go after leaving the store?"

"Toward Indian Territory," said Summerfield shortly.

"Did you trail him, or do you just feel pretty strong that he headed for the Territory?"

"Mister," Summerfield said, his face going red, "when you're in hollerin' distance of the Territory, you don't have to watch a robber ride over the line to know he's there."

"Then for all you know," said Nathan, twisting the knife, "he could have spent the night on the prairie, within sight of the fort."

"I reckon he could have," Summerfield conceded grimly. "I'm just one man, by God. Suppose you just ride out there and bring him in? When you do, I'll hand you this tin star and tell you where to stick it."

Nathan turned away, grinning. Taking his horse from the livery, he rode upriver to tent city. He had some difficulty convincing the proprietor of the mercantile to talk, and even then, he learned only one thing of value.

"He wore a mask," said the man. "When he left here, he rode south. And his horse had an XIT brand."

Nathan rode south from the mercantile, and in the first soft ground he came to, found the tracks of a single south-bound horse. He had no difficulty following the trail, but he had ridden less than a mile when he reined up. The single rider he was following had been joined by a band of other riders, all of whom had continued riding south. For ten miles, Nathan followed, and the trail never varied. He counted the tracks of twelve horses, and it soon became evident they were all bound for Indian Territory. He decided that, based on what he had learned, the man who had robbed the mercantile had been Dade Withers. Now it appeared that Withers had acted on behalf of a gang of thieves or had made their unwelcome acquaintance following the robbery. In either case, they all were bound for Indian territory. Now it was back to Nathan Stone versus a band of thieves and killers, and he had an uneasy suspicion he knew this particular band of renegades, and that they would know him. When he returned to Fort Dodge and told Mary Holden of the robbery and the strange circumstances that appeared to link Dade Withers with Indian Territory renegades, her reaction was about what he had expected.

"Nathan," she begged, "can't you just forget Dade Withers? This almost has to be El Gato's gang, and they'll kill you on sight."

"Yes," said Nathan, "I have a feeling it's El Gato, but I made a vow and I aim to keep it. But I won't be going alone. I'm going to see how serious the Kansas–Pacific is about tracking down those outlaws."

"Then please just do one thing for me," she said, "and I won't ask anything more. Wait until after Christmas. I'd like to have this to remember, if I never have anything else. I want to spend it at Eppie's place, in Kansas City."

She seemed so desperately sincere and the pleading in her eyes was so intense, it made him uneasy. She wouldn't even be eighteen until November, and she was already so much more than the girl she had been when he had met her less than a year ago.

"All right," he said, taking her hands in his, "I'll wait until after Christmas."

In the months to come, as events unfolded, it would be a decision he would never regret. His decision allowed him a kind of freedom, at least for a while, for he knew where Dade Withers was.

*   *   *

Kansas City, Missouri. July 21, 1871.

Nathan and Mary returned to Eppie's boardinghouse and settled down to an easy, unhurried life that Nathan Stone had never believed he could tolerate. He dreaded to see it end, and thus kept putting off his decision to call on Netherton and the Kansas–Pacific until events forced the railroad to take drastic measures on its own. In September, outlaws blew up the track a few miles west of Abilene, killed two railroad guards, wounded three others, and made off with fifteen thousand dollars. Descriptions given by the surviving railroad guards all pointed to El Gato as leader of the outlaws. It was too much. The Kansas–Pacific began advertising in the newspaper for men to pursue and capture the renegades, dead or alive. The pay was a hundred and fifty dollars a month, with ammunition and food furnished. Each man would take the oath of a United States deputy marshal. The Kansas–Pacific was offering a reward of five hundred dollars for each of the robbers, dead or alive. The governor of the State of Kansas would sign John Doe execution warrants.

"By God," Nathan said, "they're going too far."

"Why?" Mary asked. "I'm glad they're getting serious."

"Too damn serious," said Nathan. "I can go along with everything except the John Doe execution warrants. They allow a man, in the name of the law, to kill anybody. To positively identify a man in an execution warrant is one thing. To issue a John Doe execution warrant for a person unknown is inviting a law-sanctioned posse to become bounty hunters, killing for the reward."

"Are you ... still going with them?"

"I don't know," Nathan said. "I want to talk to Joel Netherton."

*   *   *

"The idea of the posse was mine," Netherton, "and I favor rewards, but I had nothing to do with the execution warrants. Confidentially, some of the Kansas–Pacific stock-holders became panicky and through the state legislature, put pressure on the governor."

"Hell," Nathan argued, "you'll have badge-totin' bounty hunters shootin' anybody, just to claim the reward. Can't you see that?"

"Yes," said Netherton, "and that's why I'm seeking to have you appointed U. S. Marshal in charge. All these men will answer to you."

"Don't bother," Nathan said, "because I won't accept the appointment. I'd still have to obey those damn John Doe execution warrants."

"I've been counting on you," said Netherton, disappointed.

"Don't," Nathan said. "I promised Mary to stay here with her through Christmas. I'm sure you'll make your move before then."

"Yes," said Netherton. "Like I told you, the stockholders are having conniption fits. They're demanding the heads of every one of those outlaws on a plate before the end of the year."

"I'm going to make you an offer," Nathan said. "Send your men after these outlaws. If they haven't finished the job by the first of the year, then I'll go after them. But with men of my choosing, and on my terms."

Netherton laughed. "If that bunch is still free after the first of the year, you can probably name your own terms, up to and including a piece of the Kansas–Pacific."

"Wonderful," said Mary, when Nathan told her the news, "but will you be satisfied if Withers is captured or killed by the railroad posse?"

"Yes," Nathan replied. "The only satisfaction I'd have in tracking him down is having him know why I'm about to kill him. If he's part of a gang, it won't be just between him and me. I'll have to take the varmint any way I can get him."

Now that Nathan knew where Dade Withers was, he hadn't kept track of the newspapers as before, nor had he been concerned with what came over the telegraph lines. Therefore it came as a surprise when he learned Wild Bill Hickok was marshal of Abilene. He surprised Mary with a suggestion.

"Let's take the train to Abilene. I want you to meet Wild Bill Hickok."

She laughed. "Cotton Blossom doesn't like the train. You should have seen him sliding around in that boxcar while we were taking you to the doctor."

"We'll leave him with Eppie," said Nathan. "If she puts enough food in front of him, he won't realize we're gone."

So in mid-September, Nathan and Mary boarded the only passenger coach on the Kansas–Pacific westbound and rode to Abilene. It wasn't difficult to find Wild Bill, for he was at the depot when the train stopped.

"I'm pleased to see you again," Hickok said, wringing Nathan's hand, "and especially so to see the beautiful young lady. Bill Hickok at your service, ma'am. I never realized old catawampus, here, had such excellent taste."

"Bill," said Nathan, "this is Mary. If you say anything about me, then I want your promise you'll stay as close to the truth as you can."

"Keeno," Bill replied. "I won't say nothin' about all the other women."

"I'm obliged," said Nathan, "and don't mention the red-eye and the cards, either."

Mary laughed at their banter, while Nathan marveled at Hickok's ability to be the perfect gentleman when custom demanded. They took a room at the hotel and had supper with a cold-sober Hickok. The evening was a memorable one, and when the train returned from Hays the following day, Nathan and Mary boarded it for the trip back to Kansas City.

The final event in Hickok's career as a lawman took place in Abilene on October 5, 1871. Phil Coe, with whom Hickok had already had trouble, had led a mob of Texans on a drunken spree through Abilene. Hickok had sent word to his deputy, Mike Williams, alerting him. At nine o'clock that night there had been a shot, and Hickok had gone to investigate. He had found Coe and several other Texans with guns in their hands. Coe had claimed he had fired at a dog, but Hickok had gone for his guns. Coe had fired at Hickok, hitting his coattails, but Hickok had done much better. His slug had ripped through Coe's belly and out his back. As Coe had collapsed, another slug from his gun had whipped between Hickok's legs. At that point, Mike Williams had pushed through the crowd, in hopes of helping

Wild Bill. But Wild Bill had seen only the movement, and being surrounded by drunken cowboys, he had turned and fired twice. Both slugs had struck Williams in the head and he had died instantly. Coe, mortally wounded, had died three days later. Hickok had paid the funeral expenses of Mike Williams. Hickok was to be officially discharged as marshal of Abilene on December 13, 1871.*

"How sad," said Mary. "They should have known it was an accident."

"It was the deputy's fault," Nathan said. "When a lawmen's surrounded by men with guns, he must be prepared to shoot at any movement. He has no time to distinguish friend from foe. To hesitate is to die."

*   *   *

By mid-November it had become apparent that the Kansas–Pacific's scheme for apprehending the train robbers was a colossal failure. Not only had the expensive posse not caught any of the gang, another westbound train had been robbed. Another railroad guard had died, four others had been seriously wounded, twelve thousand dollars had been taken, and the Kansas–Pacific stockholders were fit to be tied.

"Damn," said Nathan, "that bunch couldn't find a buffalo in a snowbank."

Mary said nothing, for she feared Nathan would be called upon to do what the Kansas–Pacific posse had failed to do. On December fifteenth her fears were all justified when a courier arrived with a message for Nathan. It contained just three words: *Name your terms.* It had been signed by Joel Netherton, Kansas–Pacific.

"Don't worry," Nathan said, seeing the concern in Mary's eyes. "Before I go into Indian Territory after them, I'm going to organize a welcoming committee and see if they won't come to us."

---

*After accidentally shooting Williams to death, Hickok is not known to have ever fired another shot at a man.

*   *   *

"We'll try anything within reason," said Joel Netherton.

"No more deputized bounty hunters," Nathan said, "and no more execution warrants. All I want is eleven men, armed with Colts and Winchesters. Pay them what you were paying the others. Starting with your next run, couple a boxcar directly behind the tender. From floor to roof, line the walls of the boxcar with sheet iron thick enough to withstand a rifle slug. Along both walls of the car—twelve to a side—I want three-inch cutouts, enough for rifle barrels. Riding with me I want Gustavo Beard, Kurt Cannon, Nate Sanderson, Logan Beckwith, Fin Warren, Dil Odom, Nick Klady, Chad Blake, Fletch Tobin, Cal Dooling, and Mac Weaver."

"I like the sound of it," said Netherton, "but it's our intention to do more than just defend each individual payroll by driving these outlaws away. We want them brought in, dead or alive, finished for all time."

"You haven't heard the rest of it," Nathan said. "Every man in that boxcar will have his horse, saddled and ready to ride. Once these varmints are convinced they can't get their hands on the payroll, all they can do is back off and try again. If we can't gun them down from the train, we'll trail them when they ride out."

"And if this fails?"

"Then we do it the hard way," Nathan said. "We ride into Indian Territory and flush them out. There's just one flaw in defending the payroll and trailing this bunch after we've driven them away. They always tear up the rails at some point the train won't reach until late in the day. From maps, I figure from places they're most likely to stop the train, it's at least a hundred and twenty-five miles to Indian Territory. They can't ride straight through without killing their horses, and neither can we. All they have to do is ride until it's too dark for us to follow. Then they're free to rest their mounts and escape into Indian Territory before daylight."

"Damn it," said Netherton, "we've paid men for three months to ride from one end of Indian Territory to the other, without results. Forgive me for my lack of enthusiasm, but how do we know these outlaws are *from* what we know as Indian Territory? Is it a place where men can

disappear at will, where those who ride after them are
never seen again?"

"You're close," Nathan said. "Any time you go after a
man on his ground, he has an edge. There are three rivers
across the heart of the territory, with overhangs, caves, and
brush so thick a coyote would have to belly-down to get
through it. You can't ride into Indian Territory after just a
particular band of outlaws without becoming fair game for
them all. Then there's the Indian problem. It's not known
as Indian Territory for nothing. There are Kiowa and even
Comanches. The one Indian after your scalp may have five
hundred friends who are hell-bent on seeing that he gets
it."

"But if all else fails, you intend to ride in there after
these outlaws."

"I do," said Nathan.

"Then your interest in this goes deeper than your concern for the Kansas–Pacific and the ruffled feathers of its
stockholders," said Netherton.

"It does," Nathan replied. "Six years ago, seven men
murdered my family. Only one of those men is still alive,
and he's riding with this band of renegades. You can tie
the rest of the bastards to the track and run a train over
them, for all I care, but I want that seventh man."

Netherton had involuntarily backed away, for Nathan
Stone's eyes were as blue as ice. A chill crept up the spine
of the railroad man and he felt he was looking into the
very face of death. He swallowed hard before he spoke. "I
believe you can resolve this to our satisfaction and yours.
You have my full support."

"I'm obliged," said Nathan. "There's one more thing.
We'll be aboard every train from here to Hays, not just
those carrying payrolls."

            *   *   *

Monday, Wednesday, and Friday there was a train to
end-of-track, with the train returning to Kansas City the
following day. There was no train on Sunday.

"You and Cotton Blossom will stay here in Kansas City,"
Nathan told Mary. "I'll be in Hays Monday, Wednesday,
and Friday nights."

"That's better than riding into Indian Territory. How long will you do this, if it fails?"

"If they've gotten wise, or if they're driven away empty handed," Nathan said, "I expect to cure them of robbing trains within a month. If they're smart, they'll back away from the Kansas–Pacific."

"But that won't change anything, where you're concerned," said Mary. "If I'm wrong, forgive me, but as I see it, you're only using the Kansas–Pacific manhunt to go after Dade Withers."

"Well, hell," Nathan said, irritated, "it's a little one sided, just me against a pack of renegades. Would I be more honest if I went after them by myself?"

"Of course not," she said, not looking at him. "I'm thankful you'll be among friends who can help you. It's just that ... I'm afraid this won't work, and if it doesn't ..."

"Then I'll be riding into Indian Territory," he finished.

"Yes," she said, "if you have to go alone."

* * *

For the first two weeks in January 1872, Nathan's band of armed men rode with every train to and from Hays, without any attempts to stop the trains. On January seventeenth, to everybody's surprise, the bank at Abilene was robbed just at closing time. That same night—Wednesday—Nathan received a telegram at Hays, through the Kansas–Pacific dispatcher there. On the return run to Kansas City on Thursday, Nathan had the train stopped at Abilene long enough for him to question the marshal and people at the bank. He was totally unimpressed by the new marshal, James A. Gauthie. It was he who had been instrumental in getting Hickok fired, and had then accepted the appointment as town marshal for fifty dollars a month.

"Of course I investigated," said Gauthie defensively. "There was tracks of eleven horses. Five men went into the bank, and when they left, they rode south, toward Wichita."

"You didn't mount a posse and ride after them?"

"There was no use. It would have been dark before we even got started. Besides, this is the off-season for the herds. It's hard to find enough men for a four-handed game of stud."

Nathan turned away in disgust. He was only a little more successful when he spoke to the head cashier at the bank. While the robbers had concealed their faces with bandannas, the apparent leader had fit the description of El Gato, including the Mexican sombrero and bandolier of shells over the shoulder. With nothing more to be done in Abilene, Nathan got aboard the train and it continued on to Kansas City. There he met with Joel Netherton, for he felt an obligation to inform the railroad that the outlaws were still in the area.

"They're likely expecting us to relax our guard," Nathan said.

"I suppose they've gotten word of the rewards and the execution warrants, too," said Netherton.

"By God, that's exactly what might have scared them off," Nathan said. "What damn fool allowed that to leak out?"

Netherton laughed. "It didn't leak out. Governor Harvey released it to the press to counter some of the criticism by Kansas–Pacific stockholders. It's important to him that the public—and especially KP stock holders—know he's using every resource at his command to capture these train robbers."

"Then maybe I'll just leave it to him," said Nathan angrily, "and let him lead a posse into Indian Territory after the varmints."

*   *   *

But the outlaws changed their method of operation. On January twenty-ninth, two of the renegades boarded the train on the fly, forcing it to stop by holding guns on the fireman and engineer. Nathan and his fighting men in the boxcar were prepared for anything except what happened. All were in position with their rifles, but there was nobody at which to shoot. Suddenly from beneath the boxcar came a booming voice.

"Hombres, this is El Gato. The locomotive's fireman and engineer are under the gun. A wrong move from any of you and they will die."

"Damn it," said Fin Warren, "he's under the car. Him an' God knows how many more. Now what?"

"We wait for them to ride out and then we follow," Nathan said.

But El Gato added insult to injury. Before the outlaws rode away, they shot and killed the engineer and fireman. For a long moment, the men stared at the dead bodies. The guard in the baggage coach and the brakeman in the caboose had been knocked unconscious.

"The rest of you start after them," said Nathan. "I'll have to telegraph Kansas City and report this. I'll catch up to you."

Nathan still had the telegraph key that had belonged to Benton Valentine, and he climbed a pole to make the connection. At least the outlaws had not cut the telegraph line, and he was able to reach the dispatcher. He also left a message to be sent to Mary, knowing how she would feel when she learned he was on his way to Indian Territory. He then returned the telegraph key to his saddlebag and rode to catch up to his companions.

The trail was clear enough to have been followed by starlight, and that was just about what they would be doing, Nathan thought grimly. The flaw he had mentioned to Joel Netherton came into play when darkness caught them sixty miles south of the railroad and sixty or more miles shy of Indian Territory.

"Well, gents," Dil Odom observed, "we can keep ridin' due south, hopin' they won't veer to east or west, or we can wait for daylight and keep to the trail. What's it gonna be?"

"We'll rest the horses and keep riding," Nathan said. "I look for them to cut away southeast or southwest, if only to delay us. At first light, we'll have to split up until we find their trail again."

But riding all night gained them nothing, for with the dawn came an alarming discovery. The gang had split up, and every rider they followed had disappeared, hiding his trail beneath the murky waters of the Cimarron River.

Chapter 36

❖❖❖

Nathan and his weary companions rode to Wichita, had a hot meal and continued on to Kansas City, arriving there on Sunday, February fourth.

"Where do we go from here?" Nate Sanderson asked. "Do we ride the train to Hays tomorrow?"

"I don't know," said Nathan. "All of you stay close to home tonight and tomorrow night. I'll talk to Netherton and see where we're going from here."

Nathan knew where Joel Netherton lived, but he went first to the Kansas–Pacific railroad yard. Netherton was there, and in about the frame of mind Nathan had expected. He explained how the outlaws had taken advantage of the darkness to get far ahead and how they had split up, covering their trails so that an Indian couldn't have tracked them.

"I'm tired," Netherton said gloomily. "Tired of trying to talk to board members who are so busy shouting at me they can't hear what I'm trying to say. Hell, I'm ready to resign and take a job with a section crew. Let them find another dog to kick."

"We're not beaten yet," said Nathan. "Can you hold off on payroll shipments for another week or two?"

"Do I have any choice? What kind of madman takes the money and murders two unarmed men? As things stand, I don't have a fireman-engineer team that's willing to risk their lives on a run involving a payroll."

"The only way to nail this bunch is to trap them before they can scatter into Indian Territory," Nathan said. "I have another plan, but I'll need more men."

"I can get you the men," said Netherton, "but I can't promise you a payroll for bait."

"I can't ask you to risk one," Nathan replied, "but we must lure this gang out of hiding. Suppose we posted two men with rifles in the cab. Would that make your engineers and firemen feel better?"

"I don't know," said Netherton. "I'll admit they took us all by surprise, boarding the train. I suppose if we could prevent that, the engineers and firemen wouldn't feel threatened."

"This bunch of renegades can't very well use that trick again," Nathan said. "They buffaloed us into holding back for the sake of the trainmen, and then murdered them. They can't count on that working again."

"Just for the sake of my own curiosity," said Netherton, "go ahead and lay out your other plan. I have to tell the board something."

"Suppose we had armed men less than an hour's ride from the Territory," Nathan said, "and suppose they could be contacted immediately after El Gato and his bunch commits a robbery and rides south?"

"That might be the answer," said Netherton. "Go on."

"You would send an armed guard with the train, as usual," Nathan said, "but not me and my riders. We would be waiting at Fort Dodge, and everything would depend on two factors. First, somebody from the train would have to get off a telegram to you, or one to the dispatcher at Hays. In either case, that message would have to reach me at Fort Dodge. Second, and every bit as important, nobody is to be told you have men at Fort Dodge. Nobody, by God. Especially Governor Harvey."

"Let me see what I can do," said Netherton. "I'll send word as soon as I can present this and get it approved."

Nathan got his horse from the livery and rode out to Eppie Bolivar's place. While he knew Mary was glad to see him, he sensed a change in her and was unsure as to just what it was. He hoped it was just the news of his failure to run down El Gato and his band that had upset her.

"I reckon you heard the news," he said.

"Yes," she said. "You've been given full responsibility. The newspapers are calling the Kansas–Pacific El Gato's Santa Claus."

"Let them," said Nathan. "I have one more hand to play."

Suddenly she buried her face in her hands, and big silent tears spilled through her fingers. He knelt beside her, uncertain, and she wept all the harder. She spoke little the rest of the evening, ate almost nothing at the evening meal, and virtually ignored Eppie's attempts to cheer her up. Early next morning, an hour before dawn, she was violently ill.

"I think it's time you had a visit with the doc," he said.

Despite all her protests, Nathan took her to Dr. Pendleton, recommended by Eppie Bolivar. Pendleton was in his sixties, a no-nonsense little man who didn't mince words. He spent about ten minutes with Mary, and leaving her in his consultation study, came back and spoke to Nathan.

"Nothing wrong with her she won't get over, if she takes care of herself," Pendleton said. "Come July, she's going to have a child."

"What?" Nathan shouted. "Are you sure?"

"I've been wrong a few times," said Pendleton, "but never on that."

Nathan had driven Eppie Bolivar's buckboard, and without a word, he helped Mary up on to the seat. He seated himself beside her, and she wouldn't look at him. He spoke as kindly as he could.

"You knew, didn't you? Why didn't you tell me?"

"I ... I was afraid. I promised ... not to ask anything of you. I've felt so ... alone. It's such a burden for ... one to bear ..."

"It's not yours alone," he said. "You didn't get into this by yourself. It's still early in the day, so why don't we look around and fix you up with a ring?"

"A ring?"

"It's fittin' and proper for a woman to have a ring on her marrying day," Nathan said. "It's up to you to set the date. We'll have a preacher read from the book."

Kansas City had grown to the extent that there was a jewelry store, and that's where Nathan and Mary went. Despite all Nathan had on his mind, he thoroughly enjoyed the girl's excitement as the proprietor of the store laid out a tray of rings.

"They come in sets, of course," the store manager said. "The engagement ring she can wear immediately."

"That's what we want," Nathan said. "A set."

Mary looked at the tray of rings and seemed struck dumb by such elegance. She turned to Nathan and he laughed.

"Choose the one you want," he said.

"I have less expensive sets," the jeweler said discreetly.

"No," Nathan said, "we'll go with one of these."

Mary chose a set, and the rings fit perfectly. She nodded at Nathan.

"An excellent choice," the jeweler said. "Shall I wrap it?"

"No," said Nathan. "She's going to wear the engagement ring now."

"That will be four hundred dollars," the jeweler said.

Mary's eyes went wide, but before she could protest, Nathan was paying for the rings. He slipped the engagement ring on her finger and they left the store.

*   *   *

On February eighth, a courier brought Nathan a message from Joel Netherton, and it was brief. *Proposal accepted,* it read, and Netherton had signed it.

"Kansas–Pacific's agreed to try something else I suggested," he told Mary, "and I'd like to have the marrying done first."

"I don't want to rush into it," she said. "Why don't we wait?"

"Because I have some money in a bank in Denver," he said, "and I want you to have a legal right to it."

"In case you don't come back alive," she said.

"Yes, but I didn't intend to say it like that. I have every intention of coming back alive, but I may be away for a while."

"So you want to marry before you go. Where are you going?"

He explained his plan to take his men to Fort Dodge, to cut off El Gato's renegades before they reached the safety of Indian Territory.

"Then we'll marry before you go," she said, "because I'm going with you."

"But I'd rather you were here," said Nathan. "Dr. Pendleton's near, and you'd have Eppie to look after you."

"I might have agreed to that," she said, "before today, but today I knew you wanted me, and as long as there's life in me, I'll never leave you."

It was a touching moment, and she seemed more beautiful than she'd ever been in the few short months he had

known her. He sat down beside her and took her hands
in his.

"All right," he said. "I'll see Netherton in the morning,
and we'll go find a preacher tomorrow evening."

*   *   *

"I have approval to try your plan for sixty days," said
Netherton, "and I have been instructed by our board of
directors to send you to a studio here that specializes in
tintypes. From that, an etching will be made for use in the
newspaper. The Kansas–Pacific's had so much bad publicity
as a result of the robberies and killings, they're planning to
release a story that covers some of your activities on behalf
of the railroad."

"I can't see that bein' of much help," said Nathan.
"They'd better wait until I've had some success."

He went to the studio and posed for the tintype, thinking
no more about it, not knowing until it was too late what a
profound effect a newspaper story would have on his life.

*   *   *

Nathan and Mary said their vows in the small church
that Eppie attended. Eppie was there, as was Joel Netherton and some of the men who would be going with Nathan to Fort Dodge. Afterward, Nathan spoke to
Netherton.

"The men are leaving in the morning," Nathan said,
"taking my horse with them. Mary and me will take the
train to Hays. From there to Fort Dodge, I'll rent a buckboard or we'll take the military mud wagon from Fort
Hays."

"Do you think it's wise, taking her with you?"

"She insists," said Nathan. "I'm officially recognized at
Fort Dodge, and she's been there with me before. I reckon
you've made arrangements with Fort Dodge to have my
men fed and quartered?"

"Yes," Netherton replied. "Lieutenant-Colonel Hatton
has cooperated fully. Any telegrams to you or from you
have priority."

*   *   *

On February twelfth, Nathan and Mary took the train to Hays. Cotton Blossom had made up his mind that his first train ride was going to be his last, and Nathan had to lift him bodily into the coach. Finally, resigned to his fate, he cowered on a seat, digging his claws into the fabric every time the train lurched. On February fourteenth, Nathan and Mary were taken by army ambulance to Fort Dodge. Cotton Blossom loped happily along behind.

*   *   *

On February twenty-fifth, the Sunday edition of the Kansas City newspaper featured a story on the Kansas–Pacific and its never-ending struggle with robbers and Indians. The etching accompanied the story. The story attracted widespread interest, especially in Wichita, where Breed bought one at the mercantile. When he returned to Indian Territory, he wasted no time in presenting the newspaper to El Gato.

"Bastardo," El Gato snarled. "He take my woman!"

"Married up with her, too," Breed said, laughing. "Says so, there in that newspaper."

"I will kill him," El Gato hissed. "I will kill them both. *Por Dios,* nobody makes the fool of El Gato!"

El Gato had a habit of sending a rider to Wichita, to Abilene, or even Kansas City, with instructions to keep his eyes and ears open. Once a week, usually on Saturday, one of the gang would hang around the saloons and the mercantile at the tent city, beyond Fort Dodge. Occasionally, El Gato even sent a man to Fort Dodge, to look, to listen. Thus it was Vanado who saw Nathan Stone and Mary, the girl who had once belonged to El Gato. Careful not to be seen, Vanado had ridden away, back to Indian Territory. The news he brought kept El Gato awake far into the night, pondering the reason for Nathan Stone being at Fort Dodge. He would kill this dog, but not until he had suffered, had been cut to the heart. He would take from him the treacherous bitch who had run away from him.

*   *   *

On March first, the robbers blew up the Kansas–Pacific track, stopping a westbound train that carried nothing of value. They pistol-whipped the engineer and fireman and then rode away emptyhanded. The trainmen dutifully wired Kansas City and the message was relayed to Nathan Stone at Fort Dodge. From a distance, Vanado watched the fort through El Gato's spyglass. He grunted in satisfaction as Nathan Stone and eleven other riders emerged from the fort. These men were at Fort Dodge for a purpose, and El Gato's suspicions had been confirmed. Vanado returned the spyglass to his saddlebag and rode toward the fort. El Gato wished to know where the treacherous woman was quartered . . .

*   *   *

"Damn it," Nick Klady grumbled, after Nathan and his companions had ridden for miles along the northern edge of Indian Territory, "it's like the varmints *want* us gallopin' around out here, gettin' nowhere. They're playin' cat-and-mouse with us."

"They're dead serious," Nathan said. "They didn't blow up the track, stop that train, and ride away emptyhanded for nothing. I've had a run-in with El Gato and his bunch before, and most of them would recognize me, given the chance. I reckon I've been seen at the fort. El Gato just stirred up some smoke, and now that we've come looking for the fire, he knows why we're here. We just lost our edge, whatever we had."

"Meanin' that from now on, he'll be expecting us to head him off before he can reach Indian Territory," said Logan Beckwith. "Hell, they can ride all night and get around us in the dark. They can sneak into Indian Territory over a stretch of near three hundred miles."

"I've never seen such a slippery bastard," Chad Blake said. "At every turn, he knows what we're doing. Amigos, we done hired ourselves out for a job that can't be done."

Most of the others agreed with him, leaving Nathan in a quandary. He had no answers for them, none for Joel Netherton, none for himself. He couldn't quit, however, and he spoke to them with a conviction that he did not, could not, feel. He began slowly, trying to buy himself some time, and even as he spoke, inspiration came to him.

"There's still something we haven't tried, and I'm ashamed of myself for not having thought of it sooner.

We're going back to Fort Dodge and I'm going to be on that telegraph key for a while. When I talk to you again— maybe tonight—I expect to have the kind of edge we've needed all along."

Reaching Fort Dodge, he dismissed the men and went directly to Lieutenant-Colonel Hatton's office.

"Sir," he said, "if I'm not asking too much, I'd like the use of the telegraph for a while. Perhaps as long as two hours. I know the code, and I can send much faster than I can write and have it sent."

"Permission granted," Hatton said.

Nathan made initial contact, and after relaying a prear- ranged code, was put directly on a line to Joel Netherton. An hour and fifteen minutes later, Nathan signed off and again spoke to Lieutenant-Colonel Hatton.

"The response may be pretty long. I'll just wait and re- ceive it."

The officer nodded and Nathan settled down to wait. It took Netherton less than an hour to respond, and not quite two minutes for Nathan to receive the message and ac- knowledge it. Brief, it said: *Both proposals acceptable. Pro- ceed.* Joel Netherton had signed off with his code.

"I'm obliged, sir," Nathan said to Lieutenant-Colonel Hatton.

Nathan reached the cabin he shared with Mary, only to find she and Cotton Blossom were gone. He waited impa- tiently for almost an hour, until she came in, Cotton Blos- som at her heels. She quickly noted his mood.

"I'm sorry," she said. "I wasn't sure when you'd be back. I've been to the store for some thread."

"I wish you wouldn't go out like this when I'm gone. El Gato knows I'm here, and he knows why. Whoever saw me probably saw you too."

"But how . . ."

"El Gato likely has men slip into the fort to look and listen. All of them, except for Dade Withers, would recog- nize you and me."

"Oh, God," she cried, "now they'll find a way to escape you and your men here."

"They've already done that, because our element of sur- prise is gone," Nathan said, "but I've just relayed a new plan to Netherton and had it approved. It will give us the edge we should have had from the start. By striking as late

in the day as they could, the outlaws have always used the
dark for cover, splitting up and disappearing into Indian
Territory. But suppose we had the daylight to ride them
down, giving them no chance to rest?"

"You could pin them down," she said, "but how do you
manage that? Darkness comes at almost the same time
every day."

"We can't change the time the night comes," Nathan
replied, "but we can sure as hell change the railroad schedule, forcing El Gato and his owlhoots to stop the train early
in the morning instead of the middle of the day. As of
now, all Kansas–Pacific trains bound for Hays leave at eight
o'clock in the morning. The railroad counts on forty miles
an hour, including the water stops. It's near two hundred
and sixty miles from Kansas City to Hays, and that figures
out to a little over six hours. The Kansas–Pacific has agreed
to change the schedule, having the trains leave at four
o'clock in the morning instead of eight. If the trains are on
time, they'll be arriving in Hays a few minutes after ten
o'clock, instead of sometime after two. That means El Gato
will have to stop the train no later than nine o'clock. It
also means there'll be nine to ten hours of daylight, and
while El Gato and his bunch can run, they won't be able
to hide."

"You're counting on them riding away to the south. Suppose they don't?"

"They'll have to," said Nathan, "because the guards from
the train will be pursuing them. Each of the guards riding
the train will have two horses. They can change horses
often, not allowing the outlaws or their mounts to so much
as stop for water. With nine to ten hours of daylight ahead
of them, El Gato and his renegades won't be able to escape us."

"They can still split up."

"Then so can we," Nathan said. "My outfit can match
them man for man, and so can the other force that will
pursue them from the train."

"Oh, I hope it works out as you have it planned," Mary
said. "I'm just so tired of waiting, worrying, and
wondering."

*   *   *

The change in the train schedules had a profound effect on the robbers for a while. They finally struck again on March fourth, and to the surprise of everybody, they stopped the train before it reached Abilene. The guards from the train pursued the outlaws south, toward Wichita, only to have the wily El Gato lay an ambush in which three of the railroad guards were wounded. Far to the west—a hundred and seventy miles—Nathan and his men were unable to help because of the distance.

*   *   *

Due to a lack of graze, livestock at Fort Dodge had to be grained, and on days when the weather permitted, a soldier escort was provided for those who had the time to graze their horses along the river. Mary's horse and Nathan's packhorse had been left at Eppie Bolivar's, but Mary, tired of the confines of the fort, often walked along the river while the horses grazed. It was a custom that El Gato's men were quick to discover, but Mary Stone was there only on the days when Nathan was away. That suited El Gato perfectly, for if he took the woman, would Nathan Stone not follow?

*   *   *

In Kansas City, Joel Netherton was trapped in the office of the Kansas–Pacific's board of directors. Combs and Isaacs had already raked him over the coals. Now it was Bolton's turn.

"Mr. Netherton," Bolton said, repeating the argument Netherton had heard twice, "it was our impression that this gunman, Nathan Stone, is a man who gets things done. We allowed him two months. Today is March eighth, so one of those months is gone. All we have to show for it is a pair of train holdups, a lost payroll, and three wounded men for whom we've paid medical expenses. Who *are* these outlaws, for God's sake? Do they walk on water?"

"I wouldn't be surprised," said Netherton shortly.

There was more, but Netherton withstood it. Finally he escaped, and when he returned to his office, there was a telegram from Nathan Stone. He read it, then read it again. Stone was coming to Kansas City on Monday, March eleventh. But why? There was a kind of finality to the message, as though Nathan had stepped across some line that only he could see.

*   *   *

"But why must you go to Kansas City?" Mary asked. "Can't you work everything out over the telegraph, as you've been doing?"

"Not this time, Mary," said Nathan. "I'll have some answers by the time I return. I'm riding to Hays on Monday, and I'll take the train from there."

*   *   *

Hays, Kansas. March 11, 1872.

Nathan left his horse at the livery in Hays and took a room for the night in a boardinghouse where he had stayed before. The train would return to Kansas City at four o'clock in the morning. Nathan avoided the saloons, the newspaper office, and Donaldson at the Kansas–Pacific dispatch office. He ate a lonely supper and returned to his room. He shucked his hat and boots, and hung his pistol belt on the brass bedpost. He then stretched out on the bed and began sorting out his thoughts. Reaching up, he took the gunbelt, and from the holsters he removed the twin Colts. He border-shifted the weapons from hand to hand, testing their balance, feeling them come alive. There was a tingling in the tips of his fingers and a similar one crept up his spine, as though he had been long dead and life were being restored. Now he knew, with total clarity, why he was going to see Joel Netherton and what he intended to do.

Nathan thought next of Mary, of when he had first seen her, and that snowy night in January when he had returned for her. Had he known her only thirteen months? It seemed much longer. As he thought of her becoming part of his life, it was as though his mind's eye were seeing them both from some higher plane. Like a bolt from the blue came the realization of what had happened to him and why. It had started when Eulie Prater had been killed. The flames of guilt had crackled higher with Lacy Mayfield's death, and finally, after Viola Hayden's terrible act of vengeance, he had been consumed. From the ashes had risen a new Nathan Stone: slow to anger, timid, maybe a little afraid. His mind's eye watched this new Nathan prance around for months, seeking to find the last of seven killers, and, finding him, failing to go after him with the same swift justice he had meted out to the others.

He, Nathan Stone, had surrounded himself with fighting men, supposedly to bring El Gato and his outlaws to justice on behalf of the railroad. In so doing, he would have been able to get to Dade Withers without singlehandedly facing El Gato's entire gang. He could even absolve the new Nathan of some of the blame by claiming that he had only yielded to Mary's fears for his life. But the truth of it was, he had fallen victim to his guilt, trying to make it up to her for having shortchanged all the others. Eulie, who at thirty-five had never had a man. Lacy, barely eighteen, who had never had a home; and Viola, whose life had been destroyed over one of the old Nathan's gambling debts. He lived by the gun and he would die by it, and by casting their lot with his, hadn't Eulie, Lacy, and Viola done the same? Life was short, and a man rarely had time to pay for his own mistakes. For these revelations and admissions, Nathan Stone felt a certain kind of peace. He returned the Colts to their holsters and slept soundly until time to board the train for Kansas City.

Chapter 37

It was an unseasonably warm day for March. Mary Stone walked beside the river and Cotton Blossom followed. Some of the officers' wives owned horses and were taking advantage of the favorable weather to graze the animals. The soldier assigned escort duty dozed beneath a tree. A stranger leading a horse didn't seem threatening until he came close enough to Mary to silence and subdue her with an arm around her throat. When she struggled, he clubbed her with the barrel of his pistol. Cotton Blossom lunged at him, but he swung the pistol again. It struck the dog a glancing blow to the head, stunning him. The stranger holstered his weapon, slung Mary across his horse belly down, mounted, and rode upriver. Several women had seen what had happened and were shouting. The private on escort duty scrambled to his feet and left on the run to alarm the fort. Cotton Blossom got up, unsteady on his feet, and set off after the distant horseman. By the time Lieutenant-Colonel Hatton got word of the abduction, the horseman and Mary were long gone. It was Hatton who eventually found U. S. Marshal Summerfield in the post barbershop having his hair cut.

"I'll investigate," Summerfield said.

Lieutenant-Colonel Hatton immediately sent a telegram to Nathan Stone in care of the Kansas–Pacific dispatcher in Kansas City.

* * *

Kansas City, Missouri. March 12, 1872.

Upon reaching Kansas City, Nathan wrote and mailed a letter to banker Ames Tilden in Denver. Nathan had requested that his funds be transferred to the Cattlemans and Merchants Bank in Kansas City, payable to Nathan or Mary Stone. Briefly he considered taking his packhorse from Eppie Bolivar's stable, but that would involve taking the animal back to Hays via boxcar. He wouldn't be that long concluding his business in Indian Territory, one way or another. He had until four o'clock the next morning, when the westbound left for Hays, but there was no point in delaying his meeting with Joel Netherton of the Kansas–Pacific. He purely hated being in town afoot. There was no wind, the sun was doing what it did best, and he was sweating by the time he reached the Kansas–Pacific terminal. Nathan found Netherton with a sheaf of papers in his hand, and before Nathan could speak, the railroad man handed him the telegram received just a few minutes earlier.

"I didn't know where you were," Netherton said. "I was hoping you were on your way here."

His heart in his throat, Nathan read the short message and wadded the paper in his clenched fist. It no longer mattered what he had come to tell Netherton. Instead, he had a request.

"Joel," he said, his voice trembling, "I have to get to Hays. I can't wait for tomorrow's train. I need a locomotive and a tender. I'll pay."

"You won't have to pay," said Netherton. "There's a yard engine with steam up. Come on. I'll clear it with the dispatcher and assign you a fireman and an engineer."

Nathan stood behind the engineer, keeping out of the fireman's way, begrudging every minute it took the racing locomotive to reach Hays.

"We're up to fifty and high-balling," the engineer said. "I don't dare push her any harder. Anything on the track, any damage, and we're goners."

"I'm obliged," said Nathan.

They reached Hays in just under five hours.

"Here," Nathan said, handing each of the men five double eagles. He swung out of the cab before they could refuse. It would be dark within the hour and he groaned, for he was still eighty miles from Fort Dodge. He ran to the livery, reclaimed his horse, and within minutes was riding south at a fast gallop. A horse couldn't maintain such a gait for long, and he was forced to rein up to a slow gallop.

He had to rest the horse at intervals, and he traveled the last few miles in total darkness. The sentry on duty at the gate admitted him quickly and he rode immediately to Lieutenant-Colonel Hatton's office.

"I regret having to tell you this," Hatton said, "but we were forced to abandon the trail at the Cimarron. This abduction was planned, and my patrol rode into an ambush. Men with rifles were firing from cover. One of my soldiers was killed and two more wounded. At dawn I can send a larger force."

"I'm obliged, sir," said Nathan, "but that won't be necessary. I aim to do what I should have done months ago."

"By the way," Hatton added, "your dog is still out there somewhere. He refused to leave. Magnificent animal."

Nathan felt a surge of warmth for the valiant hound. Cotton Blossom, if the outlaws hadn't managed to shoot him, might be able to accomplish what all the soldiers and fighting men in Kansas could not. The dog might be able to trail the thieves and killers to wherever they were holed up. Nathan doubted they would be found at the Cocodrilo Rancho, for he could find his way to that.

He returned to the cabin he had shared with Mary, and when he lighted a lamp, there were all the memories. Her half-finished sewing, her clothes and some of his washed, dried, and folded neatly on the bed. He feared what the outlaws would do to her, for they were spoilers, defilers. They would use her, break her spirit, perhaps destroy the child that was his. He sank down on the bed, buried his face in his hands, and wept ...

*   *   *

Mary was petrified with fear, but she refused to weep. Breed finally reined up and allowed her to straddle the horse. Her belly cramped, and while she could bear the pain, she feared what it might have done to her inside. But that, as it turned out, would be the least of her worries. She believed soldiers had been sent from the fort, because hidden men with rifles had opened fire as soon as Breed had taken her across the river. She thought of Nathan, almost three hundred miles away, fearing what he might do when he learned of her fate. That he would be coming she had no doubt, but surely he wouldn't come alone. But then dread swept through her in a wave, for that was exactly what he would do. He had always told her his business with the Kansas–Pacific, but as she thought back, she realized she had no idea why he had felt compelled to go all the way to Kansas City to meet with Joel Netherton. Thinking back, she was able to see how he must have restrained himself for her benefit. But at last he had been unable to restrain himself, and this had been a side of himself that he hadn't wanted her to see. Her thoughts were jolted back to her own plight, and she began looking for familiar landmarks. There were none. She had been wondering if the outlaws had abandoned Cocodrilo Rancho; she had been hoping they had not, for Nathan could find it without difficulty. But all her hopes were dashed when Breed reined up before a larger, more elaborate cabin than the one she had known before. Breed dismounted and handed her down. She shuddered, for when the door opened, El Gato stood there grinning evilly.

"Ah, señora, after so long, you honor us with your presence. I think before we are finished with you that you be wishing for the old days. There was a time, señora, I would have killed any man who lay a hand on you. Now, I think since you betray me, I think I give you to them to do as they wish. Then, when your Señor Stone come for you, he will be allowed to see what is left. Then we kill him, señora."

"I am a married woman," Mary said, "and I am with child. Have you no conscience, no decency, no respect for a woman?"

"For a woman, si, for a pig, no. You are a pig who has been ruined. I am sick as I look at you. Take her to the bunkhouse, Breed. She must be prepared for the coming of Señor Stone."

"No," Mary begged. "Please . . . for the love of God . . ."

El Gato laughed, and Breed lifted her back onto the horse. It wasn't far, and he walked, leading the animal. Breed pushed her before him into another log building that served as a bunkhouse. The outlaws lounged on their bunks in various stages of undress, and she closed her eyes. Breed shoved her back on one of the bunks and jerked off her boots. She felt hands unbuttoning her Levi's while others ripped the buttons from her shirt. Then she was naked, as the men shouted over her. Breed came first, and she screamed . . .

*   *   *

Nathan got up, poured cold water from a pitcher into a basin, and washed the grief from his face. He then checked his saddlebags, making sure he had some jerked beef and sufficient ammunition for his Colts and the Winchester. He then returned to Lieutenant-Colonel Hatton's office, finding Hatton about to leave.

"Sir," Nathan said, "I need to speak to the officer who led that patrol that was ambushed. I want to know where that rider crossed the Cimarron."

"That will be Lieutenant Atherton. But, my God, man, you're not going into Indian Territory tonight?"

"I am," said Nathan. "Tomorrow they'll be expecting me. Where will I find Lieutenant Atherton?"

"Wait here," Hatton said. "I'll have the sergeant of the guard get him for you."

Lieutenant Atherton was a young man who had a bloody bandage on his left arm, above the elbow.

"Lieutenant Atherton," said Hatton, "this is Nathan Stone. He needs to know where your patrol was ambushed this evening, where that rider you were trailing crossed the Cimarron."

"Ride due south," Atherton said, "bearing just a little southeast, to the sharp bend in the river. It bows up and then back down. That's where he rode across, and that's where the others were secured, on the south bank, in heavy brush. We didn't get off a shot."

"My dog's out there, too," Nathan said. "Where?"

"We left him there where the rider crossed, at the bend," said Atherton. "We tried to get him to follow us, but he wouldn't."

"Thanks, Lieutenant," Nathan said.

"You're not going after them tonight?"

"I am," Nathan replied.

"Good luck," said Atherton, shaking his head.

Nathan rode out, knowing exactly where the crossing was that Atherton had described. Cotton Blossom had known he would be coming; he just hadn't been sure when. A hundred yards shy of the river crossing, Nathan dismounted, and leading the horse, continued on. There was no moon, and in the starlight, a shadow disengaged itself from the brush. Cotton Blossom! Nathan knelt down and threw an arm around the dog. There was a lump on his head with beads of dried blood, and his coat was still damp. He had been across the river.

"Good boy," Nathan said. "Let's go."

Cotton Blossom headed straight for the river crossing, pausing at the sloping bank to be sure Nathan was following. Nathan mounted, and the water was shallow, allowing the horse to cross without difficulty. Leaving the water for the south bank, Nathan could see all the possibilities of a deadly ambush. Second-growth trees and underbrush were head high, and Nathan practically had to break trail for the horse. He couldn't even see Cotton Blossom, and only when he paused could he hear the rustle of dead leaves and grass, proof the dog was still ahead of him. Finally they were through the worst of it, the trees becoming tall enough to have choked out some of the troublesome underbrush, briars, and thorn-laden bushes. The wind was from the south, bringing the faint smell of wood smoke. Nathan drew up. It was time to leave his horse. He tied the reins to a low-hanging limb and carrying the Winchester, he continued on, with only an occasional glimpse of the shadow that was Cotton Blossom. The dog had gone looking for Mary and had found the outlaw stronghold. Nathan was amazed when he found the way in, for the camp was within a deep arroyo, with the entrance to the south. Trees and vines overhung the rims to the extent they met in the middle, creating a leafy shelter that rendered the arroyo virtually invisible. It was as near a perfect camp as Nathan had ever seen. Dimly he could see the outline of a cabin from which there was no light. Beyond it was a long, low structure with lamplight winking from a single window. The smaller cabin was where he would find the elusive El Gato, and he regretted he had not brought a Bowie knife, for the first shot would send the outlaws scattering. But he had one advantage. They must get past him to leave the arroyo, and his Winchester had seventeen deadly loads that said none of them was going to get out of there alive.

He wondered where Mary was, wondered if she were still alive; his knowledge of El Gato and his followers told him the girl was dead. Reaching the dark cabin, he touched

the door. It opened silently, probably on leather hinges.
He stepped inside. Cotton Blossom had remained outside,
wanting no part of the sinister cabin, and Nathan conceded
that between the two of them, the dog was the smarter.
There was no windows, at least in the front half of the
cabin.

"Ah," said a voice, "I have been expecting you, Señor
Stone. Only a fool would come seeking El Gato in the
dark. A fool or a brave man, and it is often there is but a
thin line between the two, eh?"

Nathan hunkered down on his knees before he spoke. El
Gato might fire at the sound of his voice.

"I came for Mary," Nathan said. "Dead or alive, I want
her. But that's not all. Before I leave here, you're going
to die."

Nathan held the Winchester out ahead of him, gripping
its muzzle, its stock braced on the floor. When El Gato
made a swipe with the knife, there was a clang of steel on
steel, as the blade struck the Winchester's muzzle. Nathan
released the Winchester, seizing the arm wielding the knife.
He came off the floor, his right knee slamming into El
Gato's groin. The knife fell to the floor, but El Gato recovered quickly and seized Nathan in a bear hug. They went
down, El Gato on top. Nathan could feel the knife at his
back, and he moved just enough to free it. Seizing it in his
right hand, he drove it with all his strength into El Gato's
back. The mighty grip relaxed, and, withdrawing the knife,
Nathan drove it in again. Humping the body off him, he
got to his knees, feeling around until he found his Winchester. While he didn't understand El Gato's passion for coming after him with a knife, he now had an edge when it
came to dealing with the rest of the outlaws. He slipped
out the door and found Cotton Blossom waiting. Taking
his time, Nathan headed for the distant bunkhouse, wondering how many doors there were. He believed it was like
the bunkhouse at Cocodrilo Rancho, with a door and a
fireplace at each end, but with the inhabitants gathering at
one end only. He crept closer to the window, for it was
low enough that he could see inside. He stood to the left
of it, lest he be outlined in the light from it. Men lay on
bunks, but he saw no sign of Mary. Was it possible she lay
dead in the darkness of El Gato's cabin? He didn't think
so. Within the walls before him was the last of the seven

men he had sworn upon his father's grave he would kill, but Dade Withers no longer seemed important.

Nathan ducked below the window, moving to the other side, so that he might see farther into the interior of the bunkhouse, and that's when he saw her. What was left of her. She lay on her back on the floor, an iron poker driven through her belly.

As El Gato had put it, there was only a thin line between a brave man and a fool, but Nathan Stone fitted into neither category. In that instant, he became a madman. He kicked open the door, firing the Winchester as rapidly as he could lever shells into the chamber. Men came off their bunks, dying with their hands on their gun butts. But not all the outlaws were caught off guard. Breed, Kirkham, Swenson, and Vanado came up shooting. Nathan took a slug in his right side and it threw him backward to the floor. He let go of the Winchester, drew his Colt, and shot Breed in the chest. He sat up and a shot from Vanado's Colt knocked him down again. Drawing his left-hand Colt, Nathan shot Kirkham. Swenson and Vanado ran toward the other end of the bunkhouse, where there was no light. Nathan sent slugs screaming after them, but they slammed open a door and were lost in the night. Nathan tried to get up, and found he had been hit five times. He could feel blood from the wound in his side soaking his Levi's. Another, high up, was soaking the front of his shirt. A third slug had ripped through his upper left arm, missing the bone. There was a bloody, painful furrow torn across each of his thighs. Somehow, he had to get to his horse. The two outlaws who had escaped might be waiting in the dark to gun him down, but he dared not remain where he was, to bleed to death.

Using the edge of one of the upper bunks for support, Nathan managed to get to his feet. He felt lightheaded and knew he was losing blood. There was death all around him, and with life leaking out of him, he wept for Mary and the child he would never see. If he made it back alive, the fort could send a burial detail. The door hung open, and he could hear the anxious whining of Cotton Blossom, for the dog was reluctant to come in. While the raw furrows on Nathan's thighs hurt like hell, he could walk, using his Winchester for support. He managed to get outside, leaning against the log wall of the bunkhouse as he tried to gain strength. He had not eaten since supper the night before, and not much then. If he could reach his horse, there was jerked beef in the saddlebag. A step at a time, he reached the cabin where he had fought El Gato. Cotton Blossom was ahead of him, guiding him. There was a rise for a hundred yards, as he left the arroyo, and in his weakened condition it seemed steeper than it was. He wondered how much farther he must go before reaching his horse. Suddenly he was so tired he had to rest. He leaned up against a pine for support, aware that he was blacking out. Slowly his knees buckled and he slid to the ground. Later—he didn't know how much later—he came to his senses, wondering where Cotton Blossom was. He must get up, go on, but he was so tired ...

                    *   *   *

"Sergeant of the guard!"

The sergeant on duty made his way to the front gate, wondering what the matter was. Sentry duty had become more hectic at Fort Dodge since the town had been laid out. He looked at the stars. Three hours to first light.

"All right, Private Fenton, what is it this time?"

"A dog, sergeant. It's Nathan Stone's dog."

"Then let him in, damn it. He's been here so often, he's practically on the duty roster."

"He won't come in."

"Then by God, leave him out there."

But Cotton Blossom wouldn't be ignored. He began barking, the irritating, incessant yapping of a dog who has a problem requiring human attention.

"He wants something," said Private Fenton. "Something or somebody."

Sergeant Haley pondered the situation. Stone wasn't on the post or the dog wouldn't be outside, refusing to come in. Nathan Stone was a civilian, but he was highly regarded by Lieutenant-Colonel Hatton.

"Walk your post, private. I'll speak to Lieutenant-Colonel Hatton."

At first, Hatton didn't answer the knock, and when he did, Sergeant Haley felt foolish, waking the post commander over a barking dog.

"Sir," Haley said, "I hesitated to wake you, but this

might be a little more serious than it appears. The dog belonging to Nathan Stone is outside the gate. He won't come in and he won't go away."

"I fear it is serious, Sergeant," said Hatton, "and we may be too late. Wake Captain Bennett and tell him I said to mount a patrol for immediate duty. He is to meet me at my office in fifteen minutes."

*　　*　　*

Nathan awoke. Through the branches of the pine he could see the stars. It was late—or early, depending on how you looked at it—past two o'clock in the morning. Again he wondered where Cotton Blossom was. His mind wasn't serving him well, and he had lost all sense of direction. While the wound in his side still bled, the bleeding of his chest wound seemed to have ceased, for the blood had dried and his shirt seemed plastered to him. He tried to rise, but his legs wouldn't support him. He longed for a blanket, something of warmth, for his teeth chattered with the cold. Maybe if he rested a little longer, he would have the strength to rise ...

*　　*　　*

Captain Bennett arrived at Hatton's office with his patrol mounted and ready to ride. There were a sergeant, a corporal, and four privates.

"Captain," Hatton said, "as foolish as this may sound, accept it in all seriousness. There's a dog at the gate, and if he'll lead, you are to follow him. It's Nathan Stone's dog. Stone rode to Indian Territory last night in search of a band of thieves and killers. Wherever he is, he's in trouble, seriously hurt or dead."

"Necessary tools for a burial detail, sir?" Captain Bennett asked.

"Later, Captain," Hatton said. "Tend to the living first. Bring me a full report of your findings and we'll take it from there. Dismissed."

When the patrol had left his office, Hatton set about building a fire in the stove from the coals of the night before. He needed coffee to sustain him for a while. From what seemed a great distance, he could hear the barking of a dog ...

*   *   *

Barely conscious, Nathan heard the chirp of birds. Suddenly they became silent, and he tried to draw and cock a Colt, but neither hand had the needed strength. There was a rustling among the leaves and grass, and Nathan felt Cotton Blossom's wet nose against the back of his hand. There were voices, and while he didn't know them, they weren't the voices of killers looking for him.

"There he is!" one of the soldiers shouted.

"Corporal Evans," said Captain Bennett, "you're in charge of getting him out of here and back across the river. You'll need two men to bear the stretcher and two to make way for it. Sergeant Goodner, you'll come with me."

Corporal Evans and his four men got Nathan on to the stretcher and while the privates began the ordeal of getting the stretcher through the underbrush, Corporal Evans led Nathan's horse. As Captain Bennett and Sergeant Goodner approached the cabin near the mouth of the arroyo, they marveled at the outlaw hideaway. Each man drew his revolver, for they knew not what might lie ahead. While the door to the cabin was open, they approached it with caution until they could see the booted foot of El Gato. They quickly learned there was nobody else in the cabin, and it was Sergeant Goodner who made an astonishing discovery in one of the small rooms.

"Lord Amighty, Captain, come have a look at this!" Goodner shouted.

It was a veritable fortune in currency and gold, much of it in the green strongboxes used by the military for transferring payrolls.

"You'll have to remain here, Sergeant," said Captain Bennett, "until I have reported to Lieutenant-Colonel Hatton. A recovery of this magnitude will turn Washington on its ear. Let's move on and be done with this."

The two men approached the bunkhouse with caution, although both doors stood open. They stepped in, revolvers drawn, and froze. Blood had pooled and dried on the floor and splattered the log walls. There were ten dead men, but the eyes of the two men were drawn to the horror that was the remains of young Mary Stone. When the soldiers turned away, it was Sergeant Goodner who spoke for them both.

"What they got was too good for them. May their souls burn in hell for eternity for what they did to her."

*   *   *

Nathan Stone was taken to Fort Dodge more dead than alive, and as he hovered near death for three days, it seemed he lacked a will to live. But there was an indomitable spark that flamed anew, and he began slowly to recover.

*   *   *

Fort Dodge, Kansas. April 1, 1872.

For the first time since he had been wounded, the post doctor allowed Nathan to get up and walk about. In the afternoon, a private came looking for him.

"Sir, you have a visitor. He's waiting for you in the post commander's office."

Joel Netherton got to his feet when Nathan stepped through the door, and offered his hand. Nathan took it.

"So that's what you came to Kansas City to tell me," Netherton said.

"Yes," said Nathan. "I'm not a man to sail under false colors, and that's what I had been doing. I thought I was holding back for Mary's sake. If I'd been a man with the strength of my own convictions, she would be alive today."

"I want you to know we made a ninety-percent recovery on every one of the robberies. I'm proposing a ten-thousand-dollar reward on behalf of the Kansas–Pacific, and you'll be getting another five thousand five hundred for the outlaws. It was an extraordinary piece of work, and you may yet receive a medal or commendation from the Congress. Your friend Byron Silver's working on that."

"I'm obliged, Joel, but I don't want any of that."

"But you've earned it ten times over," said Netherton.

"I don't care," Nathan said bitterly. "It's like ... God, it's like I've sold Mary ... put a price on her ..."

"I think I understand," said Netherton. "When you're up to it, come to Kansas City. The board of directors would like to meet you."

"No offense, Joel, but I'd rather not."

*   *   *

Fort Dodge, Kansas. April 10, 1872.

At Lieutenant-Colonel Hatton's request, Nathan met with him before leaving the post. The officer handed Nathan an envelope containing two sheets of paper.

"That's a report on the outlaws," Hatton said. "Using Washington sources, such as army records, we've assembled a background on each of them. Most of them, with the exception of El Gato, were deserters. El Gato was wanted for a variety of things, from robbery to murder, in both Mexico and Texas. Some of them were using assumed names, while some used their own."

"Thank you," said Nathan, tucking the envelope in his pocket.

"I suppose it's none of my business where you're going from here," the officer said, "but some of us feel like we have an investment in you. You have potential, son. Don't let it go to waste."

"Sir, I'm obliged for everything you've done," said Nathan. "Frankly, I don't know what I'm going to do or where I may go. How do you suddenly have the props kicked out from under you, seen your world wither and die before your eyes, and then try to start over?"

"I can't answer that," Hatton said. "Just remember, you're welcome here, and if there's anything I can do, you have only to ask. Good luck."

Nathan left the office, mounted his horse, and rode out, Cotton Blossom trotting beside him. As he rode, he read the report Hatton had given him, detailing the criminal records of the outlaws. Dade Withers had been guilty of murdering another soldier and escaping from prison. His age was given as twenty-three, and he had been born in Charlottesville, Virginia.

*   *   *

Kansas City, Missouri. April 29, 1872.

"Eppie," Nathan said, "I want you to have Mary's horse and saddle."

The old lady wept for Mary and wept for Nathan when he rode away.

* * *

Springfield, Missouri. May 15, 1872.

"I seen your picture in the paper," the kid said, "and I hear you're fast with a gun. Well, I'm faster than you, and I aim to prove it."

He wasn't a day over seventeen and he had been waiting until Nathan left a mercantile with his purchases. As though by magic, people had gathered to see one of them die. Nathan waited until the last second, his hand not moving until the kid cleared leather. The kid stood there, a hitch rail supporting his dying body, staring unbelievingly at the blood pumping from a hole in his chest. Slowly the life drained out of his eyes and he fell, his Colt clutched in his dead hand. Nathan stood there looking at him, sick to his very soul. He had been given no choice. Then, as though from far away, he heard the talk he was destined to hear again and again . . .

". . . gun-slingin' varmint's kilt little Rusty Limbaugh, from over yonder in Smelterville."

". . . never seen the like. He's a born killer. It's in his eyes . . ."

". . . kid never had a chance . . . damn killer . . . oughta be strung up . . ."

When the sheriff came, even the lawman was intimidated, and some of the onlookers laughed. Nathan rode silently away, leading his packhorse, Cotton Blossom trotting alongside. But there would be no escape, for Nathan had been branded a killer. It would become a self-fulfilling prophecy.

Nathan Stone had no illusions about what lay ahead. One who gained a reputation with a fast gun had only one means of escape, and that's when he faced a man with a faster gun. To finish what destiny had begun, Nathan rode on, the clock always ticking, toward the killing season . . .

Epilogue

1866
- The James-Younger gangs robbed the Clay County Savings Bank, Liberty, Missouri.
- Ben Thompson, after quarreling over a card game, shot a police officer in Matamoros, Mexico.

1867
- Cullen Baker shot and killed a storekeeper who demanded money owed him.
- Wild Bill Longley and his partner, Johnson McKowen, angry over a horse race, shot up a street dance in Lexington, Texas, killing two and wounding two.
- Ben Thompson pulled a gun in Austin, Texas, saving a judge from a street gang.

1868
- The James-Younger gangs robbed a bank in Russellville, Kentucky.
- John Morco murdered four people in California.
- Ben Thompson shot a man in Austin, Texas. He served two years in prison.
- Billy Thompson shot and killed a soldier in Austin. He escaped.

1869
- Cullen Baker was poisoned in Arkansas by a group of men that included his father-in-law.
- Wild Bill Hickok was wounded in a saloon brawl in Colorado Territory.
- Wild Bill Hickok, while county sheriff in Hays, Kansas, shot and killed a man who resisted arrest.
- Wild Bill Hickok, while sheriff of Hays, Kansas, shot and killed a troublemaker who had started a riot.

- Frank and Jesse James robbed a bank in Gallatin, Missouri, killing one man.
- Frank and Jesse James, holed up in a farmhouse in Clay County, Missouri, shot it out with a posse, and escaped.

1870
- Wild Bill Hickok was involved in a brawl with soldiers in a Hays, Kansas saloon. Hickok shot two soldiers, one of whom died.
- Wild Bill Longley shot and killed a soldier in Kansas.

1871
- John Wesley Hardin, being transferred from Marshall, Texas, to the jail at Waco, shot a guard and escaped.
- John Wesley Hardin shot and wounded two Mexicans in Gonzales County, after a quarrel over a card game.
- John Wesley Hardin, while on a trail drive, shot and killed an Indian in Indian Territory.
- John Wesley Hardin shot and killed a man in Abilene, Kansas.
- John Wesley Hardin shot and killed a man in Bluff City, Kansas.

Don't miss another Ralph Compton novel
featuring the ultimate gunfighter
Nathan Stone

THE KILLING SEASON

Available now from Berkley

Dodge City, Kansas. July 6, 1873.

Arriving in the late afternoon, Nathan found himself looking forward to a bath, town grub, and a clean bed. Checking in at the hotel, he bought copies of The St. Louis *Globe-Democrat* and The Kansas City *Liberty-Tribune*. As Nathan left the hotel lobby, the desk clerk studied the register and then looked at the clock. His relief would arrive within the hour. Then he would talk to Sheriff Harrington . . . .

Following his bath and a change of clothes, Nathan headed for a cafe. The cook recognized Nathan and Cotton Blossom.

"Steak cooked through," said the cook, "sided with onions, spuds, pie, and hot coffee."

"That will do for starters," Nathan said. "After feedin' Cotton Blossom and me, you may have to close up and restock. We've been on the trail for a spell, without decent grub."

Cotton Blossom headed for the kitchen while Nathan took a back table. Reading the St. Louis paper, he found little of interest, and finishing that, turned to the Kansas City edition. In an item from Wichita, Edward Beard had begun construction on another saloon and dance hall, vowing to have it in operation by October. Ben Thompson and his troublesome brother Billy had spent the night in jail, following a brawl in a Kansas City saloon. The unpredictable pair had left town the next day, traveling west.

*   *   *

When the door to his office opened, Dodge City's Sheriff Harrington looked up.

"Come in, Harley. Somebody rob the hotel?"

"Nathan Stone—the gent with the dog—checked in a while ago."

"He's at the hotel now?" Sheriff Harrington asked.

"No," said Harley. "After takin' a room, him and the dog went out. Do you reckon there's a reward?"

"I don't know," Harrington replied. "I had a telegram from the Pinkerton office in Kansas City, and all they asked was that I write them immediately if Nathan Stone showed up. They made it a point to say he has a dog with him."

"No reward, then," said Harley, disappointed. "A man wanted by the law ain't likely to be signin' his own name on a hotel register."

"I wouldn't think so," Harrington replied. "While the Pinkertons trail bank, train, and stage robbers, they don't limit themselves to that. I expect folks with money can hire them to track missing persons too. I'll telegraph them, tell them Stone's here, and we'll see what happens."

*   *   *

Receiving Sheriff Harrington's telegram, the Pinkerton office in Kansas City sent an operative with the message to a Kansas City hotel. Hate-filled eyes read the telegram and steady hands loaded a Colt revolver. The recipient of the telegram checked out of the hotel and took a hack to the Atchison, Topeka, and Santa Fe Railroad terminal. The schedule said the next train to Dodge would depart within the hour, arriving there before dawn . . . .

*   *   *

The shriek of a locomotive whistle awakened Nathan. Cotton Blossom had reared up on his hind legs, looking out the window into the darkness.

"Just a train comin' in, Cotton Blossom," Nathan said. "With the railroad through town. It's like trying to sleep next to a steamboat landing. It's a good two hours before first light."

A single passenger stepped down from the train, and taking a seat on a bench, waited for the town to awaken.

With the first gray light of dawn, Nathan arose. Leaving his room key at the desk, he and Cotton Blossom headed for the cafe. Immediately after breakfast, they would strike out north toward Ellsworth. But suddenly, from behind there came a command that drove all thought of food from Nathan's mind.

"Nathan Stone, this is Sheriff Harrington. I need to talk to you."

His hands shoulder-high, Nathan turned slowly around. Harrington's Colt was thonged to his right thigh and he looked all business. But the sheriff wasn't alone. The girl had short dark hair under a flat-crowned hat. Her boots were scuffed, her Levi's faded, and an old red flannel shirt looked too large. She looked maybe twenty-one or twenty-two, and her eyes were brimming with hatred. Before the sheriff could speak another word, she drew from the folds of her shirt a Colt revolver. There was no doubt she intended to kill Nathan.

"Hey!" Sheriff Harrington shouted. Seizing her arm, he forced the muzzle of the Colt toward the ground, and the roar of the weapon was loud in the morning stillness. But the girl was resourceful and cat-quick. Facing Harrington, she drove a knee into his groin, and using his moments of agony, wrested the Colt free.

But she now had Nathan Stone to contend with, for he no longer had any doubts as to her intentions. Before she could cock and fire the Colt, he caught her wrist, and when she tried to knee him as she had the sheriff, he seized her ankle. Using that and the hold he had on her wrist, he lifted her off the ground and slammed her down on her back. She let go of the Colt and Nathan kicked it back toward the hotel. Sheriff Harrington had regained his composure and stood there waiting for the girl to get up. She ignored Nathan, turning her anger upon the sheriff.

"You *could* help me," she snapped, struggling to her knees.

"I *could* lock you up for attempted murder," Harrington said coldly. "and I might yet, you little catamount. You lied to me. You told me you only needed to talk to Stone."

She laughed. "Oh, I *do* want to talk to him, to tell him who I am. Then I aim to kill him, because he murdered my brother."

"You don't have to tell me who you are," Nathan said. "You're from Missouri, and you're one of the Limbaughs."

"Amy, by name," said Sheriff Harrington. "Do you know her?"

"No," Nathan replied, "but I know why she's after me. I had to shoot her hotheaded brother or he'd have shot me. There's just a hell of a lot she hasn't told you, sheriff, and I aim to fill in the gaps. Then I want to know how she dragged you into this."

"We'll talk in my office," said Harrington. "We're starting to draw a crowd."

The three of them walked the short distance to the lawmen's office. There were four cells, none of them occupied. Harrington pointed to the first one.

"In there, Amy. I aim to hear Stone's side of this. Then I'll decide what to do with you."

Harrington locked the cell door, took a seat behind an old desk and nodded toward the only other chair in the room. Nathan sat down and started talking. When he had finished, Harrington got to his feet.

"What you've said has the ring of truth," the sheriff said, "but I aim to telegraph the attorney general's office in Jefferson City, Missouri. That's as much for your benefit as my own. I figure if they hear from enough lawmen, all of us raisin' hell, the state might get to the bottom of this, and clear you."

"I'm more interested in getting the Pinkertons off my trail," Nathan said. "They're after me so this female sidewinder can fill me full of lead, and she has no legal right. I'm of a mind to ride to Kansas City and pull some Pinkerton fangs."

"You would be more than justified," said Harrington. "Fact is, after I've telegraphed the Missouri attorney general's office, I'll contact the Pinkerton office in Kansas City. They should know what Miss Amy Limbaugh's intentions are, and that as a result of their being involved, you're in a position to bring charges against them. If they persist in hounding you, then I'd suggest you do exactly that. Now let's ride to Fort Dodge and send those telegrams."

"He's a killer." Amy shouted, "and I'll find him without the Pinkertons."

"He could have shot you dead and claimed self-defense," said Harrington. "Instead, he disarmed you. That's not the mark of a killer."

Reaching Fort Dodge, Harrington sent the telegrams, and in less than a quarter of an hour the Pinkertons responded. Harrington read the message and passed it on to Nathan. The telegram was simple and to the point. Sheriff Harrington was to detain Amy Limbaugh until a Pinkerton operative could question her.

"I reckon it won't stop her from comin' after you," said Harrington, "but she likely won't have the help of the Pinkertons. Won't be another train out of Kansas City until tonight. That'll give you a head start."

"Thanks," Nathan said.

They waited for almost an hour for the Missouri district attorney's office to respond, and when the telegram came, it satisfied Sheriff Harrington.

"You told it straight," said Harrington. "The shooting

was ruled self-defense and the state has no charges against you. When that Pinkerton varmint steps down from the train, I'll shove this in his face."

When they reached the jail, Nathan dismounted. "Before I ride out." Nathan said, "I have some advice for Miss Amy Limbaugh."

Unlocking the door, Sheriff Harrington went in, Nathan following. Amy Limbaugh just stared angrily at them, gripping the bars.

"Well, Amy," said Harrington, "Stone told me the truth, and the Pinkertons have asked me to keep you here until they can talk to you. If you know how, I reckon you'd better come up with some truth of your own."

"Damn you," she shouted, "you can't hold me without charges. What are the charges?"

"I don't know all the fine points of the law," said Harrington, "but we can always use attempted murder. The Pinkertons may have some of their own. Without their knowledge, you used them with the intention of committing a crime. Legally, Stone can sue the socks off them, and they know it. For that matter, when the Pinkertons are finished with you, Stone can file charges of his own. I certainly wouldn't blame him."

"No charges," said Nathan. "When the Pinkertons have had their say, turn her loose."

"Damn you," she said. "I don't want any favors from your kind."

"You've had your first and last favor from me," said Nathan. "The next time you pull a gun on me, I'll kill you."

Nodding to the sheriff, Nathan stepped out the door, closing it behind him. Mounting, he rode to the livery for his packhorse. While he expected Sheriff Harrington to truthfully present his case to the Pinkertons, he still intended to confront them personally. With that in mind, he rode eastward, toward Kansas City.

*   *   *

Kansas City, Missouri. July 12, 1873.

The Pinkerton Detective Agency was housed in a two-story brick building. As Nathan stepped into the lobby,

Amy Limbaugh and a pair of hired guns observed him from
their hiding place across the street.

"Find some cover and spread out," said the girl. "When
he leaves the building, wait until he's down the steps and
away from it. Then cut him down."

Nathan was shown into the office of Roscoe Edelman, a
regional director of the Pinkerton Detective Agency. Edelman said nothing, waiting for Nathan to speak.

"There's a gun-totin' female name of Amy Limbaugh
who aims to kill me," Nathan said, "and through Sheriff
Harrington in Dodge, I've learned the Pinkertons are responsible for her being on my trail. Now I'm here to tell
you the straight of it, that the Limbaughs have no legal
case against me, and I can prove it. If just one more sheriff
comes after me as a result of your damn telegrams, I aim
to purely raise hell and kick a chunk under it. Do you
understand?"

"I am not accustomed to being threatened," said Edelman coldly, "and I refuse to be intimidated by a mouthy
gunman. We have acknowledged our mistake, and we will
no longer concern ourselves with your whereabouts. That's
all the consideration you're going to get from this office.
Close the door on your way out."

Fighting his temper, Nathan turned and walked out, leaving the door wide open. There was little to do except return
to the livery where his horses and Cotton Blossom waited.
Nathan had left the building and was at the foot of the
steps when the first shot rang out. Lead slammed into his
left side above his pistol belt, throwing him back against
the steps. There was no way he could make it back to the
safety of the building, and he rolled off the steps, drawing
his right-hand Colt. Belly-down, he became a more difficult
target, and for just a moment, his antagonist forgot his
cover. Nathan shot him twice. A second man fired, his slug
kicking dust in Nathan's face. He fired once and had the
satisfaction of seeing the killer stumble and fall. But another slug tore into Nathan's left thigh, and he realized he
was caught in a three-way cross fire. The third bushwhacker
was to Nathan's left and much nearer. He fired once and
Amy Limbaugh screamed when the lead struck her under
the collar bone. All three bushwhackers were down and
Nathan was struggling to his knees when the sheriff and

his deputy arrived. They stood facing Nathan, their Colts drawn and ready.

"I'm Sheriff Wilhelm," the lawman said. "Drop the gun. The party's over."

"I didn't open the ball, sheriff," Nathan said. "Three bushwhackers cut down on me and they've all been hit."

"You're just hell on little red wheels with a pistol, ain't you?" the sheriff said. Then he spoke to his deputy. "Karl, see to them that's hurt."

"You that's been hit," Karl said, "hold your fire. I'm a sheriff's deputy."

Nathan staggered to his feet and Sheriff Wilhelm allowed him to keep his guns. The sheriff still hadn't holstered his weapon, waiting for Karl's report.

"He's right, sheriff," said Karl. "There's three of 'em, and one's dead. The other two are wounded, but they'll live. One of 'em's a ... uh ... female."

Before Sheriff Wilhelm could react to that, a crowd had gathered, drawn by the gunfire. One young man, a press card under his hat band, spoke directly to the sheriff.

"Sheriff, I'm Brandon Wilkes, with the *Liberty-Tribune*."

"I know who you are," Wilhelm growled, "and I got no time to talk to you."

"I'm not here to talk to you," said Wilkes coolly. "I want a story from this gentleman who seems to have survived all the shooting. Mr ... ?"

"Stone," said Nathan. "Nathan Stone."

Karl, the deputy, arrived, with his Colt cocked. Ahead of him stumbled a bearded man with the left side of his shirt bloody and a bleeding, weeping Amy Limbaugh. Nathan suspected the girl was playing on the sheriff's sympathy, and to his disgust, Wilhelm seemed to be responding.

"Ma'am," Sheriff Wilhelm said, "the doctor's office ain't far. Can you make it, or do you need help?"

"Sheriff," said Nathan, "this is the second time this little hellion has tried to kill me. By God, if you don't take that Colt away from her. I'm going to."

Ready to find
your next great read?

Let us help.

Visit prh.com/nextread

Penguin
Random
House